"You know," Roo said, "I'm really glad you came this summer."

"Yeah?"

He nodded. "I always wondered, you know? What happened to you. Because I remembered that time you came when we were kids."

"I wish *I* remembered," I said. "I lost a lot. Like, everything from this place."

"Wasn't lost," he said. "You just left it here. You know what Mimi says: the lake keeps us."

He smiled at me then, and as I felt myself smile back, I wondered if our parents had ever stood in this same spot. There were so many stories here, like every moment had already been lived once before.

But then, Roo did something different. He reached forward with one hand, sliding my fallen strap back up on my shoulder. It was a simple gesture, but I felt my heart catch in my chest. Once the strap was fixed, he left his hand there, fingers spread cool over my skin. Like a take two, second chance. The kind you don't get often.

SARAH DESSEN

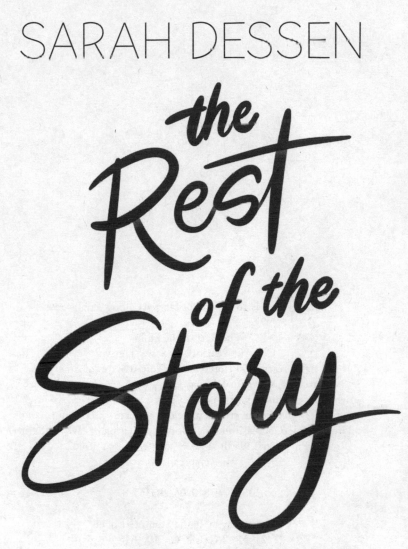

the
Rest
of the
Story

BALZER + BRAY

An Imprint of HarperCollins*Publishers*

Balzer + Bray is an imprint of HarperCollins Publishers.

The Rest of the Story
Copyright © 2019 by Sarah Dessen

ISBN 978-0-06-293363-8

Typography by Jenna Stempel-Lobell
21 22 23 24   PC/LSCC   10 9 8 7 6 5 4
❖
First paperback edition, 2020

For Leigh Feldman.
Even when words fail me, you never do.
Thank you.

the Rest of the Story

PROLOGUE

There weren't a lot of memories, especially good ones. But there was this.

"Tell me a story," I'd say when it was bedtime but I wasn't at all sleepy.

"Oh, honey," my mom would reply. "I'm tired."

She was always tired: that I did remember. Especially in the evenings, after that first or second glass of wine, which most often led to a bottle, once I was asleep. Usually my dad cleaned up before he went to bed, but when he wasn't around, the evidence remained there in the light of day when I came down for breakfast.

"Not a fairy tale," I'd say, because she always said no at first. "A lake story."

At this, she'd smile. "A lake story? Well. That's different."

That was when I knew I could lean back into my pillows, grabbing my stuffed giraffe, George, and settle in.

"Once upon a time," she'd begin, locking a leg around mine or draping an arm over my stomach, because snuggling was part of the telling, "there was a little girl who lived by a big lake that seemed like it went on forever. The trees around the edges had moss, and the water was cold and clear."

This was when I would start to picture it. Seeing the details.

"The little girl loved to swim, and she loved her family, and she loved the creaky old house with the uneven floors and the little bedroom at the top of the stairs, which was all hers."

At this point in the story, she'd look at me, as if checking to see if I'd fallen asleep. I never had, though.

"In the winters, the water was cold, and so was the house. It felt like the world had left the lake all alone, and the girl would get sad."

Here I always pictured the little girl in a window, peering out. I had an image for everything, like she was turning pages in a book.

"When the weather got warm again, though, strangers and travelers came to visit from all over. And they brought boats with loud motors, and floats of many colors and shapes, and crowded the docks through the days and nights, their voices filling the air." A pause, now, as she shifted, maybe closing her own eyes. "And on those nights, the summer nights, the little girl would sit in her yellow bedroom and look across the water and the big sky full of stars and know everything was going to be okay."

I could see it all, the picture so vivid in my mind I felt like I could have touched it. And I'd be getting sleepy, but never so much I couldn't say what came next. "How did she know?"

"Because in the summers, the world came back to the lake," she'd reply. "And that was when it felt like home."

ONE

The wedding was over. But the party had just begun.

"It's just so romantic," my best friend Bridget said, picking up the little glass jar of candy from her place setting and staring at it dreamily. "Like a fairy tale."

"You think everything is like a fairy tale," my other best friend Ryan told her, wincing as she reached down yet again to rub her sore feet. None of us were used to dressing up very much, especially in heels. "All those days of playing Princess when we were kids ruined you."

"I seem to remember *someone* who had a Belle fixation," Bridget said, putting the candy down with a clank. She tucked her short, choppy dark bob behind her ears. "Back before you decided that being cynical and depressed was much cooler."

"I was the one who liked Belle," I reminded her. We all had our roles: they were always bickering about our shared history, while I was the one who remembered all the details.

5

It had been like this since we'd met on the playground in second grade. "Ryan was all about Jasmine."

"She's right," Ryan said. "And I'll remind you again that I'm not cynical or depressed, I'm realistic. We can't all see the world as rainbows and unicorns."

"I don't even like rainbows and unicorns," Bridget muttered. "They're so overdone."

"The truth is," Ryan continued, "even with cute candy favors, the divorce rate in this country is over fifty percent."

"Oh, my God. Ryan!" Bridget looked horrified. Ryan was right about one thing: she was the biggest optimist I knew. "That is a *horrible* thing to say at Emma's dad's wedding."

"Seriously," I added. "Way to jinx my future. Was my past not bleak enough for you?"

Ryan looked at me, worried. "Oh, crap. Sorry."

"I'm kidding," I told her.

"And I *hate* your humor," she replied. "Have I mentioned that lately?"

She had not. But she didn't need to. Everyone seemed to have a problem with what I found funny. "Despite the statistics," I said, "I really do feel Dad and Tracy will make it."

"She'll always be Dr. Feldman to me," she said, glancing over to the cake table, where the couple in question were now posing for the photographer, their hands arranged together over a knife. "I still can't talk to her without feeling like I need to open wide."

"Ha," I said, although as the kid of a dentist, I'd heard

6

all *those* jokes, multiple times. What's your dad's favorite day of the week? TOOTHDAY! What do you call your dad's advice? His FLOSSOPHY! Add in the fact that my dad's name was Dr. Payne, and hilarity was always ensuing.

"No, I'm serious," Ryan said. "Even just now, when they came by to say hello, I was worried she'd notice I hadn't been flossing."

"I think she's got bigger things on her mind today," I said, watching as my new stepmother laughed, brushing some frosting off my dad's face with one hand. She looked relaxed, which was a relief after over a year of watching her juggle the details of flowers and her dress and the reception along with her own bustling practice. Even at her most stressed, though, she'd maintained the cheerful demeanor that was her signature. If my mom had been dark and tragic, Tracy was sweetness and light. And, yes, maybe flossing. But she made my dad happy, which was all that really counted to me.

"Nana incoming," Ryan said under her breath. Immediately, we all sat up straighter. Such was the power of my grandmother, who carried herself with such grace that you couldn't help but try to do the same. Also, she'd tell you if you were slouching. Nicely, but she would tell you.

"Girls, you all look so beautiful," she said as she came sweeping up in the simple rose-colored chiffon gown that she'd custom-ordered from New York. "I just can't get over it. Like little princesses!"

At this, Bridget beamed. While Ryan and I had moved

7

on, she'd never really gotten over her own years of wanting to be Cinderella. "Thank you, Mrs. Payne. The wedding is lovely."

"Isn't it?" Nana looked over to the cake table, where my dad was now feeding Tracy a bite from his fork. "It all came together perfectly. I couldn't be more thrilled for them."

"Me too," I said, and at this she smiled, reaching down to touch my shoulder. When I looked up at her and our eyes met, she gave it a squeeze.

"Are you getting excited about your cruise?" Bridget asked Nana now as the waiters began to move through the room with champagne for the toasts. "I heard you're going to see pyramids!"

"That's what I'm told," Nana replied, taking a flute from a passing tray and holding it up to the light. "And while I'm excited, I'd honestly rather be here overseeing the renovations. Travel is always good for the soul, though, isn't it?"

Bridget nodded, even though I knew for a fact she'd only been on one real trip, to Disney World a few years back. "Renovations are boring, though," she said. "We did our family room last summer. It was all sawdust and noise for *months*."

"You underestimate how ready she is to turn my room into something fabulous, like a Zen garden or formal sitting room," I said. "She's been counting the days."

"Not true," Nana said, looking at me. "You have no idea how much I will miss you."

Just like that, I felt a lump in my throat. I made a point of smiling at her, though, as a man in a suit passing by greeted her and she turned away to talk to him.

There were good changes and bad ones, and I knew that the ones ahead were firmly in the former category for both Nana and myself. After the wedding, my dad, Tracy, and I would live together in a new house they'd purchased in a neighborhood walking distance to my high school. Nana would finally get her apartment back, something she said she didn't care about one bit, but in truth I knew she wouldn't miss the clutter and noise that came along with her son and teenage granddaughter as roommates. After my parents split and my mom first went to treatment, we needed somewhere to land, and she'd offered without a second thought. Never mind that I'd probably racked up enough of a bill in broken china and scuffed floors to cover my college tuition: Nana said she wouldn't have it any other way. Her home was a work of art filled with works of art, each detail from the carpets to the wall hangings curated and considered. Now it featured a banged up bike in the entryway, as well as a huge wide-screen TV (Nana didn't watch television). After a renovation that would happen while she was floating down the Nile, she would get it back all to herself to do with as she chose. And I was glad.

I was happy for my dad as well. After the roller coaster of dealing with my mom, Tracy was the most welcome of changes. She didn't take more than she gave, or give nothing at all. She could be trusted to go to a work dinner and not embarrass him by drinking too much or telling a joke that had profanity or sex as part of the punch line. And if she said she'd be somewhere at a certain time, she was always there. It was this last thing that I think he appreciated most about her. I knew I did. After loving someone you couldn't depend on, you realize how important it is to trust someone will do what they say. It's such a simple thing, not to promise what you can't or won't deliver. But my mom had done that all the time.

In our new home in Lakeview, in the Arbors neighborhood, I would have my own suite with a big airy bedroom, as well as a bathroom and a small balcony that looked out over the rest of our street. It would be a change from our apartment, where I could look out at night and see city lights, and the noise from the street was muted but still always there: garbage trucks rumbling in the morning; drunk students walking home from the bars after midnight; sirens and car horns. I knew I would miss it, the way I'd miss my breakfasts with Nana, us splitting the newspaper—she took the cultural section, while I preferred the obituaries—and being able to step out of my house right into the world going on around me. But change was good, as Nana also said, especially the kind you were prepared for. And I was.

Before all that, though, my dad and Tracy would leave for their honeymoon to Greece. There, they were chartering a boat, just the two of them, indulging their shared love of sailing to tour the islands. It was a perfect culmination of their courtship, which, despite their shared profession, had not begun in a tooth-based setting. Instead, they'd met at a general interest meeting of the Lakeview Sailing Club, which gathered every other Sunday at Topper Lake to race dingys and knockabouts. I knew this because before Tracy, I'd had the unfortunate luck of being my dad's first mate.

I hated sailing. I know, I know. It was my *name*, for God's sake—Emma Saylor—chosen because my dad's passion for mainsheets and rudder boards had been what had brought my parents together at another lake all those years ago. My mom, however, had felt the same way about sailing as I did, which was why she'd insisted on spelling my name the way she had. And anyway, I was Emma for all intents and purposes. Emma, who hated sailing.

My dad tried. He'd signed me up for sailing camp one summer when I was ten. There, I was usually adrift, my centerboard usually having plunged into the lake below, as instructors tried to yell encouragement from a nearby motorboat. But sailing with other people was worse. More likely than not, they'd yell at you for not sitting in the right place or grabbing the wrong line under pressure. Even when my dad swore he was taking me out for a "nice, easy sail," there would be at least one moment when he got super stressed and was racing around trying to make the boat do something it wasn't wanting to do while, yes, yelling.

Tracy, however, didn't mind this. In fact, from the day they were assigned to a knockabout together at the sailing club, she yelled right back, which I believed was one of the things that made my dad fall in love with her.

So they would go to Greece, and holler at each other over

the gorgeous Aegean Sea, and I would stay with Bridget and her family. We'd spend the days babysitting her brothers, ages twelve, ten, and five, and going to her neighborhood pool, where we planned to work on our tans and the crushes we had on Sam and Steve Schroeder, the twins in our grade who lived at the end of her cul-de-sac.

But first, there was tonight and the wedding, here at the Lakeview Country Club, where the ballroom had been lined with twinkling lights and fluttering tulle and we, along with two hundred other guests, had just finished a sit-down dinner. Despite the lavishness of the celebration, the ceremony itself had been simple, with me as Tracy's maid of honor and Nana standing up with my dad as his "Best Gran." (One of the wedding planners, a dapper man named William, had come up with this moniker, and he was clearly very proud of it.) I'd been allowed to choose my own dress, which I was pretty sure was Tracy's way of trying to make it not a big deal but instead did the opposite, as who wants to make the wrong decision when you are one of only four people in the wedding party? Never mind that I was an anxious girl, always had been, and choices of any kind were my kryptonite. I'd ended up in such a panic I bought two dresses, then decided at the last minute. But even now, as I sat in my baby-blue sheath with the spaghetti straps, I was thinking of the pink gown with the full skirt at home, and wondering if I should have gone with it instead. I sighed, then reorganized my place setting, putting the silverware that remained squarely on my folded napkin and adjusting the angle of my water glass.

"You okay?" Ryan asked me. We'd been friends for so long, she knew my coping mechanisms almost better than I did. Perpetually messy herself, she'd often told me she wished she, too, had the urge to keep the world neat and tidy. But everything is welcome until you can't stop, and I'd been like this for longer than I cared to remember.

"Fine," I said, dropping my hand instead of lining up the flowers, glass jar of candy, and candle as I'd been about to do. "It's just a big night."

"Of course it is!" Bridget said. There was that optimism again. "Which is why I think we need to celebrate."

I raised my eyebrows at Ryan, who just shrugged, clearly not in on whatever Bridget was planning. Which, as it turned out, was turning to the table beside us, which had been full of young hygienists from my dad's office until they all hit the dance floor, and switching out the bottle of sparkling cider from our ice bucket for the champagne in theirs.

"Bridget," Ryan hissed. "You're going to get us so busted!"

"By who? They're already all tipsy, they won't even notice." She quickly filled our flutes before burying the bottle back in ice. Then she picked up her glass, gesturing for us to do the same. "To Dr. Payne and Dr. Feldman."

"To Dad and Tracy," I said.

"Bottoms up," added Ryan.

We clinked glasses, Bridget with a bit too much enthusiasm, champagne sloshing onto the table in front of her. I watched them both suck down big gulps—Ryan wincing— as I looked at my glass.

"It's good!" Bridget told me. "Even if you don't drink."

"My mom says it's bad luck to toast and not imbibe," Ryan added. "Just take a tiny sip."

I just looked at them. They knew I wasn't a drinker, just as they knew exactly why. Sighing, I picked up my flute and took a gulp. Immediately, my nose was tingling, prickles filling my brain. "Ugh," I said, chasing it with water right away. "How can you really enjoy that?"

"It's like drinking sparkles," Bridget replied, holding the glass up to the light just as Nana had, the bubbles drifting upward.

"Spoken like a true princess." Ryan tipped her glass back, finishing it, then gave herself a refill. "And my mom also says nobody really likes champagne. Only how it makes you feel."

"All I feel is that everything is changing," I said. Saying it aloud, it suddenly felt more true than ever.

"But in good ways!" Bridget said. "Right? New stepmom, new house, and before that, new summer full of potential . . ."

"For you two," Ryan grumbled. "I'll be stuck in the mountains with no internet, with only my dad and some drama nerds for company."

"You get to spend the entire summer at Windmill!

That's one of the best theater camps in the country—" Bridget replied.

"Where I'll be the camp director's kid, so everyone will automatically hate me," Ryan finished for her. "Except my dad."

"You *guys*." Bridget lifted out the bottle again, topping off our glasses. "It's going to be an amazing summer, for all of us. Just trust me, will you?"

Ryan shrugged, then took another sip. I looked at my own glass, then across the room at my dad, who was now leading Tracy back to their table. He looked flushed and happy, and watching him, I felt a rush of affection. He'd been through so much, with my mom and then the divorce, raising me basically as a single parent even before he really was one, all the while working nonstop. I *was* really happy for him, and excited. But the time that he'd be in Greece would be the longest we'd been apart in my memory, and I already knew I would miss him so much. Parents are always precious. But when you only have one, they become crucial.

I reached down, moving my dessert fork and coffee spoon a bit to the right. When Ryan looked over at me, I expected to be called out again, but instead, this time, she just gave me a smile. Then she turned her head away so I could arrange the vase, candy jar, and candle as well.

TWO

I'd heard a lot of words used to describe my mom both before and since her death five years ago. "Beautiful" was a big one, followed closely by "wild" or its kinder twin, "spirited." There were a few mentions each of "tragic," "sweet," and "full of life." But these were just words. My mom was bigger than any combination of letters.

She died in 2013, on the Monday of the first week after Thanksgiving. We'd actually spent it together: me, my mom, and my dad, even though they'd been split up at that point for almost five years. First love against the backdrop of a summer lake resort makes for a great movie plot or romance novel. As a working model for a relationship and parenthood, though, it left a bit to be desired. At least in their case.

I was so little when they split that I didn't remember the fighting, or how my dad was never around as he finished dental school, leaving my mom to take care of me alone. Also lost to my memory was an increase in my mom's drinking, which then blossomed into a painkiller addiction after she had wrist surgery and discovered Percocet. By the time my consciousness caught up with everything, my parents weren't together anymore and she'd already been to rehab once. The world, as I remembered it, was my post-divorce life, which was my dad and me living with Nana Payne in her apartment building in downtown Lakeview and my mom, well, anywhere and everywhere else.

Like the studio apartment in the basement of a suburban house, so small that when you fully opened the front door, it hit the bed. Or the ranch home she shared with three other women in various stages of recovery, where the sofa stank of cigarettes despite a NO SMOKING sign above it. And then there was the residential motel on the outskirts of town she landed in after her final stay at rehab, where the rooms were gross but the pool was clean. We'd race underwater across its length again and again that last summer, her beating me every time. I didn't know it was her final summer, of course. I thought we'd just go on like this forever.

That Thanksgiving, we ate around Nana's big table with the good china and the crystal goblets. My dad carved the turkey (sides were brought in from the country club), and my mother arrived with Pop Soda, her nonalcoholic drink of choice, and two plastic-wrapped pecan pies from the grocery store. Later, I'd comb over that afternoon again and again. How she had that healthy, post-treatment look, her skin clear, nails polished, not bitten to the quick. She'd been wearing jeans and a white button-down shirt with a lace collar, new white Keds on her feet, which were as small as a child's. And there was the way she kept touching me—smoothing my hair, kissing my temple, pulling me into her lap as I passed by—as if making up for the weeks we'd lost while she was away.

Finally, there was crackling chemistry between my parents, obvious even to a child. My dad, usually a measured, practical person, became lighter around my mother. That Thanksgiving, she'd teased him about his second and then third slice of pie, to which he'd responded by opening his full mouth and sticking out his tongue at her. It was stupid and silly and I loved it. She made him laugh in a way no one else could, bringing out a side of him that I coveted.

It was getting dark when I went down with her in the elevator to meet her ride. It bothered me for a long time that I never remembered this person's name, who picked her up in a nondescript American compact, gray in color. Outside the lobby door, my mom turned to face me, putting her hands on my shoulders. Then she squatted down, her signature black liner and mascara perfectly in place, as always, as she gazed into my eyes, blue like hers. People always said we looked alike.

"Saylor girl," she said, because she always called me Saylor, not Emma. "You know I love you, right?"

I nodded. "I love you too, Mama."

At this she smiled, pulling her thin jacket a bit more tightly around her. It was always windier by our building, the breeze working its way through the high-rises, racing at you. "Once I get more settled, we'll do a sleepover, okay? Movies and popcorn, just you and me."

I nodded again, wishing it was still warm enough to swim. I loved that motel pool.

"Come here," she said, pulling me into her arms, and I buried my face in her neck, breathing in her smell, body wash and hair spray and cold air, all mixed together. She hugged me back tightly, the way she always did, and I let myself relax into her. When she pulled away, she gave me a wink. My mom was a big winker. To this day, when anyone does it, I think of her. "Now go on, I'll make sure you get inside safe."

She stepped back and I took one last look at her, there on the sidewalk in those bright white sneakers. Nana had been in cocktail attire for dinner and insisted my dad wear a tie and me a dress, but my mom always followed her own rules.

"Bye," I called out as I turned, pulling the heavy glass lobby door open and stepping inside.

"Bye, baby," she replied. Then she slid her hands in her jacket pockets, taking a step back, and watched me walk to the elevator and hit the button. She was still there when I got in and raised a hand in a final wave just before the doors shut.

Later, I'd try to imagine what happened after that, from her walking to her friend's car to going back to the motel, where the pool was empty and her little room smelled of meals long ago prepared and eaten by other people. I'd see her on her bed, maybe reading the Big Book that was part of her program, or writing in one of the drugstore spiral notebooks where she was forever scribbling down lists of things to do. Lastly, I'd see her sleeping, curled up under a scratchy blanket as the light outside the door pushed in through the edges of the blinds and trucks roared past on the nearby interstate. I wanted to keep her safe in dreaming, and in my mind, even now, I slip and think of her that way. Like she's forever stayed there, in that beat between nighttime and morning, when it feels like you only dozed off a minute but it's really been hours.

What really happened was that a couple of weeks later, as I was thinking of Christmas and presents and Santa, my mom skipped her nightly meeting and went to a bar with some friends. There, she drank a few beers, met a guy, and went back to his house, where they pooled their money to buy some heroin to keep the party going. She'd overdosed twice before, each one resulting in another rehab stint and a clean start. Not this time.

Some nights when I couldn't sleep, I tried to picture this part of the story, too. I wanted to see her through to the end, especially in those early days, when it didn't seem real or possible she was gone. But the settings were foreign and details unknown, so no matter how I envisioned those last weeks and hours, it was all imagination and conjecture. The last real thing I had was her standing on the sidewalk as I pushed the elevator button, her hand lifted. Goodbye.

THREE

Middle of the night phone calls are never good news. Never.

"Bridget?" I said, sitting up as I put my phone to my ear. "Is everything okay?"

"My grandpa," she managed to get out, her voice breaking. "He had a stroke."

"Oh, my God," I said, reaching to turn on the bedside lamp before remembering that it, like most of my other stuff, had already been packed. It had been a week since the wedding: Nana's flight was midmorning; my dad and Tracy were leaving that afternoon. The next day, the movers would come. All that was left was the bed itself, a couple of boxes, and the suitcase I'd packed to bring to Bridget's the following afternoon. I looked at the clock: it was four a.m. "Is he okay?"

"We don't know yet," she said, and now she was crying, the words lost in heavy breaths and tears. "Mom's taking all of us kids to Ohio to be with him and Grandma. I'm so sorry, Emma."

"It's fine," I said automatically, although now that I was

beginning to wake up, I realized this meant I had nowhere to stay once my dad and Tracy left for Greece. "What can we do for you guys?"

She took a shuddering inhale. "Nothing right now, I don't think. Mom's just in her total crisis mode, packing suitcases, and Dad's on hold with the airline trying to find a flight. The boys are still asleep."

"I can come over," I offered. "Help get the boys up and ready so you guys can pack."

"That's so n-n-ice." She took a breath. "But I think we're okay. I just wanted to let you know, so you can make other plans. Again, I'm really sorry we're bailing on you like this."

"That's the last thing you should be worrying about," I told her. "Just take care of yourself. Okay?"

"Okay." She took another shaky breath. "Thanks, Emma. Love you."

"Love you back," I replied. "Text me an update later?"

"I will."

We hung up, and I put my phone back on the floor, where it glowed another moment before going black. Outside, the sky was still dark, the only sound the central air whirring, stirring up the curtains at my window. The last thing I wanted to do was go down the hall to my dad's room, where he and Tracy would still be fast asleep, and throw this wrench into their honeymoon plans. So I didn't. It could wait until the morning.

* * *

"Well," my dad said, rubbing a hand over his face, "I guess we just reschedule?"

"No," I said immediately. "That's crazy. You guys have had this booked for over a year. You're going."

"And leaving you to stay here alone?" Tracy asked. "Emma. I appreciate what you're trying to do, but—"

"You're seventeen, and this place is about to be full of sawdust and subcontractors," my dad finished for her. "Not happening."

Nana, sitting at the table with a cup of tea, had been quiet for much of this debate. But I could tell she was mulling this. "Surely there must be someone we're not thinking of."

I sighed—I hated that I was the problem—but not before catching my dad rubbing his eyes again under his glasses. It was his tell of tells, the one way I could always be sure he was nervous or stressed. I said, "She's right. There has to be—"

"Who?" my dad interrupted me. "Bridget's leaving, Ryan is at camp, your grandmother is about to be on a cruise ship somewhere—"

"Egypt," I reminded him.

"Actually, Morocco," Nana said, sipping her tea. "Egypt is Thursday."

"Thank you," he said. He rubbed his face again, then snapped his fingers, pointing at Tracy. "What about your sister?"

She shook her head. "Leaving the day after tomorrow to

hike the Appalachian Trail. Remember?"

"Oh, right," he said, his shoulders sinking. "We only talked about it with her at length *three days ago*." As proof, he gestured at the stack of wedding gifts and cards, some opened, some not, that had been piled into some nearby boxes for the movers to take to the new place.

"It was a wedding," I told him. He looked so down I felt like I had to say something. "You talked to a million people."

This he waved off as Tracy, seated at the table, watched him, a cup of coffee balanced in her hands. In front of her, right where she'd left them the night before, were their passports, the boarding passes she'd printed out after checking in online to their flights—"just to be on the safe side," she said—and their itinerary. Doodling at some point since, she'd drawn a row of hearts across the top, right over the word DEPARTURE.

"This is crazy," I said, looking from it back to my dad. "It's your honeymoon. I'm not going to be the reason the dream trip gets canceled."

"No one is blaming you," he said.

"Certainly not," Nana seconded. "Things happen."

"Maybe not *now*," I said. "But just think of the long-term resentment. I mean, I have enough baggage, right?"

I thought this was funny, but my dad just shot me a tired look. He took my anxiety personally, as if he'd broken me or something. Which was nuts, because all he'd ever done was hold me together, even and especially when the rest of my world was falling apart.

"We reschedule," he said firmly. "I'll call the travel agent right now."

"What about Mimi Calvander?" Nana suggested.

Silence. Then Tracy said, "Who?"

Behind me, I could hear the clock over the stove, which I always forgot made noise at all except during moments like this, when it was loud enough to feel deafening. "Mimi?" my dad said finally. "Waverly's mom?"

It was always jarring when my mom's name came up unexpectedly, even when it wasn't early in the morning. Like she belonged both everywhere and nowhere at the same time.

Nana looked at my dad. "Well, she is family. North Lake isn't too far. And Emma's stayed with her before."

"I did?" I asked.

"A long time ago," my dad said. He'd stopped pacing: he was processing this. "When you were four or so. It was during the only trip your mom and I ever took alone. Vegas."

A beat. The clock was still ticking.

"Second honeymoon," he added softly. "It was a disaster, of course."

"Well, it's just an idea," Nana said, taking another measured sip.

"You have to go to Greece," I told my dad. "It's your honeymoon, for God's sake."

"And this is your *grandmother*," he replied, "who you haven't seen in years."

"I do know her, though," I said quickly. He looked at me,

25

doubtful. "I mean, not well. But I remember her. Vaguely."

"Okay, stop," my dad said. He rubbed his face again. "*Everyone* stop. Just let me think."

It was one of those moments when you can just see the future forking, like that road in the yellow wood, right before your eyes. I knew my dad. He'd give up Greece for me. After all he'd already sacrificed, a whole country was nothing at all. Which was why I spoke up, saying, "Mimi, at the lake. With the moss on the trees. There's porch swings on the dock. And an arcade down the street you can walk to. And the water is cold and clear."

He looked at me, sighing. "Emma. You were four."

"Mom talked about it," I told him. "All the time."

This, he couldn't dispute. Every now and then, he got to hear the bedtime stories, too. "You don't understand," he said. "Your mother's family is . . ."

He trailed off, all of us waiting for a word that never came.

"And the high tourist season is just getting started," he continued. "Which means Mimi is probably too busy to take on anything else."

"I don't know about that," Nana said. "It's been so long, I bet she'd love to see Emma."

"*Sometime*," my dad said. "Not today, this second."

"But we don't know that for sure," I told him. "If she's really anything like Mom, she's not much of a planner."

He looked at me again. "North Lake, Emma . . . it's . . .

different. They're different. It's not like here."

"I wouldn't be moving there," I told him. "It's three weeks."

More silence. More ticking. "You really want me to do this?"

What I wanted was for him to go to Greece and sail that boat across the water there, with Tracy beside him. So I knew what to say.

"Yes," I said as Nana caught my eye. "Call her."

All my life I'd thought my mom grew up so far away. But after an hour and a half, we were there.

"Anything look familiar?" my dad asked.

"Every single bit!" I said, my voice bright. "Especially this part right here, the exit ramp."

He shot me a look I knew had to be sharp, not that I could tell from behind his dark sunglasses. "Hey. Don't be a smartass. I was just asking a question."

Actually, what he wanted was reassurance that this would not turn out to be the worst idea in the history of ideas. But the truth was that it was all new to me, and I'd always been a bad liar.

"Wait a second," I said now as we approached a single red light, blinking, and came to a stop. "There are two lakes?"

He peered at the sign across from us, then smiled. "No," he said. "Only one."

It didn't make sense, though. If that was the case, why

was there an arrow pointing to the right that said NORTH LAKE (5 MILES) and another to the left indicating the way to LAKE NORTH (8 MILES). "I don't get it."

"What we have here, actually," he replied, "is one of the great idiosyncrasies of this area."

"Second only to you using the word *idiosyncrasies* while sitting at an exit ramp?"

He ignored me. "See, when this place was first settled, it was pretty rural. Working-class people both lived here year-round and came to vacation in the summers. But then, in the eighties, a billionaire from New York discovered it. He decided to build an upscale resort and bought up one whole side of the lakefront to do just that."

We were still sitting there at the light, but no one was behind us or coming from either direction. So he continued.

"They had a big grand opening for the first summer . . . and nobody came. As it turned out, the rich folks didn't want to spend big money to stay at North Lake, because it was so solidly known as a blue-collar vacation spot." He put on his blinker. "By the second summer, though, the developer figured this out, and incorporated his area as Lake North."

"Which was the same place."

"But it *sounded* like a different one," he said. "So the rich folks came and bought houses and joined the country club. And from then on, there were two towns. And one lake, that sounded like two, between them."

Still not a single car had passed or come up behind us at the light. Despite different economies, neither town seemed to have much going on, at least at the current moment. "Let me guess," I said. "When you came here with Nana in high school, you went left here, to Lake North."

"Smart girl," he replied. Then he put on his blinker, and we turned to the right.

It was a short trip. Four stoplights, to be exact, and then another turn onto a two-lane road, past a big sign with blue faded letters that said WELCOME TO NORTH LAKE: YOUR FAVORITE VACATION. Just past it, the motels began.

I lost count after six different establishments, each very similar in appearance. They were all one-story concrete buildings with grass driveways and parking lots, cars in diagonal spots lining the room doors. Most had an office, identified by a hand-lettered sign or an occasional one in neon proclaiming it as such, and many featured flower and rock gardens with yard art out in front. They had names like NORTH LAKE MOTOR INN and LIPSCOMB COURT and THE JACARANDA. Mixed in here and there were trailer parks, but not the kind with big double-wides. Instead, these were the small type you attached to a car and towed, some silver and stainless, others white or painted bright colors. There was so much to see, and all of it new, that even though we were going slowly, I couldn't process much but a glimpse at a time before the scenery turned to something else.

In fact, I was looking ahead at two mini-golf courses that

faced each other from opposite sides of the street—could an economy so small sustain this, I wondered?—when my dad slowed, turning into a drive on our right. It was another hotel, this one a single story of yellow painted concrete and bright blue doors, with a big scripted sign that said only CALVANDER'S. NO VACANCIES.

We pulled in, parking outside the office. As we climbed out of the car, I got my first glimpse of the water, blue and wide. Jutting out into it were a series of long wooden docks. On the one closest to us there were two porch swings hanging by chains, and in the quiet that followed the engine cutting off, I could distantly hear them clanking.

That was the first time I felt it, that twinge of recognition as something from my long-lost past reached out from my subconscious. Splinters, I thought as I looked at the docks again. But as quickly as the memory came, it was gone.

"Matthew? Is that you?"

A woman in shorts and a faded tie-dye T-shirt had come out of the office, the door in the process of shutting slowly behind her. She had white hair cut short, spiking up a bit at the top, and she was small in stature, but formidable in the way she carried herself, like she owned the place. Which, as it turned out, she did.

"Mimi," my dad said, breaking into a wide smile. "How are you?"

"Better than a woman my age has any right to be," she told him. As they embraced, I saw she really was very small, with tiny feet, like my mom's. "You haven't changed one bit. How is that?"

"Look who's talking," my dad said, stepping back to look at her and taking her hands. "You Calvanders, I swear. You don't age."

"Tell that to my hips and my knees." Then she gave me a wink. "And this can't be Saylor. Can it?"

I suddenly felt shy, and concealed myself a bit more behind the car.

"Emma," my dad said, correcting my name kindly but clearly, "just turned seventeen. She'll be a senior this year."

"Unbelievable," Mimi said. She looked at me for a minute. "Well, girl, come give your grandma a hug. Lord knows I've missed a few."

I went, still feeling self-conscious as I approached her. As soon as I was close enough, she pulled me into her arms, her grasp surprisingly strong. I returned the hug, a bit less enthusiastically, while towering over her despite the fact that I am hardly a tall person.

After a moment, she released me, then stepped back to study my face, giving me a chance to look at her as well. Up close, I could see the effect of years of the dark tan she'd clearly cultivated in the leathery skin of her neck and face, as well as a penchant for gold braid jewelry (necklace, bracelet, knot earrings) that almost glowed against it. Most noteworthy, though, were her eyes, which were bright blue. Like mine, and my mom's.

"I'm so glad you came, Saylor," she told me, now squeezing both my arms. "It's about time."

"Emma and I," my dad said, trying again, "are both really grateful you agreed to let her come visit. We know it's literally last-minute."

"Nonsense," Mimi said. She winked at me again. "You're family. And you're not just coming. You're coming back."

A car drove by then, the first one other than our own we'd seen in ages. Actually, it was a truck, bright green, and when the driver beeped the horn as they passed, Mimi waved, not taking her eyes off me.

"Dad says I was here before, but I don't really remember," I told her, because it seemed like I should start at an honest place, considering. "When I was five?"

"Four," she replied.

"I guess I'll just have to take your word for it."

"I'm good as my word, so I'd welcome that." Then she turned back to the office door, pulling it open. "But just in case, come inside a second. I want to show you something."

As I followed her, stepping over the threshold, the temperature dropped about twenty degrees, thanks to the window A/C unit blasting cold air from across the room. I felt like my teeth would start chattering within seconds and saw my dad wrap his arms around himself, but Mimi was unfazed as she walked to the wooden counter, which was covered with a sheet of glass.

"We're almost out of room here, after so many summers,"

she said, leaning over it. "I'm thinking I may have to expand onto a bulletin board or something soon. Not that anybody prints pictures anymore, though, with all this digital this and USB that. Anyway, let me see . . . I used to know right where it was. . . ."

I stepped up beside her. Under the glass, I saw, were what had to be hundreds of pictures, from old black and whites to dingy Polaroids to, finally, color snapshots. Across them all, as the faces and clothing changed, the scenery and backgrounds remained the same. There was the water, of course, and those long docks, the swings beneath them. The rock garden under the Calvander's sign. And those yellow cinder blocks, broken up by blue doors. So many faces over so many years, both big group shots clearly taken for posterity and candids of people alone or in pairs. I leaned in closer, looking for my mom, the one face I might be able to pick out. But when Mimi found the snapshot she was looking for, tapping it with a long fingernail, all the people in it were strangers. Small ones.

"Now," she said, gesturing for me to come closer, "this was the Fourth of July, I believe. Let's see . . . there's Trinity, on the far left, she would have been, what, nine? And next to her is Bailey, she'd be four then also, and Roo and Jacky, who despite the age difference might as well have been twins . . ."

I wanted to be polite, but was so cold I was losing feeling in my extremities.

". . . and then there's you." She looked at me, then back at the picture. "Oh, I remember that cute bathing suit! You always did love giraffes. See?"

Me? I bent over the counter. Five little kids—three girls of varying ages and sizes, and two little towheaded boys—sat lined up on a wooden bench, the lake behind them. All held sparklers, although only a couple seemed to still be lit when the shutter clicked. The girl on the far left had on a bikini, her rounded, soft belly protruding; the younger one beside her, long blond hair and a one-piece with a tie-dye print. Then, the two boys, both in bathing suits, shirtless and white-blond, one of them squinting, as if the camera were the brightest of lights. And finally, me, in a brown suit with a green giraffe and the pigtails and home-cut bangs I recognized from other shots of the same period. I was the only one who was smiling.

It was the weirdest feeling, so foreign and familiar all at once, seeing my own face in a place I didn't recall. I knew the timeline, though. My parents' marriage was crumbling due to my mom's drinking and drug use, and by the coming winter, she would be in rehab and we'd move in with Nana. But sometime before all that, lost to my memory, was this trip. I'd clearly known these people well enough to be this comfortable and yet I'd still forgotten them.

"How long did I stay?" I asked Mimi.

"Two weeks, if I remember correctly," she replied. "It was supposed to be one, but your mama got sick and plans changed."

Sick, I thought, and only then did I remember my dad. I'd assumed he was listening to this. But he was standing facing the big glass window, looking out at the road, and appeared to be lost in thought.

"Where are all these people now?" I asked Mimi, who was rubbing the glass counter with the edge of her T-shirt, taking out some thumbprints on a low corner.

"Oh, they're around," she said. "You'll see most of them, I'm sure, depending how long you're here."

"Three weeks at most," my dad said now, having at some point tuned back to us. He sounded apologetic. "No change of plans this time, I promise."

"You know I wouldn't mind it," Mimi said. "She can stay as long as she likes."

There was a creak behind us: the door opening again. With it came a rush of warm, humid air, and an older man in khaki shorts and a golf shirt, a newspaper under his arm, walked in.

"There's never been peace in that house in the morning, you'd think I'd—" He stopped talking when he saw me, then my dad, standing there. "Oh, sorry. Didn't realize we had guests checking in."

"They're not," Mimi said. "This is my granddaughter Saylor, Waverly's girl. And Matthew, remember, I told you about him?"

The man smiled politely, sticking out a hand to my dad. "I'm sure you did. I'm Oxford."

"My husband," Mimi explained. When my dad looked at her, surprised, she said, "Joe died back in two thousand fifteen."

"I'm sorry," my dad said automatically. He looked shocked, and I realized again how strange it was he'd lost touch with her entirely. "God, Mimi. I had no idea."

She waved her hand, batting his apology away. "Life gets busy when you're raising kids. He had cancer and went quick, honey. And he went here, looking out at the lake, which is just what he wanted."

We all stood there, taking a moment of silence for this person, whoever he was. Then Mimi looked at me. "Let's get you over and settled, okay? Then we can send your dad on his way."

I nodded, and she led us back outside. Oxford stayed behind, settling in an easy chair by the window with a sigh I could hear as he opened his paper.

"I can't get over how much it looks the same," my dad said as I went to the trunk to retrieve my suitcase and the small duffel I'd originally packed for Bridget's. "But the dock's new, or part of it, right?"

"Two years ago," Mimi said, shading her eyes with one hand. "Hurricane Richard came through here and left nothing there but a pile of sticks. I cried when I saw it."

"Really?" he asked. He looked at the dock again. "I figured this place was indestructible."

"I wish," she sighed. "A storm can change everything."

"But you had insurance?"

"Thank goodness," she said. "Joe always was one to prepare for the worst. So yes, we rebuilt. Luckily, the house and motel stood strong, although we lost a few trees and had flooding in some of the units. Nothing new carpet couldn't fix, though."

She started down the sidewalk that ran along the motel, and we fell in behind, first my dad, then me. There were seven units by my count, each with two plastic chairs parked outside, most of which were being used as drying racks for bathing suits or brightly colored towels. Every one had a window A/C unit going full strength as well.

A cleaning cart sat outside the last room, piled with folded towels, rolls of toilet paper, and little paper-wrapped soaps. I glanced inside: a dark-haired girl in shorts, quite pregnant, was wiping down a mirror. She glanced over as we passed before going back to what she was doing.

"We're filled up this week, which is great for so early in the season," Mimi was saying as we left the sidewalk and began across the grass to a nearby gray house with white trim. "The economy rules all, as Joe used to say, but most of our yearly bookings hung in even when everything went bust."

"A lot of these motels and houses are rented by the same people for the same week, every single year," my dad explained to me. "The reservations are handed down literally in wills, so they stay in the family. A lot of people have been coming here for generations."

"And thank goodness for that," Mimi added, starting up the front steps of the house, which had a wide porch, a couple of rocking chairs facing the water. "Joe used to say that it doesn't matter what you do, everyone needs a vacation. In this business, we just happen to count on it."

My dad followed her, taking the screen door she'd pulled open and holding it for me as she went inside. Once in the foyer, though, a cluttered living room to my right, I found myself stopping short. I was steps onto a shiny wooden floor that stretched down a long hallway before opening up to a wide room full of windows. Beyond them, there was only lake, the sun glittering off it.

"Emma?" my dad asked. "You okay?"

"Yeah," I said. I wasn't sure how to explain to him, or if I even could, how I knew that this floor would tilt up slightly as I walked across it, or that the room at the end of the hall was the kitchen, even though I could see nothing of it from where I stood. Outside, this house had felt new and unknown. But standing here now, I would have bet my life I'd walked down this same stretch many times before.

"Now, I've put you in the little bedroom, if that's okay," Mimi said over her shoulder as I finally moved forward, down the hallway to come into, yes, the kitchen. A big wooden table sat against the wall of windows facing the lake and everything smelled like toast. Also, the sink was stacked full of dirty dishes. Of course I noticed. "It's the only one free and I knew you'd want your privacy. The sheets are all clean and there's towels on the bed if you want to freshen up."

"Thanks," I said. "Is it . . ."

I trailed off as my dad climbed a nearby flight of stairs, carrying my suitcase with him, then went left on the landing. Clearly, he needed no directions.

"Right up there," Mimi said to me. "You'll find it."

I thanked her, then went up the stairs myself, the middle one creaking audibly beneath me. At the top, the carpet was beige and well worn, and I could see there were three bedrooms to the left, a bathroom to the right. Only the door on the end was open, so I headed that way.

"You know your way around this place," I said to my dad when I found him in a small bedroom with a single bed, a closet, and one window facing the lake.

"Spent some time here," he replied, his voice low. I'd been so focused on my own memories, I hadn't given much thought to what he'd been feeling. But it was definitely kicking up something. He'd put my suitcase in the closet, my duffel on the bed next to two stacked towels and a washcloth. They were white with a little pink rosebud pattern, and seeing them, I felt it again, that familiarity. "This was your mom's room, way back when."

"Really?" I walked around the end of the bed to look out the window. The roof below it slanted down at an angle, ending in what looked like a porch overhang. "She used to tell me stories about this."

"This room?"

"And this view." It was gorgeous, the pane of glass capturing the lake in a perfect frame. Straight out ahead I could see a floating platform, a motorboat tethered to it. To the right, there were the motels we'd passed, as well as more docks in front of small beaches where moss hung from the trees. And far to the left, what looked like a whole other town of large houses, hotels, and other newer construction. "And the boats. She talked about those, too."

"Yes, I'm actually glad you brought that up while we were, um, alone." He sat down on the bed. "I'd like a word with you about that."

"About what?" I asked.

He nodded at the window, where another boat had now appeared, zooming past. "Boating. One of the great pastimes of North Lake. Which I enjoyed about as much as you do sailing."

"Isn't it the same thing?"

"No," he said. "Sailing is about wind. With motorboats, it's speed, which means it can be very dangerous, even if the driver of the boat hasn't been drinking. And here, they often are."

"You know I won't drink, Dad," I said.

"Yes," he replied, "but I still want to say this. I don't want you to ever go out on the water with someone who has been drinking or plans to."

"Is this like a drug talk, but aquatic?"

"Emma." That tone was like a yellow light, just before red: a warning. "Just promise me, please. It's important."

I looked out the window again. The boat had circled around and was now going back the other way. "I'll be careful. I swear."

"Okay." He sat back, resting his palms on the nubby bedspread. "And you know, now that I think about it, this would be a great place to work on your driving. I'm sure Mimi has a car you could borrow."

"Dad," I said in *my* warning voice, "I'd rather talk about boats."

"I know, I know." He sighed. "And I'm trying to be understanding. But this is your driver's license! When I was your age, I was counting the days until I could get on the road—"

"Because it represented freedom, and independence, all things already available to me via public transportation and ride apps," I finished for him. "I don't need to drive. It's just not necessary."

"But don't you *want* to?" he asked.

"Frankly, no," I said. "I like walking."

"When we move, you won't be able to walk everywhere, like you do now."

"So I'll take the bus or use GetThere."

He sighed again. I felt like I understood my dad pretty well, a by-product of it just being us two for so long. But I didn't get why, ever since I'd turned fifteen, it was *so* freaking important to him that I get my license. He'd relentlessly pushed me to take driver's ed and get my permit, then made a big deal of me getting my provisional license, followed by my full one six months later. I stuck it in my wallet, intending to forget about it, but then he was always wanting us to go out driving together, when he'd spent the entire time I was behind the wheel gripping what Bridget's dad called the "oh shit" handle over his window and pounding an imaginary brake. The whole thing just amplified my anxiety, even before I'd backed into a neighbor's SUV in our underground parking deck, which had scared me so badly I'd burst into tears.

"Dad," I said now. "Maybe I'm just not meant to be a driver. Not everyone is. Think of the accident rate."

"Driving changed my life, though," he said. "Do you know I bought my first car, a used red Audi—"

"A4 with a sunroof and leather seats," I filled in for him. This story was as familiar as one of my mom's.

"—right before I came to Lake North to work my first summer?" He sighed once more, this time happily. "Stocked shelves at AllDrug nights and weekends my entire senior year to save up for it, and drove it off the lot and straight here to my job at the Club. Or, you know, there." He nodded at the left side of the window, and the lake. "I just don't want you to miss that feeling. That you can go anywhere. It opens up the world."

I rolled my eyes. "Dad, I'm about to spend three weeks in a place that for all intents and purposes I've never been to before. Gotta say, the world seems pretty wide right now."

"Yes," he said, "but with your license you'd be free to see even more of it. Like Lake North, for example."

"Where I'd probably back Mimi's car into another, more expensive SUV. Is that what you really want?"

This was a good point. I'd hit a Range Rover in that fender bender: it hadn't been cheap. "Okay, fine. But once I'm back, we discuss. Deal?"

"Deal."

That resolved, he got to his feet, coming over to join me where I was standing by the window. "So, look," he said, putting a hand on my shoulder. "Be honest: You okay with this arrangement? It's not too late to change your mind."

"I'm fine," I said, although now that his time left here was dwindling, I was feeling a slow simmer of anxiety I could only hope wouldn't reach full boil. Did I want to change my mind?

The panic, now hitting medium high, said yes. But I had learned, over time and with various therapists we'd consulted, that it did not get to speak for me. I could do this. And I would, for my dad and Tracy first and foremost, but also, in some small way, for my mom. I worried so much about forgetting her as the years passed. Maybe spending a month in the place she came from would help me remember.

We walked downstairs, back into the kitchen, which was now empty. Peering down the hallway, I could see Mimi outside, talking to the pregnant girl out by the cleaning cart over at the motel. As they conferred, a car zoomed past on the road, beeped, and she waved her hand.

"Still the same table," my dad marveled as we passed the big wooden one against the windows. I, of course, could only see all those dirty dishes, still untouched. "But that toaster's new."

"Toaster?"

He gestured at the corner of one counter, by the sink.

Sure enough, sitting there was a huge shiny silver toaster, the kind with multiple bread slots and various dials for settings. "In a place like this, you notice change," he said to me, starting down the hallway. Appliances, too, I thought, before following behind him.

"Leaving already, Matthew?" Mimi asked when we got back outside. "You just got here!"

"He has a plane to catch," I told her. "The honeymoon awaits."

She stepped forward, giving him a hug. "Have a wonderful time. And don't worry a thing about this girl, she'll be fine."

She said this so confidently, as if she knew me, as well as the future. The weird part was how much I wanted to believe she was right.

"Thanks, Mimi," he replied. "For everything."

She smiled at him, then gave me a wink before turning and pulling open the office door. I felt a blast of cold air before it closed behind her.

"Still feel weird about this," he said when it was just us again. "It's not the way I planned to be leaving you."

"I'll be fine," I told him. "Go. Sail. Honey that moon. I'll see you in three weeks."

He laughed. "Honey that moon?"

"Just go, would you?"

Finally, he got in the car and started the engine, backing out slowly as I stood there. I made a point to wave at him, smiling, as he pulled onto the main road. Then I turned around to face the house and the lake, taking a deep breath.

As I started walking, the pregnant girl was still outside the last unit, now sitting in one of the plastic chairs, looking at her phone. She didn't say anything, but I could feel her watching me, so I picked up my pace crossing the grass, as if I had a solid plan. No matter where you are, home or the strangest of places, everyone wants to look like they know where they're going.

FOUR

"Well, shit."

I opened my eyes at the sound of voices, the first I'd heard since crawling into my bed after my dad left and falling asleep. It had still been morning then: now the clock on the bureau, analog with tiny numbers, said 3:30. Whoops.

"Why is there no bread in this house?" a woman was saying in the kitchen, the question accompanied by the banging of cabinets. "I just brought a loaf over here two days ago."

"I'm not hungry," a voice that sounded like a child said. "I told you that."

"You'll eat something if I make it." Footsteps, then a door—the screen one downstairs, I was pretty sure—slamming. "Mama! What happened to all my bread?"

"Your what?" That was Mimi.

"My bread! I'm trying to make Gordon a sandwich."

"Honey, I don't know. If there's bread, it's in the regular place."

"But that's not my bread, that I bought with my money, for *my* family to eat," her daughter replied.

"I'm not hungry!" came again from downstairs.

"I'll remind you that we are all your family," Mimi hollered, "and if you want to get picky about it, then you can stop drinking all my Pop Soda and not replacing it."

Silence. But the heavy kind. Meanwhile, I thought of my mom, who was the only person I'd ever known who had heard of Pop Soda, much less drank it. It was like a generic Diet Coke, heavy on the syrup. It had been years since I'd had one, but I could still remember how it made my teeth hurt.

"Mama, all I am asking is where is the bread," the woman said, sounding tired. "If you have some other issue with me, let's get into it, by all means, the day hasn't yet been long enough."

Mimi responded, although at this point they were apparently close enough not to be yelling, so I couldn't hear it. But I was up now, so I grabbed my toothbrush and navigated the way to the tiny bathroom at the end of the hall. Once rid of nap breath, I finger combed my hair, took a deep breath, and went downstairs.

At first the kitchen looked completely empty. Only when I'd started to the cabinets for some water—again noting all those dirty dishes, how could you just leave them like that?—did I notice a little girl standing just inside the opening to the hallway. Until she reached up, adjusting the glasses on her face, she'd been so still I'd assumed she was part of the wall.

"Oh," I said, startled. "Hi."

She studied me, her face serious. While her appearance—dark hair in a ponytail, denim shorts and thick plastic clogs, a purple T-shirt that said #AWESOME—was young, the expression on her face reflected the world-weariness usually seen in a much older woman. "Hello," she replied.

I glanced down the hallway, to the screen door. "Are you looking for Mimi?"

"No," she said. "Are you?"

"No," I replied. "I was actually trying to find a glass for some water."

Another beat as she studied me. Then she turned, crossing into the kitchen and standing on tiptoe to open an upper cabinet. She pulled out a plastic tumbler with a gas station logo on it, holding it out in my direction. "If you want ice, it's in the bucket in the freezer."

"I'm good," I said, taking the glass. "Thank you, um . . ."

"Gordon," she said.

"Gordon," I repeated. "I'm Emma."

She nodded, as if this was acceptable. Then she watched as I went to the sink, filled my glass, and took a sip. "My real first name is Anna," she said after a moment. "But nobody with two names ever uses the first one."

"I do," I said.

This seemed to intrigue her. "Really?"

I nodded. "I'm Emma Saylor, technically."

"And you get to be just Emma?"

"Well, yeah."

She looked wistful for a second. "Lucky."

The door banged again, and I heard footsteps approaching. A moment later, a woman in jeans and a polyester uniform top that said CONROY MARKET entered the kitchen. She had long blond hair pulled back in a headband and wore tall wedge sandals of the sort Nana would call ankle breakers.

"Well, it looks like you're having a quesadilla, Gordon, despite the fact I just bought—"

She stopped talking when she saw me, her blue eyes, lashes thick with mascara, widening. I put my glass down on the counter, thinking I'd overstepped by helping myself.

"Oh, my God," she said softly, putting a hand to her chest. "You look just like . . . Waverly?"

Her voice broke on the word, and I saw now she was pale, like she literally had seen a ghost. "No," I said quickly. "I'm Emma. Her daughter."

"Emma?" she repeated.

"Saylor," Gordon offered. "That's her other name."

The woman moved her hand to her mouth, still staring at me. "I'm sorry," she managed finally. "I just . . . I just didn't expect you here."

"It was kind of last-minute," I told her. "My dad was leaving the country and I didn't have any other place—"

Before I could finish, she had crossed the short distance between us and was pulling me into probably the tightest hug I had ever experienced. It felt like she was squeezing the breath right out of me.

"Oh, my God," she said again. Over her shoulder, Gordon

observed our embrace, chewing a thumbnail. "You're her spitting image—I saw you there and it was like she was back for a second."

"I'm sorry," I said.

Now, finally, she pulled away, and I saw tears in her eyes. They were so blue, like Mimi's. Like my mom's. And mine. "Do you even remember me?"

I paused, not wanting to hurt her feelings. "I—"

"Celeste," she told me, putting her hand back on her chest. "I'm your aunt. Do you remember? And Gordon there, she's your cousin."

"Oh," I said, glancing at Gordon again, then back to her. "Right. Hi."

Celeste blinked, a tear running down her face. "Oh, God, you must think I'm a total psycho, look at me."

"You're fine," I said as she reached over to a roll of paper towels and ripped one off, dabbing at her eyes. "I'm sorry you weren't warned."

"Well, that's Mama for you," she said. She blew her nose with a honk. "We've only talked on the phone three times today already. Are you hungry? I was just about to make Gordon something."

"Oh," I told her, "you don't have to do that. I can just—"

"Sit," Celeste said, gesturing to the table. She handed me my water. "Now, let me find those tortillas . . ."

I went to a chair, doing as I was told as she opened the fridge and began taking things out. A moment later, Gordon joined me, bringing a thick paperback book along with her.

"What are you reading?" I asked.

"Oh, Lord," Celeste groaned. "Don't get her started about those damn gorillas."

"They are *chimpanzees*," Gordon said. From the annoyance in her voice, it was clear this was a common exchange.

"Can I see?" I asked, nodding at the book. She pushed it toward me and I flipped it over. *The Allies, Gathering Two: Justice Begins*, it said in thick raised print on the cover. The illustration was of, yes, a chimpanzee, but with very human features, staring into a red-and-yellow-streaked setting sun. "Oh, the Allies series. I remember these. There are, like, a million of them."

"Twenty in the first gathering, fourteen so far in the second," Gordon replied. "And that's not counting all the extra editions and compilations, plus the manga and graphic novels."

"It's like she's speaking another language," Celeste added from the stove, where she was now heating up a frying pan. "I gave up trying to follow years ago."

Gordon, unfazed, flipped the book back over and opened it to a bent-down page, then started to read. After a moment, she reached up, twirling a piece of hair around one finger.

"She's gone," Celeste told me, tossing a tortilla into the frying pan. "Gets lost when she reads. Thank God for it. I give her a hard time, but I was never good in school. She is."

"What grade is she in?"

"Starting fifth in the fall. She's in accelerated reading

and math," she replied, sounding proud. "Clearly not my child, but I will take some of the credit."

"Oh," I said. "I thought she was—"

Celeste looked over her shoulder at me. "What? Oh, no. Her mama's your cousin Amber, from my daddy's side. She lives in Florida right now."

Amber, I thought. The name was familiar, but only faintly so. "Was my mom close with her?"

"Thick as thieves," she replied, pushing the tortilla with a spatula. "But we all were, back then. Growing up here, family was everything. It had to be. We only ever had each other."

It occurred to me that at some point I would need to draw up a family tree to really understand my place in all this. But as long as I had Celeste here, it was worth getting started.

"So you have . . . how many kids?" I asked her.

"Three," she said, flipping the finished quesadilla onto a nearby plate and starting another one. "There's Trinity, who you may have seen earlier, she's pregnant right now. . . ."

I thought of the girl with the cleaning cart, eyeballing me as I passed. We were first cousins? So much for family being all you had. She'd acted like she hated me. "She works at the motel, right?"

"Yes," Celeste allowed with a sigh, "but only in the broadest definition of the word. Mostly she's on her phone complaining about how her feet hurt while Mama does both their jobs because she's a damn softie."

"Right," I said.

"Then there's my son, Jack, he's three years older than you," she continued, shaking the frying pan over the burner, "and finally Bailey, who is your age."

"She's seventeen?"

"Both your birthdays are in April. Your mama and I were pregnant at the same time, our due dates just weeks apart. We spent a lot of time on the phone complaining to each other, now that I think about it. I probably shouldn't be so hard on Trinity."

She finished up the second quesadilla, then brought both plates over to the table.

"Thank you," I said as she put one in front of me.

"You're very welcome," she replied. "Silverware and napkins are—"

Before she finished saying this, I was reaching like it was a reflex to the rattan basket across from me, pulling it closer to retrieve a fork, knife, and napkin. Huh.

"Well, never mind," she said with another smile. "Gordon. Put the book away and eat."

"I can eat and read," Gordon replied, picking up her quesadilla and taking a bite, her eyes still on the page.

Celeste rolled her eyes and went to the fridge, retrieving a can of Pop Soda. Then she sat down, opening the can before kicking off her shoes, first one, then the other. "What a day. It's only early season and I'm already exhausted."

"You work at a market?" I asked.

She looked surprised I knew this, then glanced down at

her uniform top. "I forgot I had this thing on! Usually take it off the second I get in the car. Yes, Conroy Market. Only grocery store in North Lake. I'm an assistant manager."

I took a big bite of the quesadilla: I hadn't realized how hungry I was until I'd begun eating. "This is really good," I told Celeste.

"You want another one?" She started to get to her feet. "It'll only take a second."

"Oh, no," I said quickly. "I'm fine. Thank you, though."

While I ate, I could tell she was trying not to stare at me, my presence still so surprising. Finally she got to her feet, taking my now-empty plate and Gordon's. "I can do those," I said as she started to run water into the sink, crammed with all those dishes.

"Oh, no," she said. "You're a guest."

"I want to," I said, wanting to add that it had been driving me crazy all day. "You cooked, I clean. That's the rule in our house. Please?"

Celeste looked at me for a second. "Okay," she said finally. "But know this: you start washing dishes in this house, you'll never stop."

In response, I stood up and walked over to the sink, pulling the faucet aside and turning it all the way hot before beginning to sort everything into categories. I knew I probably looked like the weirdo cousin, but as I added soap to the water, finding a scrub brush in the nearby dish rack, I felt more in control than I had since that call in the dark from Bridget twelve hours earlier. I was in a strange place, feeling strange even to myself, but this task was one I knew well, and I took comfort in it. So much so that when I finished, I turned to see both Celeste and Gordon had gone, leaving the Allies book and the lake as my only company.

I always did a lot of good thinking while washing dishes, and Mimi's sink had been slam full. By the time I was done, I'd decided to look at my time here at North Lake as a kind of organizing. So back up in my room, once I unpacked my suitcase and put my clothes away, I pulled out the one note-book I'd brought with me. MIMI + JOE, I wrote at the top of a blank page, with CELESTE and WAVERLY each under a vertical line beneath. From those, I drew more lines, add-ing in my dad beside my mom's name, and mine underneath it. Then I did the same with Trinity, Jack, and Bailey under Celeste's, realizing as I did so I had no idea who her husband was. I'd be here three weeks, though. I had a feeling I could fill in the gaps.

Just then there was a whirring sound from outside, dis-tant, and I turned to see a motorboat puttering from the shore to the floating platform I'd seen earlier. Then I saw another from the corner of my eye, followed by one more, all of them converging to the same spot from varying direc-tions. The first pulled up alongside, and a dark-haired girl in a yellow bikini top and shorts jumped out, her phone to one ear. As the others docked as well, more people joined her. Within moments, between the boats and those who had arrived on them, you couldn't see the raft at all.

Downstairs, the screen door slammed—this sound was

becoming familiar—and I heard someone come into the kitchen, then start up the stairs.

". . . told you, I was at work and couldn't answer," a guy, maybe my age by the sound of it, was saying. "Taylor. Don't start. Seriously."

The bathroom door closed, and I heard water running, along with more of this conversation, now muffled. As the screen door slammed again, I thought how much this place would have driven Nana crazy: she treated her house like it was fragile, with doors and drawers eased shut, gently. You slammed, you scrammed. That was a direct quote from my dad.

"Jacky?" Mimi yelled from the kitchen. "You here?"

"One sec," the guy yelled back from the bathroom.

"Jacky? Hello?"

"ONE SEC," he replied, louder. This time, she didn't say anything, but a moment later I heard the fridge opening. I looked back at my family tree, full of gaps, and went downstairs.

"There you are," Mimi said when she saw me. Still in her tie-dye, she'd ditched her sandals and put on fuzzy slippers in their place. A can of Pop Soda was in her hand. "I wondered where you got off to."

"I fell asleep after Dad left," I told her. "And then saw Celeste and Gordon."

"Oh, good," she said, turning back to the fridge. "You want a soda?"

"No, thanks," I said. As the kid of a dentist, they'd been

56

so forbidden in my early life that when I finally could have them, I'd lost interest.

"Oxford's holding down the office until dinner, so I was just getting ready to watch my shows," she said, grabbing a bag of potato chips from the top of the fridge. "Want to join me?"

Upstairs, Jacky—Jack?—was talking again. "Sure."

She started down the hallway, to the living room we'd passed on the way in. The walls were lined with long couches—one leather, one dark blue corduroy—and there was a huge TV set, surrounded by shelves of family pictures. Off the back side of the room was the screened-in porch I'd seen earlier from outside, separated by a door with a glass pane that had been covered with a tacked-up towel. The result was a dimness that would have made the room feel cold even if the A/C hadn't been going full blast, which of course, it was.

"Does it feel hot in here to you?" Mimi asked as I thought this. I was about to say no, and try not to do it vehemently, but then she was over at the A/C unit, adjusting it from 67 to 65. "That's better. I hate a warm house. Have a seat."

She was already doing just that, lowering herself onto the leather couch and putting her soda into the built-in cup holder on its arm. Even though the couch was huge, I didn't want to crowd her, so I moved to the blue one.

"Now, let's see," Mimi said, pulling up a list of recorded programs. "What are we in the mood for?"

As I looked at the screen, scanning the titles, it was clear there was only one answer to this question: home improvement. Everything listed—*Fix and Flip*, *Contractor: You!*, *From Demo to Dream House*—shared this same subject. I said, "I take it you like renovation shows."

"They're my therapy," she replied, scrolling through the titles before picking an episode of something called *3 Flip Sisters*. "Have a hard day with everything breaking down all around you, then come and watch somebody else fix something up nice. I can't get enough."

She sighed contentedly, taking a sip of her soda as the show began. "One family," intoned the announcer as the screen showed a trio of blond women, all with long hair, wearing matching plaid shirts, "three opinions, one firm deadline. This is *3 Flip Sisters*."

Just then my phone beeped in my pocket, the first noise it had made since my dad texted from the airport an hour earlier to say he and Tracy were boarding their plane. This time, it was Ryan. She'd been incommunicado since arriving at Windmill a couple of days after the wedding.

Testing testing. Anyone out there?

I smiled, quickly typing a response. **Your phone works? I thought you were in the middle of nowhere.**

I am, she replied after a moment. **But if I climb this hill and stand on one foot, I have a signal. For now anyway. What are you and Bridget doing?**

I filled her in, as succinctly as I could, while the TV showed a montage of the sisters and Bill and Shelley looking at various properties. By the time I hit send, they'd settled on a ranch house with hideous green linoleum floor in the kitchen that Angie, the sister Realtor, said was priced to sell.

"They'll end up putting an arch in there someplace, mark my words," Mimi said as the TV cut to a commercial. "Paula loves an arch."

My phone beeped. **Holy crap. Is Bridget's grandpa okay?**

Haven't heard from her since she left, I wrote back. **So not sure.**

Are you okay? What's it like there? I've never even heard you mention having another grandmother.

Even though Mimi was on the other couch, a fair distance away, I tilted the screen to be sure she couldn't see it. The desire not to hurt her was that strong, even as I knew that I, too, could have claimed injured feelings, considering. Where had she been all this time? It was one thing if my mom had kept her at arm's length—notoriously private, she got even more so when she was using—but five years had passed since her death. Had my dad run interference, thinking Mimi and all the rest of the Calvanders would be too much for me to handle?

Plus, my mom had never talked much about her family. It was Nana—my grandfather died young in his forties—who was consistently there for holidays and birthdays. Other than the funeral, which was a blur, the only trip I'd ever taken to my mother's home was so long ago I didn't even remember it. Yes, I had the Lake Stories, but they were never about people as much as a place.

"Arch!" Mimi said, pointing at the TV. "What did I tell you?"

Sure enough, on the screen, Paula was gesturing at a small, cramped living room as a computer graphic showed what it would look like with that shape as an entryway. "You told me," I said.

She cackled, and I looked back down at my screen at Ryan's question. What *was* it like here?

Unclear, I told her. **Stay tuned.**

I heard thumping, then footsteps crossing the kitchen. A moment later, a tall, thin guy with red hair, a baseball hat, shorts, and a faded NORTH LAKE T-shirt passed by in the hallway, his phone to his ear.

"Jacky," Mimi called out, and he stopped, turning to peer in at her. "Didn't you hear me calling you before?"

"I was taking a shower," he said, sliding his phone into a back pocket.

"Well, say hello to your cousin Saylor." She nodded at me. "She's staying awhile."

It was a testament to the dimness of the room, and the dark blue couch I was on, that Jacky hadn't even seen me until she said this. He looked surprised as he lifted a hand. "Hey."

"Hi," I said. "It's Emma, actually."

"Oh, sorry," Mimi told me, her eyes on the TV, where I saw someone was now carrying a sledgehammer. "I keep forgetting you changed it."

But I didn't, I wanted to say. I'd always introduced myself

60

as Emma, even as a kid: my mom was the only one who called me Saylor. Could you literally be a different person to different people? I was pretty sure I was going to find out.

"I'm going out to the raft," Jacky told Mimi. "Back for dinner."

"We're having burgers," she replied. "I made the patties already."

"All right," he said, then started toward the door again, drawing his phone from his pocket.

"Jacky."

He stopped, exhaling visibly. "Yes?"

Mimi shifted in her seat. "Why don't you take her with you?"

"What?" he said.

"Saylor," she replied, nodding at me. "I mean, Emma. She's just got here, doesn't know anyone. You can introduce her around."

"Oh," I said quickly, mortified, "he doesn't have to—"

"They're all out at the raft this time of day," she explained, cutting me off. "Figuring out what kind of trouble to get into later."

"It's okay," I said. I had no sense of the rules here, but I did know enough to not want to be someone's burden. "I'm fine."

The TV went back to *3 Flip Sisters*. "Demo," Mimi said, nodding at the screen. "You can tell, because everyone's in goggles."

"Right," I said.

Jacky hesitated a moment more in the non-arch hallway opening, then started out the door. "Be back to grill," he called over his shoulder.

"Okay," Mimi said, taking a sip of her drink.

The door slammed, and I turned my attention back to the Flip Sisters. A moment later, though, he was back.

"Hey," he said to me. "You really want to watch that?"

I looked back at Mimi. It wasn't clear she'd heard him, but I didn't want to hurt her feelings, even if this had all been her idea.

But Jacky didn't seem worried. Instead, he just pushed the door back open, holding it for me. "Emma," he said. "Come on."

FIVE

The girl in the yellow bikini I'd seen from the window spotted me as we approached the raft. By the time I looked her way, she was already scowling.

I'd been preoccupied, smarting from various ways I had almost died of shame since leaving Mimi's house. The first involved the awkward silence as I followed Jacky across the grass and down the nearby dock to a white motorboat with red seats that was tied up to a row of cleats.

"Thanks for bringing me along, Jacky," I said finally.

He glanced up, then began loosening rope knots. "It's Jack, actually. Only Mimi calls me Jacky."

"Oh. Sorry," I said. "I understand. She's actually the only person who has called me—"

But this was lost as he turned his back again, jumping onto the boat and behind the wheel. The seats were aged and cracked, the floor covered with a few beat-up-looking life jackets. He turned a key and the engine rumbled, coming to life.

I was still standing on the dock, not sure what I was supposed to do, when he looked up at me and said, "You getting in?"

Right, I thought, my face reddening. I took a step onto the boat, but because the ropes were loose, it drifted out into the water, taking my leg with it. This led to a frantic effort not to fall in myself accompanied by, I hated to admit, a shriek. I ended up back on the dock, but just barely.

Jack observed all of this with a flat expression. Then he pulled the boat up to the dock so I could climb in. Once inside, I started to the back bench by the motor, but hit a slippery spot halfway there that resulted in me tumbling down onto the life jackets, arms flailing.

"Whoa," he said, in that same monotone. "Careful."

As we picked up speed and my embarrassment subsided—slightly—I was able to begin to appreciate the view of the lake. It was one thing to look at it from land, like a picture in a frame, another to be within it, wide and blue all around you. It's pretty here, I thought, and turned in my seat, looking back at Mimi's house to find the window to my mom's bedroom, which was growing smaller behind us.

The raft, in contrast, was larger than it had looked from shore. By the time we got there, about seven boats were tied up, either to the raft or each other, with people on them in groups, laughing and talking. As we got closer, a tall, skinny guy with white-blond hair, shirtless and in swim trunks, walked out to the back of a blue motorboat with white trim

64

to meet us. When Jack slowed the motor and walked to the bow, throwing him a line, I saw the girl staring at me.

Short, and stout, with strong-looking arms and legs, she had a deep tan, all the better to set off her yellow bikini top, which she wore with cutoff shorts. Her hair was black and long, flowing down her back, a pair of sunglasses holding it back from her face. When our eyes met, she slowly crossed her arms over her chest, squaring her shoulders.

"This is Emma," Jack said, cutting the engine. "Help her out."

The boy with the white-blond hair—it stuck up in the back, a cowlick I somehow knew he was probably always messing with—extended a hand. Cautious after how I'd boarded, and feeling awkward grabbing ahold of someone I knew not at all, I nonetheless got to my feet and gripped his fingers, stepping onto the blue boat, then the raft.

"I'm Roo," the blond boy said. He had a small gap between his two front teeth, which took the smile he gave me to another level. Gesturing to the group behind him, he added, "This is . . . everyone."

No one said hello, or even acknowledged this introduction, too caught up in their own conversations. Except, of course, Yellow Bikini, who was now glaring at Jack as he finished tying up.

"Jack Blackwood," she said in a voice that was just sharp and loud enough to make everyone else pause their interactions before stopping talking entirely, "I know we're fighting, but did you seriously bring another girl out here *right in front* of me?"

"Uh-oh. Here we go," a tall, slim black girl with short braids in an East U Volleyball T-shirt said under her breath.

"I'd stay out of it if I were you, April," another guy with a fauxhawk and tattoos covering his arms said to her.

"Yeah, because *that* will end well," April replied.

The next thing I knew, Yellow Bikini had crossed the short distance between us to stand right in front of me. Meeting my eyes, her own narrowed, she said, "Look, this is a basic lake rule. You don't just show up with someone else's boyfriend, okay?"

"Taylor," April said. "Remember your calming meditations? Breathe in, then—"

"I'm breathing," Taylor told her. "I just want answers."

"I didn't—" I said, trying to sound as assertive as she did. Unfortunately, my voice was shaking. Meanwhile, I could hear footsteps approaching, the new arrivals now also an audience to this.

"*I didn't*," she repeated in a high voice. She whirled around, looking at Jack. "Seriously? Who the hell is this girl?"

"His cousin," another voice said, sounding as confident as I wished I had. "Mine, too. So will you get out of her face, please?"

All of a sudden, a girl was standing beside me. Even before I saw she was my height, with the same color blond hair and slightly upturned nose I'd always been self-conscious about, I didn't doubt for a second that we were related. This was

66

Bailey. I remembered. Again in a way I couldn't even begin to understand, especially at that moment, but I did.

"Your cousin?" Taylor looked at me again. "You're forgetting that I *know* all your cousins."

"Not this one. Hasn't been here since we were little kids." Now, Bailey addressed me. "Hi, by the way."

"Hi," I said. This time, my voice didn't crack.

She turned back to Taylor. "Are we done? If so, let's make a plan."

Taylor looked at me again. "Jack," she said to my face. "We need to talk."

"Oh, boy," the guy with the fauxhawk said. "Duck and cover, y'all."

As someone across the raft snorted, Taylor turned on her heel and walked across the raft to climb onto Jack's boat. Jack followed, slowly, looking tired. As soon as he was on board, she started talking, although her words were lost as someone else arrived, their engine chugging.

I was no expert, but even at first glance I could tell something about this boat was different. It was longer, for starters, with a third row of seats—not worn, but shiny and clean—and a larger motor. The guy behind the wheel, tall with dark hair, was in shorts and a white polo shirt with some kind of insignia that I felt like I'd seen before. He had on mirrored sunglasses, reflecting our faces back at us.

"What's up?" he called out. "Got a plan yet?"

"Oh, great," April said with a roll of her eyes. "Look who's here."

"Stop it," Bailey told her. "I told you, he's nice."

April did not look convinced, even as Bailey crossed the raft, jumping across two docked boats—gracefully, how?—to go talk to him. To me, April said, "She knows to watch out for those yacht club boys. Not that you can tell."

"Yacht club?" I asked.

April nodded across the lake, at the distant big houses. "Over at Lake North. Everything's bigger and better there, not that it stops them from coming to our side."

I realized, suddenly, why I'd recognized the boy's shirt. It was identical to the one my dad wore in the few pictures I'd seen from the summer he'd spent here teaching sailing when he met my mom. I looked at Bailey again, now scratching one foot with the other as she spoke to the boy, who was grinning up at her.

"That's her boyfriend?" I asked.

"No," the guy with the fauxhawk replied.

"Not *yet*," April corrected, smiling. "Summer just started."

"She'll come to her senses," he told her, rubbing his arm, where a tribal-patterned tattoo covered one bicep.

"And fall for you, Vincent?" she asked him. "Keep dreaming."

"My point is," he said, his face flushing, "I just don't see them together."

"Why not? He's totally her type."

"Which is what? Yacht club?" I asked.

"Rich boy with a dazzling smile," she said. "And a nice boat. What's your name again?"

"Emma," I said. "You're April?"

"And this is Vincent," she said, pointing to the guy. "You here for the summer?"

"Just three weeks," I said.

"How you kin to this lot?" When I just looked at her, not sure what this meant, she said, more slowly, "Are you a Calvander or a Blackwood?"

"Neither. I'm a Payne." Obviously this was confusing, so I added, "My mom was a Calvander, though. Waverly."

At the name, her eyes widened. "You're Waverly's daughter? Really?"

I nodded, suddenly aware of another set of eyes on me: Roo. He'd been over near another boat, coiling some ropes, but now he turned, looking at me as if for the first time. "Saylor?" he said.

"Her name's Emma," April told him. "Keep up, would you?"

"It is Emma Saylor, technically," I said. "But mostly Emma now."

I felt like I was apologizing. Maybe because of the way Roo was still looking at me, startled, as if maybe he remembered more of that summer from the group picture than I did. It must have been confusing, for someone to reappear all those years later with a different face and name. Like the past wasn't what you'd thought. I knew that feeling.

"Okay," Vincent said, shoving his phone into his pocket. "Godfrey's at eight, then Lucy Tate's place afterward, but only if we bring our own beer and don't criticize her music."

"Since when do we have conditions?" April said. "I'd rather hang out on the dock and do what I want."

"It's high season," Roo told her. "Docks are out until August."

"Oh, right. Stupid tourists," she grumbled.

"What's the plan?" Bailey called out from the other side of the raft.

"Don't tell her," April said. "She'll just invite all the golf shirts."

"Godfrey's, then Lucy Tate's," Vincent yelled back anyway.

This seemed to be a signal that things were finalized, as everyone began saying their goodbyes and splitting off to their respective boats. Within minutes, the hum of engines filled the air and I was one of the only ones left, along with April and Vincent, with Roo alongside us behind his own wheel, motor idling.

"Let's get," Vincent told April. He looked at me. "You need a ride back to Mimi's?"

I looked over at Jack, who was still sitting on one of those red benches, Taylor standing in front of him. She'd been talking this entire time, and didn't seem to have any plans to stop soon. Meanwhile, Bailey had jumped in with the guy in the golf shirt and was already puttering away toward shore.

"I don't know," I said, looking at Jack. I still felt like a burden, this time to people I wasn't even related to. "Maybe I should wait for—"

"I wouldn't," April said flatly. "No telling how long they'll be talking. They are *always* talking."

"Right," I said. "Well . . ."

"I'll take you, Saylor," Roo said. When I looked at him, he added quickly, "I mean, Emma. It's on my way."

"Great," Vincent said as April hopped into a nearby small skiff, settling in the stern with the outboard motor there. He untied it, then joined her, his weight wobbling it from side to side. "See you at Godfrey's."

Then they, too, were gone, calling out goodbyes to Jack and Taylor as they passed. She was still talking; only he lifted a hand, waving back.

I looked at Roo, who pulled on a faded blue T-shirt before putting his boat into gear. Before, with Jack, I'd waited for permission to get in, which was the wrong thing to do. Then again, I didn't want to just go for it and risk a repeat of my earlier experience boarding. How could a single step from one floating object to another be so difficult?

I was beginning to sink into an indecisive spiral when he backed the boat up right next to where I was standing, then used one hand to pull it up to the raft's edge, making it an easy step in to take a seat beside him. Easy was good. Easy, I could take. So I did.

Once we got home, dinner was served.

"All I am saying," Celeste said as she picked up her burger, "is that I want you to be careful."

"Mom," Bailey replied. "You don't have to give me this same lecture every summer."

"Apparently, I do. Because you're already hanging out with yacht club boys."

"They're not all alike, you know."

"They're alike enough," Celeste told her. Mimi, at the head of the table, shot her a look over the bowl of potato salad between them. "What? You know what I'm worried about. I mean, we all know what happened when Waver—"

There was the sound of a thump under the table, and Celeste winced. The sudden silence that followed was awkward, not only for the kick Mimi had just given her, but the fact that we all knew it was to protect my feelings.

This was actually the second time my mom had come up since I'd left the raft. The first had been when I was riding back with Roo. Unlike when I'd gone out with Jack, we were side by side. So I was able to get quick glimpses of him, taking in the way his white-blond hair stuck up a bit in the back, the tattoo on one calf that was a series of numbers, and the way that he waved at every boat we passed, flashing a big grin. For all my own glances, he wasn't looking at me at all, instead squinting ahead, the back of his T-shirt rippling in the strong wind coming off the water. When he finally spoke, it took me by surprise.

"I'm sorry about your mom."

Even though it had been five years and some days, I worried I'd moved on too much. And then there were times like this, when just a mention of her gave me a pinch in my heart.

"Thanks," I said. "I miss her."

Now he did look at me: I could see it out of the corner of my eye, even as I watched Mimi's dock—marked with a sign that said FOR USE BY CALVANDER'S GUESTS ONLY—approach. "She and my dad were friends in high school. Chris Price."

I nodded, as if I'd heard this name, even though I hadn't. "He still lives here?"

He looked at me for a second. "No, not anymore. I live with my mom." He pointed to a line of houses down the shore from Mimi's, each painted a different bright color—yellow, blue, pink, red, and green—and trimmed with white. "Ours is the green one."

"Who has the pink?"

"Renters, usually," he said. "Season just started, though."

"How many people live here year-round?" I asked.

He was slowing the engine now. "More than you'd think. A lot, like Celeste, have houses they rent out for summer."

"I thought she lived with Mimi," I said.

"Only from June to August," he replied. "The rest of the time they have a place up by Blackwood Station, right on the water."

"Blackwood Station," I said. "I feel like I've heard of that."

"You probably have. It's the only boatyard in town. Plus, the arcade is right there, and the public beach."

I looked in that direction, getting my bearings, then back up at Mimi's house, now right in front of us. As I did, I saw

Celeste, standing in the grass, one hand shading her eyes as she looked out at us. I couldn't make out her expression.

"And Celeste is a Blackwood, right?" I asked.

"She was. Her ex-husband, Silas, runs the boatyard and gas station. Been in his family for generations."

Now I had something else to add to my family tree. "But you're not a Blackwood or Calvander," I said, clarifying.

"Nope." He cut the engine, letting us drift up to the dock. "Silas, Celeste, my dad, my mom, and yours all went to high school together. There's only one, the same one we all go to now."

I tried to picture my own parents at my school, Jackson High, walking the same halls I did with Ryan and Bridget. I couldn't. Nana Payne and my dad lived in Massachusetts when he was in high school, and my mom was, well, here.

"It's a lot, all this new information," I said. "I'm honestly having some trouble keeping up."

"Well, then you need to start asking people their five sentences."

I raised my eyebrows. "Their what?"

"It's a lake thing," he explained. "The basic idea is that since you meet a ton of people at the beginning of every summer, everyone has to condense their bio down to the main ideas. Thus, five sentences."

"Right," I said slowly. "What's yours?"

He cleared his throat. "Born and bred here at North Lake. High school senior this fall. Work multiple jobs. Want to go to journalism school. Allergic to shellfish."

"Wow," I said. "Didn't see that shellfish part coming."

"An element of surprise and oddity is crucial with this," he told me. "Hit me with yours."

"I need five in all?"

"Start with one."

"Okay," I said, thinking it over. "Well, I'm from Lakeview. Also about to be a high school senior."

"Coming out strong," he said as we hit a wave, water splashing over the bow. "I like it. Go on."

"My mom grew up here at the lake," I continued, "but this is my first real visit. I came once as a kid, but I don't really remember."

"Nice," he said. "Facts *and* intrigue. Now you need something random and memorable."

I thought for a second. "People don't get my humor."

"Meaning?"

"I think I'm funny, but other people often don't laugh."

"I know that feeling," he said.

"You do?" I hadn't met anyone who could relate before.

"Yep," he said. "Okay, now for the strong finish. Your shellfish allergy, so to speak. What's it going to be?"

I had to admit, I was feeling the pressure. Especially as the seconds ticked by and nothing came. What could I say? I was nervous to the point of obsessive? I liked organizing things?

Roo did not rush me. He just waited.

Finally, I had it. "I read the obituaries every day."

His eyes widened. "Seriously?"

I nodded. "Yep."

"Okay, that is *good*," he said, then held his hand up for a high five. I slapped it. "You, in five sentences. Nicely done."

Me, in five sentences. All facts, some informative, some colorful. Not really all that different from the obits themselves, now that I thought of it. Only shorter, while you're living, and still have time to add more.

Roo slowed the engine, then stopped it entirely, and we drifted up to the dock. As he hopped off the boat, pulling the line with him, I heard the thump of footsteps coming down the dock. Looking up, I saw Trinity approaching, now in a flowing black maxi dress, her hair wet. She looked grumpy, but considering this had been a constant each time I'd crossed her path so far, maybe it was just her face.

"Hey," Roo called. "What's up?"

"Mimi says you should stay for dinner," she replied. "Since you brought her in, and everything."

Her was me. Apparently. While I was not sure what five sentences Trinity would pick, I was pretty sure one would cover the fact that she *really* didn't like me.

"You know Trinity, right?" Roo said to me.

"We haven't been reintroduced formally," I told him. To her I said, "Hi. I'm Emma."

"Hi," she said, her voice flat. She turned her attention back to Roo. "Where's Bailey? She's not answering her phone."

"Rode off with some yacht club guy," he replied. "Maybe up at the Station?"

"Of course she is." Trinity rubbed a hand over her belly.

"Like I have the energy to go all the way up there."

"I can go find her," I offered. "I need to learn my way around anyway."

"I'll walk you," Roo said. "If I'm coming for dinner, I should go home and change."

"Will you just drive me?" Trinity whined. "I need to go to the store and I can't reach the clutch anymore."

"Sure," he said agreeably. "Emma, you want to ride along?"

"She should go help with dinner," Trinity said. Now I was *She*. "Mimi said to tell her to."

Roo looked at me. "Oh. Right. Well, rain check."

"Sounds good," I said, making a point to act like it was no big deal. Still, as Trinity and Roo started down the dock without me, I felt another sting, this one a sort of shame. Despite all my mom had told me about the lake, none of it explained why so far at least half the females I'd met had disliked or outright hated me on sight.

Now, back at the table, I looked out the window to the sandy beach below the house, where Roo, Trinity, and Jack were sitting in lawn chairs, eating their own dinners. We'd all fixed our plates together, assembly-line style, but it was only after I'd sat down that I realized the table was too small for everyone, and this contingent was eating outside. Which left me with Celeste, Mimi, and Bailey, as Gordon was again lost in her Allies book.

"So," Mimi said to me. "You getting situated? Meet everyone out at the raft?"

I nodded, finishing my bite of potato salad before saying, "A few people, yeah."

"Taylor got up in her face," Bailey said, adjusting the tomato on her burger.

"What?" Mimi said. "Why?"

"Because she was with Jack, and Taylor's got major jealousy issues." She rolled her eyes. "Even when they're together, they're fighting."

"It's not easy to disconnect from someone totally in a place as small as this," Celeste pointed out.

"Says the woman who married and divorced the same man twice," Bailey said.

I blinked: this was news to me. Another thing to add to my family tree.

Mimi chuckled. "She's got you there, Celeste."

Celeste, hardly bothered, reached for the bowl of potato chips. "I've got to tell you, Saylor, when I saw you coming in with Roo, man, it brought back some memories. Wild to see you two together, after how close you were as kids."

"Wait, what?" I said. Now I felt even worse about our first meeting at the dock, when he'd looked so surprised. "We were?"

"You don't remember?" I shook my head. "Well, I guess maybe you wouldn't. You *were* babies. But yeah, that time you stayed here, you two were like frick and frack. Always together."

"Remember the best friend hug?" Mimi said, smiling.

"The what?" Bailey asked.

"Whenever Roo and Saylor had been together and then had to split up, they did their best friend hug. Just clung to each other. Lord, it was the cutest."

Bailey, bemused, glanced at me, and I was pretty sure I blushed. Evidently, embarrassment had no statute of limitations.

"It got me thinking about Waverly and Chris, which of course got me in the gut," Celeste said to Mimi. "Those two really were inseparable."

"He did mention that, actually," I said. "How my mom and his dad were friends."

"Those Prices. All such sweet boys," Mimi said, looking out the window. Roo was saying something to Jack, who was grinning, as Trinity, still sour-faced, looked on. "I just hate all Roo's been through, with his daddy and everything."

"He said his dad doesn't live here anymore," I said. "Where is he?"

There are all kinds of silences. Natural ones, when conversation just ebbs after a flow. Awkward, just after someone's said something they shouldn't. The worst, though, are shocked silences, when no one can speak at all. This was one of those.

"He died, honey," Mimi said finally. "Before you two were born. Boating accident."

I didn't know what to say. All I could do, in fact, was look at Roo again while running through my mind again the moment earlier when I'd asked if his dad was still local. There had been a silence then, too, but only the briefest one,

79

like a song missing a beat. He hadn't wanted to make me feel bad for being so ignorant. The way I felt right now.

"Oh, my God." I put my hand to my mouth, horrified. "I had no idea. I'm such an idiot."

"It's okay," Mimi said. When I just sat there, blinking, she added, "Saylor. You didn't know."

Down below the house, Jack was now on his feet, his plate empty except for a crumpled napkin. Roo got up as well, then extended a hand to Trinity, pulling her to a standing position. For him, she smiled.

"So. Saylor," Mimi said. "You going out with the kids tonight?"

I looked at Bailey, who was back on her phone. She didn't say anything, and the last thing I wanted was to yet again be forced on anyone. "I'm pretty tired, actually."

"Well, in case you change your mind," Celeste said, "Bailey, give Emma your number."

Bailey sighed. "You guys. Seriously. This is getting ridiculous."

I felt my face blush again. Here I'd thought this cousin was the nice one, but clearly even she was sick of dealing with me. I said quickly, "She doesn't have—"

"I mean," Bailey continued, over me, "is it Emma or is it Saylor? Because so far I'm hearing both, interchangeably. It's super confusing."

Everyone looked at me. So it wasn't me that was annoying. Just my names. I said, "At home, I've always been Emma.

Except if my mom was talking to me."

"Which is why I keep calling you Saylor," Mimi said softly. "Sorry. But she loved that name."

I bit my lip, hearing this. It had been a long day indeed, if this was the thing that would make me cry.

"How about this," Bailey said to me. "You think about it and let me know. Whatever you say, it sticks. Officially. Deal?"

I nodded. In time, maybe I'd figure this out.

"And give me your phone," she added. "I'll put in my number."

I swallowed, trying to pull it together, as I took my phone out of my pocket, unlocking the screen and sliding it over. BAILEY, I watched her type, then the digits.

"There," she said, returning it to me. Across the table, Mimi was watching us, but I couldn't read her expression. Half-sad, half-happy, all hard to explain. Like she was seeing something I wouldn't have, even from the same vantage point. "We're leaving here at eight. Let me know if you change your mind."

"Okay," I said. "Thanks."

After dinner, I went to my room, where I opened my notebook again to the family tree I'd started. SILAS, I wrote, next to Celeste, then drew a line through it. Twice. (There had to be a story there.) I added Amber under Joe, with a question mark, and Anna Gordon below her. So many gaps still to fill, but I was getting there.

Downstairs, I could hear Bailey and Trinity as they got ready in the kitchen and then the screen porch that functioned as their bedroom. There were other noises, too. Mimi's TV, most certainly showing another fixer-upper show. Jack on his own phone on the other side of the wall, speaking quietly, maybe to Taylor. But as darkness fell and I found myself nodding off earlier than I had in ages, it was those who were not there that filled my mind. Roo first, and the secret, not so much a secret, that he'd kept from me. My mom, in this same room. And the frick to her frack, Chris, gone as well. The past was always present, in its way, and you can't help but remember. Even if you can't remember at all.

SIX

I woke to the smell of toast.

It was actually the second time I'd been up. The first had been at four a.m., when my dad, obviously so worried about how I was faring that he forgot about the seven-hour time difference, called me from Greece.

"Dad?" I answered, after fumbling for the phone in the dark for a moment. "Is everything okay?"

"What's not okay?" he replied.

"What?" I said.

"Did you say you're not okay?"

"No," I said. "I asked if *you* were okay, since you're calling me so early."

A pause. Then, "Oh, no. What time is it there? I'm all turned around."

"It doesn't matter," I assured him, even as I noticed the little clock on the dresser said 4:15 a.m. Which made this the second morning in a row I'd been awakened by a phone call at this hour, something I could only hope wasn't a trend. "How was the flight?"

"Good," he said. "Long. But we're here now, in a taxi on our way to the hotel."

"Hi, Emma!" Tracy called out.

"Tell her hi," I said to my dad.

He relayed the message. "The important thing is, how are you? Is it all right there?"

I looked at the clock again, weighing how to answer this. Of course I didn't want him to worry. I was fine, just a bit discombobulated. Also I had a lot of questions, most of which he probably couldn't answer. "It's good," I said. "I had dinner with Celeste and her kids."

"Great." Hearing the relief in his voice as he said this one word made it clear how worried he'd been, and I was glad I'd chosen carefully. "How is Celeste?"

"She's good," I told him. "Raising a cousin's kid, this ten-year-old named Gordon. Her mom is in Florida. I think her name is Amber?"

"Amber? No. She's, like, ten years old herself." A pause. "Or, she was the last time I saw her. Which I guess was about twenty years ago, now that I think of it. Keeping up with your mom's family always made my head hurt. Glad to know some things don't change."

"Guess not," I said. "Look, I'm fine. Go enjoy your trip."

"Honey that moon," he said, chuckling. "Call me when it's a decent hour there, okay? We're supposed to have service on the boat."

"Okay," I told him. "I love you."

"Love you too, Emma. Bye."

I put my phone back on the bedside table, rolling over to face the window. I could just see the surface of the water, the moon overhead. I looked at it, thinking of my dad and Tracy, speeding across a city I'd never seen and couldn't even picture, until I fell asleep.

And now it was eight a.m., and there was toast, or at least the smell of it. Also, possibly coffee. Hopeful, I got up, pulling on some shorts and a clean T-shirt, then brushed my teeth and went downstairs.

"Morning," a voice said as soon as my foot hit the bottom step. Startled, I jumped: Oxford, Mimi's husband, was sitting at the table, a newspaper open in front of him. Otherwise the kitchen was empty, although when I glanced at the toaster, I saw the indicator light shone bright red, signaling it was on.

"Good morning," I replied. I walked over to the counter, where, sure enough, I found a coffeemaker with half a pot left. Score. "Okay if I take some of this?"

"Help yourself." He turned a page of the paper. "Milk and cream are in the fridge, sugar's over here."

I found a mug, filled it, then came over to the table, finding a spoon and adding some sugar before taking a seat. As I did, the toaster binged cheerfully, six slices popping up. Oxford didn't seem to notice.

"You want some of the paper?" he asked me.

"Sure."

"What section?"

I took a sip from my mug. Perfect. "Do you have the obituaries?"

He didn't bat an eye, rifling through to pull out the local news. "One of my favorites. Always good to start the day making sure I'm not in there."

"I'll let you know," I said, smiling at him.

"Do that."

We sat there, reading in companionable silence, which was a strange thing to do with someone you'd only barely met. But reading the paper I *did* know, since Nana and I did it together every morning. After all the newness of the day before, it was nice to have something familiar. Of course, the moment I felt relaxed, Trinity showed up.

At first she was just shuffling footsteps, coming down the hallway. Then she appeared, looking half-asleep in sweatpants and an oversized tank top, her pregnant belly stretching it out. She did not look at or address either Oxford or myself, instead just walking to the toaster, where she retrieved the six pieces of toast, piling them on a paper towel, before going to the fridge for a tub of butter.

"If you take that, bring it back," Oxford said, still reading. She did not reply, instead just going back the way she'd come, leaving us alone again.

The obituary section in the *Bly County News*—North Lake was too small for its own paper, clearly—was much smaller than the one in the *Lakeview Observer*. Which I supposed made sense: fewer people, fewer deaths to report.

Today there were only two, starting with Marjorie McGuire, 82, who had gone to meet her Lord and Savior the previous week. In her picture, she had a beauty shop hairdo and was smiling.

The fact that I was interested in the obits made my dad uneasy. He worried it reflected my anxiety, fear of death, not dealing with my mom's passing, or the triple bonus, all three. But it wasn't about that. When Nana and I had first started our breakfast-and-paper tradition, I'd cared about comics and not much else. The obits were always there, though, on the opposite page, and at some point I'd started reading them as well. Then my mom died. She'd had no obit, for reasons I could never understand, so I got even more interested in how people chose to be, or were, remembered.

Most obituaries, I'd found, shared the same basics. The opening paragraphs rarely gave specifics, other than the person had passed "after a long illness" or "unexpectedly." Occasionally someone died "at home," which sounded like it might be a way of saying it was on purpose without using those exact words. The religious ones often contained scripture, if not a mention of where the deceased planned to go and who they hoped to see there. Next up was usually a summary of the life itself, with education, marriages, and children and a listing of career high points. The final paragraphs usually touched on a hobby dear to the person who had passed—travel was big, and volunteering for good causes—before providing funeral info and suggesting where to donate in lieu of flowers.

I always made a point to read each word of every obit. This would be the last way this person was remembered: Was I really too busy to take an extra three seconds to read about their commitment to the March of Dimes? Also, I felt reassured when all the day's listings were people like Mrs. Maguire, who had lived a good, full life. An obit for a younger person, like my dad's age, always made me sad. A teen or a child was heartbreaking. It just didn't fit, like a rule had been broken, and I'd find myself trying to piece together the part of the story that wasn't told.

When I'd first started reading the obits, they never mentioned overdoses or drugs as causes of death. In recent years, though, as more opioid crisis stories hit the front page, they made this section as well. Occasionally it was spelled out, with the deceased having "struggled with an addiction," or similar. More often, though, you had to read between the lines, finding the references to battling demons, pride in a previous period of sobriety, or a family request to donate to Narcotics Anonymous.

Would it have made a difference, having a clipping from a paper with my mom's name and dates, a recap of the things and people she loved, and those who were missing her? It would have been at least more closure than that night outside the building as the elevator doors closed. Maybe that was what I was looking for, all those mornings with Nana and now.

"Morning," I heard a voice say. I looked up to see Bailey come into the kitchen in shorts and a red T-shirt that said BLACKWOOD on it, her hair pulled back in a ponytail.

"Morning," Oxford said. "You working today?"

"At nine," she replied. She went over to the counter, where she opened a loaf of bread, taking out six slices and dropping them into the toaster before turning it on. "Why?"

"Mimi's knee is acting up," he replied, folding down the top part of the sports section.

"Oh, no." Bailey came over, sliding into the chair beside mine. "How bad is it?"

"Doc says he wants her off her feet for at least a week, but we all know that's not happening. You want any of the paper?"

"Horoscopes, please."

He handed her a section as I went back to my own reading about Wallace Camp, 78, who had passed surrounded by loved ones after a long illness. His photo was from his military days.

There was a thunk from upstairs, then the sound of a door opening. Jack yelled, "Can someone put in some toast for me?"

"On it," Bailey called back.

"Thanks." The door shut again.

"I can try to trade shifts with someone for tomorrow," Bailey said, running her finger down the horoscopes before landing on Aries, which was my sign as well. "But it's late notice for today."

"Don't worry about it. We'll work it out somehow."

The timer sounded—BING!—and she jumped up, taking a plate from the cupboard and bringing it over to the toaster. As she plucked the pieces out, one by one, the screen door slammed and Mimi came in. Gordon was behind her, in shorts over a bathing suit, a backpack over her shoulders.

"Oxford," Mimi said, dropping a cordless phone receiver on the table beside him. "Answer this if it rings. I've got to take Gordon to camp."

"Where's Celeste?"

"Early shift. She left at six." Mimi looked at me. "Emma, honey, did you eat breakfast?"

"Not yet. I'm fine, though."

"Let me make you some before the bread's all gone," she replied, crossing the kitchen to load the toaster up with slices again. "If the Sergeant's spending his money on this fancy thing, we should use it."

The toaster being idle couldn't have been an issue. By my count we were at eighteen slices now and counting. I asked, "The Sergeant?"

"Trinity's fiancé," Oxford explained, not looking up from his own section of the paper. "Deployed right now."

"Where's the butter?" Bailey, now peering into the fridge, asked.

"Your sister took it," Oxford told her.

Bailey sighed. "Trinity! Bring back the butter!"

"I'm getting dressed," her sister replied. "You can come get it."

"Honey, I've got to take Gordon to camp!" Mimi yelled in the direction of the hallway, starting the toaster again. "So you'll be starting on your own today."

"Are you *serious*?" Trinity replied. "I'm huge. I can't even bend down to get under the beds."

Mimi exhaled, looking at the ceiling. "We'll talk about it when I get back. Gordon, come on."

"Trinity!" Bailey yelled as they left, the door again slamming behind them. "I need the butter."

"I told you, I'm getting dressed. Damn!"

"You two stop yelling, before you chase me out of my own kitchen again," Oxford warned.

"Fine," Bailey said, ripping a paper towel off the roll and folding two slices up inside it. "I'll eat it dry on the way to work. If I choke to death on the way, you'll know who to blame."

With that, she was gone, the door banging again behind her. A beat later, the toaster popped up: BING! Oxford reached over, extracting the slices and dropping them on the plate Mimi had left for this purpose. Then he put it on the table between us, taking one before looking at me.

"You want butter?"

I smiled. "Nope."

"Wise move," he said, and went back to his paper.

The two obits read, I pulled over the horoscopes to read Aries for myself. Apparently, Bailey and I were both going to savor something delicious in the day ahead. My thoughts drifted back to Trinity, who was coming back down the hallway, dressed now in shorts and a tie-dye, carrying the butter. She went straight to the toaster, loading it up again with what I could not help but notice was the last of the bread. Suddenly Celeste's frustration the day before made sense.

"Here," she announced, dropping the butter in front of me, as if I'd been the one demanding it. I didn't say anything, instead just picking up my dry toast and taking a pointed bite. I was pretty sure she didn't notice. "Is Bailey going to come clean today?"

"She's got to work," Oxford replied.

Trinity's expression, already sour, grew more so. "Great. So it'll just be me turning over four rooms before check-in."

Oxford did not reply to this. I said, "I can help you, if you want."

"You?" She narrowed her eyes, as if I was so small she couldn't see me otherwise. "You're on vacation."

This stung, for some reason. "Not really."

"Well, tell it to Mimi. That's what she said."

Oxford glanced at her, then me. I thought he was about to say something, but was glad when he didn't.

BING! went the toaster, six slices popping up. Trinity retrieved them before bringing them to the table on a paper towel. She reached across me for a knife, which she then used to briskly butter each slice, the scraping sound hard to ignore.

"I'm late," Jack, also in a BLACKWOOD T-shirt, said as he came down the stairs. "Is there any—"

Wordlessly, Trinity picked up two pieces of buttered toast, holding them over her head. As Jack passed, he grabbed them. "Thanks."

"No problem."

"We're short a cleaner," Oxford said as he started for the door. "Mimi's knee. Ask Roo if he wants some hours."

"Will do," Jack said, heading for the door. "Thanks for the toast."

"Thank the Sergeant," she replied. "He's the one who bought that huge thing."

I looked at the toaster, remembering how my dad had remarked that it was new. Apparently, there was a military aspect to it as well. In this house, even the appliances were complicated.

"Trinity?" I heard Mimi yell from outside. "Best get started on those rooms."

In response, Trinity sighed loudly enough I literally felt a breeze from her direction. Then she pushed back her chair, grabbing a piece of toast. Oxford said, "Mimi's got no business cleaning. Her knee can't take it."

"I'm *pregnant*," she replied unnecessarily. But she got to her feet, yelling outside to Mimi, "Coming!"

As she left, I looked at the table. Only three pieces of toast remained. On the counter, the bread bag, defeated, was crumpled into a ball. The clock on the stove said 8:58 a.m.

I stood up, carrying my plate over to the sink, which was again full of dishes. They don't want your help, I told myself, even as the urge hit, then grew, to start washing them. But I rinsed only my cup, putting it on the (empty) dish rack as Oxford grabbed a final slice of toast and the phone, taking both with him as he left. After so much noise and commotion, the house felt so still suddenly, with only me in it and the whole day ahead. What do you do when no one wants you to do anything? I wasn't sure. But I did put the butter away.

* * *

It's so boring, oh my God. I mean, I'm happy Grandpa's ok. But I am so sick of hospital cafeteria food and trying to keep my brothers quiet.

It was late morning now, and I'd finally heard from Bridget. Her grandfather was recovering in the hospital, the boys were driving her nuts, and there was nothing to do in Ohio. These were the headlines.

I understand, I wrote back. **So glad he's getting better, though.**

Me too. What are you doing?

What *was* I doing? At the moment, sitting on the front steps of Mimi's house, wondering how to keep myself busy while everyone else was at work. So far, that had entailed reorganizing my already neat clothes, reading part of an Allies book Gordon had left in the living room—the sixth book from the second series, according to the back cover, but I'd had no trouble dropping right into the mythology—and, now, watching the hotel guests converge on the beach for the day.

Guests emerged with beach bags, wheeled coolers, and more children as they made their way down the plank walkway to the water. They set up camp on the covered part of the dock or the sand, spreading towels and dragging chairs into position as kids were wrangled, protesting the application of sunscreen.

The office of Calvander's, in the opposite direction, was the other center of activity. All morning long, people had been coming and going: Mimi, of course, even though she was supposed to be off her feet. Oxford, wiping down the glass door with Windex and weeding the sparse garden. I even glimpsed both Taylor and April popping in before they walked off down the street, out of sight. Between the constant activity of both the beach and the office, I felt even more frozen where I sat on the steps.

Getting used to this place, I finally wrote back to Bridget. **What's the boy situation?**

Immediately, I had a flash of Roo the day before, shirtless, holding out a hand to me at the raft. That gap in his teeth. Which was ridiculous, I knew.

All related to me. Or might as well be.

Seriously?

Just then, I saw Mimi coming down the motel sidewalk, pushing a cleaning cart. She now wore a Velcro brace on one knee and had the office phone between her ear and shoulder as she stopped by a door marked 7 and pulled a ring of keys from her pocket. She let herself in, and a moment later the front blinds were rising, revealing a streaky window.

I thought of how I'd offered help to Trinity earlier and the way she'd so easily grouped me with the guests now out on the beach. She'd said it was Mimi who made this clear, and possibly she had. But maybe sometimes you had to ask twice. I walked over.

"No kidding," I heard her saying as I approached the door to room seven. "In a perfect world, my body wouldn't be breaking down. But this is the world we're in."

The room was dim, and it took my eyes a second to

adjust. Once they did, I saw the walls were made of cinder block painted white, the carpet a dated flat orange. There were two double beds, both stripped, a rattan bedside table between them. The TV was one of those ancient kinds, huge and mounted up high on the wall, a bunch of cords snaking out of the back. Against the far wall was a small fridge and stovetop, a microwave and a sink, three skinny cabinets above. The only other furniture was two faded canvas chairs, and between them a low table with a flyswatter and an ashtray on it. Who even smoked inside anymore?

". . . okay, well, keep me posted," Mimi said as she stepped out of what had to be the bathroom. Her arms were full of towels, which she dumped onto a pile of sheets already under the TV. "I'd better run. We've got two check-ins today plus housekeeping. Okay. Bye."

She sighed as she hung up, still not seeing me. I didn't want to startle her, so I knocked on the door lightly. When she didn't hear me, I did it again.

"Oh, hey," she said, breaking into a smile. "You need something?"

"No," I replied. "I just . . . I heard you could use some help."

"I always need help," she said, starting toward the door. Her brace creaked with each step. "It's an ongoing condition in a resort town. But nothing you can do, I'm afraid."

I stepped aside as she came out to the cart, grabbing a stack of paper bath mats and a handful of individually wrapped soaps. "I can clean. I'm actually pretty good at it."

She looked at me. "Oh, honey. You don't want to do that. Motel work is gross."

As if to emphasize this point, Trinity emerged from room six, carrying a plunger. "Got out the clog, not that it was pretty. There's a damn sign saying not to flush anything other than toilet paper. Can't people read?"

"Shhh," Mimi told her.

"Nobody's listening to us." She leaned the plunger against the cart. "You have linens yet?"

"Nope," Mimi replied. "Grab some, would you? Get them for six too, we'll do all the beds at once."

Trinity nodded, then turned, walking to a nearby door that said STAFF ONLY and pushing it open. As she did, the smell of chlorine bleach filled the air, along with the banging of what sounded like a dryer.

Mimi turned back to me. "Why don't you walk down to the Station, see what's going on there? There's usually a group at the arcade or the snack bar."

She turned me down so easily; it was frustrating. "I can help you," I said, emphasizing the words this time. "Really."

"Honey, I don't *want* you to," she replied. I felt unexpectedly hurt, hearing this. Which must have shown on my face, because she added, quickly, "Saylor, you haven't been here in over ten years. I want you to enjoy it. That's what your mom would have wanted, too."

Trinity walked past me, carrying a stack of folded linens, and went into room seven, dropping them onto the bed closest to the door. On the cart the phone started to ring and

Mimi picked it up, just as a white van that said ARTHUR AND SONS WINDOWS pulled up to the office.

"Hello? Oh, hey, Tom. Yes, it's unit ten. Okay. Meet you there in five minutes." She glanced at the van, then sighed again. "Lord, and there's Artie coming for an estimate. Everything's happening at once today."

The man in question was climbing out of the van now, carrying a clipboard. He lifted a hand in our direction, and Mimi, looking stressed, waved back. As she started making her way to meet him, I opened my mouth to say something, then closed it. Three times might have been the charm, but it could also mean not taking a hint.

"Why do you really want to help?"

I turned around to face Trinity. "Why?"

"Come on," she said. "You're the spoiled rich cousin and everyone's been told to make sure you have fun here."

I'd been tiptoeing around her so much the flare of temper I felt, hearing this, was welcome. "Not by me," I said, an edge to my voice.

"Who cares? Why not just kick back and enjoy yourself? I would."

"Well, that's you," I told her. She raised her eyebrows. "Look, you don't have to like me or the fact I'm here. But don't pretend you know me. Mimi let me come stay here with zero notice. The very least I can do is help her out when *she* needs it."

"Yeah, but have you ever actually *held* a job?"

I'm only seventeen, I wanted to say. Just as I thought this, though, I realized she'd probably been working for years. Things were different here. Out loud I said, "I can help you, if you'll let me. It's up to you."

She looked at me for a second, and I leveled my gaze back at her. Finally she said, "Go by the office and tell Mimi you need the keys to room ten. Then go let Tom in. Don't give her a choice."

"Okay," I said, surprised at how victorious I felt. "Then what?"

"You need something else?"

"What I need is to not feel I'm just sitting around doing nothing while she's working on her bad knee," I told her. "That's something I'm pretty sure my mom wouldn't have wanted."

She glanced out the door, toward the office. "Okay. Come back here after. I'll show you how to do the beds."

I nodded, then started down the sidewalk. Of course she hadn't denied not liking me, not that I really expected her to. But I'd take her offer. Since arriving, I'd felt like not family and not a guest, the sole inhabitant of this weird place in between. It felt good to have a job and task at hand. Like the chaos that was this trip could actually get a bit more organized, and I might just find my place in it.

SEVEN

"You know, it's not exactly that I don't like you."

"No?" I asked Trinity, spraying down the mirror in front of me, then starting to wipe it from the center out, as she'd showed me earlier.

"Not really." She added two folded dish towels to the dish rack, hanging them just so. "It's more the *idea* of you."

I looked over at her. "That's supposed to make me feel better?"

"It's not supposed to make you feel anything," she replied. "It's just the truth."

"You called me the spoiled rich cousin," I pointed out.

"Okay, well, I can see how that might have seemed bitchy."

Might? I thought. But I stayed quiet, taking my annoyance out on a stubborn streak.

"But look at it from my point of view," she continued. "Here I am, hugely pregnant and uncomfortable—"

"Not my fault," I pointed out quietly.

"—and alone, because my fiancé is still deployed even though he was supposed to be back last month," she continued. "And I'm on my feet all day doing this incredibly physical job, because no one else but my grandmother wants to hire someone almost eight months along at the beginning of summer."

"Again, not my fault," I told her. "Also technically not legal."

"And then," she went on, spraying some cleaner with jabs of the bottle, "here you come, with your hot dad in a fancy car, just to chill out for a while and take it easy. And we're told that, specifically. That you are here to have a good time, like that's our responsibility."

I turned to look at her, surprised. "You think my dad's hot?"

She shrugged. "Yeah."

Ugh. I made a face, then turned back to the mirror. Behind me, she laughed—which also took me by surprise, as I'd hardly even seen her smile—then said, "My point is, I made up my mind about you based on the information I was given. That's not mean. It's science."

"Science?" I repeated.

"What?" she replied, running some water into the sink. "Lake girls can't be good in school?"

"Just didn't peg you as a science nerd," I said.

"I'm not." She turned off the faucet. "Math is my favorite. And half my double major."

"What's the other?"

"Education," she said, wiping a bit of something off the stove handle. "I want to teach middle school algebra. I mean, once the baby comes and I finish my degree."

Hearing this, I realized she wasn't the only one who had made assumptions. I was embarrassed—ashamed, really. "I bet you'll make a good teacher."

This seemed to please her. "Yeah?"

"After that cleaning tutorial you gave me earlier? You bet."

Now, she did smile—briefly—and we both went back to work. It had been like this all day, into the late afternoon. Us working together, talking sometimes, but just as often, letting silences fall.

After our standoff by room seven—as I had a feeling I'd be remembering it—I'd done as she said, going down to the office, where I found Mimi deep in discussion with the window guy. Not surprisingly, it was freezing.

"Saylor?" she said as the wind chimes hanging from the door handle clanked behind me. "You need something?"

I took a breath. "Trinity said I should get the keys to room ten to meet the A/C repair guy?"

Mimi looked at me a moment, then walked over behind the counter, grabbing a set of keys from the board hanging there. "Here," she said. "Tell him it's been blowing warm since last weekend."

I nodded, taking the keys. That was easy, I thought, as I left to help Tom access the A/C. When I returned to Trinity, she was shaking a clean sheet over one of the double beds. As it billowed out and the edges fluttered down, our eyes met across all that whiteness.

"Grab the other side and pull it tight," she instructed me. When I did, she said, "Tighter."

Thus began my course in motel room cleaning, which was short, harsh, and brutally to the point, much like Trinity herself. Luckily, she wasn't the only one who was a good student.

There were two types of room cleaning at Calvander's, she told me as we made those first beds. Housekeeping, which was for rooms with guests staying on another night, and turnover, for rooms that had been vacated and needed a full clean before being occupied again. Both included what I'd come to think of as the defaults: vacuuming, emptying trash cans, cleaning toilets and wiping down sinks, replacing towels, and so on. For turnover, you then added changing the bed linens, wiping down the kitchen, mirror, and shower, and putting away all dishes and silverware, plus cleaning out whatever was left in the small fridges provided for guests. Which, so far, had been mostly beer, soda, and, in one case, a to-go box with a piece of leftover something, coated with mold.

"Turnover is mandatory," Trinity said as we loaded fresh towels onto the racks in the bathroom. "New guests, clean room. Housekeeping, however, is a courtesy. But people always want it, as long as they're not inconvenienced. Like exhibit A over there."

This referred to a woman staying in room four, who had been sleeping when we knocked, then let ourselves in. She woke up yelling, keeping it up until we beat a quick retreat, Trinity cursing back under her own breath. An hour later, she found us and said the room was ready to be serviced, and not to forget extra towels and to vacuum under the beds. As she departed, she nicked a bunch of our soaps from our cart, something Trinity clearly viewed as an insult.

"People will steal anything from a motel room," she said, nodding at the woman retreating. "I mean, those soaps are tiny and cheap. She's driving a Cadillac. Really?"

I didn't say anything to this, because I'd already figured out I had two jobs here other than my actual one: listen to what my cousin said, and retain that information. The commentary—and there was lots, sprinkled throughout— was just a bonus.

"You *will* be disgusted, daily," she informed me as we stood in the open doorway of our first truly dirty bathroom. Towels were everywhere, the trash can overflowing, and the toilet itself full of something I wasn't going to look at unless I had to. "There are rubber gloves on the cart. Do not be afraid to use them."

"Right," I said, bending down to grab the towels as gingerly as possible. Already, it was unspoken that we'd divide and conquer, with me doing the low stuff and her reaching the higher things.

"Clorox, and all its forms, is your friend," she continued, spraying an arc from her own bottle—which said TRINITY on it in pink marker—into the room ahead of us. "Ditto for the blue goo."

"The what?"

She nodded at the toilet. "Flush that first."

I looked at it, and the contents, reminding myself I had been warned away from this job. The spoiled city cousin wouldn't do it. So I had to. I started to reach for the lever.

"Not with your HAND," she bellowed, and I jumped. "Use a foot."

"My foot?"

In response, she stepped past me, kicking out a leg so one beat-up sneaker hit the handle, flushing the contents. As it swirled away, she sprayed the Clorox again in its direction. "Blue goo," she continued, grabbing another bottle from the counter beside her, "is this toilet cleaner. Major disinfectant. Lift the seat—"

"With my foot?"

She nodded. I did. "Good. Now, line that bowl with this stuff. Don't be dainty, load it in there. Then we leave it to do the hard work for us before we come back with gloves on."

I followed these instructions, the bottle squirting loudly as I did so. When I was done, she handed me the bleach again. "Now, the shower."

And so it went, as we covered everything, from the stacking of soaps—"Two in two places, the holders built into the shower and sink"—to checking the toilet paper supply— "one on the roll, one extra if it runs out. Any more, they'll just get stolen."

"People steal toilet paper?"

"I told you, people steal everything," she said. "Aren't you paying attention?"

This continued throughout the day, with us covering the polishing of mirrors (newspaper worked best for streaks), using caution when cleaning under beds (always look before you reach for something you see, you have no idea what else is there). With turnover, it was all about being thorough but quick, as people usually showed up early, eager to begin their vacation.

Housekeeping, on the other hand, involved an added layer of conscious, careful awareness. When working around people's possessions and luggage, you were to treat them pretty much the same as toilets: don't touch unless you absolutely must, and then, do it quick.

"We are always the first to be accused," she explained, delicately moving a tablet aside to retrieve an empty box of tissues. "Something goes missing, we stole it. And God forbid it's medication. If you go into a bathroom and there's a bottle with pills falling out of it? Leave it as is. Even if it means missing a spot. Do you hear me?"

I nodded. "Look me in the eye," she said. I did. "Understood?"

"Understood," I repeated. When she kept looking at me, I added, "Never touch a pill or meds. Ever."

"Good girl."

Not for the first time that day, I thought of my own stays at hotels with my dad over the years. Had I left a big mess, toilet unflushed, something gross? I didn't recall doing so, and certainly hoped not. Nevertheless, I felt a wave of shame as I realized I'd never given much thought to the people who cleaned our rooms, even after seeing them or their carts in the hallways. It was just like magic: messy became clean. Except it wasn't.

While we cleaned, people continued to come in and out of the office, the clang of the wind chimes on the door marking each departure. But I wasn't really paying that much attention when someone knocked on room five. I was fighting with the vacuum, which had a frayed cord and cut off every time I moved it. When I turned, there was Roo. I literally jumped, I was so startled.

"Hey," he said. "Surprised to see you here."

"Let me guess," I said, sighing. "You were also told I'm the spoiled cousin who is on vacation."

He just looked at me for a moment. "No," he said finally. "Because Mimi asked me to clean this room, but you're already doing it."

Whoops. I pushed my hair out of my face, taking a breath. "Sorry," I said. "It's just been frustrating. Nobody has wanted my help."

"Really?" He stepped inside, picking up my spray bottle. "Weird. We always need an extra set of hands."

"Not mine, apparently. Until I forced the issue."

He sprayed the table by the window, then grabbed a clean rag, wiping it down. "Well, you're in it now. Once you start, you're one of us. No escape."

I smiled at this, starting up the vacuum again as he

dragged the smaller garbage can over to the bag I'd left by the door. For a moment we worked in silence, him emptying another can. Then I said, "Do you work here a lot?"

"I fill in as needed," he said. "Like everyone else."

There was a loud crackle, followed by a squeak. Then a girl's voice said, "Breaker breaker. Who's got their ears on?"

Roo reached to his back pocket, pulling out a beat-up walkie-talkie. He pushed a button as he put it to his mouth, then said, "You've got Rubber Duck and Saylor, go ahead."

I just looked at him. "Rubber Duck?"

He grinned. "That's my handle."

"Your—"

"Roo and *who*?" the girl's voice crackled over the handset again.

There was another buzz, followed by a different girl's voice. "Taylor, it's the girl you were so awful to yesterday. Did you already forget?"

I must have looked as confused as I felt, because Roo explained, "April and Taylor. They work at the mini-golf places down the block."

That explained why I'd seen them that morning. "And you guys communicate?"

"The power of the walkie. Works all the way up at the Station." He grinned, then pushed the button again. "So, yeah, Daffodil. You want to apologize to Saylor now or do it in person later?"

No reply. Finally April said, "Taylor. We can hear you breathing."

"I'm thinking!" Taylor said.

"I thought they worked at the same place?" I whispered to Roo.

He shook his head. "Nope. Both mini golf, but two different places, right across the street from each other."

There was another beep, and then I heard a voice say, flatly, "I am sorry for my behavior yesterday. I am working on my jealousy and anger issues and I hope you can accept my apology."

Roo looked at me, his eyebrows raised. Then, slowly, he pushed the handset's button, holding it out to me. I leaned toward it, clearing my throat. "I do. Thank you."

"See?" April said. "That wasn't so hard, was it? Now we're one big, happy family again!"

"Which should last for about five seconds," Roo added into the walkie. "Okay, everyone. Catch you later."

"Bye, y'all!" Taylor said. She sounded different when she wasn't so angry.

Roo shoved the handset back into his pocket and glanced around the room. "I should get back to the Station—they're short-staffed today too. You want me to come back when I'm off? Or you guys got this?"

"You should ask Trinity, but I think we're okay," I said as he bent down, picking up a crumpled piece of paper and chucking it in the trash can. "So you guys are all really close, huh?"

He shrugged. "Guess so. Sort of inevitable when there aren't that many of you."

"You're all the same age?"

"Nope," he replied, picking up the trash bag and shaking it. "Trinity's the oldest: she's five years ahead of me. Jack graduated two years ago, and April's a sophomore at East U. Me, Taylor, Vincent, and Bailey are all seniors this year."

"Is Jack in school, too?"

He looked at me, surprised. "No. He's running the Station with his dad. Family business, remember?"

I did. But in Lakeview, everyone at least tried to go to college. Once again, I'd assumed it was the same here. Just like a rich cousin would.

"Okay, so I'm going," he said. "See you later?"

I had no plans to cross paths with him again that day, as far as I knew. But I still said, "Yeah. See you later."

Now, it was four thirty, and Trinity and I were on the last room of the day. By my count, we'd been at it six and a half hours, with only a thirty-minute lunch break, when we made and ate quesadillas in Mimi's kitchen. My arms ached from reaching up to polish mirrors, the smell of bleach was seemingly lodged permanently in my nose, and I understood for the first time the expression "bone tired." I knew hanging with her to the end would surprise Trinity. What I didn't expect was that I'd be so proud of myself. Putting things in order, even other people's things, felt familiar and soothing. Like my anxiety had found a good place to land, too.

"Go all the way out the door," Trinity instructed me as I cleaned the carpet to the threshold, stepping myself onto the sidewalk outside. "Then unplug and we're done."

I yanked out the cord, pulling the vacuum over to my side, and shut the door. "Now what?" I said to Trinity, who was wiping a smudge off the outside of the window.

"We put the cart back, deal with laundry, and fill bleach bottles for tomorrow. Then we get the hell out of here before anyone asks for anything else."

She led the way back to the door that said STAFF ONLY, opening it. The room inside was narrow, with a row of washers and dryers tumbling the sheets and towels we'd collected earlier. I followed her to a small countertop, lined with spray bottles. All of them were labeled with names, some in recent marker, others faded almost to the point of being unreadable. ESTHER. DAWN. MARIKA. CARMEN. It made me aware, suddenly, that the one she'd given me off the cart said nothing.

"We're possessive about our bottles," she said, clearly having noticed this. She pulled a huge container of bleach off a shelf. "If you find one you really like, you have to claim it."

"Aren't they all the same?"

She screwed off the top of her own. "At a glance, yes. But there are subtle differences. Tautness of handle, for example. And some have an adjustable spray, but others don't."

Again, I looked at my own bottle, which I was still holding, and gave it a quick squirt. It did feel a little loose.

"You don't get your own for just one day," she told me, filling up her TRINITY-marked one with water. "They're earned, not given."

"It's a spray bottle," I pointed out.

"Not here," she replied. "Here, it's a badge of honor. Now hand that over so I can refill it."

I did, then watched as she filled it up with the same mix of water and bleach. Then she put it on the shelf with all the others before placing her TRINITY one beside it.

"How long have you been doing this?" I asked.

"Officially? Since June. But I started helping clean when I was Gordon's age," she replied. "Bailey and Jack, too. We didn't have a choice, same as with the Station."

Family business, again. My dad had his own practice, not that I'd ever worked a day there. I'd spent my summers at various camps and traveling with my father or Nana. None of my friends worked real jobs yet. But things were clearly different here.

"A lot of people have passed through, huh?" I said, again scanning the names.

"It's a lake town," she replied. "Nobody stays for long unless they have roots here."

We put in some more sheets, then folded a load of towels before she pronounced us finished for the day. As we walked down the sidewalk toward Mimi's, we passed a family of guests heading up from the dock. The dad was pulling a cooler stacked with beach toys, the mom carrying a beer in one of those foam insulated holders. Their kids trailed along behind them, bickering and smelling of sunscreen.

As they all disappeared into room six, which we'd left pristine, I wondered how long it would take for them to mess it up again. Already I was tired. But thinking about this made me exhausted.

I was too wiped out to go out to the raft that afternoon, even if someone had invited me. Which they didn't.

"Lake North Pavilion at eight, then over to Colin and Blake's," Bailey reported as she came down below the house with her plate, joining Trinity and me at the picnic table there. Mimi, also worn-out, had asked Oxford to pick up two buckets of fried chicken for dinner and was eating hers in front of the TV. There was no sign of Jack anywhere, at least not so far.

"That's the plan?" Trinity asked.

"It's what I said, isn't it?"

"Sounds more like *your* plan," her sister replied. "Lake North and yacht club boys."

"Anyone who doesn't like it doesn't have to come," Bailey said, putting her glass of milk down with a thunk. "Nobody's got a damn gun to their head."

"Let me guess," Trinity said. "You're snapping at me because I'm not the only one who expressed a lack of enthusiasm."

"I'm not snapping at you," Bailey replied. "I'm just tired of putting things together every night only to have people bitch and moan."

"Summer just started, Bay."

"Exactly. Too early to be so damn picky."

They were both silent for a moment, during which I took

a bite off my own plate, wondering if it was possible to have any meal in this house without some sort of friction. Finally I asked, "Did I meet Colin and Blake?"

"Not unless you're taking sailing lessons at the yacht club," Trinity said.

Bailey shot her a look. "Colin was out at the raft yesterday. He gave me a ride in. Blake's his roommate."

"Oh, right," I said.

"And they've been over here every night this week," Bailey said. "So it only seems fair that we reciprocate and go there for once."

"Or," Trinity said, picking up a biscuit from her plate, "we could just stick with our own kind the way nature intended."

"That is such bullshit," Bailey shot back. "You know as well as I do that the kids from both sides have hung out since this place was settled."

"I'm not saying they haven't. I'm saying maybe they *shouldn't*."

"Why? Because we're not exactly alike?"

"Because we have nothing in common with those rich kids! And even if you do find one you like, do you think it's actually going to end up being anything that lasts? Every time some girl we know gets tangled up with one of them, she gets dumped at the end of the summer. It's like clock-work."

"Not every time."

"Every time."

"My mom didn't," I said.

That shut them up. Which had not been my intention, really. I was just contributing, because for once I had something to add. Now that I'd done that, though, I realized this subject was a fraught one.

"She didn't?" Trinity said after a moment. "They got divorced."

"Trinity," her sister said, her voice like a warning shot.

"After seven years," I replied. "And it was a mutual decision, from what I've heard."

Again, silence. Down at the shore, some ducks quacked as they walked along the small waves breaking there.

Trinity sighed, then looked up at the sky overhead. "Saylor. I don't mean to insult you or your mom and dad."

"It's never your intention," Bailey grumbled. "You just do."

"I'm not insulted," I told her. And I wasn't. I just knew so little of the history around here: when something came up I could claim, I wanted it to be correct. "But for what it's worth, my dad's a good guy. Even if he was a yacht club boy once."

"Fine, they're all probably wonderful," Trinity said. "I still don't want to hang out with them. Which is a moot point anyway because the Sergeant and I are doing a HiThere! tonight."

"We just went through all that and you're not even going with us?" Bailey asked.

"You know I haven't gone out since I got huge." Trinity

swung her legs around, off the bench, then grunted as she got to her feet. "But Saylor is."

"I am?" I asked.

"You have to," she replied, starting up to the house. "Otherwise she's going alone, and cousins don't let cousins do that. Especially with yacht club boys."

With this, she started up the hill to the house. I looked at Bailey, who was angrily picking at her chicken leg again. "You don't have to include me," I said. "She's just being nice."

She looked up at me. "Trinity? Nice? Since when?"

"Since I worked with her today," I said. Hardly convinced, she went back to her food. "And maybe it's more like nice-ish. I don't think she hates me anymore, at any rate."

"You cleaned rooms?" she asked. "Wow. I'm surprised."

This again. In a tired voice, I said, "Because you thought I was the spoiled rich cousin just here to relax and hang out?"

She blinked, hearing this. "Well . . . that is kind of what Mimi said."

"Well," I said, "I'm not. At least, I don't want to be."

We were both quiet a moment. Up at the house, the screen door slammed.

I picked up my drink, taking a sip. "So tell me about these boys."

She smiled. The change in subject was like that in the weather, the equivalent of a sudden cool breeze. Everything just felt different. "They're nice. Roommates at East U, just finished their freshman year."

"How'd you meet them?"

She wiped her mouth with a paper towel. "Where I meet everyone: the Station."

"You work there every summer?"

"Since I was fourteen. That's how it goes with a family business. You pitch in as soon as you can," she replied. That sounded familiar. "Trinity only ever worked the arcade and the snack bar, which is why she's so narrow-minded about Lake North folks. But like I said, working the pumps is different. You meet everyone there."

I put down my fork. "When my mom used to talk about this place, she never mentioned there were basically two different lakes. I had no idea."

"Well, it probably wasn't a bad thing as far as she was concerned, right? I mean, she did meet your dad that way."

She stopped talking then, clearly not sure whether this topic was all right to return to or still needed to be avoided. Taking out the guesswork, I said, "Do people here hate him?"

She turned to face me. "No. I mean, I don't think so. Why would they?"

I shrugged. "Because he was a rich yacht club boy. And he took her from here, and then she died."

"Because she was an addict," she replied. Immediately, she put her hand over her mouth. "Oh, shit, Emma. I can't believe I just said that. I'm—"

"It's okay." I bit my lip, then took a breath. "She was. The truth hurts, but there it is. I just wondered if everyone thought that might be Dad's fault, too."

"No." She said this so flatly, so quickly, I immediately believed her. "Look, again, I don't mean offense or to dishonor anyone's memory. All I've ever heard was how much everyone loved Waverly. But they also know she had problems long before and after he came along. I mean, that night with Chris Price, your dad wasn't even here."

Chris Price. It took a minute. "Roo's dad," I said finally.

She nodded. "He was her best friend. And she was with him that night, you know, when the boat crashed."

I didn't know. For all the stories, she'd never told this one. "What happened?"

Just then, though, I heard it: boys' voices, coming from the lawn above us. When I looked up, there were Roo and Jack, climbing out of a beat-up VW that had pulled up by the back steps.

"Yo!" Jack yelled. "I hear there's no plan for tonight. What gives?"

Bailey, too annoyed to even answer, just sighed and went back to her dinner. As she did, I watched the boys disappear into the house before re-emerging in the bright kitchen above, where they grabbed plates and descended on the chicken that remained. Clearly, the moment had passed to get the answer to my question and the story I'd not yet heard. Now, I turned back to the lake, looking past the church and that big white cross, over to the other side. From the way Trinity acted, it was another world. But really, how different could it be?

EIGHT

"Moment of truth," Bailey said, tying the boat up tight. "Who are you tonight: Emma or Saylor?"

Emma was the logical choice, of course. It was the name I knew, the one I'd always answered to as long as my mom wasn't the one calling. And she'd been gone five years now, almost six. Maybe I could just say she took Saylor with her. At the same time, though, she had picked that name based on the summer here when she'd met my dad. So if I was going to go by it, this was the time and place. Emma was the rich cousin from Lakeview who organized things and worried. Saylor, well, she could be anyone.

Even and especially this girl I was tonight, arriving at a pavilion adjacent to a yacht club in a new-to-me outfit and more makeup than I'd worn, well, ever. That was Trinity's doing.

"I'm huge and can't wear anything," she'd said as she dragged me onto the back porch that was her and Bailey's bedroom. "Just indulge me."

What this meant, I discovered, was standing there in my normal, chosen outfit of cutoff shorts and a JACKSON TIGERS T-shirt while she assembled other options on the unmade bed. Apparently, she had quite the wardrobe, pre-pregnancy, as well as a signature look: just about everything she owned was short, had cutouts, or both.

"This is really not my style," I told her, after she'd badgered me into a silky blouse, run through with gold thread, over a tight black skirt. "I don't think I can even sit in this."

"Who has to sit?" she asked, stepping back to look at me. "You're going out, not to church."

Bailey, across the room brushing her hair, snorted. Sure, it was funny to her. She was wearing jeans and a tank top, of her own choosing.

"I'm not wearing this," I said, tugging off the skirt. "It's cutting off my circulation."

"Fine." She pushed a minidress at me in its place. "Try this one."

It had a deep scoop neck, plus sleeves that billowed open to reveal my wrists and upper arms. "No," I said flatly.

"Why? It's perfect!"

"If I was giving blood," I said.

This time, Bailey laughed out loud. "You're funny," she said. "Do people tell you that?"

"More often I'm told my humor isn't for everyone," I told her. "Or, you know, anyone."

"Let's try shoes," Trinity said, heading over to a box by the end of the bed. There were no closets, the only storage a few suitcases and a couple of cardboard boxes. The bulk of their possessions were piled on the beds and other surfaces. I'd had to move a laptop, two bottles of shampoo, and a big hardback book called *Pregnancy and You* just to make enough room to sit down. "How do you feel about stilettos?"

"Strongly opposed," I told her.

"Trinity, we're taking the boat," Bailey told her. "Not going to prom."

"Well, never mind, they're not here anyway." She stood up, putting her hands on her lower back. "None of my good shoes are, now that I think of it. I left them all at the storage unit at the house when we were cleaning out for the renters. It wasn't like I was going to be wearing them."

"That's got to be weird," I said as, undeterred, she went back to picking through the piles of clothes on the bed. "Having to move house every summer."

She picked up a red blouse, squinting at it. "With the two divorces, we're used to moving around a lot. It's not so bad."

"I hate it," Bailey told me. "People we don't know living in our room, sleeping in my bed. It gives me the creeps."

"Also makes Mom money," Trinity pointed out.

"You can't put a price on peace of mind."

"I can. Eleven hundred a week."

To this, her sister rolled her eyes, turning back to the small mirror that was propped up on a nearby bookshelf. "Well, you don't even have to worry, since this is your last time doing it."

"Really?" I asked Trinity, who was now holding the red shirt up against me.

"Yep," she replied. "Once the Sergeant is back, he and the baby and I will have our own place over in Delaney, closer to the base. And start planning the wedding. I can't *wait*."

She sounded so happy, her voice a contrast to Bailey's expression in the mirror, which was hesitant, worried. Change is hard, I thought, thinking of Nana saying this to me. When Bailey saw me watching her, though, she looked away.

Now, back on the boat, I watched my feet carefully as I stepped up from the seating area to the deck. Even so, I felt unstable, miles away from the easy grace that Bailey and all those other lake girls possessed doing the same thing. Clearly, it wasn't a genetic trait.

"You can take off those shoes, if you want," Bailey said as I joined her on the dock. "I won't tell Trinity."

I looked down at the red wedge sandals her sister had picked out. They were espadrilles, with cork soles, a twist of leather fastened by a tiny gold hoop between the big toe and the rest. I had to admit, they were unlike anything I'd ever worn. But once on, with my own cutoffs and the peasant blouse with the gold threads, they worked.

"I'm good," I told her.

"Your feet, your funeral," she said with a shrug. "Come on. The Pavilion's over here."

I followed her down the dock to where it made a T into a small boardwalk, about a block or so long, dotted with shops and restaurants. WELCOME TO LAKE NORTH! said a big painted sign on one end, a graphic of a little wave beside it. At the other, built out over the water, was a covered area crisscrossed with string lights. Beneath it, a band made up of older men in tropical print shirts and khaki shorts was playing beach music.

The ride from Mimi's dock had taken ten minutes, maybe fifteen. But as we began walking toward the Pavilion, I felt more like we'd gone a million miles. It wasn't just the boardwalk itself, which was lined with planters sprouting perfectly landscaped flowers, expensive cars parked along it. Or the stores we passed, with names like Sprinkles (an ice cream parlor with a madras theme), Rosewater Boutique (offering fancy, flowing resort wear of the type Nana had packed for her cruise), and Au Jus (a dim steakhouse with leather booths, antique blown-glass lights hanging over them). Compared to what I'd seen of North Lake, everything seemed new and, well, expensive. And that was even before I got to the Tides.

Calvander's was a motel. This was a resort. Several stories high, it had been built to resemble a Spanish villa, with the walls a terra-cotta color, moss spreading across them. Now, it was lit up, illuminating the crowded open-air bar and restaurant below, as well as its own dock and private beach. No plastic floats or wheeling coolers dotted the sand, much less unattended children. Instead, there were rows of wooden beach chairs, each with a folded white towel on its seat.

"Crazy, right?" Bailey said, nodding at it. "I heard the

rooms have whirlpool baths and a menu for pillows. Can you even imagine?"

I shook my head, remembering the rooms I'd cleaned earlier, with their cool cinder-block walls and those tiny, thin soaps. "Can't be cheap to stay there."

"Three hundred a *night*," she replied. "And that's just a basic room. Who has that kind of money?"

The answer: these people all around us. Women in flower-print tailored dresses and diamond stud earrings, wearing what my grandmother called a "statement" watch and carrying purses I knew cost more than that single room rate, easily. An army of men in golf shirts in all colors and dress pants paired with loafers. Even the kids looked polished and effortless, as they ran past us to the Pavilion, their shoes thumping across the decking. I looked down at the wedges I was wearing, which now seemed too red in this place where understated made the biggest statement of all.

"And there's the yacht club," Bailey said. "Which used to be the fanciest place on this side of the lake, before the Tides came along."

She pointed at a long white building with columns, with a big deck and steps leading down to a large dock. Inside, it was brightly lit, and I could see people moving around, as well as seated at tables, each covered with a white cloth, on the outside patio. The beach below had two lifeguard stands, and rows of boats were moored at the dock and just beyond it out on the water.

"There they are," Bailey said now. Up ahead at the

Pavilion, two guys—the dark-haired one I recognized from the raft, as well as a redheaded friend who was taller and skinnier, both in shorts and T-shirts—waved from where they were standing against the rail, the water behind them. "You okay?"

"Fine," I said, even as I felt a little zing in my stomach. The truth was, for all Bridget's talk and enthusiasm, neither she, nor Ryan, nor I had actually gotten as far as dating someone yet, instead sticking to groups and packs when we went out. This was looking more like a double date, which I hadn't exactly planned on. Not that I could bail out now. Could I?

"Hey there," Colin, the guy from the raft, said with a wide smile as we came up to them. He had a red plastic cup in his hand. "Where's everyone else?"

"They'll be along eventually," Bailey answered, so smoothly I kind of believed her, even as I knew this was a lie. "Probably meet us at your place."

"Great," he replied. He looked at me. "Hi. I'm Colin."

I certainly didn't feel like the same old Emma, not right then. "Saylor," I said.

"My cousin," Bailey explained. To me she said, "And this is Blake."

The redhead had a shell necklace around his neck and a nice smile, as well as freckles that made him seem younger than he was. "Hey."

"Hi."

"How's the music?" Bailey asked Colin.

"Terrible," he replied. "Like it always is."

"The yacht club runs this whole boardwalk," she explained to me, "so the Pavilion bands are always selected for their demographic."

"Which means three types of music," Colin said. "Beach, beach, and swing."

"Not always," Blake pointed out. "Spinnerbait's playing for the Fourth."

"Seriously?" Colin asked.

"It's probably as a favor to someone in the band's grand-mother," Blake said. "Since I've never seen that kind of music here. And I've been coming my whole life."

The song ended, and there was a smattering of applause. Bailey hopped up onto the rail beside Colin and he handed her his cup. She took a sip, tucking a piece of hair behind her ear with the other hand.

"You from around here?" Blake asked me.

I shook my head. "Just visiting. From Lakeview."

"Oh. You at the U?"

Before I could answer, the band started up again. "Every-one, let's SHAG!" the lead singer said into his mike. A few couples took to the floor, whooping as they twisted and turned to the music.

"I can't take it," Colin said to Bailey. "If everyone knows where the party is, let's just go."

She nodded, hopping down, then gestured for me to follow them as they cut through the crowd around the bandstand, then down the boardwalk until it ended. As we stepped onto the sand, Blake bent down, retrieving his own plastic cup from where he'd apparently left it hidden under the decking and taking a gulp.

"Gin and tonic," he said to me, holding it out. "Want some?"

I shook my head. "Nah, I'm okay."

He seemed hardly bothered by this, sipping again as we started toward a parking lot. LAKE NORTH YACHT CLUB said a large sign stuck in the grass. MEMBERS AND THEIR GUESTS ONLY.

"Saylor's dad worked here when he was in college," Bailey said to the guys.

"Yeah?" Colin asked. "What did he do?"

"Sailing lessons," I said.

"Did he live on Campus?" Colin said.

I blinked. "What?"

"Campus," Bailey repeated. "It's what they call the apartments they rent to the employees for the summer."

"I don't know," I said. My mom was the one who always talked about the lake. "If he did, he never mentioned it."

"Then he probably didn't," Blake said as we stopped at the side of a road, waiting for a BMW to turn into the Club entrance. "You don't forget Campus."

Once across the street, we approached an L-shaped building made up of several units. It actually kind of reminded me of Calvander's: plastic chairs outside the doors piled with swimsuits and towels, a full garbage can with a pizza box poking out of it. As Blake pushed open the door to the unit F1, though, I saw the inside was actually nicer than the rooms I'd cleaned all day, with more modern fixtures and a bigger kitchen area.

"Home sweet hovel," Colin said, kicking aside a plastic garbage bag as he crossed the threshold. "Who wants a beer?"

"Me," Bailey said, following him across to the kitchen area, where he bent down to open a small fridge. "Saylor?"

"I'm okay," I called out as Blake flopped down on one of the unmade beds, grabbing a nearby remote. The flat-screen TV flashed and came on, showing a baseball game. "Thanks, though."

Across the room, I heard Bailey laughing, and turned to see her leaning against the stovetop, now with Colin's arms around her waist. She looked perfectly at ease, while I couldn't figure out if I was supposed to join Blake on his bed or just stand there. I was still wondering when the door opened again.

"Is this the party?" a girl's voice asked, and the next moment two were entering. One was a tall brunette with long legs and cheekbones to die for. Her friend was a cute Asian girl with red lipstick and a high ponytail. They both had on black shorts and yacht club shirts, white sneakers on their feet. "Because we need one. Badly."

"*Very* badly," the second girl added, heading for the kitchen. "The monsters were in top form today. And by top,

I mean at their worst."

"Hannah," Blake said, nodding at the taller girl, "and Rachel's got the ponytail." Both girls looked at me and nodded. "They work at the kids' camp."

"I almost quit today," Hannah said, pulling a beer from the fridge as Rachel plopped down on the other bed, leaning back onto her elbows. "Between the vomit and the lice scare, it was almost too much."

"Did you say lice?" Blake asked, rearing back from her, even though she was across the room.

"False alarm," she replied. "Although my head is still itching."

"But the vomit was real?" Colin said, coming across the room with Bailey behind him.

"Sadly, yes." She sighed. "The make-your-own-sundae bar seemed like a good idea, except Braden Johnson is a total glutton."

"Put the whole container of gummy worms on his," Rachel added, then shuddered. "The puke was blue and slimy."

"See, this is why you guys need to be working at the docks," Blake said as Rachel took a seat on the end of his bed, crossing her legs. "No puke and people tip."

"And deal with the parents of these children?" Rachel asked, pulling out her phone. "No thanks. They're even worse."

Listening to this, I couldn't help but think of Trinity and the similar sentiments she'd expressed as we cleaned that day. Not that she'd ever think of herself as having something in common with this group. I barely knew her, but this I was sure of.

"Where's everyone else?" Hannah asked now, taking a sip of her beer.

Colin gave her a look. "Do you mean everyone, or just Roo?"

Roo? I thought. My Roo? But he wasn't mine.

"Everyone," Hannah replied, her pretty, angular face reddening a bit. "And Roo."

Bailey, sitting with Colin on his bed close enough that their legs were touching, pulled out her phone. After glancing at the screen, she said, "They should be here soon. I think work ran late."

"Then I have time to change," Hannah said, getting to her feet. "Rachel, you coming?"

They both got up and started for the door. "Back in five," Hannah said. "Don't let anything fun happen without us."

This didn't seem likely, especially considering that the moment they left, Colin and Bailey turned to each other and began talking in low voices. Their conversation was obviously private even before he reached out, smoothing her hair back with his hand, and she closed her eyes. Meanwhile, I was left with Blake and the baseball game, which had cut to a commercial.

"So," he said, jabbing the remote at the TV as he flipped channels. "So you said you go to the U?"

I shook my head. "No. Just live in Lakeview. I have

one more year of high school."

"High school," he said. "Wow. That brings back memories."

"You're a freshman, right?"

"Going into sophomore year," he corrected me. "*Big* difference from high school."

"I bet," I said, although privately, I wondered. "What's your major?"

He sat up a bit. "Business. Although I don't know if I'll actually stay long enough to get my degree. I'm going to do this startup, sooner rather than later."

"Like a company thing?"

"Yep," he said, taking another sip of his beer. "Me and two of my friends, we've got this great idea for an app. We've got backing and everything."

"Like an app for your phone?" I asked.

"You got it." He sat up suddenly: it was clear this subject energized him. "Want to hear the idea? You can't steal it to develop yourself. We've already applied for patenting."

This would never have occurred to me, but I said, "Sure."

He muted the TV, then held up both hands. "Okay. So you drive, right?"

Already, I wasn't thrilled with the turn this conversation had taken. "Um, yeah."

"And what's the one thing everyone told you a million times when you got your license?"

I thought for a moment. "Wear a seat belt."

"No," he said. "The other thing."

"Don't drink and drive," I said.

"No." He sighed. "The *other* other thing."

I was still clueless, which must have been obvious, because he pulled out his phone, holding it up.

"Don't text and drive?" I said.

"Exactly!" he replied. "It's, like, the most dangerous thing for any driver, but especially new ones. So imagine if there was a way to turn off that function anytime you were in a car. Not only *should* you not text: you *couldn't* even if you wanted to. That's the power of I'M DRIVING. Not only can your messages wait until you get from point A to point B: they will."

He sat back, clearly pleased with himself. I said, "Wow."

"Right? It's great. I mean, just imagine the market for parents, what they'd pay for that peace of mind. You can't even put a number on it, really."

"No?"

"Well, we're thinking four ninety-nine, actually," he admitted. He really did look like a little kid with those freckles. "Again, though, we're only in the early stages. It's going to take a lot of development, since it has to work with different operating systems and stuff. Luckily, we've got a programmer on our team."

"And you're funded already?"

"We had a connection," he explained. "Taz, my suitemate? He's the real driving force behind all this."

"So to speak," I quipped. Blake looked confused. "Never mind."

"Anyway," he went on, "his dad runs Hermandos Foods, which invented the Zapwich."

"Seriously?" Zapwiches, which were like frozen calzones, had been a staple of my childhood, when I'd been allowed them. "I love those things!"

"So does everyone. Which is why they are big money." He held up two fingers, rubbing them together. "We came up with I'M DRIVING in a programming class we took fall semester, me and Taz and our other friend Lucas. The assignment was to create an app that made something safer."

"Like driving," I said, as if I was a person who did this, and worried about such things, instead of, you know, driving itself.

"Got an A, of course," he continued. "But what we were really working toward was the pitch to Taz's dad over winter break. He loved it: totally in. So now, it's just a matter of development, getting it up and running. Our long-term plan, though, is to be bought out so that I'M DRIVING becomes standard on *all* phones."

This was more than he'd said to me all night, so I took a second to catch up. "Wow," I said again.

"I know." He leaned back into the pillow behind him, picking up the remote again. "It's kind of crazy, being nineteen and knowing you've probably already made your first million. Definitely makes college seem like less of a priority."

I didn't even know what to say to this. I mean, we were well-off, as was Nana Payne, from my grandfather, who, although not the inventor of an iconic frozen food item, had also been a successful businessman. Even so, though, we never talked about money this confidently, or at all, really. It made me uncomfortable, and not just because I'd spent the day cleaning motel rooms. Although that really made me aware of it.

"This game's done," Blake announced, glancing at the TV. "You up for some beer pong?"

"I'm not much of a drinker," I told him. "But I'll cheer you on if you play."

"Yeah?" He seemed surprised by this, even touched.

"Sure," I said.

He smiled, then got to his feet, picking up his cup. Before moving, though, he waved a hand in front of him, signaling I should go first. That's sweet, I thought. As was the touch of his hand, which I felt briefly on the small of my back as I started toward the kitchen. Was this what it really felt like to have a boy interested in you? Girl falling in love at the lake was my mom's story. But maybe it could still be mine as well.

"Great minds," Blake said, waving a hand between us. "It's hot as balls in there."

That wasn't exactly how I would have put it, but he wasn't wrong. Hannah and Rachel had returned, the beer pong game began, and I watched as Blake lost three rounds in a row. Meanwhile, a bunch of servers and waiters, off their shifts from the Club restaurant, began to show up, taking the room from crowded to outright packed. Unlike at

Mimi's, the A/C couldn't keep up. I'd basically had to leave before I melted.

Still, I hadn't expected Blake to follow me outside, as this was technically his party. Then again, he had downed several beers in a short period. He probably needed air even more than I did.

"Having fun?" he asked. "I mean, aside from the hot-as-balls part."

"Yeah," I said.

"You sure you don't want a beer? We have plenty."

I shook my head. "No thanks."

"Why not?"

"I'm sorry?"

He cleared his throat. "Sorry. It's just in college, when people are sober, there's usually a reason. Religion. A problem. Parents super strict. Or something."

"Nothing like that," I said, and he nodded. I thought maybe I should explain more, tell him about my mom. But something stopped me. "Just not my thing."

"Ah. Got it." He snapped his fingers. "Speaking of parents, I wanted to show you something."

"Is it *your* parents?" I asked in a deadpan voice. "Because if so, you might want a mint. And some coffee. And a chance to make better choices."

"What?" he said.

Again, I thought of Roo, nodding as I discussed my humor. Clearly, Blake was not of our people. "Never mind," I said. "Show me."

I followed him down the sidewalk. At the end of the row, there was a laundry room, a dryer inside banging loudly, as well as a bulletin board with the clearly ignored rules of NO PARTIES and NO GUESTS. After that, the walkway ended, but Blake kept going, hanging a left into the dark behind the building. We passed a row of shrubs before coming up on a blank bit of wall, a pair of floodlights shining down it.

"I give you," he said, "the Campus wall."

What I was looking at was a square expanse, maybe six feet by eight feet, weather-worn and streaked with dirt. It looked in need of a power washing, not our attention. "It's nice?" I ventured.

"Nice?" He sighed, then stepped closer, right up to it, gesturing for me to do the same. "It's history. Look."

I stepped up beside him. As I did, I saw what I'd thought was dirt and blotches were actually signatures, tons of them, stretching from one side to the other. KENT RAMENS KITCHEN WARRIOR! CLASS OF 1987. ELIZABETH WAS HERE '94. ALEX AND EVIE, 7/20/2000–4EVER. It reminded me of the pictures under glass in Mimi's office, all these memories, but in words, not images.

"When was your dad here?" Blake asked me now. "Do you know?"

I thought for a second. "The late nineties, I think."

He bent down to study something scribbled by one of the bushes. "I've seen some from then here for sure.

Unfortunately, they're not in any order. You just sign where you find a spot."

"Have you?" I asked.

"Yep. It's up there." I looked where he was indicating, scanning the scribbles above us to the left. Finally, I found it: BLAKE R., DOCKS Y'ALL! '18. Colin's signature was below.

"You do it every summer," I said, clarifying.

"At the *end* of summer. The bash on the last night. It's a ritual."

I looked back up at all those names and dates, wondering if my dad's really was up there someplace. It was weird, picturing him at Blake's age, maybe with my mom nearby. And now here I was, brought to this same place all these years later. It seemed crazy, and fated, hitting me all at once, so that I felt unsteady even before I turned to find Blake right there, his face close to mine.

"Hi," he said softly. Up close the freckles weren't so noticeable, which was weird.

"Hi," I replied. I could see a name in my side vision— MARY!—with a heart, but only for a second, because then I was closing my eyes and he was sliding his arms around my waist and kissing me.

I'd waited so long for this moment, my first real kiss, and envisioned it in a million different ways. None of them, however, involved a wall, the thought of my mom and dad, and then, just as I'd managed to push these things away, the sudden sound of someone yelling.

"Did you hear that?" he asked, pulling back from me.

"Yeah. What was it?"

We were both quiet. His arms were still around my waist. A beat later, I heard a girl's voice, distant but clear. "I always do what you want! The least you can do is return the favor *once*!"

"That sounds like Bailey," I said softly, not sure why I was whispering.

"You want me to let you drive the boat home when you've been drinking," a male voice replied.

"Goddammit, Jack. I didn't say that!"

Blake looked at me. "Her brother," I explained. "I should probably—"

"Yeah," he said, stepping back to wave me past him. "Let's go."

Quickly, I made my way around the building and into the light of the Campus. As my feet hit the sidewalk and I passed the bulletin board, I realized how loud their voices actually were.

"I set this whole thing up," Bailey was saying. "I told everyone you guys were going to be here, and then you finally show up and just want to take the boat—"

"Because you're not driving it," Jack shot back. "Look at you! You're slurring!"

"I am not slurring!" she shouted, and she wasn't, to my ears. "I'm pissed!"

Now, coming around the final corner to the row of

units, I could see a small group—Colin, Rachel, some of the servers—gathered around my cousins, who were face-to-face. I hurried over.

"Give me the keys to the motor," Jack said now, sticking out his hand.

"You couldn't just hang out for an hour," she said, and I thought of how she'd organized this from the start to bring both sides of the lake together, folding Colin in. "For me."

He wiggled his hand at her, impatient.

"You're an asshole," she said.

"Whoa, whoa." Colin stepped up beside her. "Let's take it down a notch."

Jack pointed at him. "You stay out of this. It's your fault she's drunk in the first place."

"Me?" Colin objected. "I didn't force anything on her."

"She's underage!" Jack said. "Still in high school. Did she tell you that?"

In response, Bailey surged forward, slapping both hands against his chest and pushing him backward. As he stumbled, then caught himself, I spotted Roo just behind him, watching all of this with a tense look on his face.

"Bailey," I said to her softly.

"Just get out of here," she told Jack, her voice cracking. "You don't want to be here, go."

He held out his hand again. "Give me the keys and I will."

She shoved a hand into her pocket, pulling out a key ring and winging it at him. "Fine. Here."

Even though she was upset, her aim was good enough that he had to shift right at the last minute to avoid getting hit. The keys hit the ground with a clank. He bent down, snatching them up, then turned and started to walk away.

"You'll thank me tomorrow," he said over his shoulder. "When you realize how close you came to doing something stupid."

"I wasn't going to drive home!" she replied. "We both know I wouldn't do that."

"What we know," he replied, "is that death is no joke. So stop fucking around."

Furious, Bailey started to charge at him again. I looked at Colin, who was beside me, but he just stood there, so I reached to grab her, pulling her back. She was shaking, an actual heat coming off her skin as I tightened my grip around her wrists. On Jack's other side, Roo was watching, too.

"Take a breath," I said into her ear. "Bailey."

After fighting me for another moment, she finally went limp. Jack was almost to the road now, his own pace brisk, but Roo remained where he'd been.

"I wasn't going to take the boat home," Bailey said to him, her voice tight. "Roo. I wasn't."

"Okay," he said quietly.

She exhaled a half sob, half breath, running her hands through her hair. I'd been so caught up on what was happening I hadn't noticed everyone else had gone back into Blake and Colin's place, leaving the three of us alone. I watched as Bailey saw this as well, processing what it may or may not have meant, before she spoke again.

"I'm leaving. Come on, Saylor."

I looked back at the guys' apartment, where the door was half-open, voices and music drifting out from inside. It seemed rude to just take off, especially since I'd been lip-locked with one of the hosts only moments earlier. And didn't she want to say goodbye to Colin?

Apparently, the answer was no. She was already halfway to the road.

I looked at Roo again. "What just happened?"

He was watching Bailey crossing the grass. Jack was long gone. "Depends on who you ask, I guess."

"I'm asking you," I said.

Now, he did meet my eyes. "She wanted him to stay. He wanted to go. And drinking and boats don't mix."

The accident. I blinked, it only just then hitting me that we were talking about his dad, and that night all those years ago, when my mom was with him.

I squinted through the dark, to the road. Bailey was about a block down now. "I should go, I guess." I kicked off Trinity's shoes, picking them up in one hand, then started across the grass.

"Hey," Roo called out. I turned. "See you later?"

I told myself it was just what they said here. And yet. "Yeah," I said. "See you."

I had to jog to catch up with Bailey, leaving me breathless. Finally I reached her, the lights of Campus dimmer now behind us. "Hey," I said. "You okay?"

"No," she replied, still walking. "Yes. Maybe. I don't know."

We walked in silence for a bit, passing the back of the Tides—PRIVATE! GUESTS ONLY! said several signs— as well as the boardwalk, which was pretty much deserted. It was clear that North Lake and Lake North had many differences, but neither was a late-night town.

"I wasn't going to take the boat home, just so you know," she said suddenly as a gated neighborhood called Bellewether came up on our left.

I didn't say anything.

"Seriously! I wasn't." She tucked a piece of hair behind her ear. "I figured Roo would bring them over, Jack would take our boat back, and we'd catch a ride with someone. It would have worked out fine if he'd just not been such a jerk. But lately he's always a jerk because my dad is putting all this pressure on him about taking over the Station."

A car was coming toward us now, moving slowly, headlights bright in my eyes. I started to move out of the road, but then it turned, leaving just us and the dark again.

"I'll be honest," I said. "I don't really understand what happened back there."

She sighed, shoving her hands in her pockets. "Jack's the oldest of all of us. He knows that what he does, everyone else will do. He's hung out with Rachel and Hannah before on our side. If he'd come over here in good faith, it would have been just like any other night. Only the setting is different."

"But he didn't do that," I said, clarifying.

"Of course not. He had a chip on his shoulder, the way he always does about guys from the yacht club, and everyone from Lake North, for that matter."

"And it probably doesn't help if they're into his little sister," I added.

She glanced at me. "That's irrelevant. He'd rather I date a certified douchebag from our side than a saint from over here."

"Is there really a verification process for that?"

She rolled her eyes. "Ha, ha."

I smiled. "So maybe he's biased. But it seems like what you were actually about to come to blows about was the whole drinking-on-the-boat thing."

"Because he knows that subject negates anything else!" she replied, loudly enough so I stopped walking for a second, startled. "Sorry. It's just we've heard about that accident our whole lives. It's the cautionary tale of all cautionary tales and had nothing to do with all this. And the fact that he brought it up in front of Roo just makes me look more like a jerk, because . . ."

She trailed off, her flip-flops slapping hard against the pavement as we passed a third gated neighborhood in a row, by my count, on this tiny deserted road. What were they keeping out? Civilization?

"Because it was his dad," I finished.

"Which, again," she shot back, "had nothing to do with Jack sabotaging my night and this thing I had going with Colin!"

"I know," I said carefully, holding up a hand. "I'm new here, remember? I'm just trying to catch up."

She ducked her head down, not saying anything for a minute. Up ahead, the road was widening as we approached an intersection, a single red blinking light above it.

"Your mom never talked about it?" she asked me finally.

"The accident?" She nodded. "No. She told a lot of stories, but not that one."

"Whereas my mom," Bailey said, "couldn't forget. Everything was a reminder. The summer starting, their group hanging out together, even the lake itself. It was like a ghost, haunting her."

"What happened?"

We were almost to the light now. Just beyond it, there was a sign: NORTH LAKE 3 MILES. An arrow pointed the way.

"You really want to hear it?" she asked.

"Yeah."

We passed under the light. Blink. Blink. Blink.

"All right," she said. "So it happened in July."

NINE

July 9, 2000, was my mom's twenty-first birthday. She'd been with Dad for a year by then, dating long-distance during the school months. By Christmas, they'd be engaged, and she'd be pregnant with me.

But in June, as summer began, she didn't know any of this. She was just missing her boyfriend, and more nervous than she wanted to admit about starting a new life almost two hours west. She dealt with it the way she did most things, back then. She tried to forget.

Most lake kids liked to party—in that small of a town, there weren't a lot of entertainment options—but even with this as the norm, my mom had always stood out. Whatever she liked to do, she did to excess. What she was best known for, though, was her disappearing act.

The gist was this: they'd all be out on the water at night, having a few beers at the raft, when someone would notice she was gone. The first time, of course, panic ensued, especially when despite zigzagging the water and yelling, she couldn't be found. Until Celeste, near hysteria, got back to the shore to call 911 and found my mom sitting there wrapped in a towel, sucking on a cold Pop Soda. She'd swum all the way back, in darkness, then sat and watched as they searched for her.

My dad hated the disappearing act. One time she did it while they were sailing with his friends on the Lake North side, and he was so angry he broke up with her as a result. It took a full week of profuse apologizing before she finally convinced him to change his mind.

Her birthday that year fell on a Sunday, but my mom planned to celebrate all weekend, starting with when my dad arrived on Friday from Lakeview, where he'd been taking summer classes for dental school. She'd been so looking forward to his visit, literally crossing the days off the calendar she kept on her bedroom wall. That morning, though, he called: the mandatory study group for one of his classes could only meet that weekend. He wasn't coming.

My mom, hurt and furious, screamed at him over the phone before slamming every door on her way out of the house to her car. The next time anyone saw her was the following afternoon, when she came home hungover, slept until noon the next day, then started up again to celebrate her first legal birthday in earnest.

Her party was being held at Celeste and Silas's new place. By then they'd been married two years and had Jack, who was just starting to walk. The house was small, but homey, and they'd planned a cookout and game night. There were stations for cornhole, pin the tail on the donkey, Texas

Hold'em, and others. Celeste wanted everything to be perfect.

My mom arrived at the party with Chris Price and an open beer in her hand, then proceeded to down some shots of tequila in quick succession. As her sister began to explain the protocol of game night, my mom heckled her. When she crumpled up her hand-printed scorecard and chucked it at her, Celeste threw her out.

Chris and Silas tried to negotiate a peace, but Calvander girls, stubborn as a rule, were not budging. So Celeste locked herself in her room, crying, while Waverly and Chris Price left together to go to Splinkey's, the only bar in town. They drank a pitcher of beer and played darts, cutting up, until the guy serving them told them to go home. Instead, they went to the lake.

At twenty-two, Chris was a year older than Waverly, and had a kid on the way with his on-and-off girlfriend, Stephanie. At that moment, they were split, having broken up after fighting about money, impending parenthood, and his own partying. Like Waverly, Chris was known for his love of a good time as well as a sense of humor that bordered on the annoying. Celeste said there were lots of reasons he and my mom were best friends, but a big one was that sometimes, no one else could stand to be around them.

They were alone, then, that night, as they climbed onto Chris's boat with a six-pack they'd grabbed from the market. It probably felt like old times, high school days, when they'd had nothing to worry about but curfew. But beyond that buzz, the real world was looming: Chris was going to be a dad, and my mom was moving away. Bailey said Celeste had always wondered what they talked about that night, alone on the raft in the dark. But Waverly had never said. She never talked about it at all.

What we did know was this. At some point, Waverly pulled her disappearing act, slipping into the dark water. When Chris realized she was gone, he started shouting for her, first half laughing, then angry. By the time he got into the boat to search, he was enraged and, as blood alcohol tests would later show, way over the legal limit. He had to be, everyone said, to forget the contours and landmarks of the lake he knew by heart, and run at full speed into the mooring that was a hundred feet from the Calvander dock. Chris wasn't in the boat as it began to sink. He'd been pitched into the water, breaking his neck. It might have all started with Waverly wanting to vanish, but in the end, he was the one who was gone.

Emma? You there?

I picked up my phone. It was early morning, the sun not even up, and I'd assumed it was my dad calling from Greece again across time zones. But it was Ryan.

Why are you awake right now? I asked.

Sunrise hike with cast and crew. Bonding experience. My legs are screaming.

I blinked. **Cast and crew?**

For the musical. South Pacific. I told you, right?

148

No. You're in a show? I'm impressed!

Downstairs, I heard a door slam. Even at this hour, someone was up. Probably making toast.

Well it is a drama camp, she wrote back. **Dad strongly suggested I stop moping in my room and get involved. Please never tell him I said this but it's actually kind of fun.**

So you're acting? I wrote back.

I'm not. Tech crew. Everyone's pretty cool, though.

There was a pause, and then two pictures popped up on the screen. One was of Ryan at a picnic table with a bunch of other campers, all of them making stupid faces for the camera. The next was of her standing over a lightboard, a girl with long black hair in an army cap beside her.

How's the mystery grandmother?

I'd only texted with Ryan a few days earlier, and this had been what we'd talked about. But already, North Lake felt like something bigger than just Mimi and me seeing each other again, or even me coming to stay. But I wasn't sure how to word it for myself yet, much less someone else.

Good, I wrote. **Learning my way around.**

Oh crap, we're going back down the mountain. Pray for me. Talk soon???

I sent her a thumbs-up. When she replied with a heart, I rolled over, closing my eyes again. Ryan was doing shows. I was cleaning rooms. When Bridget had predicted a different summer, she'd been onto something. Even if I'd never expected anything like this.

* * *

"Hungover?"

I looked at Trinity, who had just come in from the porch, still in her pajamas. "No," I said. "Why?"

"You and Bailey were out pretty late," she replied, picking up the bread from the counter.

"Jack came and took the boat," I explained. "We had to walk back."

"In my shoes?"

"I took them off first." I nodded at the steps, where I had left them neatly lined up. "My feet were filthy."

"Ugh. I bet." She loaded the toaster and pushed down the lever. Then she leaned against the counter, her belly poking out in front of her. "So how was it?"

I shrugged. "Fine. We just hung out until Jack showed up and wanted the boat. The guys were nice."

She scoffed at this, blowing her hair out of her face. "Let me guess. They're both rich and in college."

"Don't know about rich," I replied, although I didn't doubt it. "But yeah, they're roommates at East U."

Another snort, although this time she saved me the commentary. A moment later—BING!—the toast popped up. After she quickly moved the slices to a plate, cursing at the heat on them, she said, "You want to work this morning?"

"Sure," I replied.

She went to the fridge, collecting the butter, then came to the table to grab a knife. "We'll start at nine sharp. Meet you over there?"

"Sounds good."

She shuffled off, toast and butter balanced on the plate. I pulled over the paper Oxford had left behind and flipped to the obits. Just as I was about to start reading about Hazel Walker, aged 85, who had passed away surrounded by her loved ones, my phone beeped again. Blake.

At the docks today. You should come by.

So he'd gotten my number. Which meant that despite my nerves, I'd clearly made a good impression. Plus, he wasn't bad to look at, and the kiss (my first!) had been nice while it lasted. Maybe I just needed to give this a chance.

Have to work. Will try, I wrote back. A beat later, he sent me a smiley face. A redhead. Cute.

"Morning."

I jumped, startled to find myself there in my seat at the table, the obit for Hazel Walker still unread in front of me and Jack crossing the kitchen to the toaster.

"Hey," I said in return.

He loaded up some bread before coming over to sit. "Obituaries, huh?" he asked. "Kind of a morbid way to start the day, isn't it?"

"Death is no joke," I pointed out.

He smiled, a bit ruefully. "I did say that, didn't I?"

"Among other things."

A sigh, and then he ran a hand over his hair. "Well, it's the truth. I was in the right, whether she sees it that way or not."

To this I said nothing, focusing again on Hazel as I took another bite of my toast.

"Okay, fine." He sighed. "I was in the right but *might* have handled it a bit more diplomatically."

"A bit?" I asked.

"How pissed was she, really?"

I looked up at him. "On a scale of one to ten? Twelve."

BING! went the toaster. He got up, plucking out the slices and dropping them onto a plate, then went to the fridge. "Where's the butter?"

"Trinity took it." I pointed. "The porch."

He glanced down the hallway, then came back to the table. Picking up a piece of toast, he said, "What about you?"

I swallowed. "What about me?"

"How pissed are *you*?" he replied. "At me."

Surprised he'd care either way, I was nonetheless truthful. "Not at all. It was a nice walk."

"Except for Bailey being at a twelve."

"Well, there was that," I agreed. "She cooled down after a mile or so, though."

He sighed again. Then, nodding at the paper, he said, "One more question and I'll leave you to your death notices."

"Shoot."

"How much is she really into this yacht club guy?"

I thought of Bailey's face the night before, streaked with tears, as we made our way down the middle of the empty road that led home.

"I think it was pretty obvious," I said finally. "Don't you?"

Jack bit his lip, and for a second I could see just what

he must have looked like as a little kid, getting caught for something and instantly sorry. Just as quickly, though, he was getting to his feet, taking his breakfast to go. "Tell her the boat needs gas," he said over his shoulder as he dropped his glass in the sink. "Not sure she realizes."

I nodded, and then he was gone, down the hallway to the door. As he went to push it open, I saw him pause, glancing at the entryway to the living room and porch beyond where Bailey was still sleeping. I thought he might go to her or say something. No. He did, however, ease the door shut slowly behind him, so for once it didn't slam.

TEN

I was working in room three that morning, while Trinity tackled four, her vacuum banging against the wall separating us. I'd just started changing the sheets when Roo passed by, carrying a ladder.

The walkie-talkie was stuck in his back pocket again, and he was whistling cheerfully, as he passed room four, then five, before finally stopping in front of six to set up the ladder. I watched, silent, until he started to climb it. Then I couldn't help myself.

"Be careful!" I yelled, realizing too late I'd startled him. Whoops. "You need a ladder buddy."

He just looked at me. "A what?"

"A ladder buddy. So you don't fall." God, I was such a dork. I put down my spray bottle, walking toward him. "You know, to hold it. My dad . . . he has this rule."

That was putting it mildly. If my mom had been one to throw caution to the wind, my dad had always held it close and tight. We walked with scissors. At even the smallest intersection we looked both ways. Twice. And when it came to ladders, you never went up alone.

"Ladder buddy?" Roo repeated. He looked amused. "I have never heard of that in my life."

"Maybe it's a dentist thing," I suggested, assuming my normal position on the other side of the ladder, both hands gripping it tight. "Okay, you're good. Go ahead."

"You're going to stop me from falling?"

"No," I replied, a bit huffily, "but I will keep the ladder from collapsing underneath you, which would pitch you off to your death."

"Death?"

"I'm a Payne," I explained. "We're a careful people."

He considered this, and me, before saying, "Well, I'm a Price. We're mostly known for sticking our fingers into light sockets."

"All the more reason to make safety a habit," I said. He snorted. "Just climb, would you?"

He laughed. "Okay, buddy."

Up he went, while I, still gripping, contemplated when I'd escape the long shadow of my father's safety practices. Not yet, apparently. As Roo pulled his phone from his pocket, I said, "What are you doing, exactly?"

"Mimi needs some roof work done, so Silas sent me down to grab shots of what needs repairing," he replied, snapping one photo, then another. The ladder wobbled, and I gripped it harder.

"I thought Silas and Celeste were divorced," I said.

"Twice," he replied, lifting one foot to scratch it. "But he's still family to Mimi. They take care of each other."

"Both feet on the ladder, please," I said before I could even stop myself.

He turned, peering down at me again. "You really are nervous about this, aren't you?"

"I told you," I replied. "It's genetic."

"Maybe," he said, examining a shot he'd already taken on his screen, "but you are also part Calvander. And they leap off ladders. For fun."

"Are you done?"

"Not yet," he said cheerfully, turning the phone to landscape mode. He looked down at me. "Question: Does it make you nervous when I do this?"

Gingerly, he jumped on the ladder step once. Then twice. With both feet.

"You stop that," I said in my sternest voice.

"What about this?" He widened his eyes, then dangled one leg off entirely. "Oopsie!"

"Roo. Just—"

"Boy!" Oxford bellowed from the porch of the main house. I jumped where I was standing. "Don't you be acting a fool on that damn ladder, you want to crack your head open?"

Roo pulled all his limbs back on, quick, as I laughed out loud. Then he looked at me. "Some buddy you are," he said. "What happened to *support*?"

"I'm supporting!" I said. "You're the one acting a fool."

BEEP, went the walkie suddenly. "Rubber Duck! You got the keys to the prize case? Someone just hit the jackpot on the bonus tickets and they're getting antsy."

"On my way," Roo replied, taking his hands back. He signed off with a beep, then looked at me. "Duty calls. Thanks for the support, buddy."

"You're welcome," I said.

"Saylor!" I turned to see Trinity, in the doorway of room four with the vacuum. "Are we working or are we flirting?"

My face went red-hot, but Roo just laughed. "Some buddy you are," I said. "What happened to support?"

"I'm supporting," he said, folding up the ladder. "You're the one flirting." Then he grinned at me, stuck it under his arm, and started toward the office. Again my face was flushed. But for different reasons, now.

"Now, what I want us all to do is to breathe together," Kim, the leader of the birthing class, was saying from the front of the room. "Okay? Inhale on three. One, two, THREE."

I drew in a shallow breath, not sure how me doing this would actually help this process. Trinity, who was leaning back against me, sucked in enough for both our lungs, before letting it go when instructed with a whoosh that blew her bangs sideways. Impressive.

"When the baby comes," Kim was saying now, "there will be moments to push and moments to rest. But no matter what, you want to be breathing."

"Seems like a good rule for anytime, really," I muttered.

"Hush." Trinity shifted her position, elbowing me in my stomach in the process. "You're supposed to be the Sergeant, remember?"

"He doesn't make jokes?" I asked.

"Not stupid ones, no."

Originally it was Celeste who had been Trinity's partner, as the Sergeant's delayed homecoming meant he wasn't around when the birthing classes began in early June. But then Celeste's boss at the grocery had quit, so she'd had to take over running everything, and Mimi stepped in. With the season beginning and the hotel still down a housekeeper, though, soon she too had her hands full. The only other ones with free time were me and Oxford, who claimed he'd faint at even the mention of the word *uterus*, much less a whole class about its capabilities.

So here I was, in the partner position, breathing and reassuring and watching incredibly disturbing birth videos that I could not forget despite really, really trying. If all went well, the Sergeant would be home by the end of July, in time for the birth itself, if not the last few classes. I didn't know him at all, but I was still pretty sure he'd be better at it than I was.

Until then, though, it was my job to tote the nursing pillow, water bottle, and pad that Trinity used to jot down notes. She was so big it was all she could do just to drive us there and walk in, and that day, she'd decided maybe she couldn't even manage that.

"You drive," she'd said as we'd come out to Mimi's

Toyota, parked by the Calvander's office. "It's just too hard for me these days."

I hesitated. "I can't."

Already at the passenger door, she glanced over at me. "You don't have a license?"

Lie, I told myself. But out loud I said, "No, I do."

"Great," she said, starting to ease herself into the seat. It was a multiphase process: backing in her rear end first, then a pivot to a sitting position, followed by pulling in her legs. When she finished and I still hadn't moved, she said, "What's the problem?"

"I don't like to drive," I said, or rather blurted. "It makes me nervous."

"Nervous?" she repeated. "This is North Lake. We'll be lucky if we even pass another car."

"I know," I said. "But I've never liked it, and then I backed into a car in the parking deck—"

"That happens to everyone," she replied, shifting to get both feet more in the center of her floor mat. "Rite of passage. Now get in, we're going to be late."

She shut her door. I stayed where I was. A moment later, she rolled down the window. "Are you serious about this?"

"I don't like driving," I said again.

"Well, I don't like that my fiancé isn't here for birthing class, but I'm doing it anyway," she replied. "You have your license on you?"

"Yeah."

"Then come on." She tossed the keys into the driver's

159

seat. "If I can get in the goddamn car at my size, you can do this."

I wasn't sure what it was about Trinity, exactly, that caused me to find myself doing things I normally thought impossible. Maybe that it wasn't her faith in me as much as her frustration. She just had no time for my neurosis, which made me wonder if maybe that was an option for me, as well.

I walked over and pulled open the driver's-side door. "I'm going to be nervous."

"Great. You'll drive carefully. Let's go."

She pulled out her phone as I picked up the keys, and then I slid behind the wheel. It felt weird, and I wished I was in her seat, where the view was familiar. I was trying to figure out another way to get her to switch with me when she took a pointed view at the clock on the console.

It's North Lake, I thought. We'll be lucky if we even see another car. I put the key in and turned it.

She was partially right. After we turned out of Calvander's—a Payne, I looked left, right, then left again, and would have done another round of this if she hadn't sighed, loudly—we were the only ones on the road for a good ten minutes. Then, though, we came up on construction and a row of cars backed up as a bored flagman held up a sign that said STOP. With people suddenly ahead of and behind me, I felt my palms begin to sweat against the wheel.

"The thing is," Trinity, who'd spent the entire trip so far detailing various grudges she had with the army, her pregnant body, and the world in general, was saying, "this isn't the way I would have done this, given the chance. No one wants to be knocked up before the wedding, you know?"

I nodded, realizing I was clenching my teeth. The flag guy, bored, was looking at his phone.

"But it is what it is, and I am," she continued, rubbing a hand over her stomach. "And honestly, I just want the Sergeant here when the baby comes. Even if he shows up literally the night before my water breaks. It's one thing to be pregnant alone. I don't want to start my life as a parent that way, too."

Breathe, I told myself, as someone beeped behind us. It didn't work, so I went for another way to distract myself. "So how did you guys meet?"

At this, she smiled. It was a rare thing, as I'd noticed soon after meeting her, and happened mostly when the subject turned to her fiancé. "He and one of his buddies rented a room last summer for his twenty-first birthday. But really, it all started with toast."

I glanced in the rearview just in time to see the guy behind me shake a fist at the flagman. I said, "Toast?"

"Yep." She sat back, now with both hands on her belly. "The morning after they checked in, he was outside the unit when I went to work at the office. I had my two slices with butter, and they were burnt, because our toaster then was a fire hazard. He made a joke about it and we started talking. Been together ever since."

"That's cute," I said, because even in my anxious state, I had to admit it was.

"I know, right?" she replied. "We got engaged in the fall, and I found out about this one"— she patted her stomach— "a month later, about the same time he got his deployment orders. Right before he left, he bought me the toaster. It's a good thing, too, because I was so sick the first trimester, and bread was all I could eat."

I'd figured there was a story behind all this, and under any other circumstances I would have been glad to finally hear it. As it was, though, I couldn't focus because traffic was moving again, this time around the construction in the opposite lane. Trinity kept talking about the Sergeant, but I was too busy white-knuckling it until we were back on the right side of the road to really listen.

Now, back at birth class, I took a deep breath as I grappled with the fact that in less than a half hour, I would have to drive back. Normal people don't do this, I thought as Kim encouraged all the mamas to visualize an ocean with the contractions as waves. But I'd never been "normal," especially when it came to being in my head. Although other people's worries still seemed to be freeing me from my own a bit. Which was a nice surprise.

I also appeared to, maybe, have something going on with Blake. To find out, I'd turned to another expert.

"Tell me *everything*," Bridget had said when I finally got hold of her a few days after that first trip to the Campus. "And go *slowly*."

I glanced at my watch. I was sitting on Mimi's side steps, with thirty minutes for lunch before I had to go back to cleaning with Trinity, who was currently stretched out across a bed in an empty room eight, resting her feet. But Bridget could drag out a story like no one else: with her questions, follow-ups, and then follow-ups to the follow-ups, I could see this easily taking the entire afternoon.

Still, I did my best. By the time I was done, we still had ten minutes for analysis. She got right to it.

"Well, it's obvious he's into you," she said as I finally ripped open the pack of peanut butter crackers that was my lunch. "The wall, that kiss . . . it's like textbook. But what's happened *since* the kiss? That's important."

I thought for a second. There had been the texts that morning following the night at Blake's apartment. Also, the invite to come visit the docks, which didn't happen, as I'd instead ended up at my first birth class. Two nights later, however, I'd ridden out to the raft in the late afternoon with Jack. When Blake had shown up with Colin and a few other guys from the Club, he'd immediately climbed off the boat to come over to talk to me, in full view of everyone. Then, when we met up later at the Station, he'd again sought me out, issuing a challenge to a Skee-Ball tournament. I lost, but he let me choose the prize when we cashed in tickets. I picked a small stuffed bear wearing an even tinier pair of board shorts in a Hawaiian print, which he insisted I name Blake for its shock of red hair. Currently, it sat in my room by the clock, although we'd agreed to share custody from week to week.

"Okay," Bridget said when I finished detailing all this. "That's all three of the IFS. Total boyfriend behavior."

"The IFS?" I asked.

"Initiative, Future thinking, and Sweet," she replied. "It's the checklist. Initiative: he reached out first by text and came to find you. Twice. Future thinking: he's assuming you'll still be hanging out when it's time for the bear to go to him. And sweetness, because guys who are only wanting a quick fling or even less don't bother with that."

"Where did you hear this?"

"I didn't. It's my own invention." When I laughed, she said, "Hey, I'm being serious! I've watched just about every rom-com from the last twenty years, read all the great romances. . . . I've retained things. Studied patterns. There's a science to this."

I smiled. "You know, you should be the one sort of dating someone. Clearly, you're the expert."

"Right?" She sighed. "Unfortunately, I'm living here in a senior community in Ohio for the time being. There's plenty of shuffleboard, but not a lot of opportunity to test my theories."

"Summer's not over yet," I pointed out.

"At least Grandpa is doing better," she said, "which means I may get back home to pursue the twins solo before school starts. You have to admit, I will have earned it by then. But anyway, tell me again about the kiss. I feel like you're leaving things out."

I hadn't, not that I was aware of. It didn't matter anyway, because just then Trinity emerged from room eight, moving slowly and rubbing her eyes. When she started to push the cart down to the next room, I'd said goodbye to Bridget, grabbed my spray bottle, and went to join her. The first room we opened was a shambles. Just what I needed.

Since then, Bridget and I hadn't talked. If we had, though, I was sure she'd probably have another acronym, if not multiple theories, about how well things were developing between Blake and me.

Maybe it was just that I had high expectations, thanks to all the romantic movies and books I myself had consumed. But I'd always thought that if and when this finally happened, I would have that whooshing, tingly feeling, almost an out-of-body experience.

I wouldn't have been so aware of this if it wasn't for Bailey. After that night at Lake North when we'd walked home, I thought things would have cooled between her and Colin. I mean, he hadn't exactly stood up for her with Jack, and then went inside when things got really ugly between them. In her mind, however, he hadn't been a disappointment: she had.

"What could he do?" she asked me the next night, as we sat in her bedroom. "My brother shows up and the next thing Colin knows, we're outside screaming at each other. It's so embarrassing. I would have taken off, too."

"No, you wouldn't have," I said, thinking of her sticking up for me on the raft.

"And all those people were there!" She sighed, as if this was the worst part. "My dad always says if you want to really know someone, look at how they act when *no one's* watching. That's the true test of character."

I had to think about this a moment. "But that doesn't make sense. I mean, if you can see them, then someone's watching: you. Right?"

"The point is," she continued, missing this or choosing not to hear it, "he did me a favor. The last thing I wanted was for him to see me get so upset. It's not who I am."

It made my head hurt, trying to follow this logic. But to her, it made sense. It had to, because the only other option was that Colin didn't care about her the way she did him, and that she wouldn't even consider.

As a result, her feelings for him had only grown more intense. If not at Campus or planning how to get there, she was on the phone with him, texting him or—more often—waiting for him to respond. At all other times she was visibly distracted, with any question posed to her needing to be repeated, often more than once. I'd never seen anything like it.

It wasn't like that with Blake. At least, not yet. But sometimes, you just need something to get you there. I was counting on Club Prom.

Around as old as the Club itself, it was held every year, just as the season was reaching full swing. The ballroom would be decorated according to a chosen theme, a band brought in, and everyone attending had to dress up in what was referred to as "resort finest." At the beginning, this had meant bathing suits with corsages, the whole thing more of a joke than anything else. But in the last ten years or so, it had become more of a real formal dance. It was a big deal to go, and if you weren't a Club member, you had to be asked.

I was well versed in all of this because lately, Bailey was obsessed, spending what free time she had looking for dresses at Bly County Thrift and the discount stores, as well as dog-earing pages with makeup looks in Trinity's fashion magazines. Colin hadn't yet formally asked her—nor Blake me—but she assured me repeatedly this didn't mean anything, since it was over two weeks away. When he did extend the invitation, she'd have everything ready along with her yes, and thought that I should, too.

"But what if he doesn't ask me?" I'd said the previous evening, after we'd ridden with Vincent, who I'd met that first night, out to the raft in late afternoon. "Then I have a dress and makeup and everything, and I'm pathetic."

"You're sharing custody of a stuffed animal," she said, squinting in the direction of the yacht club. "He's going to ask you."

"Stuffed animal?" Vincent said. "What kind of weird stuff are you into, Saylor?"

"Leave her alone," Bailey said. "It's romantic."

"Really weird stuff," I told him at the same time. "Would put hair on your chest."

"I could use that," he said, then laughed, hard enough that his sunglasses, which he kept parked on his head, slid off and hit the dock with a bang. "Damn, my shades!"

"You need one of those things to hang them around your neck," Bailey told him.

"You offering to buy me one?" he replied.

She rolled her eyes, but I saw her smiling. I thought back to that first night I'd been out to the raft, how Vincent's face flushed when April alluded to a possible crush. Maybe she was onto something.

"I cannot wait to see the Club at Prom," Bailey said to me.

"You've never been?" I asked.

"Nope. But this girl from the Station went last year, with a guy she was dating who was a valet over there." She sighed happily. "She said it was beautiful."

"Oh, please," Vincent said with a snort. "Who wants to dress up at the lake?"

"I do," she said, and he made a face. To me she added, "Just wait. You'll see. It's going to be great."

She, at least, was sure of things. I supposed it was good that one of us was.

Now, back at birth class, Trinity turned around, looking up at me. "Hey. Saylor. Are you breathing?"

I blinked, surprised to find myself with her and not with Vincent and Bailey. "Yes," I said quickly, blowing out some air as proof. "Of course I am."

"Well, you're the only one. So stop." She turned back around, elbowing me sharply in the stomach again as she did so. "The movie's about to start."

"Movie?" I looked at the front of the room, where, sure enough, Kim had rolled in a cart with a TV and DVD player on it. On the screen, a title page: STAGES OF LABOR AND DELIVERY. "Oh, God. Is it okay if I wait—"

"Nope," she said as the lights went dim overhead and the video began. The camera zeroed in on a woman in a hospital bed, hugely pregnant, her feet up in stirrups. She was smiling, as was her husband, sitting beside her.

I looked at the clock: there were twenty minutes left of class, and then I'd have to drive us home. When faced with two not-so-good options, there really isn't even a point in choosing between them. Still, I did cover my eyes.

ELEVEN

"Hey. Do you want to go to Club Prom with me?"

Every movement in the guys' apartment did not screech to a halt as Blake said this. It just felt that way.

"What?" I said, although I'd heard him. So had Bailey, who was now looking squarely at us from where she was sitting on the other bed with Colin.

"It's this dance," Blake said casually, taking a sip from his beer. "They have it every year at the Club. Kind of a joke, kind of not. It's usually fun."

I looked at Bailey again, feeling helpless. She'd talked about this so much, it seemed wrong that I'd get asked first, and I wanted to give Colin a chance to make his move. But when I looked at him, he was studying his phone, his eyes narrowed.

"Um," I finally said to Blake. "Yeah. Sure. I'd love to go."

"Cool," he said, so nonchalantly I wondered, briefly, what he would have done if I'd said no. "It's next Saturday, and you'll need something kind of formal, just FYI."

"That's fine," I said. "I'll figure something out."

"I have procured a date to Club Prom," Blake yelled toward Hannah and Rachel, who were by the doorway, huddled over their phones. "So you can stop nagging me."

"Thank God," Rachel said. "Nothing like waiting until the last minute."

"Last minute? It's Monday. The dance is next Saturday," Blake told them.

"We're girls," Hannah informed him. "We need time to prepare for things like this."

"Which is why," Rachel said, "we asked our guys ages ago."

At this, Colin got to his feet and walked back into the kitchen, where he opened the fridge, taking out another beer. He popped the tab, then just stood there, holding it and looking out the back door.

"You already have dates?" Bailey asked the girls now. "Who are you taking?"

Rachel shook the ice in her plastic cup. "These German exchange students from the kitchen."

"Who are super cute but don't speak English," Hannah said. "And we don't know German. Should be fun."

"You," Rachel said, "are just pissed because Roo said no. Don't take it out on Gunther and Konrad."

Bailey, surprised, said, "You asked Roo to Club Prom?"

Hannah blushed. "Oh, God. Yes. He shot me down, but at least he was nice about it. Said he had to work."

"He probably does," Bailey told her. "He has, like, four jobs."

"That's what he said," she replied. "Truthfully, though, I don't think he's into me. Which stinks, because he's totally my type."

"Your type," Rachel repeated. "What's that, blond and handsome?"

"And *nice*," Hannah added. "The other night at Lucy Tate's, I lost my shoes and he spent like a half hour helping me find them. What's not to like?"

Shoe buddy, I thought. It was hard not to wince.

Bailey stood then, walking back to the kitchen, where she said something to Colin I couldn't hear. He replied, his voice also low, and then they were going out the back door, the screen swinging shut behind them.

"Someone seems tense," Rachel said to me. "Everything okay with them?"

"As long as he's asking her to the Prom right now, yes," I said.

Hannah's eyes widened. "He hasn't asked her yet?"

"No," I said.

"Who else would he take?" she asked Blake.

He held up his hands. "Whoa. Don't look at me. I know nothing except I needed a date and now I have one."

I couldn't help but notice this was the second time I'd been referred to as his date, not by name. When everything comes easy, I guess you learn not to sweat the details.

"Boys are so weird," Rachel observed, shaking her drink again. To me she said, "Hey, you need a dress? We brought a few options that should fit."

This was a nice offer, I knew, extended in kindness. And maybe I'd been spending too much time with Trinity—okay, I was definitely spending too much time with Trinity—but I wondered about her motivation. I was a North Lake girl going to a Lake North Prom: of course they'd think I wouldn't have something suitable to wear. And the truth was, here, I didn't. But at home, my closet held a number of expensive dresses, most purchased by Nana for dinners at *her* club. Not that they'd know that, though. They only knew Saylor, not Emma.

The back door opened again then, and Bailey came in, followed after a beat by Colin. Now, she was smiling and so flushed that I guessed what had happened even before she plopped down beside me and said, "He asked me! Finally."

I looked at Colin, who was still in the kitchen, getting another beer, his face, unlike hers, neither relieved nor overjoyed.

"That's great," I said as Blake stood and also walked back to the kitchen.

"Better than great," she replied, taking my hand and squeezing it. "See? It's all coming together."

"Club Prom?" my dad asked. "Man. That brings back some memories."

It was seven thirty a.m., the time my dad had taken to calling me to check in. Which was great for him, because in Greece, it was midafternoon. I, however, was always only (barely) waking up.

"You went to Club Prom?" I asked him now.

"Oh, yeah." He was quiet for long enough for me to picture him on the boat, with a faraway look on his face, smiling. "Twice, actually. And both times with your mom."

"*Mom* went?" I asked. "She never mentioned that."

"Because it wasn't a great night," he replied with a sigh. "Either time."

"What happened?"

Another pause, but this one felt different, like he wasn't thinking as much as deciding how best to answer this. "Well, you know, she always felt out of place at the Club. Even though she knew a lot of people there. And when she was nervous, she . . ."

". . . drank too much?" I finished for him.

"Well," he said. "Yes."

Even after all this time, it was hard for my dad to talk about my mom's issues. He preferred to avoid the subject as much as possible, as if bringing it up did some disservice to her or her memory. This was in marked contrast to what I'd seen of Celeste, Mimi, and the rest of the family at the lake, for whom my mother's problems were as much a part of her story as, well, I was. There were lots of ways to love someone, I guessed, both by remembering and forgetting.

"I wish you'd taken pictures," I said now.

"I'm sure somebody did," he replied. "All I remember is that even barefoot in a borrowed dress, your mom was gorgeous."

"Until she got drunk," I said.

Another pause, this one to let me know I'd crossed a line. "Anyway," he said a moment later, "you must need something to wear. I left you a credit card, didn't I?"

He had, for emergencies: it was tucked in a spare pair of sneakers in my closet. "I should be able to borrow something from Bailey, I think."

"Well, if not, buy something," he replied. Then, quickly: "Within reason, of course."

"Of course," I agreed. How hard could that be?

"I just filled it up, so there's plenty of gas," Mimi said, handing me her keys. "Bly Corners is pretty much a straight shot once you get into Delaney. You can't miss it."

"Great," I said. "Thanks."

"Oh, I remember when Waverly and Matthew were going to that dance over at the Club," she said, somewhat wistful. "Ancient history, but it feels like yesterday."

Then she just stood there, clearly waiting for me to get behind the wheel. So with dread building in my gut, I did.

In a perfect world, driving Trinity to birth class would have been just what it took to get me over my fear of being behind the wheel. In reality, though, it just made everything worse.

Sure, I'd gotten us there and home alive. But between the traffic jam and near panic attack going, followed by having to slam on brakes to avoid hitting a car that stopped suddenly on the way home, I'd stepped out from behind the wheel swearing I'd never return. Which wouldn't be a big deal, I figured, because this was North Lake, a place small enough to get anywhere on foot. Except, as it turned out, a place to buy a dress for Club Prom.

It had all started innocently enough. That morning, I'd been minding my own business, having breakfast and reading the obits, when Bailey came down to go to work.

"It's dress day," she informed me as she loaded slices of bread into the toaster.

"Actually, it's Thursday," I replied, still reading about Daniel Polk, 74, who had left this earthly plane after a long illness.

"I just wish I didn't have to work," she said, ignoring this. "I'm worried about you picking out something at the mall on your own."

"Well, don't," I said, "because I'm not doing that. I'll just find something around here that will work."

She turned, looking at me. "Here? What are you going to wear, a Calvander's tie-dye? One of Trinity's maternity dresses?"

"Maybe." I felt her glare at me. "Look, you have your dress, so what are you worried about?"

"*Your* dress," she replied, as if I was stupid. "We're going together, remember? And this is a big deal."

"I'll find something," I said again.

"I know you will." BING! went the toaster, spitting out her slices. "Because I told Mimi you were borrowing her car to go to Bly Corners today."

This got my attention. "You what?"

She walked to the fridge, pulling it open. After scanning the contents, she sighed, then shut it. "I told her you needed to borrow her car to go buy a dress. She's fine with it. Said to come grab the keys whenever you're ready to go."

"Never," I said. "That's when I'll be ready."

"You don't like shopping?"

"It's not that," I said.

"Then what is it?"

I just sat there, not wanting to get into the whole driving thing with another Blackwood sister. "Well, I have to work, for starters."

"No, you don't." She took a crunchy bite. "Mimi says there's no turnover and only three rooms for housekeeping. Trinity can do it."

"She can't even bend over," I pointed out.

"So she'll do it standing up. You need a dress," she replied. I sighed. "Look, I'm not taking no for an answer, Saylor. Just go."

She made it sound so simple to get in the car and drive miles into a town I'd never been to before, all by myself. In practice, though, everything was more complicated.

"Have fun!" Mimi said now, stepping back from the car. "Can't wait to see what you come home with!"

I smiled, waving as I cranked the engine. Then, gripping the wheel and with her watching, I drove—slowly—out of the Calvander's lot. A block later, when I was sure I was fully out of sight, I pulled into a gas station. There, I cut the engine and wiped my sweaty palms against my shorts, trying to calm the thudding of my heart in my chest. Finally, I just leaned my head against the steering wheel, closing my eyes.

A few weeks earlier, I'd been planning a summer at Bridget's, every detail organized and in place. Now, here I was, at the lake with my mother's family, sort of dating a college boy and needing a formal dress. Also, driving, or trying to. Even with my imagination, I never would have pictured this.

Knock. Knock.

Startled, I jumped, my eyes springing open. There, standing on the other side of my closed window, was Roo Price.

"Hey," he said. He had on a green collared shirt and shorts and was squinting in at me, eyes narrowed. "You okay?"

I turned my key, then put down the window. "Do I not seem okay?"

"You're in a gas station parking lot collapsed over your steering wheel," he pointed out.

"I was resting my eyes," I replied.

He glanced around at the nearby pumps, the blinking neon sign out front that said COLD SODAS. "Interesting spot for a nap."

"Well, life is busy," I said, smiling. "Sometimes you have to take them where you can."

A car drove by and beeped. Roo raised his hand in a wave. Did everyone know everyone here? Lately I felt like the only stranger.

"What are you doing?" I asked. "I mean, other than policing people taking naps in public places."

"Just got off work," he said, bending down so he was level with the window.

"I hear you have a ton of jobs."

"Not really," he replied, running his fingers through his hair, which was short and the whitest of blond. When he was done, a single tuft stuck up, and it was all I could do not to fix it. "Just five."

"That's four more than most people," I pointed out. "I bet you could use a gas station nap."

"I prefer to grab my shut-eye at grocery stores," he replied.

"Different strokes for different folks," I said. "What are the jobs?"

"Well, there's the Station arcade. Fifteen hours a week." He held up four fingers, then folded one down. "Then I work the night desk at the Park Palms when they need someone to fill in."

"That's a hotel?"

"Nursing home," he said, folding down another finger. "The grocery store, with Celeste. That's another fifteen a week, usually."

"Okay if I rest my eyes again? I'm getting tired just hearing this."

"And finally," he continued, "there's the Yum truck."

"The Yum truck?"

Instead of replying, he turned, glancing behind him. There, parked only a few spaces away, was a white food truck, plastered with pictures of various frozen desserts. YUM! was painted across the hood in hot-pink letters. It was a testament to my level of distraction that I hadn't even noticed it.

"You drive an ice cream truck?" I asked. "Seriously?"

"It's the lake," he replied. "Ice cream is big business."

"Can I see?"

He stepped back, waving a hand. "Be my guest."

Suddenly energized, I got out of the car, following him over. "Are you selling right now?"

"Not a lot of takers at ten a.m.," he said. "The truth is my car broke down again, so I took this to work last night."

I raised an eyebrow. "You drove an ice cream truck to a nursing home?"

"I'm very popular with the residents," he said, flashing that gap in his teeth again.

"I bet you're popular with everyone."

"That's my charm, though," he corrected me. "Not my access to frozen desserts."

"Keep telling yourself that," I replied, patting his back.

"Oh, I will."

I was too busy laughing, at first, to realize how easily we'd fallen into this rapid-fire exchange. Like when I was with him, I wasn't a stranger after all.

"Why *do* you work so much?" I asked. "Are you saving for something?"

"College," he replied.

Of course. I felt my face get hot: I was always getting this wrong. "Oh, yeah. You mentioned journalism school in your five sentences."

"Yup," he said, pulling a hand through his hair again. "I'm the editor of the paper at school this year. It got me into it. There's a good program at the U, actually, if I stay in-state. Which I probably will. It's cheaper."

I was beginning to realize that not thinking about money was a luxury, and one I should have been appreciating more.

"With all these jobs," I said now, "how do you even remember where to be and at what time?"

He pulled his phone out of his pocket. "Alerts. Lots of them. If you hear a beep, it's probably me."

"Good to know," I said as he walked over, sliding open the door to the truck and stepping back.

"Watch your step," he said. "It's perennially sticky."

I climbed in, my footsteps clanking on the metal floor. "This is so cool."

"It is," he agreed. "Until you get mobbed by a bunch of damp kids all screaming for sugar. Then, not so much."

"Tell me there's a little song you turn on as you drive."

He smiled, pointing to a white box with some buttons installed above the driver's seat. "Four melodies total, with a choice of tempos."

"Can you play one now?"

"No, because someone will want ice cream and I'm not on the clock," he said.

I looked out the window. The lot was empty. "There's no one around."

"Doesn't matter. It's like a dog whistle. If you play it, they will come." He stepped around me, into the narrow walkway that led back into the truck. "You can have something, though, if you're an ice-cream-at-ten-a.m. person."

"Who isn't?"

"Well, me, for one. But again, different strokes." He bent over a built-in cooler, turning a handle and then pushing it open. "Pick your poison."

I stepped closer, peering inside at a huge selection of offerings, all individually wrapped and organized by category: frozen candy bars, push-ups, cookie sandwiches, Sundae in a Cup. Even if you didn't like ice cream—and I did—you'd have to be excited by such a selection, at ten a.m. or, really, anytime.

"This one," I said, pulling out a Choco-wich, two chocolate chip cookies with vanilla ice cream between them. It was cold in my hands. "Thank you."

"No problem," he replied, sliding the cooler shut. He leaned back, arms crossed over his chest, as I unwrapped it and took a bite.

"So you want to tell me what you were really doing collapsed over your steering wheel in a parking lot?"

"Waiting for the Yum truck," I replied, grinning. "And it came!"

He just looked at me.

"Fine." I swallowed. "The truth is, I'm supposed to be driving to Bly Corners."

"The mall?" I nodded. "So what's the problem?"

"I don't like to drive."

"You drove here," he pointed out.

"And I drove Trinity to birth class on Saturday," I said, sighing. "What I'm saying is I didn't *like* it."

"You went to birth class?" he asked. "Did Kim show one of those videos?"

"She did."

He shuddered. "See, now *that's* something to be scared of. You can handle a full dilation shot, you can handle anything."

"You went to birth class?"

"Filled in for Celeste once, when she had to work." He reached down, rubbing a smudge on the cooler top. "Fair to say it traumatized me."

I tried to picture Roo in that little room, Trinity elbowing his gut as she tried to practice her ocean breathing. It actually wasn't that hard. At this rate, we'd all be trained to help push when the baby came.

"See, that's me when it comes to driving," I said. "Like, I literally panic when I have to get behind the wheel."

"Since when?"

"Always. Although it got worse when I hit another car in a parking deck." Even as I cringed, saying this, I felt a sense of relief. The truth felt good. "I freaked."

"Understandable."

"Not to my dad." I took another bite of my Choco-wich. "He's always been so pushy about me getting my license, even when I was adamant I didn't want to. He won't let up. I don't get it."

Roo considered this for a second as I chewed. "Well, that

probably has more to do with your mom than you, though, don't you think?"

"My mom?"

"Because she didn't drive," he said. "She wouldn't. Right?"

It was like time just stopped, my breathing as well, as I stood there, the Choco-wich melting down onto my wrist. Could this be true? I'd been in a car with my mom behind the wheel. Hadn't I?

"Wait," I said. "She was afraid to drive? Are you sure?"

He opened his mouth, then quickly shut it before pulling a hand through his hair again, this time leaving a different tuft vertical. "That's just what Celeste said."

"Celeste," I repeated.

"I'm sorry," he said quickly. "Obviously, you know your mom better than—"

"I don't, though," I said. I heard the catch in my voice, and hoped he didn't. "That's what I'm realizing. I didn't really know her at all."

We just stood there for a second, the truck dark and cool all around us as a car drove by, beeping.

"I'm sorry," Roo said quietly. He looked back down at his hand, spread on the cooler. "And for what it's worth, I can relate to having more questions than answers. My dad died before I was born."

"That's harder," I pointed out. "At least I had her for a little while."

"Or, easier," he countered. "You can't miss what you never had."

I looked out the window at Mimi's Toyota, parked where I'd left it, in the perfect center of a space, no cars anywhere nearby. "I guess everyone's afraid of something."

"Yeah." He was quiet for a minute. "With me, it's clowns."

"Shut up," I said, hitting him.

"What? I thought we were having a moment."

"You," I said, "are not really afraid of clowns."

"I am. And before you mock, I'll remind you that clowns are much more avoidable than driving."

"Not if you work at the circus."

"Joke's on you. That's my fifth job."

We looked at each other, slightly breathless. Then, together, we cracked up, the sound amplified by all the metal surfaces around us. I laughed until I cried, harder than I had in years. Or maybe ever. There was something almost primal about it, this moment of near hysteria with a boy I'd just met and yet, again, felt like I knew.

It was hard to stop, taking some deep breaths, not making eye contact with Roo, and throwing away my mostly melted Choco-wich to get calmed down. Even then I was still sputtering a bit. "I should go," I said finally. "I'm not going to find a dress store within walking distance standing here in the Yum truck."

"You're not going to find one, period," he replied as I turned and started toward the seats up front. "Bly Corners is pretty much the only option."

I sighed as he reached around me, sliding the door open. Immediately, I felt the heat of the day, bouncing off the asphalt and thick with humidity, smack me in the face. "What's your real fifth job?"

"What if I said it was driving instructor?"

I just looked at him. "I'd say you were full of crap."

"And you would be right." He grinned, shutting the door with a bang. "It's actually landscaping with my uncle. That said, I would be happy to ride along with you for moral support, if you want. I'm told I have a very calming presence."

"Just as long as we don't see any clowns."

"Well, obviously," he said. "Then you're on your own."

I snorted, then looked over at Mimi's car again, remembering how happy she'd been waving at me as she left.

"How about this," I said. "You drive my car. I'll watch out for people in face paint wearing big shoes and spraying water bottles."

"How about *this*," he countered. "I drive there. You drive back. And we don't talk about the other thing."

"Clowns?"

"Watch it," he warned me. "You want to drive both ways?"

"Nope." I grabbed the keys, holding them out to him. "Let's go."

TWELVE

"I *love* it when boyfriends come to help pick out for formals," the salesgirl said with a sigh as I turned sideways in front of the mirror, trying to decide if I liked the long black sheath I had on. "It's the cutest."

I knew I should tell her that Roo, who was standing nearby examining a leather cuff with a quizzical expression, was not my boyfriend. That he was just being nice—"What's not to like?" I heard Hannah say, in my head—tagging along, not to mention driving me, at least halfway. But for some reason, I didn't correct her. He didn't, either. I couldn't help but notice.

"What's your feeling on feathers?" he asked me.

"Opposed," I replied. "Unless it's on a bird, in which case, fine. Why?"

"I'm intrigued by these shoes," he said, gesturing to a pair of green sandals that had, yes, feathers woven into the straps. "Do people really wear stuff like this?"

"Sure!" the salesgirl, a skinny redhead in a too-short minidress, said as she hurried over. "That's part of our new

Femme Tropicale line. It's all about being uninhibited and wild."

Roo looked into the mirror he was facing, right at me. "Hear that? Uninhibited and wild."

"Sounds exactly like Club Prom," I said. "Grab them before someone else does."

"What's your size?" the girl asked me.

"She's kidding," Roo told her.

"What?" She looked at me, confused. "You don't want the shoes?"

"No," I said, narrowing my eyes at my reflection again. "Or this dress, actually."

"Good call," Roo said. "I didn't want to say anything, but you kind of look like the Grim Reaper."

"You think I *literally* look like death, and you weren't going to mention it?" I said.

"Well," he replied. "Yeah. I mean, what's with the cape?"

"It's not a cape, actually," the girl told him cheerfully. "It's a detachable midi top to add flow to the piece."

I faced the mirror again, and they both looked at me. Roo said, "Looks like a cape."

I sighed. "This is, like, the millionth dress I've tried."

"Then I bet number million and one is the charm." He glanced at his watch, then added, "No pressure, but it kind of has to be. I'm supposed to be in the Yum truck doing the motel circuit by one at the latest."

I walked back into the dressing room. "You know what

would save us lots of time?" I yelled over the door. "If you drove back."

"About as likely as someone not thinking that's a cape," he said. "Nice try, though."

Standing there alone, in front of yet another mirror, I smiled at my reflection. Normally, two hours of shopping for anything would try my patience to a point of rage. This outing, however, had been different. It was actually fun.

First, there was the ride over, during which I got to relax in the passenger seat as Roo drove, entertaining me with stories about his interactions with the residents of Park Palms, the nursing home where he worked the night shift. Then, our arrival at Bly Corners, which was less a mall than three stores and a food court surrounded by a huge parking lot in which we were one of only four cars. I counted.

"Is this place even open?" I asked as he pulled right up to the main entrance, taking one of many empty spaces.

"Careful with the judgment, Big City," he replied. "For Delaney, this is mobbed."

As we got out of the car, the only sound was Roo shutting his door and, I kid you not, a pigeon I could hear cooing from atop a nearby light pole. "Seriously, how do they even stay open if no one comes here?"

"Selling overpriced dresses to desperate out-of-towners," he replied. "Now, watch your purse. Pickpockets thrive in crowded places."

I laughed as we walked to the main entrance, where he

pulled the door open for me. Nice, I thought again. This time, I heard it in my own voice, not Hannah's.

Our first stop was TOGS!, a narrow store blasting loud music where everything was neon and priced at twenty-five bucks or less.

"NO!" Roo said when I presented him with the only thing I'd even slightly liked, a royal-blue dress with a pink ruffle underneath. "You look radioactive. Next."

That was Claudia's Closet, a women's boutique that specialized in flowing, loose-waisted clothing for women of a certain age that was *not* seventeen. Still, I tried on a maroon dress with a full skirt that swished when I walked.

"Might look good with a high wind," Roo observed when I emerged from the fitting room. "But we can't count on that. Let's move on."

We had, to Douglas Arthur, the department store, where we'd been ever since. Everything was fun and games until you were out of time, though. And we almost were.

"All that is left is the green-and-white one," I reported, again over the door. "With the halter neck."

"You know how I feel about that," he said. "I told you when you picked it out."

"What did you say, again? That it makes me look like I'm—"

"Being strangled," he finished. "So that's a no. Try this."

I stepped back, startled, as a dress was flung over the top of the door, its hanger clanking. The top had thin, gauzy straps, the skirt ending in a series of layers, all of it a pale rose color.

"Pink?" I said.

"Don't be gender biased. Just try it."

I slipped out of the black one, then pulled the dress down, removing it from the hanger. Looking at it up close, I had more doubts: it was so simple as to be almost plain, the fabric delicate and thin.

"I don't think this is me," I said. "How strongly are you opposed to the cape?"

"I'm not answering that," he replied. "Put it on."

I did, turning my back to the mirror as I slid it over my head, easing the straps over my shoulders. When I looked down, all I saw was pink.

"This is a no," I reported.

"But we haven't seen it yet!" the salesgirl said. "And he picked it out himself!"

I sighed. At this point I'd leave with nothing to wear and Roo would have himself an actual girlfriend, not just a pretend one. Oh, well, I thought, and opened the door.

He was standing right outside, the salesgirl a few feet behind him, a grin on his face. When he saw me, however, he immediately stopped smiling.

I looked down at myself. Was there a cutout I had missed, exposing me? Could the entire thing be not just thin and delicate, but transparent?

A quick, panicked check confirmed neither of these was the case. But he was still staring at me. "What?" I said, crossing my arms over my chest anyway. "What's wrong with it?"

He blinked at me. "Nothing," he said. "It's—"

"Perfect," the salesgirl sighed. "You look incredible."

I did? I turned, facing the mirror on the dressing room door to see for myself. And while I wouldn't have said perfect—nothing was, in clothing or otherwise—I did have to admit that it worked. The color, which warmed up my skin and the beginnings of a tan I'd gotten since I'd been here. The cut, which emphasized my waist and made me look tall, even in bare feet. But there was something else, too, that had nothing to do with the dress itself. Roo had seen something in it, and recognized a part of me that matched. How could someone know you better than you knew yourself? Especially if they really didn't know you, not at all.

"I'm not convinced," I said after a moment. "The fact it's lacking a cape is kind of a deal breaker."

"You want a cape?" the salesgirl asked, dismayed. "Well . . . I guess we could look for something. . . ."

"She's kidding," Roo told her. Again. Like a translator I never knew I needed. To me he said, "Seriously, though, you should get that. You look great."

I felt my face flush, hearing this, and quickly turned back to the mirror. Which was stupid, because of course he was still there in the reflection, although he immediately turned his attention back to the shoe rack. What was happening here? We were friends. Not even that. Acquaintances whose parents had been closer than close. But

192

relationships were not passed down like hair or eye color. Were they?

I looked down at the tag, hanging from my armpit. The dress was ninety bucks, which I knew was a lot more than Bailey had spent on hers from Bly County Thrift, even with the alterations it had needed. Nana Payne, though, would have plunked down three times that without hesitating, for herself or me. It's important to remember this, I told myself, whether I was here three weeks or always. Don't forget.

"Okay, I'll take it," I said. "But only because we have ice cream to sell."

"And you don't want a cape," the salesgirl said, clarifying.

"No," Roo and I replied in unison. Then he looked at me in the mirror again. And smiled.

After I paid, it was back to the parking lot, where we were still one of the only cars present. Which did not make me any less nervous about having to drive out of there.

"You know," I said as Roo slid into the passenger seat, "you can drive if you want."

"Not our deal," he reminded me, shutting his door. I stayed where I was, outside on the driver's side. A moment later he swung it open again. "Are you getting in?"

"Eventually," I replied.

"Can't drive from outside." Still, I didn't move. "Saylor. Come on."

"I'm nervous!"

Now he got out of the car, so we were both standing by our open doors. "About what?"

I thought for a second. "Crashing."

"What else?"

"That's not enough?"

"Planes crash. You still fly."

"You don't know that. For all you know, I've never even been on a plane."

He considered this. "Okay, fine. How about this: pedestrians get struck by cars. You still walk. And I know, because I have seen you."

"That is not the same."

"As the car thing or the plane?" he asked.

"Neither," I replied. A seagull flew by, cawing above us. "Look. I never wanted to drive. I was fine without it. Then my dad forced me, and I hit that car. It was traumatic."

"Trauma can be educational," he pointed out in that same maddeningly reasonable voice. "And even if you fail, at least you tried."

"Fail?" I said. "Do you think I can't do it?"

"You won't even get in the car," he said.

I slid behind the wheel, feeling like I'd show him. Until I realized that was probably exactly what he wanted. By then, though, I'd already shut my door. Crap.

"Okay. Put your foot on the brake." I did, and he reached over, turning the key I'd put in the ignition so the engine revved to life. Like one of Pavlov's dogs, just the sound made my heart jump. "Now, tell me what you're feeling."

I was too scared to go into more detail than "Terrified."

"Why?"

"Because I might kill someone."

Roo took an exaggerated look around the mostly empty parking lot. "Who?"

I tightened my grip on the wheel, right at the ten and two spots. "You. Me. Everyone."

"The only way to overcome a fear is to face it," he said. "You have to knock down the power it has over you."

"Have you done that with clowns? Because if not, I don't see why I have to do this."

"Because," he shot back loudly, over the A/C, which had just come on and begun blasting us, "as we discussed earlier, clowns are location-specific. I see them on TV or at the circus. My fear of them does not prevent me from fully living my life."

"I am living my life!"

"We've been sitting here for seven minutes," he said, poking a finger at the clock on the dashboard. "Seven minutes, spent in fear, that you won't get back."

Great. Now I was a failure *and* a waste of human energy. "You know, a lot of people don't drive. They are just happy and grateful passengers."

He sat back, looking at me. "Yes, but when you only ride, you're never in control. You get taken from point A to point B through no volition or work of your own. It's like drifting. If life is a journey, wouldn't you rather be the person behind the wheel than the one just being carried along?"

I bit my lip, looking out the window at the empty row of spaces beside us. Put like that, I couldn't help but think, again, of my mom. So willful, so strong in so many ways, and yet in the end she succumbed to something that drove her, so to speak, and not the other way around. I'd worried for so long about all the ways we were alike and what that meant for my own future. Here was a way to make one choice, at least, to be different.

"Fine," I said. And I turned the key.

Since the engine was already on, however, it made a loud, screeching noise, sending another nearby gull into sudden flight. Shit. My face flushed, bright red I was sure, and I felt tears in my eyes.

"Engine's on," Roo said cheerfully. He was not looking at me, but straight ahead. "Now let's just get into reverse so we can back out of here."

I did, swallowing a huge lump in my throat as I did so. Then I hit the gas, gently, moving out of the space in a very slow, wide arc.

"Tip number one," he said as I switched gears. "Never back up more than you have to."

I looked around the empty lot. "We're, like, the only ones here."

"True. But everything is practice. So you should do it right. Try again."

"Get back in the space, you mean?"

"Yep." He sat back, crossing one leg over the other. "I'll wait."

I pulled back in, then reversed out once more, this time keeping the car tightly between the empty spaces. "Better?"

"Great," he said. "Now: the road."

It wasn't easy. I got beeped at as I turned out of Bly Corners ("Not your fault, they're being an asshole," Roo said) as well as when I was merging onto the road home ("Okay, that one was your fault, watch your blind spot next time"). But unlike my dad, who did commentary on my driving between obviously clenched teeth, and Trinity, who ignored my panic while looking at her phone, Roo actually was, as he'd claimed, a calming presence. He watched everything, from what I was doing to the traffic around us, correcting and praising as necessary. Even when I froze as we approached a huge pothole—I drove right into it, almost taking Mimi's muffler off in the process—he just said lightly, "And *that's* why we steer around road hazards."

Even so, by the time I got him back to the Yum truck, I was soaked with sweat, my shirt sticking to my back and my nerves jangled. "I can't believe I did that," I said. "I think that's the farthest I've driven, like, ever."

"You still have to get back to Mimi's," he reminded me. I slumped a bit. "But hey! It's the perfect way to cap this off. Solo drive to celebrate. A win-win."

I just looked at him. "Are you always this positive about everything?"

"Me?" I nodded. "No. In fact, about a year ago, I went through a real doom-and-gloom phase. Wore black, sulked, shut myself in my room. Good times."

"I can't imagine that," I said, because I really couldn't.

"I was working through stuff. Thinking about my dad,

how I never knew him. You know, woe is me, et cetera." He pulled a hand through his hair, leaving a bit sticking up. Something I was already thinking of as his signature look. "But then I realized me being all down was really a drag, not just for me but for my mom. She's had enough darkness already. For her, at least, I figured I should at least try to look for the good in things."

"And it was that easy?" I said, doubtful.

"It was a process," he admitted. "I also got my license. That helped."

I gave him a look. "How convenient for this story."

"No, seriously!" he said. "Once I could drive, I could literally go places. This small town, my dad's accident . . . I could get out of it all. Even if it was just for a little while. Like a trip to Bly Corners."

I considered this. "You could also walk there to clear your head, though."

"You could," he agreed. "But the trip would take a *lot* longer."

I had to admit, he had me there. Not that I wanted to tell him this, so instead I said, "Can I ask you a question?"

"Sure."

"Why does everyone call you Roo?"

He sighed. "My real name is Christopher. When I was little, I was super into kangaroos. Some might say obsessed. I couldn't say the whole word for a while, so I called them roos. It stuck."

I smiled. "That's pretty cute."

"To everyone else," he agreed. "Now I have a question for you."

"Shoot."

"*Have* you ever been on a plane?"

I bit my lip. "Yeah. A bunch of times."

"I knew it!" He snapped his fingers. "I could tell."

"How can you tell something like that?"

He shrugged. "Dunno. Maybe you just look like you're going places."

It was so stupid and corny, but still, I laughed. And now, on the porch with Bailey and Trinity, I felt myself again begin to grin, remembering this, before I quickly rearranged my face into a neutral expression. This had kept happening over the last few days, my mind drifting to one exchange or another from the trip to Bly Corners even when I tried to stay focused. Stop it, I thought. Blake is the boy you're going to Club Prom with.

Right.

Celeste squinted into her camera, a Pop Soda dangling from her other hand. "Okay. Now let's take one of just the girls. Gordon, get in there."

"Mom," Bailey groaned. "I think you have enough pictures."

"What? I've barely taken any," Celeste said, gesturing for us to move in closer in front of the gardenia bush chosen as the backdrop for this documentation. "Gordon. Put down the gorilla book and get between them."

"It's *chimpanzees*," Gordon said, getting to her feet and coming over to join us. She brought the book with her.

"Whatever." Celeste peered at her camera again. "Now, hold on, I think I've been in portrait this whole time . . ."

"You need landscape," said Mimi, who was off to the side with a Pop Soda, observing. "Turn it sideways."

"Mama, I know."

Beside me, Bailey sighed loudly. "I just want the guys to get here. Where are they?"

"It's only seven fifteen," I told her.

"Yeah, but we said seven."

"You can't smile while you're talking!" Celeste said. "Now, everyone look here. Say cheese!"

We did, as she took several without a flash, some with, and then a few in portrait mode just to be on the safe side. "Perfect," she said as Gordon returned to the steps, reopening her book to her marked place. "Now we just need a few with the boys and we'll be set."

"No," Bailey said flatly. "We are *not* doing that."

Celeste looked up from her camera, where she'd been examining the shots she'd taken. "What do you mean? Of course we are. It's a formal dance, we need pictures with your dates."

"You don't, actually," Bailey replied. "Because I'm sure we'll take some once we're there, as a group. And anyway, we're running late. There's no time for anything else."

Celeste looked at Mimi, who shrugged. "Fine," she said. "But I want to meet these boys before you leave with them. Especially the famous Colin."

Bailey rolled her eyes. Then she pulled out her phone, quickly firing off another text. When I glanced at her screen and saw it was the fourth in a row with no response, I quickly messaged Blake, asking for an update.

Be there in ten, he wrote back immediately. **Meet me outside.**

"Look," I said, showing Bailey. "Everything's fine."

"Why does he want you to meet him outside, though?" she asked worriedly, squinting at the message.

"You're the one who just said they're running late," I pointed out. "Bailey. It's fine."

She did not look convinced, though, as Mimi and Celeste headed into the house, telling us to yell when the boys arrived. Gordon stayed on the steps. "I just want to get there," Bailey said, looking at the Club, which we could see, lit up across the water, from where we were standing. "I hate all this waiting."

"It's fifteen minutes," I assured her, but this she ignored, already checking her phone again.

A moment later, a car did turn into the Calvander's lot. It wasn't Colin and Blake, though, but Jack, returning from work at the Station with Roo in tow. As they made their way toward us, I suddenly felt shy, standing there in what he'd picked out for me. But when he saw me in it, he grinned.

"Really like the dress," he said, looking me up and down.

"But you know what it's missing?"

"A cape?" I asked.

He gave me a thumbs-up. "You got it."

I laughed, but Bailey just looked at him. "Shut up, Roo. She looks great."

"Whoa," he said, holding up a hand. "I was—"

"It's an inside joke," I explained.

"Yeah, I'm just kidding around, Bay," Roo told her.

"Well, don't," she told him. "You can't just show up when someone's done all this work to get ready and make fun of them. That's a jerk move."

"Nobody's making fun of anyone," Jack said to her. "What's wrong with you?"

"Nothing. I just don't know why you're here if you can't be nice."

"Because I live here?" He shook his head. "Man. Talk about self-centered. It's not just about you all the time, you know."

Bailey looked like she was about to respond to this—and hotly—but then another car slowed, turning into the lot. It was Blake, in a black Toyota, and the first thing I noticed was that he looked nice in his tux. The second was that he was alone.

"Where's Colin?" Bailey yelled at him, as soon as he parked. When he didn't hear her, or pretended not to, she started walking up the sloping grass toward him. Gordon, a finger now marking her place in her book, watched her go.

"What's her problem?" Jack asked me, but I didn't answer,

202

my eyes only on Bailey as Blake got out from behind the wheel. When she said something to him, he just shrugged, then waved at me.

"We're late," he called out. "Come on."

"Where's Colin?" I replied, but he didn't hear me over Bailey, who was now repeating this same question, but with more emotion. Enough, in fact, that he started to get back in the car, shooting me another look first.

"Something's up," Jack reported, his eyes on both of them. I started walking.

"Look, enough with the bullshit," Bailey was saying, her voice cracking slightly, when I came up. "Just tell me what's going on."

"I told you," Blake replied. Seeing me, he reached over, pushing open the passenger door. "I'm not part of all this."

"Actually, you are. You're his best friend."

"Saylor," Blake said to me across the empty seat. As if she wasn't even there, breathing hard, close to tears. "Let's go. We're meeting everyone there."

"I can't go with you," I said, and I did look at Bailey, who bit her lip. "Not without her."

"Well, fine. Then you can both stay here," he replied. "It's not worth all this trouble."

Trouble, to expect someone to do what they said they would. Then again, he was someone to whom things came easily, always: a job, a future, a girl. I said, "Yes or no: Is Colin coming?"

Blake, still avoiding looking anywhere near Bailey's

direction, closed his eyes for a second. "No," he said finally. "He's not."

I heard Bailey exhale, a shaky, long breath. Back by the steps, Jack and Roo were still watching us.

"Why not?" Bailey said to him now.

"I don't know," he replied, cranking the engine. To me he said, "Can we go, please?"

"Answer her question," I said.

"Because he's with the girl he asked a month ago!" Blake said. "His girlfriend, from school."

I was stunned. Bailey said, "Colin has a girlfriend?"

"Yeah," he said, as if we were stupid for not knowing it. "They have an understanding, just like he had with you."

Bailey was just standing there, eyes wide, her phone in her hands. She turned to me. "What does that even mean?"

"That he's an asshole," I replied.

"Enough about Colin, Jesus!" Blake said. He looked at me. "Are you getting in or not?"

I looked at my cousin, in the dress on which she'd spent so much time and effort, her makeup applied so carefully it was perfect. She didn't deserve this. Nobody did.

"Not," I told Blake.

In response, he threw up a hand, then hit the gas, spraying some gravel as he pulled away. I watched him turn out onto the road, cursing us, and kept my eyes on him until he was out of sight. Only then did I turn back to Bailey, who was now standing with her arms around herself, her face streaked with tears. What could I even say at this moment?

What words would even make any difference? I didn't know where, or how, to start. But as it turned out, I didn't have to.

"Bailey," Jack said. He was standing there, his own keys in hand. Roo was coming up the grass behind him. "Let's get out of here."

THIRTEEN

"I can't believe this," Bailey said. She turned around, her face tear-streaked, and looked at me. "Can you?"

I shook my head as, distantly, I heard her phone beep again. About five minutes earlier, Celeste had realized we'd left without saying goodbye. Seriously pissed, she was making her displeasure clear with a series of angry texts, none of which Bailey had responded to so far. All she had been capable of, really, was sitting in the passenger seat and crying while Jack drove us, well, someplace.

The phone beeped again. Bailey leaned her head against the window, closing her eyes. "I can't tell Mom what happened," she said. "It's so humiliating and she'll just say she told me so."

"No, she won't," Jack said, glancing in the rearview.

"Yeah, right. All she and Trinity have done all summer is say how Colin is going to break my heart. And now he has. They'll be thrilled."

"More likely, they'll want to kill him," Roo, who was

beside me in the back seat, said. "I'd be more worried about that. Trinity's temper these days is off the charts."

Bailey, reaching up to wipe her eyes, didn't smile at this comment, but I did. "He'll just need to stand still," I said, thinking of her struggling cleaning with her huge belly. "And not be on a low or high shelf."

Roo snorted, which made me laugh out loud, and then we were both cracking up. Bailey turned around to look at us again.

"You guys aren't funny," she informed us as we composed ourselves, or tried to. "And Saylor, you just got dumped as well, in case you didn't notice."

"Easy come, easy go." I couldn't think of a phrase that fit the situation more.

"I thought you liked Blake!" she said.

I shrugged. "It was fun and all, but . . . I think I'll be fine."

Her phone beeped. Then once more. If it could have screamed, it would have.

"Give me that," Roo said to Bailey, holding out his hand. "I'll explain to Celeste what happened."

She handed it over to him and he started typing a response. With him and Jack both on the same side of the car, dressed in shorts and T-shirts, and Bailey and me in our formal wear on the other, we looked like we were headed to very different evenings. Which made me think of something.

"Where are we even going?" I asked Jack. We'd turned left out of Calvander's, heading toward the main road, but at some point we had entered a neighborhood with narrow streets and trees strung with moss. Through my open window, I could smell the lake, but not see it.

"Green house," he said, as if I knew what this was.

O-kay, I thought. Bailey sniffled, wiping her nose with the back of her hand. "I can't believe I spent all this money and time on this dress. I'm so stupid."

"You're not," Roo said, still typing.

"He has a *girlfriend.*" Her voice broke on the final syllable. "Why did he even ask me if he already had a date?"

I thought back to that night at the Campus apartment, how Colin had gotten up and left when the subject of Club Prom came up, only to finally invite her when they were outside. He probably figured he'd just dump her before the dance, so it wouldn't come back to bite him. And now he was at the Club, far away from the pain he'd caused.

Jack slowed the car, turning down a dirt driveway. It was long, and bumpy with tree roots, but as we came over a rise, I saw a little green house, the lake behind it. A skinny dock extended out into the water. April and Vincent stood on it, a cooler on a bench nearby. The sun was just going down.

"I can't do this," Bailey said as we parked behind a blue pickup. "It's so embarrassing."

"These are your friends," Jack told her. "Nobody gives a shit."

She sighed, but pushed her door open. Then she bent down, undoing the strappy sandals she'd been so excited to find almost new at Bly County Thrift. She left them on the floorboard as she climbed out, shutting the door behind her.

I kept my shoes on. "What is this place, again?" I asked.

Roo, a few steps ahead, turned back to look at me. "My house. Come on."

I raised a hand to cover my eyes just as Bailey started down to the dock, her dress flowing out a bit behind her. When she got to the end, April, who was standing there, looked up at her.

"Boys STINK," she announced, then opened her arms. Blinking fast, Bailey stepped into them. Vincent, standing just nearby with a beer in his hand, looked at them for a second, then out to the lake.

"Yacht club boys," Jack announced as the rest of us made our way out to the end. "Get it right, please."

"I'm so stupid," Bailey groaned, now resting her head on April's shoulder. "I thought he was a good guy."

"Because you are a trusting, wonderful person," April told her, patting her on the back. "Vincent, get this girl a beer. She needs it."

Vincent complied, kicking open the cooler and pulling out a dripping can. He wiped it on his shirt, then handed it to Bailey, saying, "I'm sorry. For what it's worth."

"Nothing," she replied, and he laughed. "But thanks anyway."

"Great dress," April said to me.

"Thanks."

"I picked it out," Roo said, helping himself to a beer. When he held one out to me, I shook my head.

"Really?" April cocked her head to the side. "Wow. Since when are you a stylist?"

"Sixth job," he said, popping the beer.

She looked at me. "Is he kidding? I can never tell if he's kidding."

Suddenly, I was the expert. I didn't mind. "I think so," I told her. "But again, I'm new here."

She smiled at me, then turned back to Bailey, who was now facing the water, looking at the yacht club in the distance. "Hey," she said, "don't torture yourself, all right? You're better off. When Dana went to Club Prom last year, she said everyone was super snooty and into themselves. Who wants to deal with that?"

"Me," Bailey said softly. "For just one night, anyway. And I couldn't even get that."

"There will be other dances," April said. "Trust me."

"What?" Bailey scoffed. "Prom in the gym with some guy I've known my whole life? Sorry, not the same."

Vincent, hearing this, turned and looked back up at the house, putting his own can to his lips. I caught his eye and smiled. A beat later, he smiled back, although his mind was clearly on other things.

"Then let's have a dance," April said.

"Where?" Jack asked.

"Here." When we all just looked at her, she sighed. "What? I'm on the party committee at my sorority. All we need is some lights and music."

"You want to throw a dance in my house?" Roo asked. "Have you forgotten how small it is inside?"

"We'll move the furniture," she told him.

"Where?" Jack asked again.

"Outside," she replied, sounding annoyed. "Look, our friend is sad and this will make her happy. Saylor, too."

"I'm not really sad," I pointed out.

"But you are all dressed up for a magical night, and you should get one," April told me. She clapped her hands, grinning. "Okay, I love this idea. It's perfect."

"Perfect would be us over there, where we're supposed to be," Bailey said morosely. "And anyway, I'm not in the mood."

"But you *are* in a dress," Jack said. "What else are you going to do?"

"Drink away my sorrows," she replied.

"You can still do that while you're pushing the couch outside," April told her. "Follow me."

When Taylor arrived a little later, I was nervous, considering our first face-to-face encounter had almost ended with her kicking my ass. But her apology had obviously been for real. So far, she was being perfectly nice.

"Okay, who needs a corsage?" she asked from the small kitchen table where she was sitting, bent over a bowl of gardenia blossoms and some stickpins. "If you don't look too closely, they're actually not bad."

"If this was a real dance—" April said.

"It's not," Bailey told her from the couch, which she'd only left long enough for the guys to move it outside to the front porch. The house was tiny, though, and the door open, so she might as well have been inside.

"—then we wouldn't be putting on our own corsages," April finished. "The boys would do it for us."

We all looked out at the deck, where Jack, Vincent, and Roo were still all gathered around the cooler. "I am not," Bailey said, "going to let my brother pin a corsage on me for this fake dance. It would be even more humiliating than anything else that's happened so far. Which is really saying something."

"Jack's with me, remember?" Taylor told her. "So you don't have to worry about that."

"Great." Bailey took a gulp of her beer. "Now I don't even have a fake date to the fake dance."

April raised an eyebrow. "Slow down with those beers over there. The night is young."

"This night sucks," Bailey replied.

Taylor, piercing a stem with a pin, sighed. "Fine. Be that way."

I actually felt kind of bad for her. "I'll take one," I said. "If that's okay."

She looked up at me. "Sure! Whichever you want, although the smaller ones are holding together better."

I went over to the table, where she had laid out three little bundles of gardenias and stems so far, each pierced with a pin. The tiny kitchen smelled of nothing but their scent.

I picked one from the middle, holding it up to the strap of my dress.

"Too small," Taylor said, handing me a larger one. "Try this."

"I wish I'd known I was going to a formal tonight," April said. "I would have worn something else."

"You could run home and change," Taylor suggested, bent over the flowers again.

"No, I like the DIY aspect of this. Making do with what we have." April, her hands on her hips, surveyed the room. "Okay, so we have the lights up—"

"It looks like Christmas," Bailey, continuing her role as the dark shadow of the evening, observed. "Which is also depressing."

"Bailey. Enough with the gloom and doom, okay?" April said.

"Yeah, listen to your party planner. They'll be great once we turn them on," Taylor said. Bailey, unconvinced, looked out at the water again. "Wasn't Roo supposed to be finding a power strip?"

"He was," April replied. She walked over to the open door. "Roo!"

Outside, he turned his head. "Yeah?"

"Power strip?"

"Oh. Right." He put down his beer on the bench. "Coming."

As he jogged up the dock, then came in the back door, brushing his feet on a mat, I took another look around me.

Where Mimi's house was big, airy, and full of windows, the place where Roo lived with his mom was small and cozy. The tiny kitchen, with its metal countertops and collection of sea glass lining the windowsill, opened into a bigger space, which held the couch (now outside) and a worn leather recliner, both facing a small TV. The table where Taylor sat, plain wood with four chairs, made up the only dining area somewhere in the middle.

Normally, small spaces made me anxious. But I felt different here. I had since the moment I'd stepped inside, following April with Bailey dragging along, complaining, behind me. There was just a comfort to it, even before I saw the fridge.

It wasn't the appliance itself, which was white with a few rust spots. What drew me were the pictures that were scattered among the receipts and lists also adhered to the surface. Unlike the counter in the Calvander's office, there were only a handful here, which made each of them seem that much more important.

The first I saw was a school picture of Roo, from what looked to be maybe second grade. Smaller and skinnier, he was still unmistakable, with that same white-blond hair, cut short and sticking up in the back. The grin on his face showed he was missing a top tooth, a gap in its place.

A little over from that one was a shot of who I assumed were his parents. Chris Price, shirtless and with the same blond hair and squinty smile, was sitting on a bench on the dock, a pretty girl with short red hair in cutoffs and a bathing suit top on his lap. He was looking right at the camera, while she had her head thrown back, caught in the middle of what looked like a big belly laugh.

Picture three, a little lower down, was of Roo and his mom, and more recent. Dressed in a gray EAST U sweatshirt, he was taller than her. She had on a black dress, her hair shorter now, one hand resting on his chest as she smiled proudly.

The last one was the oldest of the group, stuck high in one corner of the fridge door with thick brown tape. There are those pictures that are clearly posed, where the subjects were told to stop what they were doing and gather together. Then there were the ones when the photographer just aimed and shot. This had to be why Roo's dad, in shorts and a baggy T-shirt, was slightly blurred: he'd been in the process of moving. The girl in the picture, though, was still facing him, and in profile, one hand held up as if making a point. She had blond hair spilling down her back and blue eyes with long lashes. My mom.

I leaned in closer, startled and not sure why. She was everywhere at the lake so far, so why not here as well? Maybe because you never think, leaning into a snapshot in a stranger's kitchen, that you'll see the person who probably knew you better than anyone. Like she'd been waiting there for me all this time, and now here I was.

"That's one of my favorites," I heard someone say. "It's such a lousy picture, but so real."

I turned, facing Roo, who was now standing right behind me, a power strip in his hands. "That's your dad, right?"

"Yep." He squinted, leaning in a bit closer. "My mom

says it was at a cookout at someone's house. She'd just gotten into photography and was driving everyone crazy snapping pictures. That's why Waverly isn't even looking. She'd had enough."

I looked at my mom again. She had on white shorts and a blue halter top, drugstore flip-flops on her feet. "Mimi said they were inseparable, her and your dad."

"Yeah." I watched as his gaze flicked to the other pictures, then came back to the one of our parents. "But our moms were actually super close as well. When mine moved here senior year, Waverly was the first person she met. She introduced her to Chris."

"Where's your mom now?" I asked.

"In the bedroom," he said.

I looked at all the beers on the table in panic, not to mention the mess we'd made moving things around. "Seriously?"

"No." He grinned at me. "She's an ER nurse in Delaney and works nights. She'll be back in the morning."

"Ah," I said. I looked at the shot of Chris, the redhead in his lap. "It must have been hard for your mom, losing a husband and one of her closest friends."

"Yeah." He was quiet for a second. "It was."

I looked at the picture again. It seemed crazy that after all these years, I had never known about the accident until this summer. For so long I'd questioned why she was in such pain, what could have been so awful that haunted her. The answer, like this picture, had been here all along. I'd just had to come find it.

"You going to wear that?" Roo asked me now.

I blinked, unsure what he was talking about until he nodded at the corsage I was somehow still holding in my hand. "Well, it is a dance," I said.

"You don't put on your own corsage, though." He placed the power strip on the kitchen counter, then reached out, taking the gardenia bundle from me. "Stand super still so I don't stick you, though. I can't take the sight of blood."

"Blood?" I repeated, but he just smiled, gesturing for me to step closer. So I did.

And then he was reaching out to me, sliding a finger under my dress strap and putting the corsage flush against it. Then, with his other hand, he carefully removed the pin before sticking it into the stem and around it. It all happened so quickly, but I was aware of every single detail. His hand against my skin, the way his eyes narrowed, lashes lowering, as he concentrated on fixing it tight. In movies and in life whenever I'd seen this done, it had been awkward, but here, now, the action felt almost sacred in a way I couldn't explain. Which was maybe why I felt like I had to make a joke.

"Thanks, Corsage Buddy," I said.

"Safety first," he replied, his eyes right on mine.

I cleared my throat. "Thanks."

"No problem." He turned around, grabbing the power strip. To April he said, "Where do you want this?"

"Um," she said, looking at me, then him. "By the door."

"Got it," he said, walking over and bending down. He

got it set up, then started plugging in the lights one strand at a time. We stood there watching, the tiny dim room coming alive as they came on, soft and white and twinkling, all around us.

"It's beautiful," April sighed. "If I may say so myself."

"Looks great," Taylor agreed. "Clearly, you are learning something in college, party planner."

"You doubted that?" April replied, giving her an indignant look. "I'll remind you I've got a 3.9 this semester. I contain *multitudes*."

I glanced over at Bailey, still on the couch, her feet now tucked up underneath her. She looked at the decor but didn't say anything, instead taking a sip of her beer as she turned back to the water.

"How's the prep coming?" Jack asked as he came through the kitchen door, pitching a beer can into the bag for empties there.

"You mean the stuff you guys have been absolutely no part of?" Taylor said.

"Not true. We moved the couch," Vincent told her as he joined us. "And if you are lucky, I will bless you with one of my playlists."

"No!" Taylor and Jack said in unison. April snorted.

"What?" Vincent said, pulling out his phone. "It's a dance. I have great dance music."

"What you have," Jack told him, "is heavy hair metal. No one wants to dance to that."

"Heavy metal is great for dancing!" Vincent said. "It's

loud, there's a beat, and you can scream. What's not to love?"

"You scream while you dance?" Roo asked him.

"Sure," Vincent said easily. "Who doesn't?"

"Here's what I think we should do," April said. "Let's set up the room, then go outside and come in again."

"It will still be Roo's living room," Jack pointed out.

"Yes, but it will *feel* different," she told him. She reached down for a bag hanging off one of the chairs, digging around for a moment, then pulled out a bottle of liquor. "Especially if we take a shot first."

"Now, I'm in," Jack said.

"You're driving," Bailey said.

"Actually, I'm not," he told her. "I'm staying with Roo. But even if I wasn't, I could walk home. Just like you did the other night."

"That wasn't my choice," she said, glaring at him. "It was because you were being an—"

"And we're going outside!" Taylor announced in an enthusiastic voice, getting to her feet. She gathered up the corsages in her hands, holding them against her. "Everyone, follow me."

We all traipsed out the door and gathered around the couch, where Bailey still sat, her expression dark. Roo fetched some plastic cups, pouring a little bit from the bottle—rum, I saw now—into seven and lining them up on the porch rail. When everyone took one, only a single cup remained.

"Who are we missing?" April said, glancing around.

"Saylor doesn't drink," Jack told her.

"Oh. Sorry!" Taylor said. "I'll just—"

Before she could finish this thought, Bailey reached over and picked up the shot. Then, as we all watched, she threw it back, then tossed the cup over the rail.

Taylor raised her eyebrows. "O-kay then. What should the rest of us drink to?"

Roo handed me an empty cup, then held out his own shot to the middle of the circle. "To summer. And to us."

Even though I'd never been one to imbibe, I knew that normally, toasts were taken all at once. Here, though, like so much else, it was different. Lake rules.

"To summer," Jack repeated, pressing his own cup against Roo's. "And to us."

Slowly, we went around the circle to April, Vincent, and then Taylor, each of them following suit. Then it was Bailey's turn.

"Fine," she said, adding her own shot to the cups pressed together.

"Do it right or don't do it at all," Roo told her.

She sighed, rolling her eyes, then said, "To summer and to us."

Now, I was the only one. From where I was standing, through the nearby window, I could see the fridge and the picture of my mother, although the specifics were blurry at a distance. Still, I knew she was there, caught in that beat of time as I was in this one.

I held out my empty cup, putting it in the circle. "To summer, and to us."

Everyone drank. Then April put her hand on the door-knob. "Okay. Everyone ready?"

"Yes!" Taylor said.

"No," Bailey grumbled at the same time.

Ignoring her, April opened the door. "Welcome," she said, "to the first annual North Lake Prom."

She stepped back, waving an arm for the rest of us to enter: Jack and Taylor first, laughing, then Vincent, with Bailey, Roo, and me bringing up the rear.

"We were just in here," Bailey said. "How different can it really look?"

A lot, actually. Maybe it was really the change in scenery. Or the fact that I'd been busy examining the pictures and worrying about Bailey instead of watching April and Taylor work their decorating magic. But as I came in, Roo's living room seemed transformed.

There were the lights, of course, tiny and white and strung across all four walls, then meeting in the center of the ceiling, where they were bound with gardenias. The furniture had been pushed to the corners and covered with white sheets, leaving an empty stretch of hardwood floor. Off to one side was the kitchen table, which held a speaker, a punch bowl, and the rest of the corsages, laid out neatly in a row. To someone else, maybe it could have been a room where we'd just been. But I was new here, and could see it as something special. Because it was.

"Is this a punch bowl?" Jack asked, peering down at the table. "Seriously?"

"Formals always have punch!" April told him. "Take it from a party planner. It's like a rule."

"Right," he said as he picked up a corsage, holding it out to Taylor. She grinned, then stepped closer, watching as he affixed it to her tank top. "Hey, does this mean we can skip your prom this year now? Because that would be—"

"No," she replied flatly. She took his hand. "Dance with me."

"There's no music."

"I can fix that," Vincent, by the door with Bailey, offered.

"No!" Roo and April said together. Then she pulled out her phone and tapped it a few times. A moment later, as a pop song filled the room, Taylor stepped into the center of the floor, pulling Jack with her and grabbing April with her other hand. As she began to shimmy, grinning, and he clapped his hands, April let out a whoop.

I could feel my cheeks flushing as the small room got warmer and louder. Vincent slipped around me to the table, picking up a corsage, which he then brought back to Bailey, holding it out to her.

"You don't have to," she told him.

"I want to," he said. "Okay if I put it on?"

"Fine," she said.

Vincent carefully removed the pin, then attached the small bundle of flowers and stems to her dress as she watched. This was not the corsage she'd wanted, nor the place she'd planned to get it. Still, I hoped so much she could still see it for the sweet act it was.

"Wanna dance?" he asked her once he was done.

Bailey looked at her brother, who was spinning Taylor out as she tilted her head back and laughed. To Vincent she said, "Are you going to scream?"

"I'll try not to," he replied.

They joined the group, Vincent pumping his hands over his head while Bailey, less enthused, shifted from side to side. When April saw her and stuck out a hand, however, she took it, doing a little spin. When everyone else applauded, I saw her smile, but just barely.

Back against the wall, alone, I wished I could have captured this moment like those ones on the fridge. Posed, or spontaneous, I wouldn't have cared. I just wanted to remember it, every detail, long after this night was done.

"Saylor."

I looked up: Roo was standing in front of me. "Yeah?"

"Want to dance?"

I felt myself blink. Of course he'd think I'd want to be part of this: I was here, too. But all my life I'd felt more like an observer than an active participant. Beside the wheel, not behind. It was safer there, but could be lonely too, or so I was now realizing. Maybe there was a middle ground between living too hard and living at all. Maybe, here, I was finding it.

"Sure," I said. Then he stuck out his hand, I took it, and he pulled me in.

I danced. We all did, there in that small dark room lit with tiny white lights, spinning and bumping each other

223

and laughing. We made our way through a couple of April's playlists, then one of Jack's, before finally Vincent was allowed to take over DJ duty. Two songs later, when my head was throbbing with happy screaming and my dress literally stuck to me with sweat, April threw open the door and announced we were going swimming. No one hesitated except for me.

"But you *can* swim," Roo said. "Right? Because if not, you should have told us that first night out at the raft. Strong lake rule, that one."

"Yes, I can swim," I told him. "I just haven't here. Yet."

And why was that? Because no one else had been swimming and invited me. Once again, it was all the actions of other people, like Bailey, that made my own life happen: Blake, my first kiss, even the prom I'd almost attended that night. I was like those pieces of litter I sometimes saw swept up on windy days and carried down entire streets. You just look up and there you are.

I watched now as Taylor took off her corsage, carefully laying it on a porch rail. "I'm going in," she announced before shaking her hair back and running down the grass to the dock. At the end, she leaped off with a shriek before disappearing into the dark water. We all cheered.

"My turn," April announced, kicking off her shoes. "Dare me to belly flop?"

"Don't do it," Vincent said. "Remember last time!"

"What happened last time?" I asked as she barreled down the dock before launching outward flat, arms outstretched, with a scream. A beat later, we heard the slap of skin against water.

"She'll feel that tomorrow," Roo said.

"She's not the only one," Jack said, turning to look behind him at Bailey, who was sound asleep on the couch, her dress tangled around her legs and bare feet dirty, flecked with sand. All the time and money she'd spent to make this night perfect, only to end it passed out, alone.

"She'll be okay when she sleeps it off," I said, to him as well as myself. Then I stepped inside the door, grabbing a blanket I'd seen earlier from a chair there. When I shook it out over Bailey, she slapped it away, muttering as she curled deeper into the cushions. I left it at her feet in case she changed her mind.

"Hey!" April called out from the water. "Y'all coming in or what?"

"On the way," Jack replied, then pulled off his shirt, dropping it to the grass. After a quick check on Bailey—I saw it, if no one else—Vincent did the same. Those already in increased their volume as Jack dove in sideways and Vincent did his own cannonball. Splash. And then there were two of us. Who were conscious, anyway.

"You know I was just giving you a hard time before, right?" Roo said as I watched Taylor splash Jack, and him dunk her in return. "I understand not wanting to swim in that dress."

I looked down at it, the corsage he'd pinned on now wilted, hanging feebly by its pin. Like it, my dress had lived the evening hard, the hem now dirty and one strap, loosened by a particularly enthusiastic conga line, hanging down over my shoulder. I pulled it back up; it fell again. This time, I just left it there.

"It's not the dress," I said, looking back at the water. "I think it's more that it's nighttime. I've never gone swimming in the dark."

"Some people might say night swims are a lake rite of passage," he pointed out.

"I guess." I crossed my arms. "But maybe my mom did it enough for both of us."

He bit his lip, ducking his head as he turned to look at the water, dark except for the moon and thrown light from the motels and houses along the shore. "Right," he said finally. "I wasn't even thinking about that. Didn't mean to make it awkward."

"You couldn't," I said, and smiled, to prove I meant it.

Behind us, Bailey shifted, talking in her sleep, but I couldn't make out what she was saying.

"You know," Roo said, once it was quiet again, "I'm really glad you came this summer."

"Yeah?"

He nodded. "I always wondered, you know? What happened to you. Because I remembered that time you came when we were kids."

"I wish *I* remembered," I said. "I lost a lot. Like, everything from this place."

"Wasn't lost," he said. "You just left it here. You know

what Mimi says: the lake keeps us."

"I've never heard that before."

"Sure you have," he replied. "Just now."

He smiled at me then, and as I felt myself smile back, I wondered if our parents, the best of friends, had ever stood in this same spot. There were so many stories here, like every moment had already been lived once before.

But then, Roo did something different. He reached forward with one hand, sliding my fallen strap back up on my shoulder. It was a simple gesture, but like earlier, with the corsage, I felt my heart catch in my chest. Once the strap was fixed, he left his hand there, fingers spread cool over my skin. Like a take two, second chance. The kind you don't get often.

Maybe this was why I stepped a little closer, lifting my chin as I looked up at him. His eyes widened a bit, but he stayed where he was.

"Hey!" someone yelled from the water. "What are you guys doing up there?"

We both jumped, him turning his head at the noise while I took a full step back, putting space between us again.

"One sec," he called back. Turning back to me, he said, "Look, I didn't mean to—"

"It's fine," I said quickly. I could feel my heart beating in my chest, as well as the weight of his hand on my shoulder, even though it was now gone.

"Roo! Get in here!" Jack yelled.

He reached up, tugging his own shirt off and tossing it

onto the grass with the others. Then, with a final look back at me, he jogged down the dock as everyone else whooped and clapped, and dove off.

"Shoulda done it."

Again startled, I looked over to the couch, where Bailey was now curled up on one side. "What?"

"Kissed him," she said, her voice muffled by her hair. Her eyes remained closed. "Had the perfect chance. Shoulda taken it."

"I panicked," I said, looking out at the water. Familiar story. "Why do I always do that?"

She didn't answer, as her breathing had steadied: she was asleep again.

Back inside, the room was still hot, one of the light strands had fallen down, and a leftover corsage lay flattened on the floor. No one had touched the punch. When I realized the speaker was buzzing steadily, not connected to anything, I went over and turned it off. That was when I heard my phone.

It was in my bag, which I'd left in the kitchen on the counter. By the time I went over and pulled it out, it had gone silent as well, although a message remained on the screen. My dad.

Just got off the boat. Great time but EXHAUSTED. See you Friday! Can't wait.

No way, I thought, rereading this a second time. But when I flipped over to my calendar, scanning the month of June into July, I saw it was true: my trip was almost over.

Before long, I'd be going back to Lakeview to move into our new house and begin another life. But what about this one?

I started down the steps, and when I felt grass beneath my feet, my instinct was to stop, stay where I was. Instead, I started moving faster, enough to blow my hair back and feel a breeze on my skin. I knew I must look ridiculous, a girl in a formal dress, running alone down the grass. But at least I was doing it myself, each step a choice as I got closer to the water.

"Saylor?" April called out, spotting me, but I didn't look for her, or anyone else, as I banged down the dock, gaining speed. I just had my eyes on the end, that leap to come, and in my mind I could see it as jumping past so many other things as well: the view behind the wheel, my neatly organized closet and room, Trinity's judging face. Blake leaning in for that kiss, then Roo fixing my strap so carefully while I stood by, frozen. You can make your life, or life can make you. Was it really that simple of a choice?

As I hit the dock's end and jumped, I wanted to see it, that change from passenger to driver, Emma to Saylor, watching to doing. So when I hit the cold lake and went under, I kept my eyes open.

FOURTEEN

Things move fast once you decide to get behind the wheel. Or maybe it just seems that way.

"Good. Now, wipe it with those newspapers. Rub in circles."

Gordon did as she was told, her skinny arm moving across the mirror as Trinity, stretched out across the bed with her feet up, watched. "Like this?"

"Yes," I said as I passed behind her with the bathroom trash can, then dumped it into the garbage bag by the unit's door. "Be sure to take all the dust to the edge and off. That way you don't leave any."

"Listen to you," Trinity said, turning a page in the magazine she was reading. "You sound like an expert."

"I had a good teacher," I said.

"Puh-leese," Bailey groaned from the bathroom, where she was scrubbing the shower. "Don't flatter her. She's already acting enough like a princess."

"I'm *pregnant*," Trinity pointed out, unnecessarily. Her

stomach was like a mountain when she was prone, blocking the view of her face from the end of the bed.

"And I'm working two jobs and we have Gordon on as child labor," her sister replied. "So everyone's suffering, not just you."

It was true. Not so much about the suffering, but the extra hands on deck. The morning after the first official North Lake Prom, Trinity had woken up with some light spotting, which prompted a panicky trip to the ER. She wasn't in labor, but they did put her on bed rest. That left only Mimi and me to clean rooms, so Bailey had been coming in afternoons after her shift at the Station as well as her days off, with Roo and Jack filling in as they could as well. When Gordon got strep throat and couldn't go to camp, she'd been recruited as well. Somehow, we were getting both turnover and housekeeping done, although with two beginners and one super-reluctant veteran, I wasn't exactly sure how.

The truth was, everything had been chaotic since that morning, and not just because of the bed rest and new workload. There was also the issue of my dad and Tracy's return from Greece, scheduled for late that evening. The plan had been for them to return to Nana's, who had just gotten home from her own trip, then come fetch me so we could all move over to the new house. But the "easy" remodel of Nana's condo had hit a permitting snag. With our new house also still needing some work to pass inspection, I was now the only one with someplace to stay.

"I mean, we can do a hotel," my dad had said the day

before, calling from Athens, where he was about to board his plane. "But your grandmother . . ."

He didn't finish this thought, not that he had to. Nana was used to a certain level of comfort. All she wanted to do was get back to her newly redone home, and now she couldn't even do that.

I, however, felt like I'd been given a break by the universe. If the house wasn't ready, I could just remain here for a while longer. When I floated this by my dad, though, he was not convinced.

"You've been there three weeks," he told me. "We don't want you to outstay your welcome."

"I'm helping," I pointed out. "They need me to clean rooms at the motel anyway."

"You're cleaning rooms at Calvander's?"

Whoops. I bit my lip, realizing I shouldn't have shared this. "Just because they're short-staffed. With the baby coming and everything."

"Baby?"

"Trinity. Celeste's daughter? She's having a baby really soon."

"Who?"

I sighed, switching my phone to my other ear. Downstairs, I could hear Oxford in the kitchen, making coffee and rustling around with the paper. Even though it hadn't been that long since I'd arrived, it was already hard to imagine a morning now that didn't start this way. "The point is, I'm happy to stay here and I'm sure it's okay with Mimi."

"But what if I don't want you to stay?" he replied.

"Why wouldn't you?"

I heard some friction on the line. "Because," he said, his voice quiet, "we're starting a new life in a new house, as a new family. It seems only right we do it together."

"But you just said the house wasn't ready."

"Well, it isn't."

"So how are we going to stay there?"

"Emma." Before, he'd sounded tired. Now, irritation was creeping in. "Just let Mimi know you'll be leaving by the end of the week."

"But—"

"Let her know," he repeated, as in the background, an announcement began. "That's our group. I'll call as soon as we're back in your time zone. Okay?"

"Okay," I replied. "Fly safe."

We hung up, and I flopped back against my pillow, looking at the ceiling above me. After sulking a bit, I went downstairs for toast and the obits, and when I saw Mimi, I told her nothing. My dad was in the air, over an ocean. I still had some time, and there were rooms to clean.

Now, I pulled out my spray bottle, pumping the handle until the small glass table I was standing over was covered with bleach solution. As I started to wipe it clean, Trinity said, "Who are you today, Saylor?"

I looked down at my bottle, where a name was written in pink Sharpie, surrounded by plump hearts. "Vicki," I said.

"Oh, right," she replied. "Big on pink, not so much on

working. I think she lasted one season."

"And a half," Bailey said, banging against something in the bathroom. Thump. Thump. "She took off with that trucker, remember?"

Trinity thought for a second. "God, you're right!"

"Of course I am," Bailey said. "I remember everything. All details, every story. You know that."

"Is this good?" Gordon, now at the edge of the mirror, her face red with exertion, asked.

"Missed a spot," Trinity told her, pointing to the left side.

As Gordon started rubbing again, I asked, "Is that true, Bailey? Do you really remember everything?"

Another thump. Then, "Yeah. It's like a gift. Or a curse."

"It's seriously creepy sometimes," Trinity added. "She remembers the stuff she wasn't even here for, because she's heard Mom tell *her* stories."

"Do you remember hearing about when I was here?" I asked Bailey as she threw a pile of towels out the bathroom door. "When we were four?"

"Yeah," she said. Her voice carried out as she added, "Your mom and dad were going on a trip and they left you with Mimi."

"Second honeymoon," I said, adding the pillowcases to my own pile. "That's what he said."

"They didn't seem like newlyweds," Bailey said. I could hear her own spray bottle. "Pretty tense, as I recall hearing. Your mom hadn't been here since Chris Price died, so there was that, too."

"She never came back, all those years?"

"Nope." More spritzing. "Mom said Mimi went to visit her, with Joe, when you were born and a couple of other times. But she was weird about this place. It was like there were—"

"Ghosts," I finished for her.

"Yeah." She came out, gathering the towels in her arms and crossing the room to add them to the pile of linens. "She just wasn't herself, according to my mom. And then when Steph came over, she kind of lost it."

"Steph?" I asked.

"Roo's mom," Bailey said. "It was the first time Waverly had seen her since the funeral. And she'd never met Roo."

"That, I remember," Trinity said, turning a page. "Waverly started crying, just standing there watching you and Roo together."

I plumped the pillow I was holding, then replaced it. "I wish I could remember."

"This was *your* mom, though, and she was really upset. Your mind is probably doing you a favor by forgetting."

"I'd rather remember," I said. "There are enough holes."

"But lots of pictures," Bailey said.

I looked over at her, now standing by the front door scraping what looked like gum off the carpet. "What did you say?"

"The pictures," she replied, not looking up. "Because of Steph."

I just looked at her.

"Because she was so into photography," she continued.

235

"She documented everything."

"Are you saying there are more pictures of that visit than the one in Mimi's office?"

"Which one is that?"

I told her about the snapshot I'd seen under the glass my first day, of all of us kids together on the steps. "Oh, yeah," she said. "Steph definitely took that. She lined us all up, too, while your mom was off to the side watching."

"Bribed us with candy," Trinity added, sniffing a perfume insert.

Hearing this, I sat down on the bed, the pillow I'd been about to cover in my arms. I wasn't sure what compelled me at that moment, but I heard myself say, "My dad wants me to come home."

It was quiet for a second. Even Gordon, wiping the TV, stopped in mid circle. Trinity said, "You just got here, though."

"It's been almost a month," I pointed out. "That was how long I was supposed to visit."

"Yeah, but that was when you were just here because you needed a place to stay," Bailey said, standing up and tossing a paper towel with the gum in it toward the trash bag.

"Isn't that why I'm here now?"

"No." She picked up her bottle from the windowsill, then looked at me. "You're learning your history. Before it was just a visit, yes. But now it's personal."

"Sounds like news to her," Trinity observed. "So maybe not *so* personal."

"My history," I repeated. "How do you figure?"

Bailey sighed, looking at the ceiling. "Hello, what were we just talking about? Filling in the holes in your memory. Getting the rest of the story about your mom. I mean, you didn't even know about the accident!"

"Bay, where are you going with this?" Trinity asked.

"I'm making a *point*." She looked at me again. "You were just saying how you don't have any memories of the lake before this summer. But you do, because we're helping you fill them in. Part of grieving is letting go of the past. But how can you let go if you never knew it in the first place?"

Outside, a man, a motel guest, walked by shirtless, his flip-flops thwacking. He glanced in at us, but only briefly, as he passed by.

"People should wear shirts if they're not *right* on the beach," Trinity said, once he was out of earshot. Gordon snickered.

"My mom's been gone five years," I said to Bailey, ignoring this. "I don't think I can claim to be grieving anymore."

"Of course you can!" She picked up the garbage bag, shaking it. "Look. Saylor. My mom still cries for yours at least once a week. No joke. It's not like you just snap your fingers and move on."

Now I felt even worse. I didn't cry that much anymore. In fact, I couldn't remember the last time. Which, as I thought about it, made me feel close to tears myself. "I don't want to leave yet," I said, swallowing. "I'm not sure it's for the reasons you're saying or something else. All I know is that

I wish some of these were *my* memories, not just everyone else's. Like there's more to the story, but I'm not there yet."

"You should ask to see the pictures."

Gordon spoke so softly, at first I wasn't even sure it was her who had said this. When we all looked at her, though, she blushed a deep red. "What did you say?" I asked.

She cleared her throat. "The pictures. That Roo's mom took. Bailey said there were tons of them. Maybe they'd help you remember."

Trinity and Bailey exchanged a look. Then Bailey said, "That is a great idea, actually."

Gordon, pleased, turned back to the TV and started dusting again.

"You think?" I asked Bailey as she headed back to the kitchen.

"It can't hurt," she said. "And neither can asking your dad again if you can have a little more time. For your mom, and her memory, if nothing else."

I wasn't so sure about that. My dad had always been selective about my mom's legacy, what we remembered and what we didn't. I truly believed he thought he was doing me a favor by keeping the bad stuff out.

"Just ask him," Bailey said, spraying down the stovetop. "The worst he can do is say no."

"No."

The answer came so quickly—mere moments after I'd gotten up the nerve to ask—that I wasn't even ready. "But you didn't even think about it!"

"Emma—"

"You asked me to come here so you could go on your honeymoon. I did," I said, pacing across the sand below Mimi's house, where I'd come to make this call while everyone else got dinner together. "And I'm learning a lot about Mom, and myself, and just don't understand why, if I have no place to stay, I can't—"

"Because you *do* have a place to stay," he finished over me. "And if you'd just let me talk for a second, I'll tell you about it."

I bit my lip, then sat down at the picnic table. Now that I'd pledged to try to take control of my life, the last thing I wanted was to hear more plans that had been made for me. Unfortunately, I didn't have a choice.

"What I was going to say, before you started in about this—" he began.

"It's my history," I blurted out. "My memories. I'm already here, I should be allowed to finish what I've started."

"Emma. Please just let me talk for a second." He sounded tired. "As you know, we are currently between residences, as is your grandmother. After some discussion, she's suggested a temporary solution that I think will work for all of us."

Whatever it was, I was sure I wouldn't like it. But I stayed quiet. For now.

"Nana has a friend with a resort in Lake North," he continued. "He's been offering her use of a suite of rooms for ages, and now seems like a good time to take him up on it."

It took me a second to process what he was saying. Finally I said, "Wait. You're coming *here*?"

"We," he replied, "will be spending two weeks at Lake North, all of us. Then we'll head home to our hopefully finished homes."

"You're coming to Lake North," I said again. "Great. So I'll just stay here. Everyone's happy."

"No. You've been with Mimi, and we're very grateful. But it's time to be together as a family now."

"This is my family, too."

"Emma." He sighed. "I know you're having fun. But I don't think these people are at the same level as Tracy, Nana, and myself."

"Why do there have to be levels?" I asked, getting to my feet again. "I went from a four-person unit to discovering all these cousins and aunts and uncles I never even knew I had. I don't want to just forget them now."

"No one is asking you to forget anyone."

"But why didn't we ever visit here, except for that one time before you and Mom split and the funeral? Why didn't she ever come back, with me or just by herself?"

He groaned. "Do we have to get into this now? I'm so jet-lagged I can barely think."

"I know about the accident," I told him. "What happened with Chris Price. But only because of Bailey. It makes me wonder how much else I don't know."

"You don't need to know everything," he said. Now there was an edge to his voice.

"Maybe I do," I replied. Silence. I pressed on. "Look, Dad. I know you want me to remember only the good stuff about Mom. But it's okay that she was human and flawed. You don't have to hide that fact from me."

"I couldn't even if I wanted to!" he said. He exhaled. "And that's just my point. Despite everything, *you* are okay. My one job is to protect you. I tried to do that by building our lives in Lakeview. There just wasn't room for anything else."

"You can protect me without keeping secrets," I said. "She was my mom. And this, here, it's part of my life. And you kept it from me."

"We both did," he replied, sounding frustrated. "Look, Emma. Your mom never went back to the lake because by then it meant nothing but tragedy to her. It was where her problems started, the drinking, the addictions. Her bad choices led to the death of her best friend. She never got over that."

"Then why did you guys bring me that summer?" I asked. "What was the point?"

"We were trying to save our marriage," he said. I could hear the fatigue now in his voice, although whether it was literal or just this subject was hard to say. "Nana couldn't help with you and we had no other options."

"Just like this time," I said. "So they're family when you need a babysitter, and strangers when you don't. That makes sense."

He was quiet for what felt like a long time. As for me, I felt sick: I rarely, if ever, argued with my dad. Finally, he spoke.

"It's not my intent to take you away from your family." He said this last word slowly, as if it was difficult to pronounce. "But if we're talking about what's fair, you've spent three weeks there with her experience. It doesn't seem wrong to ask you to do the same with mine."

"You?" I said. "You're not a lake kid."

"No," he agreed. "But I did spend summers working at the Club and met your mom there. It was a big part of my life, too."

Not the same, I thought. But I didn't say this aloud.

"How about this," he said now. "You agree to come stay at the Tides. But you can still visit Mimi's, as long as you make time for us as well. Get a bit of both worlds. Is that fair?"

"You're staying at the Tides?" I said, remembering the ritzy resort Bailey had pointed out to me on my first trip to Lake North.

"It's your grandmother," he said helplessly. "And it's not like we have a lot of choices."

So that's what it comes down to. Choices. Good and bad, right and wrong, yes and no. Like being behind the wheel, there are some that are instinctive, others you have to think about. It was only three miles to the other side, a distance I'd covered by foot already. Before I went back, though, there was one more trip to take. Luckily, it wasn't far.

FIFTEEN

When I got to Roo's, the Yum truck was parked outside, an extension cord stretching from it to the small garage. As I passed and heard the coolers humming, I thought of all that ice cream inside.

I went around the house to the screen door and peered in, but didn't see anyone. There was a pair of sneakers kicked off on the floor, though, as well as a phone and some keys on a nearby table. When I heard a shower running, distantly, I sat down on the steps to wait.

It had only been a day since the conversation with my dad, and the fact that I was going to be moving to Lake North was just beginning to sink in. Partly this was because I hadn't exactly told anyone about my dad's directive. Yet.

First, Gordon went back to the doctor, who said she needed another round of antibiotics, making day camp still off-limits. Since I was the only one without a full-time job who wasn't hugely pregnant, I'd offered to keep an eye on her. I hadn't imagined it being that big of a task, until she attached herself to me like a shadow. If I was cleaning rooms, Gordon, her own spray bottle in hand, was right there. At lunch, she waited for me to make her a quesadilla after my own, then sat beside me at the table, reading her Allies book until we were done, at which point she followed me back to the motel. In the evenings, while Bailey worked late at the Station—since the breakup with Colin, she'd focused on making money and not much else—Gordon sat next to me on the couch as I watched house remodeling shows with Mimi, cheering when the hard hats came out and demos began. The only time we parted ways was when she went to bed, and I was pretty sure she would have stayed in my room if I'd offered. Which I didn't.

"I think it's cute," Trinity had said that morning as we sat eating toast together in her room. In a rare moment, we were alone: Gordon had gone with Mimi to open up the office, although I knew she'd find me as soon as I started cleaning. "She looks up to you."

"Yeah, but why?" I asked. "She barely knows me."

Trinity shrugged, slathering butter onto one of the four pieces of toast I'd brought her. Her bed, which was basically her home until the baby came, was piled with magazines, dirty plates, and her laptop, which she used to alternately HiThere! with the Sergeant and watch *Big New York*, her favorite reality show. Although I'd managed to quell a lot of my organizing urges, I was dying to get her out of the room just long enough to do a deep clean.

"Well, think about it," she said. "Her mom's out of the picture. So is yours."

"My mom is dead, though."

"True. But if you're ten and live in another state from your only parent, it probably feels like a death, right?"

I thought about this. "What's Amber's story, anyway?"

She finished chewing. "Grew up here, followed some deadbeat guy to Florida, where she got hooked on pills. Social services was going to take Gordon until Mama and Mimi got involved."

I thought of Gordon, so small in her glasses. My heart just broke for her. "Sounds kind of familiar."

"You're more alike than you know," Trinity continued, shifting herself and rubbing a hip. "There's also the fact that you both have two names but only go by one."

"You think that bonds us?"

"It doesn't hurt."

I thought of that first day, when I'd told Gordon about my name and she'd called me lucky. It made me think maybe I should call her Anna once in a while. "I just don't think I'm much of a role model. It makes me nervous."

"Are you kidding?" she snorted. "You're a good student with a bright future who lives in a big house with a nice, normal family. Forget Gordon. *I* want to be like you."

It said something that this description, so easily put, did not describe me in my mind at all. "I'm also an anxious person with a dead mom who was an addict, trying to figure out what that means for me in my own life."

"In your big house with your normal family," she added, raising an eyebrow.

I made a face, just as over at the motel, Gordon came out of the office, shutting the door behind her. She had on shorts and an oversized Calvander's tie-dye, just like mine, her short hair gathered back in an identical ponytail. When she saw me on the porch, she immediately started over.

"If I were you," Trinity said, having observed this as well, "I'd enjoy it. You'll notice nobody is wanting to emulate me right now."

I smiled at her. "Pretty soon, you'll have someone who loves you best, though."

"Here's hoping." She put a hand on her belly. "I was so hard on my mom, though. Still am. With my luck, the payback is going to be *brutal*."

She'd started saying this kind of thing a lot lately, as the due date got closer and she grew increasingly nervous. And a couple of weeks earlier, I might have privately agreed that maybe she didn't have the most tender, motherly touch, though I never would have had the nerve to tell her to her face. Now, though, I'd caught enough glimpses of her good heart to know it was in there somewhere. A tough mom was better than none at all. Gordon and I, of all people, could vouch for that.

Now, sitting on Roo's steps, I heard whistling. When I turned around, he was walking into the living room, in shorts and bare feet and a Blackwood T-shirt. "Hey," he said. "How long have you been there?"

"Not long," I told him, getting to my feet. "Got a second?"

"Sure." He walked over, pushing open the screen door with a creak. "Come on in."

I did, feeling strangely nervous by this formality, plus the fact it was just us. Since the night of Club Prom, we'd barely seen each other, a result of my increased work schedule and his beginning a (yes) sixth job. Or was it seventh?

"How's work going?" I said, thinking this.

"You'll have to be more specific," he replied, gesturing for me to have a seat on the couch.

"The new one," I told him. "What was it again?"

"Driving for RideFly," he said.

"Is that like GetThere? A ride-sharing thing?"

"No, it's an airport shuttle," he said. "Fifty bucks round trip from Lake North or North Lake to the Bly County airport. Plus, you get a free water and some mints."

"There's an airport in Bly County?"

"And here you thought it was just a mecca for formal wear," he said, picking up his phone from the table and sliding it into a pocket. "Yes, there is an airport. It's about the size of a dentist's waiting room, but it exists."

"Wow," I said. "I had no idea."

"Don't feel bad. Nobody I know has ever flown out of it," he said, plopping down beside me. "It's mostly Lake North people who have money, and there aren't much of those unless there's a big event going on. This weekend it's a wedding. We're scooping up the out-of-towners."

"Sounds like you could do that in the Yum truck," I said.

"Is that an ice cream joke?"

247

"Couldn't resist," I said, and he laughed. As he sat back, stretching his feet out to rest on the buckled trunk that functioned as a coffee table, I said, "You know, it's funny you mention Lake North. I'm actually going there tomorrow."

"Are you attending the Janney-Sipowicz wedding?" he asked. "Because if so, I've already met the father of the groom. He likes jokes that start with someone walking into a bar."

"Sadly, no." I took a breath. "I'm actually moving over there. My dad and his new wife and my grandma are all coming down and we're staying at the Tides, together."

"The Tides? That place is super fancy. When are you coming back to stay at Mimi's?"

"I'm not."

He raised his eyebrows. "What? You're leaving for good?"

"I can still visit," I said. "For two weeks, anyway. After that, we all go back to Lakeview."

"Wow." He reached up, running a hand through the back of his hair. Another tuft sprang to attention, sideways. "I thought you were here all summer."

"Nope," I said. "Really, I was only supposed to be here until now. The Lake North thing just sort of happened because our house and Nana's are still under construction. So I guess I should be happy."

"Are you?"

"No," I answered, honestly. "I mean, a month ago I had no plans to come here. I didn't even think about this place. Now that I have to leave, I can't imagine not being here to help with Calvander's and see the baby come."

We were quiet for a second. Outside, on the water, I could hear a motorboat chugging by.

"So you came to say goodbye," he said. He looked at me. "That *sucks*."

Hearing this, I felt a pang I didn't expect. "Not goodbye yet. First I have a favor to ask."

"You want some complimentary RideFly mints? I've got a whole bag."

"No." I took a breath. "Bailey said your mom took a lot of pictures that week I was here, when I was a kid. Do you guys still have them?"

"I'm sure we do," he replied. "The tricky part will be finding them."

He got up, crossing the room quickly over to a low cabinet beneath a window. When he bent down, pulling open the doors, I saw it was jammed full of photo albums of all types, sizes, and colors.

"Like a needle in a haystack," he said, taking out a small flowered one that was wedged at the top and opening it. After scanning a page, he said, "Well, this one documents my awkward stage. So we can rule that out."

"Can I see?"

"No," he said flatly, putting it on the cabinet and taking out another one that was deep green, square, with an embossed cover. Opening it, he said, "Oh, here's a picture of Waverly. So at least we're getting closer."

He handed the album to me. Sure enough, in the right-hand corner was a snapshot of my mom, in rolled-up jeans and a Blackwood Station T-shirt, bent over one of the dock pumps. "I wonder when this was."

Roo, now rummaging through the rest of the cabinet, glanced over my shoulder. "Well, that's the old Pavilion. It got taken out by a hurricane in 1997, so it had to be before that."

"She met my dad in 1999," I said. "And I guess she left for Lakeview in—"

"2000," he finished for me. "That fall, after my dad died."

I looked at the picture again. In it, my mom would have been around the same age I was now, although she looked like much more of a grown-up than I felt. What was it about pictures that aged people?

"Okay," Roo said suddenly, putting another album, this one burgundy-colored, on the top of the cabinet and opening it. "I think we're getting somewhere. Look."

It was a picture of three little girls with blond hair, sitting at the picnic table below Mimi's. They were all in swimsuits, eating Popsicles, and turned in the same direction, as if they'd been told to look at whoever was taking the shot. I immediately picked out myself, in the red tank suit with a giraffe on it. It took a second of looking this time, but only that, to realize the other two were Bailey and Trinity.

"That's the summer," I said. "2005. My parents split up that fall."

"So we were four."

"Yep." I looked to the next picture, also of the beach area

at Mimi's, but this one was of a skinny little boy in a skiff, holding a set of oars. "Is that you?"

"Nope. Jack. He's always been skinnier and taller." He pointed to the row below. "That's me."

I leaned in closer, taking him in: towheaded and skinny as well, in baggy shorts and a T-shirt with a dinosaur on it. He was sitting on the hood of a car, feet balanced on the front bumper. Behind him, you could see the driver's-side door was open, an arm—thick and hairy—cut off by the frame.

"Who's that?" I asked, indicating the driver.

"Some boyfriend of my mom's," he said with a shrug. "There was a string of them for a while there. Then she went back to school and didn't have time to date."

"Did she ever remarry?"

"Nope." He squinted down at the shot again. "I think I remember that car, actually. It was huge. The guy was small. Probably compensating."

I looked again as well, but you couldn't really tell much by just an arm. "My dad was the opposite. Didn't date anyone for years, just threw himself into work. Tracy was the first woman he brought home, and now they're married."

"You like her?"

I nodded. "She's nice. She makes him happy. Plus, she likes to sail, which I hate."

"Ticks every box," Roo said.

"Exactly." I picked up the album. "Okay if I look at this one over on the couch?"

"Sure. I'll keep digging, see if there's another one."

251

I got through two full pages before I saw something that brought me to tears. Weirdly, it was not the shot of Bailey and Jack with my parents in the background, my dad with his arm over my mom's shoulders. Or the one of Celeste and my mom, posing together in front of what I was pretty sure was the same gardenia bush where we'd taken our pictures before Club Prom. Instead, it was a picture I'd almost passed over. It was of an older woman in a lawn chair, taken from behind, and the composition was weird, everything in the picture over to one side and just empty lake on the other. It was only when I looked more closely that I saw she had a child in her lap, blond-headed, and that they were holding hands. You could see a gold bracelet, braided and thick, on the woman's wrist. The child held a stuffed giraffe in her arms. Me, Mimi, and George.

By this point I'd seen my own face and that of my parents, cousins, aunt, and grandmother repeated in square after square of snapshots. But there was something about seeing my beloved giraffe there as well that made this one picture feel like the ultimate proof that the trip really happened. When things were hard between my parents, and later, when my mom moved out, he was the one I cried to most, burying my face in the soft, nubby fur of his neck. He'd stayed on my bed all the way up until high school before I'd moved him across the room to a shelf, where he remained close enough for me to see before I fell asleep every night. Even now, I knew exactly where he was: in the final box I'd packed up from my room at Nana's, with my books and favorite

252

pictures. It would be the first one I would unpack in the new house, once I got there.

"I think that's the only album you'd want," Roo said now. I swallowed over the lump in my throat, turning the page as he walked over and sat down again. "Although you're welcome to keep looking. My dad's albums are someplace as well. Probably tons of shots of your mom there."

"This is great, actually," I said, studying a shot of Celeste, my dad and mom, and another man, with Jack's same nose and slim frame—Silas, I assumed—sitting at the picnic table. "These are all new to me."

"Really?" he said. "That's crazy. I've probably looked at them all a thousand times."

"Yeah?"

He crossed one leg over the other. "I had a lot of questions about my dad when I was old enough to finally ask. My mom usually just showed me these for her answers. That's why I was kind of freaked out that first day Jack brought you out to the lake."

I thought back. "I'm sorry."

"Don't be. It was just when I heard your name," he said, shifting slightly. His shoulder bumped mine. I didn't move, even as he did to add space again. "It was like you were actually real. Or something."

"I'll take that as a compliment, I guess," I said with a laugh.

"Okay, maybe that's the wrong word." He turned, looking at me. "It was just, you know, those pictures were part of a narrative for me. So you were, as well. Does that make sense?"

I wanted to say yes. It wasn't like I hadn't spent a fair amount of time lately thinking about stories, the ones we told and those we didn't. But the truth was, it didn't exactly track.

My face must has shown this, because he said, "Okay. So when I was nine or ten, I started to get really interested in my dad. I wanted to hear all about him, what he was like, all the time. It wore my mom out, so she'd often just give me these albums and tell me to go nuts. But of course, when I dug through them, I had other questions. Like who you were, and what happened to you."

"Why me?"

"Because, like him, you were in all these pictures. Until you weren't. Here, I'll show you." He pulled the album over into his lap. "See, this one of you with Bailey and Trinity at the table? That was the day your parents brought you. You just appear, after all these books filled with other faces I still knew. A stranger."

I looked down at myself, the Popsicle gripped in one hand. "You didn't remember me."

"I sort of did," he said. "But we were four. Like I said, I was in a thing. I had questions."

I felt my face get a little warm, suddenly, knowing I'd been discussed. It was the same finding that shot of my mom on the fridge: like I, too, had been here all along, even if I hadn't known it.

"And then," he went on, turning a page, "this was the first time we met, which was probably a few minutes later. She literally got the exact moment."

I looked at the picture. It was of the shoreline, littered then as it was now with various floats and beach toys. I was standing at the water's edge in the same bathing suit, holding a plastic flowerpot, as Roo, crouched in the sand, gripped a shovel and looked up into my face. Behind us, a white boat was sliding past, out of frame.

"I look skeptical," I said.

"You had good instincts. I was shady."

I laughed, glad for the release. This felt heavy in a way I couldn't explain. "Are there more?"

He turned another page, pointing to the bottom corner and a shot taken on a bumper car. The two of us were side by side, me behind the fake wheel while he had his arms up in the air, a gleeful look on his face. "Well, here we have evidence that you used to drive just fine."

"Maybe that's where I got traumatized," I suggested.

"Entirely possible." Another page turn. "I think we did better off four wheels. Look."

I did, following his finger to a picture of him and me in the grassy stretch behind Mimi's house, Calvander's office in the distant background. I had to look more closely to make out that it was bubbles, tons of them, floating up over us as we stood together. I had one arm looped around his neck, my eyes cast downward while he looked straight ahead.

"Wow," I said softly.

"I know." He leaned in a little bit more: now our shoulders touched again. "I've always really liked this shot, for some reason. It just looks—"

"Magical," I finished for him. As soon as I said the word, I felt silly. But that was what had come to mind.

"Yeah." He turned his head, smiling at me, and I wished more than anything, right then, that I did remember. That day, that shot, those bubbles. But especially him.

"Anyway," he said, "there are others, too. But those are the ones I remember. As well as that group shot, the one you already saw. Which is . . . here."

He turned a few more pages until it appeared, this time blown up bigger: me, Roo, Jack, Bailey, and Trinity, all on the bench, side by side. The day I had arrived and seen it beneath the glass in Mimi's office, every other face had been a stranger. Now, looking at them, I could see things I immediately recognized: the recognizable wry annoyance of Trinity's expression, how Bailey looked so serious, sitting with elbows propped on knees, framing her own face with her fists. Jack, the oldest, already focused on what would come after the shutter clicked, while Roo's grin was the same. I looked at myself last, thinking there would be no surprises there, at least. But this time, I did see something different. It was the way I was sitting, leaning against Roo, our knees bumping each other: the ease and comfortableness that comes with familiarity. It was, actually, much like we were sitting now.

"After that," he said, "you just vanish, never to be seen again. Poof. You can see why I was confused."

Like I was the ghost, I thought. "Did you think I was dead, too?"

"I was a kid, so it wasn't that cut and dry. It was more . . ." He sat back again, thinking. "I wondered about you. But it had been a while. And then you show up, at the dock, and you're Emma but really Saylor, and you don't know me. . . ."

"I'm sorry," I said instantly.

"Not your fault." He turned to look at me. "Look, the point is . . . I'm glad you came this summer. To see you again."

I stared back at him, feeling a tug in my chest. "I'm real now," I said.

"Yeah," he said, smiling. We were so close, I could see him breathing. "You are."

It was perfect, that kind of moment when time just stops. Until my phone, in my pocket, buzzed suddenly. When I pulled it out, I had a text from Bailey.

Where are you? Come find me. It's important.

Of course it was.

"Everything okay?" Roo asked.

"Think so." I shut the book. "I should go. Thanks for letting me look at this."

"You can take it, if you want," he offered.

"Really?"

"Sure," he said with a smile. "I know where to find you."

Lake North, I thought. The Tides. Sighing, I stood up, pressing the book to my chest. "Thank you. Really. You have no idea . . ." I trailed off, not sure how to put this. "It means a lot."

"No problem." He stood up. "You want a ride? I've got the Yum truck. I can play the music."

I shook my head. "Thanks. But I want to walk. Soak up the ambience while I can."

"At this hour, it's more likely to be mosquitoes."

"I'll be okay."

"It's your skin," he said amiably, pulling out his keys. I stepped out on the porch, with him behind me. "But we'll catch up later, right?"

He always said this, and I loved it. But later, like so much else, was now in shorter supply. I held the album closer to my chest, picturing us in all those bubbles. Magic. "Absolutely," I told him. "We will."

When I reached Mimi's dock, it was early evening, some guests from the motel gathered on the swings, while others cooked something on a grill, the smell of charcoal in the air. Just another summer night, to be followed by another, and one more after that. By then, though, I'd be at the Tides, a vantage point from which all of this would look much different, because it was.

I walked up to the house, stepping around a rather rowdy-sounding game of cornhole—"YESSSSS!" someone yelled as I passed—on the way. Gordon was on the steps with her book, alone. She wasn't reading, just holding it shut on her lap.

"Hey," I called out as I approached. It was prime home-improvement viewing hour, so I was surprised to see her. "What's going on?"

She looked up at me. "You're leaving."

I just stood there, not sure what to say. Finally I asked, "Who told you that?"

"Mimi," she replied, reaching down to scratch a violently red bug bite on one knee. "She said your dad says he's coming to get you."

I wasn't sure why I'd just assumed my dad would let me break this news by myself. Maybe because it was, well, mine? Clearly, though, he'd suspected I might not mention it, so calls had been made.

"It's true." I moved over to sit beside her. "I'm leaving tomorrow."

It wasn't until she rubbed a fist over her eyes, then looked away from me, that I realized she was crying. And as I looked at her, so small in her pink shorts and T-shirt with a unicorn on it, glasses smudged, her beat-up Allies book in her lap, I felt like I might, too.

"Hey," I said, reaching out for her, but she quickly moved, out of reach. "You'll still see me. I'm only going to Lake North."

"That's the whole other side," she said, and sniffled.

"It's not that far."

"It's not *here*."

She was right about that. I sat back, stretching out my legs, elbows on the step behind me. Inside, I could hear Mimi and Celeste talking, the TV on low behind them. "You know, I wasn't even supposed to come this summer," I told her finally. "I feel really lucky I got to meet you, and spend time with Bailey and Trinity and everyone else. It's been great."

"So you're not sad you're leaving?"

"Of course I am," I replied, reaching out to her again. This time, she let me slide an arm over her shoulder. "But I'll be back."

"When?"

It occurred to me there was no real way to answer this question. But I had to try.

"I don't know for sure," I said. She slumped a bit. "But listen. It's just like the Allies. There is always the rest of the story, right? Even if you don't know right now what it is."

She looked down at the book she was holding. "Twenty volumes in this series."

"See? And that's just a book!" I said. "In real life, the chapters go on forever. Or a long time, anyway."

I watched her face as she considered this. Then, out of nowhere, she said, "Do you miss your mom?"

I didn't know why this question hit me like a gut punch. Maybe because it was unexpected, or since she was young, closer to the age I'd been when my mom died than I was now. "Yes, very much," I said. "Do you miss yours?"

She nodded, silent. "Do you think I'll have to leave here, too?"

So that was what this was really about. Not me, but her fear that someone might take her away unexpectedly as well. "Is that what you want?"

"No," she said, reaching down to run a finger over the face of the chimp on the book's cover. "I like it here."

"I know that feeling," I said. She shifted a bit, my arm still over her shoulder. When I went to move it, though, she surprised me by leaning in closer, resting her head against my chest. "But you know what Mimi says. Even if you do have to go someday, the lake keeps you."

To this she said nothing. I could feel her warm face against my shirt, accompanied by that little-kid feral smell of sunscreen and dirt. After a moment she said, "What's that book?"

I'd forgotten about the album, which I'd set on the step beside me. Picking it up, I said, "It's photos from the first time I came here. Want to see?"

She nodded, sitting up again, and pulled the book into my lap, opening it up. "That's Mimi," she said, pointing to one of the first shots.

"Yep," I said. We looked at it quietly for a moment. "You said the pictures might help me remember. So I borrowed this from Roo."

Hearing this, she looked pleased. "Are there a lot of them?" she asked as I turned the page.

"Not really," I said. "But there are enough."

Now we were on the page with the shot of me with Trinity and Bailey with our Popsicles, as well as Jack in the boat and Roo on the car. "That's you," she said, putting a finger right in the center of my swimsuit. "Right?"

"Yep, that's the first one," I said. "Now we just need to find the others."

As she leaned in a little closer, squinting, I heard footsteps behind us in the hallway. When I looked through the screen, Mimi was standing there, watching us. I'd have to talk to her now about leaving, and how grateful I was for the time I'd spent here. There were other things I wanted to say, too. But for now, I turned back to Gordon, who was flipping a page with one finger, her eyes scanning the photos there. Everything changes tomorrow, I thought, but then again, that was always the case.

I wanted to tell Gordon this, share with her the things I was learning, these rules for us outliers. Instead, I got settled, the album square in my lap, and searched with her for my own face among the others that now, I finally recognized. But it was she who spoke first.

"Look," she said softly. "There's another one."

SIXTEEN

The day I was leaving, I woke up before the sun and everyone else. Or so I thought.

"Well, look who it is," Mimi said as I came into the kitchen. She was at the table, a mug in front of her. The paper was there as well, but still rolled up, waiting for Oxford, I assumed. "Isn't this a nice surprise."

"Didn't sleep well," I told her. "Are you always up this early?"

"Oh, honey, I've never been much of a sleeper." She picked up her drink, taking a sip. "Plus I love having the house and lake all to myself. I'm selfish that way."

"You're anything but selfish," I told her, crossing to the cupboard to take out a glass. At the sink, I filled it with water, then went to join her.

"I don't know about that." She smiled at me. "I'm wishing you could stay here awhile longer when I know your daddy is more than ready to have you back."

"I wish I could stay, too," I said with a sigh. "I feel like I'm just starting to figure things out."

"Things?"

I sat back in my chair, pulling a leg up underneath me. "I never really understood what this place meant to me. I mean, I knew my mom loved it, because she talked about it. A lot."

"I'm sure that's true," she said. "What did she say?"

"It was mostly stories." I looked out the big window in front of me at the water, which was still and quiet, the sky streaked with pink above it. "About a girl who lived at a lake and hated the winter. But in the summer, she was happy."

"Sounds like Waverly," she said. Her face looked sad, and again I wondered if I shouldn't have gone into detail. "She had a complicated relationship with this place. And a lot of things."

"My dad never wants to talk about her problems," I said, surprising myself. "It's like he feels like he has to present this sanitized version of her life for my sake. I mean, I never even knew about the accident with Chris Price until Bailey told me."

"Don't be too hard on your dad," she said. "Everyone grieves differently."

"Part of grieving is remembering," I pointed out. "He just wants to forget."

"I don't think that's true," she replied. She looked down at her mug. "If it was, you wouldn't know anything about her, and it sounds like you do."

"But it's selective, only what he chose to share." I looked

at my fingers, spread out on the table in front of me. "I feel like I missed so much. Like knowing you, and Celeste and her kids, and the lake. All the stuff I only found here, in these last three weeks."

Mimi slid her hand, tan and knotted with veins and sunspots, across to cover mine. "We never stopped thinking about you, honey. I hope you know that."

"That's just the thing, though," I said. "I wasn't thinking about *you*. Because I didn't know to."

"But now you do. So you will."

I swallowed, hard, and she gave my hand a squeeze. Finally I said, "Thank you for having me. I don't know how to repay you."

"By coming back," she said, and smiled. "And when you do, we'll be waiting."

Tears filled my eyes, and I blinked, just as Oxford came downstairs, whistling softly as he did so. Seeing us, he said, "What's everyone doing up so early?"

"I'm always up at this time, you know that," Mimi told him, getting to her feet. "You hungry?"

"Wouldn't say no to some toast," he replied. As he reached for the paper, he said to me, "You want the obits?"

"I will," I said as he shook out the main section, glancing at the front page. "But first I have something to do."

Mimi glanced at the clock over the stove. "You know it's only six a.m., right?"

"Yeah. I'll be back soon."

I pushed back my chair and took my glass to the sink,

which still had dishes in it from the night before. Had they even noticed the times I'd washed everything and put it away? Maybe not. But it had made me feel good. Like I was part of all this, in my own fashion.

"You want to borrow the car?" Mimi asked when I came downstairs after grabbing my shoes and wallet and pulling a brush through my hair. "I can get the keys."

"No, I'm good to walk," I told her. Then I waved and started down the hallway before she could ask any more questions or, God forbid, insist I drive.

At Calvander's, all the guest-room doors were closed, the beach empty. When I got to the road, instead of going left, I turned the other way. About a block ahead, just beyond a sign that said LAKE NORTH, 3 MILES, I could see Conroy Market, brightly lit and open. It wasn't a long way, but enough to at least try to clear my head, which I needed, especially after what had happened between Bailey and me the night before.

"Where have you *been*?" she'd demanded when she appeared in my room after I got back with the album. "I sent you a text. We need to talk."

"I went to see Roo," I told her. "What's going on?"

She shut the door behind her, then came over, climbing up to sit opposite me. "Colin called."

I just looked at her. "And?"

"And," she said slowly, tucking a piece of hair behind her ear, "we talked."

"Talked?" I repeated. "About what? The fact that he's a jerk?"

Clearly, the answer to this was no: instead of replying, she scooted a bit closer, lowering her voice. "Look. What he did was awful. But he did explain."

"You can't explain blowing someone off for a formal dance," I said, surprised at how angry I was getting. "It's horrible."

She looked doubtful, as if this was in question. "Well—"

"Bailey. He had a girlfriend the *whole time* you guys were hanging out."

"It's more complicated than that," she protested. "See, they were basically on a break for the summer, except that he'd mentioned Club Prom to her months ago, and she wanted to come see the lake, so . . ."

"He asked *you* to go with him," I said.

"Because he didn't think she'd actually follow through and come! But then, you know, she did. And he was stuck."

"Huh," I said.

"I know!" she said quickly, encouraged, as if I'd agreed with her, which I hadn't. "He's not a bad guy, Saylor. He just screwed up. And he's really sorry."

"Bailey." I narrowed my eyes at her. "You're not going to get back together with him, are you? Because that's—"

"We're *talking*," she said again. I already hated this phrase. "And he invited us over tonight, because they're having a Campus party. Will you come?"

267

"No," I said.

She blinked. "You didn't even think about it!"

"I don't have to," I said. "I don't want anything to do with those guys."

"Saylor," she groaned, adding syllables to my name to draw it out. "If you don't come, I have to go alone. Is that what you want?"

"What I want," I replied, "is for you to realize that you deserve better than someone who would stand you up when you are all dressed up for an event *to which they invited you* and then not apologize for, like, days."

"Saylor."

"I'm not going," I said, and she sighed, rolling her eyes. "Besides, this is my last night. I want to spend it here."

She looked at me, surprised. "Your last night? What do you mean?"

"I'm leaving tomorrow," I said, gesturing at my barely packed bag, which sat on the only chair in the room, symbolizing my ambivalence. "My dad's coming and we're going to stay at the Tides."

Now she was shocked silent, at least for a moment. "Are you serious?"

I nodded. "I found out a few days ago, but now it's really—"

"This is great!" She sat up straighter, suddenly energized. "You'll be over there right by the Club, so you can be my eyes and ears. You can tell me if he's serious about wanting to get back together."

Forget denial: this was delusional. "Did you hear me say I'm leaving?"

"For the Tides, though!" she said. "You can't be upset about that, it's like a dream."

Of course she'd see it that way. "I just want to stay where I am."

"God, why?" she said. "Saylor, you're going to hang out in the nicest hotel in the area."

Who cares? I wanted to shout. Out loud I said, "I like it here."

"Only because you don't know any better." She sighed wistfully. "God. You are *so* lucky."

I could admit to already being emotional. But something about her using that word, at that moment, made my temper flare. "*Lucky?*" I repeated. "Just because I'm going to stay someplace nice?"

"Well . . . yeah. I mean, Saylor, come on. It's kind of a first world problem. If it's a problem at all."

"You've had the lake your whole life," I said, my voice rising a bit. "You take it for granted. I only had three weeks to meet you, and Trinity, and—"

"We're not going anywhere," she said. "You can come back anytime. But the Tides? That's, like, special. Can't you see that?"

Always about the place. Never about me. "What I see is that you don't care at all that I'm upset," I said. "When you aren't telling me I'm spoiled for feeling that way."

"You are spoiled!" she shot back. Then, immediately, she said, "I mean—"

I swallowed, hard. "Yeah. What *do* you mean?"

"You don't know what it's like to live here! How dead it is all winter, nobody around. And then summer comes and yeah, it's nicer, but most of us have to work all the time, because that's when you make money. For you it's a fun getaway, discovering your history or whatever. The rest of us don't get that luxury. Nobody does except for you."

I thought back to the first days I'd been here, when I'd found out Mimi had said I was on vacation and that everyone should let me relax. Since then I'd worked my butt off cleaning rooms, not to mention being Bailey's wing person as she made one bad choice after another. Clearly, though, it made no difference. I was the rich spoiled cousin then, and the rich spoiled cousin now.

"I need to pack," I said flatly, sliding off the bed. "Are we done here?"

"Are you coming to Campus?"

I just looked at her. "You just called me spoiled! Why would I go anywhere with you?"

"Saylor." She exhaled softly. "I didn't—"

"Yeah, you did," I told her. I walked over to the door, opening it. "Have fun. Maybe you can find someone else to date Blake this time."

She looked at the door, but didn't budge. "Okay, I think

things have gotten a little twisted. All I said was—"

"I know what you said," I told her. Then I walked over to my bureau, pulling open a drawer, and started to pack again.

For a while she just sat there, watching me. Waiting for me to say something, or reverse this. By the time I moved on to my closet, though, she'd gotten to her feet and started over to the door.

"Hey," she said. "Look. I'm sorry."

"Me too," I said. But I didn't turn around. "I'll see you around."

She stayed there another minute, waiting for me to look at her again, but I didn't. I was just so hurt, and frustrated, so close to crying I could feel the sobs in my chest. That first day, knowing me from no one, it was Bailey who'd stood up for me to Taylor, claiming family trumped everything. Back then, I hadn't expected such loyalty and had been touched. When I really needed it, however, she could only think of herself. I was putting the album in my bag when I heard her leave and go down the stairs.

Now, walking the silent block to Conroy's, I thought of Bailey and not much else. How we'd covered this same distance, but going the other way, on our own walk home together. We'd talked the entire time. Now it seemed entirely possible, if not likely, that I'd leave without even saying goodbye to her. It wasn't like we were sisters, only cousins. But it still made me sad.

When I reached the market, I crossed the parking lot

and pushed open the door. Immediately, I was hit with a blast of A/C like a wind gust, sending goose bumps springing up on my bare arms.

"Welcome to Conroy's," a distant female voice said in a monotone. I looked over to see Celeste behind the register, flipping through a sheaf of papers on a clipboard.

"Good morning," I said.

"Good—" That was as far as she got before she finally looked up. "Saylor! Sorry, I was focused on my BOGO."

"BOGO?" I asked.

"Daily discounted item," she replied. "Which today is . . . sticky buns."

Indeed, there was a display across from the register: they were buy one, get one, fifty cents each. "That's a bargain."

"I guess, if you like sticky buns." She sighed, putting down the clipboard. "What brings you in so early?"

"Couldn't sleep," I said. "I'm leaving today."

"I heard." She cocked her head to the side, smiling. "But at least you aren't going far. Thank goodness. I don't think Bailey could take it if you were going home for good."

That answered the question of whether she'd been told about our argument. "I wasn't sure I'd see you," I said. "I wanted to come say goodbye."

"Goodbye?" She came out from behind the counter, adjusting her CONROY MARKET apron. Beneath it, she was wearing jean shorts and, again, platform wedges with a thick heel, showcasing her bright toenails. "You're only going to the other side of the lake, though, right?"

"Yeah," I replied. "But it won't be the same."

"Oh, honey." She reached out, pulling me in for a hug. Her grip was still strong, but this time I leaned into it, holding on tightly as well. "Even if you were going all the way back to Lakeview, you couldn't get rid of us that easily. You're stuck with us now. You know that, right?"

I nodded, worried that a verbal response might get me teary again. "I'm sorry, Celeste."

She loosened her grip, holding me out away from her and looking at my face. "Sorry? Whatever for?"

"For never coming here before," I said. "All those years since my mom died. I didn't realize . . . what I was missing."

"How could you have?" She shook her head. "Honey. I know all you kids think you are long grown, but you are still children, for the most part. Which means adults make the decisions. The road runs both ways. We could have come to you."

"But you didn't," I said, and as she opened her mouth to protest, I added, "because of my dad, and how he probably would have reacted. He could have brought me here, too."

She gave one of my arms a hard squeeze. "Now, now. Family is complicated. You factor in a loss that's particularly hard to bear and it just makes it more so. I'm sure it wasn't your dad's intent to keep you from us. Being a parent is tough. Being a single parent, sometimes impossible. He was just doing the best he could."

"Which now is two weeks at the Tides," I said.

"Hard punishment." She smiled. "And, as we said, three

miles from here and a place we all are dying to see in person. Good luck keeping us away. You can't."

"Bailey was excited when I told her," I said.

"That child and the other side of the lake. It's like your mom, all over again. I couldn't keep her here even if I wanted. And I do, especially after what happened with that boy."

There was a chime as the front door opened and a tall, slouching guy with a nose piercing came in. "Morning," he mumbled, more into his collar than to us.

"Morning, Edgar," Celeste replied. Once he ambled past us behind the counter, she added, "Bless his heart. I've never seen anyone move so slowly. It's like a glacier or something."

Just then, somewhere, a phone began to ring. Edgar didn't seem to notice.

"I've got to take this, hold on a sec," Celeste said with a sigh.

"I should go," I told her. "I have packing to do."

"All right, then." She pulled me in for another hug, the phone still ringing. "You come back anytime, you hear? To Mimi's or the Station or even here. We'll be waiting."

"Thank you," I said. The phone was starting to make me nervous, but she squeezed me again before walking to the door marked EMPLOYEES ONLY and disappearing inside.

Which left just Edgar and me. Outside, a truck pulled in, a bunch of guys in orange T-shirts saying DOT piling out. I was going to slip out as they came in, but right by the door I saw a shelf lined with loaves of bread, which gave me an idea.

I grabbed three of them, then crossed to the coolers lining the wall, scanning the groceries there until I found the
tubs of butter. I took one and then, after thinking about it,
another, adding them to what was already in my arms as I
walked over to the register to pay. When I got home, I'd
put it all where everyone at Mimi's could find it. Like the
dishes, they'd notice or wouldn't. But either way, there would
be plenty of toast for a while. Maybe it was the best way to
say goodbye.

Gordon swung her feet back and forth on the bench where
we both sat, by the Calvander's office. It was eight thirty
a.m. and my dad would be here any minute.

Back at the house, everyone else would be finally waking
up and eating breakfast, maybe even breaking into the loaves
I'd bought at Conroy's earlier. I'd had enough of farewells for
one day, though, so I'd taken my duffel and the rest of my
stuff up here to wait. If it was true what Celeste and Mimi
had both said, I wasn't really leaving anyway, just changing
locations. Even so, I hadn't wanted to deal with seeing Bailey
after our argument, preferring to leave as I'd arrived, basically alone. But then Gordon showed up.

She moved silently, like a cat: I hadn't even realized she
was approaching until she was right beside me. She was in a
purple terry-cloth romper, her pink plastic jelly sandals on
her feet. In her hand she carried an Allies book.

"What are you doing?" she asked, once I'd gotten over
being startled.

"Waiting."

She slid onto the bench beside me, putting the book squarely in her lap. "I will too, then."

Behind me, I heard the familiar sound of Mimi's screen door banging shut. I tensed, sure it was Bailey, but when I looked, I saw Jack instead, crossing the grass to his car. A moment later, he pulled up next to us.

"What are you two doing?" he asked.

"Waiting," Gordon told him.

"For what?"

"My dad," I said. "I'm leaving today."

"Leaving?" He raised his eyebrows. "You're going home?"

"No." Another car drove by, an older VW, the muffler sputtering. "To Lake North."

He considered this as Gordon picked up her book. "But you'll come back to visit, right? I mean, it's only three miles."

The was true. But sometimes even the shortest distance can be impossible to navigate, whether you went road or shore or some other route. In all her recovery attempts, my mom had never lived far from us. But sometimes, when someone's not right there, they might as well be a million miles away.

"I'll be back at some point," I said to Jack. "You'll see me before I leave for good."

"Let's make sure of it," he told me. "Come to Taylor's birthday party. We're planning it as we speak."

"Am I invited?" Gordon asked.

"No. Sorry." She slumped, disappointed. To me he said, "It'll be at April's this weekend. Bailey will give you the details."

"I'm not sure I'll see her," I said as the A/C unit cut off. Just like that, I was shouting. I lowered my voice. "We had an argument."

"You're cousins. It happens," he said, sounding hardly bothered. "Ask Trinity. Or Roo. Or anyone, really. No gifts, but beer is welcome." He looked at Gordon. "You didn't hear that."

"Hear what?" she said. I couldn't tell if she was being clever or just hadn't been listening that closely.

"And you," Jack said, turning to me. "Don't be a stranger, because you aren't. You hear?"

Hear what, I wanted to say to be funny, but this was so unexpectedly sweet I found myself instead just nodding.

"And don't stay in Lake North too long," he added, starting to roll forward. "It's different over there."

I thought of that first night I'd crossed the lake with Bailey. The world changed in those three miles, for sure. Would I?

"I'll be careful," I promised him. "Thanks, Jack."

He smiled, then gave me a salute with two fingers, stuck his tongue out at Gordon, and pulled away. As he started to accelerate, he beeped, and I waved. Finally, not a stranger anymore.

I was watching him disappear around a curve, thinking this, when I saw my dad's silver Audi approaching. Even

277

though I'd missed him, and was excited to see Tracy, I felt my heart sink a bit.

"Is that them?" Gordon asked.

"Yep."

A moment later, they were pulling in and parking, so I picked up my bag and purse and got to my feet. Gordon did the same, carrying her book, and we walked over together.

"Emma!" Tracy called out, jumping out and rushing over to give me a big hug. She had on a white sundress, all the better to emphasize a deep tan. "I missed you!"

"I missed you, too," I said, meaning it. "How was the trip?"

"An adventure," she replied. "I can't wait to tell you all about it."

"And if you're worried about her not having enough pictures, don't," my dad said as he walked over to join us. "The entirety of Greece was fully and thoroughly documented."

"Oh, stop," Tracy said as he gave me a once-over—did I look as different as I felt?—before pulling me in for a hug. "Everyone takes pictures on vacation."

"True," he said, smoothing a hand over my head, "but not everyone chooses to spend the entire trip seeing things solely through the camera lens. Who's this?"

I'd temporarily forgotten Gordon, who was still right beside me. "Dad, meet Anna Gordon. My cousin."

Hearing this, Gordon looked pleased. But I knew the name you used first was the one people remembered.

"Well, hello, Anna Gordon," my dad said, extending a

hand. She took it, shyly, not meeting his eyes. "It's nice to meet you. Is Celeste your mom?"

"No," I said. "Amber. From Joe's side."

"Amber," he repeated, still shaking Gordon's small hand. "Right. I remember her."

"And this is Tracy," I said to Gordon. "My . . . stepmom."

At this, Tracy and I both looked at each other. "Wow," she said with a smile. "That's the first time I've heard that. I like it."

"Me too," I said.

She bent down a bit. "So, Anna Gordon. What are you reading?"

Gordon held out her book. "It's the Allies series."

"That's the chimpanzees, right?" Tracy took the book, flipping it over. "I have patients who are nuts for these books."

Gordon looked at me. "Tracy and Dad are both dentists," I explained.

Instantly, she looked worried, biting her mouth shut.

"But not for another two weeks," Tracy said quickly, handing the book back. She took a look around. "Wow, it's great to finally see this place. It's gorgeous, just like your dad said!"

"Well, we're not going to be here," I pointed out. "Lake North is different."

"Not that much," my dad said. To Tracy he explained, "It's three miles down the road, with more new construction, bigger houses. But basically it's all the same no matter where you are on the lake."

It wasn't, though, and he'd been the first one to tell me so, when we first pulled up to the sign with two opposite arrows. But I chose not to point this out. "It's too bad we aren't staying here," Tracy said, looking at the Calvander's office, with its rock garden and blinking VACANCY sign. "It's charming."

"You could," I offered quickly. "There are rooms available."

"But Nana made her own plans," my dad said. "We'll come visit, though, when it's a more decent hour. Is Mimi up yet? I'd love to thank her in person."

"She went to Delaney," Gordon informed him. "Room ten needed new screens."

"Well, we'll definitely be back to visit," my dad said, looking at Tracy. "But for now, we should probably—"

"Yes," she agreed. "I'm sure your mother is wondering where we are."

And just like that, it was time to go. My dad took my bag, opening the trunk, while Tracy shaded her eyes with her hand, again looking at the big trees along the water.

"Anna Gordon, it was very nice to meet you," he said as the hatch closed with a click. "We'll see you soon, I'm sure."

I squatted down so I was at her level, then said, "You take care of everyone for me, okay? I'll be back before you know it."

"Promise?"

I nodded and she stepped forward, hugging my neck so

tightly I almost lost my balance, her book bumping my back.

"Bye, Saylor," Gordon said.

"Bye, Anna Gordon."

Tracy waved and started over to the car. I smiled, lifting a hand myself as I followed. When I climbed inside, the car was cool and smelled of leather, the seat sinking beneath me.

"She called you Saylor," my dad said as he started the engine and began pulling out of the drive. "Why is that?"

There was no traffic, but we stopped anyway, long enough for me to glimpse Mimi's house one more time in the side mirror, where it already was starting to look far away.

"Because it's my name," I said, and I saw them exchange looks as we turned onto the road. The sign said Lake North was three miles. A passenger again, I settled in for the ride.

SEVENTEEN

"Welcome to the Tides!"

The staff said this every time you walked through the main door, even if you'd only stepped out moments earlier. I'd been there less than twenty-four hours, and already I was sick of it.

Still, I nodded and smiled as I crossed the lobby, the copy of the *Bly County News* I'd just picked up under one arm. At the hotel restaurant, the Channel Marker, they offered a variety of newspapers at breakfast: *New York Times*, *Washington Post*, *Wall Street Journal*. For the local news—which was to say, obits—I had to walk across the street to the Larder, a glorified convenience store that sold gas and ice cream but also expensive wine and packages of cheese straws that cost six bucks each. I was a long way from BOGO sticky buns, not that I didn't realize this already.

That first morning, as Dad and Tracy and I drove away from Mimi's, I kept telling myself the same things, on repeat: it's only three miles. Not that different. But even as I did,

I was aware of the visible transition happening outside my window. After we passed Conroy Market, the squat concrete motels began disappearing, replaced by bigger neighborhoods. North Lake Estates, Fernwood Cove, the Sunset. And that was before we even pulled into the hotel itself.

"Welcome to the Tides," the young, cute valet—he looked familiar, making me think I might have seen him at one of the Campus parties—said as he opened my door. Two others, also both in white golf shirts and black shorts, were already helping my dad and Tracy out and getting the luggage. "We're glad to have you."

"Um, thanks," I mumbled, sliding out of my seat. He immediately shut the door behind me, then jogged back to help one of the other guys as they unloaded the hatch.

"Wow, this is nice," my dad said, looking around. "How long has this place been here?"

"The Tides opened in two thousand sixteen," another one of the valets, who had dark, shoulder-length hair, told him. "It's the vision of the Delhomme family, owners of the Lake North Yacht Club. They saw a need for a place where members could stay that allowed the same level of service. That's our goal."

He said this so easily I assumed the answer was company-dictated. "Well," Tracy said, "it's lovely. Although I guess I shouldn't have expected any less, since it *is* Grace who planned all this."

That would be Nana, who was already up in our suite, having been brought straight from the airport late the night

283

before. She didn't drive either, but with her declining eyesight, she at least had a good excuse.

"Welcome to the Tides," the woman behind the desk said as we approached. "Checking in?"

"Yes," my dad said. "The last name is Payne. I believe my mother is already here."

"I can't wait to go for a swim," Tracy said to me. "And eat something. Are you hungry?"

I was, although I hadn't been aware of this until right at that moment. "Yeah, actually. I am."

"The Channel Marker, our restaurant, is open for breakfast, lunch, and dinner," the woman said, sliding some cards to my dad. "The hours are here on your keys. And room service is available twenty-four hours a day."

"Room service it is," my dad said, and Tracy grinned. He turned to face us. "Ready to go up?"

In the elevator, there was a screen showing a video, on repeat, of the highlights of the Tides. Here was the pool, blue and empty. The beach, with a clearly posed photo of a single child digging in the sand with a bucket. Even the lake, which I'd seen every day for weeks now, looked different in the sunset picture that appeared.

"Floor five," the voice announced as the doors slid open. Like "Lake North," it was all in the order you said it.

"Five fourteen," my dad said, glancing at the key card in his hand. "So that's—oh. Right here."

It wasn't hard to spot, as the door marked with these numbers was the only one on the short hallway where we were standing. On the other side of the elevators was 515. So we basically had half of an entire floor? Was that even possible?

My dad waved his card at the door, which clicked, and he pushed it open, standing back to hold it for Tracy and myself. "Hello?" Tracy called out as she stepped inside.

"In here," I heard Nana say. At the sound of her voice, I smiled.

I loved my grandmother. With her, everything was always, effortlessly, Just So, from the thin teacup she drank her coffee from every morning—in a matching robe and slipper set, hair combed perfectly—to the simple, but perfect, bouquet of seasonal flowers that always stood on her dining room table. Everything outside Nana's apartment might have felt fragile and already falling apart, but with her, there was always a sense that things were as they should be.

"Emma," she said when she saw me, holding open her arms. After all the foot dragging of the morning, now I felt like I couldn't move fast enough. "You are a sight for these sore eyes! How are you?"

"Good," I said, giving her a tight squeeze before she gestured for me to sit in the chair next to hers. "How was the cruise?"

"Oh, it was wonderful," she sighed. "The pyramids must be seen to be believed. Are you hungry? I have a few things here, but we can easily order more."

This was an understatement: I saw a pot of coffee and a plate stacked with pastries, as well as fresh fruit and berries, arranged beautifully in a bowl. There was toast, too, four pieces perfectly browned, balls of butter dotted with salt beside them.

"Have some," Nana said, seeing me notice this. She picked up the plate, putting it closer to me. "You look hungry."

"Thanks," I replied, reaching for a piece and putting it on the plate in front of me.

"It looks delicious," Tracy said after also greeting Nana. "This place is amazing."

"It's lovely, I agree," Nana said, looking around the room. Like the lobby, the floor was white tile, the room open, with a small kitchen tucked away in a corner and a living area to the right of where we were sitting. The real centerpiece, though, were the sliding doors, open now to let in the breeze, that framed both a patio and a gorgeous, wide view of the lake. "So," she said. "How are Mimi and the rest of the family?"

"Good," I said. "It was nice to get to know everyone. I just wish I'd had longer there."

"I told her she's only a couple of miles away," my dad said. "Easy to visit while we're here."

"And we'll have to have them, as well," Nana said, picking up a piece of toast and putting in on her plate. "Matthew, let's plan on that. A thank-you dinner. I'll talk to the desk about booking a table at the Club."

"Oh, you don't have to do that," I said quickly. While Bailey would lose her mind at the prospect, I could only imagine everyone else would be less than enthused.

"I think it's the least we can do since they took such good

care of you. Ask Mimi what night is good, will you? And how many will be coming. The more the merrier."

My phone beeped, the sound distant in my purse, which was on the back of my chair. Nana, who hated screens at the table, gave it a pointed look, making it clear I should not check it. So I didn't.

"I'll talk to her," I said instead. "But she's really busy with the motel and everything."

"All the more reason for a nice dinner out," Nana replied as, outside, a large boat puttered across the water, pulling a float behind it. "Now, what's the plan for today? Pool? Lake? A nap?"

"I vote pool," Tracy said. "Although once I eat, I have a feeling a nap might win out."

"They both sound good to me," I said. "I'll get settled and then decide."

"Perfect. Your room is the one at the end of the hall, with the twin bed."

I smiled, thanking her again, then grabbed my purse and headed that way. My room was small, but immaculate, everything white—walls, floor, sheets, and comforter. A fan turned slowly overhead. I walked around the bed, to the sheer white curtain, pulling it aside to reveal yet another sliding glass door with the patio beyond it. Another room with a view of the lake. If it was all the same, really, why did it feel so different?

It was a question I was still asking myself, these two days later, as the elevator opened again, depositing me in the empty

hallway outside our room. My dad, Tracy, and Nana had easily moved into vacation mode and a schedule of late breakfast,
pool, naps, and dinners at the hotel restaurant, but I was still
getting adjusted. It didn't help that out every window was
the lake, and the other side: from this height, through the
big hallway window, I could actually sort of make out Mimi's
house if I squinted. And I did, every morning.

I waved my key at the door, heard the click, and then
pushed it open. Nana had not emerged from her room, and
my dad and Tracy, swearing they needed to work off all the
great Greek food they ate on their honeymoon, had gone out
for a morning run. The quiet made my phone sound even
louder as it signaled a new message.

Without even looking, I knew it was Bailey. Despite the
fact that we hadn't exactly left things on the best note, she'd
texted me at least five times since I'd left Mimi's. Our fight
was still on my mind, but she had apparently gotten over it.

Promised I'd take Gordon tubing early afternoon. You in?

As coercion went, this was next-level. It was one thing
to claim to want to hang out with me: another, entirely, to
bring Gordon into it. As she intended, though, it gave me
pause, especially after the conversation I'd had with Trinity
the day before.

"You've got to come over here and see Gordon," she'd
announced in lieu of a hello. "She's driving me nuts."

"Trinity?" I asked.

"I mean, if she could go back to camp, it would be different," she continued. "But instead she's home and sulking

288

around. I'm a sitting target because I am literally bed-bound. You need to do something."

"Me?" I said. "I'm on the other side of the lake."

"It's three miles," she pointed out. "Also, can you take me to birth class this afternoon? Everyone else is working."

"I don't know," I said slowly. "I'm kind of stuck here with my family."

"I am *also* your family," she said. "Remember?"

I sighed. "I'll see what I can do."

Which had turned out to be not much, as my dad was determined to use the time we had together to bond us as a new family. While Nana stayed in the A/C of the room, reading, he was busy organizing activities to the point that I was, honestly, kind of exhausted. We'd done mini golf, attended a Pavilion concert (beach music, surprise!), and taken part in a low-country boil the Tides staff arranged on the beach for all the guests. But today was what I'd been dreading.

"An easy morning on the water," my dad had said the night before, presenting this idea as we sat on the wooden beach chairs, our plates of shrimp, potatoes, and sausage on our laps. "I reserved a day sailer and a picnic lunch from the kitchen. We'll just tool around, then find a beach to pull up to for a bit to swim and eat."

"Wait," I said, "are we all doing this or just you guys?"

"All of us," he replied, wiping his mouth with a napkin. "I mean, we three. Not Nana. She's never been a boat person."

"Neither have I," I pointed out.

"You said before you were out on boats all the time with

your cousins these last few weeks," he reminded me.

"Motorboats," I corrected him. "And that was just transportation. Sailing is different."

"Yes, because it's great," he replied. Tracy, beside him, smiled. "Emma, just be open-minded. You might actually really like it."

I doubted this. But it did give me a good reason to tell Bailey no to her invitation, which I did now, explaining I already had plans for the water. She wrote back right away, probably because it was the first time I'd responded so far.

Later today, then?

I sighed. All these invitations and requests, but not one from the person I really wanted to see.

I missed Roo. Which was weird, I knew, because with his multiple jobs and my work at Calvander's, it wasn't like we'd spent that much time together even when we'd been on the same side. But when we were hanging out, there had just been that ease, a shorthand, not to mention that moment with my dress strap that might have led to something else. But didn't, I reminded myself.

There was still Taylor's birthday party, that evening. April had texted me the details, and I'd told Jack I'd be there. It was one thing to say this, however, and another to actually find my way there, to a house I'd never been to, and walk in alone. Knowing Roo would be there was an incentive, but the truth was, I'd feel better if I was with Bailey. So maybe I had my own selfish reasons for making up as well.

Maybe, I wrote back to her now. A single word, without

weight in either direction. Immediately, she texted back a thumbs-up.

"Emma?" My dad was outside, his voice clear through the thin door. "Are you in there?"

"Yes," I called out, sliding my newspaper under a pillow. "Coming."

When I opened the door, he was standing there, in an ATHENS T-shirt and swim trunks. Sunscreen streaked his face. "Ready to sail?"

"No," I replied.

"Great," he said easily, too happily distracted to notice this. "The boat is ready for us. Tracy went to grab the cooler from the Club. Walk down with me?"

Clearly, I wasn't getting out of this. I took my stuff and followed him.

"Breakfast?" Nana asked as we passed by, gesturing to the expanse of room service plates that sat before her. "Sailing requires energy."

"No time," my dad said, plucking a muffin from a tray of pastries. "We're headed out right now."

I kissed her cheek as I passed her, taking a doughnut after she told me again to help myself. Once out in the hallway, as my dad pushed the button for the elevator, I wrapped it in a tissue, stuffing it deep in my bag.

"I think you'll really like this," he said as the doors slid open and we got in. "Going down," the voice informed us. "It won't be like those days at Topper Lake back at home, so choppy. Just an easy sail."

"I can't stay out long," I told him. "Bailey wants me to do something with her later, and then there's this party."

"Party?" he asked. "When?"

"Tonight," I said. "I told you, my friend Taylor. It's her birthday."

"I don't know," he said. "We're supposed to eat with the Delhommes tonight."

I'd forgotten. Nana's friends, who owned the Tides, had invited us to dinner at the Club. "I don't have to be there, though, right? It'll be all you guys drinking wine and talking."

"I think it's the least we can do to thank them for this vacation," he replied as we reached the lobby. "Plus, they're expecting you."

"Dad," I said. Before, I hadn't been that into going to Taylor's party. Now that it seemed I might not be allowed to do so, it felt imperative. "I'm going sailing. You have to let me do something I like today. It's my vacation, too."

He looked at me. "Emma. You've already spent a month with your friends. I think you can miss one party."

"But it's her birthday!"

"Maybe," he said, and having this same word as my answer felt like payback after all of Bailey's pleadings that I'd ignored. "We'll see. For now, let's just have a good time, okay?"

Sure. Because that was what *always* happened when we went sailing. I bit this thought back, though, as we stepped outside. The heat was like a thick wall, even with the chill of the A/C still on my skin, and I immediately dug in my bag for the baseball hat I'd brought, pulling it down to shade my face.

"Great day to be on the water," he announced, leading me down a side set of stairs to the pool area. The beach was just beyond, a girl in a white Club shirt sitting in the lifeguard chair, swinging a whistle on a chain. The sand was dotted with beachgoers, some with their chairs in groups, kids digging with shovels and pails nearby, others alone, soaking up the sun. A waiter moved through them with a tray in hand, taking orders. "The dock is just this way, I think . . . yes. Look, that's ours!"

I followed his finger, which was pointing at a small sailboat bobbing just off to one side. Staring at it, I felt a nervousness not unlike what I felt when I had to drive, a mix of dread and fear.

"Great," I said as another white-shirted Club worker came around from behind the sail, wiping his hands on his shorts. It was Blake, not that I had time to react, as in the next moment my dad was walking right up him.

"I think that's for us," he said, nodding at the boat. "Payne?"

"That's right," Blake replied, hopping onto the dock. "All ready for you as promised. Do you need a quick lesson?"

"No, no," my dad said as I pulled my hat down a bit farther. "I know what I'm doing. Actually taught sailing here when I was your age."

"Really?" Blake asked. "That's cool. Did you live on Campus?"

"Room fourteen," my dad told him proudly. "All four

years. Could still find my name on the wall, I bet, if I looked. Matthew Payne."

"Nice to meet you. I'm Blake." He stuck out his hand and they shook while I stood off to one side, willing myself to be invisible. "I've left a card with our number here at the docks and a backup Club one, just in case you run into any trouble."

"Hopefully not," my dad said. "We're just doing an easy sail. My daughter, Emma, here isn't exactly a fan."

Blake gave me a quick glance, nodding, then turned back to the boat. A beat later, though, he looked at me again. My hat had covered my face some, but not enough. Damn. "Saylor? Is that you?"

My dad, surprised, looked at me as well. "You guys know each other?"

Silence as neither one of us confirmed or denied this. Finally I said, "He's friends with Bailey."

"Oh, right," my dad said, as if I'd mentioned this before, which I hadn't. "Small world. Oh, there's Tracy."

With that, he was walking down the dock to the Club, where I could now see my stepmother emerging, a basket hooked over one arm. Blake and I both watched him go, if only to not look at each other.

"So," he said finally. "Um . . . how have you been?"

"You mean since you guys ditched us for Club Prom?"

He sighed. "Hey, *I* showed up. Remember?"

"Did you really expect me to leave Bailey, too, and come with you?"

"I don't know!" He lowered his voice, stepping closer to me. "Look, what Colin does is his thing. Don't hold it against me. What was I supposed to do?"

"Well," I said as a motorboat approached, puttering, "you could have been honest with me so I could be honest with her. That would have been a start."

"He's my best friend," he said. "And it was a crap situation. I'm sorry. What can I do to make it up to you?"

"Tell him to leave Bailey alone. It's not cool that he's calling her."

"I know." He slid his hands in his pockets. "But again, that's him. Anything else?"

I considered this, looking at the boat beside us, sails still fluttering. "Declare this thing unseaworthy so I don't have to go sailing?"

He cocked his head to the side. "It's a lake, though. Not a sea."

"Unlakeworthy, then," I said, giving him a smile. "Help a girl out."

"The thing is, I'm kind of here to help the guests get *on* the water, not hinder them," he said. "Sorry."

I shrugged. "It's okay."

"What about dinner?" he asked. "Tonight. Wherever you want, on me."

Suddenly I'd gone from no plans to being in high demand. But again, he was not the person I was hoping would be doing the asking. "I can't," I said. "I have a party to go to."

"For that girl Taylor?"

"You know about that?"

He nodded. "Rachel and Hannah are invited, too. Said we could come along."

"Bailey will be there," I warned him.

"I know. So does Colin. I think that's why he's going." He sighed again. "Let me give you a ride, at least?"

I bit my lip a second, considering this. Blake wasn't inherently a bad guy. As he'd said, *he* had showed up for Club Prom.

"Okay," I said, and he grinned so quickly I was immediately angry at myself for making yet another thing simple for him. "A ride. But if Colin's along, I'm out."

"He won't be," he promised. "He's covering the last couple of hours of a valet shift as a favor to someone. I'll text you when I get off work?"

I nodded, just as my dad and Tracy stepped back onto the dock, now carrying the basket. "Okay."

"Great," he said. "And have fun out there. Just remember the first rule of sailing: duck when they tell you to."

"Sounds like good advice for life in general," I cracked.

"You're funny," he told me, as if he'd forgotten this. He turned to Tracy, holding out a hand. "Ready to board?"

She climbed on, stepping down by the rudder, and I followed without an assist. My dad handed over the basket, which Tracy took and put in the small covered cargo area while he jumped on as well.

"Feels so small after weeks on *Artemis*," he said, gathering up the mainsheet as I found a seat on one of the flat cushioned areas. To me he added, "That was the boat we had in Athens, Forty-two-footer, slept six."

"This is nice, too, though," Tracy said, as if the boat might be offended. "Shall I go raise the front sail?"

"Yep," my dad replied, busy futzing with the rudder. "I'll get this one."

With that, they were in motion, her jumping up to walk down the boat's deck to the bow while he pulled the mainsail the rest of the way up. All around me, things were luffing, lines clanking, the side of the boat thumping against the dock with the waves. Even worse, over it all, I could hear my dad muttering, something he always did while sailing. I pulled my legs to my chest, trying to get small and out of the way, and looked out on the water.

"About ready?" Blake, up on the dock, asked.

"One second," my dad said from the center of the sunken part of the deck, right in front of me. "I'm having trouble with this centerboard."

"You just pull straight up and push down."

"I'm doing that," my dad replied. "But it won't —"

"Let me try," Tracy suggested, jumping down from the upper deck to where he was. "I think you just—"

"I've got it," he said, but she reached in anyway, and then he was grumbling again, both their hands on it, before it fell into the slot with a bang. "See? I had it. You have to let me do things if I say I am doing them."

"I would have," Tracy replied cheerfully, "but it seemed like you needed another pair of hands."

My dad grumbled again. Then to Blake he said, "Okay,

push us off. We're ready."

"Yes sir," Blake said, handing the line to Tracy, who shot me a smile. At least one of us was having fun. "Enjoy the lake!"

And with that, we were drifting toward the swimming area, the sails still ruffling, as my dad got himself by the rudder. Blake, on the dock, gave us an enthusiastic wave.

"All right," my dad said as we came close to bumping a float shaped like a huge toucan. He grabbed the mainsheet, pulling it tight, pushing the rudder over at the same time. "Ready about, hard a lee!"

Tracy bent her head down. I did not until the boom came swinging right for my face. We were now moving away from the shore at a fast clip, the sails suddenly full and creaking.

"Oh, yeah," my dad said, nodding up at the mast. "Feel that speed?"

"Watch out for the buoys," Tracy called out. "There's one right up here to starboard."

"I see it." My dad eased the rudder a bit to the right. To me he said, "Great, right? You can go up to the bowsprit if you want a better view."

"No thanks," I said.

"Keep the buoy on your right," Tracy told him. "There's a red one to port, about a hundred feet."

As we passed it, though, the traffic of swimmers and other boats began to clear out, leaving us an open path ahead. The water was glittering, sun bouncing off it, and

I let a hand dangle in as waves peeled off the sides. I had to admit it was nice, if you liked that sort of thing.

My dad pulled the mainsheet even tighter, leaning back as my side of the boat lifted up a bit. "Now we're cooking with grease! Emma, pull up that centerboard."

"What?" I asked.

"The centerboard." He pointed. "Grab it with both hands and pull straight up."

I scrambled over, grabbing for the centerboard handle. It didn't budge. Meanwhile, we were now moving what felt like even faster, the wind whipping in my ears.

"Pull straight up," he repeated.

"I am!" I replied, doing just that. Tracy got to her feet, coming over to join me. "It's stuck!"

"She's right," Tracy reported, after trying herself. "Maybe if we wiggle it again . . ."

"Emma, take the rudder and this mainsheet," he directed me. Which was even worse. Now I was steering?

"But—" I said.

"Take it." He stood, holding it out to me, and I grabbed it, moving into the spot where he'd been sitting, the mainsheet clutched in one hand. "Just steer us toward the other side, keeping all buoys on your left."

"Or right, if it's red," Tracy added.

"Is this thing broken?" my dad asked, his face flushed from his efforts to budge the centerboard. Tracy, trying to help him, pulled from the other side. Meanwhile, we were flying across the water, the sails I was holding full to the point of straining. It was scary enough even before I saw the Sunfish.

It was small, with an orange sail that had a smiley face on it. A guy and a kid, both in life vests, were sitting on it, staring at us openmouthed as we raced toward them.

"Um, Dad?" I said.

"Just keep us pointed in the direction I told you."

"But—"

Then, Tracy saw the Sunfish. "Emma! Come about!"

"What?" I said. On the Sunfish, the kid's eyes were wide, his dad now scrambling to get out of the way.

"Wait, what?" my dad said quizzically. Then he looked up. "COME ABOUT!"

But I didn't know how to do that. I didn't even really know what the centerboard was. And now we were almost at the Sunfish.

"Move!" my dad yelled. I did, jumping out of the way as he grabbed the rudder, pushing it away from us, hard. There was a jerk and the boom came swinging around: this time, I ducked. The mainsheet, caught on a knob between my dad and the mast, was pulled so tight I could see it straining. As I watched, helpless, as my dad tried to loosen it, we dipped even farther to the side, then farther still.

We're capsizing, I thought, panicked, but it was all happening so slowly it was surreal: the boat tilting, scooping up water, the sails all flapping, their lines thwacking.

"MAYDAY!" screamed the kid on the Sunfish, which

didn't really help anything.

"Hold on!" my dad yelled. "I'm getting her upright. Find life jackets!"

Tracy dove into the cargo hold, returning seconds later with three orange life preservers. As she handed me one, my dad cursing behind her, she said evenly, "Everything's fine."

Fine, I repeated to myself as I pulled it over my head, tightening the straps. We were upright again, although water was inside the boat now, rushing over my feet. That couldn't be good.

"Matthew?" Tracy asked. "Should I call someone?"

"Just give me a second," he said, wiggling the centerboard, which finally came loose. "There. Okay. Now, let me just—shit, did we take in all this water?"

That wasn't encouraging. Trying not to panic, I turned, orienting myself with the shore by finding Mimi's again. There it was. There was the boat. And there were Bailey and Gordon, walking down the dock toward it. I didn't even think. I just yelled.

"BAILEY!"

At the sound of my voice, she turned her head, scanning the lake, then put a hand over her eyes.

"OVER HERE!" I yelled. "HELP!"

"Emma," my dad said sternly. "You never yell that on a boat unless it's an emergency."

"Matthew," Tracy said delicately, "there is quite a bit of water here."

She was right. What I'd thought had only been a bit

splashing around my toes was now up to my ankles. And we had a broken centerboard. But sure, yes, let's take our time asking for a hand.

Bailey was still looking in our direction, although clearly not sure what we needed. So I put my hands over my head, waving them wildly, the international sign for WE NEED RESCUING. She jumped into the boat, Gordon climbing in after her, and started the outboard.

"This is ridiculous," my dad said, kicking around the water at his feet as he went back to the rudder. "Who puts a useless knob right where it will catch the mainsheet?"

"Someone," Tracy said, still so calm. I don't know what we would have done without her. "I'm going to call the Club."

"You don't have to," I said. "Bailey's coming."

"Who?" my dad asked.

I pointed to where she was right then pulling away from the dock, already coming toward us. Gordon was in the bow.

"What happened?" she yelled once closer. Gordon waved excitedly.

"Just took in a little water," my dad replied.

"And broke the centerboard," Tracy added.

"Everyone have a life jacket?" Bailey asked, circling now to come up our other side. I gave her a thumbs-up. "Good. You want a tow back to the Club?"

"Just to that raft," Tracy replied as my dad grumbled something. "If you don't mind."

"Sure," she said. "Saylor. Throw me that."

She did another pass, coming up close, and I tossed her the line. Quickly, she tied it to the back of her motorboat, tugging to make sure it was tight.

"If you can pull up the centerboard, do it," she hollered as she took the motor again. "Less resistance. It'll be slow no matter what, though."

Personally, I didn't care. We could have been barely moving at all and it still would have been an improvement on the outing so far. My dad, however, looked glum as she started to the raft, tugging us slowly behind.

"We really could have just bailed out the boat on our own," he told Tracy. "We were fine."

"I know." She reached out, patting his leg. "But Emma was scared. This is better."

"I'm going to try to get you as close as I can!" Bailey yelled then from the motorboat. "Then I'll untie you so you can drift up alongside."

"Great," Tracy said. "Thank you!"

Bailey nodded, then turned back to face forward as we approached the raft. She and Gordon went just a bit past it, then cut the engine. A moment later, we floated right up. Tracy grabbed hold, jumping out, as Bailey undid our line, throwing it to her. Within seconds she had us tied up to a post, safe now. Scrambling down off the bow, I was never happier to feel deck planks beneath my feet. My dad, however, stayed on the boat, beginning to bail with a scoop he'd found in the cargo hold.

"Whew," Tracy said as Bailey came back around, pulling up to the other side. "That was exciting."

"That's one word for it," I said.

As soon as she could, Gordon hopped out as well, running over to give me a hug. I could feel her glasses poking my stomach.

"Hey," I said, smoothing a hand over her head. "How are you?"

"Good," she replied, into my shirt. "When are you coming back to Mimi's?"

This I didn't answer, although I saw Tracy heard it as well. Bailey, having tied up her own boat, now joined us. "What happened out there?"

"Combination of factors," Tracy told her. "You are a godsend, by the way. I'm Tracy."

"My stepmother," I said to Bailey. "Tracy, this is Bailey. And that's my dad."

"Hi," Bailey called out.

My dad lifted a hand in a wave, nodding at her. He looked sheepish, almost embarrassed, and I found myself both angry and sorry for him at the same time. God, I hated sailing.

"So," Bailey said as Tracy went over to join my dad. "Now you have to go to that party with me, right?"

"Because you gave us a tow?"

"Because I *saved* you. You owe me your life now." I just looked at her. "What? That's how this works!"

"I subscribe to none of these boat rules," I told her. "That said, I do thank you for the help. But I'd say that we're actually even. You owed me, and now you paid up."

"I owed you? How do you figure?"

"Because you didn't even care I was leaving!" I said. "It was all about Colin this, and Colin that, and how you could use me to get to him. You didn't even say goodbye."

"You snuck out before the sun was even up!"

"Not true," I said flatly, and she sighed, rolling her eyes. "You could have found me. We're supposed to be friends."

"No," she said. "We're cousins."

Now I was exasperated. "That's different?"

"Of course it is!" She pushed her hair back from her face. "Look, Saylor. The first time we met, neither of us remembered. The second, you were about to get your ass kicked. We never had formalities, you and I. We're blood. It's messy. But we don't need goodbyes, because we're going to be stuck with each other forever. That's what family is."

This made me well up. And when I spoke, I actually started to cry.

"You hurt my feelings," I said, my voice breaking.

"I'm sorry." She bit her lip, then tucked a piece of hair behind her ear, lowering her voice. "Look, I know I've been stupid and crazy. I'm lucky that you've stuck with me. But you just don't understand what it's like to be really into someone so much that you make terrible choices. It's like . . . beyond my control, or something."

"He's going to hurt you again," I told her as my dad chucked the bailer into the cargo hold and hoisted himself onto the raft.

"Maybe," she said. "But this time, I'll only have myself to blame."

This was not altogether encouraging. I mean, why go into anything if you think there's a decent chance you'll get your heart broken? You don't risk what you don't want to, I supposed. Not that I could get into it, as my dad and Tracy were now joining us. She had the picnic basket over her arm.

"Who's hungry?" she asked.

"Me!" Gordon said. When Bailey shot her a look, she added, "I mean, only a little."

"You can have whatever you want from here," Tracy said, putting the basket down and opening it. "It's the least we can do since you saved us."

"We weren't in danger," my dad said. "It was just a little water."

Instead of responding, Tracy pulled out a bottle of wine, glistening with ice, fetching an opener from a side pocket. Deftly and quickly, she got out the cork and poured them each a plastic glass full before handing out thick bottled sodas to the rest of us.

"Wow," Gordon said, taking the bottle she handed her. "Is this a cola?"

"It's not Pop Soda," Bailey said, examining her own. She tipped it up, taking a taste. "Oh, my God. This is incredible. Where did you get it?"

"The Club made the basket for us," Tracy replied, digging farther in. "We have a cheese plate, too, as well as some sandwiches. Why don't I get everything out and we'll have a picnic?"

"Here?" my dad said. "I was hoping to get us to a beach spot away from everything."

"Well, we have the second part," Tracy said. "And I think we're better off not sailing the boat anymore today. I'll call the Club and have them tow it in."

"Oh, don't do that," Bailey said automatically, as I knew she would. "I can just pull you back."

"We're getting to go to the Club?" Gordon asked. "Can we see your hotel room?"

"No," Bailey told her. "We'll just get them safely to the dock. Then we need to get home to take Trinity to the doctor."

I turned to look at her. "Is everything okay?"

She nodded. "They just want to see her every week now, to check if she's dilated."

"What's *dilated*?" Gordon asked.

"Ready to have the baby," I explained. Then I looked up to see Dad and Tracy staring at me. I said, "She's due in like, a month."

"Who is this, again?" my dad asked, taking a cracker from the tray Tracy had unwrapped.

"My sister," Bailey told him. To me she said, "You can come back with us, come along to the appointment, and then we'll go to the party."

"Party?" my dad said.

"Our friend's birthday is tonight," Bailey explained. To me she said, "You can stay over with me, if you want. That way you don't have to get all the way back."

Already, she had a plan. I supposed I shouldn't have been surprised.

"Sounds great, but Emma is supposed to eat with us and our friends this evening," my dad said.

To me, this might as well have been a brick wall: my dad said no, end of topic. But I'd again forgotten about Bailey and the power of persuasion. Or cousinhood. Or something.

"Point taken," she said. "But the thing is, Saylor didn't really get to say goodbye, you know, when she moved over to be with you guys. It was just like, poof! And she was gone. Everyone's asking where she is. So can she come to something, you know, just for closure?"

"She's here for two weeks," my dad pointed out.

"I know! But it's already been a minute and we haven't heard from her. I mean, until now. Which was not the best of circumstances." Bailey smiled at Tracy, who immediately smiled back. "The longer she's at the Tides, the less inclined she'll be to make the trip all the way over to our side. I mean, the boys are *really* cute there."

Now my dad looked at me. I kept my face impassive, not wanting to get my hopes up, although it was hard not to show my relief when he said, "Okay, I suppose that's fine. But I want you to stay at the hotel, with us."

"Great! The party is at April's, which is just down from the Station," Bailey told him. "It starts at around seven. And we'll have Roo drive her back. He's got to leave early too, for work."

Okay. Now I *really* wanted to go.

"Roo?" my dad said. "Is that a person?"

"His real name is Christopher," I explained. "He's Chris Price's son."

"Price," my dad repeated. "Wait. Chris Price?"

"Yes," I said. Tracy raised her eyebrows, not following, and I added, "He was a friend of my mom's."

"Really." She smiled at me. "Well, I'm sure Matthew will agree, if he's a good driver and—"

"I don't know," my dad said. "Maybe it's not the best night for you to go out."

Roo was the deal breaker? That wasn't fair. "You just said it was okay," I protested.

He snapped his fingers. "Hey, I know. Why don't we go back during the day, when I can take you. Or we can drive together! Get in some practice. I'd like to see Mimi anyway."

"Mr. Payne," Bailey said, still in her best-behavior voice, "Roo's really reliable, if that's what you're worried about. He works for my mom doing night stocking at Conroy Market, and he has to be there at midnight. So he won't be drinking or anything."

I winced. Crap.

"Well, I would hope not," my dad said. "You are all underage, last I checked. Are you saying there will be beer at this party?"

"No," I said quickly. "But even if there was—"

309

"Saylor doesn't drink," Bailey finished for me. "Like, at all. You know that, right?"

Now, my dad looked at me. "She's not supposed to. She's seventeen."

"Dad, I can't control what other people do!" I said.

"If there's beer there, you're not going." When I opened my mouth, he repeated, "That's it. End of discussion."

There was that wall again, but this time, I could see it, not just sense its presence. Bailey, however, was not giving up that easily.

"It's your call, of course," she told my dad as Tracy, choosing wisely to stay out of this, bent back over the cooler and began to unpack sandwiches. "And we'll miss her. But for what it's worth, Saylor's a good girl, Mr. Payne. The kind of girl my mom wishes I was, if I'm honest."

"Her name is Emma," my dad told her.

I knew, in my rational mind, that he was just correcting her. I was Emma to him, I always had been. But as I heard him say this with such certainty, I could feel my temper rising. He could keep me from the other side of the lake. From Roo. But I would not let him take the weeks I'd already had, and the girl I'd been then, as well.

"It's Emma Saylor," I corrected him. "And I told you. They know me here as Saylor."

My dad looked surprised, although whether by this statement or my tone was hard to tell. For a moment we just looked at each other, both of us silent. "Why don't we have lunch," he said finally. "I'm starving."

I felt tears spring to my eyes as I turned, walking across to the other side of the raft so my dad wouldn't see. A moment later, Bailey stepped up beside me.

"You can always say you're going to the Pavilion and then come over," she said in a low voice. "We'll get someone to pick you up."

"Blake already offered me a ride," I said.

"Really?" Realizing she'd almost yelped this, she lowered her voice, shooting my dad a glance. "He's coming?"

"Taylor invited Rachel and Hannah, and they invited him," I told her.

A pause. Her unasked question boomed between us, loud to the point of deafening. I sighed.

"Colin, too," I added. Her face lit up. "But he's showing up later. I said I wouldn't ride with him, because I still hate him."

"Well, sure," she said easily, waving this off with one hand. "But seriously, now you really *have* to get there. I need you! It'll be the first time we've seen each other since Club Prom, and you know Jack and Roo will be all shitty to him, and—"

"Bailey?"

She stopped, mid-sentence. "Yes?"

"Do you remember when I said it seemed you only cared about Colin and not about me and my problems at all?"

"Oh, right." She exhaled. "Sorry. But look, if you want to go to the party, you can absolutely do it. Just tell them you're doing something else, take up Blake on the ride, and make it back before they check. No one is the wiser."

311

"This already sounds like a bad idea," I said.

"Why?" Which is what the planners of bad ideas always say. "Look. There's a movie outside on the beach at eight. Tell them you're going to that. It'll give you till at least ten. Oh, and make sure you mention the crappy reception on the Lake North side, so if he does demand you come home, you can say the message took a while to come through."

"How do you even know all this?"

She shrugged. "I like the Club. I may absorb any and all facts about it for that reason."

I looked back at my dad, who was now sitting with Tracy, eating as he sipped his wine. I turned back to the water. "What if he comes looking for me?"

"He's still jet-lagged, right? He probably won't even make it to ten."

This was clever, I had to admit: the last two evenings my dad and Tracy had both been out cold long before I turned in. "I'll try it," I said as my stomach grumbled. Turned out I was hungry after all. "But if I am coming, it's for me. Not for you and Colin."

"I know, I know," she said quickly. "Hey, do you think I can really have something to eat? I'm starving."

I nodded, getting to my feet and walking over to the basket, which Tracy pushed toward me, saying, "Help yourself. There are six sandwiches in there—I thought we might want extra."

I dug around a bit, finally finding two turkey and roasted red peppers as described by the custom, handwritten labels with the Club insignia. "Gordon," I called out. "Want a sandwich?"

"She doesn't like anything," Bailey warned me, taking one.

"We have turkey with red pepper," I told Gordon anyway. When she made a face, I turned to Tracy. "Are there chips or anything?"

"Um . . ." She dug around a bit. "No, just crackers and cheese, I'm afraid. But—"

Then I remembered something. "Hold on," I told Gordon, walking over to the sailboat and my bag, which I'd left on the seat. I pulled out the doughnut I'd taken from Nana's breakfast table, still wrapped in a napkin. "How about this?"

She looked over, expectations clearly low. Seeing the pastry, she brightened instantly. "You don't want it?"

I handed it to her. "All yours."

Grinning, she immediately took a bite, getting chocolate on her face. Chewing, she said, "Are you coming back to our side?"

With kids, you never wanted to make promises you couldn't keep. I'd learned that early, when my dad was often the bad guy, reining my mom in from her pie-in-the-sky promises. He wanted to protect me, I knew, and Emma would have let him. But Saylor, with her Calvander blood, had other ideas.

"Yeah," I told Gordon as we sat there. "I am."

EIGHTEEN

I met someone.

When my phone first beeped with this text, waking me from an afternoon nap, I just assumed it was from Bridget. Only she could declare a place hopelessly boring one day, only to find a dreamy summer romance the next. When I rubbed my eyes and looked at it again, I saw it wasn't her, but Ryan. My eyes widened.

What? How? Who is he?

She didn't respond for a bit, and it made me wonder if she'd already left that one spot where she had reception on the mountaintop. But then, finally, this.

Not he. A she.

I rubbed my eyes again, wanting to make sure I was reading this correctly. Even though these were only four words, and small ones at that, the message was big. I sat up, shaking my head to clear it. What I said now was important.

That's awesome. Details?

This time, she answered right away.

Her name is Liz. She's from Maine. Drama geek. But I think I might be too now?

This was almost as surprising as the fact she was crushing on a girl. **You?**

The tech stuff is actually really fun! Getting a crash course in a bunch of things, but I might want to do it at home, too? Anyway, she's the lead.

Wow, I wrote. **Picture?**

A pause. Then, with a beep, a shot of Ryan and the same girl with the olive skin and long, curly dark hair who'd had the army cap on in the shot she'd sent earlier. This time, though, it was just the two of them making faces, goofing for the camera, but even so, I could see something in my long-time friend that was different. A happiness, almost a glow.

She's pretty! You have a type, clearly, I wrote.

????

I laughed out loud. **Ry, she looks like Jasmine!**

A beep. Then another.

I am laughing so hard right now

Omg you're right!

Beep.

I didn't even make the connection!

Good thing you have me, I replied.

A pause. I tried to picture her on some steep hill, surrounded by scrub brush, away from camp to share this with someone. And she'd picked me, which felt like a gift.

I'm glad we're cool, she said now.

I am very cool, I agreed.

Not really, she replied. **But about this, yes.**

Then: **Don't tell Bridget, okay? I want to.**

Of course.

How about you? she wrote. **Found a prince (or princess)** yet?

I knew I should tell her about Blake, the prom, and everything else. But as she said this, I only thought of Roo.

Not yet, I typed back.

Beep. **Okay, I need to get off the mountain. Dress is tonight. Talk soon?**

Definitely.

A row of smiley faces appeared on the screen, followed by a bright red heart. I smiled, putting my phone back on the floor before stretching back out across the bed with a yawn. I couldn't say I was totally surprised by Ryan's news, as she'd always had a lack of interest when it came to Bridget's incessant chatter about boys. As one of her two closest friends, though, maybe I should have asked a few more questions. Instead, I'd just assumed she was straight because I was. What kind of a friend did that? I picked up my phone again and started a new text to her.

Hey I'm sorry

No, that wasn't right.

I didn't realize, I should have

Even worse.

The cursor just sat there, blinking. I looked out at the water outside my window. There was still time to come up with the right words, and probably better to say them

316

face-to-face anyway. So I just sent her a heart back, and left it at that.

"So you'll be a senior this year," Mrs. Delhomme said to me as the waiter refilled her wineglass. A woman about Nana's age, she was deeply tan, with short white hair she wore so spiky it resembled plumage. "Do you have college plans?"

"We've taken a couple of tours while traveling," my dad said from my other side. "But she hasn't narrowed down a real list, have you, Emma?"

"Not yet," I said. "I want to keep my options open."

At this, my dad smiled. I'd never been great with other kids, but I could hang at any adult dinner party. The gift and curse of the only child.

"Options are good," Mrs. Delhomme said. "It's how we ended up with the Tides. The land went up for sale when Wilton was in college, and his dad snapped it up for what he called 'a rainy day.' Which is so funny, because I swear it never rains here! One reason why it's such a great place to get away."

I'd realized, over three courses and now dessert, that Mrs. Delhomme, like my grandmother, had a story for everything.

"Well, it's absolutely stunning," Nana said now from her seat, next to Tracy. "We're having just the best time. I can't thank you enough."

"Nonsense," said Mr. Delhomme, who was on my dad's other side. His wife was the talker of the two of them, while he spent most of the meal on the phone. "We're thrilled you finally came down to see us."

"And you're here for two weeks?" Mrs. Delhomme asked me.

I nodded, scooping up the last of my vanilla ice cream with chocolate sauce. "I was over in North Lake before this, with my mom's family."

"Really?" She smiled. "I didn't know she was from this area. Where do they live?"

"Her grandmother owns a motel called Calvander's," my dad replied before I could answer. "Just over the line."

"Such a lovely community, North Lake," she told him. "There's just so much history there, those families that have been coming for generations." She took a sip of her wine, leaving a lipstick mark on the glass. "It's what we really aspired to when we developed Lake North. That sense of tradition."

"That said, it's not someplace I'd want to spend my vacation," Mr. Delhomme added. "I'm a fan of modern comforts. The places there are a bit . . . antiquated."

I was pretty sure this was a burn. I couldn't help but say, "I think for some people it's just what they want."

My dad shot me a look. I pretended I didn't see.

"Coffee?" asked a voice right behind me. I turned to see a girl with two long braids I sort of recognized from a Campus party, holding a pot.

"No, thanks," I said, and she nodded, moving on.

"Are you going to the Pavilion this evening?" Mrs. Delhomme asked me. "I hear there is a great band playing.

Swing music, I believe. Sadly, my dancing days are behind me since my hip operation, but it might be fun for you."

Hearing this, I glanced at my dad, but now he was leaning into a conversation with Nana, nodding.

"I actually heard there might be a movie?" I said, a bit louder than necessary. "A friend mentioned it."

"Well, let's find out." She turned to the girl with the coffeepot. "Mila? Do you know anything about a movie here tonight?"

Mila smiled politely. "Absolutely. They do it on the beach. There's popcorn and everything. It's great."

"Oh, good," Mrs. Delhomme said. "You'll have a wonderful time."

"Did you say eight?" I asked Mila, making a show of checking my phone. "Because I don't want to be late."

"Go, go," Mrs. Delhomme, who probably needed coffee but was still downing her wine, said to me. "Grace, I'm giving your granddaughter permission to be excused. She's put up with our chatter all evening and wants to be with some people her own age."

"Oh, not at all," I told her. "I'm fine to stay."

"No, you go," Tracy said to me. When my dad looked at her, she said to him, "I mean, of course it's up to you, I just feel like she's been here all night with us . . ."

"Where is this movie, again?" he asked me.

"On the beach," I said, pointing out the back doors. "It will be over at ten."

"I'd go," Tracy said, stifling a yawn, "but this jet lag

319

is killing me. I'll be lucky to make it home without falling asleep on the way."

Bailey was good. I had to give her that.

My dad, however, was still thinking. Or pretending to, if only to torture me. Finally he said, "Okay, fine. But I want you home by midnight. And answer your phone if I call."

"Will do," I said, getting to my feet before he could give me any other addendums. "My reception isn't great on the beach, though, just so you know."

"Oh, it's horrible everywhere on this side," Mrs. Delhomme said to the table. "We're working on a tower. If we can get the permits."

A good time to make my escape. "Thank you so much for dinner," I said to the Delhommes, then walked over and kissed Nana's cheek before waving at Dad and Tracy and heading for the door. Outside in the hallway, I checked my phone. I had three messages from Bailey.

I'm here.

Where are you?

Remember to mention the bad reception!!!

I couldn't handle the nagging, so I turned it off again. Then I went into the bathroom, which had neatly stacked real hand towels, as well as complimentary lotion and perfume dispensers (ALL PRODUCTS AVAILABLE AT CLUB GIFT SHOP!). Five minutes later, smelling like honeysuckle rose, I brushed my hair, put on some lipstick, and took a deep breath. I was going to do this, consequences be damned. Although if I chose to believe Bailey, there might not be any at all. But how often was she right?

Just as I went to push the door open, it swung back the other way. I stepped back just as Mila, she of the coffeepot and braids, came in, bumping right into me.

"Oh, sorry!" she said, jumping back as the door shut behind her with a quiet swish. "I totally wasn't looking where I was going."

"It's fine," I said, stepping to the side so she could get around me and to a stall. As she stepped inside one, I reached to push the door open again, but then I heard her voice.

"You're friends with Blake and Hannah, right?"

"Um . . . yeah," I said. "I am."

"Then you should go to the party in North Lake tonight instead of the movie. It will just be all families there anyway."

"Oh," I said. "You think?"

The toilet flushed. A moment later, she emerged, walking to the sink. "Totally. Anyway, everyone's going to this party either now or when they get off work. I can give you the address, if you want. I know that guy Hannah's all into is going to be there."

"Hannah has a boyfriend?" I asked.

"Well, they're not there yet, but that's her goal," she said, turning off the faucet and picking up a hand towel. "He's cool. And really cute. His name's Roo."

Hearing this, I felt like I'd been punched. I'd only been gone two days: How had this happened? "I know Roo," I said quietly. "I didn't realize they were talking."

"Like I said, it's early days." She glanced at me through

the mirror. "She and Rachel are going over there pretty soon. Maybe text them and grab a ride? You won't regret missing the movie. I promise."

"Maybe I'll do that," I said, inching slowly toward the door again. "Thanks for the heads-up."

"Anytime," she replied. "See you over there!"

Back out in the Club lobby, I suddenly felt tired, the weight of the whole day—arguing with my dad, the sail—hitting me. Did I really now want to go all the way to North Lake, risking serious punishment, just to see Roo with another girl? Sure, I'd always have Bailey, but if things went her way, she'd be caught up with Colin. Maybe it was just better to take this enforced separation as a sign.

"Saylor! Over here."

I turned to see Blake just inside the doors of the Club, waving at me. On the other side of the glass door behind him was his car. Hannah was in the front seat, looking effortlessly gorgeous as usual, Rachel in the back. Great.

"Hey," I said, walking over to him. "What's going on?"

"You mean, other than assuming you'd bailed on me?" When I just looked at him, he added, "You didn't answer any of my texts."

Whoops. I pulled my phone out, powering up, then was immediately hit with a series of alerts. "Huh," I said. "According to this, you'll pick me up at eight just outside the lobby."

"Really?" he said. "Imagine that."

I smiled. "Sorry. Long day. So long, in fact, that I'm

322

thinking maybe—"

"Nope," he said flatly.

Stopped in mid-sentence, I paused before trying to speak again. "It's just, we were out on the water today, I'm really—"

"Nope."

"Nope what?"

"Nope," he said, "you're not going to bail on me right in front of my face. This ride, and party, is my apology. You accepted it. Therefore, you have to come."

I looked out at the car again. Hannah had the mirror visor down and was checking her lipstick, while Rachel laughed at something in the back seat. "I don't know," I said. "I'm not sure it's my thing."

"It's your *side*," he said. "Come on."

Sighing, I went, following him through the doors, which swung open automatically, and outside, where the valets were running around as cars came and went. When Rachel saw me, she squealed.

"Oh, good, you're coming!" she yelled. "Let's go!"

This enthusiasm was seconded by Hannah, who reached around for me once I was in the back seat and gave me a sloppy hug that smelled like beer. "*So* glad you're here," she said, her voice hot in my ear. "This is the night it all happens. I'm sure of it!"

She sounded so excited. But if she meant her getting with Roo, I wasn't.

Blake slid behind the wheel, starting the engine, then beeped at the valets as we pulled around the circle in front of the Club. Just as we pulled out on the main road, I caught a quick glimpse of a white screen set up on the beach beyond the pool. This is probably a bad idea, I thought. But then we were accelerating, the wind picking up through the windows, and it was done.

"This neighborhood is like a maze," Blake complained as we crept down yet another street, looking for house numbers. "And all the houses are so *tiny*."

Hearing this, I felt a flare of annoyance. They weren't that small, actually. I guess it just depended what you were comparing them to.

"Roo says it's a white house with a carport," Hannah said, reading off her phone's screen. "And that he'll come out so we can see him if necessary."

This was the fifth time she'd mentioned his name in the short trip over. And yes, I'd been counting.

"I swear, we've already been down this road," Blake muttered as we turned onto another dark stretch. "Unless it's at the very—"

"Roo!" Hannah yelled. Six. "There he is."

It was indeed him, standing at the end of a cul-de-sac right by a wooden staircase, waving at us. He had on jeans and a white T-shirt that said NORTH LAKE TIGERS, and seeing him, I felt my stomach drop. He couldn't really be into Hannah. Could he?

"Where should I park?" Blake yelled out his window.

"Anywhere up here's fine," he replied. "The driveway's already packed."

Blake pulled up next to a mailbox. He hadn't even cut the engine before Hannah was out of the car, slamming her door behind her.

"*So* ready to blow off some steam," she said to Roo, and I watched his face for signs he was equally enamored with her. He *was* smiling, but then he always smiled. "We brought beer."

"Great," he said as she gave him a hug. Don't, don't, I thought, surprising myself with how much I really did not want him to return this gesture, even as he gave her what seemed to be a quick, friendly squeeze in return. "I wish I could drink it. But I'm sure someone will be happy to."

"Do you really have to work?" Hannah said, cocking her head to the side.

"Money won't make itself," he replied cheerfully as Blake got out of the car, followed by Rachel. I was dragging my feet, enjoying being hidden in the dark of the back seat, like as long as I stayed put, this whole scene wasn't happening. Then Blake was popping the trunk, though, so Roo came over, lifting out the cases of beer there. Just as he was about to shut it again with a bang, he looked through the window and saw me. His eyes widened.

"Saylor?" he asked.

"Hi," I said, opening my door and getting out. "How are—"

This was as far as I got, however, before it happened: Blake, who'd been just off to my side, came over and took my hand, easily sliding his palm against mine and intertwining our fingers. And for some stupid reason, I didn't stop him. I just stood there, like on the boat earlier, watching it happen like I was helpless against it, too.

Roo noticed. It was clear in the way his eyes narrowed on our now-joined hands, quickly processing what this meant. Then, the beers in his arms, he turned back to Hannah. "Let's go," he said. "It's this way."

They started down a wooden staircase that led off the cul-de-sac, with Rachel right behind them. Down below, I could see people were crowded on the small porch, the steps, and the dock, their voices rising up to us. I suddenly remembered Blake was holding my hand.

"What are you doing?" I asked, finally coming to my senses and pulling it back. "This is an apology. Not a date."

"Oh, come on," he said. I just looked at him. "Fine. Kill me for trying. I had a chance, I took it."

"Well, we're not like that anymore," I told him. "Understood?"

"Yeah, sure. You just wanted a ride. I get it."

"That's what you offered!"

"Because I was trying to get back with you!"

I stopped walking, halfway down the stairs. Roo, Rachel, and Hannah had already gotten to the porch, their arrival (or that of the beer) celebrated with a burst of applause. "Why?"

He just looked at me. "What do you mean?"

"Why?" I repeated. Like his "nope" earlier, I wasn't backing down. "*Why* do you want to be with me?"

"I don't know," he replied, frustrated. "Why wouldn't I want to be with you?"

"You can't answer my question with a question. Try again."

He sighed, leaning back against the rail behind him. "What do you want me to say?"

"I want you to explain why you want to hold my hand. Why you want to date me. Why this"—here, I ran a hand through the air between us, to him, me, then back to him again—"is appealing to you."

"Well, right now, it's not," he said. I made a face. "What? Look, I'm an assertive person, okay? I go with the flow. And the flow treats me well. So what's not to like?"

I could not even begin to understand this. Yes, I'd been a person who'd benefited also from the actions of others: because of my dad and his hard work, I lived in a nice house and basically wanted for nothing. But people weren't things you just came across. They had to mean more.

"Colin liked Bailey. Bailey brought me along. And you dated me because I was there," I said to Blake. "This isn't a relationship, it's a coincidence."

"Who wants a relationship?" he asked.

Me, I thought, surprising myself. But not with someone who's been given everything. How could you value something if you never fought for it?

But what had *I* fought for, before this summer? All the

things I didn't want to do, a battle of prevention: driving, thinking too much about my mom, keeping the world as I knew it small, safe, and organized. Then I'd come here, where I was thrown in with little notice and no manual, forced to figure it out on my own. North Lake had changed me. And I wasn't sure I wanted to change back.

And then, of course, there was Roo. Who'd recognized me when I felt surrounded by strangers that first day. Who'd picked a dress that made me feel beautiful, made me laugh and think and, most of all, remember. He was right there in that house below us, nearby once again, and I should have been able to make this my moment to return the favor, find him and say everything I hadn't that night of Club Prom. *Shoulda done it*, Bailey had said. And for every moment since, I'd known she was right.

"I don't want to be part of your flow," I said to Blake now. When he opened his mouth to reply, I continued, "And you shouldn't want that either. Life is big and huge and scary. But you have to go and take your part of it. There's a reason the saying is 'Seize the day,' not 'Wait for it to come along at some point.'"

"Hold on, so you want me to seize you? I just did! I took your hand."

"But I'm not the one for you!" I said, exasperated. "I'm just the one who's right here."

He was quiet for a second. "So . . . are you saying you don't even want to walk in with me? You want, you know, me to wait out here until you go in?"

"No," I said. "We walk in together, as friends. Because we are. Right?"

"I hope so," he said quietly, and I could tell he meant it. Then he gestured for me to go ahead on the stairs, and I did, hearing him follow in the next beat behind me.

April's house was right on the water, with a great view of the lake. As we approached, I could see her through the window, adjusting some twinkling lights in the kitchen. The party planner at work.

"It's my BIRTHDAY!" Taylor, who was sitting on a cooler by the house's front door, wearing a light-up crown with feathers that said PRINCESS—slightly crooked—and only one shoe, said when she saw us.

"I heard," I told her, bending down to give her a hug. "Happy birthday."

"Thank YOU!" She looked at Blake. "Who's this?"

"Blake," I said, stepping back so he could say hello. "He works over at the Club."

"Blake from the Club," she said cheerfully. "You want a beer?"

"Sure," he replied. She slid off the cooler, opening it and taking out a can, which she handed him. Then she looked at me. "Saylor?"

We weren't even in the party proper yet, still outside. But through the screen door ahead of me, I could see Vincent, messing with a speaker up on the fireplace mantel. Two girls dancing together, laughing. And in the kitchen, Hannah sitting on the counter, Roo right in front of her. She was saying something, gesturing widely, as he listened, a smile on his face.

"Sure," I said, keeping my eyes on them. "I'll take one."

"You don't drink," Blake said as Taylor handed me a dripping can as well.

"Not usually," I said, popping the tab. "But it's her birthday."

"Hell YEAH it is!" Taylor yelled, hopping up and holding out her own beer to tap mine. "Let's drink to THAT."

She did, and I followed suit, even as I felt Blake's eyes on me. While the beer was cold, it still tasted awful, making me wince as I swallowed it down. Still, with a last look at Roo and Hannah—or what I hoped would be—I forced another one. Then one more.

"We should dance," I said to Taylor.

"Um, YEAH," she replied, keeping up the streak of shouting every few words. "I have a playlist I made just for this moment. Seriously! Let me just—hey, Vincent! Don't you dare pair your phone with that speaker. I'm not kidding!"

With that, she was opening the door to cross the floor to the fireplace, pulling her own phone from her pocket as she did so. Vincent, busted, slipped out the back door, leaving what I was pretty sure was, yep, heavy metal blasting behind him.

"Hey," Blake said to me as we came inside. "I know I'm not your boyfriend, but watch it with the beer. It can hit you fast when you're not used to it."

"I'll be fine," I said, taking another sip. "I'm only having this one."

And that was the plan. Just a few sips to loosen me up and take my mind off Roo and Hannah, as well as my dad. But as the alcohol began to hit, blurring the edges of this stressful day, and Taylor, after cursing Vincent loudly for a moment, put on a song with a whirly, pumping beat that Ryan, Bridget, and I loved, I was already thinking how another one would have to make me feel better. This would probably be the last party I'd attend on this side this summer. Or ever. I might as well make it one to remember.

"Isn't this AWESOME?" Taylor shouted in my ear a little while later. We'd started dancing just by ourselves, then pulled in the other two girls who'd been moving solo as well as April, who was now doing the bump with vigor. The room suddenly felt packed with sweaty, moving bodies, the music barely audible, even though the speaker was right there.

I nodded—it was too hot to speak—taking a swig from my third (fourth?) beer before pressing it to my temple. The taste wasn't bothering me anymore: really, nothing was. There was just the music and Taylor swaying in front of me, barefoot now, her own hair sweaty and sticking to her neck. I closed my eyes, thinking of my dad on the boat that day, shouting out orders to me when he knew I hated sailing. Telling Bailey my name was Emma, not Saylor.

"Whoa," I heard someone say, just as I realized I was stumbling and had bumped into the person behind me. I opened my eyes, but still felt dizzy as I stopped where I was to get my bearings. So hot. So loud. I pressed my can against my face again, but it was warm. And empty.

"There you are," said another voice from behind me, but this one was familiar. That said, I didn't realize it was Bailey specifically until I turned around to see her there. She had on a black maxidress, her hair pulled back, silver hoops hanging from her ears. "I've been looking all over!"

"We're dancing," I said, grabbing her hand. I went to spin, still holding it, feeling a flush creep up my neck—it was so hot—but then got tangled as she just stood there, elbow rigid, looking at me. "What?"

"Are you drunk?" she asked.

"No," I said automatically. "I just had one. Or two."

"Still two more than I've ever seen you drink," she replied as I dropped her hand, moving into a shimmy as Taylor did the same beside me. "Let's go get some air."

"I'm fine," I said, making a point to e-nun-ci-ate this carefully. "I'm just having fun, like you have basically every time we've gone out."

"Yes, but that's me," she said, eyeing me as I stumbled. Wait, *was* I drunk? Suddenly I wasn't so sure. "Saylor. Come on. Now."

She sounded strict, like a mother. Although not my mother. If anyone could understand blowing off a little necessary steam, it was Waverly. "I'm fine," I told her. "Since when are you the party police?"

"Since I found you drunk for the first time, like, ever,"

she said. And then, without another word, she grabbed my wrist and started to literally drag me toward the back door. Immediately, I resisted, surprising myself, yanking my arm from her. A bit too hard, as it turned out, because it flung back behind me, whacking Taylor, who was doing some low-down twist move, right in the face. I felt her eyebrows.

"OUCH!" she yelled, over the music and all the noise.

"Oh, sorry," I said, "I didn't mean—"

"Saylor." Bailey had me again, this time so tightly I knew there was no point in fighting her. "Let's go."

I went, although I told myself it was my choice. When we neared the kitchen, where Roo and Hannah were, I tried to stop, wanting to collect myself. But the momentum worked against me, suddenly and surprisingly, and just like that, I was down.

"Oh, shit," Bailey said as I hit the floor. In the next beat, a wave of dizziness hit me, just as I was trying to get up again. Maybe better to stay where I was, I thought. The tile was actually kind of cool. Above me, I heard Bailey say, "Can I get a little help here?"

"What's wrong?" a boy's voice said. Roo. I needed to get up. Off the floor. I was on the floor, right?

"Drunk," Bailey said flatly. "Help me get her outside."

After all of Bailey's dragging me and literal arm twisting, what happened next was smooth and quick: I felt hands beneath my arms, and then I was on my feet. But only briefly, because they didn't seem to want to hold me. Luckily, I collapsed into someone's side. Oh, right. Roo.

"Careful there," he said, locking an arm around my waist. "One foot in front of the other."

"I'm fine," I said.

"I know." Then, loudly, he said, "Make way, you guys! Coming through!"

Somehow, we got to the back door. I wasn't sure of the specifics because I kept my eyes closed, due to the fact that this was super humiliating. Also, I was suddenly feeling a tiny bit sick. I just need air, I told myself, and a second later, like a wish granted, I felt myself surrounded by it.

"Where are we going?" Roo asked before pausing briefly to scoop up my legs so he was carrying me outright. "Just on the porch?"

"Let's go down to the dock," I heard Bailey say. She sounded far away. "Just so we have some space to think."

At first when I got outside, I could hear voices and music, the party still close by. Now, though, we were moving away, all of it condensing to a distant hum beyond Roo's footsteps. Finally, he put me down.

"Ah," I said, spying the water nearby and reaching out to dip my hand in. Again, though, I misjudged my own weight and felt myself starting to tumble, until someone grabbed me by my hair. "Hey, OUCH that hurts!"

"Too bad," Bailey said, pushing me into a sitting position. Then she bent down in front of me. "What are you trying to do? Drown while we watch?"

"I'm hot," I moaned.

In response, she dumped the cup she was holding,

scooping up some water, and flung it on me. I went from sweaty to soaked in seconds.

"Hey!"

"Sober up," she commanded. "I don't like you this way."

"Bailey, come on," Roo said, and from the sound and direction of his voice, I realized what I was leaning against was actually his legs. I turned, looking at them in the light thrown from the house, as he said, "She can't help it. She won't even remember this."

"She will, because I won't let her forget."

"How many times have I pulled you out of parties?" he asked her. "Have a little compassion."

"I'm compassionate," she said, sounding just about anything but. "I just don't understand how she got like this."

"I'm guessing it was the beer," he told her, deadpan. "How many have *you* had?"

"Yes, but," she replied, "I'm not lying on the dock on my back, staring at your calves."

I laughed. Oh, wait, she meant me. I said, "What are these, anyway?"

A pause. Then Bailey said, sounding exhausted, "What's what, Saylor?"

"These," I said, pointing at the numbers on the back of Roo's leg. "I saw them the first day, on the boat. And I've been wondering ever since."

"Nautical coordinates," he told me.

"For what?"

"For the lake's center," he said.

I looked at the numbers again, which were blurring slightly. "So you can find it, always."

Roo gazed down at me. "That's right."

"Oh, Jesus," Bailey said. "I'm going to get her some water."

I heard her walking away, the deck bouncing with each step. And then it was just Roo and me and the lake, gurgling under the dock between us.

"She's mad," I observed.

"More like worried," he said as he took a seat. "Funny thing about always being the one out of control. You tend not to like it when other people are."

"I am not out of control," I stated. "I just had a few beers."

"Right," he said. "Of course."

Sitting there, though, I suddenly felt very fuzzy-headed, not to mention tired. And, apparently, honest, as I heard myself say, "Do you know that, at home, I always have to organize everything? My closet, the mail on the counter, even my toothbrush and toothpaste on the shelf. It doesn't matter what it is. It's, like, I can't control it. I've done it for as long as I remember. I was doing it when I first got here."

When he answered, he didn't sound like he found this weird or notable, just saying, "Really."

I nodded. "But then I started cleaning rooms, and hanging out with you guys, and I don't have to do it so much anymore. It's like this place is changing me."

He looked over. "That's good, right?'

"I guess. But now I'm gone and everything's different.

It's just going to come back."

"You're not gone," he said. In the dark, behind my closed eyes, his voice was all I could hear, like a lifeline I was still gripping, keeping me conscious. "It's just the other side of the lake."

"It's so different," I murmured, curling into him. "I miss you."

I mean, I miss it here, I thought, realizing too late what I'd said instead. But then it was fading, too, and I couldn't reach it to take it back.

"It's okay, Saylor," he said, smoothing a hand over my head. "Just rest."

But with this touch, this contact, I suddenly wanted to say something else, even as I knew I was fading. "I didn't know you were into Hannah. I wish—"

A pause, but maybe just my sense of time. Then he said, "You and Blake were holding hands."

"That was all him," I said. "I had no idea. I came here to see you."

It felt good, I realized, being this honest. At least now, whatever else happened, he would know. That day at his house, he'd said I'd always been part of his story. Now he would know that whatever happened from here, he, too, was in mine.

The dock was bouncing again as someone approached. So tired, I thought, closing my eyes. I was just about to drift off, leaning into his shoulder, when I heard Bailey speak.

"Okay. So we have a problem."

NINETEEN

"Just do me a favor. Don't puke again."

I blinked. I was in an enclosed space, and moving, by the feel of it. Also sitting on something very cold. But how did I get here?

"I threw up?" I managed to say. The thought of doing it was bad enough, but not realizing? I was horrified.

"Yep," Bailey said. She was beside me, one hand thrown across my midsection like a makeshift seat belt. "Luckily, Roo gave me that bucket, so you didn't make a mess."

I looked down at my lap: there was a plastic sand pail between my legs, the word TIPS APPRECIATED written on it in black marker. Inside was a bit of liquid I chose not to examine closely, instead turning again to my surroundings. White. Metal. Rattling and in motion. And my ass was *freezing*.

"Wait," I said. "Are we in the Yum truck?"

"Yep," I heard Roo say, from somewhere to my right. "And on our way to the Tides."

The Tides? Oh, shit. My dad. "What time is it?"

"Eleven," Bailey said, handing me my phone. "Which would be an hour after your father first texted asking you how the movie was."

Movie? Oh, right. I grabbed the phone from her, then opened up my texts. My dad had sent his first message at 9:58.

How's the movie? Want company? Can't sleep!

Then, at 10:05.

Hello? Are you getting this? Let me know please.

I was starting to panic now. I gave a sideways look at the TIPS APPRECIATED pail, swallowing down a bad taste in my mouth. 10:21.

Concerned. Coming down to find you.

"Oh, shit," I said. I thought I might puke again.

"No joke," Bailey replied, craning her neck to look ahead, out the windshield. "Where are we now? I can't see anything from back here."

"Still in North Lake," a girl replied. "But we're getting close to the line."

Oh, that's Hannah, I thought as I recognized her voice. A beat. Then I remembered. Everything. Oh, God. Shame went over me like a wave.

It's so different, I'd said. I miss you, I'd said. I wish, I'd said.

Panicked, I made myself turn my head and look at Roo, who was bent over the steering wheel, squinting in the headlights of an oncoming car. How could I take it all back, now, after the fact? I'd been drunk, I didn't know what I was saying.

But I did. And I'd meant every word.

"Okay," Bailey said, pulling me back from this crisis to the other one at hand. "Now, the key is what you say to him first. It sets the precedent for the entire incident."

"Incident?" I said.

"Well, he is pissed and, to use his word, concerned," she said, gesturing to my phone. "Which means that once he sees you are safe, he's just going to be pissed."

"I'll tell him I didn't have reception."

"And that might work," she agreed, "if he does not see you arrive in this ice cream truck but instead finds you somewhere on the beach, ostensibly just finishing the movie."

"Movie's been over for an hour, though," Hannah added from the front seat. I felt surprised by the rush of anger I felt toward her. What was wrong with me? "So you might want another plan."

"How about this," Bailey said as we went over a pothole, the entire truck rattling. "You were at the movie, then you bumped into Hannah and went to her place for a bit, where you had one beer, immediately regretted it, and returned to the Club, but the movie was over, so you just sat down on the beach to contemplate your bad choices."

"This sounds like something we'd watch in health class," Roo observed.

"Then come up with something better!" she barked at him.

340

"Okay, you don't have to—" Roo stopped talking, suddenly, and I saw him look out his window. "Oh, crap. Pit stop ahead, at the market."

"What?" Bailey asked. "We don't have time for that!"

"We also don't have a choice," he replied, slowing down now and starting to take a left turn, widely, which almost threw both Bailey and me off the cooler and onto the truck floor. "It's your mom with Gordon. She's waving us over."

"My mom?"

We stopped with a jerk. The lights in the back of the truck immediately came on, bright all around me, and I caught a glimpse of the contents of that bucket for real. Ugh.

"Thank goodness!" I heard Celeste say. She had to be standing outside in the lot. "My arm's about to fall off from waving."

"I'm coming right back to work," Roo explained. "Just have to drop someone off. Everything okay?"

"Oh, yeah," Celeste said. Beside me, Bailey opened her own purse, pulling out some breath mints and tossing a handful into her mouth. Suddenly everything smelled like wintergreen. "I just saw you coming and Gordon really needs a YumPop."

"What's Gordon doing up this late?" Bailey hissed to me, cracking her mints in her teeth.

"She's up late," Roo noted to Celeste.

"Joe and Mimi went to Bly County for the night and Trinity's too grumpy to be around anyone," Celeste explained. "Poor Gordon, she's tired and bored. I've been texting Bailey and Jack, but of course neither of them are answering their phones."

"Can you turn this light off?" Bailey whisper-hissed from beside me. Roo, still focused on Celeste, shook his head almost imperceptibly.

"I think we can manage a YumPop," he said, pulling the truck's brake and getting up. "What flavor, Gordon?"

My head was hurting now, and I was pretty sure I had never in my life been so thirsty. Gordon's voice sounded very small as she replied, "Chocolate?"

"Move," Bailey said to me, giving me a shove as Roo came toward us, pointing at the cooler. I started to slide down, then fell instead, landing with a bang on the floor. Ouch.

"What was that?" I heard Celeste say.

"Just some junk falling," Roo told her, shooting me an apologetic look. "Chocolate, you said?"

"Oh, crap," I heard Celeste say. "That's the store phone. Can you just give it to her, and I'll see you when you get back? And if you hear from Bailey, tell her to call me and that she's in trouble."

"What?" Bailey whispered. "What did I do?"

"You're hiding from her," I pointed out from the floor. She ignored me.

"Chocolate!" Roo announced, pulling a wrapped cone from the cooler. "I'll bring it to—"

Before he could finish this thought, however, his driver's-side door creaked open and Gordon stuck her head in, looking down into the truck at us. "Saylor? Are you okay?"

"She's fine," Bailey told her. "And keep it down. You didn't see us, you hear?"

Solemnly, Gordon nodded. She was still looking at me. "Are you sick?"

I shook my head, but even as I did so, I felt it: shame, thick and hot, creeping up from my chest to my face. Here I was, in front of the only person who probably would ever think I was perennially awesome, drunk and sprawled on the floor of an ice cream truck with what I was realizing was probably vomit on my shirt. It was a horrible impression to make on anyone, but especially a kid. They were supposed to be protected from things like this, their world consisting only of chocolate YumPops, swimming, and a warm, safe place to sleep at night. Not this. I knew how scary it could be. Because I'd been that kid.

"I'm fine," I said to her, but even to my ears my voice sounded rough, uneven. "I'm just not feeling great right this second."

"Now take your ice cream and go act like you never saw us," Bailey added as Roo walked back up to the front, handing it to her. "Can you do that?"

"Yes," Gordon said. She was still watching me.

"Good girl," Roo told her. "See you when I get back, okay?"

Gordon nodded as Roo took his seat, cranking the engine again. The lights went out. But I could still see her, the market lit up behind, as we drove away.

"What's the over-under of her telling Celeste everything

anyway?" Roo asked as we pulled out onto the main road.

"About even," Bailey told him, hopping up on the cooler again. "But either way, she'll wait until she's done with the ice cream. So step on it."

He did, the engine rattling as we accelerated. From the floor, I watched the Lake North sign approach in the wind-shield, then disappear over us. I couldn't get Gordon's face out of my mind. Luckily, Bailey was not so distracted.

"So we'll drop you at the Pavilion," she was saying. "From there, you go back to the Tides and say you've just been out enjoying walking and thinking and had no reception. Okay?"

"Right," I said. I sat up, locating my purse, then dug through until I found my hairbrush and an elastic. My head was pounding as I pulled my hair up in a high ponytail, securing it, then accepted the mints that Bailey was already holding out to me.

"Don't make any rookie mistakes," she said. "I'm sensing this is your first time doing this."

"What? Being drunk in an ice cream truck?" I asked.

"Trying to explain yourself out of a punishment," she corrected me. "The most common screw-up is giving too much detail or information. Stick to facts in simple statements."

"Like five sentences," I said.

She looked at me. "What?"

"Five sentences," I explained. She still looked clueless. "What you say to introduce yourself, you boiled down to the basics. It's a lake thing."

"Says who?"

"Roo," I told her.

"It's true," he said from the front seat.

"I have *never* heard of that," Bailey said. "But sure, great. Five sentences. Keep it short and sweet. Like, 'I went to the movie. I saw a friend. We had a beer. I felt bad about it. So I've been out here thinking.'"

"Wow," Roo said, and I looked at the rearview mirror just as he did, our eyes meeting. To me he said, "She's a natural."

"Went to a movie, saw a friend, had a beer, felt bad, been thinking," I repeated. "Got it."

"Tears are helpful, too," Hannah added. "I always cry when I get busted. Sometimes the sympathy vote is all you have going for you."

"Not *too* many tears, though," Bailey warned me. "If you're blubbering, it just pisses them off more. Or it does Celeste. I don't know your dad, though."

When it came to this sort of thing, I didn't really know him either: I hadn't ever had to lie to him about where I'd been or what I was doing. There'd been no need to until now. Which was probably just what he would say, I was sure, if none of this worked.

"Getting close," Roo reported, slowing for a stop sign. He looked at Hannah. "You want to hop off at Campus?"

"Can you come back by and hang out before you go to work?" she asked. "We can watch a movie or something."

He glanced at the clock on the console. "Probably not. Sorry."

She bit her lip, clearly unhappy. "I thought we were

345

hanging out tonight. I mean, you invited me to this party—"

"Everyone was invited," Bailey said under her breath. But I could hear her. "Not just you."

"—and then, when I get there, all you do is take care of Saylor and leave early." She sighed. "I just don't understand."

"Hannah." Roo looked at her. "She was in over her head and we're friends. What do you want me to do?"

"Let someone else take over," she replied, nodding at Bailey.

"I'm kind of in this, now," he pointed out.

"Yeah, but you don't have to be," she said. "I mean, you don't have to save everyone just because you lost your dad."

Silence. Except for the truck rattling, the sound of which also seemed quieter after this statement.

"This is not about my dad," he said evenly. "Just trying to help out."

"Almost there," Bailey reported, and I looked up to see she was right: the Tides and the Club were lit up brightly just ahead. "You want to hop out, Hannah?"

"Fine," she said, sounding like she didn't. She looked at Roo. "Stop by for a second on your way back, okay? Just to talk."

"I have to work," he said.

"You always have to work!" she said as she jumped out, her feet hitting the ground with a slap. "God. What happened to summer being about having fun?"

Apparently, this was a rhetorical question, as she was walking away. As Roo watched her, Bailey said, "It's called real life. She should look into it."

"Let's go," Roo said, pulling away from the curb. "The Pavilion is just up here."

He was right: I could see it approaching, all the lights on, although there was no longer anyone there. How late was it now?

"We'll just pull up and you hop out," Bailey told me as Roo took a turn that sent me sliding toward the other side of the truck. "Then start walking toward the hotel. Remember to look regretful and contemplative."

"Right," I said, feeling a shot of adrenaline wake me up. I could do this. Five sentences. The truck suddenly slowed considerably.

"Wait, this isn't the Pavilion," Bailey said, squinting out the back window. "This is . . . Roo, what are you doing?"

"Stopping," he replied.

"Why?"

But then, we spotted the red and blue lights. LAKE NORTH SECURITY, it said on the car parked just a few hundred feet ahead, a man in uniform standing beside it. Next to him, phone to his ear, was my dad. I broke into a sweat.

"Oh, shit," Bailey said, which didn't help.

"Is that the police?" I asked.

"Worse," she replied. "It's Later Gator."

"What?"

"Crocodile Security Company," she said, taking a quick glance out the back windows. "They're the police at the

Club, the Tides, and around these parts. But everyone calls them Later Gator, because if you don't run and they catch you, you're screwed."

"Great," I said. "What do we do now?"

"I don't know," Bailey said, and while her endless instructions this evening had been wearing on my nerves, hearing this was worse. "But the thing is, I'm not supposed to be here."

I turned. She was looking out the back door again. "Where?"

"Lake North," she replied, as if it was perfectly normal to be banned from an entire town. "Since I got busted drinking at the Pavilion last year, I'm kind of, um, banned from city limits."

"But you've been coming here the entire time I've been visiting," I pointed out.

"Well, yes," she agreed. "But very stealthily! You'll notice we never came across security once."

"This is insane," I announced. We were now close enough to the Gator that the lights were bathing us in blue and red, and Roo had dropped the speed to where I was pretty sure we were just getting pushed along by the wind off the water. "Are we both going to get arrested?"

"You're not. You're just late and irresponsible." She kicked off her shoes, stuffing them in her purse, then strapped it over her chest, cross-body style. "I, however, need to get out of here. Think you can handle this like we discussed?"

"Out of here?" I repeated. "Where are you going?"

"Five sentences," she said, shooting Roo a look in the rearview. He nodded, slowing even more. "You were tired of his rules. You went to the party. You had a beer and it made you feel even worse. You feel awful now. You're sorry."

As she said this, she was sliding the lock open on the double doors, one hand moving slowly down to the handle.

"Are you jumping out of the truck?" I asked. "Seriously?"

"Shh," she said, easing the left-side door open. It creaked, but only barely audibly. Then she looked at me. "Text me when it's over, whatever happens. I'm sorry I have to go like this. But you can handle it. You're a Calvander."

But my dad, a Payne, was now standing right on the other side of the windshield, still holding his phone, eyes narrowed on Roo. The man in uniform, Later Gator, unnecessarily held up a hand to signal we should stop.

"Now, Bailey," Roo said under his breath, his lips barely moving as he started to roll down his window, Gator approaching from the other side.

It happened fast: one second she was there, perched by the half-open door, and then she was jumping out, noiselessly, into the dark behind us. I scrambled over, pulling the door shut again as Roo finally covered the last few inches between now and whatever was about to happen.

"Evening," Later Gator said through the open window. He had a slim flashlight in his hand, the beam of which he pointed in the truck, moving it around. "License and registration, please."

"It's me you want," I said, getting to my feet. I had one

hell of a head rush as I started walking, but pushed through anyway. "Let him go."

"Whoa," Later Gator said, aiming the light at me. "How many people are back there? Don't make another move. Understood?"

I nodded, standing there as his light shone bright in my face. "I'm Emma Payne," I said. "It's just me. That's my dad right there."

"Emma Payne?" he repeated.

Hearing this, my dad let his phone drop, coming up to the window as well. "Emma? Are you okay?"

"I'm fine," I said. "Can I please get out so I can explain?"

Later Gator nodded, gesturing toward the passenger-side door. To Roo he said, "You stay where you are and give me those documents. And keep your hands where I can see them."

"He didn't do anything," I protested. "He's just driving me home."

"Saylor, it's okay," Roo told me, digging into his pocket for his wallet before reaching across to pop open the glove box. To Gator he said, "The registration is in here somewhere. This isn't my truck—I've never had to find it before."

"Not your truck?" Gator said suspiciously. "Then whose is it?"

"It's an ice cream truck," I said. "He's a teenager. Of course it doesn't belong to him!"

"Emma," my dad barked through the window. "Get out. Now."

350

Gator gave him a look. "Sir, I'll ask you to step back so I can handle this."

My dad, annoyed, took a tiny step backward. Gator, satisfied, turned back to Roo, taking his documents. After studying the license for what felt like a long time, he said, "Christopher Price. You're from North Lake?"

"Yes, sir," Roo said. God, I hated that I'd gotten him into this.

"Anything in the truck I should know about?"

"Other than Emma?" Roo asked. Gator nodded, humorlessly. "Just ice cream, sir."

"Christopher Price?" my dad said. He looked at Roo, then me. "You're the one who's responsible for my daughter not being where she said she would be?"

"No," I said. The bright light, still shining at both of us, was making my eyes water. "I left of my own accord, with someone else. He just brought me back."

"You went to that party?" my dad demanded, now right back beside Gator despite his previous warning. "After I specifically told you not to?"

"I was upset," I said, thinking of Bailey for the first time since she'd jumped ship. I hoped for her sake she was halfway to the town line by now. "I saw some people who offered me a ride. I went. I drank a beer. I regretted—"

Roo winced, biting his lip. Oh, shit. I'd just made things worse without even trying.

"You've been *drinking*?" my dad said. Now he wasn't just

mad: he was furious. "What are you even thinking?"

"I'm sorry!" I cried out, my voice breaking. Six sentences. But who was counting? "I was angry and stupid."

Gator flipped the flashlight back so it was squarely on Roo. "Have you been drinking, Mr. Price?"

"No sir. I have to be at work at midnight. I was the DD tonight."

"And if I have to call the mobile unit for a Breathalyzer, it will confirm that?"

"He hasn't been drinking!" I protested. "He's just driving me home. It's me who screwed up—I'm the reason you're all here—just let him go!"

"Emma," my dad said. "Be quiet and let the officer do his job."

"But Roo isn't part of this!"

"Miss." Gator turned the flashlight back to me. "Calm down and be quiet or you'll have another problem. Understood?"

Roo glanced at me. I nodded and said, "Yes, sir."

Gator looked back down at the license and registration in his hand. "Now, Mr. Price, you say you're headed to work. Where is that?"

"Conroy Market, in North Lake. My boss is Celeste Blackwood. She's there right now."

"And where are *your* parents?"

I saw Roo swallow. "My mom is at work at the Bly County hospital. And my dad is deceased."

Gator nodded, then looked at the registration again. "Okay. Sit tight. I'll be right back."

With that, he turned, walking over to his cruiser and sliding behind the wheel. My dad came back up to the window, pointing a finger at Roo.

"You have a minor under the influence in your car," he told him, his voice thick with anger. "I don't care if you're sober or not, I'll still be pressing charges."

"For what?" I demanded.

"Saylor—" Roo said.

"Her name is Emma!" my dad exploded. His face was inches from Roo now: I could see spit flying from his mouth when he spoke. "And she doesn't go to parties and drink, or at least she didn't until she came here and started hanging out with all of you."

"Dad, stop it!"

"Look, I know what goes on with lake kids," he continued. "I married a lake kid, for Christ's sake. And I watched her destroy herself. I won't do it again."

Roo, my dad's finger inches from his nose, didn't say a word. He just sat there, taking this, and that was the worst thing of all.

"Mr. Price checks out," Gator announced to my dad, coming back from his car and sticking Roo's documents through the window. "Ms. Blackwood says she's expecting him at midnight and that he's a good kid. Said I should let him go."

"He gave my daughter beer!"

"No, he didn't!" I said. "God, are you even listening to me?"

"I don't have evidence of that," Gator explained to my dad. "Not much I can do."

"Go bust the party! Then you'll have your proof!"

"Well," Gator said, considering this, "the problem is it's in North Lake. And I only police Lake North. So—"

"Do not tell me this is out of your jurisdiction," my dad warned him. "This entire place is six miles long."

"Sir, I'll ask you to lower your voice," Gator replied.

"All he did was drive me home," I said. "Look, I understand you're pissed and you want to punish me—"

"You're damn right," my dad replied, but he was glaring at Roo as he said this.

"But leave Roo out of it," I finished. "Dad. *Please*."

My dad didn't say anything for a moment. When he did speak, it was very quietly and very clearly. "Fine. But hear me when I say this: I do not want you around my daughter ever again. Whatever has been going on, it's over as of tonight. Are we clear?"

"Dad," I said. "You can't just decide—"

"Actually, I can." He pointed at me. "Get out of that truck. Right now."

I glanced at Gator, thinking he might step in, but no. He just stood there with his stupid entirely too bright flashlight, watching along with the rest of us.

"I'm sorry," I said to Roo. But he didn't respond, the beam still bright in his face. Of all the ways I thought the night would end, I never could have guessed this. There had always been invisible lines between the two sides and the two communities. But my dad had drawn another, his own. And even though I was right next to Roo, I could feel it between us.

"I'm sorry," I said softly to him. "I—"

"It's okay," he replied, still looking straight ahead. "Just go."

I nodded, feeling a lump rise in my throat. Then I got up and walked to the passenger door, pushing it open to step out onto the road. It was late, almost midnight, and thankfully, most of Lake North was asleep. But I thought of all those windows at the Tides, each with a person or people on the other side. How did I look, leaving this truck with a cop car, lights spinning, beside it? Maybe, like Waverly herself.

My dad was coming around the front bumper now, and I heard the Yum truck start as we began to walk back toward the hotel together. I wanted to turn and watch it, get this last glimpse of Roo to last me until . . . well, I wasn't even sure. But just as I was about to, I realized I couldn't bear it. It was easier, somehow, to just walk toward those doors already opening to reveal the night desk clerk, cheerful and oblivious.

"Welcome to the Tides!"

Neither of us responded as we walked to the elevator, where my dad pushed the button for our floor. The elevator chimed. We went in, the doors sliding shut behind us.

TWENTY

My summer had come to a full stop. But Bridget's was finally beginning.

"So then," she was saying, "Sam asks if I'm going to the pool fireworks. And I'm like, yeah, I should be there. And Steve says, 'What about Emma? Will she be home then?'"

Silence. Too late, I realized she'd paused for maximum dramatic effect. "Wow," I said quickly.

"I know!" She sighed happily. "I mean, granted, the first part of this summer did not go as I planned with Pop Pop's stroke and our detour to Ohio. But then to come back, and have this happen within days . . . it's like fate. It's what we've always wanted!"

She was right. And five weeks ago I would have been just as excited. Now, though: not so much.

"I hate that I'm not there," I said to her. "Although I'd probably be grounded anyway."

"Yeah, about that," she replied. "I have to admit, I'm kind

of impressed. The Emma I know won't even take a drink. Now you're getting pulled over by the police."

"It was security," I corrected her. "Which is *really* not the same thing."

"Still, very exciting," she told me. "The part about your cousin jumping out of the back of the truck . . . I mean, who does that?"

Calvanders, I thought, getting off my bed and walking over to the window. "I'm so stupid," I said. "If I just hadn't drunk . . ."

"He still would have freaked out, Emma," she said. "I mean, come on. Think about it. You weren't answering his calls or where you said you'd be."

"It made it worse, though," I said, thinking of Roo, his face in that bright light of Gator's flashlight.

She was quiet for a second. Then she said, "Have you heard from him at all? How did you guys leave things?"

Bridget was one of my two best friends for lots of reasons. But I especially loved that she knew what I was thinking, even when I didn't say it out loud.

"Not good," I said. "I know I should text him, but I'm so embarrassed. He must hate me."

"He doesn't hate you," she said automatically.

"Bridget. I almost got him arrested."

"*Almost*," she said, like this was hardly anything of note. "Not the same thing."

I watched a motorboat pass by, a girl with long hair

gripping the float as it bounced over a wake. Fun in the sun, all summer long. I sat back down on my made bed.

"Anyway," Bridget said now, "have you talked to Ryan? I can't get through to her except an occasional text. All she's thinking about is that show! And the *girl* in that show."

So there it was. "She told you," I said.

"After telling me she called you first!" She sighed again. "This is HUGE. And as the romance expert among us, it stings a little bit that I'm the last to know."

"Sorry," I said.

"I'll get over it. What's important," she continued, "is that she told us. I just hope this girl's good enough for her. If she's not, she'll hear from me."

I laughed. "I think Ryan can take care of herself."

"True." She thought for a moment. "Really, it's ironic. I was the one who was so sure this summer was going to be fabulous, full of amazing potential. And now you guys have romance for real, while I'm left standing, unkissed."

"I have a feeling you'll be fine in that department, though."

"Well, yes," she agreed. "But it better happen soon!"

I laughed. "I'm so happy for Ryan, though," I said, thinking of how she looked in the pictures she'd sent. "She's, like, giddy."

"No kidding. God, I feel so bad about all the times I dragged her along, trying to meet up with the twins. Assuming she'd want that."

"I feel the same way," I said. "Like we should have known or something."

"Ryan's always been private, until she decides not to be. And she told us when she was ready, which is all that matters."

It was true. I'd had two more top-of-mountain texts from her, and they were all about dress rehearsals and tech runs. There'd been a couple more pictures as well, of her hanging at camp with her castmates. Liz was beside her in every single one.

"Do you think they'll stay together when she's home?" I asked her.

"Long-distance? Oh, man. I don't know. Does that ever work?" she replied. "I mean, in the movies, summer romance tends to be location-specific."

I had a flash of Roo, then immediately pushed this thought away. We didn't have a relationship. And now, thanks to me, we never would. "My mom and dad remained a couple during the year," I pointed out.

"Yes, but they were only two hours apart. Ryan's dealing with entire states between her and Liz. It'll be a challenge." She was quiet for a minute. "But if it's meant to be, it will be. Things work out, that's what I'm saying. Look at Sam and me!"

"True," I said, choosing not to mention that right now what she had was an invitation, not a relationship. Which was still more than I could claim at the moment.

"Just promise," she said, "that even with all these new cousins and boys and everything else, you won't forget about me. When my time comes, you guys have to listen and be excited."

"I can't wait," I said. "I'll scream from the rooftops."

"Okay, that might be a bit much," she said, laughing.

"You think?"

"I'll let you know."

When I hung up, I looked at the digital clock on the bedside table: it was only ten a.m. Then again, I'd been awake since six, tossing and turning as I went over the events of the previous days. Normally I would have just slipped downstairs to walk over to the Larder for a copy of the *Bly County News* and a muffin. But I wasn't even allowed to do that. Because now, there were rules.

My dad had been clear: from now on, I couldn't go to North Lake. I couldn't go to the raft. Really, all I was allowed was to sit in the hotel room, which got boring quick. Which was why I'd found myself reorganizing my sparse belongings: folding and stacking shirts in my drawers, lining up my two pairs of shoes in the mostly empty closet, and making my bed the way Trinity had taught me, sheets pulled so tightly I could barely wedge myself beneath them.

It was in the midst of this routine—now repeated a few times—that I'd found the family tree I had begun my first day at Mimi's. I'd immediately sat down, flipping it open to read over the names that had once sounded like strangers, but were now as real to me as my own face. Now, I looked at those Calvanders, neatly organized on the page, then at my shoes, lined up against the wall, and shut the notebook again.

Suddenly there was a soft tapping on the other side of my

closed door. When I opened it, Nana was there, a *Bly County News* in her hand.

"Come have some food," she said, giving it to me. "I want to talk to you."

When I nodded, grateful, she smiled, pulling her lavender robe a bit more tightly around herself as she made her way down the hallway. There, on the table by the window, was her daily breakfast—already delivered and arranged by a Tides employee—as well as a plate of toast and butter for me. Lately it was all I'd been eating each morning, and of course she noticed.

"Thank you," I said, sliding into the chair beside her.

"You're more than welcome," she said. "I just feel like we haven't had a proper catch-up since . . . everything happened."

She was right: after the night of Taylor's party, I'd only left my room a handful of times, and each one I'd been so concerned about how my dad would react—not speaking to me, as it turned out—I hadn't had time to think about anyone else. Nana and Tracy had basically been tiptoeing together in the spaces between us, shooting me sympathetic looks he couldn't see. This also meant I hadn't formally apologized to her for causing all this trouble and tension, something I wanted to remedy now.

"I'm sorry," I told her as she poured coffee into a mug. "I know you hate conflict and seeing Dad upset. So this must be your worst nightmare."

She reached over, giving my hand a squeeze. "Don't you

worry about me, I'm fine. And your dad will be, too. He's just adapting. It's what we parents have to do, even when we aren't feeling up to it."

"I shouldn't have had those beers," I said, feeling embarrassed even saying these words in front of her. But I knew she was aware of the whole story. "I really let him down."

"Your father loves you so much," she said, pushing the plate of toast over to me. "He's always been overprotective because of what he went through with your mom. But you aren't Waverly, and he knows that. You just gave him a scare, is all."

This was classic Nana, the ability to break down anything to simple phrases that made sense and helped you feel better. She was like the original five sentences.

"I feel like I messed everything up," I said. "If I'd just waited a bit, he probably would have let me go back to Mimi's whenever I wanted."

"Maybe," she agreed. "But I think you're aware now that how your dad sees North Lake and how you do are very different things. For him, it was always just about your mother, her family, and her problems. He couldn't separate them. But you've had your own experience now, and redefined it accordingly. He's still looking with the same eyes. You have to remember that."

"So, what?" I asked. "I should try to show him it's not what he thinks?"

"Ideally, yes, that would be good," she said. "But I think we both know he might not be so fully open to it. Which is why even before this happened, I was thinking of ways to ease him into it."

I chewed my toast, which was delicious, as I tried to follow this. Then it hit me. "Oh, the dinner? Is that what you mean?"

She pointed at me, smiling. "Yes. It was my hope that by bringing Mimi and the rest over here to thank them for their hospitality, we could maybe begin a dialogue about something other than Waverly. A fresh start, as it were."

"And then I screwed it up," I said glumly. "I'm so stupid."

"Now, now." She dabbed at her mouth with her napkin, then folded it and put it back in her lap. "It's not too late."

I put down my toast. "You're going to invite them all over here, still? Really?"

"Well, yes," she said. "The planning will just require a bit more finesse, as we have to get your dad on board."

Immediately, I felt the wind go out of every sail in this plan. So to speak. "Yeah, well. Good luck with that. He hates them."

"Nonsense." There was an edge to her voice as she said this. "Your father doesn't hate anyone. He's just worried and frustrated."

"You're right," I said quietly.

"So," she continued, "what I'm thinking is we give him a bit of time. We could all use that, I think. So I've been looking at July thirteenth. Next Friday."

I raised my eyebrows. "Friday the thirteenth? Seriously?"

"Oh, now, don't be superstitious," she said. "By then

enough time will have passed since what happened between you and your dad for clearer heads to prevail. I've already spoken to the concierge about getting a table at the Club."

I wasn't surprised that Nana had thought things through to this extent. Her attention to detail was legendary. But it was one thing to design a good plan, another for everything to come together to make it work. Factor in several different people and personalities—and a dinner at the Club, no less—and disaster seemed even more possible, if not likely. But what was the other option? Sitting here in this suite stewing and angry until it was time to go home?

"I'm in," I said. "What can I do?"

She smiled. "For now, follow your dad's rules. Can you do that?"

"Yes." I nodded. "Thank you, Nana."

"Of course." She pointed at the *Bly County News*, which was next to my plate. "Now, tell me what you love so much about that paper. I glanced at your copy the other day and it seems to be nothing but ads and classified listings for boats."

"It's the obits, really," I said. "In the paper at home, there are at least eight to ten obituaries every day. Here, because it's smaller, usually they only run one or two. But they do a *lot* more In Memoriams, I've noticed."

"In Memoriams?"

I opened the paper. "They run on what would have been the person's birthday, or the anniversary of the day they died. They talk about how much they're missed and loved and all that. Like a letter to the beyond, but in the paper."

"Interesting," Nana said. "It's similar to lawsuit settlements, when you're often required to post terms in the classifieds. If it's in the public record, everyone sees it."

"Even the dead," I said.

"Even them."

As we sat there together, eating and reading in companionable silence, I thought of Mimi's kitchen, far across that water just outside the window, and my mornings there. It was possible I'd never get to wake up again to the smell of toast, arguments over butter, and a day of housekeeping ahead of me. But maybe I would. Even with all that had been taken from me, I still had time.

TWENTY-ONE

The one good thing about being in the same place all the time is that you're easy to find. Or, you know, call.

"How bad is it?" Bailey asked, skipping a hello. She'd been texting me nonstop since the night of Taylor's party, but I hadn't had the heart or energy to reply, so she'd been forced to reach out to me with an actual call. Which she hated. I was kind of touched, to be honest.

"Well, I'm grounded," I said. "I can't go anywhere."

"At least it's a nice place," she replied. "What else?"

"My dad is pissed. He's not talking to me. Still."

"Did you cry?"

"Yes. Didn't help."

"Damn." She sighed. "How long are you punished for?"

"He didn't say," I told her. Another loud exhale. "Is that bad?"

"Well, it's not good," she said. "Personally I prefer a date range for all my punishments at the time they are given. Otherwise extensions get tacked on again and again for even the smallest thing, and the next thing you know, you have no life whatsoever."

That was encouraging. I said, "My grandmother is trying to help, though. She wants to have you all over for dinner."

"Who's all of us?" she asked, sounding suspicious.

"Well," I said, "Mimi and Oxford, I guess, and you and Trinity. Celeste and Gordon and Jack."

"Is she thinking, like, a restaurant or something?"

"The Club, actually. She's looking at next Friday."

"The Club?" Now, I had her full attention. "Are you serious?"

"Yep," I said. "Do you think you all will come?"

"I'll be there," she said automatically. "Are you kidding? I've always wanted to eat at the Club. I hear they have specific forks just for oysters. Have you seen those yet?"

"I don't like oysters."

"Who cares? They're specific little forks just for ONE FOOD. I mean, what is that?" She laughed. "Oh, God, and what will I *wear*? And will we come by boat, or drive? Because if we come by boat, then I might see Colin, and—"

Hearing this name, I realized I'd been so caught up with my experience at Taylor's party I hadn't even thought of hers. Who was selfish now? "What's happening with Colin? Did you see him at the party?"

"Briefly," she replied, her voice coy. "I mean, it was kind of hard for us to talk with my drunk cousin about to be busted by her dad, but—"

"I'm sorry," I said.

"It's okay. I think me being busy was actually a good move. He, like, won't stop texting me."

"You're welcome."

She snorted. "I'm still mad at you for drinking. It's one thing for me to be messed up, but I didn't like seeing you that way. I need you compos mentis."

"You need me what, now?"

"Compos mentis," she repeated. "It's Latin. Means of sound mind."

"You took Latin?"

"Yeah, one semester," she said.

"Wow," I said, surprised.

"What? It's not easy for lake kids to get into a good college. We need all the credits we can get." So she was going to school, even if she never talked about it. I hated I'd just assumed otherwise. "Anyway, the point is you're not a party girl, Saylor. It doesn't suit you."

"No kidding." Just the thought of alcohol brought back a wave of shame that was hot and awful. "I've learned my lesson, don't worry. From now on I'll be the DD, every time."

"But first you have to, like, drive," she pointed out.

"Well, yes." By now, even getting behind the wheel sounded appealing compared to drinking. "I'm working on that. Or I was, before all this."

There was a chime sound, distant. "Oh, crap. That's Mimi, telling me to come do turnover. With you gone, I'm the last one standing. Or cleaning."

"I'd love to be doing that," I said wistfully. "I miss it."

"Are you crazy? You're at the Tides, for God's sake!"

"*Grounded* at the Tides," I reminded her.

"Which is still a million times better than wiping pubic hairs off a motel sink."

I cringed. "That was quite the visual."

"I know." Another chime. "God, I'm coming. I'll text you later. Reply this time, you hear? You know I hate talking on the phone." Then she hung up, again without a goodbye.

It was now two thirty, which gave me three hours until dinner. I was contemplating a nap, just to help the time pass, when my phone lit up again. This time, it was a HiThere! from a number I didn't recognize. Normally I would have ignored it, but what else was I doing? I hit ACCEPT.

There was that signature swooshing sound, and then a picture appeared. It was Trinity. Her belly, huge and rounded, took up all of the foreground.

"What is this I hear about you drinking?" she demanded. Did none of these Blackwood girls believe in greetings? "Are you crazy?"

"I made a mistake," I said, sighing.

"Damn right you did," she replied. "I expected more from you, honestly."

I wasn't sure if I should be flattered or ashamed by this scolding, considering not so long ago, she couldn't stand me. "I'm paying the price, believe me. I'm grounded until further notice."

"At the Tides," she said. "Boo-hoo. I'm here on the

porch, a million weeks pregnant with a fan on me and still sweating."

"What's the latest on the Sergeant?" I asked, wanting to get away from this tit-for-tat topic.

"Supposedly," she said, shifting slightly so that her belly eclipsed the entire screen, momentarily, "he is getting home on the eighteenth. Which is a week before my due date."

"That's great, Trinity," I told her.

"I'll believe it when I see it." She fanned her face with one hand. "At this point I honestly just want him here when the baby comes, even if he walks in the door when it's coming out of me."

I winced. "He'll be there."

"I hope you're right." She shifted again. "In the meantime, you need to come visit me. I need someone to paint my toenails."

"I'm grounded," I reminded her. "Maybe ask Gordon?"

She groaned. "Oh, God. No thanks. She's terrible with polish. Gets it everywhere. Besides, all she's doing is moping around since you left anyway. She's so pathetic Roo had her holding a ladder for him the other day."

I blinked. "A what?"

"I looked out there," she said, "and he's got her supporting the ladder while he climbs, like she's going to keep it steady or something. As if! She's ten. But you should have seen her face. You would have thought he'd trusted her with the world."

Ladder buddy, I thought, smiling. And in the next beat,

what Bailey had said: if you really want to know someone, look at what they do when they don't know you're watching. Oh, Gordon.

"She saw me," I said, remembering all over again. "When I was drunk. I feel awful about that."

"Yeah, well." Weirdly, I appreciated that she didn't tell me I shouldn't, or that it was okay. It wasn't. "It won't happen again."

"No," I said. "It won't."

We were both quiet for a moment, the only sounds the distant puttering of a motorboat and some kid shrieking from the beach.

"Just get back over here," Trinity said suddenly. "Okay? We need you. Or, my toenails do."

"I will," I promised. "And thanks."

"For what?"

Even though I'd been the one to say it, now I wasn't so sure how to answer this question. "Just being there."

"I'm bedridden," she reminded me. "Where else would I be?"

After hanging up, I walked back to the window. It was now three p.m., and the beach was crowded, almost every chair taken. Earlier, Tracy had invited me to go for a late afternoon swim with her at the pool, something I supposed she'd cleared with my dad. At the time, I'd said no. But Trinity and Bailey were right: this wasn't a bad place to be stuck at all. I went to look for my swimsuit.

I'd just put it on, and tied my hair back, when my phone

buzzed again. It was another number I didn't recognize, so at first I just ignored it, assuming it was a spam call. As it kept ringing, though, I got curious and answered it.

"Hello?"

"Good afternoon! My name is Chris and I'm calling from Defender Storm Shutter Solutions. How confident are you in your window protection?"

Nope, I thought, moving my finger to the END button. Just as I was about to push it, though, he spoke again, much more softly this time.

"Saylor. It's me."

I blinked, startled. "Who?"

"Roo."

Roo? I almost dropped the phone. "Oh, my gosh," I finally managed. "How are—"

He cleared his throat, then said loudly and confidently, "Well, then it's a good thing I called! For just a moment of your time, I can tell you why Defender Storm Shutters are the best choice for your home."

Slowly, I was starting to understand. "Hold on. You're selling storm shutters now?"

"Yes!" he said in that same loud, cheerful voice.

"What are you up to, now? Six jobs?"

In his normal voice, he said, "Actually, I'm back to four. Had to give up the airport job when they realized I'm not twenty-one. And then the Park Palms hired someone on salary for the overnight shift. I was panicking until I saw this open up."

Of course he was. "So now it's the Station, Conroy Market, Storm Shutters—"

"And the Yum truck," he finished for me. The next beat, he was back to his booming salesperson voice, saying, "Well, then, let me tell you about our in-house financing! With our easy payments and credit offer, you can focus on safety, not paying bills."

"Am I supposed to respond?" I asked.

"No," he said loudly. Then he added, in his normal voice, "I've been here since nine and have cold-called the entire list Juan gave me. Not one nibble. I think I suck at this?"

"Nobody buys anything over the phone," I told him.

"Clearly." I heard someone in the background, distant, say something. Returning to his big voice, Roo said, "Oh, no, ma'am, installation is simple! We do all the work so you can rest easy, knowing you and your home are protected."

"Let me guess," I said. "You're being watched."

"Yes!" he boomed. A pause. Then, in a normal tone, "Juan's a great guy. And he's paying me by the hour to sit here. He just passes through every now and—well, ma'am, of course! Our bonded installers will arrive at your home, do the work, and leave everything as they found it. No stress for you. Just peace of mind!"

"Sounds great," I said, trying to play along. "Unfortunately, I kind of live in a hotel now. So—"

"I heard you're grounded," he said, back to his regular voice.

"News travels fast."

"Well, I asked Bailey for your number," he explained. "I was worried about you."

Hearing this gave me a little twinge in my chest. He wasn't mad. He'd been thinking about me. "I'm so sorry," I said to him now. "I never meant to get you into trouble."

"You didn't," he replied, then added, "That's right, ma'am! I can easily run a credit check to find out if you qualify for our winter payoff plan. Get the shutters now, rest easy all year long!"

"You got pulled over by the police," I pointed out to him, once he'd finished.

"By Later Gator," he corrected me. "And I was sober as a judge. You, on the other hand, had reason to be worried. Your dad was *pissed*."

"No kidding. He's not speaking to me."

"Still?" He gave a low whistle. "Ouch."

"I know." Trying again, I said, "Seriously, though. I feel really bad. About you having to help take care of me, and Hannah getting upset—"

"It's not necessary!" he said, so loudly I had to pull the phone away from my ear. "We handle all removal and recycling, if pertinent, of your old shutters!"

"It's necessary for me," I continued, finally getting a rhythm between these two very different conversations. "You never signed up to be my caretaker."

"There was a sign-up period?" he asked, back to normal. All I could do was hope Juan would stay away for a bit, if only for my sanity. When I sighed, he said, "Look, Saylor. We're ladder and corsage buddies, remember? We help each other out."

"I didn't exactly help *you*."

"Well, I'll tell you what comes next!" Here we went again. "First, we'll set up a time convenient for you to have one of our trained sales teams come to your home for an estimate."

I waited.

"And at that time, we can also discuss the current specials we are running." His voice faded out on this last part, then he was back, speaking normally again. "You're helping me now. I have two hours of this left to go and I'm here all week, until Kenyatta comes back from Barbados."

"What?" All this back-and-forth, now with detail, was making my head swim.

"She's the normal cold caller," he explained. "I'm just filling in, which stinks because this is an inside job, in A/C, where I get to sit down all day. It's the best."

"Except for the whole selling window protection over the phone thing."

"Ma'am, I am glad you asked!" he replied. "All of our shutters are American-made, guaranteed, and come with a ten-year warranty."

I felt like at some point, I should play along. "Do you take checks?"

"No, we do not!" he boomed back in reply. "But your credit card or bank draft is more than welcome, and again, we do offer our Winter Payment Plan, for ease of mind. Okay, we're clear. Sorry about that."

The switch was so quick this time I almost didn't notice. I was still waiting for more details about the installment plan. "He's gone?"

"Went to the bank. Which gives us about ten minutes to talk about things other than shutters."

So here it was. I'd apologized—or tried to, he certainly hadn't made it easy, or accepted it—and now we had time, uninterrupted, to get out everything else that had been on my mind. Maybe, if I was really brave, I'd tell him I'd been missing him, and how often I replayed that moment on the night of Club Prom, when we'd almost gone from friends to something more. But when I spoke next, I was surprised to find it wasn't about any of these things.

"I miss the other side so much; I was only there three weeks," I said. "I can't imagine my mom just swearing it all off when her whole *life* was here. Why didn't she ever come back, except that once?"

He was quiet for a moment, considering this. Finally he said, "Well, I've heard a lot of theories over the years. But I think it had to do with the accident. I mean, would you come back?"

"Probably not," I said, looking again at the lake, so pretty and blue with the sun glinting off it. But the water had moods and moments, like everything else. I could understand how after something like that happened, you'd never see it the same way again. "I just don't know what's worse. Not having any idea of any of these stories or history before last month, or only learning some to have them taken away."

"The stories haven't gone anywhere," he pointed out. "They, like me, remain in convenient central North Lake."

I smiled. "True. So maybe I should ask you to tell the rest to me."

"What? Your mom's history?"

"Yeah." According to the clock, it was now three thirty: I was going swimming with Tracy at four. "Or at least, some of them. I mean, I have the album you lent me, but—"

"Pictures only tell half," he finished. "I had my mom to tell me the rest, what was going on in the pictures."

"Maybe I should talk to your mom."

"Maybe. Or, you could just talk to me. I mean, I do know that album by heart. At bedtime it was that and *Goodnight Moon*. Which I can also remember perfectly."

"Really," I said, getting up and walking over to my bureau, where I'd left the album in the back of a top drawer. I reached in, pulling it out, then sat down on the carpet. "So what's the first picture?"

"Shot of my dad as a kid in footie pajamas," he replied. "They have yellow ducks on them."

I opened the album to look: he was right. He and his dad had the same face, those blue eyes and white-blond hair. "And the story?"

"My dad was an only child," he said. "Grandparents had him late in life, after they thought they could never have kids. And he was *wild*, full of energy, always keeping them running. See that guy in the background, on the plaid sofa?"

I hadn't before, too focused on the cute baby to notice.

Now, I looked, saying, "Yeah."

"That's my grandfather. He was about fifty in that picture."

I studied it again. The man had white hair, his face tired. "Really? He looks much older."

"Exactly. Takeaway: my dad aged people, he was so exhausting."

"*That's* how the album of stories begins?"

"Yep. I guess it was both history and, for me, a subtle warning." He laughed. "Now, see, after that there are, I think, a bunch more of my dad as a kid. School pictures, holding up a fish, at Halloween dressed like a Ninja Turtle . . ."

I was following along as he spoke, running a finger over each of these. "Impressive."

". . . until finally, on the top of page two," he said, "we have the arrival of Waverly Calvander. They met at summer day camp at Church of the Lamb, just after kindergarten."

I turned to that page, finding the picture. Chris and my mom were in the center of a group of about six kids standing on a dock. Everyone was wearing LAMB CAMP T-shirts, and he and a few others were smiling. My mom, however, held her mouth in a thin line, clearly displeased.

"She looks mad," I observed.

"She hated camp," he told me. "Too many rules. I don't think she even lasted the summer."

I zeroed in more closely, taking in every feature I could. My mom's bangs, blowing slightly sideways. The rope bracelet around one wrist. How adult she seemed, in comparison with the rest of the kids, like she'd discovered something they wouldn't for many years. And without Roo's voice in my ear, that would have been me, as well: I'd have the image, but as he said, that was only half. And I'd had enough of bits and pieces.

"Okay, so below that," he said now, "like, two or three rows and to the right? That's them on the Fourth of July with Celeste. It was my dad's first time over to Mimi's: she's the one who took the picture."

My mom wasn't smiling in this shot, but she didn't look openly hostile, either. She had on a jumper and sandals with little block heels, one arm thrown around Celeste, who was looking off to one side, her mouth open as she was saying something. Chris, excited, was holding a lit sparkler out to the camera, sparks falling off it. I recognized that same clump of gardenia bushes behind them.

"Your dad looks fiendish with that sparkler," I said.

"Good catch. He loved blowing things up and the Fourth. Later it was him who organized the fireworks out at the raft every year," he replied. "In fact, if you turn to the next page, on the right—yes, ma'am, that's correct! We're based in convenient North Lake, a quick trip to all of Bly County, and we offer a wide variety and price range of both hurricane and storm shutters."

Juan was back. I looked back at the picture, the goofy way my mom hung on her sister, hamming it up. I'd never known her to be silly. I guess by the time I came along, there was a lot less to laugh about.

Outside in the suite, I could now hear voices: my dad and Tracy were back from whatever outing they'd taken, and soon enough I'd need to go on that swim. But for now, with Roo still reciting his cold-call points in my ear, I studied the other shots on the page. My mom and Chris on the back of a tube, in life jackets. At the table at Mimi's, eating hot dogs with Celeste and another boy around the same age whose features looked a lot like Trinity, Bailey, and Jack.

". . . of course, I'd be happy to follow up with some more information when it's more convenient to talk," Roo was saying now. "I'll just take down your info and be back in touch. Will that work?"

Yes, I thought, although I stayed silent. At least until he stopped talking in that voice, his normal tone filling my ear. "You still there?" he asked.

"For a minute," I said. Which I hoped was long enough. "Can you tell me another one?"

That was how it started. The calls, and the stories. Before I knew it, I'd gone from watching the clock all day to watching my phone. Because every time it rang, there was a chance for a bit more connection with Roo, as well as everything I'd left on the other side. His voice was the conduit. All I had to do was listen.

"Top of page, three or four over," he said that evening, after I'd slipped out early from dinner at the Tides restaurant and come home while my parents and Nana shared a nightcap. "Middle school dance. Also known as the only time your mom and my dad ever tried to be more than friends."

Everything about the picture screamed awkward. First, there was the stiff button-down Chris Price was wearing that made him look like a kid playing dress-up. My mom, in a periwinkle dress with spaghetti straps, her hair loose over her shoulders, seemed years older and, solely by the twisty smile on her face, like she might be trouble. They were standing side by side outside of Mimi's house, not touching.

"It looks like a date."

"Mom always said my dad called it the worst one ever," he replied. He was in the arcade at Blackwood Station: in the background, I heard a siren, which meant someone had won from the bonus ticket machine. "Picture it. Eighth grade. Since Celeste and Silas had paired up the year before, they thought maybe they were meant to do the same. But it felt weird and they bickered all night except for one kiss, which was disappointing for everyone involved. So that was that."

"Makes me wonder if you ever thought about dating Bailey," I said. I couldn't imagine it, but I also didn't want to.

"No." He replied so quickly, and flatly, I was reassured. "Her brother would have killed me. Also, there's Vincent. Who has been hooked on her since middle school."

So it was true. "I *thought* he was into her!"

"He's obsessed." I heard a cash register beep: he'd told me his main job was making change for the arcade. "Unfortunately, he's also too scared to let her know or make a move. It's like watching paint dry, but more frustrating."

"I bet he'd be a great boyfriend," I said.

"Yeah? Maybe you should date him."

Hearing this, I had to think how to respond. Was he kidding? Trying to find out more information? Finally I said, "He's sweet. But not my type."

"No?" he asked. The siren went off again. "And what's that, exactly? Yacht club guys?"

"No," I said. "I got set up with Blake because of Bailey. Left to my own devices, I'd choose differently."

"You would? Like how?"

"I can't say exactly," I said, running my finger around the edge of the picture we'd been talking about. "But when you know, you know."

"Well, that's frustratingly vague," he replied.

I grinned, sitting back against my bedroom door with my legs stretched out in front of me. "But it's like my mom and dad, right? She didn't know what her type was until he showed up. We're not to that part of the album yet."

"But there aren't any pictures of her with your dad in there," he pointed out. "I know it by heart, remember?"

"True. I'm speaking of it in a larger sense."

"The big album in the sky," he said, clarifying.

"No," I said, stifling a snort, "just that, like history, it's ongoing. Just because the pictures stop doesn't mean the story does."

He was quiet, long enough that I wondered if we'd been cut off. Then he said, "You're right. I guess we all have those invisible pages, so to speak."

"Exactly," I said. "Like, say, for you, there will be shots

from in college, you working on the paper there, thanks to all those hours working at Defender and every other place in town."

I swore, I could hear him smile at this. "You think?"

"Sure," I said. "And Bailey's pictures will have her, like, running the Tides or something after college. And Trinity pushing her baby across a different campus, when *she* gets back to school."

"You've thought about this," he observed.

"It just makes sense, right?" I said. "A life isn't just the pages you know, it's everything. We just can't see what's happened yet."

Somewhere near him at the Station, there was a burst of laughter, loud and sudden. When it died down, he said, "Okay, then. What's your picture?"

"Of what?"

"The future," he replied. "What's the rest of your story?"

I thought for a second. What did I see, or want to see, ahead? "Something having to do with this place," I said finally. "Proof that it's not over, that I'll come back. That's what I want."

He was quiet again. But this time I could hear him, just there on the other end of the line. "Well, for what it's worth, nobody here's forgetting you."

I felt my face flush. It wasn't nobody I was worried about. "I hope you're right," I said. "Now, tell me more about this picture and that terrible kiss."

Just as he was about to launch into the story, though, I

heard a knock on my door. I scooted aside so it could open and my dad stuck his head in. "Hey," he said. "You busy?"

"Um," I said, gesturing at the phone at my ear. "Kind of. What do you need?"

"Just thought we could take a walk," he replied. "Five minutes?"

I nodded. "Sure."

He gave me a thumbs-up, then shut the door again. Slightly stunned, I said, "My dad wants to take a walk."

"So he's talking to you now?"

"Apparently," I said, still wary. "I wonder what he wants to discuss."

"Talking is good either way," he said. "But mark our place, okay? Up next is some good stuff, including but not limited to when your mom and my dad became obsessed with the California look and tried to lighten his hair."

I couldn't help it: I flipped ahead until I found a shot of Chris sitting in a chair, a towel around his neck and his head over the sink while my mom was shaking up a plastic bottle. I recognized a framed needlepoint by the sink that CLEAN UP AFTER YOURSELF: it was still in Mimi's bathroom. "Was it bad?"

"Awful," he told me. "You'll love it. Bye, Saylor."

"Bye," I said. But even after he hung up, I kept my phone where it was for another second of connection between us. Then I put it down, turning back to the album.

I grabbed all the pages that were left, turning them all in one motion to the back cover opposite that final one. If there was more room, how would this story go on?

In that moment, I hoped to see my dad and me together, side by side, talking. Beyond that, who knew. I closed the book and went to find him.

At first, it was awkward. So we started walking.

"I've been meaning to explore around here a bit," my dad said as we left the front entrance of the Tides and started toward the main road. "I bet a lot has changed in nineteen years."

"It's been that long?" I asked.

"Since I was on this side, yes," he replied as a BMW with tinted windows drove past us, barely making a sound. "When we came back with you that summer, we only went to Mimi's. And left quickly, as I remember."

This seemed like an opening. "The second honeymoon didn't take, right?"

"Nope," he said, wiping his brow. Even though it was dark, it was still hot. "Truthfully, I think we both knew things weren't salvageable at that point."

"But you went to Vegas anyway?"

He shrugged. "Well, yeah. I mean, I loved your mom so much. I wanted it to work. It just . . . didn't."

"Roo's been telling me some stories," I said quietly, hoping it wasn't too risky to mention his name. "About Mom and his dad, growing up here."

"Hmm," he said. I wasn't sure what that meant. "They were very close."

"You met him, right?" I asked. "Chris Price?"

"Oh, yeah," he replied. We were across from the Tides now, heading toward Campus, which I could see up ahead. "We all met the same night, actually. At a party on the raft."

"Our raft?" I said.

He looked at me, amused. "Well, we considered it *ours*, but yes. The very same."

"You guys had parties out there?"

"Yep," he said, nodding. "It was the gathering place back then too, especially in the evenings. Tons of boats, tied together, and everyone moving between them."

I would have bet the rest of my grounding there was beer there, too. Not that I felt I could say this out loud.

"How did you guys meet?" I asked.

He gave me a sideways look. "We didn't come here to talk about your mom and me."

"I don't know why we came here," I replied. "You're the one who invited me."

"True," he said mildly. We walked a little farther, until Campus, its low block buildings dotted with chairs heaped with towels, was right beside us. He stopped, looking at it, then said, "My unit was around back. Should we try to find it?"

I looked at the buildings, wondering who I might run into. Then again, it was better than being in the suite. "Sure."

He stepped up onto the grass and I followed him, crossing over to the first building. The door to Blake and Colin's place was closed, but Hannah and Rachel's was ajar, and I could see someone's feet up on the bed as we passed by. Then my dad turned down the short hall by the laundry and bulletin board where Blake had taken me all those nights ago.

"See, the back rooms were better," he explained as we popped out on that side and started passing doors. "More shade, so they weren't as hot."

"There's A/C now, though," I said, pointing at one.

"Ha! These kids don't know how good they have it," he said. "We melted all summer, every summer. Let's see . . . here it is. Fourteen."

It was the last door of the building, no chair or towels marking it. Just a single-bulb light, bugs circling it, and the strong sound of peepers coming from the nearby woods. This close up, they were deafening.

"Guess a tour is out of the question," my dad said, peering in the one, dark window. "But man, do you hear those frogs? Those first few nights, I couldn't sleep it was so loud. By the end of the summer, though, I didn't even notice them. It's funny what you can get used to."

"It is," I agreed, just as I heard footsteps on the other end of the walkway. By the time I looked, though, a door was just shutting, whoever it was having slipped inside.

"There used to be a wall," he said, glancing back down the way we'd come. "Everyone signed it, every summer. I wonder—"

"It's over here," I told him, walking around the corner.

"You know about the wall?" he asked.

Whoops. "Um, Bailey had to run over here one time for work. I rode along and she showed me."

He followed me until he was facing the wall himself. "Wow," he said, looking up at all the names. "Now it really doesn't feel like nineteen years."

There was a sudden hiss, followed by a popping sound, from somewhere in the neighborhood to our right. Fireworks. The Fourth wasn't until the next day, but everyone always started early.

"Did you—" I began to ask, but already he'd stepped up closer to the cinder block, squinting at all the names there. After a moment, he moved his hand over to the right, and down a bit, holding his finger to one small spot.

"Right here." He pushed his glasses up, squinting through them. "Your mom signed right below, even though she technically wasn't supposed to."

I moved closer as well, and he stepped aside, making room, his finger still holding the place. MATT PAYNE, SUMMER 1999, it said in black Sharpie in the same neat, block printing he still used for shopping lists and the notes he left for me. Underneath, smaller and scrawled: just WAVERLY, a chubby heart with an arrow through it right above. Both looked so clear in front of my eyes, but I knew I never would have found them alone.

"It must have been a lot of fun, working here," I said.

"It was." He dropped his hand, but kept looking at the spot. Then, suddenly, he said, "Emma, I'm not trying to ruin your life, even if you think I am. You know that, right?"

"Yeah," I said. "I do."

He turned, facing me. "Do you know how much you

scared me the other night? When I was calling and couldn't find you? It just brought so much back, all those nights with your mom when she disappeared. . . ."

"I didn't know that! I wasn't here in nineteen ninety-nine; I don't know all these stories."

"But you *did* know your mom, and are old enough to remember what she put us through when she was using."

"I had a couple of beers!" I cried, frustrated. "It's not the same."

"It's how it starts!" he shot back. Then, lowering his voice, he said, "Look, Emma. You have to be vigilant. We both do. There's a history there."

"I'm not going to do what she did, though."

"You don't know that!" he said. "You're seventeen. We don't know anything except what's already happened. The only thing we can do is prevent it from happening again."

"You make it sound like it's inevitable," I replied. "Maybe I'm different."

"Oh, honey." He looked so pained, stepping closer to me and taking hold of both my arms. "You are different. So different. But being here, especially on the other side, hanging out with those kids . . . we can't tempt fate. It's too dangerous."

"Roo's nice, Dad."

"I'm sure he is." He dropped his hands. "I just . . . I feel like you've been through so much. The divorce, then losing your mom. And you're great, you're perfect. I just want to be sure you stay that way."

"I'm not perfect, though. Nobody is." That would be true even if I'd never laid a foot in North Lake again. "And anyway, what about you? Were *you* perfect back then? Did you make all the right choices?"

"Me? God, no." He sighed. "I was young and stupid. But I didn't have a parent who was an addict. You do. It's an added responsibility."

"One I don't want," I grumbled. We were quiet for a second. Then I said, "So what did you do?"

"When?" he asked.

"When you were young and stupid."

He looked at me as if I was kidding. When it was clear I wasn't, he said, "We don't really need to get into that, do we?"

I shrugged. "I don't know. Stories help sometimes. That's something I've learned this summer."

"You want to hear my irresponsible stories," he said.

"I want to know what you went through," I said. "I know all about Mom. But not you."

There was another pop. We both looked up to see a firework shooting up above the trees, then split into a shower of sparks. Somewhere, a dog started barking.

"Give me some time, okay?" he said finally. "I'll work up to it. Or try to. Is that fair?"

I nodded. "Yeah."

Now, he smiled. Would this really happen? Time would tell. "We should probably get out of here," he said. "Don't want Later Gator to show up because someone reported a couple of prowlers."

I looked at him, surprised. "*You* know they call him Later Gator?"

He gave me a grin. "I'll explain another time."

Back out at the road, it was fully dark now, the Tides all lit up as well as the Club beside it. I could hear another pop as we crossed the street, but this time I didn't turn around to look. "Fourth is tomorrow," he observed. "The Club's having a cookout on the beach, followed by fireworks. You up for going?"

"Can I?"

"Tracy and I are," he said. "I think Nana will probably watch from the room."

"I'd love it," I told him.

He looked at me then, seeming surprised. "Great. I'll let the Club know. We'll have a nice family evening."

I nodded, just as we approached the main doors of the hotel. "Welcome to the Tides!" someone yelled as we came inside, the A/C feeling freezing after the humid night. Glimpsing the lake out the windows, I looked for the raft, trying to picture my mom and dad, just a little older than me, riding out on a similar night to meet cute on the water. I never had gotten the whole story out of him, but I knew how it ended. Us together, two instead of three, stepping into another elevator on a different night, this one.

TWENTY-TWO

"More toast?" Nana asked me, breaking the silence that we'd sat in together for the last half hour or so with our respective breakfasts and papers.

"I'm fine," I told her. "But thanks."

She dabbed her mouth with her napkin, moving her coffee cup to one side. "I heard you and your dad come in last night. It sounded like you were actually talking."

I nodded. "Yeah. We went for a walk and worked some stuff out."

"I'm glad to hear it," she said, giving me a smile. "In other news, the dinner is coming together nicely. I've got us a reservation at the Club for next Friday at six p.m. Large table, so we can invite whoever we like."

"It's really happening?" I asked, surprised.

"What's happening?" I heard my dad say as he came down the hallway from his suite in his trunks, carrying his goggles. An all-state swimmer in college, he'd begun starting every day with a dive off the dock, followed by a quick mile, before breakfast.

I looked at Nana, who said, "Oh, well, Emma and I were just talking about this dinner I want to plan with the Calvanders."

My dad, who had started to peel his banana, now stopped, looking at her. "The Calvanders? You mean Mimi and Joe?"

"Joe died," I reminded him. "Oxford is her husband now."

Nana said, "I was thinking Mimi and her husband, yes, and Celeste and hers, and then the kids. Maybe one or two of Emma's other friends, too, if they were free."

"Mother." He was still holding the banana. "Emma is grounded."

"And this is happening Friday, at which point I was thinking you may have revisited that issue." She picked up a napkin, holding it out to him, even though from what I could tell, the banana was barely messy. Nice touch. "Of course, if you feel strongly, then I can cancel the reservation. I just thought that after they had Emma all that time, it would be a good gesture."

"It is," he agreed. "But I'm not sure a Club dinner is the best way to express our gratitude. It might make them . . . uncomfortable."

"Not Bailey," I said. I couldn't help myself. "She's already excited about the oyster forks."

They both looked at me. Dad said, "Excuse me?"

"She's always wanted to eat at the Club. It's, like, her dream."

"Well." Nana smiled. "Now we're making dreams come true. That's nice!"

"Mother, maybe you and I should discuss this privately," my dad said, putting the napkin back on the table. "We certainly don't want to invite someone to something that will be stressful for them."

"The girl is excited about the forks," Nana pointed out.

"Maybe it would be better if I offered to do something at their place," my dad said. "On the beach, say. I could find a caterer, and—"

"Or," Nana said, "we could leave it all to the Club and just show up. That sounds easier, doesn't it?"

My dad did not look convinced. But instead of saying so, he looked at me. "So. Think you'll be leaving the suite today?"

I was confused. "I'm grounded."

"Yes, but that doesn't mean you have to sit in your room all day long," he said. "Tracy says there's a band you might like playing at the Pavilion for the Fourth."

More confusion. "I can go to the Pavilion?"

"Yes," he said, and while it was all I could do not to get to my feet right that second, before he changed his mind, I resisted. "But there are ground rules. Number one, you will stay on Tides or Club property. And if at any point I can't reach you, then you *will* be inside until we leave. Are we clear?"

"Crystal," I said. Across the table, Nana had her eyes on me. "Thanks, Dad."

He nodded, and then I did get up, thanking Nana as well as I pushed in my chair, then headed back to my room. The last thing I saw before going inside was him sitting down, then speaking in a lowered voice to my grandmother, who said something quietly in return. Probably better I wasn't there anyway. Nana worked best on her own.

In my room, I put on my bathing suit, then a sundress, before digging my flip-flops out from the closet. Through the window, I could see the Club attendants down on the sand, distributing towels to the chairs. It was only just after eight a.m., but I figured I should go while I had the chance, as there was no telling when my dad might change his mind.

Both he and Nana were gone when I came back through the living room, their plates being cleared by a woman in a Tides Golf shirt and a black skirt. "Happy Fourth of July," she said as I slipped past to the door.

"To you, too," I told her. Outside, a cleaning cart was parked by the elevators, and I looked it over, thinking of the rickety ones back at Calvander's, which usually sported at least one loose, wobbling wheel. This one might as well have been a sports car, chrome and sleek. Linens were folded below, toiletries and room supplies above, everything separated into neat, labeled categories. The spray bottles had Tides logos, but no names.

Downstairs, out on the back patio, I slipped on my sunglasses, then looked around, getting my bearings, before starting out to the pool. I was scoping out the perfect chair when I heard someone call my name. I turned around to see Colin and Blake heading down to the Club dock via a walkway that was right behind me. Great.

"Heard you were staying here," Colin said, clearly oblivious to the fact that I outright disliked him. Blake, behind him, remained silent, making me think he was still annoyed from the night of the party.

"Yep," I said mildly. All I wanted was to get away from them.

"Well, Fourth of July means it's going to be nuts. And that's not even counting the fireworks tonight. You going to the cookout?" Colin asked.

I nodded. "I got sprung, finally. Been grounded in the room for the last few days."

"Well, we're having a door party at Campus after the fireworks, if you want to come. Kind of a tradition."

"What's a door party?"

"Like bar golf, but with rooms, basically," he replied. "Different drinks in each room. There's a scorecard. Hit them all, get a prize."

"What's the prize?"

"Being wasted," Blake said, finally joining in the conversation. "And bragging rights."

"Yeah, I can't see that happening," I said as a man in madras shorts and a pink shirt passed by, talking into his phone in an irritated voice. "Drinking and parties is what got me grounded in the first place. I kind of have to lay low."

"Oh, right," Colin said. "Well, there's also this great band at the Pavilion midday. Spinnerbait. Should be fun. You heard of them?"

I shook my head. "Nope. My stepmother mentioned it, though."

"They play all the time at East U. You'll like them." He said this so confidently, like he knew me well, that I decided right then that I wouldn't. "You know if Bailey's coming?"

I just looked at him. So that explained the friendliness. "No."

"Well, if she does, you guys should come by the docks," he said. "Say hello."

"Better hop," Blake said to Colin, nodding at a motor-boat that was approaching the docks. "We were supposed to be on two minutes ago."

"Right," he replied. To me he said, "Good seeing you, Saylor."

"You, too."

Blake didn't say anything as they headed down the walkway, now at a faster clip, to meet the boat that had just arrived. Jerks, I thought, just as my phone rang. It was the toll-free number I'd come to recognize, and I smiled before I even answered it.

"Good morning, ma'am! My name is Chris and I'm calling to talk about your home's defense against the coming storm season. Do you have a moment?"

"I do," I said, settling into a beach chair I'd picked and stretching out my legs. "Go right ahead."

"Perfect! Well, I'll begin by telling you a little bit about . . . okay, sorry about that. We're only open for a half day today for the holiday, but Juan still thinks someone sitting home feeling patriotic might bite."

"Could happen," I said, pulling some sunblock out of my bag. "So only half a day, huh? Are you off too, or just going to another job?"

"Driving the Yum truck around all the beaches until five," he said. "Then I promised Silas I'd come by the Station for backup in case he needs it before the fireworks start. But *then*, I am free and clear."

"Which will be when? Like, ten or so?"

"Probably," he said, and I laughed. "But still, it's something. Which is good because everyone knows the Fourth is my favorite holiday."

"Just like your dad, huh?"

"You remembered," he said. I remember everything, I wanted to say. "Yeah. My mom always talked about how much he loved the fireworks. The Fourth was one of the times we always remembered him, with the whole sparkler thing."

"What sparkler thing?"

"You haven't heard about that?" he asked. Then, before I could reply, he said, "Well, I guess you wouldn't have. It's kind of a lake thing."

So many lake things. Even if I'd had a whole summer, I was pretty sure I wouldn't learn them all.

"When my dad died, my grandparents planned the

whole funeral," Roo explained as I hoped against hope Juan was gone on a long errand this time. I wanted to hear this. "Church service, very formal and sad. But my mom felt like it didn't capture him as he really was, you know. So that evening, she had a service of her own."

"With sparklers?"

"Hundreds of them," he said. "She, Silas, Celeste, and Waverly bought every box they could find in the entire county. When people arrived, they got a handful and some matches. Then, after everyone said what they wanted to, they lit them all at the same time."

"Wow."

"I know." He was quiet a second: I could hear buzzing on the phone line between us. "The thing about sparklers? They're cool but quick. You light them, they go like crazy, and then it's all over. So it always seemed fitting to me, you know, that they did that for my dad. A big life lived, gone too soon. That sort of thing."

I was quiet for a moment. Then I said, "Like my mom, too."

"Well . . . yeah," he said. "After she passed, they did it again. Same beach, same crowd. And every Fourth since, that I can remember anyway."

"Sparklers."

"Yep. All year we buy them up wherever we see them. It's one of our few family traditions."

Out by the pool, the sun was growing stronger, people arriving to the chairs around me with their beach bags and floats. "I was already sad I was missing the fireworks with you guys," I said quietly. "Now I'd give anything to be there."

"You will be, in spirit," he said. "And if you're watching from the Tides, you'll probably see it. Hard to miss, especially if you know when to look."

"Which is . . ."

"At the very end, when the last big blasts are over," he finished for me.

I pulled my legs up to my chest. "I'll be watching," I told him. "And Roo?"

"Yeah?"

"Thanks."

"For what?" he asked.

"For the stories. And the album. And just calling."

"Don't thank me, it's mutual," he said. "I'd go nuts if this was seriously about windows all day long."

I smiled. "I will listen anytime."

"I appreciate that," he said. We were both quiet a second. "So, look. When you're free to come and go as you please—"

"If," I corrected him.

"When," he repeated, "do you think you might want to . . . well, I'm glad you asked! Once we run the credit check, we'll go ahead and set you up for a visit by one of our knowledgeable, bonded technicians. They'll take measurements, then discuss the best options for protection of your home, at which point . . ."

He kept talking, but I couldn't think about windows. I couldn't think about anything but those words he had been saying, leading to what I thought was a question, now unasked. Would I what? Want to buy storm protection? Light sparklers together? Or something else?

Just then, there was a burst of feedback from the Pavilion and Tracy appeared, now in her own swimsuit, to take the beach chair next to me. In between covering my ears and greeting her, I lost Roo. Sadly, with this job he could only call out. I'd have to wait. And I knew I would.

It was around six, as I walked across the lobby with Tracy and Dad, headed to the cookout on the beach, when the concierge called out to us. "Mr. Payne?"

My dad stopped, looking over at the desk. "Yes?"

"Something was left for you earlier," he said, reaching under the counter to pull out a small brown bag. "Or, for Saylor?"

"Emma?" he said.

The concierge looked at the bag, then back at us. "Perhaps I misunderstood? This says Saylor Payne, but . . ."

"That's me," I told him, stepping forward.

He handed me the bag. "Have a wonderful evening."

I thanked him, taking it, then carefully opened the flap. Inside was a box of sparklers and a pack of matches. I smiled.

"What is it?" Tracy asked. My dad, suspicious, was watching me, too.

"Nothing," I told them, dropping it into my purse. "Let's go."

We did, out to our reserved spot on the sand, where three chairs, an ice bucket with beverages, and a full view of the lake awaited us. As we sat and ate, I tried to focus on my dad, happily devouring a burger and fries from the plate on his lap, and Tracy, who was telling a series of honeymoon sailing stories.

Finally, after the ice cream sandwiches were served and the anthem played, the fireworks began. Set off from a Tides boat anchored near the raft, they were gorgeous and loud, with color exploding across the dark sky and reflecting in the water. All around me, people oohed and aahed, waiting for the next big burst. After the extended, no-holds-barred finale, everyone applauded.

But as my dad gathered up our trash, and people began dragging their tired, sugar-filled kids back to the hotel, I walked the other way, down the shoreline until I could see, distantly, Mimi's dock and beach.

"Emma? You coming?" my dad called out.

"I'll be there in a sec," I replied, then pulled out my box and the matches, getting a sparkler ready. I was worried the wind would blow out the flame, or it wouldn't catch at all. But as I saw the lights appear on that beach, shimmering and sudden, I dipped the tip of my own offering into the flame and watched it spark for all those big lives lived, gone too soon, and all the unanswered questions. I let it burn all the way down.

TWENTY-THREE

Finally, it was the day of the Club dinner. I was nervous and excited, but all anyone could talk about was the tropical storm that was supposed to hit the coast that evening before heading our way. While what it would do then was anyone's guess, everyone had an opinion.

There was the *Bly County News*, which ran pictures of destruction and damage from other storms, including Richard, which had taken out Mimi's dock two years earlier. The TV anchors had gone from occasionally breaking into programming to taking over the air entirely with footage and discussion of preparations, even though nothing had even happened yet. At the Tides, though, no one seemed concerned.

"There's absolutely no need to worry," I overhead the concierge saying to a woman in a brightly colored caftan and a straw hat that morning. "The Tides was built with more storm protection than any other structure on the lake. You could not be in a safer place."

This was the party line, clearly, as I heard it repeated multiple times before breakfast, including from my dad, who had talked to the hotel's general manager on his way back from his daily swim.

"Some tracking models have it not even coming this way," he assured us. "The dinner should go on as scheduled, no problem."

"Well, that's good," Nana replied, turning a page of her *Times*. "With all the planning for the menu and coordinating schedules, I'd hate for the weather to force us to cancel."

"You won't be able to keep Bailey away even if the Club is the only thing left standing," I told her. "She won't miss those forks for *anything*."

"Good," she replied, sipping her coffee. "Because I had them put oysters on our menu just for her."

This I couldn't wait to share. Did Bailey even like oysters? Did it really matter?

"Speaking of the dinner," Nana continued as I perused the day's obits, which consisted of one passing (Marlene Ficus, 55, after a brave fight against ovarian cancer) as well as an In Memoriam (John Davers, gone now five years, and missed greatly since he's been up in heaven), "I'm confirming the numbers this morning at nine. Did you hear from your friend?"

That would be Roo, who she'd told me to invite after asking who I'd been chatting with on the phone so regularly. Nana had never been one to miss much, but I was really glad this time she'd been paying attention.

"He says he'll be there," I said.

"Who's this?" my dad, chewing, asked.

I paused, hesitant. "Roo Price."

"Wait, he's coming to the dinner? After what happened at the party?"

"That was not his fault, remember?" I said.

"I thought this was a dinner for Mimi and her family."

"To thank them for all they've done for Emma this summer, yes," Nana said. "It sounded like this boy was part of that, so I said to include him. Is that a problem?"

Instead of answering her, my dad looked at me as if I was up to something. Which was so not fair, because I had followed his rules completely, not leaving the Tides except for short nearby outings, usually with him or Tracy. In fact, the only contact I'd had with the other side of the lake, other than my calls with Roo, hadn't even really been contact at all.

It had been a couple of days earlier when, after a particularly slow shift at Defender, Roo and I finally made our way through the entire photo album. Even though we'd been through so many pictures and stories from the first page to the last, I'd gotten used to there being another one to turn, one more reason for us to keep talking. I wanted it to keep going, like that big album in the sky we'd discussed. The final picture was him at the Station by the pumps, grinning, in a Blackwood T-shirt. The end.

"And now you're all caught up," he said as I sat there with the album on the bed in front of me. Outside, I could hear kids in the pool, playing Marco Polo. "You know as much as I do."

Which did not explain why I felt such a loss. I swallowed, then said, "I need to return it to you. Although I'm not sure how to get it over there."

"Don't even think about it," he said. "The last thing I need is you in trouble again because of me. Just bring it to the dinner."

The album meant so much to me, though: I could only imagine he felt the same way, even if he knew it by heart. Also, I didn't want to have to explain it to my dad or anyone else. "How about this. I'll leave it at the desk, like you did with the sparklers."

"Saylor. You really don't have to do that."

"I want to," I said. "I'll take it down right now. And then when you pick it up—"

"I will grab it and run before I bump into your dad," he finished for me.

"I was going to say I'd meet you in the lobby."

"No way." He was firm. "I'll see you at the dinner, when it's authorized. Until then, it's just the—Yes, ma'am, we do offer a ten-year guarantee on any work we do as well as all windows!"

And that was that. Now that the storm was building, suddenly people were very interested in home window protection. The phones were ringing so constantly that Roo was kept on even after Kenyatta returned from Barbados. He'd been so busy, in fact, that we'd barely talked other than him letting me know he got the album and confirming the dinner that night. But all that mattered was that I would finally see him.

"Well, it should be a nice evening," my dad said now as I got up, folding my paper. "Six, right?"

"That's right," Nana said. "We'll have a lovely time."

I hoped she was right. I had so much riding on this dinner, if only as a way to bring these two sides of the family, and the lake, together. Would drinks, appetizers, a salad, entrees, then dessert and coffee be enough to start to mend the tear of my mom's problems, the divorce, and the past? Maybe with oysters, and special forks, the answer was yes.

"I don't know," Bailey said about an hour later, as I put on my bathing suit to go down to the pool with Tracy. "I have a bad feeling."

"What?" Everyone on my end had been so positive, I was surprised. "Why?"

"This storm is a *lot* like Richard," she replied. "Same path in the Atlantic, same general size, same place it's supposed to come in. And it almost leveled us."

"But here at the Tides, they're saying it's nothing."

"They don't know anything!" She sighed. "That place was still under construction two years ago, and most of the people there aren't from the lake anyway. I've been watching my dad, and he's worried. So I'm really worried."

I got chill bumps suddenly, springing up along my arms. "Really?"

"Yep." She was quiet for a moment. "Listen to me, okay? Don't wait for them to tell you guys to take cover. Do it when the sky starts to darken. Get low and inside and away from doorways and windows."

I looked outside again. It was sunny and bright, with a breeze that was ruffling the awnings of the restaurant downstairs. Motorboats dotted the water.

"If it comes, I'll be careful," I told Bailey. "Although it's gorgeous now, so I'm pretty sure I'll be seeing you and everyone else at six."

"Hopefully," she replied, sounding anything but. "But for now, I've got to go help put plywood over the windows and drag in all the outside furniture."

Now I sighed. "I wish I could help."

"Don't. Wish for the storm to miss us. And then wish it again."

She sounded so serious. "Okay. I will. See you later?"

"Yeah." A pause. "Be careful, Saylor."

After hanging up, I sat there a second, then turned on the small TV in my room, flipping from an infomercial for a slow cooker to the local news. A guy in a windbreaker was reporting from Colby, a beach town about two hours to the southeast, where it was also still sunny, although the waves were starting to build behind him in the live shot. When a bullet list of Smart Storm Prep appeared, I turned it off.

As Tracy and I headed to the pool, there was little to no sign of any weather concerns other than a pile of sandbags that had appeared on the back patio. When I eyed them, a girl behind the outdoor bar in a Tides Golf shirt was quick to reassure us.

"Standard operating procedure," she said. "The Tides is more prepared for this storm than any other place on the lake, if it even comes. For now, can I get you a cool beverage?"

I declined, taking my bag to two chairs over by the far corner of the pool. When Tracy joined me a moment later, she had a tall pink drink in a frosted glass, a little yellow umbrella poking out of it. "To the storm," she said, holding it up. I did the same with my bottled water. "Let it stay far away."

"Amen," I said. We clinked, then drank.

About an hour later, my phone rang, the Defender Windows' familiar toll-free number popping up on the screen. I answered, readying myself for whatever pitch I would get this time. But when Roo spoke, it wasn't to some fake customer about credit checks. Just me.

"Saylor?"

"Hi," I said. "How's work? Still really busy with the—"

"Are they prepping over there? Do you have a place to go when the storm comes?"

I looked around again at the pool: a group of kids in goggles were wrestling in the shallow end, while the bar was already packed, even though it wasn't noon yet. "No . . . I mean, it's still gorgeous here."

Behind him, I could hear a phone ringing. "Which doesn't mean anything if you look at the forecast. They should already have told you where to go when it starts to get bad—it's Storm 101."

"According to them, this place is hurricane-proof. All

I've seen are a few sandbags."

"And they haven't said anything about shelter?"

"Well . . ." I looked at the bar again. "No. Not yet."

"Get low," he said. "Bottom floor, ideally a room with no windows if you can find it. Stay away from all glass. Bring your valuables and medication. And if you haven't charged your phone, do it now. Tell your dad and Tracy, too."

"Okay," I said, "but seriously, maybe they're watching a different forecast track over here, because they're really not worried."

"Then they're stupid," he replied. "Look, get ready and then hopefully it will all be for nothing. But if it isn't . . ."

He let this thought trail off, even as I waited for him to finish. Finally I said, "Are you scared?"

"I'm concerned," he said. Another phone rang. "And busy, so I should go, even though only morons think they can get storm windows put in before this afternoon. I just wanted to make sure you were safe. I'll call again later, okay?"

"Yeah," I said. "And you'll be at the dinner, right? At six?"

"Sure," he assured me, but he sounded so distracted I wondered if he'd even heard my question. "Talk to you soon."

When I hung up, Tracy turned her head, looking at me over her sunglasses. "Everything okay?"

I nodded. "Roo's just worried about the storm."

She tilted her head back, looking up at the blue sky, white clouds drifting across it. "It hardly looks like hurricane weather, though, does it?"

When I shook my head, she stretched out, then lowered

her sunglasses again. But the truth was, behind the Tides, over the trees, I could now see a row of darker clouds, shorter and squatter, piling up on the horizon. As I lay back, I called on my imagination to picture us all at dinner that night, with oyster forks and candles, Mimi and Nana and Bailey and Roo. But when I closed my eyes, all I could see were those clouds. By the time we left the pool an hour later, there were even more of them.

At four p.m., I was sitting at the table with Nana, looking out at the sky. By then, it was dark as dusk.

"Looks ominous," she observed mildly. She turned to my dad, who was watching the TV, now all storm coverage. "Should we double-check with the hotel that dinner is still going to happen?"

"They're saying they'll be fine no matter what the weather does," he replied, not taking his eyes off the screen, where the reporter in the windbreaker from earlier was being thrashed by rain and wind as he tried to describe the conditions. "But I'm wondering if we should have a shelter plan, just to be safe."

"Roo says so," I told him as I yet again tried Roo's number, only to have it ring and ring before going to voicemail. It was the same with Bailey. "We need to be downstairs, away from windows."

"You'd think they'd set up *something*," my dad muttered, walking over to the phone in the kitchen. "I'll call down, see what's happening."

"It's going to be okay," Nana told me. "If the dinner gets canceled, we'll reschedule."

But for the last few hours, I hadn't been thinking about the dinner anymore. It was Mimi's house and Calvander's that were on my mind: that big kitchen, with the shiny toaster. The gardenia bushes by the door. Each of those rooms I'd learned to clean, the tiny fold on the toilet paper at the beginning of a roll. I'd just gotten it all back. What if it was lost for good?

My phone rang then, startling me after so long of not being able to reach anyone. I jumped on it like it was alive. "Hello?"

"Can you get over here? Do you have a car?"

Trinity. She sounded like she was moving, her voice coming in and out. "What's wrong?"

"I just want to be at the hospital," she said, her voice breaking. "If this baby decides to come during the storm, I swear to God I will clamp my legs SHUT. I want my fucking epidural!"

Nana glanced over at me. Whoops. I stood up, putting some distance between us before saying, "Are you having contractions?"

"No," she said, "but I'm so uncomfortable and I can feel the barometric pressure dropping. Storms make weird things happen, and I do not want my kid to be one of them."

I looked at my dad, who was on hold with the front desk, still watching the TV. Outside, I could see several Tides employees in white golf shirts hurriedly folding up the chairs on the beach.

"I have a car," I said. "But I don't think—"

At first, I didn't recognize the sound she made in response to this. Then I realized it was a sob. "I just can't do this, I'm already alone without the Sergeant and everyone's freaking out here. Even if I just sit in the hospital parking lot, I'll feel better, I swear to God, I'll walk there if I have to. . . ."

"Can you call Roo?" I asked, turning my back to Nana and my dad. "Or Vincent?"

"Everyone's at the Station," she wailed. Good God. "Mimi and Oxford boarded up the hotel windows and went to help down there—it always needs a ton of storm prep. So it's just me and Gordon here, and she was all nervous, so I yelled at her, and now she's God knows where feeling sorry for herself, even though she is NOT a million years pregnant."

I heard a beep: another call coming in. Bailey. "Hold on," I said to Trinity, who was sniffling in my ear. "I've got Bailey on the other line."

"Tell her to get over here and take me to the hospital!" she yelled, loud enough to make my dad, halfway across the room, turn and look at me.

"One sec," I said in my best measured voice, to compensate for her near hysteria. Then I clicked over. "Bailey?"

At first, all I heard was whooshing. Then, finally, her voice. "Are you downstairs yet?"

"No, they haven't said anything," I told her. "I've got

Trinity on the other line. She's kind of—"

"Freaking out," she finished for me. "I know. But she's not in labor, so there's no point in trying the roads. One way or another, this will be over by tomorrow."

Well, that didn't inspire much confidence. I said, "She's all alone, though."

"Gordon is there."

"She yelled at Gordon."

"Well, my dad's yelling at everyone. It's a storm," she replied. "Look, the wind is really picking up here: we've already got some branches falling. Tell her I said to find Gordon and get to the TV room. They've already reported a tornado touching down in Colby."

"What?" I said, looking back at the TV, where the wind-breaker reporter was now literally getting pushed sideways by the wind. "Really?"

"Saylor, wake up. This is a storm. It's going to be bad." She cleared her throat. "Look, just get your dad and grand-mother and Tracy and get safe, okay? I'll check back in with you in a bit."

"What about you, though?" I asked as Nana looked at me. "Are you safe?'

"Safe enough," she replied. In the background, I heard a male voice, bellowing. "Shit, I better go. Just stay low and away from windows, okay?"

Before I could answer, the line cut off, bouncing me back to Trinity. Who was still crying.

"I just hate this so much," she said when I told her I was

back. "Being alone this whole stupid pregnancy, and now—"

"You're not alone," I told her.

"I am literally standing in this room all by myself!" she yelled so loudly I pulled the phone from my ear. "Nobody cares! If this is like Richard, the house will probably come down around me and my unborn child!"

"Emma?" my dad asked. I looked at him. "What's going on?"

Now Trinity was sobbing, her breath coming in ragged jags. I said, "It's Trinity. She's alone and really pregnant and she wants to go to the hospital."

"Hospital? Now? They're saying to stay off all the roads for emergency vehicles to get through."

Trinity, hearing this, wailed even louder. "I know. But she's so upset, and no one is there to drive her. So she asked if I—"

"You?" Now he gave me his full attention, turning from the TV entirely. "Absolutely not. You're not leaving this hotel."

"I know," I said. More sobbing, louder, and now I felt tears prick my own eyes, I felt so helpless. "But I just—"

He came over, holding out his hand. "Let me talk to her."

I handed it over. He put it to his own ear, blinked at the sobbing, and then cleared his throat. "Trinity? Hello? This is Emma's dad, Matthew. You've got to calm down, okay? This isn't good for you or the baby."

There was a blast of response from the phone, none of which I could make out. He said, "I understand. It's scary.

But the storm will pass and you will be fine. Deep breaths."

I didn't hear breathing, though. Just yelling.

"Is there someone who can keep you company?" my dad was saying now. "Sit with you until the storm passes?"

More wailing. Tracy emerged from the bedroom, where she'd been taking a shower. "Um, I just got a tornado warning on my phone. Should we be worried about that?"

I looked at Nana, who said, "According to the hotel, no."

Outside, there was a crack of lightning, followed by a gust of wind that made the windows creak. "We need to go downstairs," I said. "Now."

"Agreed," my dad said. To Trinity he said, "What? No, we're just discussing if we should take shelter. I'm going to give you back to Emma—"

He pulled the phone away from his ear as she sobbed, loudly, in response to this. He covered the mouthpiece and looked at me. "Does she really not have anyone there?"

I shook my head. "Just Gordon."

"Jesus." He looked out at the lake, which looked mean now, ominous, whitecaps dotting the water, the dark clouds low and thick. "Okay. Look. I'll get you all downstairs and settled, and then I'll ride over there."

"What?" I said. "I want to go."

"No." He looked at Tracy. "Gather up your phone and charger, your purse, anything you might need in the next few hours. Mom and Emma, you too."

"But—"

"*Now*," he said, sounding so firm that I jumped. Tracy

went back into the bedroom, moving quickly, while Nana got to her feet as well. I just stood there, though, as he put the phone back to his ear. "Trinity. Breathe. I'm coming over. Just give me a few minutes, okay?"

I couldn't hear her response, because at that moment another wind gust hit. Then the power went out.

"Go," my dad said to me, and I ran into my room, grabbing my purse, a charger, and my shoes. By the time I got back to the living room, Nana and Tracy were at the door, ready, my dad scrambling for his own things. When we went out into the hallway, it was dark except for the emergency lights, blinking.

"Elevator's out," my dad reported, after trying the button. He turned to Nana. "Mom, can you handle the stairs?"

"Certainly," Nana replied, but I took her arm anyway. "Lead the way."

We went into the stairwell, which was also illuminated by blinking lights, and started down, my dad and Tracy in front, Nana and me following. We'd gone down two flights—slowly—when my phone rang again. Trinity.

"A tree just fell on the porch!" she screamed. "It took out one of the windows and now the rain is pouring in!"

"Okay, okay," I said, reporting this to my dad. "Are you in the middle room? Where's Gordon?"

"I can't find her!" she said. "I've been yelling, but you know how she gets when you scream at her, she just vanishes. My mom's at work freaking out, but she can't leave. God, why is this happening?"

A door on the landing we were passing opened suddenly, a Tides employee with a silver room service tray stepping through. People were ordering food right now?

"Good evening," he said, flashing us a toothy smile. "On your way to dinner?"

"The power's out," my dad told him. "What are you all doing about it?"

"The generator is *just* about to come on," the guy replied cheerfully. "But even if it didn't, we'd be totally safe. The Tides is the most storm-ready structure—"

"Right, right," my dad said, pushing past him. To me he said, "What's happening with Trinity?"

"Tree hit the house," I told him. "And now she can't find Gordon."

He sighed. "Jesus. Okay. Let's get a move on. Mom, you all right?"

"Fine," Nana replied, but she did grip my hand a little harder as we began down the next flight. I squeezed back.

Finally we reached the lobby, where Tides employees were scurrying around, moving plants away from windows and herding guests into a nearby ballroom. "It's a hurricane party!" one girl in a golf shirt told us, waving at the open door. "We have drinks and food and activities for the whole family. Join us, won't you?"

My dad looked in the ballroom, where a total of about eight people, mostly kids, were grouped around one table. The rest were empty. "You need to get everyone down here. This storm is no joke."

"Oh, sir, this is just a precaution," she said as a wall of rain hit the windows, the sound drowning everything out for a moment. "You'd be perfectly safe in your room, as the Tides is—"

My dad hurried past her. "Emma, you and your grandmother get settled. Tracy and I will run over to Mimi's just to check on Trinity and Gordon."

"But—"

"Emma. Do not question me right now."

"Honey." Tracy put her hand on his arm. "It's Emma's family. Her cousin. You can understand why she might want to—"

"This is an emergency," he said.

"Which is why I think it would be better if I stayed with your mother," Tracy replied, more firmly now. "You take Emma and go. Safely. Okay?"

At the desk behind us, all the phones were ringing at once as rain lashed the windows. Someone came in the automatic doors. No one yelled, "Welcome to the Tides!"

"Fine," he said. Then he gave her a kiss. "We'll call once we're on our way. Stay here, yes?"

"Yes," she said, walking to a nearby table and holding out a chair so Nana could sit down. My phone, in my pocket, buzzed again. Trinity.

"We're coming," I said as I answered. "Hang tight."

"I can't find her!" she said. Her voice was high, scared. "I've looked everywhere!"

"Okay, okay," I said, glancing at my dad, who had

overheard this. "Just . . . we'll be there soon."

It was, after all, only three miles. But when we went to the valet stand for the car, no one was there. The rain was coming down sideways.

"Well," my dad said, glancing around for a moment. Then he opened the door to the valet stand, which held all the keys, scanning them until he found his own. "I guess we'll go look for it ourselves."

I followed him down a path to the parking garage. Inside, we looked up at the two stories of cars, some of them double-parked. "Any idea where to start?" I asked.

"At the beginning," he said, starting to jog up to the next level. "Come on."

The good news: we found his Audi at the very start of level two. The bad: it was parked right against a wall and blocked in by a huge SUV directly behind it.

"What the *hell*," he said, eyeing it. "This is insane. We'll never get it out."

My phone was ringing again, but I couldn't stop to answer it. Instead, I walked around to the Audi, which actually had some space ahead of it. "I think I can back it out."

"You can't even get in there!"

"I can try," I said, gesturing for him to throw me the keys. He did, and I unlocked the car, then stuffed myself in the small space on the side away from the wall, inching down between it and the car beside it, a Mercedes. "I think I can crawl in the window, if I can get it open."

"This is crazy and stupid," he said. "We shouldn't even

be trying to get out of here. Doesn't she have family that can come help her?"

"We *are* her family," I said.

He just looked at me as, although my insides felt compressed to the point of flattening, I finally made it to the passenger door. I eased it open about an inch, which was all the give there was, before sticking my hand in and wiggling it around until I found the window button. Because the key was in my hand, it went down. Thank God. I pitched myself in, crawling behind the wheel.

"There's not enough—" my dad was saying, but I ignored him as I started the engine. We'd practiced parking endlessly before my test, in the garage under Nana's building, before I'd hit that car and gotten spooked. No time for fear now. I put the car in reverse, easing back a tiny bit.

"Okay," my dad said, coming around to the front. "That's as far as you've got before the bumper. Now go for—"

I already was, inching up, the wheel turned as far as it would go. Then back. Then up again. Slowly, I began to make a space between the Audi and the SUV, although it took another ten passes or so before it was wide enough to reverse out entirely. But I did it. My phone was ringing the entire time.

"All right," my dad said. He looked as surprised as I'd ever seen him. "Now, let me behind the wheel."

"I'm already here," I said. "Just get in."

He paused, as if he was going to resist this, but then climbed into the passenger seat. I hit the gas as soon as his door swung shut behind him.

Out in front of the hotel, it was crazy windy, the trees bent sideways, rain pelting the glass as I tried to peer through it. We passed a couple of Tides employees, running toward Campus, as I turned onto the road. A layer of water was running across it.

"Flooding," my dad said. "Go very slow and don't brake."

I did as he said until we were past it, then sped up. My phone rang again. "Can you get that?" I asked. "It's probably Trinity."

He picked it up. "Hello? Trinity? Look, we're on our way . . . Celeste? It's Matthew."

I had to slow again to drive over a power line, broken and wiggling like a snake. Yikes. "Ask her if they found Gordon."

". . . yes, we're going there," he said. "Trinity is very upset and Gordon . . . well, she's probably hiding. We'll find her. What? No, we just left the hotel. We should be there . . . what's in the road?"

I waited to hear the answer to this question, but there was none: the line went dead, and he lowered the phone, looking worried. "Sounds like there might be a problem," he said. "We'll see."

A couple of miles later, we did: a tree had fallen across both lanes, bark and leaves scattered all around it. The sky was as dark as I'd ever seen it in my life, and suddenly, probably much later than I should have, I felt my heart begin to race. I was scared.

"Dad," I said as we stopped. "Now what?"

He took a breath. We'd gotten this far—extracting the car, dealing with the weather—and now it was all for nothing. I thought of Trinity, crying in the dark of the TV room. I was about to turn to him and say we should just run the rest of the way when I heard it.

Music.

It was distant, and barely audible above the whipping wind and the rain. But it was there, tinkling piano music, growing louder and louder. It seemed nuts I didn't put together that it was the Yum truck until it appeared on the other side of the tree, its lights blinking.

"Roo," I said, feeling a rush of relief. I pushed my door open.

"What?" my dad asked.

"Just come on." I jumped out and started to run, going around the tree with him following. The rain stung my skin, the howl of the wind filling my ears: it felt like the storm might just carry me away, like Dorothy when *The Wizard of Oz* is in black and white. But then Roo was holding open the door, and I was climbing in. The music was still going.

"It's stuck," he said by way of explanation as my dad piled in behind me. I moved to the cooler, my spot, while he took the front seat, putting on his belt as Roo backed up. "But at least people can hear us coming."

We started driving the final stretch, passing Conroy Market, where the power was also out. Roo stuck his hand out the window and gave a thumbs-up to Celeste, who was standing outside, her phone to her ear. Then she, like everything else, was lost in the wind and rain behind us. But still the music kept playing.

"Apparently, there's a huge tree down on the highway," Roo said as he leaned forward, trying to see through the windshield. The wipers were going full speed, but only pushing the water around. "So Trinity can't get to the hospital."

"She's not in labor, just scared," I said. "And Gordon—"

"Is going to be in *so* much trouble once I find her safe," he finished for me. My dad glanced at him, saying nothing. "Okay, we're almost there. Once we are, you go find Trinity. I'll look for Gordon."

"You take cover," my dad said. "I'll handle looking for Gordon."

Roo jerked the wheel to the right, suddenly, to dodge a branch that was in the road, and I almost slid off the cooler, catching myself at the last minute. The music made it sound like a wacky caper, not an emergency.

Finally, we were at Calvander's, where all the windows facing the water were boarded up, debris from the beach—a shovel, a plastic bag, a beer can—blowing across the yard. Roo jerked to a stop and we all jumped out, running to the main house. The tree that had so scared Trinity was across the porch, water pouring in the one window it had hit, reminding me how serious this actually was.

"Trinity!" I yelled as I came up the steps, throwing the door open. The house was quiet except for the wind, wheezing through any and all cracks. "Where are you?"

"In here!" she said.

I pushed open the door to the TV room to find her on the couch, holding a pillow, tears streaming down her face. "She's not anywhere!" she said. "I've looked all over the goddamn place."

"It's okay," I said, going to her as Roo and my dad took off to the kitchen and the rest of the house. I heard them yelling Gordon's name as I grabbed a blanket from the couch, shaking it out over Trinity, who was trembling. "We'll find her."

"Don't leave me!" she yelled, but I had to, running down the hallway to the kitchen, where the windows were all rain: I couldn't even see the lake. Outside, I could still make out the tinkling music of the Yum truck, or at least I could until another sound grew loud enough to drown it out: a humming, like an engine. Growing closer.

My dad, coming back down the stairs, heard it too. "Tornado," he said. "Into the middle room, both of you. Now!"

I hadn't even realized Roo was there, behind me, until he said, "I can't. We have to find Gordon."

"I will find Gordon," my dad told him. "GO."

I looked at Roo, who nodded and then ran back down the hallway, me following. In the TV room Trinity was rocking back and forth, her eyes squeezed shut.

"Oh, my God," she said as I sat down beside her, taking her hand. Her grip was like a vise, tightening with each boom of thunder from outside. "Where's Gordon? If she's outside, she'll—"

"Shh," Roo said, taking her other hand. "Emma's dad is on it."

He said this so confidently, as if he had all the faith in my father, despite what had happened between them. My dad would handle this. He had to.

Before, the wind had been howling; now, it sounded different. Trinity whimpered, twisting my fingers, and I sucked in a breath, trying to stay calm. Then I heard a crack just outside, followed by a crash.

"Shit," Roo said.

"My dad." I stood up, running to the door. "I should—"

"Saylor!" Roo yelled. "Don't open that!"

I did; I couldn't help it. Nothing can happen to him, I thought, as I ran to the front door and opened it as well, feeling the wind push back against me, hard. "Dad!"

But I couldn't see him. And I knew there was no way he could hear me, over the wind and the howling and the rain smacking the windows. I turned, looking down at the shore: the water was rushing over the dock, foam stuck to everything, and I couldn't make out a single thing. The howling was getting louder.

"Dad!" I yelled again, into the storm. No answer. I stood there, tears in my throat, thinking of the last time I'd seen my mom. That white lace shirt, the way she touched my face. The elevator doors closing as she watched me disappear. Was this another ending I'd remember forever? Where would I imagine him?

"Saylor!" Roo came running up behind me. "Come back inside."

"My dad is out there!" I said, my voice breaking, and then I was crying. "He's—"

There was a whoosh, pushing me back from the door, and I felt Roo grab me, his arms around my waist. The rain was pelting us sideways as I buried my face in his chest, eyes tightly closed, just wanting to hold on to something, someone, as the world seemed to come loose all around me. He put a hand on the back of my head as I turned, looking out in the storm again, and I could hear him speak but couldn't make out the words he was saying. Still, I strained to hear them, holding on tight, and then finally, there was this.

"I see them."

I opened my eyes. He was looking at the shore, so I did too, squinting into the rain and bending trees. At first, I saw nothing, but then, after a beat, then one more, movement in the distance at the dock. I blinked. Twice. And then there was my dad, carrying Gordon as he walked away from the water.

"Oh, my God," I said. She had her arms looped at his neck, legs locked around his waist, as he jogged up the grass, head bent against the storm. In one of her hands, Gordon was holding her Allies book.

Roo let me go, rushing out to open and hold the door as they came up the steps.

"Let's go," my dad said, ducking into the TV room. Gordon was still holding on tightly, her own eyes squeezed

427

shut, as Trinity shrieked, relieved, upon seeing them. "Saylor. You okay?"

I paused. He had never called me that. "Yeah. I'm fine."

He reached out, touching my hair, but couldn't do much more with Gordon attached to him like a spider monkey. Roo shut the living room door. "It's coming," he said as we all got back on the couch, together. We were so close, crammed in together, that I felt like I had a piece of everyone: Trinity's hand in mine, my dad's leg pressed against me, Gordon's skinny elbow at my ear. And then, Roo, sliding in behind me. He took my other hand, squeezing it, as if he'd done it a million times. Maybe, in the deep, lost part of my memory, he had. But it still felt new and familiar all at once as I squeezed back, pressing myself against him. I thought of my mom in that hotel room, on another night years ago, leaving this world with no one even knowing. There were a million ways to go, but the worst would be alone. And I wasn't.

I'd never heard the wind the way it sounded at that moment. Sometimes I still hear it in my dreams. But even then, I have that sense of being part of a greater whole. All of us on the couch, Roo's breath in my ear. Together, we held on.

TWENTY-FOUR

"This is so nice," Bailey said, looking around the room. "You didn't have to."

"Oh, I think I did!" Nana replied, gesturing for us to take our seats at the table before she did the same. "Of course, it's not the Club. But there are oyster forks. See?"

I did. There they were, on the little card table Oxford had brought into room seven, along with three folding chairs. I'd found the tablecloth and napkins in a drawer in Mimi's kitchen, while Nana picked a bunch of gardenias and put them in water for the centerpiece. She was right, it wasn't the Club. It was better.

The Club wasn't an option anyway, as, like the Tides, it had suffered so much damage from the storm it was closed until further notice. Which meant all the guests who'd been so reassured about the hotel's storm readiness suddenly had to find other places to stay, causing everything to be fully booked up. Luckily, we had a connection.

It was Calvander's we'd come to, the night of the storm, after we'd picked up Nana and Tracy, who'd been evacuated as the water rushed into the Tides lobby. We'd taken the Yum truck, me on the cooler seat with Tracy, while Nana rode up front, next to Roo, delighted by the music, which was still playing.

On the day of the storm, Calvander's had two vacancies, so Nana and I bunked in seven while Dad and Tracy took number ten. I'd been a little worried about how my grandmother would adapt to her new digs. But she took easily to walking over to the main house with me for breakfast each morning with Oxford, who split his paper with her and made all the toast we could ever want. Usually Gordon joined us as well, with her book. She'd become fascinated with everything Nana, which I could understand, following her around the way she once had me. Sometimes I'd see them in our room, sitting together and talking quietly, and wonder what they were discussing. But I'd never ask.

The motel itself had withstood the storm with only a little damage, and within a day or two the other guests were back on the beach, slathering themselves with sunscreen as they spread out their towels. From across the lake, we could hear bulldozers and construction equipment going all day long as the Tides and the Club tried to get back up and running. But it would be a while.

And by then, we'd be gone. Back in Lakeview, Nana's remodeled apartment and our new house were both done and waiting for us, as well as the new school year. But I was determined to stay at North Lake, both literally and figuratively, as long as I could.

Which was why we'd scheduled this, our oyster fork meal, on the evening of the second-to-last day, before the chaos of packing and leaving really set in. It wasn't the big group dinner we'd planned, but it didn't matter, as by that point we'd had plenty of those. In the first days after the storm, when the power was still out, we'd sat together at Mimi's big table, eating meals made with everything perishable from the fridge. Oxford grilled hot dogs outside while Mimi and Nana drank boxed wine they'd found in the pantry, sharing stories. Even Trinity was there, still hugely pregnant, counting down the days until the Sergeant arrived home. I was hoping I'd be there when the baby came, but I knew even from the distance of Lakeview I'd still feel part of it, whenever it happened.

A lot of this was because of Roo. That day of the storm, we'd all stayed in the living room, on the couch, until the wind died down and we were sure the danger had passed. Only then did my dad get up, helping Trinity to her feet while Gordon stuck close to his other side.

"Bound to be a lot of branches and power lines down," he told us, crossing the room and opening the door to squint out. "Nobody touch anything, understood?"

Gordon, solemn, nodded, although Trinity was already going to the front door. "Oh, crap," she said a moment later. "That same office window that blew out in Richard is gone again. Mimi is going to be *pissed*."

"Better a window than a person," my dad pointed out. He looked at Gordon, then bent down to her level. "You okay? That was kind of scary."

Hearing his voice as he said this—low, calm, invested—I felt a lump rise in my own throat. We Paynes were a safe people, for sure. And my dad had lots of experience: he could take care of anyone.

Everyone else left to check damage then, leaving just Roo and me on the couch in the dimness of the living room. Distantly, I could hear a siren, as well as someone's phone ringing. But as I turned to face him, his hand still in mine, I blocked that all out. All I could think of were the moments the wind had wailed, the house literally shaking, and we held hands so tightly I could feel both his pulse and mine.

I looked up at him. All those pictures I'd seen of him, from the group shot until the very last one, by the pumps at the Station, and yet this was what I knew I would remember best. This moment, uncaptured, but just as real.

"You okay, storm buddy?" he asked.

I smiled. Then, instead of replying, I leaned in and kissed him. Lightly at first, trying it out, before going deeper, pulling him closer. His lips were so soft as he smoothed a hand over my head, gazing steadily into my eyes while I reached up to touch his face, every bit of us fitting neatly together. It was so perfect—the world falling away, just how I thought a real first kiss should feel—I knew I didn't need a picture, that I would remember it always. Even now, when I thought of it, my heart jumped.

Since then, we'd just sort of slipped easily, wordlessly, into being a couple. A few days later, as we sat on Mimi's steps, he told me he had something for me, picking up the bag he'd brought with him.

"What is it?" I asked.

He handed it over. "Look and see."

It was a photo album, a new one, with a red cover and stiff pages. At first I was confused, until I opened it up to see that same first picture, his dad in his duck pajamas, at the very top.

"Is this—"

"Yep," he said. His leg was warm, pressing against mine. I just felt better with him close by. "Same pictures, same order. I made copies."

"This is incredible," I said, flipping pages.

"I thought you deserved your own album," he told me. "Since the stories are yours, too."

I turned a couple more pages: they were all there. The shot of my mom, somber at day camp. Her dyeing Chris Price's hair. That ill-fated middle school dance. Then Roo and me as kids. Each picture another step toward here, where we were now. I wouldn't be leaving everything behind. Now, I could take the lake with me.

But when I got to the last page, and that final shot of him with his mom and the Christmas tree, I noticed something. "Wait. Are there more pages?"

He grinned. "Look and see."

I turned past the final photo, and sure enough, instead of

the back cover, another page was there, with more behind it. Empty slots, waiting to be filled with the rest of the stories I would tell. I was so touched, moving through them, that at first I almost missed the single picture he'd already included.

It was the two of us, at our makeshift prom, a shot I hadn't even realized was being taken. I was in my dress, barefoot, him holding a hand to spin me out as we danced. I was laughing, my head thrown back, someone blurry and in motion behind me. Like the moment was already passing, even as whoever took the shot captured it.

"This is incredible," I said, barely even able to speak.

"The big photo album in the sky," he replied. "It's like good storm windows. Everyone should have one."

I turned to face him, moving my leg between his. "You are the best."

"I am not," he replied, sliding his arms around my waist. "But I will take the compliment anyway."

I leaned in then, kissing him as the wind blew over us, ruffling the nearby gardenia bushes. I wanted it to last forever, but then I heard Gordon tittering, the way she did when she caught us like this together, and she always caught us like this together.

"Gordon," Roo said, pulling away but keeping his eyes on me. "Don't you have a closet to get into or something?"

"It wasn't a closet!" she shot back as she did every time he said this, which was equally as often. "It was a shed and I was fine."

"Fine." Roo snorted. "You were by the water with a

hurricane coming in and no one could find you."

"Except my dad," I pointed out. I looked at Gordon. "Lucky he knew that place, huh?"

She nodded, solemn. "Lucky."

But it wasn't, not really. I'd assumed he'd found her that day by process of elimination, hunting around the dock until he discovered the small shed built into the side of the motel where, after Trinity had yelled at her, she'd gone to barricade herself with her book. It was only later, when I'd finally had a chance to sit down with my dad, that I found out the real story.

It was a few days after the storm and we were at Mimi's table, having breakfast. Tracy and Nana had gone back over to the Tides to collect our things, so it was my dad and me and my *Bly County News*, where I was reading the obits (Ellis Murdock, 67, died at home with his family around him) while he stared out the window. When Gordon emerged from the motel office, we both watched her walk down to the dock, carrying her book, then take a seat with her legs dangling in the water.

"You saved her life," I said as he nibbled some toast.

"Oh, I don't know about that," he said. "That shed is pretty tough. That's why your mom liked it."

I looked at him. "Mom?"

He nodded, swallowing. "You know how she was into disappearing. She could hide anywhere. But she loved that shed. She told me she always went there when Mimi and Joe were fighting."

435

I looked back at Gordon, kicking her feet as she read. "And you remembered?"

He looked surprised. "I remember everything about your mom, Emma."

I turned the page of my paper, over to sports. "Me too. But I want to hear all your stories, remember? I mean, sometime."

For a second, he was silent. Then he said, "Right. Yeah, I've been thinking. I'd like that too."

I looked at him. "Really?"

"Really." He smiled, then reached up, rubbing his hand under his glasses. "We can start with this table, right here. Do you know that was my seat?"

He was pointing at the one I was in, to the left of the head. "It was?"

"Yep. Right next to Joe, who did not like PDA of any sort. Your mom sat across from me, but kicked my leg under the table throughout every meal. I had a permanent shin bruise."

I tried to picture him with his own seat in this place I thought *I* knew so well. "Really."

"Oh, yeah." He smiled, a little sadly, looking out at the lake. "It was like a whole new world, being in this crazy house after living with your grandmother. I loved it."

Me too, I thought. Then I kicked him under the table, and he laughed.

The last few days we'd spent packing, getting ready to leave. I slipped my notebook with my family tree in the bottom of my bag, then threw my shoes in on top of it, all jumbled together. Then I took them all out again and put them in neatly. You couldn't change everything all at once. It was good we had time.

The album was one of the last things I packed. Before I did, though, I'd gone up to the office, where I found Mimi standing behind the counter facing the window, her hands on her hips.

"What are you looking at?" I asked her as I came in, the cold air smacking me in the face.

"Oh, just the traffic going by," she said, even though there were no cars at that moment. "Helps me think. What are you up to?"

"I wanted to show you something," I said. "If you have a minute."

"For you, honey?" She gave me a wink. "Always. What is it?"

I walked over, putting the album on the counter between us. As she leaned over it and I opened the cover, I said, "Roo gave me this. But there's something in it I want you to have."

"Oh, my," she breathed softly as I turned the page to that first picture of my mom scowling at church camp. "That brings back some memories."

She was studying the page so intently, her eyes moving across the pictures, that I stayed quiet for a moment. When I saw her eyes get wet, I said quickly, "I didn't mean to upset you."

"Oh, no." She waved her hand in front of her face, turning another page. "I'm not upset. Just remembering."

I looked down too, at all those pictures Roo had told me about, wondering if she recalled the same things. Because the story can change so much, depending on who's telling it. I hoped, over time, I'd hear more of hers.

"This is the one I wanted to give you," I said, flipping to the page I'd marked. There, at the bottom, was the picture of us together on my first visit, sitting in that lawn chair. I'd driven to Delaney to a drugstore to get a good copy of it, which I pulled out now from behind the original. "I thought maybe you could put it under the glass."

She was still for a second. Then, slowly, she moved her hand forward, taking the picture from me. "Well, what do you know," she said, then smiled. "If it isn't George."

We made room for it beside an old shot of Celeste and my mom, right by the register. If I couldn't be there, I liked knowing it was.

Now, back in room seven, I looked around as Nana unpacked the meal she'd ordered from the Club, which was running a shoestring kitchen to try to accommodate all the displaced members. "Oyster salad," she said, handing the container to Bailey, "and cucumber and cream cheese sandwiches. Not too fancy, but it's something."

"It's perfect," Bailey told her as I heard her phone buzz. She glanced down at it, balanced on her bag, then smiled, helping herself to oysters. I looked too: VINCENT, it said on the screen. Apparently, Roo and I weren't the only ones who had found each other during the storm. At the Station, Bailey and Vincent had taken shelter in the snack bar, even as a piece of roof metal blew against the doors, trapping them there. By the time Silas and Jack got them out, something had changed. All I knew was I hadn't heard a word about Colin or Campus since.

"Let's have a toast," Nana said, once we'd each helped ourselves from the carry-out containers and I'd filled our glasses with Pop Soda. She lifted her glass. "To family."

"To family," Bailey said, looking at me.

"To family," I repeated, and I had that feeling again, of being complete, as we clinked our glasses and drank. The next day I'd go home, see Ryan and Bridget, move into a new house and new neighborhood. Even with my wild imagination I couldn't picture it, not yet, but that was okay. The details would come, and then I'd capture and add them, image by image, onto the pages of the book Roo had given me.

What would they be? At that moment, I couldn't say. Only later would I know they would include the In Memoriam I'd write for the *Bly County News*, sending it in so it ran on the Monday after Thanksgiving, the day my mom died. My dad would help me find a picture of her when she was sober and happy. Also to be in those pages, eventually: the day I left, when Trinity and Bailey presented me with my own spray bottle, EMMA SAYLOR—I'd decided to go by both names, not choosing between them anymore— which would be waiting for me the following summer when I returned.

But first, I had to go, and I would. But not as a passenger this time.

Even with all the progress I'd made, my dad wasn't thrilled with the idea of me driving home alone. But Nana had a car coming, and plenty of room for him and Tracy and all their bags, and I had more goodbyes to say than he did. So finally, begrudgingly, he agreed, waving at me as they drove off from Calvander's in a black town car, the blinker flashing as they turned left onto the main road. Which left just Roo and me, my packed bags, and one more thing. A lake thing.

"Hold it out," he said as I gripped the sparkler in my hand. I did, and he put his against it, tip to tip, before striking the lighter. As he waited for them to catch, I took the opportunity to study him. Blond hair, sticking up a bit in the back. The gap in this teeth, trademark. And those numbers, where to find him, across one calf. There were no guarantees of what would happen to us in the coming year, but as my mind started to consider it, there was a spark, another, then a shower between us. I thought of my mom and his dad—both big lives, gone too soon. I was leaving, too. But I knew I'd be back.

P9-DHT-545

THE INSIDER'S GUIDE TO

NEW ENGLAND

U.S. IMMIGRATION
160-LOS C-4125

MAY 23 1992

ADMITTED_____
UNTIL   (CLASS)

THE INSIDER'S GUIDES
AUSTRALIA • BALI • CALIFORNIA • CANADA • CHINA • EASTERN CANADA • FLORIDA • HAWAII •
HONG KONG • INDIA • INDONESIA • JAPAN • KENYA • KOREA • NEPAL •
NEW ENGLAND • NEW ZEALAND • MALAYSIA AND SINGAPORE • MEXICO •
RUSSIA • SPAIN • THAILAND • TURKEY • WESTERN CANADA

The Insider's Guide to New England
First Published 1992
Hunter Publishing Inc
300 Raritan Center Parkway
CN94, Edison, N.J. 08818
by arrangement with Novo Editions, S.A.
53 rue Beaudouin, 27700 Les Andelys, France
Telefax: (33) 32 54 54 50

© 1992 Novo Editions, S.A.

ISBN: 1-55650-455-1

Created, edited and produced by Novo Editions, S.A.
Editor in Chief: Allan Amsel
Original design concept: Hon Bing-wah
Picture editor and designer: Jane Pinel
Text and artwork composed and information updated
using Xerox Ventura software

Printed by Samhwa Printing Co Ltd, Seoul, Korea

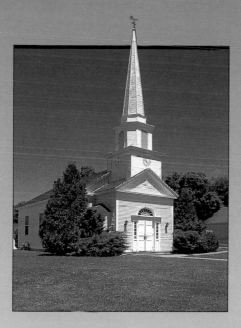

THE INSIDER'S GUIDE TO

NEW ENGLAND

By Richard Bond
Photographed by Robert Holmes

HUNTER PUBLISHING, INC.
Edison, N.J.

Contents

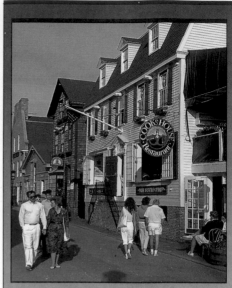

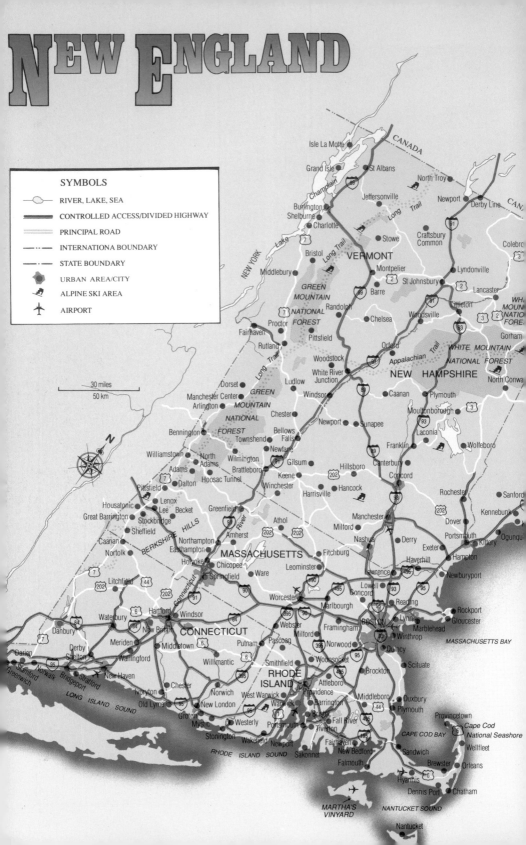

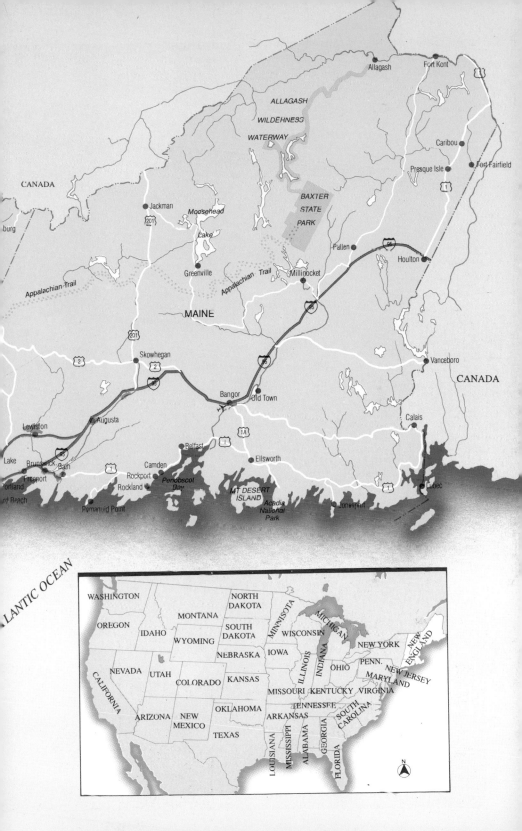

CANADA

ALLAGASH
WILDERNESS
WATERWAY

Allagash   Fort Kent

Caribou

Presque Isle   Fort Fairfield

BAXTER
STATE
PARK

Jackman

Moosehead
Lake

Greenville

MAINE

Appalachian Trail

Pallen

Houlton

Millinocket

Appalachian Trail

Skowhegan

Bangor   Old Town

Vanceboro

CANADA

Lewiston   Augusta

Calais

Brunswick
Freeport
Bath
Portland
rd Beach

Belfast

Ellsworth

Camden
Rockport
Rockland

Penobscot
Bay

Pemaquid Point

MT DESERT
ISLAND
Acadia
National
Park

Lubec

Jonesport

LANTIC OCEAN

WASHINGTON

OREGON   IDAHO

MONTANA

NORTH
DAKOTA

SOUTH
DAKOTA

MINNESOTA

MICHIGAN

NEW YORK

NEW
ENGLAND

WYOMING

NEBRASKA   IOWA

WISCONSIN

ILLINOIS

INDIANA

OHIO

PENN.

NEW JERSEY

NEVADA   UTAH

CALIFORNIA

COLORADO   KANSAS

MISSOURI   KENTUCKY

MARYLAND

VIRGINIA

ARIZONA   NEW
MEXICO

OKLAHOMA

TENNESSEE

ARKANSAS

SOUTH
CAROLINA

TEXAS

LOUISIANA

MISSISSIPPI

ALABAMA

GEORGIA

FLORIDA

N

New England

A PLACE APART

There are so many reasons to visit New England that no book can enumerate them all. It is truly a place apart, an often-beautiful land of lakes, seashores, mountains, river valleys, villages, towns, and bustling cities. Not only the best of America's past, it is also much of the cultural, educational, and technological promise of its coming centuries. In a nation bereft of a long historical tradition, New England keeps a way of life, architecture, and culture linked to America's earliest days, and to the Europe which preceded them.

Composed of six states, including five of the original thirteen colonies, New England is so steeped in the history and culture of the United States it is difficult to imagine an America without New England. Although geographically small when compared to the rest of the nation, New England has had perhaps the strongest impact of any region on the country as a whole.

Named "New" England by the early explorer Sir John Smith, it is the New World's strongest link, historically and culturally, to the Old. Yet it is also profoundly American, from its colonial villages, farmsteads, and elegant Victorian city streets to the bold commercial vigor of its modern skylines. And if New England is the land where American liberty was born, it has also nurtured this liberty with its continuing commitment to education and culture, expressed today in a concentration of many of the nation's best colleges, universities, museums, theaters, and concert halls.

But these are not the best reasons to come to New England. The best reasons are countless, and include the multicolored splendor of the autumn hills, the crystalline purity of the northern lakes, the salty smell of the sea, the beauty of villages couched in emerald pastures and peaceful river valleys, the glitter of trout streams emerging from spring snow, the towering granite peaks, the vast forests of spruce and pine, the taste of America as once it truly was.

A LAND FOR ALL SEASONS

And New England is a land for all seasons. In winter the earth lies beneath a blanket of white; wood smoke rises from the chimneys; skaters flit across the frozen ponds while on the lakes fishermen huddle in their huts and drop their lines through holes in the deep ice. Children sled on steep back streets and country slopes; the hills are alive with skiers; snowshoers and cross-country skiers wander back-country

trails through forests whose silence is broken only by the occasional chatter of a chickadee.

Spring, the rebirth of life, is magical in New England. After months of cold, the warm March winds melt the snow and in April the buds burst forth, transforming the gaunt gray branches to brilliant green. The geese, ducks, and first songbirds begin to return; boys follow the thawing trout streams, and early blossoms paint the apple orchards.

Summer brings hot days, and the lakes fill with swimmers, water skiers, and boaters. Fishermen cast and troll for trout, lake salmon, pickerel, bass, and other game fish. The ocean bays are a kaleidoscope of sails and spinnakers; surf and sandy beaches glimmer in the warm sun. Rafters, kayakers, and canoers ride the rivers and hikers wander the peaks, hills, and forests.

Ocean fog OPPOSITE and rolling hills ABOVE characterize New England's scenic charm.

But it is fall that is the glory of New England. From north to south the woodlands blaze with countless shades of scarlet, crimson, vermilion, yellow, gold, and orange; as the leaves fall the white birches and tan beeches and oaks stand out against the darker firs, spruce, tamaracks, and pines. Hunters go forth to seek deer, pheasant, moose, and other prey to stock their larders. The rural air has a scent of apples and coming snow, and families draw closer round the hearth, conscious of the ending of the year.

PEAKS, BAYS, AND RIVERS

New England occupies an area of only 66,672 sq miles (172,680 sq km) in the northeast corner of the United States, bordered by New York to the south and west, by Quebec and New Brunswick to the north, and by the Atlantic Ocean to the east. In size it is somewhat smaller than Great Britain, less than half the size of California, and slightly larger than Michigan or Illinois.

New Hampshire's White Mountains are ideal for river fishing ABOVE, and in the autumn display an array of vivid fall colors OPPOSITE.

Maine is the only New England state which was not part of the original thirteen colonies, because it was part of Massachusetts until 1820. At 33,265 sq miles (86,156 sq km) Maine is also half the total area of New England, and more than three times the size of Vermont, New Hampshire, or Massachusetts, and nearly six times the size of Connecticut. At 1,212 sq miles (3,139 sq km), Rhode Island is New England's, and the nation's, smallest state.

The Appalachian chain dominates much of western New England, from Mt Katahdin in northern Maine down through Maine's Rangely Mountains and the White Mountains of Maine and New Hampshire. Further west, the lower, forested Green Mountains span the entire length of Vermont and continue into Massachusetts as the Berkshires, and on across Connecticut to join the Taconic Mountains of New York.

Like New England's mountains, its rivers run primarily north to south, swinging east to meet the sea at wide, island-filled bays from Maine's Bar Harbor to Connecticut's shores of Long Island Sound. Many of New England's rivers keep the names given to them by the original New Englanders — the Merrimac, Penobscot, Kennebec, and the 400-mile (644-km) Connecticut, which runs almost the entire length of western New England, separating Vermont from New Hampshire and bisecting Massachusetts and Connecticut to reach Long Island Sound.

Because eras of glaciation have given it relatively poor, rocky soil, New England has never been an agricultural center, although its sheep-raising industry was a significant national resource in the nineteenth century, and Maine's potatoes remain the nation's best. Endowed with a magnificent coastline and hundreds of bays and harbors, New England first derived its prosperity from ship-building and fisheries. In the nineteenth century, New England's textile, leather, and other manufacturing became the nation's most predominant. In recent years, electronics, computer and data communications technologies, weaponry, banking, and a growing tourist industry have become major aspects of New England's commercial vitality.

THE NEW ENGLANDERS

New Englanders have learned to live with the various stereotypes which have been assigned to them — the shrewd Connecticut Yankee, the imperturbable Boston Brahmin, or the terse and taciturn inhabitant of Maine, New Hampshire, or Vermont. These characterizations, once more valid, have become blurred over the years by the mixing of Irish, Italian, Polish, and other European genes. The beliefs and traditions that these immi-

whose ancestors came to the region in southward migrations from the Bering Straits about 12,000 to 15,000 years ago. These people hardly modified the land in which they lived, finding adequate sustenance in the forests, lakes, rivers, and ocean. Some tribes also grew pumpkins, beans, corn, and other vegetables.

As human migration from Europe turned from trickle to torrent between the seventeenth and twentieth centuries, the ecological diversity and bounty of the land was diminished and in many areas totally de-

grants added to a population traditionally English and ethically Puritan brought a welcome infusion of renewed vigor and broader cultural tolerance.

The population of the six New England states is unevenly distributed. A majority inhabits the southern half of the region, in cities such as Boston, Providence, and Hartford, swelling their hubs and sprawling suburbs to house almost three-quarters of New England's 13 million inhabitants. In the three northern states, the cities and towns are smaller with greater distances between them, and there remain large areas of wilderness, particularly in Maine.

The original settlers of New England's wilderness were the Algonquin Indians,

stroyed. Once flocks of geese truly darkened the sky, covering it in a solid cloud from one horizon to the other. Fish were so plentiful in the streams they could be literally scooped out by hand or net. The forests were filled with animals that are now legend: caribou, wolf, eastern buffalo, and panther.

But the Europeans, with their conviction that anyone not a Christian was a "Devil," had little interest in or respect for New England's inhabitants, or for its wildlife. The environment took a back seat to buccaneering. Whenever possible, the colonists cheated the Indians out of title to their lands by devious and meaningless agreements; when the Indians refused such stratagems, the colonists simply overwhelmed them withtheir firepower, leaving smallpox and alcohol to further reduce their numbers. Today, the names for lakes and rivers, for islands and mountains, are almost all that connects New England with its tribal past.

By the late seventeenth century, the English Puritans had established a theocracy that imposed upon their new world, and was to impose upon their descendants, a prevailing sense of order, discipline, and frugality. These qualities were to remain strong in the New England Yankee temperament until the spiritual earnestness that had

and Virginia and the Carolinas, moved ever westward, its numbers increased by a steady flow of immigrants from across the sea. By the late 1840's, after worsening English repressions and "the great hunger" in Ireland, the Irish came to New England in great numbers. In time, their political and oratory skills and gave them a strong hold on local governments, particularly in Massachusetts, where they have continued to exercise an active role.

French Canadians, too, emigrated from neighboring Canada to work in the many textile mills that rose beside New England's

accompanied them diminished in the eighteenth century. Under the influence of the practical elements of the Puritan ethic, fleets of merchant and fishing ships, including slavers and privateers, expanded and brought increasing prosperity to New England and with it the accumulation of wealth.

This wealth, and the independence derived from it, caused bitter resentment toward the "mother country" when England arbitrarily imposed a number of trade edicts and taxes upon this, her most affluent North American possession.

In angry response, the colonists rose up in successful rebellion, drove the British into the sea, and formed a new nation. This fledgling nation, born in New England

rivers, bringing with them their own language and customs. Portuguese fishermen augmented the region's fishing fleets, Italians came to labor on construction sites and formed a "little Italy" of their own in many a New England town. The Jews came, so did the Poles, the Russians, and the Swedes, all forming distinctive communities where, for a time, their cultural heritages could be celebrated and preserved. Although they have been long since absorbed into the mainstream of New England life, their ways and the ways of those who came before them together create the human pageant that is now New England.

Faces of today's New Englanders display a warmth and friendliness at odds with the taciturn reputation of their forebears.

TRAVELERS AND TOURISTS

Among the millions who visit New England every year are both travelers and tourists, those who come to enjoy it as it is, and those who are contented with the largely superficial attractions of its tourism industry. Needless to say, the traveler, he or she who is willing to investigate beyond the cliche, who is willing to change a little in order to learn, will have more fun and profit more from a visit than will the simple tourist.

trails, or to wander the beaches, promenades, scenic villages, and historic city tours. Like Europe, New England was built at a different pace than today's — before the automobile came to endanger the pedestrian and fill the cities with clamor and pollution.

And rather than seeing New England as a 66,000-square-mile shopping mall, attempting to validate one's visit by what one carries home, it is simpler to see it as New Englanders do — as a place to *be* at home, to most of them the best place on earth. Thus there's wisdom in avoiding the tourist

Like many popular areas, New England has created a tourism industry that portrays it not as it is, but as it would like to seem, or as it thinks the visitor would like to see it. Because tourism is much the same everywhere, the tourist is therefore deprived of many of the unique resources and fascinations of this extraordinary, beautiful, and historic place.

Thus there are better and worse ways to visit New England. If possible, one should avoid the main highways except for transit, take as much time as possible, and avoid the noise and hubbub of the cities for the relaxation and harmony of country life. To the extent feasible, it's wise to walk as much as possible, to enjoy a few of the many hiking

trinket zones, the high-priced shops and restaurants dedicated to the superficial distracting of the summer crowds, and instead go for the heart and soul of New England, the back roads and quiet country inns, the shores, peaks, and vistas, a way of life that was born with America.

Many people come to New England to "get away from it all", the stress, urban ugliness, crowded conditions, and discord that characterizes much of the late twentieth century. Others come to revisit the birthplace of American liberty and culture, to seek a common heritage, a place that reminds us of what America was once and hoped to be.

Because New England truly has it all — ocean, beaches, islands, mountains, rivers, streams, lakes, Indian memories, American history, colonial and Victorian architecture, education, museums, music, art, hiking, fishing, hunting, skiing, swimming, boating, canoeing, and a hundred other recreations — one's visit should be predicated on what one wants to see and do.

NEW ENGLAND ITINERARIES

Although small by comparison with the rest of the United States, New England is so

are simply too many interesting roads, towns, and byways to list them all here.

THE FULL CIRCUIT

The best of all New England: Connecticut's **Litchfield Hills**, crossing into Massachusetts and traveling north up the **Housatonic River** into the **Berkshires** and the western **Mohawk Trail** to the Vermont border. From here one can swing northwest to **Lake Champlain** then east through the **Green Mountains**, across New Hampshire, with a stop in

topographically and culturally diverse that one could not hope to know it in detail without spending many weeks, if not months, there. But a series of highlights, itineraries to discover the best of New England, can give the visitor a marvelous sense of the beauty, complexity, and history of this land.

To be sure, your itinerary will naturally be based on your place of entry. The most common entries to New England are by car from New York state, often from the greater New York City area, by plane at Boston, or by car from Canada. Depending on your entry, you may want to try one or a combination of the following itineraries. In each case, general areas only are noted here, with detail provided in the following text. There

its stunning **White Mountains**, and then east to the Maine coast. Continuing northeast along the coast, with a stop at scenic **Portland**, to **Camden** or **Bar Harbor**, one can then turn inland toward **Mount Katahdin State Park** and back south through the villages and forests of the **Rangely Mountains** and Maine's rolling southern hills.

From southern Maine one hops the border for a look at historic **Portsmouth** and lower New Hampshire, then crosses into Massachusetts to explore the **Boston** area and **Cape Cod**, and from there south along

The attractive Atlantic shores OPPOSITE and lakes ABOVE of New England provide livelihood and recreation for the millions of inhabitants and visitors.

the coast into **Rhode Island** and back along the coast of Connecticut.

This circuit can be begun at any point, and can take anywhere from several weeks to as long as you want. For outdoors people, the best season is summer, for the swimming, beach strolling, boating, fishing, and hiking. For those who love the fall colors, this entire itinerary is resplendent in September and October.

THE BERKSHIRES

Nationally famous music, art, architecture,

and history among the superb green hills and precipitous granite crests of western Massachusetts. Enchanting country inns, exhilarating hiking, rafting, fishing, swimming, and a host of other activities are possible in one of the most beautiful areas of the United States.

SAILING THE COAST

For boating afficianados, New England's 6,130 miles of shoreline, its thousands of islands, and its lovely bays and many harbors all provide unique opportunities for summertime sailing. Bring your own boat if you have one, or, providing you can attest to your abilities, rent or lease a craft at one of New England's many yacht basins.

A HISTORICAL TOUR OF NEW ENGLAND

It's all historic, so you can hardly go astray. But from the old cities of **Boston**, **Portland**, **Portsmouth, Providence**, and **New Haven**, to the thousands of centuries-old towns from

southern Connecticut to northern Maine, there is more than enough history to fill a library and a lifetime of travels.

A TOUR OF NEW ENGLAND'S FINEST ART MUSEUMS

Among the best areas for art museums are **Boston**, **Providence**, **Portland**, **Williamstown** and the **Berkshires**, **Hartford**, and **New Haven**, as well as many smaller towns with both international and regional collections.

DOWN THE HISTORIC CONNECTICUT AND HOUSATONIC VALLEYS

Both the Connecticut and Housatonic Rivers flow north to south across wide areas of natural beauty and historic interest.

THE WILDERNESS

A Week in Maine's Baxter State Park
One of the finest parks in the eastern United States, Baxter is centered around magnificent Mt Katahdin. In addition to climbing the main peak, there are many smaller peaks and miles of hiking trails through superb pine, spruce, and fir forests. Mt Katahdin is also the northern end of the Appalachian Trail, which can be followed down through New Hampshire, Vermont, Massachusetts, and Connecticut.

VERMONT'S LONG TRAIL

Considered one of the world's ten best hiking trails, the Long Trail is situated in Vermont's Green Mountains. They are less precipitous and therefore easier hiking than the White Mountains of New Hampshire. A mix of hardwood and conifer forests and open meadows, with plenty of water, camping places, and vistas, this area makes a fine excursion.

WANDERING THE COAST OF MAINE

Maine has 3,500 miles of shoreline, more than any other Atlantic state, and even more than California! Much of the southern section, between the New Hampshire border and Portland, has been developed, but north of Portland to the Canadian border it is often completely undeveloped and stunningly beautiful. Many small towns add scenic variety.

THE WOODLANDER: THE BACKWOODS OF MAINE — SWIMMING, CANOEING, HIKING

No other place east of the Rocky Mountains has the backwoods variety of Maine. With its 10,000 lakes and over 5,000 trout streams and rivers, its mountains and rocky coast-

White Mountains, and from there westward into southern Vermont, down into the Berkshires of Massachusetts, and back to Boston.

A TWO-WEEK ITINERARY OF NEW ENGLAND

Again, the northern half is best, from Boston northward through Newburyport, Portsmouth, the southern Maine coast, including Portland and as far north as Acadia National Park, across Maine into

line, Maine is the last vestige of the outdoors experience left in the eastern United States. Best choices include the Allagash, Penobscot, and St John Rivers, the Moosehead Lake region, Mt Katahdin, the northeast coast from Acadia National Park to the Canadian border, and all the top half of the state.

ONE WEEK IN NEW ENGLAND — THE VERY BEST

If you have only a week in New England, go for the northern half — a day in Boston, then a drive up the coast to Portland (if it's summer, continue on, to Sebago Lake State Park). Then turn west toward the

New Hampshire and down to the White Mountains, across to the Green Mountains and Lake Champlain, then down to the Berkshires and back to Boston, with stops, if there's time, in Connecticut's Litchfield Hills and then Rhode Island.

The important thing to remember about any New England itinerary is that the destination is never as important as the journey, and that sometimes wandering with no destination is the best journey of all.

OPPOSITE: The lighthouse of Eastham, Massachusetts was built at a time when the ocean was New England's lifeline to the world. ABOVE: Lake Sunapee, New Hampshire, a popular tourist destination, was once the home of Indian tribes.

Eastern Massachusetts, Boston and Cape Cod

THE HEART OF NEW ENGLAND

The geographical "middle" of New England, Masssachusetts is an irregular rectangle of 8,257 sq miles (21,385 sq km) bordering Rhode Island and Connecticut in the south and Vermont and New Hampshire in the north.

In the west, the rolling, and at times massive, Berkshire Hills are one of the nation's loveliest mountain regions. The Connecticut River flows from north to south across the western middle of the state, its wide channel and tree-bordered banks offering tranquility and beautiful vistas. The Massachusetts coast offers a variety of natural beauty to those who love the sea. Though not as impressive as Maine's, it is best exemplified by the sand dunes, beaches, and cranberry bogs of Cape Cod. The offshore islands, Nantucket and Martha's Vineyard, have a unique charm that draws many thousands of visitors each year.

But it is to the Massachusetts villages and towns, with their superb colonial architecture, and to modern and historic Boston, that the visitor is drawn.

TOURIST INFORMATION

The **Massachusetts Office of Travel and Tourism** (13th floor, 100 Cambridge Street, Boston, MA 02202; ☎ (617) 727-3201, toll-free (800) 623-8038) provides a free travel kit that can be useful in planning a vacation in its historic cities or picturesque countryside. For travel information, call toll-free (800) 624-MASS.

BACKGROUND

Long before Europeans reached the shores of Massachusetts, a variety of Indian tribes, belonging mostly to the Algonquin federation, peopled the land. They first welcomed these strange, white-skinned people, sheltered them from the cold winter, and fed them in times of hunger. But it soon became clear that these European guests did not intend to go home, would not respond with friendship in kind, but rather intended to take over the Indian lands, betray and enslave the tribes, and force them to accept this strange religion which insisted that humans had crucified the Great Spirit. Courageous and independent, the Indian tribes one by one chose annihilation in war over serfdom, or died pitiably by the thousands from diseases introduced by the new immigrants.

THE FIRST EUROPEANS

Probably someday archaeologists and historians will discover incontrovertible proof that Scandinavian or other European explorers reached New England well before Columbus came to the New World. Some now claim it was the Viking Eric the Red, or his son, Leif Ericsson, who was the first European to reach Cape Cod. Records do show that the English explorer John Cabot visited the Massachusetts coast in 1497, only five years after Columbus discovered the New World. Yet it was well over a century before there were any permanent settlements here.

PILGRIMS AND PURITANS

Four days before Christmas, 1620, a shipload of pilgrims from Southampton, England, weighed anchor off what is now Plymouth. They had left England on September 15, intending to go Jamestown, but had first reached land at Cape Cod on November 19. Before disembarking at what they were to call Plymouth Rock, they drew up a charter which they termed the Mayflower Compact. This document established a temporary government based on the principle of the will of the majority; as such it set the stage for the American Revolution and the writing of the Constitution of the United States 150 years thereafter. Little could these first settlers have imagined that by the end of the century nearly 100,000 men, women, and children would have crossed the ocean from England to settle in the Massachusetts wilderness.

In 1630, a second settlement, based on theocratic principles, was founded at Massachusetts Bay by John Winthrop and his

OPPOSITE: On July 4, Bostonians dress up to commemorate their Colonial past.

hard-working, God-fearing Puritans. It was in this spirit that "the good town of Boston" was established — a town which quickly became, as the city remains today, the hub of New England business, cultural, and intellectual life.

THE SEEDS OF REVOLUTION

In subsequent years, British mismanagement of its American possessions created mistrust and anger in the colonies. Nowhere was this more notable than in Massachusetts. A stubborn king and a politically unwise Parliament burdened the colonies with unreasonable taxes. The Acts of Trade required that the colonies trade only with England and its markets. The Tea Act, the Stamp Act, the Townshend Acts, and the Intolerable Acts — all were perceived in the colonies as either oppressive or punitive, and created reactions of increasing defiance. "No taxation without representation" became the rallying cry that carried the colonists to revolution.

By 1775, under the uncompromising leadership of Bostonians like Samuel Adams, James Otis, and John Hancock, Massachusetts had become a catalyst uniting the thirteen colonies. Their speeches provoked protests that eventually exploded into action and bloody revolution. Indeed, "the shot heard 'round the world" and the first battle of the revolution took place on Massachusetts soil.

On April 19, 1775, British soldiers fired on the minutemen, as the patriot soldiers were termed, on the green in Lexington, Massachusetts — the first time mutual hostility became open warfare. Two months later on June 17, the Battle of Bunker Hill was fought, actually not on the hill for which it was named but on nearby Breed's Hill. In this battle, the colonial militia were defeated by British regulars. Nonetheless it fired the fighting spirit of the Continental soldier and the determination of the colonists to sustain the revolution until independence was achieved.

As a consequence of this revolution a new nation was born in 1776, a nation that was to name itself the United States. Its cornerstone was laid in Massachusetts.

OPPOSITE: A replica of the *Mayflower*, the clipper that brought the pilgrims to Plymouth in 1620, is anchored in the Plymouth harbor.

26

THE MARITIME MERCHANTS

Although Massachusetts experienced some political problems after the Revolution, it survived economically by exploiting the seas. Fishing, whaling, and the China trade made fortunes for daring seafarers and enterprising merchants. Those fortunes stood the state in good stead when the nineteenth century saw a decline in the maritime economy. Fortunes brought home to Boston in the sleek hulls of sailing ships were, during the industrial revolution, wisely invested in new industrial endeavors, notably textile manufacture. Textiles were to become the state's economic backbone as mill towns were quickly built along Massachusetts rivers. By 1850 the city of Lowell was a world leader in textile production.

THE TWENTIETH CENTURY

When, in the early years of the twentieth century, cheap labor in the southern states and abroad began to draw the textile industry away from New England, Massachusetts sought out new sources of income. By mid-century, the state regained economic stability in electronic and related industries — the high-tech revolution.

Since its earliest beginnings, Massachusetts has been the cultural and intellectual center of New England. In politics and government, its statesmen, once pre-eminent in the struggle for independence, became active thereafter in the affairs of the new nation. For more than two hundred years Massachusetts statesmen have continued to exert creative leadership in the nation's subsequent existence, as recently as the Presidency of John F. Kennedy and the Presidential campaigns of Robert Kennedy and Michael Dukakis.

Massachusetts is the home of more institutions of higher learning than any other state in the Union. Among them are two of the world's most prestigious universities — Harvard University and the Massachusetts Institute of Technology (MIT), as well as five of the nation's most academically outstanding colleges — Williams, Amherst, Smith, Mount Holyoke, and Wellesley.

Throughout the years Massachusetts has retained, in some measure, the ethical standards that characterized its beginnings: a capacity for independent thinking, a strong moral sense, a consistent faith in the power of education, a capacity for hard work, and a commitment to frugality.

BOSTON

It is easy to fall in love with Boston. Beautiful and sophisticated, it represents an almost

neighborhoods — elegant Beacon Hill, fashionable Back Bay, and historic North End.

Boston's nearly three million citizens, if one includes the city's outlying suburbs, is half the population of the state. They are a mix of blue bloods and blue collars, of sixth generation "Brahmins" and first generation Irish, the wealthy and the disadvantaged, the gentry and the homeless.

Over the centuries, Boston has provided more than its share of scholars, writers, and statesmen, men and women who have profoundly influenced the life of the nation.

perfect marriage of historic preservation and economic revitalization. The union has created a marvelous skyline of contrasts. Tall skyscrapers and the imposing modern Government Center alternate with the steeple of the Old North Church, the clock tower of the Customs House, and other historic landmarks.

BACKGROUND

The city founded by the Puritans in 1630 is inextricably associated with America's first role as a British colony. It remains proud of its part in the struggle for independence. Narrow streets, much as they were in colonial times, twist and turn haphazardly through famous

Indeed, Boston could be said to combine in its history and people the classic elements of America's heritage and its promise for the future.

Shawmut Peninsula

John Winthrop and his Puritans are said to have "stolen" much of the Shawmut Peninsula from hermit preacher Reverend William Blackstone to establish the city of Boston. The city owed much of its rapid growth to its fine deep water harbor and its fishing and merchant fleet that, by the eighteenth century, was the third largest in the English-speaking world.

Settlers in ever-increasing numbers came to Boston, making it the hub of trade and commerce in the English colonies and the most prosperous city in the English colonial empire. However, when the Crown and Parliament grew greedy and imposed upon the colonies a series of oppressive taxes and trade regulations, Boston led the break from the Mother Country.

Cradle of Independence

Years before the Revolution, the Massachusetts House of Representatives denied the right of Parliament to tax the colonies without representation, and it was Boston's revolutionaries whose speeches at meeting after meeting rallied their compatriots to unite against British oppression.

In March, 1770, one such group gathered outside the Old State House loudly protesting British tax policies. British soldiers fired into the crowd, killing five people. News of the "Boston Massacre" spread through New England, everywhere fanning hotter and hotter the flames of rebellion.

In meetings at Faneuil Hall and the Old Meeting House, Sam Otis and Samuel Adams continued to call for independence. One meeting, in December, 1773, led to the "Boston Tea Party," when about 90 colonists disguised as Indians boarded English ships by night in Boston Harbor and dumped more than three hundred chests of tea into the sea. In retaliation, the English closed the harbor and, in May, 1774, sent troops to occupy the city, forcing Boston's citizens to house the hated British soldiers in their homes.

The festering anger and resentment came to a head on April 18, 1775, when Paul Revere traveled to Lexington on his famous "Midnight Ride" to warn patriot leaders that British troop were on their way to nearby Concord to confiscate arms stored there by colonists. Bloody skirmishes the next day at Lexington Green and later at Concord gave the colonial militia its baptism by fire and marked the beginning of the Revolution.

George Washington, formerly a colonel of the Virginia militia, assumed general command of the Continental forces at Cambridge in July, 1775. He proved to be a brilliant soldier and politician. In less than a year he had wrested Boston from British control. The city continued free for the remaining years of the Revolution and, thereafter, exercised a major role in the affairs of the new nation.

From the time of the Revolution and well into the nineteenth century, Boston's ships sailed the seas of the world reaping great riches. Wealthy merchants transformed Beacon Hill and Back Bay into showplaces, featuring splendid mansions and elegant townhouses. The city became known as the "Athens of America" and the "Boston Brahmin," a symbol of the ultimate in human culture and refinement.

The Immigrant Wave

When, in the middle of the nineteenth century, Boston's maritime eminence began to fade, a manufacturing economy gradually took its place. In the same period, new waves of European immigrants reached the shores of America. Thousands of Polish, Irish, and Italian workers came to Boston, as well as to other New England cities, eager to begin life anew and to find work in this burgeoning industrial economy. With the rapid influx of people of different customs and nationalities, Boston's population tended to become segregated. Enclaves of Irish or Poles or Italians grew up in older neighborhoods while the "proper" Bostonians kept to themselves in their own enclaves on Beacon Hill and Back Bay.

Decline and Revival

By the end of the nineteenth century, Boston and all of Massachusetts lost much of their manufacturing base to southern states, which

OPPOSITE AND ABOVE: Boston's Fourth of July festivities.

CENTRAL BOSTON

N

★ Bunker Hill Monument

Warren Street

Monument Avenue

Winthrop Street

Adams Street

Chelsea Street

Mystic River Bridge

Constitution Museum

Constitution Road

★ U.S.S. Constitution

Charlestown Navy Yard

Rutherford Avenue

New Charles River Dam Visitors' Informations

Freedom Trail

Charlestown Bridge

RIVER

CHARLES

Science Park

Charles River Dam

Museum of Science

Commercial Street

Copp's Hill Burial Ground

Hull Street

Old North Church

Salem Street

Paul Revere Mall

Paul Revere Statue

Prince Street

Charlesgate Yacht Club

LEVERETT CIRCLE

Boston Garden and North Station

Causeway

John Fitzgerald Expressway

Washington Street

Hanover Street

Fleet Street

Paul Revere House

Charlesbank Playground

Massachusetts General Hospital

Merrimac Street

State Service Center

New Chardon Street

Sudbury Street

Black Stone Street

Marshall Street

North Street

Richmond Street

Marina

Cambridge Street

Stanford Street

Somerset Street

Congress Street

J.F. Kennedy Federal Building

Boston City Hall

Union Street

Columbus Park

Central Wharf

Louisburg Square

Bowdoin Street

Pemberton Square

Court Sq.

Faneuil Hall

Quincy Market

Mt. Vernon Street

State House and Archives Museum

Granary Burial Ground

Ben Franklin Statue Old City Hall

Boston Massacre Site

Central Street

State Street

Charles Street

Beacon Street

Freedom Trail

Park Street

School Street

Old City Hall

Old South Meeting House

Milk Street

Congress Street

Frog Pond

Tourist Information

Park Street Church

Devonshire Street

Boston Common

Washington Street

Winter Street

Arlington Street

Public Garden

Boylston Street

Tremont Street

Essex Street

Boston Tea Party Ship and Museum

Summer Street

Boylston Street

South Station Amtrak

INNER

Northern Av.

Atlantic Avenue

Dorchester Avenue

Museum Wharf

0.31 miles

500 m

could offer cheaper labor and lower taxes. The city's decline continued well into the twentieth century. In the 1960's, the area's incredible reserve of "brain power" at Harvard and MIT attracted high technology industries and research and development, which in turn fueled an urban revolution. Under the leadership of MIT-alumnus and architect I. M. Pei, Boston began to regain part of its former splendor. Expansive skyscrapers, government centers, and office complexes mingled with the historic buildings to create a "new" Boston look — one of urban sophistication infused with the charm of an earlier era.

Today Boston is one of America's most livable cities. It remains the financial, commercial, intellectual, and cultural hub of New England. The cobbled streets twist and turn, while an emerald necklace of parks and greenbelts (designed last century by the renowned landscape architect Frederick Law Olmstead) encircles the city. Ethnic neighborhoods break up any tendency toward urban sprawl, with each enclave having its own distinct appeal.

TOURIST INFORMATION

In advance of your trip the **Greater Boston Convention and Visitors Bureau** (Prudential Plaza, P.O. Box 490, Boston, MA 02199. ℂ (617) 536-4100, telefax (617) 424 7664) will send its free planning guide. After your arrival, you can pick it up at the **Prudential Visitor Center** in the Prudential Center Plaza, open daily from 8:30 am to 5 pm, or at the **Boston Commons Visitor Information Center** at Tremont and Winter Streets, also open daily, from 8 am to 5 pm. In the downtown historic center, the National Park Service, which manages the Freedom Trail, keeps its Visitor Center at 15 State Street open from 9 am to 5 pm.

TOURING BOSTON

The Freedom Trail

Boston is a city to be explored on foot and the **Freedom Trail**, a three-mile (five-kilometer) walking tour has been laid out by the National Park Service. It winds through the city and across the river into Charlestown, passing along its route 16 major historic sites and buildings related to the Revolu-

tionary era. It also goes through the varied neighborhoods that characterize the city: the Italian North End, the "Old Boston" section of Beacon Hill, and the Irish community in Charlestown. Do not worry about getting lost; signposts and a red line painted on the sidewalk point you in the right direction. It takes about half a day to see all the sights if you are in a hurry; allow an entire day for a leisurely stroll.

To start your Freedom Trail tour, go to the information kiosk on the Boston Common off Tremont Street. This is an area with souvenir

vendors hawking Boston memorabilia and food carts offering hot-dogs, ice-cream, and sweets. Inside the kiosk you can pick up a map of the Trail, along with information about the city's other attractions.

Now follow the red line into the **Boston Common**. This handsome, 45-acre (18-hectare), city green was purchased for $150 by the Puritan city fathers in 1634 as a militia "trayning field" and for the "feeding of Cattell." Under law, the Common can still be used for these purposes.

The Common has always been the pride of the city, even though in the beginning it was used for public hangings and punishments. In fact, the Puritans had a pillory built here to make an example of transgressors; the first to be pilloried was the carpenter who built it, who was accused of charging too much money for his work.

During the Battle of Bunker Hill, the British used the Common as an encampment and

Swan boats for rent at the pond in Boston Commons.

embarked for Charlestown from its grounds. Today, the Common is filled with hilly knolls and winding paths, statues and gurgling fountains. Noontime office workers often stroll through the park to enjoy the open space; in summer, outdoor concerts are held here. Sadly, however, like most urban open spaces in the United States, the Common is decidedly less appealing at night; even in daytime panhandlers and drunks are a common sight, and one should, needless to say, be on guard against pickpockets.

teenth-century granary that used to stand here. Established in 1660, it contains the graves of several notable Americans, including John Hancock, who signed the Declaration of Independence; the Revolutionary leader and orator Samuel Adams; the revolutionary Paul Revere; Peter Faneuil, who gave the city Faneuil Hall; and the victims of the Boston Massacre. Also interred here is Mary ("Mother") Goose, who concocted nursery rhymes to entertain her grandchildren.

Farther along the Trail at Tremont and School Streets is **King's Chapel**, completed

You can follow the Trail across Beacon Street to the "new" **State House**, designed by Charles Bulfinch and completed in 1795 on land that originally belonged to John Hancock. Its golden dome gleams like the harbor beacon that once topped this hill, and gave the neighborhood its name. The archives here contain valuable historic documents, including the original Charter of the Massachusetts Bay Colony.

Across the street from the Common is the lovely **Park Street Church**, its tall steeple a familiar Boston landmark since it was built in 1809. Abolitionist William Lloyd Garrison gave his first anti-slavery speech here in 1829.

Next to the church is the **Old Granary Burying Ground**, so-named for the seven-

in 1754; it was the first Anglican church in New England. In pre-Revolutionary times, the church was graced with gifts of silver and vestments from Queen Anne and King George III. The old cemetery next to the church contains the graves of John Winthrop, the first Puritan governor of the colony, and Elizabeth Pain, a seventeenth-century woman accused of adultery and said to have inspired Nathaniel Hawthorne to write his classic novel, *The Scarlet Letter*. Also on School Street is the statue of **Benjamin Franklin**, the first portrait statue erected in Boston, and the **Old Corner Bookstore**, a red brick house dating to 1712 that was the center of literary Boston in the nineteenth century. Noted authors, including Hawthorne,

Longfellow, and Emerson, gathered here to discuss their craft.

The **Old South Meeting House**, built in 1729, was the largest building in colonial Boston. It frequently hosted town meetings, especially in the years leading to the Revolution, when men such as Samuel Adams and John Hancock rallied the townspeople against the British. One of those meetings (held December 16, 1773), called to discuss the new British tea tax, led to the famous Boston Tea Party.

The **Old State House**, at Washington, Court, and State Streets, is located in the heart of downtown Boston, overshadowed by the towering steel and glass behemoth of **Government Center**. Built in 1713, it was the seat of colonial government and public life. In 1761, James Otis railed against unfair British regulations, prompting John Adams later to write, "then and there, the child Independence was born." And on July 18, 1776, from the east balcony, the Declaration of Independence was first proclaimed to the citizens of Boston.

A circle of cobblestones in the street just outside the Old State House marks the site of the **Boston Massacre**. Paul Revere's famed engraving helped to make the Massacre a key event in the growing popular resistance to British rule.

Follow the red line into **Dock Square**, with its boutiques, food-stands, markets, and bricked plaza. Also located here are **Faneuil Hall** and the **Quincy Markets**.

It is ironic that the Hall known as the "Cradle of Liberty" — because its second-floor meeting house hosted several important (and vociferous) protests against British colonial policies — was donated to the city in 1742 by Dutch slave trader Peter Faneuil. The first floor of the Hall has always been a market; however, stalls that once offered fresh meat, vegetables, and dairy products to colonial Bostonians have been transformed into modern boutique stands and food booths catering to tourists.

Note the grasshopper weather-vane atop the hall dome; for over two centuries it has been the symbol of Faneuil Hall. Fashioned in 1742 and a fine example of colonial artistry, it was inspired by similar weather vanes on the Royal Exchange building in London

and is the only part of the original Faneuil Hall which remains totally unmodified.

The Trail passes next through riotous **Haymarket Square**, a sprawling open-air food market with booths offering everything from fresh meats to hand-polished fruits and vegetables. Use the pedestrian underpass to cross Fitzgerald Expressway. This brings you to the **North End**, Boston's famed Italian neighborhood

The North End, not Back Bay, is the city's oldest neighborhood. In fact, until the nineteenth century, this section of

narrow, twisting streets was about all there was to Boston. When landfill and reclamation projects created new city dwellings, wealthy Boston families moved out of the crowded North End, and waves of immigrants moved in.

Today, it is a colorful area with its streetside restaurants featuring noontime plates of homemade pasta, sausage, and pizza. It also contains two of the most revered historic shrines along the Freedom Trail.

If **Paul Revere** were alive today, he would still have a **home** in Boston. That home, in North Square, is where the Revere family

Faneuil Hall OPPOSITE and Paul Revere's House ABOVE are preserved as memorials to America's fight for independence.

lived from 1770 to 1800. The clapboard building was built in 1680 by a wealthy merchant on the site of Puritan minister Increase Mather's home, which was destroyed by fire in 1676. In its time a fashionable townhouse, it is today the oldest wooden house in Boston.

While living here, Revere produced his famous Boston Massacre engraving, took part in the Boston Tea Party, secretly carried important revolutionary dispatches to Philadelphia, and participated in numerous other radical causes.

On April 18, 1775, Revere left his house, slipped out of the city in a rowboat, borrowed a horse in Charlestown, and rode to Lexington to warn revolutionaries there that the British were marching from Boston to seize munitions hidden in Concord.

The interior of the house has been restored, and many Revere artifacts — including some of his exquisite silversmith work, his old rocking chair, and saddlebags — are displayed.

"One if by land and two if by sea" is a phrase familiar to all American schoolchildren. It was the signal to be given from the **Old North Church** (at the foot of Hull Street near the end of Paul Revere Mall) to warn revolutionaries of a British invasion aimed at Lexington and Concord. In April 1775, a church sexton hung two lanterns from the steeple's highest windows to indicate British troop movements.

The 190-ft (58-m) white steeple has been a city landmark since the church — the oldest in Boston — was built in 1723. Inside the church, pew 54 once belonged to Paul Revere's son,

and was occupied several times by Revere himself. The church bells were cast in Gloucester, England, the first made for Britain's North American empire; they sound now only on Sunday mornings before services.

Up Hull Street is **Copp's Hill Burying Ground**. The earliest graves here date from 1660 and include those of Increase, Cotton, and Samuel Mather, important figures in early Boston history. One of the more interesting graves is that of the revolutionary Daniel Malcolm, who defiantly requested that "he be buried 10 feet deep, safe from British Musket Balls." He got his wish, but six years later, British soldiers got the last laugh when they used his tombstone for target practice. Even today you can see the marks on the stone.

Copp's Hill was also the site of a British cannon, which was trained on Bunker Hill across the Charles River during the battle. You can see the same view of Bunker Hill that British General Burgoyne had when he directed cannon fire at the entrenched revolutionaries.

Here you cross the Charlestown Bridge, and then either walk up Monument Avenue to Bunker Hill, or keep to the waterfront along Constitution Avenue to visit the *SS Constitution*, the Navy's oldest fighting ship.

A 221-ft (67-m) white granite obelisk stands as a memorial to the men who fought at the Battle of Bunker Hill. The **Bunker Hill monument** is actually on Breed's Hill, where the misnamed clash took place on June 17, 1775. About 1,200 Americans and 3,000 British troops took part in the battle. The first English attack failed, and British troops twice required reinforcements.

The revolutionaries eventually were forced to withdraw; colonial General Prescott ordered a retreat only after all ammunition had been used. The toll: for the Americans, 140 killed, 271 wounded, 30 captured; for the British, 226 killed, 828 wounded.

Even though the revolutionaries were defeated, the Battle of Bunker Hill proved to the revolutionaries that they measured up well in battle against the British regulars. Said General Washington of the clash: "I am content. The liberties of the country are safe."

The monument's observation tower offers a panoramic view of Boston, the harbor, its islands, and the *SS Constitution*; its spiral staircase has 294 steps leading to the top, with no elevator. An excellent audiovisual presentation explaining the battle in detail, as well as the events leading up to it, can be seen at the **Bunker Hill Pavilion** on Hoosac Pier, just off Constitution Avenue.

Along the harbor front is the **Charlestown Navy Yard**, one of the first naval shipyards in the nation, and the last stop on the Freedom Trail.

A tour of the yard's exhibits spans nearly 200 years of maritime history. At the Visitor Information Center, you can view a 10-minute slide show, and receive information on guided walking tours.

Beginning in 1800, the yard built, serviced, and supplied ships for the Navy. Workers swarmed over the dry docks, rope walks, and shipways cluttered with maritime equipment. The yard reached peak operation during World War II, when it employed more than 50,000 men and women who built and repaired a record number of vessels. You can tour the *SS Cassin Young*, a destroyer of the type built here, which saw extensive action in that war.

Attractions include Pier 1 (one of the 11 original wharves that serviced ships), the 1833 dry dock (one of the first of its kind in the country), the Maritime Society Museum, and the Commandant's House.

But the centerpiece of the yard is the magnificent *SS Constitution*, the oldest commissioned warship in the Navy. ((617) 426-1812; admission free; open daily from 9:30 am to 3:30 pm. The foundations of the U.S. Navy were established by Congress in 1794 upon authorization of six new frigates. One of these was the *SS Constitution*, a 44-gun warship built at the nearby Hartt's Shipyard and launched in 1797.

She sailed against the Barbary pirates, fought the British in the war of 1812, and engaged in 40 sea battles without a loss. When a British sailor saw shots bounce off the *SS Constitution*'s planking, he shouted, "Her sides are made of iron!" Thus the ship gained its renowned nickname, "Old Ironsides."

The *SS Constitution* is still a commissioned warship; members of its present crew take visitors on tours of the spar deck with its huge cannons that fire 32 lb (15 kg) shells, the gun

deck with its 30 24-lb (11-kg)-long guns, the captain's quarters below decks, and the berthing deck where the crew slept in hammocks. At the rear is the ship's wheel, which required the strength of four men to control. Sailors also climbed the ropes to the "fighting tops" positioned on each mast to fire on enemy ships.

Beacon Hill

The Beacon Hill neighborhood, with its narrow gas-lit streets, elegant townhouses and tall shade trees, is like a city-within-a-city

with turn-of-the-century splendor. This has not always been the case. In the late seventeeth-century, the Trimount neighborhood (Beacon Hill's old name) was a wild no-man's land referred to by some Bostonians as Mt Whoredom. But when the State House was built here in 1798, many of the city's wealthiest families rushed to commission State House architect Charles Bulfinch to design Federal mansions and elegant bow-fronted Greek Revival row houses. Beacon Hill had arrived, and it remains one of the most desirable districts in which to live.

OPPOSITE AND ABOVE: Clapboard and red-brick houses, typical of Boston's Colonial architecture, are much admired for their style.

Today, a walk along the bumpy side-walks of Beacon Hill is reminiscent of a more elegant, peaceful era. It is a splendid oasis of fine period architecture and tranquil surroundings yet within a stone's throw of busy downtown Boston.

Start your tour at the Common on **Beacon Street**. Numbers 39 and 40 are Bulfinch-designed twin mansions that house the Women's City Club of Boston; guided tours of the homes' elegant Greek Revival interiors are by appointment only. Also note the Beacon Hill "purple glass" in the windows, caused when sunlight reacted with impurities in the imported English glass, turning it a distinctive purple color.

Go north on Spruce, past old servants' houses, to **Mount Vernon Street**. This is

arguably the most beautiful street on "the Hill," as locals now call it. The **Nichols House Museum**, another 1804 Bulfinch design, is typical of Beacon Hill's architecture from its golden era. It is one of the few private homes on the Hill open to visitors, and is lavishly furnished in period decor.

Just off Mt Vernon is **Louisburg Square**. Its ornate homes frame the elegant green, creating the ultimate in traditional Boston-style charm; a home in this idyllic enclave remains the dream of many Bostonians. Louisa May Alcott, author of *Little Women*, lived here, as did novelist William Dean Howells. One of Howells' books, *The Rise of Silas Lapham*, relates the life of Boston's wealthy in the mid-nineteen hundreds.

Paris, while the streets are lined with beautiful Victorian brownstone row houses. Since the 1870's, a Back Bay address has been a coveted status symbol.

Copley Square is the heart of Back Bay, and displays some of Boston's best nineteenth- and twentieth-century architecture.

The 1877 **Trinity Church**, designed by Henry Hobson Richardson, is a magnificent Romanesque design some consider the best church architecture in America. Inspired by the great cathedrals of France and Spain, it is massive in scale. Inside, the intricate details include rich wall murals, carvings, and friezes.

Across Dartmouth Street is the **Boston Public Library**, the world's oldest free library. The Library, with its collection of six million books, is approached through an elegant central courtyard with a fountain and a spectacular entry fashioned after a Greek temple and graced with a grand Siena marble staircase. The library is enriched by murals, bronzes, and paintings by some of the world's most renowned artists and is a tranquil retreat from the bustle of Boston.

Cross St James Avenue to reach the **John Hancock Tower**, a striking, glass-covered 60-story skyscraper designed by I. M. Pei. New England's tallest building, it is the corporate headquarters of the John Hancock Mutual Life Insurance Company. It often acts as a giant mirror, reflecting the Back Bay cityscape in its tall glass walls. It has long been plagued by the not insignificant problem of its glass sheets falling off; this however, seems to have recently been remedied.

One of the best ways to see Boston is from the Tower's 60th-floor **observatory**. High-speed elevators carry visitors the 740 ft (226 m) from the street to the observatory in about 30 seconds, from where they can see a panorama embracing the gold-domed State House, the gracious townhouses of Beacon Hill, Boston Harbor's islands, Cambridge, the North and South shores, and the distant White Mountains of southern New Hampshire. Observatory exhibits include "Boston 1775," a light and

Christmas is a great time to visit Beacon Hill, when strolling carolers are a holiday tradition. With its nineteenth-century ambience, you almost expect Whittier or Longfellow to pop up on the green.

Other Beacon Hill streets of interest to visitors are narrow, cobblestoned **Acorn Street** and, for its coffee houses, galleries, and chic shops, **Charles Street**.

If you prefer a guided tour to simply wandering around, Boston By Foot, ((617) 367-2345, offers one-and-a-half hour walking tours of the Hill, as well as walks along the Freedom Trail and through historic Copley Square.

Back Bay and Copley Square

Back Bay's wide Commonwealth Avenue is fashioned after the grand boulevards of

During the summer, Bostonians are drawn to the city's many parks and pedestrian walkways.

sound show about Revolutionary Boston. ((617) 247-1976.

Down Stuart Street is **Copley Place**, a $500 million shopping and eating emporium. Along Huntington Avenue are the 22-acre (nine hectare) grounds of the **Christian Science Center** (the 1894 Mother Church here has a square shaped bell tower) and the offices of the *Christian Science Monitor*, the highly respected national daily newspaper.

Backtrack to reach the **Prudential Center**, another corporate insurance headquarters skyscraper with its own 50th-floor Skywalk, an observation tower from which 360-degree views of the city with accompanying historical commentary can be enjoyed. Sunset is the best time to visit.

Government Center

Rising in the middle of the city like a fortress of brick, steel, and glass is Government Center, an urban renewal program designed by I. M. Pei that transformed 60 acres (24 hectares) of tattoo parlors and girlie stores which only a decade ago dominated the squalid Scollay Square district, into some of the most imposing buildings in Boston, and created a new focus for the city. The district's centerpiece is the new **City Hall**, designed by Kallman, McKinell, and Knowles. It is a massive inverted pyramid resting on a plaza of brick resembling "an Aztec temple on a brick desert."

Surrounding the Hall are several modern buildings that add to the district's futuristic feel: the tall twin towers of the **John F. Kennedy Office Building**, the **Center Plaza Building** with its contours that curve to the slope of Beacon Hill, and the **State Service Center**, whose sharp architectural lines cut the horizon northwest of the Hall.

In fact, the only historic nineteenth-century building that survived Government Center's transformation is the **Sears Crescent**, notable for the huge 200-gallon (909-liter) steaming tea pot that hangs from one corner of the building to mark the site of what was the largest tea store in Boston.

The district's display of modern architecture is on a grand scale and its huge open spaces a welcoming oasis from the crowded city neighborhoods.

The Harborwalk

Harborwalk is a two-mile (3.2-km) trail that loops around Boston's historic waterfront, providing a bird's-eye view of the wharfs, boats, and islands. It begins at the National Park Service Visitor Center (on State Street near the Old State House) and ends at the Boston Tea Party Ship and Museum. Along the way are some interesting historic and commercial buildings, as well as sights and sounds of maritime Boston. Highlights include:

The **Boston Children's Museum** (300 Congress Street; ((617) 426-8855, admission $6.00 with reductions for children and senior citizens; open every day but Monday, 10 am to 5 pm, Friday until 9 pm), on Museum Wharf across the Fort Point Channel, has been called "the country's best museum for kids." Its varied displays, exhibits, and special events are guaranteed to entertain children of all ages. Toddlers jump over steps and slide down platforms in Playspace; older kids climb like monkeys from platform to platform within a futuristic sculpture; and teens can even try out the latest dance steps at the Clubhouse. There are replicas of an Indian wigwam, a country street, a two-story Japanese house, and a television studio equipped with TV monitors.

The **New England Aquarium** (Central Wharf, off Atlantic Avenue; ((617) 742-8870; admission $7.00 with reductions for children and senior citizens; open Monday, Wednesday, and Friday, 9 am to 5 pm) contains a four-story ocean coral reef glass tank filled with sharks, turtles, and more than 600 other sea creatures. Dolphin and sea lion shows are offered daily on the *Discovery*. One of its newest exhibits, "Wired for Sound," demonstrates just how noisy the underwater world can be. From here you can board whale-watching cruises on the wharf, which head to Stellwagen Bank, one of the East Coast's prime whale habitats.

The **Computer Museum** (Museum Wharf; ((617) 423-6758; admission $5.00 with reductions for children, students, and senior citizens; open every day but Monday, 10 am to 5 pm, Friday until 9 pm) features state-of-the-art computer technology

OPPOSITE: Boston's high-tech Computer Museum captivates visitors of all ages.

in interactive displays. You can play games, create art, write music — in fact almost anything is possible here, including a computer that not only talks, but can carry on a "conversation."

Another pleasant option is the **Boston Tea Party Ship and Museum** (near South Station at Congress Street Bridge; ((617) 338-1773; admission $5.00 with reductions for children, students, and seniors; open daily 9 am to dusk). It is a full-scale replica of the British brigantine *Beaver*, and costumed guides relate the history of the 1773 Boston

Tea Party. Museum artifacts include a tea chest reputed to be among those tossed into the water on that fateful night.

CULTURAL ATTRACTIONS

Museums

The best known of Boston's museums is the **Museum of Fine Arts** (465 Huntington Avenue; ((617) 267-9300; admission $6.00 adults, $5.00 seniors, free to children under 16, free to all on Saturday 10 am to 2 pm; open Tuesday to Saturday, 10 am to 5 pm, Wednesday 10 am to 10 pm). It was originally beneficiary of artifacts gathered by Boston's wealthy Brahmins as they traveled the world in the nineteenth century; those objects still form the centerpieces of its varied collections.

It is today considered one of the world's great museums. The handsome 1909 Greek temple-style building contains more than 200 galleries. The Oriental collection is one

ABOVE: In downtown Boston, American history is at your fingertips. OPPOSITE: The John Fitzgerald Kennedy Library and Museum.

of the most remarkable in the country, with Buddhist paintings and sculptures, some dating to the twelfth century, dominating the Japanese displays; ceramics, including objects from the Han dynasty (third century), highlight the Chinese section.

The Egyptian artifacts are largely the bounty of a 40-year Middle East expedition sponsored by the Museum and Harvard University. It is reputed to be the finest collection of 4,000-year-old antiquities outside Cairo.

The European galleries display a large selection of Monets; in the American collection are Gilbert Stuart's portraits of George and Martha Washington. Twentieth-century art is displayed in the museum's new glass-roofed wing.

Just a short walk away is the **Isabella Stewart Gardner Museum** (The Fenway; ((617) 566-1401; admission $5.00 with reductions for children, students, and seniors; open Wednesday to Sunday, noon to 5 pm, Tuesday noon to 6:30 pm), a Venetian-style palazzo which houses the personal collections of the eccentric nineteenth-century millionairess. Isabella Stewart Gardner commissioned agents to travel the world in search of fine art, and they purchased six million dollars worth which included Matisses, Whistlers and Titian's *Rape of Europa*, painted for Phillip II of Spain. Other treasures include beautiful tapestries, centuries-old mosaics, and sculpture. Its courtyard, with Venetian-style windows and balconies, flowering plants and trees framing a Roman floor mosaic from Livia that dates to the second century, is a delight.

The **John F. Kennedy Library and Museum** (Columbia Point, off Morrissey Boulevard; ((617) 929-4523; admission $3.50 for adults, $2.00 for seniors, free under 16; open daily from 9 am to 5 pm) is another of architect I. M. Pei's designs and some consider the sleek concrete and glass structure to be one of his best.

Nine exhibit halls, filled with family and presidential memorabilia encircle a central room containing the president's desk as it was on November 22, 1963 when he was assassinated during a motorcade ride through the streets of Dallas. A 35-minute film chronicles his life and times. Other displays feature artifacts from his PT-109 days and the

Cuban missile crisis. An eight-story gray glass contemplation pavilion contains only an American flag, a bench, and a Kennedy quotation engraved on the wall.

Another **Kennedy** museum is his **birthplace** in suburban Brookline, Z (617) 566-7937. The house has been restored to the way it looked in 1917, the year Kennedy was born, and offers audio guided tours narrated by his mother, Rose Kennedy.

The **Museum of Science** and the **Charles Hayden Planetarium** (Science Park, along the Charles River; ((617) 723-2500; admission $6.00 with reductions for children and seniors; open Tuesday to Sunday, 9 am to 5 pm, Friday 9 am to 9 pm) are hands-on delights, and feature a life-sized model of an Apollo space capsule, a 20-ft (six-meter) plastic tyrannosaurus rex, and a "lightning-making" machine.

Finally, **Fenway Park** is also a museum of sorts. Located just off Brookline Avenue, in Back Bay, it is home to the Boston Red Sox, the city's major league baseball team. Fenway is also one of the oldest, most charming, and intimate of baseball stadiums, which brings the fans so close to the action that they can almost reach out and touch the players.

Music

The world-famous **Boston Symphony Orchestra** performs in **Symphony Hall** (Massachusetts Avenue; ((617) 266-1492); and the **Boston Pops** performs outdoors at the **Hatch Memorial Shell** on the Charles River Esplanade during the summer, as does the **Boston Ballet Company**. Theaters and performing arts centers are found throughout the city.

SHOPPING

If you were born to shop, get your credit cards ready, because Boston has it all. **Back Bay** is one of the leading shopping districts; its **Newbury Street** is the city's equivalent to New York's Fifth Avenue with its ultra-chic boutiques, clothiers, and galleries. Alan Bilzerian, Divino, Daree, Martini Carl, Settebello, and Parachute offer the latest fashions from designers such as Gianni Versace, Kendo, and Armani. Also down the street is Burberry's, makers of the renowned British

trench coat that helps to keep Bostonians warm during their often-bitter winters.

Copley Place, a new $500 million shopping and dining palace, showcases the international fashions of Gucci, Louis Vuitton, Jaegar, and plenty of others. New England's only Neiman-Marcus department store offers a Texas-sized selection of high-quality merchandise. And if you are in the mood for something gold, try Tiffany's. Just down the block is the **Prudential Center**, for Saks Fifth Avenue and Lord and Taylor.

Downtown Crossing is unquestionably the city's most popular shopping area for all walks of Boston society. Jordan Marsh, the venerable 135-year-old Boston department store, offers designer-label clothing for both men and women, not to mention a fine selection of silver and china.

Then there is **Filene's**, a sophisticated fashion emporium whose basement sales are a Boston tradition. All sorts of designer items are sold here at bargain-basement prices, with prices further slashed at regular intervals until the remaining merchandise is sold or finally donated to charity.

Beacon Hill's Charles Street is the neighborhood's commercial center. Its many art galleries, antique stores and coffee houses make it an interesting place for browsing.

Finally, **Bloomingdales**, of New York City fame, is located in nearby Newton, Massachusetts, just west of Boston.

WHERE TO STAY

As in most major American cities, Boston hotels tend to be expensive and many cost over $150 for a double. However, Boston does offer value for the price. By shopping around you can frequently book a weekend package that includes a room on Friday and Saturday night for about two thirds the weekday rate. These offer vary with the season, but don't hesitate to ask about weekend rates when you call for reservations. You can find yourself in Boston without a room if the Red Sox are playing or during graduation time at the numerous colleges in and around the city.

OPPOSITE TOP: Boston's Red Sox baseball team has an avid local following. OPPOSITE BOTTOM: Food stands and boutiques line Quincy Markets.

Super Luxury Hotels

For elegant old-style Boston hospitality, one cannot beat the **Copley Plaza Hotel** (138 St James Avenue; Z (617) 267-5300, toll-free (800) 225-7654; 394 rooms), the **Ritz-Carlton** (Arlington and Newbury Street; Z (617) 536-5700, toll-free (800) 241-3333; 287 rooms), and the Omni Parker House (60 School Street; Z (617) 227-8600, toll-free (800) 843-6664; 541 rooms). These are "luxury" hotels with double room rates in excess of $150.

A very classy luxury hotel, decorated with murals by N.C. Wyeth (the father of Andrew), is the **Meridien** (250 Franklin Street; ((617) 451-1900, toll-free (800) 223-9918; 326 rooms), now owned by Air France. Another superb hotel is the new **Four Seasons** (200 Boylston Street; ((617) 338-4400, toll-free (800) 268-6282; 228 rooms).

In this same category is the European-style **Bostonian Hotel** (Faneuil Hall Marketplace, Dick Square; ((617) 523-3600, toll-free (800) 343-0922; 153 rooms) which is centrally located near Faneuil Hall, Government Center, and the open market; children under 12 stay free. Toward the waterfront is the ultra-modern **Boston Marriott Hotel at Long Wharf** (296 State Street; ((617) 227-0800, toll-free (800) 228-9290; 400 rooms).

Expensive

More moderately priced, but still on the high end of expensive, are **Back Bay Hilton Hotel** (40 Dalton Street; ((617) 236-1100; 367 rooms); **The Westin Hotel at Copley Place** (10 Huntington Avenue; ((617) 262-9600, toll-free (800) 228-3000; 804 rooms) and **Lafayette Swissotel** (1 Avenue de Lafayette; ((617) 451-2600, toll-free (800) 992-0124; 500 rooms).

Located near the Prudential Center is **The Lenox Hotel** (710 Boylston Street; ((617) 536-5300, toll-free (800) 225-7676; 225 rooms).

If you are attracted to large scale hotels, there is the **Marriott at Copley Place** (110 Huntington Avenue; ((617) 236-5800; 1,147 rooms).

The **Holiday Inn — Government Center** (2 Blossom Street; ((617) 742-7630, toll-free (800) 238-8000; 304 rooms) is attractive for families as children under 18 stay free.

Moderate

Howard Johnson's operates three establishments in the city that are among the best of the moderately priced hotels: **Howard Johnson's Motor Lodge** (Andrew Square; ((617) 288-3030, toll free (800) 654-2000; 180 rooms); **Howard Johnson Lodge Fenway** (1271 Boylston Street; ((617) 267-8300, toll-free (800) 654-2000; 94 rooms); and **Howard Johnson's Hotel Kenmore Square** (575 Commonwealth Avenue; ((617) 267-3100, toll-free (800) 654-2000; 179 rooms).

If you are flying out early in the morning

or arriving late at night, the **Ramada Inn — Boston Airport** (225 McClellan Highway; ((617) 569-5250; 209 rooms), is a good standby.

Inexpensive

Finding an inexpensive hotel in Boston is not an easy task. In fact, I hesitate to suggest any. However, there is an alternative — a bed-and-breakfast. A double room will cost between $45 and $90. You can book a bed-and-breakfast through the **Bed and Breakfast Associates Bay Colony, Inc.** (P.O. Box 57166, Babson Park Branch, Boston, MA 02157; ((617) 449-5302; telefax: (617) 449-5958).

OPPOSITE: Sightseeing buses tour elegant downtown Boston. ABOVE: Downtown dining out of doors.

EATING OUT

In Boston you can find a bit of everything when it comes to cuisine, but no one should visit New England without tasting its seafood specialties — creamy clam chowder, fresh lobster, fish chowder, fried or steamed clams, and fried cod. These are served at several of the moderately priced restaurants listed below. Reservations are advised for evening meals at all restaurants.

It may come as a disappointment, but you will be hard-pressed to find the famous Boston baked beans in a restaurant. Once the staple of the New Englander's diet, this wholesome, tasty dish is now considered low-brow and uncouth. Also sadly absent from the menus is the traditional New England boiled dinner — a joint of ham boiled for hours with cabbage, carrots, onions, turnips, and potatoes.

Expensive

Most of the top-of-the-line restaurants in Boston specialize in European fare except for the **Hampshire House** (84 Beacon Street;

ABOVE: Street chess challenger in Cambridge. OPPOSITE: The Colonial buildings of Harvard University dominate Cambridge.

((617) 227-9600). It was known for its fine cuisine long before its Bull & Finch Pub, which inspired the television series, *Cheers*, thrust it into the national spotlight. Here you can dine on New England clam chowder and lobster, or steaks and chicken prepared with a French or Italian twist.

For French cuisine, Boston has several restaurants from which you can choose. **Another Season** on Beacon Hill (97 Mount Vernon Street; ((617) 367-0880) has a weekday (Monday to Thursday) fixed price, four-course menu that is moderately priced. Downtown at **Maison Robert** (45 School Street), weather permitting, one can lunch or dine outside. Here you can order New England food, such as a New England lobster in champagne sauce. **Aujourd'hui** in the Four Seasons Hotel (200 Boylston Street; ((617) 338-4400) and **Le Marquis de Lafayette** in the Lafayette Hotel (1 Avenue de Lafayette; ((617) 451-2600) also serve French-style meals.

For a change of pace, **Cafe Budapest** in the Copley Square Hotel (47 Huntington Avenue; ((617) 266-1979) serves, as its name suggests, Hungarian meals. **Jasper** (240 Commercial Street; ((617) 523-1126) prepares superb Continental meals in an elegant ambiance.

Moderate

Along the waterfront are the best seafood restaurants. Recommended are **Anthony's Pier Four Restaurant** (140 Northern Avenue; ((617) 423-6363), and **Jimmy's Harborside Restaurant** (242 Northern Avenue; ((617) 423-1000). Nearby is the **Ye Olde Union House** (41 Union Street; ((617) 227-2750).

Famous for its "fresh" lobster stew is **Durgin Park Market Dining Room** (340 Faneuil Hall Marketplace), which also claims to have been established "before you were born." As no reservations are accepted here, it is wise to arrive early on weekends.

In Boston, you can also find excellent Italian restaurants. **Cricket's** (Faneuil Hall Marketplace; ((617) 720-5570) and **Davio's Ristorante and Cafe** (269 Newbury Street; ((617) 262-4810) are highly recommended.

For good food served with elegance at a reasonable price, there is the **Cafe Plaza** in the Plaza Hotel (138 St James Avenue; ((617) 267-5300).

Inexpensive

Like its hotels, Boston's restaurants are pricey. However, many of the above establishments serve a lower price luncheon menu, and the thrifty traveler, who wants to sample the "high life" of Boston, would do well to eat a late lunch and a light dinner.

For lighter meals, Boston abounds with establishments serving Italian sandwiches and pizzas. The Italian sandwich, originally a long hard roll filled with salami, tomato, lettuce, onions, black olives, and topped

Massachusetts Institute of Technology

MIT, situated along the Charles River just off the bridge, is world-famous for its research in science and engineering, and for the Nobel laureates among its numbers. Tours of the campus are offered daily. Two of the most interesting buildings are the triangular roofed Kresge Auditorium and the moated **MIT Chapel**, both designed by Eero Saarinen.

with olive oil, now comes in a wide variety of fillings. Some have even become so "yuppie" as to include bean sprouts. An Italian sandwich is a meal in a bun. Along the same line are meatball and Italian sausage sandwiches, which are filling and tasty.

CAMBRIDGE

Cross the Harvard Bridge from Boston and you will enter Cambridge, a small and unassuming industrial city that is home to two of the world's greatest institutions of higher learning: the Massachusetts Institute of Technology and Harvard University.

Harvard

Continue down Massachusetts Avenue and you will head directly into **Harvard Yard**. This is the heart of **Harvard University**, the oldest college in the United States, established in 1636 to train young men for the ministry. Six American presidents graduated from Harvard and its alumni include countless statesmen and renowned thinkers in every field and from every corner of the world.

The Harvard Information Center (1350 Massachusetts Avenue; ((617) 495-1573) provides maps and materials outlining the campus highlights; guided tours are offered from June through September.

Harvard itself, with more than 400 buildings, resembles a small village rather than a typical campus. **Massachusetts Hall** is the oldest building on campus, dating to 1720; its handsome red brick walls adorned with ivy provided the architectural inspiration for other buildings on the grounds. During the Revolution, the Hall headquartered colonial troops.

Nearby are **Harvard Hall** (1776) and the very English Holden Chapel (1744), complete with its own coat of arms. But **University Hall**, a white granite building completed in 1815 from a Charles Bulfinch design, is one of the most striking structures

on campus. In front of the building is Daniel Chester French's statue of university namesake John Harvard, a seventeenth-century minister who willed a large sum of money to the fledgling college. (The model for the work was not actually Harvard at all, but rather a nineteenth-century student whom Chester thought fit the ideal of what John Harvard should have looked like.)

The many-columned **Widener Memorial Library**, containing more than 10 million volumes in its collections, is an imposing building.

Do not overlook Harvard's fine museums. Van Goghs, Renoirs, and Picassos can be found at the **Fogg Art Museum**; in the **Sackler Museum**, just across the street from the Fogg, are one of the finest collections of Chinese jade in the world; and German Expressionists dominate at the **Busch-Reisinger Museum**.

Other interesting displays include the **Peabody Museum of Archaeology and**

Ethnology (North American Indians, with relics from Lewis and Clark's 1803 explorations), and the **Botanical Garden's** German glass-blown flowers, depicting nearly 800 different species of flowering plants. However, the **Museum of Comparative Zoology** has the most fascinating collections, including a 225-million-year-old egg, a six-million-year-old turtle shell, the 25,000-year-old Harvard Mastodon (found in New Jersey), a 180-million-year-old dinosaur, and a genuine giant sea monster.

For a break from touring, head to **Harvard Square**, with its fine selection of coffee houses and bookstores. Don't leave Cambridge without a brief walk through its historic district. The handsome **Common** was the encampment site for George Washington's colonial army for nearly a year. **Brattle Street** is notable for "Tory Row," named for homes built by wealthy British sympathizers during the Revolution. (Most of the houses date back to the nineteenth century.) Also on Brattle is the house of Maine poet Henry Wadsworth Longfellow, who lived here for nearly 50 years. The 1759 structure was also Washington's army headquarters during the British attack on Boston.

WHERE TO STAY

Cambridge hotel rates tend to be high and reservations will be essential during graduation season (mid-May to early June) and college registration (late August and early September).

Luxury and Expensive
For ultra-modern, luxury lodging in either Boston or Cambridge, try the **Hyatt Regency** (575 Memorial Drive; ((617) 492-1234, toll-free (800) 233-1234; 471 rooms). Patterned after the Hyatt Regency in San Francisco, it has a glass elevator that carries you to the revolving Spinnaker Restaurant, which serves Italian meals.

For night life without having to leave the hotel, you can stay at the **Charles at Harvard Square** (1 Bennett Street; ((617) 864-1200; 299 rooms) whose **Regattabar** is one of the top jazz clubs in Boston.

Of equal quality and price are **Boston Marriott Cambridge** (Kendall Square; ((617)

Phoning home from Harvard Square.

494-6600, toll-free (800) 228-9290) and **Royal Sonesta** (5 Cambridge Parkway; ((617) 491-3600, toll-free (800) 343-7170; 400 rooms).

Moderate

Howard Johnson's Motel (777 Memorial Drive; ((617) 492-7777, toll-free (800) 654-2000; 205 rooms) is reliable. At the **Quality Inn** (1651 Massachusetts Avenue; ((617) 491-1000; 134 rooms) children under 16 stay free.

EATING OUT

Cambridge, like Boston, has fine dining establishments, but the Cambridge coffeehouses, which serve food along with coffee, tea, and hot drinks, have a style of their own. They abound in the university area and rise and fall in popularity with the whims of the college crowd. Ice cream parlors are popular here. Hit Harvard Square on a hot summer's day for the best ice cream treats in Boston or Cambridge.

Expensive

Panache (798 Main Street; ((617) 492-9500) serves excellent lobster as well as the best lamb in the area. At **Upstairs at the Hasty Pudding** (10 Holyoke Street; ((617) 864-1933), you can get a fixed-price three-course English or French dinner. The **Spinnaker Restaurant**, atop the Hyatt Regency (575 Memorial Drive) serves Italian cuisine.

LEXINGTON AND CONCORD

BACKGROUND

"Bloody Butchery by the British Troops" screamed the headlines of the *Salem Gazette*, describing the fight that took place between 77 colonial militiamen and 700 regular British troops on April 19, 1775. These were the "shots heard round the world."

Word of the battles at Lexington Green and at Concord bridge and of the skirmishes back along the 20-mile (32-km) road to Boston spread quickly through the American colonies, uniting the colonists as no words could do, in a resolve to fight for their independence.

What had begun as a struggle between English authorities determined to enforce the will of Parliament, and the people of Massachusetts, who were just as determined to retain their rights as English citizens, soon escalated into a war for independence which lasted more than eight years. By 1775, Britain's oppressive economic policies had transformed America into a seething powder keg of discontent.

The English government suggested that General Thomas Gage, governor of Massachusetts and commander of the British forces, jail revolutionary rabble-rousers like Sam Adams and John Hancock. But Gage knew where such actions would lead and decided on what he thought was a less inflammatory engagement: to seize the revolutionaries' arms supplies stored in Concord. His mission's success depended on secrecy to ensure little resistance by the townspeople. Despite his precautions, Boston's revolutionaries knew of Gage's plan before his troops left the city, and sent Paul Revere and William Dawes to Lexington with news of the advancing soldiers.

In Lexington, revolutionaries gathered at Buckman's Tavern on the Common to await the arrival of the British troops. When the 77 minutemen saw the Redcoats, they formed two long lines. Militia Captain John Parker exhorted his men, "Stand your ground. Don't fire unless fired upon. But if they mean to have a war, let it begin here!"

Soon British officer Major John Pitcairn ordered the patriots to disband; in the face of more than 700 British regulars, there wasn't much else they could do. As the militiamen slowly obeyed, a shot rang out, no one knows from which side. Then British troops, many of them inexperienced in actual combat, began firing wildly at the revolutionaries, ignoring their commanders' orders to stop. When it was over, eight Americans lay dead, and the first battle of the Revolution had taken place.

The British continued to Concord where they searched all buildings for arms; what they found they burned or tossed into ponds. When the revolutionaries saw smoke coming from Concord, they thought the British were burning the town, and advanced to attack them at Concord's North

Bridge. "Fire, fellow soldiers, for God's sake, fire!" yelled revolutionary Major Buttrick of Concord. Having been joined by minutemen from the surrounding countryside, the militia soon outnumbered the English by four to one.

The battle raged on. The British were driven into retreat along the road back to Boston, where they were attacked constantly. One British officer said it "seemed as if there was a musket behind every tree." Some of the heaviest fighting took place at Menotomy, with more than 5,000 troops on both sides. Eventually, the arrival of British reinforcements saved Gage's troops from annihilation, and they retreated to Bunker Hill in Boston.

The final toll: for the British, 73 dead, 173 wounded, 26 missing; for the revolutionaries, 49 dead, 40 wounded, five missing. Now England knew that the American rebellion ran deeper than dissatisfaction over taxes; the American people were prepared to fight for their freedom.

WHAT TO SEE

Lexington is a good place to begin your "Revolution" tour. Often called the "cradle of American liberty," nearly 100,000 visitors a year trek **Battle Green** where troops and patriots fought. The battle line is marked by a sculpture of the *Minuteman*.

On the Green is the **Buckman Tavern**, where revolutionary militia gathered before the battle. The tavern's old front door has a bullet hole made by a British musket ball during the fight. Inside, you will find the original seven-foot (two-meter)-wide tap room, along with many other historic artifacts.

The seventeenth-century **Hancock-Clarke House** is where Paul Revere and William Dawes warned Sam Adams and John Hancock of the British advance. The nearby **Munro House** served as British headquarters and a field hospital for troops after the battle. Other historic sites are detailed in walking tour maps available at the Lexington Historical Society, on the Common, ((617) 861-0928.

From Lexington, you can follow the battle road down Massachusetts Avenue. At the **Fiske House** site, intense close-quarter fighting took place; it also marks the boundary of **Minuteman National Historic Park**, which encompasses the battlegrounds.

Your first stop in the park should be at the Battle Road Visitor Center (Route 2A), where a film and maps portray the skirmish. During summer months, reenactments of the battle are sponsored by the National Park Service. Up the road is the **Paul Revere Capture Site**, where Revere was taken by British troops when he, William Dawes, and Dr. Samuel Prescott were surprised by an English patrol as they rode on from Lexington to Concord to warn of the British advance. The captured Revere later escaped, Dawes fled back to Lexington, but Prescott eluded the British to carry word of their march to Concord.

Continuing west is **Bloody Angles**, so-called for two sharp turns in the road which provided ambush points for the militia. Eight British soldiers were killed here during their retreat. Just before reaching Concord is **Meriam House**, which gave cover to minutemen as they fired on fleeing British troops crossing a narrow bridge.

Finally, Concord's **North Bridge** is where the American revolutionaries first fired a volley against British soldiers. It is difficult to believe that these beautiful surroundings could have been host to such bloody undertakings. You can walk the battle route, and even cross over the North Bridge itself. Daniel Chester French's statue, the *Minuteman*, stands here, a memorial to the citizen-soldiers of 1775 who led the fight for freedom. You get a panoramic overview of the battleground from the North Bridge Visitor Center, ((617) 369-6993.

WHERE TO STAY

In Concord it is possible to stay in Henry David Thoreau's former home, now the **Colonial Inn** (48 Monument Square; ((508) 369-9200; 60 rooms; moderate to expensive). It has a good restaurant with seafood, continental specialties, and home-baked breads and pastries.

Another place to stay is the standard **Howard Johnson's Motor Lodge** (740 Elm Street; ((508) 369-6100; 106 rooms; moderate to expensive).

EASTERN
MASSACHUSETTS

NEW HAMPSHIRE

PLUM ISLAND

Newburyport

Haverhill

CAPE ANN

Rockport

Lawrence

Gloucester

Lowell

Danvers

Fitchburg

Beverly

Reading

Salem

Leominster

Peabody

Marblehead

Concord

Lynn

Swampscott

MASSACHUSETTS BAY

MASSACHUSETTS

Revere

Winthrop

Marlborough

BOSTON

Steamer (no autos)
Summer Only

Worcester

Framingham

Quincy

Passenger Ferry Summer Only

Scituate

Norwood

Milford

Brockton

Duxbury

Plymouth

RHODE ISLAND

Attleboro

Middleboro

CONNECTICUT

N

Fall River

New Bedford

Steamer (no autos)
Summer Only

Passenger Ferry

BUZZARDS BAY

ELIZABETH ISLANDS

Falmouth

10 miles

16 km

Steamer (summer only)

ISLAND SOUND

ATLANTIC OCEAN

Cuttyhunk

VINEYARD SOUND

THE WORCESTER AREA

WORCESTER

Industrial Worcester is the second largest
city in Massachusetts. Situated 50 miles
(80 km) west of Boston, it is not a major
tourist destination, but the **Worcester Art
Museum** (55 Salisbury Street; ((508) 799-
4406; admission $3.50 with reductions for
students and senior citizens, free for children under 18; open year-round daily except
Monday, times variable) houses one of the
finest collections of art and antiquities in
New England.

One of the museum's displays is that of
the priceless artifacts from Antioch, dating
from the second to the sixth century AD. The
collection resides in Worcester because the
museum sponsored a series of Syrian ex-
cavations in the 1930's which unearthed
these ancient treasures.

For the serious history buffs, the **American Antiquarian Society** (Salisbury Street
and Park Avenue; ((508) 755-5221; admission free; open Monday to Friday 9 am to
5 pm, closed holidays) has the largest collection of source materials covering the nation's first 250 years of history. This collection includes copies of the *Massachusetts
Spy*, the inflammatory anti-British newspaper printed in Worcester between 1700
and 1776, which boldly supported the push
for independence.

Tourist Information
The **Worcester County Convention and
Visitors Bureau** (33 Waldo Street, Worcester, MA 01608; ((508) 753-2920) can provide
information about the city.

Where to Stay
There are many hotels in Worcester, particularly in the moderate to expensive range.
If you want to make reservations in advance,
you can call **Howard Johnson–College
Square** (800 Southbridge Street; ((508) 791-
5501; 137 rooms; moderate to expensive).

"FRUITLANDS"

The youth movement's "return to nature"
in the 1960's could have been inspired by a
curious nineteenth-century settlement
in **Harvard** Massachusetts, called **Fruitlands** about 22 miles (35 km) north of
Worcester on Route 110. Established in 1834
by transcendentalist Bronson Alcott (father
of Louisa May Alcott, author of *Little Women*)
and English activist Charles Lane, the little
farm community attracted Utopians who
gave up material goods, embraced vegetari-
anism, and spent much time communing
with their natural surroundings — the hilly
beauty of the Nashua Valley. The community soon disbanded, but the old farmhouse
at Fruitlands now houses a transcendentalist
museum with displays of artifacts belonging
to Alcott and other nineteenth-century transcendentalist writers and philosophers such
as Thoreau and Emerson.

Other museums on the grounds include
a 1794 **Shaker House**, moved here after
Harvard's Shakers (see also THE SHAKERS,
page 85) left the village in the early twentieth
century. It is now filled with exhibits of
handsome Shaker handiwork.

THE NORTH SHORE

SAUGUS

Many an eighteenth and nineteenth century
New England sea captain harbored his merchant ship in ports along the North Shore. A
trip north from Boston can be a journey
through history. The **North of Boston
Tourist Council** (P.O. Box 3031, Peabody,
MA 01960; ((508) 532-1449) has prepared a
wealth of literature on the area's museums
and historic houses and public buildings.

Just north of Boston, off U.S. 1, is the **Sau-
gus Iron Works**. A replica of an iron works
built in 1650 by early Puritans, it demonstrates how settlers made and forged iron.
Its workers toiled 12 hours a day, six days a
week, in the white heat of the blast furnace,
to the constant clanging of great hammers.

Today the iron works looks much as it did
in the seventeenth century, complete with

water wheel pits and slag piles. You can tour the furnace, forge, iron house, and blacksmith shop; only the iron works house is original, dating to 1646.

SALEM

Background: The Witch Trials
"At first the girls would not answer, for fear of being discovered. They simply screamed and writhed or did blasphemous things, such as dashing a Bible against the wall. But gradually they began to give names."

Thus begins an inquisitor's account of Puritan Salem's 1692 Witch Trials, an American inquisition and reign of terror and hysteria. By the time it was over, 19 people had been hanged on Gallows Hill in one of the most notorious episodes in American history.

What to See
This town, settled in 1626, leans heavily on its "be-witching" legacy. (Even its tourism slogan chips in with, "Stop by for a Spell.") If witches grab your fancy, head to the **Salem Witch Museum** (admission $3.50 with reductions for children and senior citizens; open daily 10 am to 5 pm), where 13 life-sized stage settings present a historically

accurate drama examining the hysteria (Washington Square; ((508) 744-1692).

The 1642 **Witch House** (on Essex Street; admission $2.50; open daily 10 am to 4:30 pm) is the restored home of Jonathan Corwin, one of the judges at the witch trials; preliminary examinations of more than 200 people accused of witchcraft were held here. The **Burying Point** (Charter Street), dating from 1637, is interesting for its seventeenth-century gravestones; the graves include those of judges of the witchcraft trials and a *May-flower* passenger. The **Rebecca Nurse House** (in Danvers) belonged to a woman who was hanged as a witch; it overlooks a field where she is buried in an unmarked grave. And Gallow Hill is still here.

From the early eighteenth century, Salem was an important port and shipbuilding town, home of many wealthy merchants. Its seafaring legacy is apparent in the **Peabody Museum**, begun in 1799 by 22 sea captains who founded the East India Marine Society. By 1821 they had collected 2,000 items from all over the world for the growing museum; today, the collection numbers more than 300,000 artifacts and works of art exhibited in seven buildings and 30 galleries. Included are ships' figureheads and models, paintings, gold, silver, and textiles (on East India Square; ((508) 745-1876).

Of Salem's seafarers, Nathaniel Hawthorne wrote, "They sailed where no others dared to go, anchored where no one else dreamed of making a trade." Native son Hawthorne was a leading celebrity in the mid-1800's during the flowering of American literature. He was fascinated by both Salem's witch and sea legacies: he harbored a brooding sense of guilt about one of his ancestor's involvement in the witch trials, and had turned to the sea for an occupation when he served as officer of the Custom House.

At one time, 40 wharves stood on Salem's harborfront; the longest was **Derby Wharf**, which still stands today. Across the street, the 1819 **Custom House** (((508) 744-4323; open 8:30 am to 5:30 pm every day of the year except Thanksgiving, Christmas, and New Year) contains restored offices, including Hawthorne's. Both Derby Wharf and the Custom House are managed by the National Park Service, which offers daily guided tours in July and August. But the **House of the Seven Gables** ((Turner Street; ((508) 744-0991; admission $5.00 adults, $2.50 children under 16; open daily 10 am to 4:30 pm) is the major Hawthorne relic. Featured in his novel of the same name, the 1668 house contains original Hawthorne furnishings, and its share of secret stairways and passages. Other houses on the grounds include the 1750 Hawthorne birthplace, and the 1655 Retire Becket house. The **Essex Institute** (Essex Street; Z (508) 744-3390) preserves six houses spanning three centuries (the earliest dating from 1627) and its museum includes original witchcraft trial records.

Salem's new **Heritage Walking Trail** maps supply an itinerary that includes most of the town's historical attractions; the path is marked by a red line drawn on the sidewalk.

Tourist Information
The **Salem Chamber of Commerce** (Old Town Hall in Derby Square; ((508) 744-0004) can provide you with maps and other information.

Where to Stay and Eating Out
In downtown Salem is the **Hawthorne Hotel on the Common** (18 Washington Square; ((508) 744-4080; 89 rooms; moderate to expensive) and nearby is the **Lyceum** (43 Church Street; ((508) 745-7665) which serves inexpensive to moderate Continental menus. It was here that Alexander Graham Bell first demonstrated his telephone.

CAPE ANN

Cape Ann's rocky promontory and wild seas lure weekending Bostonians to its coastal villages, harbors, and artists' colonies. Named for the Queen of England in 1614 by Captain John Smith, the Cape has always looked to the sea for its livelihood.

GLOUCESTER

The first settlement on the Cape and the oldest seaport in the nation (1623), Gloucester continues to be one of the busiest fishing ports in the world, with a fleet of nearly 300 boats. Huge fish-processing plants line its shores, packaging the catch for shipment across the country.

The **statue** of the Gloucester fisherman (*Man at the Wheel*), which appropriately faces the sea, is a New England landmark. The statue's inscription simply reads, "They that go down to the sea in ships."

More than 10,000 Gloucester men have been lost in three centuries of fishing, and almost every year another Gloucester boat and crew is claimed by the sea. Each June, the Blessing of the Fleet ceremony takes place during St Peter's Fiesta.

Whale-watching cruises board at the docks in downtown Gloucester. For

additional Cape Ann whale-watching cruises, contact **Cape Ann Chamber of Commerce**, (33 Commercial Street, Gloucester, MA 01930-5034; ((617) 283-1601).

For a completely different perspective of this fishing village, head to the **Rocky Neck Art Colony** (East Main Street, East Gloucester), the nation's oldest working art colony, with galleries and shops.

Where to Stay
The best hotels are along the beach on Atlantic Road. The **Bass Rocks Motor Inn** (119

OPPOSITE: Witches were taken seriously by early New Englanders, but in Salem today their legacy is a tourist attraction. ABOVE: Placid waters at the fishing village of Rockport.

Atlantic Road; ((508) 283-7600; 48 rooms) is expensive, but the view is rewarding. In the moderate to inexpensive price range is **Gray Manor** (14 Atlantic Road, East Gloucester, MA 01930; ((508) 283-5409), a large summer home converted into a guest house.

Where to Eat

For good New England seafood, stop at **The Easterly Restaurant** (87 Atlantic Avenue; ((508) 283-0140; inexpensive to moderate).

ROCKPORT

Rockport is a fishing village, artists' colony, and tourist attraction rolled into one. Its streets are busy with people during the summer season, and parking space is but a dream, and its folksy style attracts families, the elderly, and tour buses.

Rockport is well known for its shops. Galleries, crafts, and restaurants are crowded into both old and new fishing shanties along the narrow winding lanes of **Bearskin Neck**, a favorite gathering place for artists.

The quality of natural light on Cape Ann attracts artists and photographers to this picturesque village. Late afternoon is an especially popular time, as the setting sun focuses its fiery colors on the landscape and casts fleeting shadows over the craggy outcroppings along the shoreline.

A Rockport landmark is **Motif No.** 1, a weathered red lobster shack, a favorite subject for countless painters. It is actually a recent replica of the original, which was destroyed in a storm a few years ago.

Continuing around the head of the Cape, the shoreline scenery from Pigeon Cove to Annisquam is dotted with picturesque hidden bays and tiny coves.

Where to Stay

The best is the **Peg Leg Inn** (2 King Street; ((508) 546-2352; 29 rooms). It is almost as old as the town itself and has moderate and expensive rooms depending on the view.

Eating out

No alcohol is served in Rockport; it is a "dry" town. You can, however, bring your own

Picturesque Rockport Harbor.

wine into any of the restaurants that line Bearskin Neck. Seafood is the standard fare and prices are inexpensive to moderate.

IPSWICH

A colonial town about 21 miles (34 km) north of Rockport on Route 1A, Ipswich still has nearly 50 homes built before 1725, with several from the 1600s. One of the finest is the **John Whipple House** (on Main Street), which dates back to 1640.

The **Richard T. Crane Beach Reservation**, at the end of Argilla Road on Ipswich Bay, is popular with the area's artists, and the sandy beach which stretches for five miles (eight kilometers) is among the East Coast's finest. Here the **Pine Hollow Trail** leads hikers on an hour-long trek along the shore and through a red maple swamp. Follow up a walk with a feast of a regional favorite, delectable Ipswich clams, available at any restaurant in the village.

NEWBURYPORT

At the mouth of the Merrimack River, less than six miles (10 km) from the New Hampshire state line, is Newburyport. During the eighteenth and nineteenth centuries, the town's large merchant vessel fleet made local sea captains wealthy. Their Federal-style mansions lining High Street are a testament to their success. Tours around one of the finest, **Cushing House**, built in 1808 for Caleb Cushing, first U.S. envoy to China, show some of the artifacts he brought back from his tour of duty in the Orient.

Note the "widow's walks" atop many of the historic homes. Historians are divided as to their origin. Some say they were built for sea captains' anxious wives, who could gaze over the harbor and out to sea from their lofty perch, searching for their husbands' returning ships. Others contend that they were simply an affectation of style — an ornamental ironwork favored by one wealthy sea salt, and then copied by his contemporaries.

The riverside **Market Square District** is also newly restored, its cobblestoned streets lined with handsome historic brick buildings which now house shops and restaurants.

Less than three miles (five kilometers) east of Newburyport is **Plum Island**, a national wildlife refuge where more than 250 species of migratory birds stop to rest along the Atlantic Flyway each spring and fall. Vistas of the island's dunes, marshes, and its six-mile (10-km)-long beach can be enjoyed from an observation tower. In the fall, wild beach plums and cranberries can be found along the shore.

THE SOUTH SHORE

While some visitors might make a quick stop at Hingham's Old Ship Church (1681), Scituate's Lawson Tower and Light, and the Hull Lifesaving Museum, most travel the South Shore along Interstate 93 and U.S. 6 only as a route from metropolitan Boston to Cape Cod. However, there are at least three sightseeing detours that should not be missed.

QUINCY

Just south of Boston across the Neponset River, this former shipbuilding center was home to both John Adams and John Quincy Adams, the only fatherson tandem to become presidents of the United States (they were the second and sixth presidents, respectively).

The **John Adams National Historic Site** (Adams Street; ℂ (508) 773-1177) is the home bought in 1787 by the president and his wife Abigail. The varied styles of its original furnishings are the result of occupancy by four generations of Adamses. The **John Quincy Adams Stone Library** has more than 14,000 books in nine languages. On Franklin Street, guided tours lead you through the birthplaces of the Adamses, modest seventeenth-century colonial saltboxes containing family artifacts, including some of the famous letters Abigail wrote to John when he was a member of the Continental Congress in Philadelphia and, later, a negotiator at the Paris Peace Talks. (ℂ (508) 773-1177; open daily from mid-April to mid-November.) Finally, the resting place of two presidents — John and son John Quincy — is the **United First Parish Church** (Hancock and Washington Streets; ℂ (508) 773-1290).

PLYMOUTH

Next stop is Plymouth, about 30 miles (50 km) south. Every American schoolchild knows about **Plymouth Rock**, the boulder where the Mayflower Pilgrims first stepped onto American soil on December 21, 1620. What is traditionally regarded as "The Rock" is covered by an elaborate Greek Classical pavilion on the Water Street Harbor shore, and marked with a plaque.

Across the street, you can climb the 37 steps to the top of **Cole's Hill** to the burial place of the Pilgrims who died during that first bitter winter in the New World and to a great view of Plymouth Harbor. Also on the harbor front, at State Pier, is the *Mayflower II*, a full-scale replica of the vessel which brought the 103 settlers from England (admission $5.50 adults, $3.75 children ages 5 to 12; open daily, April to November, 9 am to 5 pm, July to August, 9 am to 7 pm). Guides, dressed in period costumes and playing the roles of the passengers and crew who made the treacherous crossing, demonstrate seventeenth-century skills, and answer questions about the first colony of Pilgrims.

Tablets on **Leyden Street** mark the sites of the Pilgrims' first houses; however, the 1666 **John Howland House** (on Sandwich Street) is the only remaining Plymouth home where original Mayflower Pilgrims actually lived. The **Richard Sparrow House** (on Summer Street) is Plymouth's oldest, dating from 1640. In nearby Kingston is the 1674 **Major John Bradford House**. Possessions of the first Pilgrims are on display at the **Pilgrim Hall Museum** (Court Street; ((508) 746-1620; admission $4.00 with reductions for children and senior citizens; open daily 9:30 am to 4:30 pm).

About three miles (five kilometers) south on Route 3A is **Plymouth Plantation** (admission $12 adults, $8 children 5 to 12; open daily, April to November, 9 am to 5 pm), a living-history museum that recreates the 1627 settlement of the Pilgrims. Men and women portray the dress, speech, and manner of actual residents of the historic community, bringing to life the routines and activities of seventeenth-century Plymouth.

You will get a good overview of the village, with its many thatch-roofed cottages, from the **Fort Meetinghouse**, ((508) 746-1622.

Plymouth County

Southern Massachusetts produces more than 50 percent of the nation's cranberry crop. **Cranberry World** (off Route 44; ((508) 747-1000; admission free; open daily, April to November 9:30 am to 5 pm, and July to August 9:30 am to 9 pm) traces the history of this tangy red berry from colonial times to the present; features include tours

of working cranberry bogs and cooking demonstrations.

Another way to enjoy the cranberry region is to board the **Edaville steam train** in nearby **Carver**, one of the state's cranberry capitals with more than 3,000 acres (1,200 hectares) under cultivation. The train takes you through six miles (10 km) of a 1,800-acre (730-hectare) cranberry plantation. The ideal time for a trip is during the fall harvest. (Rochester Street; ((508) 866-4526; admission $12.50 with reductions for children and senior citizens; open April to December, times variable.)

At Plymouth Plantation, seventeenth century lifestyles are reenacted.

Tourist Information

The **Plymouth County Development Council** (P.O. Box 1620, Pembroke, MA 02359; ((508) 826-3136) provides tourist information free of charge.

Where to Stay

The **Sheraton Plymouth Hotel at Village Landing** (180 Water Street; ((508) 747-4900; 177 rooms) is in the expensive range and offers high-quality service and rooms with a water view.

For a change of pace and an intimate look at New England living, **Be Our Guest** (P.O. Box 1333, Plymouth, MA 02360; ((508) 837-9867) will book you a room in a moderately priced guest house or bed-and-breakfast.

Eating Out

With a charm all its own, the **Lobster Hut** (Town Wharf; ((508) 746-2270) fixes simple seafood meals for less than $10.00. On hot summer days you can eat outside on the picnic tables.

New Bedford

In the second chapter of his classic novel, *Moby Dick*, Herman Melville says that Nantucket may have been the romantic home of whaling, but that it was New Bedford which made whaling an industry.

Indeed, New Bedford, a deepwater port on Apponagansett Bay, was once the greatest whaling center in the world, providing work for more than 10,000 men. By the 1850's, it harbored more than 400 whaling ships, some of whose voyages lasted up to five years. Each whaling fleet alone was valued at more than $10 million.

Whaling built New Bedford. As Melville wrote, "all these brave houses and flowery gardens came from the Atlantic, Pacific and Indian Oceans. One and all, they were harpooned and dragged up hither from the bottom of the sea."

A good example of the prosperity derived from whaling is the many elaborate mansions of sea captains and maritime merchants along **County Street**, at the crest of a hill overlooking the harbor. The **Gilbert Russel House**, built in 1800 and remodeled in

elaborate Italianate style in 1868, is one of the most spectacular.

The discovery of oil in Pennsylvania in the late 1850's marked the beginning of the end for New Bedford. With its whaling fleet badly depleted by the Civil War and losses in Arctic waters, New Bedford's whaling slowly gave way to manufacturing.

But much of the whalers' presence remains in New Bedford. The town's fishing fleet ranks first in the nation in value of fish and scallops landed. More than 200 vessels moor at the downtown waterfront.

From the New Bedford Visitor Center on North Second Street it is a short trip up Johnny Cake Hill to the world's largest whaling museum, the **New Bedford Whaling Museum** (admission $3.50 with reductions for children and senior citizens; open September to June, Monday to Saturday 9 am to 5 pm, Sunday 1 pm to 5 pm, summer hours variable ((508) 997-0046). For 175 years, New Bedford's whalers were known throughout the world, and their legacy is preserved here. Perhaps the most interesting exhibit is the bark, *Lagoda*, the

ABOVE: New England's seafaring legacy is on display in New Bedford's Whaling Museum. OPPOSITE: Full-scale replica of the *Mayflower* moored at Plymouth.

largest ship model in the world, built in 1915. This half-scale replica of a vessel that made 12 whaling voyages is outfitted with whaleboats, harpoons, and other equipment. In the Panorama Room gallery, there are two 50-ft (15-m) sections from a quarter-mile (400-m)-long painting depicting one year aboard an 1847 whaler. The original crew list of the whaleship *Acushnet* bearing Herman Melville's name are also on display here. The museum library contains more than 1,100 logbooks from whaling journeys, and the theater shows a film of an actual whaling expedition, complete with a "Nantucket sleigh ride," or whale chase.

Across the street from the Whaling Museum is the **Seamen's Bethel**, the whaleman's chapel of Melville's *Moby Dick*. Built in 1832, it contains a pulpit resembling the hull of a ship, and memorial tablets dedicated to sailors lost at sea.

New Bedford's flourishing nineteenth-century glass industry is represented at the **Glass Museum**, housed in a 1821 Federal mansion filled with more than 2,000 pieces of Pairpoint and Mt Washington glass (Second Street; ((508) 994-0115; admission \$2.00 with reductions for children and senior citizens; open 10 am to 4 pm, closed Sundays).

Tourist Information
New Bedford Visitor Center (North Second Street; ((508) 991-6200).

Where to Stay
Pineapple Hospitality (P.O. Box F821; ((508) 990-1696) operates a bed-and-breakfast booking service (open Monday through Friday from 9 am to 5 pm). It specializes in the New Bedford area but does have some listings for other parts of New England and will happily help you lay out an itinerary and bookings for each night.

On the outskirts of New Bedford are many moderately priced motels, including the **Comfort Inn** (171 Faunce Corner Road; ((508) 996-0800; 85 rooms).

CAPE COD

A long spit of sand that curls out into the Atlantic Ocean for about 70 miles (113 km), Cape Cod is one of New England's premier resort areas, with 300 miles (480 km) of sandy beaches, coastal villages, and isolated islands.

The Cape extends about 30 miles (50 km) into the warm Gulf Stream before it turns up at its "elbow." The weather is much milder here than on the mainland, with summers cooled by sea winds and winters warmed by Gulf Stream air.

The peninsula was a sleepy amalgam of small colonial fishing villages before the advent of the automobile. Then mobile visitors from nearby cities (Boston is only 70 miles

Tidy villages and natural harbors contribute to Cape Cod's summer popularity.

or 113 km to the north and New York City is less than 250 miles or 400 km away) discovered its charm. Now swamped by visitors each summer, Cape Cod is a more intriguing destination in off-season months.

Cape Cod has preserved much of its beauty due largely to the **Cape Cod National Seashore**, 27,000 acres (10,930 hectares) of dunes and beaches, salt marshes, pine forests, and cranberry bogs set aside to protect a remnant of the fragile ecosystems of the Lower Cape.

TOURIST INFORMATION

In the summer, the **Cape Cod Chamber of Commerce** (Routes 6 and 132, Hyannis, MA 02601; ((508) 362-3225) keeps its visitors center open daily from 9 am to 7 pm. There you can pick up maps, guides, and hotel information. The **Bed & Breakfast Cape Cod** (P.O. Box 341, West Hyannisport, MA 02672; ((508) 775-2772) will help you in finding a moderately-priced room, if one is available, on the Cape.

A DISAPPEARING LAND

A succession of glacial depositions and wind and wave erosion formed Cape Cod's present hook shape. This geologic history, and ongoing ocean and climatic changes, spell a doubtful future for the Cape, one all too well known to its 175,000 residents. Studies seem to indicate that the roaring sea and northwest winds of the Atlantic are

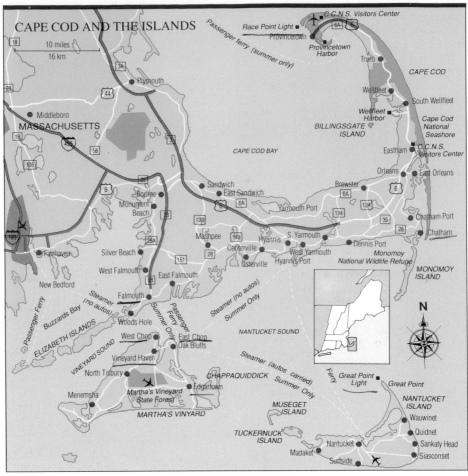

CAPE COD AND THE ISLANDS

eroding the Cape a little more each year, and that the land itself may be sinking into the sea.

Over the last century, entire communities have been lost to the ocean. One report tells of Billingsgate Island, a fishing village off Jeremy's Point that once held a lighthouse, school, and 35 family homes. By 1935, it had been completely washed into the sea. "Now all that is left of this island, which was first explored in 1620 by the Pilgrims, is a sand bar that surfaces at low tide — a grim reminder of Cape Cod's tenuous future," the report read.

Scientists say that generations from now, the Cape will be only a memory, worn away to a few sandy shoals, and that there is nothing modern-day technology can do to stop it. There are more alarming statistics: "Parts of the Cape are losing five acres (two

hectares) a year to marine erosion," wrote Greg O'Brien, an expert on Cape Cod and the islands. "Chatham, on the Mid Cape's south coast, lost 10 ft (three meters) of shoreline a day to marine erosion during a recent winter."

A greater threat to the Cape is the rise in sea level brought about by the "greenhouse effect" — automobile, power plant, and other human pollution melting polar ice caps. Scientists predict that within the next 40 years, shorelines from Provincetown to Bourne will retreat an average of 100 ft (30 m), and according to O'Brien, by the year 2100 more than 1,200 ft (366 m) of shoreline could be underwater. "Adding to this problem is the fact that while sea levels are rising, some coastal areas of the Cape, formed from silt sediments, are actually sinking — slowly compressing under their own weight."

Provincetown, at the Cape's tip, finds itself in a most precarious position; the U.S. Geological Survey in Woods Hole predicts that the town "is headed for real trouble" which can be measured "in tens of years, not hundreds."

This is happening all over the Cape. The cliffs at Falmouth Heights are washing into Vineyard Sound; West Barnstable lost 15 ft (4.5 m) of Sandy Neck beach in one recent winter storm; even the land in Wellfleet, where Marconi transmitted the first transatlantic cable 85 years ago, rests more than 200 ft (61 m) out in the sea. Geologists give Nantucket Island only 700 years before it disappears under the ocean.

PILGRIM BEGINNINGS

Cape Cod was inhabited by the Wampanoag Indians when explorer Bartholomew Gosnold landed in 1602. He named the peninsula for the great schools of cod found in the surrounding waters.

In 1620, the Mayflower Pilgrims landed at today's Provincetown before moving on to Plymouth, just across Cape Cod Bay. The Pilgrims stayed there for more than a month, exploring the area and working on what was to become the Mayflower Compact, the governing constitution of the Massachusetts Bay Colony.

By the 1630's, settlements had sprung up along the Cape, with fishing the mainstay industry. A whaling industry evolved, and the Cape's fishermen commanded a fleet of vessels that sailed out of the ports of Truro, Wellfleet, and Nantucket Island.

OVER THE BRIDGE

On summer weekends, traffic to the Cape may be backed up more than an hour at the bridges spanning the **Cape Cod Canal**, and cars line up bumper-to-bumper along U.S. 6 and 6A, which together stretch the length of the Cape.

The Cape Cod Canal, which eliminates the need for ships to circumnavigate the peninsula, took 11 years to build, and was finished in 1919 at a cost of $16 million. Because of it, there are only two road accesses to the Cape.

If you select the Bourne Bridge at the southern end of the canal, Route 28 will lead you first into the "Upper Cape," that part of the peninsula closest to the mainland, past West Falmouth and Falmouth and Marstons Mill before reaching Hyannis. If you cross at the Sagamore Bridge, at the canal's northern end, you can either continue on U.S. 6, a four-lane highway across the "Mid Cape" to Orleans, or Route 6A, a two-lane scenic road through several Mid-Cape towns. Highways 6 and 6A meet near Orleans and continue up the "Lower Cape" to Provincetown as rural Route 6.

THE UPPER CAPE

The southwestern end of Cape Cod, on Buzzard's Bay, has spectacular coastline, historic houses, and the Nobska Lighthouse overlooking Vineyard Sound. It was originally settled by Quakers in the seventeenth century; its first house was built in 1685.

Falmouth

The main town on the southwestern elbow of the cape, Falmouth expanded around its village green, where many sea captains built fine houses at the height of the whaling

Fences decrease the erosion of Cape Cod's dunes.

industry's prosperity. The **Falmouth Historical Society Museum** (55/65 Palmer Avenue; ((508) 548-4857; admission $2.00 adults, $0.50 children; open mid-June to mid-September, Monday through Friday 2 pm to 5 pm), which occupies two eighteenth-century houses on the Green records the town's whaling legacy. Also on the village green is the birthplace of Katherine Lee Bates, who wrote the lyrics to *America the Beautiful*.

Around Falmouth

From Falmouth one can bicycle along the

old railbed from Falmouth to **Woods Hole**, a principal port on the Cape, and a former whaling town from where ferries depart daily for the islands. It is also home to the **Woods Hole Oceanographic Institute** (WHOI), the **Marine Biological Laboratories**, and the **National Marine Fisheries Service** — some of the world's most prestigious marine research institutions. The successful search for the *Titanic* was planned and launched by WHOI from Woods Hole in 1986. Only the Marine Fisheries Service is open to the public, allowing visitors to view its aquarium during the summer.

From the **bluff** where Nobska Lighthouse stands, one can see the boats

traveling between Woods Hole and the islands, as well as those en route to New York and Boston.

North Falmouth's **Old Silver Beach** on Buzzard's Bay, and Falmouth's **Surf Drive Beach** on Vineyard Sound, are two of the best beaches on the Upper Cape.

Tourist Information

The **Falmouth Chamber of Commerce** (P.O. Box 582; toll free ((800) 526-8532) has a visitors center in downtown Falmouth in the Lawrence Academy building.

Where to Stay

EXPENSIVE

On the outskirts of town, overlooking a lake, is **Coonamessett Inn** (Jones Road; ((508) 548-2300; 24 rooms), a former New England farm.

More modern, and less homey, are **Holiday Inn — Falmouth** (24 Main Street; ((508) 540-2500; 121 rooms), **Sea Crest Resort and Conference Center** (Old Silver Beach; ((508) 548-3850; 266 rooms), and **Quality Inn Falmouth** (291 Jones Road; ((508) 540-2000; 98 rooms).

MODERATE

The **Capewind** (34 Maravista Avenue; ((508) 548-3400; 31 rooms) offers quality rooms on a small scale, and **New Seabury**

Resort (Rock Landing Road; ((508) 477-9111) does it on a grand scale with 368 rooms.

Eating Out

If you are not staying at the **Coonamessett Inn**, (Jones Road; ((508) 548-2300) consider having a traditional New England seafood meal there. Prices run from moderate to expensive.

Another choice is the **Regatta** (217 Clinton Avenue; ((508) 548-5400) overlooking the harbor. It specializes in seafood prepared in French and American styles. Reservations are essential at this expensive restaurant.

mill still stone-grinds cornmeal. The **Heritage Plantation** (Grove and Pine Streets; ((508) 888-3300) offers more antiquities, including the 1931 Duesenberg used by actor Gary Cooper, and a large selection of Currier and Ives paintings.

Mashpee

At Mashpee, on the southern shore, live the few surviving descendants of the Massipee Indians, who lived on the Cape before the first European explorers arrived. The **Old Indian Meetinghouse and Burial Ground** dates back to 1684, making it the oldest in the state.

Sandwich

Sandwich, on the northwestern corner of the Cape just a few miles past the Sagamore Bridge, is the oldest town on the peninsula, dating from 1637. It is renowned for its Sandwich glass, produced between 1825 and 1888 in the workshops of the Boston and Sandwich Glass Company. The exquisite, lacy patterns are collectors items and quite valuable; see also the glass displays at the **Sandwich Glass Museum** (Town Hall Square, across from the village green; ((508) 888-0251; admission $2.50 with reductions for children and senior citizens; open April 1 to October 31, daily 9:30 am to 4:30 pm).

The **Hoxie House** and **Dexter Grist Mill** (on Water Street) are two of the village's restored seventeenth-century buildings; the

MID CAPE

Barnstable

Barnstable is just over 12 miles (20 km) along the Cape's north shore from Sandwich and faces Cape Cod Bay. It has a fine beach on **Sandy Neck**, a seven-mile (11-km) spit of sand that protects the harbor. Cabin cruisers, schooners, and other boats are often docked here. The old **Custom House** (now called the **Donald G. Trayser Memorial Museum**), located on Main Street at Cobb's Hill, has interesting displays of the town's maritime history.

ABOVE: Beach huts stand like sentinels along the Cape Cod coast. OPPOSITE: Parking attendant looks out for business at a Barnstable beach.

As a county seat, Barnstable is the political hub of the Cape. The two cannons in front of its courthouse were brought by oxen from Boston during the war of 1812. The **Sturgis Library**, built in 1644, is the oldest library in the country; among its collections are genealogical records of the Cape's families.

Yarmouth Port and Dennis

Yarmouth Port has a row of sea captains' homes on Main Street; botanic trails past Miller's Pond can be found off Route 6A.

Martha's Vineyard. National attention focused on the Cape in the early 1960s when native son John F. Kennedy became President. "I always go to Hyannis Port to be revived, to know again the power of the sea and the Master who rules over it all and all of us," said the President, whose family still owns a large estate in this exclusive waterside village. The estate is protected by a tall fence and is not open to the public, but the **John F. Kennedy Memorial** is located on Ocean Street.

The **Cape Cod & Hyannis Railroad** provides daily excursions of varying time

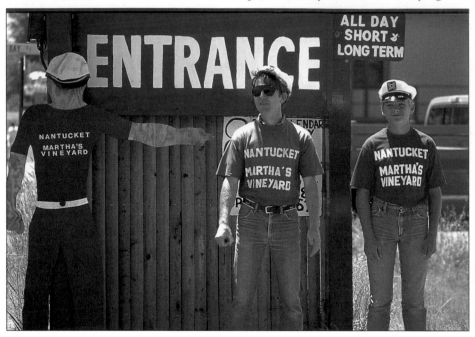

Dennis is less than five miles (eight kilometers) to the east. From its **Scargo Hill Tower** there are fine views of both the bay and ocean; when the weather is clear you can see from Plymouth to Provincetown at the tip of the Cape. Dennis is also where Henry Hall developed commercial cranberry growing in the early eighteenth century; now cranberry bogs are common on the Cape landscape.

Hyannis

Flights to the Cape arrive here and Hyannis is the Cape's main vacation and shopping center, and a good base for visits around the Cape. Ferry services leave from here (summer season) to Nantucket Island and to

lengths around the Upper and Mid Cape's spectacular coastline, salt marshes, and cranberry bogs (Main Street, Hyannis; ((508) 771-1145).

Centerville

Just west of Hyannis, Centerville is adjacent to **Craigville Beach**, the most popular swimming spot on Nantucket Sound.

LOWER CAPE

Chatham

Located on the southeastern tip of the Cape, Chatham is protected from fierce ocean storms by Morris Island, part of the nationally-protected seashore. **Fish Pier**, off Shore

Road, is home to the large fishing fleets that unload their catches in the late afternoon.

The **Chatham Lighthouse** Beach offers panoramic views of the bay and **Nauset Beach**, the Cape's first true ocean beach and among the most popular. Just off the coast is **Monomoy Island**, a 10-mile (16-km)-long sand spit protected as a wildlife refuge, with more than 250 species of birds.

Cape Cod National Seashore

Established in 1961, this 27,000-acre (11-hectare) refuge of wind-sculpted dunes, deserted ocean beaches, spectacular cliffs, and salt pond marshes dominates the seashore from Orleans to Provincetown.

The **Salt Pond Visitor Center** in **Eastham** and the **Province Lands Visitor Center** provide literature on the Seashore, schedules for guided nature walks, and pamphlets on biking and hiking trails; the Seashore's headquarters is located in **South Wellfleet**, ℂ (508) 349-3785.

Seashore highlights include nine scenic hiking trails, including **Nauset Marsh Trail**, a beautiful 30-minute walk among salt ponds and marshes; **Atlantic White Cedar Swamp Trail**, a 35-minute trek through a white cedar swamp, beginning near Marconi Station; **Beech Forest Trail** near Provincetown, a 40-minute walk through sand dunes and beech forests; and **Cranberry Bog Trail**, east of Truro, which leads through natural wild cranberry habitat.

Wellfleet

Historic towns also edge the seashore. One of the most picturesque is **Wellfleet**, once a great whaling port. It is still home port for a large fishing fleet. In true seafaring spirit, the downtown church tolls "ship's bells."

PROVINCETOWN

At the tip of the peninsula, Provincetown is a strange amalgam of tacky tourist shops, chic boutiques, fishing fleets manned by burly Portuguese sailors, whale-watching cruises, wide beaches, wind-swept dunes, an artists colony, and more recently, a meeting place for gays.

For all its freak-show atmosphere, P-Town, as locals call it, looks out on some of the Cape's most spectacular scenery. The **Pilgrim Monument**, at Town Hill off Bradford Street, is a 252-ft (77-m)-high Italianate bell tower commemorating the Pilgrims' "landing" at Provincetown in 1620 (they were blown off course); the view from the tower's observation deck takes in all of the Cape. Nearby hiking trails take visitors past marshes, ponds, and pine forests. **Herring Cove** and **Race Point** beaches provide a spectacular setting for swimming and sun bathing.

A tour of Provincetown begins on **Commercial Street**, the main village thoroughfare, lined with galleries, shops, restaurants, and bars. The population swells from less than 4,000 to nearly 80,000 at the height of the summer season, and it seems that everyone is walking along this street at the same time; sometimes it is simply impassable — a tangle of people, cars, and bicycles.

Once it was the third-largest whaling port in the world. Today, its fishing village legacy continues, with boats arriving during late afternoon at **MacMillan Wharf** to unload their catches.

OPPOSITE: Would-be dummies in Nantucket.
ABOVE: Memento artist in Cape Cod.

Early this century, artists and writers were drawn to this isolated outpost on the Atlantic Ocean by Charles Hawthorne's Cape Cod School of Art. In 1916, the Provincetown Players launched the careers of playwrights Eugene O'Neill, Tennessee Williams, and Sinclair Lewis.

Whale-watching

Whether sailing off Cape Ann, north of Boston, or near Cape Cod to the south, **whale-watching cruises** have been cited as a great way to "witness the miraculous." One little girl on a cruise marveled that a whale once came so close "he sprayed us when he blew." A chance to see these marvelous mammals at close range is a thrilling adventure indeed.

You will also quite likely see schools of porpoises and dolphins, sea turtles, sharks, seals, and sea birds playing very close to the ships.

However, all whale-watching operations are not alike. Some boats are no more than floating hotdog and souvenir stands that happen to ply the waters the whales frequent. Others offer marine biologist-led narrated tours of prime whaling areas, video replays of the day's sightings, and good food. A few more enterprising cruise operators "guarantee" whale sightings, claiming a 95 percent success rate; if you fail to spot any whales, you are offered a free trip to try again.

If time permits, choose a whale-watching cruise off Cape Cod. Daily morning and afternoon cruises, offered April to October, last anywhere from three to four hours. While many cruise operators vie for your dollar, the **Whale Watch Dolphin Fleet**, ☎ (508) 255-3857, of Provincetown on the tip of the Cape, likes to claim that they are the cream of the crop.

The Dolphin Fleet originated whale-watching on the East Coast, and it is also the largest and most successful of all the operations, having made more than 6,000 trips since 1975. Their boats, built especially for whale-watching, are exceptionally stable. (The boats' seating capacity is 270 passengers, but only 145 people are permitted on each cruise to ensure a satisfying trip.) Cruises are led by scientists from the Center for Coastal Studies, one of the world's leading whale research and conservation organizations, and acknowledged authorities on the humpback whales that live in local waters. A portion of each ticket sale is donated to help "save the whales."

Dolphin Fleet ships head offshore about six miles (10 km) to the Stellwagen Bank, the main whale feeding ground in Massachusetts Bay. Through years of research, Coastal Studies scientists have identified several hundred individual humpbacks, and will offer you their individual histories, as well as stories of the finback and right whales found here. There are morning, afternoon, and sunset cruises lasting four hours; reservations are recommended.

For additional information about Cape Cod whale-watching cruises, contact **The Massachusetts Department of Commerce and Development**, Division of Tourism, (100 Cambridge Street, Boston, MA 02202; ☎ (617) 727-3201).

Getting There

By car from Boston, take Interstate 93 south to Route 3; continue south to U.S. 6, and follow that up the Cape to Provincetown at the tip.

To reach the Whale Watch Dolphin Fleet office, turn left on Conwell Street, right on Bradford, then left on Standish.

It is only 114 miles (184 km) from Boston to Provincetown, but allow at least three hours to get through the sometimes maddening traffic on the Cape.

THE ISLANDS

MARTHA'S VINEYARD

"Island in Troubled Water" screamed the headline in the *Vineyard Gazette*, the 131-year-old weekly newspaper that serves Martha's Vineyard, the bucolic island seven miles (11 km) off the Cape Cod coast. The piece was in response to a decision of the state legislature that would allow private developers to run wild over the island's South Beach.

Developers as bogeymen have always been a rallying point for the island's 12,000 full-time residents, who include celebrities such as former first lady Jacqueline Kennedy Onassis, newsmen Walter Cronkite and Mike Wallace, singer Carly Simon, and cartoonist Jules Feiffer. As a result of the concern expressed by such influential residents, the decision was reversed and the island's spectacular beauty and miles of beaches and woodlands remain comparatively unspoiled.

The triangular shaped island was named by the explorer Gosnold in 1602, when he found wild grapes growing everywhere. The grapes are gone, but what remains is a fascinating landscape dotted with little fishing villages and summer resorts.

Vineyard Haven, the main port of entry for visitors, is an old whaling town, much of which was destroyed in the Great Fire of 1883. Some pre-1883 houses can still be found on Williams Avenue, and the Seamen's Bethel is another original harborfront building. Along Main Street, you'll find shops and cafés, along with a Daughters of the American Revolution museum.

Two of the Haven's most familiar landmarks are the **West and East Chop Lighthouses** on the cliffs at the entrance to the harbor.

However, many visitors head straight for **Edgartown**, the oldest town (1642) on Martha's Vineyard. This whaling port of the early nineteenth century is charming, with elegant sea captains' houses (complete with widows' walks) and weathered saltboxes lining North and South Water Streets, overlooking the harbor.

Other architectural delights include the 1840 **Fisher House** on Main Street, called by many the most elegant residence in town; the 1843 **Methodist Church**, with its massive pillars and tower; and the **Cooke House**, a 1765 shipbuilder's house that is now home to the Dukes County Historical Society.

Board the *On Time* ferry (an island joke — it has no regular schedule, and can transport only three cars at a time) at Edgartown to reach **Chappaquiddick Island**, 200 yds (180 m) across the harbor. The island is a paradise of thick woodlands, wildlife refuges, and unspoiled beaches.

Oak Bluffs, located between Vineyard Haven and Edgartown, has a unique his-

tory. In the 1830's, Edgartown Methodists came to Trinity Park each summer to meet and pray at extended revival meetings. By 1850, the revival, held in an oak grove at the town's north end, was drawing 12,000 people. Soon tents were replaced with small cottages — the so-called **Cottage City.** Today, these colorful cottages with their gingerbread turnings, fish scales, and lacy fretwork remain one of the most charming symbols of Vineyard living.

Up-island towns are few and far between. **Chilmark** offers excellent views of Vineyard Sound; and **Menemsha** is largely a working fishing village, but renowned for its picturesque moors.

Martha's Vineyard State Forest, in the center of the island, has hiking paths through dense stands of pines.

However, the westernmost tip of the island is the most spectacular. The brilliantly colored **Gay Head cliffs** rise 150 ft (45 m) above the stormy Atlantic. Ripples of blue, red, white, and orange run through the clay, whose strata contain fossils of camels, whales, and other animals millions of years old. Because of erosion problems, one can no longer walk down the face of the cliffs to the beach below, but a winding path eventually gets you there.

The small towns around Gay Head are peopled by Wampannoag Indians, descendants of the island's original inhabitants.

Getting There

Access to Martha's Vineyard is by the **Steamship Authority** ferry, ((508) 540-2022, which provides daily services between Woods Hole and the harbor at Vineyard Haven; the trip takes about 45 minutes. (Car ferries fill up quickly, so you should call well in advance to reserve space on the boat.) Or you can fly with the **ProvincetownBoston Airline,** ((508) 693-2070.

NANTUCKET ISLAND

Some 30 miles (50 km) south of Cape Cod is Nantucket Island, for almost 100 years — until the 1830's — the world's greatest whaling port. Today it is one of the most charming and picturesque destinations on the East Coast, its streets lined with well-preserved houses, and its landscape graced with long stretches of lovely beaches and open green moors.

Visitors arriving by ferry from Woods Hole (a three-hour ride) are often confronted with a mysterious, fog-shrouded island seascape that obscures the main port, **Nantucket Town**. But once ashore the beauty is astounding. As one writer put it, "This is not just an island; it is an experience."

Early Nantucket settlers were taught by the Indians how to harpoon whales from the shore, and soon the settlers were setting out to sea to do their whaling.

By the early 1800's, Nantucket Town had more than 10,000 residents. Its cobblestone streets, elegant houses, and tall elm trees were testament to the successes of its sea captains, shipowners, and merchants.

When the new, larger ships could no longer dock in shallow Nantucket Harbor, the island lost many of its whalers to the deep port in New Bedford. After the Pennsylvania oil boom hit in the 1840's, Nantucket's fortunes declined even further, along with the whaling industry's. Today, its year-round population numbers around 3,500.

Fine seventeenth- and eighteenth-century houses can be seen on Main Street. The local **Historical Association**, ((508) 228-1894, provides pamphlets outlining a self-guided walking tour of the town.

One of the best preserved is the **Hadwen House** (Main and Pleasant Streets), a Greek Revival mansion built in 1845 for a whale oil merchant; it contains original furnishings of the whaling era.

The oldest existing house in the village was built in 1686 by **Jethro Coffin** on Sunset Hill. This **saltbox** is a fine example of seventeenth-century colonial architecture. The horseshoe-design in the chimney brick was meant to ward off witches and other evil spirits. And the **Old Mill**, on Mill Hill, built in 1746 by wood salvaged from wrecked ships, is still used to grind corn.

To learn more of Nantucket's seafaring legacy, visit the **Whaling Museum** (Broad Street; admission $3.00 adults, $1.00 children; open daily 10 am to 5 pm, May 28 to October 12), located in a factory that once made candles from whale oil. On display are

excellent collections of harpoons, ship and whale models, and other artifacts from the town's whaling days.

At **Straight Wharf**, at the beginning of Main Street, is the *Lighthouse Nantucket*, a double-masted lightship formerly moored offshore to guide ocean vessels around the island's dangerous shoals. The wharf's fishing sheds have now been transformed into shops and restaurants.

Around the Island

Just outside the town, the **Nantucket Moors** are windswept hills of bayberry, wild rose, heather, and brambles that burst into vibrant color in summer and fall. Nestled among these hills are the villages of Wauwinet, Quidnet, and Siasconset.

Wauwinet is the gateway to the **Coatue**, a 10-mile (16-km) sand spit that protects Nantucket Harbor from the more turbulent Nantucket Sound. One can walk along the spit to its northern tip, where the 1818 **Great Point Lighthouse** marks the site of treacherous sandbars in the Sound.

Siasconset sits on the easternmost edge of the island. By the end of the nineteenth century, this village, which became a popular destination for both artists and tourists, was linked to Nantucket Town by a railroad.

Nantucket beaches offer something for everyone — **Jetties Beach**, located near the channel leading into Nantucket Harbor, has warm Sound swimming and gentle surf; **Children's Beach**, with broad shallow flats, is a protected swimming area for bathers.

The beaches of the island's south shore are often washed by powerful breakers. **Surfside** and **Cisco Beaches** are popular with surfers; **Madaket Beach**, at the island's western end, is good for surf casting.

OPPOSITE TOP: Many of the Cape's vacationing visitors take advantage of its relatively undeveloped shorelines and relaxed atmosphere. OPPOSITE BOTTOM: A short distance off the coast of Cape Cod, the island of Martha's Vineyard is a world unto itself.

Eastern Massachusetts, Boston and Cape Cod

Central Massa- chusetts and the Berkshires

CENTRAL MASSACHUSETTS

Leaving historic Boston, the coastal region, and Cape Cod, central Massachusetts offers a quite different ambiance. An area of lakes, trails, colleges and cornfields, it stretches north to New Hampshire and west to the foothills of the Berkshires.

SPRINGFIELD

Springfield is a sprawling industrial city, home to more than 200 factories and manufacturing plants. The city is located in the geographical center of the state at the crossroads of two interstate highways (Interstate 90 and Interstate 91).

Springfield is best known as the home of America's largest weapons arsenal, **Springfield Armory**. The Armory manufactured the first American musket in 1795, supplied Union weapons during the Civil War, and produced the famous Springfield rifle. It now houses the **Benton Small Arms Museum**, with displays of weapons dating from the fifteenth century.

The Armory, on the Quadrangle (Chestnut and State Streets), is part of a cultural complex that includes the **Museum of Fine Arts** (European and American primitive paintings) and the **Smith Art Museum** (Oriental and American art and furnishings).

Also worthy of attention is Springfield's massive **Eastern States Exhibition**, or "Big E" as it is called, which is held each September to display the year's agricultural and industrial achievements.

In 1891, Dr James Naismith of Springfield College invented a game whose object was to toss a ball into a peach basket. He called it basketball, and after he realized that removing the basket bottoms would add momentum to the game, it became wildly popular.

Now basketball is part of the American way of life and its heroes and their hours of glory are the pride of The **Basketball Hall of Fame** (Springfield Center, off Interstate 91; ℭ (413) 781-6500; admission $5.00 with reductions for children and senior citizens; open year round, times

variable) which is the nation's shrine to hoops.

The inventor is honored with a large memorial and a replica of the original YMCA gymnasium where the first game was played. It differs from other major sports' halls of fame in that it honors great players from amateur, college, and professional ranks — not just the professional. Besides old balls, jerseys, trophies, and videos, the hall offers a "shooting gallery" with basketballs delivered on a conveyor belt to visitors who stand behind a rail and "shoot some hoops."

Tourist Information

Always willing to provide information on the area is the **Greater Springfield Convention and Visitors Bureau**, (56 Dwight Street, Springfield, MA 01101; ℭ (413) 787-1548).

Where to Stay

For reliable quality with a little personal attention, try the **Best Western Black Horse** (500 Riverdale Street, West Springfield; ℭ (413) 733-2161; 50 rooms; moderate to expensive). One can also count on **Howard Johnson's Motor Lodge** (1150 Riverdale Street, West Springfield; ℭ (413) 739-7261; 112 rooms; moderate to expensive), **Quality Inn and Conference Center** (296 Burnett Road, Chicopee; ℭ (413) 592-7751; 185 rooms; moderate to expensive), and **Sheraton Inn — Springfield West** (1080 Riverdale Street, West Springfield; ℭ (413) 781-8750; 265 rooms; expensive) for comfortable lodgings.

OPPOSITE: Flower market in the Pioneer Valley.
ABOVE: Picnicking near the Mohawk Trail.

AROUND SPRINGFIELD

Old Sturbridge Village

Just 30 miles (48 km) east of Springfield is **Old Sturbridge Village** (℃ (508) 347-3362; admission $14.00 adults, $6.00 children; open daily 9 am to 5 pm, closed holidays and Mondays from November to April), a living-history museum that recreates life in an 1830's rural New England town. More than 200 acres (81 hectares) of rolling landscape, woodlands, country pathways, a

working historical farm, and more than 40 historic buildings form part of the village, which opened in 1946. Guides in historical dress demonstrate nineteenth-century skills, and share the customs, work, and celebrations of early Massachusetts with visitors.

Center Village is the heart of Old Sturbridge. Its Common is lined with historic homes such as the rustic 1704 Fenno House, the 1740 Richardson House Parsonage of a saltbox design, and the Center Meeting House, which dominates the head of the Common with its Greek Revival columns and tall white-clapboard spire.

The living-history museum of Old Sturbridge Village in central Massachusetts recreates nineteenth-century New England life.

Take one of the footpaths leading off the Common to the **Pliny Freeman Farm**, which demonstrates typical 1830's community life in New England. It is one of the liveliest spots in the entire village, with costumed men and women performing daily farmstead tasks. The seasonal rhythms are also very evident — with the birth of baby lambs and calves and the plowing and planting of fields each spring; crop harvesting in the fall; and preparations for the long New England winter.

In addition to their daily tasks, village residents recreate special events such as the festive Fourth of July celebrations which include a parade, music, and a reading of the Declaration of Independence. There are also programs, seminars, and workshops for those with an interest in field archaeology, spinning, and blacksmithing.

Where to Stay

Hotels here are more reasonably priced, and smaller, than in Springfield: **Old Sturbridge Village Motor Lodge** (U.S. 20; ℃ (508) 347-3327; 59 rooms; moderate) and **Quality Inn Colonial** (U.S. 20; ℃ (508) 347-3306; 64 rooms; moderate).

QUABBIN RESERVOIR

The Quabbin Reservoir covers 128 sq miles (332 sq km), and supplies drinking water to the Boston area. To build the reservoir, engineers dammed the Swift River, flooding four river valley towns and in the process, created a recreational wonderland offering fishing, hiking, and scenic shore drives along U.S. 202, Routes 9 and Alt. 32. From an observation tower off **Windsor Dam** (Route 9, two miles or just over three kilometers from Belchertown) there is a wonderful view of nearly 50 reservoir islands, created by valley hills that rise above the water line.

THE PIONEER VALLEY

Several well-known college campuses can be visited in the Pioneer Valley.

In **Amherst**, the Amherst College campus is a tree-shaded green; the high-rise University of Massachusetts towers above the

surrounding corn fields. The town itself was home to three celebrated American poets — Robert Frost, Emily Dickinson, and Eugene Field. One University of Massachusetts French professor is reputed to have the state's most extensive private library.

In nearby **Northampton**, Smith College, founded in 1875 to produce "intelligent gentlewomen," is now co-educational. Just north of town are many restored homes, including the 1658 Parsons House and 1796 Shepherd House. With Hampshire and Mount Holyoke colleges as well, the Pioneer Valley is blessed with cultural attractions and college-style nightlife.

THE MOHAWK TRAIL

The Mohawk Trail follows the trace of an ancient Indian footpath from New York's Finger Lakes to central Massachusetts. One of the first historical references to the trail notes that the Pocumtuck Indians, under pressure from the expanding colonists, retreated from their villages on the banks of the Connecticut River near what is now Greenfield, Massachusetts, in 1663 to invade the lands of the Mohawks, in the area of what is now Troy, New York. In the ensuing war, the Mohawks annihilated the Pocumtucks, virtually wiping out their legacy in North America. Later, pioneers traveled along the Mohawk Trail from the Massachusetts Bay Colony to the Berkshires, then on to Dutch settlements in the Mohawk and Hudson valleys.

The Mohawk Trail became a major path for moving colonial forces to New York to defend British outposts during the French and Indian wars. These troops included a young Paul Revere, then making his first trip away from his Boston home.

Soon after Independence, the Mohawk Trail was used by covered wagon trains moving west, as it provided the easiest way over the mountains. In 1786, it became America's first toll-free interstate road.

The nineteenth century brought stagecoaches to the trail, as more and more settlers moved westward. But it was not until

After wiping out nearly every Indian in the state, Massachusetts now attempts to capitalize on its native American heritage.

1914 that the Mohawk Trail was opened to automobile travel.

Today, the Mohawk Trail extends 63 miles (100 km) along Massachusetts Routes 2 and 2A, from Millers Falls on the Connecticut River to Williamstown, near the Massachusett–New York state line. It is one of the nation's prettiest highways, ascending from the Connecticut River valley past farms and orchards into the rugged forested slopes of the Berkshires, and ending, at Williamstown, in one of New England's most renowned villages.

ALONG THE TRAIL

Millers Falls
Spanning the Connecticut River just west of Millers Falls is the **French King Bridge**, 750 ft (228 m) long and 140 ft (43 m) above the water. The northern side of the bridge provides an excellent view of the River and of **French King Rock**, supposedly the site of the first planting of the French flag in this region by French explorers.

Greenfield
Farther west, Greenfield is known for its involvement in the Indian wars and for its fine colonial architecture. There is a panoramic view of the lush Greenfield Valley from the **"Poet's Seat Tower"** on Greenfield Mountain (east on Main Street toward High Street, then follow the signs). The town also has a covered bridge over the Green River.

Deerfield
South of U.S. 5 and settled in the mid-1600s this famous colonial town has Indian and Revolutionary War monuments and pre-Revolutionary War houses lining its Main Street, with many open to visitors. Deerfield was the site of two attacks in the French and Indian wars, the Massacre of Bloody Brook in 1675, and the Deerfield Massacre in 1704.

The restoration of Deerfield's historic structures was the first project of its kind in the United States. Period artifacts can be viewed at **Old Deerfield Village and Memorial Hall Museum**. The Museum also offers guided tours of a street lined with 12 colonial-era houses.

Back on the Mohawk Trail, you can stop in **Shelburne Falls** to see the **"Bridge of**

Flowers," an arched trolley bridge that has been maintained as a "hanging garden" by the Shelbourne Women's Club since 1929. Flowers cover the bridge from spring to fall. The 400-ft (122-m), five-arch concrete bridge was built in 1908 across the Deerfield River to carry trolley tracks between Shelburne and Buckland, but was abandoned in the late 1920s as transportation patterns changed.

Also worth seeing are the geologically impressive glacial potholes visible at **Salmon Falls** (follow the signs from the bridge), reputed to be some of the largest in the world.

Charlemont

The trail's half-way point, this town, settled in 1749, offers "Mohawk Trail concerts" featuring classical American and European chamber music (May to October) in the historic, yet acoustically perfect, **Charlemont Confederated Church**.

Charlemont's landmark is the 900-lb (409-kg) bronze cast statue (at Indian Bridge spanning the Deerfield River) "Hail to the Sunrise," depicting an Indian with arms outstretched to the "Great Spirit," a 1932 memorial to the Mohawks. Unfortunately, commemoration of America's original inhabitants occured only long after they had been annihilated.

Bissell Bridge, a recreated covered bridge built in 1951 across Mill Brook, is just off Route 2 on Heath Road.

Charlemont to North Adams

West of Charlemont, the Mohawk Trail climbs into rugged **Hoosac Range**, a wall of granite

(once nicknamed the "Berkshire Barrier") that isolated the northern Berkshires from the rest of Massachusetts until 1875, when the Hoosac Tunnel was blasted through the rock. Soon after, one enters the superb mountain scenery of the **Mohawk Trail State Forest**. There are plenty of excellent hiking trails, including an easy one to the top of Forbidden Mountain, as well as picnic areas and campgrounds.

Whitcomb Summit, just north of the town of Florida, offers the Trail's highest viewpoint (2,200 ft or 670 m) with a panorama of the Deerfield River and the Hoosac Tunnel.

Built to reduce the grade for trains traveling between Boston and Troy, New York, the **Hoosac Tunnel** is four miles (six kilometers) long. It took 25 years to complete, finally opening in 1873 after taking the lives of nearly 200 men and costing more than $15 million. It had to be blasted through solid granite, and involved the first working use of nitroglycerin; constant accidents earned the Tunnel the nickname of the "Bloody Pit." It is now considered by many local residents to be haunted by the ghosts of the men who died building it.

To reach the Tunnel's eastern entrance, take Whitcomb Hill Road south to the Deerfield River, then turn left on River Road until you reach the railroad tracks.

Just west of Florida is the **Western Summit**, with fantastic views of North Adams, Williamstown, the Hoosac Valley, and the Green Mountains, along with Mt Greylock, the highest mountain in the Berkshires. Hang gliders launched from the summit often reach altitudes of more than 3,500 ft (1,067 m).

As the Trail descends toward North Adams, be careful to slow for the Hairpin Turn, a 180-degree curve memorable for its configuration and its spectacular views of the surrounding countryside. Off-the-road parking provides access to an observation platform. Here the Golden Eagle Restaurant has a second-story, outdoor veranda with panoramic views of three states: Massachusetts, Vermont, and New York. The Trail continues down to the factory town of North Adams.

North Adams

Once a busy nineteenth century mill town, North Adams has seen its commercial prominence vanish with the textile industry. It is now a year-round recreation center, with **ski**

ABOVE: Deerfield's historic church has long been one of the town's most prominent attractions.
OPPOSITE: Fall colors on the Mohawk Trail.

areas minutes away, and abundant summer activities. It also puts on a **Fall Foliage Festival**, when the surrounding hills are a palette of scarlet, gold, and crimson.

Its 150-year-old **Cider Mill**, one of the largest restored mills in New England, makes tasty golden apple cider. The **Natural Bridge**, located on Route 8 North, is another North Adams attraction. A rock formation about 550 million years old, it is a marble chasm 475 ft (145 m) long and 60 ft (18 m) deep. This unique geological feature is the only natural, water-eroded bridge in North

WILLIAMSTOWN

Williamstown is only five miles (eight kilometers) west of North Adams on Route 2, but it is a universe apart. Hawthorne once remarked that Williamstown is "a white village and a steeple set like a daydream among the high mountain waves." In the late nineteenth century, it was a spa and summer resort. Set in a hollow of the surrounding Berkshires and in the shadow of Mt Greylock, Williamstown remains one of New England's

America, and can be traversed from May through October for a small admission charge. North Adams has also recently created the $72 million **Massachusetts Museum of Contemporary Art**, located in a 28-building industrial complex.

High over the town looms the magnificent granite bulk of **Mt Greylock**. At 3,491 ft (1,064 m), it is the highest point in Massachusetts. From its rocky barren summit the hiker is rewarded with a fine vista of the Berkshires and western Massachusetts, the Green Mountains of Vermont, and the Hudson River Valley of New York. The surrounding peaks and forests have many well-marked hiking trails, including part of the Appalachian Trail, which crosses Mt Greylock.

loveliest villages. The 1793 **Williams College**, long rated the country's best liberal arts college, is situated in this town. Known for its stringent intellectual requirements and brilliant, demanding professors, Williams College is well worth a visit by those whose children might someday seek the best American education has to offer.

Williamstown's **Sterling and Francine Clark Art Institute** (South Street, just west of the town center) houses one of the world's largest private collections of Renoirs, as well as works of other Impressionists, and is one of the finest small art museums in the country.

At the information booth, Main and South Streets, you may obtain a self-guiding map to explore Williamstown's rich past. On Main

Street, many of the large and lovely homes date from the 1750's. One of the most interesting college buildings is Lawrence Hall, part of the **Williams College Museum of Art**, an octagonal Grecian rotunda inspired by Thomas Jefferson's *Monticello*.

The **Williamstown Summer Theater Festival**, founded in 1955, is an annual event featuring some of the country's most celebrated actors.

The main venue is at the nation's finest summer theater, Williamstown Theater on Main Stage. In addition there is Williams

Pittsfield, Massachusetts, Shakespeare & Company in Lenox, Massachusetts, and the Berkshire Theater Festival in Stockbridge, Massachusetts, to name a few. You can watch a different theater production in Williamstown or one of its neighboring towns every night of the week, at less than half the cost of a ticket to one of New York's Broadway shows.

Where to Stay and Eating Out
Williamstown has many hotels and restaurants for a college town. Reccommended

College's Adams Memorial Theater on Main Street. The festival has featured actors such as Christopher Reeve and Richard Thomas, directors such as Joanne Woodward, and playwrights like John Guare. Other choices include: Adams Memorial Theater's "Cabaret," which presents an early revue and a late cabaret that often includes stars from the Main Stage, Thespis Productions, now almost 10 years old, at the Clark Institute; the Calliope Theatre Company; a women's theater group; and the Spring Street Ensemble Theatre, which showcases experimental productions.

Just a half-hour drive away are the Oldcastle Theatre Company in Bennington, Vermont, The Theater Barn in New Lebanon, New York, the Berkshire Public Theatre in

hotels are **The William's Inn** (on the Green; ((413) 458-9371; 103 rooms; expensive), and the **Four Acres Motel** (213 Main Street; ((413) 457-9731; 30 rooms; moderate). The best restaurant is **Le Jardin Inn** (777 Cold Spring Road; ((413) 458-8032) which specializes in lamb and duck meals.

THE BERKSHIRES

"There's no tonic like the Housatonic," said Oliver Wendell Holmes about the river that snakes through the Berkshire Hills and winds into Connecticut. It creates an idyllic setting for the well-preserved little towns that dot the **Berkshires** in the westernmost county of

Massachusetts. Village greens are surrounded by stunning colonial architecture; white clapboard church steeples pierce the blue skies; and tall shade trees line quiet residential streets. A plethora of cultural activities include nationally-renowned theater and music festivals.

However, its extraordinary variety of landscapes — open meadows and rolling farmlands, valleys dotted with shimmering lakes, wooded hills and green mountains, rushing rivers and plummeting waterfalls — is a major ingredient of the Berkshires' magic; this area is also the heart of Massachusetts' ski country.

Stretching from the Vermont border in the north, down the old "York State" line to the south, the Berkshire Hills remained a wilderness until 1725, when pioneer Matthew Noble erected a log cabin in what is now the town of Sheffield. Soon dense forests were cleared for farmland, and towns appeared along the Housatonic River. In the nineteenth century, the Berkshires were mined for iron used on the railroads. Marble was also quarried here and transported to construct such edifices as the Capitol dome in Washington, D.C.

The Berkshires attracted urban dwellers wishing to "escape" into the country, including some of America's wealthiest families (such as the Carnegies and the Vanderbilts), who built elegant mansions (quaintly called summer "cottages") and used them for less than three months of the year.

From Williamstown you can continue north to Burlington, Vermont, or turn south on Route 7 toward the lower Berkshires.

Along the way you will pass the popular **Jimmy Peak** and **Brodie Mountain** ski areas near the town of Hancock.

THE SHAKERS

A detour off U.S. 7 onto U.S. 20 at Pittsfield brings you to **Hancock Shaker Village**, an authentic community of the Shaker religious sect that thrived from 1790 to 1960. It is today a living, working museum of Shaker rural life, with 20 restored buildings on 1,000 acres (405 hectares).

The Shaker movement started in England in 1747 as an offshoot of Quakerism. Manchester's Ann Lee first led eight followers to the American colony of New York and founded a settlement near Albany.

For a time, they were known as "shaking Quakers" because "dances" during religious services made their bodies shake and tremble. Eventually, the Shakers' pronouncements and beliefs in four principle doctrines (separation from the outside world, common property, confession of sins, and celibacy, with separation but equality of the sexes) took hold. By the mid-nineteenth century, the Shaker movement reached its zenith, with 19 communities in the United States.

Strolling through the village on a guided tour, you will notice that the buildings are

austere but elegant and the craftsmanship outstanding. Shaker ways of coping with the material world are sometimes ingenious, while their keen grasp of the concepts of purity and functionalism have raised the design of their buildings, furniture, and common utensils to an art form.

The village's finest example of Shaker architecture and genius is the magnificently restored **Round Stone Barn**. Built in 1826, the barn's upper level could be accessed by horses and wagons, which unloaded their harvest into a central haymow and then proceeded around a track to another exit. This eliminated the problem of backing hitched teams out of the barn, an often difficult task. Cows were stabled on the ground floor.

It is also interesting to note how separation of the sexes was carried to an extreme. **The Brick Dwelling** (community dining room, sleeping rooms, and kitchen) which

OPPOSITE: The Chapel of Williams College, one of the nation's highest-ranked liberal arts colleges. ABOVE: Hancock Shaker Village is a study in simplicity.

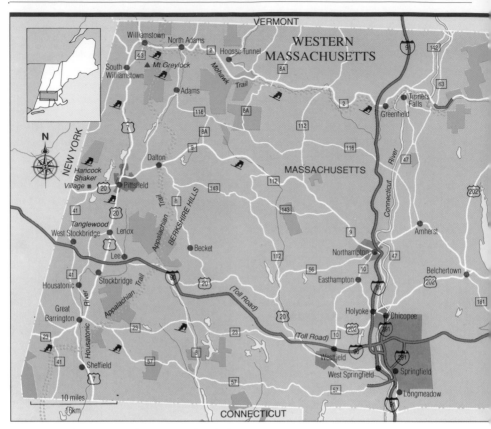

housed 100 brothers and sisters, is divided exactly in half; it is also very light and airy, with more than 3,000 windowpanes.

Hancock tours also include nineteenth-century **craft demonstration** and a walk through the site's farm and herb garden (the seed industry was a Shaker specialty).

PITTSFIELD

Returning toward U.S. 7, you will arrive at **Pittsfield**, whose **concert hall** has been the scene of distinguished music since 1918 and is now home to the South Mountain Concerts series. Artists who have appeared here include Leonard Bernstein, Leontyne Price, Rudolf Serkin, and the Tokyo Quartet. Concerts are held during late summer and fall. The Berkshire Ballet offers a six-week series of classical, modern, and contemporary dance at the **Koussevotzky Arts Center** on the Berkshire Community College campus.

Pittsfield is also home to the **Berkshire Museum**, a fine collection of nineteenth- and twentieth-century American paintings and Hawthorne memorabilia. The **Berkshire Athenaeum's Melville Room** has a unique selection of books, letters, and pictures of the author. Melville's home, "Arrowhead," in Pittsfield, is filled with personal artifacts from his time in the house (1850–1863). Melville wrote part of *Moby Dick* here, where he could gaze out over the Berkshire Hills, which he said reminded him of rolling waves and gray humpback whales.

Where to Stay

The **Berkshire Hilton Inn** is on Berkshire Common (☎ (413) 499-2000; 175 rooms; expensive) or you can stay at the smaller, cozy **Heart of the Berkshires Hotel** (970 West Housatonic Street; ☎ (413) 433-1255; 16 rooms; moderate).

LENOX AND TANGLEWOOD

Lenox became popular as a summer resort when the Boston Symphony Orchestra

One can enjoy, as well, one of the many non-Boston Symphony concerts, recitals, and full orchestra presentations; nearly 50 of these performances are held throughout the summer. The **Popular Artists' Series** consists of rock, pop, and folk concerts, while the **Stockbridge Chamber Concerts** at Seven Hills offers a year-round program of music in the great estates, halls, and historic churches of the Berkshires.

On Lenox's Main Street is the 1805 "Church on the Hill." Several other streets offer glimpses of mansions once owned by business and industrial magnates (Harrimans, Biddles, Stuyvesants) who had summer "cottages" in Lenox. Most of these houses are not open to the public, although one — Wheatleigh — now operates as an elegant country inn and restaurant.

Where to Stay

Wheatleigh (West Hawthorn Road; ((413) 637-0610; expensive), **Village Inn** (16 Church Street; ((413) 637-0020; 28 rooms; moderate to expensive) and **Quality Inn** (330 PittsfieldLenox Road; ((413) 637-1100; 120 rooms; moderate to expensive) are recommended in the area.

Around Lenox

Nearby the **Pleasant Valley Wildlife Sanctuary** is a Massachusetts Audubon preserve of native plants and landscapes, including beaver ponds, open meadows, and more than seven miles (11 km) of walking trails.

BECKET

Jacob's Pillow Dance Festival, which takes place in Becket over 10 weeks each summer, offers some of the country's best dance and music. Since its inception more than 50 years ago, the program has commissioned new dance works from many innovative and renowned choreographers. Performers have included Martha Graham, Merce Cunningham, and the Alvin Ailey Repertory Ensemble. Besides main theater performances, the Pillow's "Inside/Out Series" presents a free, hour-long show on an outdoor stage that includes works in progress, discussions with dancers and choreographers, and audience questions.

chose it in 1939 as the site of its annual **Berkshire Festival of Music**. The festival is held at **Tanglewood**, one-and-a-half miles (just under three kilometers) south west on Route 183. The 210-acre (85-hectare) estate is where Hawthorne once lived and wrote *The House of Seven Gables*. The site takes its name from *Tanglewood Tales*, which he also wrote here.

The Boston Symphony and guest artists perform here every July and August. The main "Music Shed," designed by Eero Saarinen, seats only 6,000, but an expansive lawn allows thousands more to enjoy the evening's music.

During Boston Symphony concert nights, Tanglewood is a mass of traffic and humanity. It is best to arrive early to find a spot in the parking lot, and maybe bring along a picnic meal; it is not unusual for people to arrive more than three hours before a scheduled performance. Special bus excursions to Tanglewood concerts are offered by a number of local tour agencies.

STOCKBRIDGE

Stockbridge is a stately New England town with fine houses, quaint shops, historical attractions, and a lively arts community. Established as an Indian mission by preacher and theologian John Sargeant (whose 1739 home, the **Old Mission House**, is open for tours), the town has evolved into a grand summer resort. The **Norman Rockwell Museum**, a restored eighteenth-century mansion in the Old Corner House (on Main

Street; ((413) 298-3822; admission $4.00, children $1.00; open year-round except January 15 to 31, times variable), exhibits a large permanent collection of his paintings.

Other attractions worth visiting include **Chesterwood**, off Route 183 in Glendale, the summer estate of Daniel Chester French, sculptor of the Lincoln Memorial in Washington, D. C., and the *Minuteman* in Concord, Mass. His mansion, studio, barn gallery, and period garden are open to guided tours, along with nature trails that offer views of Monument Mountain.

ABOVE: The studio and estate of reknowned sculptor Daniel Chester French in Stockbridge. OPPOSITE: Antiques and objets d'art can be found in New England's many antique shops.

The **Berkshire Theatre Festival**, one of the nation's top summer theaters, has performed here for more than 60 years. Classical works with name actors are staged June through August in the large Playhouse; new plays and children's theater from around the world are set in the barn, as part of the Unicorn Theater Company.

Where to Stay

The antique-filled rooms, flower-laden courtyard, and front porch lined with comfortable rocking chairs of the **Red Lion Inn** have made it a regional favorite for years. (Main Street; ((413) 298-5545; 100 rooms; moderate to expensive). Smaller and of equal quality is **The Inn at Stockbridge** (U.S. 7; ((413) 298-3337; 7 rooms; expensive).

Around Stockbridge

Just west off Interstate 90, **West Stockbridge** is a replica of a New England town, as if there were not enough real ones in the area. Its Main Street is lined with 1800s-style storefronts housing galleries, specialty stores, antiques, and other tourist traps. A number of fairs and festivals are held here during the year. The **Williamsville Inn** (Route 41; (9413 374-6118; expensive) has an excellent dining room.

Berkshire Scenic Railway is a "rolling museum" that operates over a portion of the historic New Haven Housatonic Valley Line with vintage railroad equipment and comfortable 1920-vintage coaches. It rambles at a leisurely 10-mph (16-kph) pace for 15 miles (24 km) between **Lee** and **Great Barrington**. With an open or round trip ticket you can stop anywhere you wish along the line and board a later train to complete your journey. The train follows the path of the Housatonic River, past mills, waterfalls, meadows, and mountains. Although the train is stationed at Lee, you can also board in Stockbridge, Housatonic, and Great Barrington.

Tyringham, about five miles (eight kilometers) south of Lee along Tyringham Road, is noted for its **Gingerbread House** and **Tyringham Art Galleries**. The thatched cottage with rock pillars and grottoes, built in the 1930's by sculptor Sir Henry Hudson Kitson, now houses several art galleries. There are also beautiful sculpture gardens and woodland walking trails.

GREAT BARRINGTON

A short scenic drive south on U.S. 7 leads to Great Barrington, the largest town in the southern Berkshires resort area. The Mohican Indians built their "Great Wigwam" at a ford here in the Housatonic River. The village gained prominence in 1774 when its residents seized the courthouse from the British, committing the first act of open rebellion in the colonies against the Crown. And William Stanley (founder of General Electric) helped to light up the town with electricity as early as 1886. A booth on Main Street in the center of town provides visitor information.

Great Barrington was a station on the Underground Railroad transporting fugitive slaves to freedom. W.E.B. du Bois, the author and editor, lived here, as did James Weldon Johnson, co-founder of the National Association for the Advancement of Colored People (NAACP).

This part of the southern Berkshires is an antique hunter's delight. Scores of antique shops can be found in Great Barrington, South Egremont, Sheffield, New Marlboro, and along the winding backroads of the Berkshire farm country nestled cozily in gentle hills. As with all antique shops, beware of fakes and inflated prices.

Where to Stay

The best of Great Barrington's hotels are **Wildflower Inn** (Route 23; ℂ (413) 528-2720; 12 rooms; moderate to expensive); **Monument Mountain** (249 Stockbridge Road; ℂ (413) 528-3272; 18 rooms; moderate to expensive); and **Briarcliff Motor Lodge** (U.S. 7; ℂ (413) 528-3000; 16 rooms; moderate to expensive).

Around Great Barrington

Sheffield, founded in 1733 and the oldest village in the Berkshires, is the only Massachusetts town with two **covered bridges**.

Farther south, off Route 7A, is **Ashley Falls**, location of Berkshire County's oldest home, the 1735 **Ashley House** (open for tours May to mid-October), and **Bartholomew's Cobble**, a national natural landmark renowned for its native ferns and wildflowers.

There are also six miles (10 km) of hiking trails skirting the banks of the Housatonic River.

About 12 miles (19 km) past South Egremont (off Route 41, then follow the signs almost to the New York state line) is **Bash Bish Falls**, a 275-ft (84-m) waterfall plunging down a steep gorge. Legend has it that an Indian girl jumped to her death here; her spirit is said to haunt the pool beneath the falls.

Less than five miles (eight kilometers) north of Great Barrington off Route 7, is

Monument Mountain. Two trails lead to the summit. An easy two- to three-hour round trip offers spectacular views of Squaw Peak. Monument Mountain is also known as the site of an 1850 meeting between Melville and Hawthorne, which began their friendship.

ANTIQUE HUNTING IN THE BERKSHIRES

The Berkshire Mountains offer some of the best antique-hunting grounds in the region. Colonists who settled in New England in the seventeenth century tried to duplicate those styles which were popular back home in England. But very few had the skills or services of a master carpenter or furniture maker. Thus, you will find that the earliest "early American" antiques might be rudimentary pieces of furniture — often large, squared-off pine and oak cupboards, broad flat tables, and smaller boxy furnishing, (see SHOPPING in TRAVELERS' TIPS Chapter).

Maine

BY FAR the largest New England state, Maine is also in many ways the purest remnant of the old New England spirit of hard work, honesty, thrift, and personal ethics — in a word, the "soul" of New England. Looking down on its neighbor states as too soft, too modern, too flamboyant, and too money-oriented, Maine has been hardened by its long, cold winters and constant battle with the sea.

Although the state's stunning beauty, lovely architecture, and largely undeveloped back country continue to draw more and more visitors (and new residents) each year, native Mainers still retain a certain sense of privacy which seems to exclude newcomers — a newcomer being anyone whose family has not lived in the state for at least several generations. And although in recent years there has been a rise in "anti-outsider" sentiment, the traveler is still welcomed for himself more than for the money he might spend.

"DOWN EAST"

A fabulous landscape of 10,000 lakes and 10,000 offshore islands, Maine is as far east as the traveler can go without leaving the United States. For a Maine resident, to travel northeast toward Canada is to go "down east" a term that has come to be identified with the state itself. Maine's coastline juts north and east into the cold, stormy Atlantic; to the north Maine is bounded by the endless spruce and fir forests of the Canadian provinces Quebec and New Brunswick. Only on its western border does Maine touch the United States, along the state line with New Hampshire.

In his famous journal of exploration, *The Maine Woods*, Henry David Thoreau termed the state the last remaining wilderness east of the Mississippi. Even then, however, most of the towering white pines that gave the state its nickname had been cut down for ships' masts. Today, nearly 90 percent of Maine remains uninhabited spruce, fir, and pine forests, which are, however, heavily overlogged by the paper industry, furnishing, as one Maine conservationist complained, "half of America's toilet paper."

THE MAINE ETHIC

Maine's wild coastline is the longest and most varied in New England, stretching for 3,500 miles (5,600 km). A jagged panoply of inlets, islands, peaks, peninsulas, bays, reefs, and stony headlands washed by the cobalt sea and hammered by white surf and crashing winter storms, the Maine coast has given rise to countless legends and tragedies of the north Atlantic, and has prepared many thousands of young fishermen and sailors for a life at sea.

Similarly so, the back woods of Maine, which gave rise to generations of lumberjacks, woodsmen, trappers, and guides, remain a marvelous experience for the more adventurous and hardy visitor — the largest undeveloped forest area in the United States east of Montana. For those willing to take the time and trouble, Maine's extensive northern river system offers perhaps the best long-distance canoeing in the lower 48 states, where the traveler can lie at night under the undimmed stars and hear the lonely, half-mad laughter of the loons across vast and silent lakes.

OPPOSITE: At anchor in Rockport, one of many excellent harbors along the Maine coast.
ABOVE: Local flair at the Fryeburg Fair.

Less well known is Maine's major, though lessening, agricultural role. Before the United States took over the Indian lands west of the Mississippi, Maine provided sheep and cattle for much of the northeast. And until federally-subsidized irrigation projects made it possible to grow potatoes cheaply on arid western farmlands, Maine potatoes were known as the nation's finest — which indeed they still are.

As with most unique places, Maine suffers from numerous cliches: rough-and-tumble lumberjacks and log cabins, salty lobster fishermen and tight-lipped natives whittling wood on the porch of a century-old general store while they talk about the "comin' nor'easter," of wandering moose, howling wolves, and L.L. Bean.

But the lumberjacks have been largely replaced by huge belching combines that grind their way through the north woods, uprooting trees and snipping off their tips and roots. Like most of their fellow Americans, unfortunately, the natives are more likely to be watching television than whittling wood, and the general store is probably filled with trinkets for the tourist trade. The moose still wander, except in hunting season when they try to keep their heads down, but no wolves have howled in Maine for nearly a hundred years — although their ecological niche is being taken over by coyotes, wilier and less afraid of man.

And sadly, L.L. Bean, once the purveyor of fine outdoors gear for Maine hunters and fishermen, is now a catch-all, trendy cloth-

downhill ski, skate, or ice fish. And in spring again there is fishing, hiking, wandering, and enjoying the outburst of blossoms and flowers that foretells the coming summer.

For warm-season vacationers, late June through August is best, when the temperatures generally hover between 70 °F and 80 °F (21 °C and 27 °C) during the day, and slightly lower at night. For skiers, Maine's cold winter weather is a blessing, for it brings heavy falls of snow. Western Maine's ski retreats, mountains surrounded by lush forests, provide a magnificent wilderness setting in which to enjoy the slopes.

TOURIST INFORMATION

To help plan your trip, the **Chamber of Commerce & Industry** (126 Sewall Street, Augusta, ME 04330) will provide free maps and brochures. For travel information, call (out of state) toll-free (800) 533-9595, or (in-state) ((207) 289-2423.

BACKGROUND

THE DAWN PEOPLE

Maine's first known inhabitants were the tribes of Paleo and Algonquin Indians who, 10,000 to 25,000 years ago, wandered down from what is now Canada and the western United States, probably along the St Lawrence River, until they reached the sea. Called "the dawn people" because they had traveled so far east, toward the dawn, they were divided, in Maine, into roughly Algonquins in the south, Penobscots in the middle, and Micmacs and other coastal tribes in the north.

They tended to winter along the coast and travel inland in the late spring, summer, and fall for hunting and gathering. The Penobscots, whose name means "the rocky place," describing a bouldered series of rapids on the river of the same name, spent their winters along Penobscot Bay, where they lived off the shellfish, fish, and shore animals. In warmer months they traveled in

ing mall and catalog store full of high-price goods for those who prefer the image of the back woods to the reality of being there.

YEAR-ROUND VACATIONS

For vacationers, the 33,215 sq mile (86,050 sq km) Maine offer unique experiences on a year-round basis. In summer one can swim in its crystalline, unpolluted lakes, swim and sail on the coast, fish the lakes, streams, and ocean, visit its lovely colonial towns, canoe its rivers, or hike its mountains. In the fall there is Maine's wonderland of autumn colors to enjoy, as well as hiking, hunting, and fishing. In winter the visitor can cross-country or

The Fryeburg Fair is a "Maine" event in late September or early October of every year.

small clans and hunting groups far up into the vastness of the Allagash and upper Penobscot watersheds, even into what is now Canada, returning with moose, caribou, and deer. Although they apparently lived in relative peace among themselves, the Maine tribes were threatened by raiding parties of fierce Mohawk warriors from upper New York state, and later by the colonists, who massacred them with the efficiency befitting Christian religious superiority.

EUROPEAN EXPLORERS

Tenth-century Norsemen were probably the first European explorers to land on Maine's shores. But the region was largely ignored until John Cabot passed in 1497. In the 1600s, colonists began to move north from what is now Massachusetts, and the French started to travel south from Acadia into Maine; there were soon frequent skirmishes between British and French troops, which continued until an eventual British victory in 1763.

The colony of Massachusetts bought what is now Maine for $6,000 in 1677; and this area remained part of Massachusetts until 1820, when it entered the Union as a free state under the Missouri Compromise. The young state quickly distinguished itself in its opposition to slavery, its commercial power, and the contribution which its brave regiments made in several major Civil War battles. It had some moral surprises in store for its sister states as well: in 1851, Maine became the first state to enact a law prohibiting the manufacture of alcoholic beverages; the law remained in force until 1934. More recently, in 1949, Maine voters sent their Congresswoman Margaret Chase Smith to the Senate, making her the first woman to serve in both houses of Congress.

THE SOUTH COAST

Maine's south coast draws many of the state's visitors to its wide beaches and sparkling surf. There are many lovely beaches along the coast, with the water gradually getting colder as one moves northeast. Well-known is the 11-mile (18-km) **Old Orchard Beach**, a traditional haven for families from Quebec; it is the smoothest, hardest sand beach in Maine.

KITTERY

Most travelers enter Maine at its southernmost point, from Portsmouth, New Hampshire. The first town on the Maine side of the border is Kittery, once the home of pioneers and Revolutionary War heroes. This sea village — Maine's oldest community, established in 1623 — was once the backbone of the young nation's shipbuilding industry. Its legacy can be traced to Kittery's Portsmouth Navy Yard, which built John Paul Jones' ship, *Ranger*, in 1775. The *Ranger* was the first ship to fly the Stars and Stripes, and took to France the news of General Burgoyne's surrender, thus receiving the first salute ever given an American ship by a foreign power.

Today, the shipyard builds primarily submarines, and no visitors are allowed. But at the private boat yards on the Piscataqua River, the visitor can watch pleasure craft being built. The **Kittery Historical and Naval Museum** (Rogers Road, off U.S. 1; ((207) 439-3080; admission $2.00 with reductions for children, families, and senior citizens; open Monday to Saturday, 10 am to 4 pm, closed October 15 to Memorial Day except Saturdays, 1 pm to 4 pm) has an interesting collection of artifacts from Kittery's past.

Another Kittery landmark is **Fort McClary** (1809) on Kittery Point, which defended the townspeople against Indian attacks. A restored hexagonal blockhouse and the original granite sea walls remain standing.

The **Isles of Shoals** can be seen just off shore. They once harbored pirates who plundered ships after luring them to their doom along the rocks by placing false lights near the shallows.

Around Kittery

Historic sites north of Kittery include the **Sarah Orne Jewett House**, birthplace and home of the noted nineteenth-century novelist, and the **Hamilton House**, a fine 1787 Georgian mansion overlooking Salmon

Kittery, just north of the New Hampshire border, is Maine's oldest community.

96

Maine

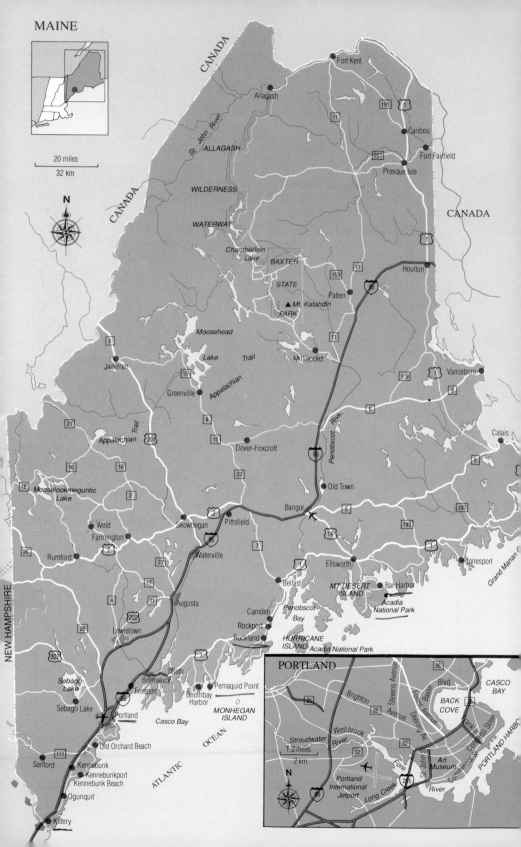

MAINE

CANADA

Fort Kent

Allagash

181

Caribou

227

Fort Fairfield

Presque Isle

CANADA

ALLAGASH

WILDERNESS

WATERWAY

Chamberlain
Lake

BAXTER

STATE

159

11

Houlton

95

▲ Mt. Katahdin

Patten

PARK

71

Millinocket

1 9

1

Vanceboro

6

Moosehead

Lake

Trail

St. John River

Penobscot River

5

6

Jackman

15

Greenville

Appalachian

6

15

Dover-Foxcroft

95

Calais

6

27

Appalachian

201

23

Old Town

Bangor

192

6

193

16

16

2

Skowhegan

2

Pittsfield

1A

Weld

Farmington

Ellsworth

1

Jonesport

26

Rumford

2

Waterville

7

MT DESERT
ISLAND

Bar Harbor

Grand Manan

17

Augusta

Belfast

Acadia
National Park

4

11

Camden

Penobscot

Rockport

Bay

202

26

Lewiston

Rockland

HURRICANE
ISLAND

Acadia National Park

302

Bath

Brunswick

Pemaquid Point

Sebago
Lake

Freeport

Boothbay
Harbor

MONHEGAN
ISLAND

95

Sebago Lake

Portland

Casco Bay

Old Orchard Beach

OCEAN

111

Santford

Kennebunk

Kennebunkport
Kennebunk Beach

ATLANTIC

Ogunquit

Kittery

20 miles

32 km

N

NEW HAMPSHIRE

PORTLAND

26

Stevens Avenue

CASCO
BAY

Brighton

25

Deering Av

BACK
COVE

95

Forest Avenue

Baxter Blvd

22

PORTLAND HARBOR

Westbrook

River

22

Art
Museum

Stroudwater

Franklin St

Commercial St

Congress Street

St John

River

1.2 miles

2 km

Portland
International
Jetport

Fore

295

Long Creek

N

95

Falls River, both in Berwick. But perhaps the most notable historical complex is **York Village** (York StreetU.S. 1ALindsay Road; ℂ (207) 363-4974). A self-guided tour includes several historic buildings and a colonial-period cemetery.

Well worth a visit is the **Old Gaol**, a stone jail built in the 1600s on a knoll overlooking York, complete with dungeons, cramped cells, jailers' quarters and a most gruesome pit—an oozing, wet hole in the ground used for unruly prisoners. It continued to be used as a jail until the 1860s.

Other local attractions include one-mile (1.6-km) **York Beach**, **Wild Kingdom Amusement Park**, and a never-ending string of fast-food seafood restaurants.

On leaving York, you have the choice of touring Maine via Interstate 95, making quick loops at various exits to harbor towns and other attractions, or taking U.S. 1, a two- to three-lane highway that bisects the commercial districts of most coastal communities.

Where to Stay
Hotels in the area are usually booked in the summer season. However, several days in advance you can usually reserve a room: **Charter House Motor Hotel** (Route 1, Kittery; ℂ (207) 439-2000; 56 rooms; expensive); **Days Inn** (Route 1, Kittery; ℂ (207) 439-5555; 108 rooms; moderate).

Eating Out
Fresh seafood is the standard fare at Kittery's restaurants. There are good restaurants in each price category: **Warren's Lobster House** (Route 1, Kittery; ℂ (207)439-1630; expensive); **Bill Foster's Down East Lobster and Clambake** (Route 1A, York Harbor; ℂ (207) 363-3255; moderate); and **Weathervane** (Route 1, Kittery; ℂ (207) 439-0330; inexpensive).

OGUNQUIT

Going north on U.S. 1 along the coast, the next major community is Ogunquit, whose Indian name means "beautiful place by the sea." The name is well-suited, as the beach here is a three-mile (five-kilometer) stretch of white, inviting sand. The town itself is also lovely, with shady streets and fine colonial architecture.

Not to be missed is **Marginal Way**, a one-mile (1.6-km)-long path along the ledges high above the Atlantic. It follows the 100-ft (30-m) crest of Bald Head Cliff, linking the promontory with **Perkins Cove**, a fishing port with lobster shacks and shops. Along the path there are superb vistas of the ocean and shoreline tidal pools.

With its cliffs, sandy beaches, and peaceful backdrop of rolling dunes, it is no surprise that Ogunquit and Perkins Cove became an attractive destination for artists at the turn of the century. A number of small

art galleries (along with a jumble of shops) can be found in the village.

The **Ogunquit Summer Playhouse**, ℂ (207) 934-2091, the oldest in Maine, stages a different play each week during the tourist season. Started half a century ago in a local garage, it has become one of the premier summer stock theaters on the East Coast, with its drama school attracting students from around the country.

Where to Stay
The Cliff House (Bald Head Cliff; ℂ (207) 361-1000; 94 rooms; moderate to ex-

The Kittery Point Lighthouse marks the entrance of the Piscataqua River to the harbor.

pensive) sits atop a bluff and most rooms have sea views. The **Sparhawk** (Shore Road; ((207) 646-5562; 82 rooms; expensive) also has excellent views and good service.

Eating Out

It is not unusual for diners to travel from nearby New Hampshire and Massachusetts to eat at **Whistling Oyster** (Perkins Cove; ((207) 646-9521; expensive).

For less expensive Maine seafood dinners, there are **Clay Hill Farm** (Agamenticus Road; ((207) 646-2272; moderate to expensive), which also serves prime rib, and **Old Village Inn** (30 Main Street; ((207) 646-7088; moderate).

THE KENNEBUNKS

Since the election of George Bush as president, the next set of villages along this picturesque coastline — Kennebunk, West Kennebunk, Kennebunk Beach, and Kennebunkport, collectively called The Kennebunks — have attracted even more attention than usual, although the area was already a vastly popular vacation spot in its own right. **Kennebunk**, settled in 1650, was once the shipbuilding capital of York County. But as the boatwright trade declined, the town became a fishing and tourism center. What remains of those affluent days when shipbuilders were king are some imposing homes, stately trees, and typical New England churches, including the 1772 **First Parish Church** (on Main Street) which has a bell cast by Paul Revere & Sons.

Perhaps the town's most beautiful and unusual building is the **Wedding Cake House**. It was apparently built by a sea captain who, about to marry, was suddenly called on duty. With little time to spare, the wedding took place but without a wedding cake. The captain promised his bride that when he returned he would build her a house frosted like the cake she had wanted. The ornate gingerbread trim on the spectacular two-story, 1826 house does indeed make it look like a lacy wedding cake. It is not open to public tours, but is one of the most photographed buildings in Maine.

For an inside look at Kennebunk's historic houses, some dating back to 1724, take

the **Brick Store Museum**'s 90-minute architectural walking tour (117 Main Street; ((207) 985-4802), offered during summer only.

Kennebunkport, another picturesque town at the mouth of the Kennebunk River, is the summer hometown of President George Bush. In summer, Kennebunkport is transformed into a vacation boom town. It has the standard quota of quaint shops, old inns, and fancy private estates. Historical attractions include the **Seashore Trolley Museum** (on U.S. 1, just north of town; ((207) 967-2712; admission $5.50 for adults with reductions for children, families, and senior citizens; open daily 10 am to 5:30 pm, June 23 to September 4, or Saturday and Sunday, 12 to 5 pm in spring and fall). It displays 150 antique streetcars from the United States and abroad. There is good swimming at Arundel, Cleaves Cove, and Goose Rocks beaches.

Where to Stay

Since George Bush became President, prices have gone up and reservations are hard to come by. If you must stay here, the following are recommended: **The Captain Lord Mansion** (Pleasant and Green Streets; ((207) 967-3141; 18 rooms; expensive); **The Colony** (Ocean Avenue; ((207) 967-3331; 139 rooms; a deluxe resort); **Inn at Goose Rocks** (Dyke Road; ((207) 967-5425; expensive; near saltwater marshes and woods); a **Old Fort Inn** (Old Fort Avenue; ((207) 967-5353; 16 rooms; expensive); and **Village Cove Inn** (South Maine Street; ((207) 967-3993; 32 rooms; overlooks a private cove; expensive).

Eating Out

It is easier to get dinner reservations here than hotel accommodations, and there are several excellent restaurants.

The Kennebunk Inn (45 Main Street; ((207) 985-3351; moderate to expensive) is a classic seacoast inn, providing fine continental dining.

Olde Grist Mill (Mill Lane; ((207) 967-4781; moderate to expensive) serves traditional Maine seafood diners in its converted mill.

White Barn Inn (Beach Street; ((207) 967-2321; moderate to expensive) is popular for its sirloin steak *au poivre*.

OLD ORCHARD BEACH

Ten miles further north on U.S. 1, just east of Saco, is **Old Orchard Beach**, Maine's answer to Coney Island. Its seven-mile (11-km) strip of flat, sloping sand was once the departure strip for early attempts to fly across the Atlantic, and was long known for its stylish promenade and boisterous dance halls. Today its traditional boardwalk is lined with arcades and carnival rides. Perhaps because it is the first large saltwater beach south of Montreal, Old Orchard attracts large numbers of French Canadians. Many of the hotels and restaurants here employ bilingual staff to make these visitors feel at home.

Tourist Information

During the summer season, Old Orchard has many open air concerts and special events. The **Old Orchard Chamber of Commerce** (P.O. Box 600, Old Orchard Beach, ME 04064; ℂ (207) 934-2091) has a complete schedule of events, maps, and other useful travel information.

Where to Stay

There are many hotels, good and bad, in Old Orchard Beach; the following are recommended: **Brunswick Inn** (West Grand Avenue; ℂ (207) 934 2171; expensive); **Edgewater** (57 W. Grand Avenue; ℂ (207) 934-2221; 35 rooms; moderate to expensive); and **Royal Anchor** (East Grand Avenue; ℂ (207) 934-4521; 40 rooms; moderate to expensive).

Eating Out

For seafood and steaks, **Joseph's-by-the-Sea** (55 W. Grand Avenue; ℂ (207) 934-5044; moderate to expensive) is a local favorite.

PORTLAND

Often called the San Francisco of the East, Portland dominates a long peninsula jutting into magnificent Casco Bay, with a panorama of the Bay's hundreds of islands. At both ends of the city, the land rises gently, forming excellent viewpoints, the Eastern and Western Promenades, from which to view the islands to the east and the hills and mountains to the west.

Background

First settled in 1631, Portland has been burned to the ground three times—by raiding Indians in 1676, by invading British troops in 1775, and by accident in 1866. Longfellow commented that the smoldering ruins of 1866 resembled the rubble of Pompeii.

Each time, Portland has rebuilt itself on its ashes, stronger than before. Today it is Maine's largest and most populous city (62,000 people), providing a center of culture and urbanity in a state best known for its back country and natural beauty.

From its very beginnings, the city was an important commercial and shipping center, its natural deep-water harbor being 100 miles (160 km) closer to Europe than any other port in the United States. From Portland's docks sailed many of the finest sailing vessels and clipper ships built in the United States; in the eighteenth and nineteenth centuries the city was a major center for lumber export, fisheries, and the West Indies sugar and molasses trade. Until the completion of the Saint Lawrence Seaway, much of Canada's wheat sold overseas was shipped from Portland; the city's large

Portland's famous Observatory, one of the nation's first.

oil depots supply a regional network of pipelines. The Bath Iron Works has established a ship repair facility in Portland which has a constant stream of U.S. Navy vessels in its drydocks.

Overfishing of Atlantic fisheries and lobster beds, however, has cut into Portland's trade, and many of the docks along the port have been turned to non-fishery uses. But the city continues to grow and diversify as many professionals from lower New England, New York, and the Atlantic states arrive each year in search of a more peaceful,

crime-free and pollution-free life. A not insignificant number still commute by plane to offices in New York and Boston; others find the technological revolution of telefaxes and computers has made it possible to live in Portland while keeping in daily contact with clients elsewhere.

Portland remains a lovely city with its historic waterfront district, a magnificent skyline and architecture, and many other fascinations for the traveler.

ABOVE LEFT: State Street in Portland. ABOVE RIGHT: Relaxing in the shade of Portland's tree-lined streets. OPPOSITE: Portland's docks harbor fishing boats, tankers and cruise ships alike.

Tourist Information

The city's **Chamber of Commerce**, ((207) 772-2811, and **Visitors Bureau**, ((207) 772-4994, both at 142 Free Street, supply brochures outlining a self-guided **"Portland History Trail"** walking tour of nearly 40 historic buildings.

The History Trail

Parts of the waterfront district, now called the **Old Port Exchange** (Exchange and Pearl Streets), have been saved and resuscitated into a thriving commercial and tourist

center of historic buildings and brick sidewalks, with cafes, good restaurants, bookstores, clothing stores, and boutiques of all shapes and sizes amid lawyers' offices, ship chandlers, and seamen's bars.

Portland also contains some of the most exquisite historic homes of New England, including the 1785 boyhood **home** of the poet **Henry Wadsworth Longfellow**, which was also the first brick building in the city (admission $3.00 with reductions for children; open Tuesday to Saturday, 10 am to 4 pm, from June 1 to Columbus Day). The **Maine Historical Society**, a repository of information on four centuries of the city's life, is next door.

Also extraordinary is the **Victoria Mansion** (109 Danforth Street; ((207) 772-4841;

admission $3.00 with reductions for children; open Tuesday to Saturday, 10 am to 4pm, Sunday 1 to 4 pm, from June 1 to Labor Day, with shorter hours in September).

Both the Eastern and Western Promenades offer views of many large and impressive mansions; nearly any downtown street has its share of colonial or Victorian masterpieces.

The city is a major educational center as well, with both the **University of Maine's** southern campus and **Westbrook College** — the nation's first coeducational college, dating from 1831. The latter, located on

Homer, Edward Hopper, and Andrew Wyeth. Another fine museum is Westbrook College's **Payson Gallery**, with its collection of impressionist and New England art.

The **Portland Civic Center** offers a variety of prominent sports events, conventions, and concerts staged by the **Portland Concert Society**. The Visitors Bureau has schedules and ticket information.

Where to Stay
EXPENSIVE
Portland Regency, in the Old Port (20 Milk

Stevens Avenue, is a lovely tree-shaded campus of brick buildings.

Outside Portland, near the airport, the **Tate House**, built in 1755, offers a detailed view of life in the eighteenth century (1270 Westbrook Street, off outer Congress Street at the airport turnoff; admission $2.50 with reductions for children; open Tuesday to Saturday, 11 am to 5 pm, Sunday, 1:30 to 5 pm, from June 15 to September 15).

Museums And Entertainment
The art scene is also well represented here. At the **Portland Museum of Art** (7 Congress Square; ((207) 773-2787), a new wing designed by I.M. Pei houses a fine selection of paintings by Maine artists like Winslow

Street; ((207) 774-4200), is superbly situated in the Old Port, with lovely rooms in a restored nineteenth-century armory. Outside the old town are the **Holiday Inn West** (81 Riverside Street; ((207) 774-5601; 205 rooms) and the **Ramada Inn** (1230 Congress Street; ((207) 774-5611; 149 rooms). Near the new Maine Mall is the **Sheraton Tara Hotel** (363 Maine Mall Road; ((207) 775-6161; 218 rooms).

MODERATE
Susse Chalet Motor Lodge has two locations, at 340 Park Avenue near the Maine Medical Center; ((207) 871-0611, and off the Maine Turnpike at Exit 8, Brighton Avenue; ((207) 774-6101. Both can also be reached at toll-free (800) 258-1980.

Eating Out

DiMillo's (121 Commercial Street; ((207) 772-2216; moderate) serves excellent food, including fresh lobster and other sea fare, amid pleasant decor and interesting views aboard a large docked cruise ship. Unfortunately it does not accept reservations, but is one of the very best restaurants in Portland.

Boone's (6 Custom House Wharf, ((207) 774-5725; moderate to expensive) and **Seamen's Club** (375 Fore Street; ((207) 772-7311; moderate) also serve fresh seafood meals.

The Village (112 Newbury Street; ((207) 772-5320; moderate) has fine seafood, New England and continental cuisine, with emphasis on the Italian.

The Good Egg (705 Congress Street near Longfellow Square; ((207) 773-0801; inexpensive) has excellent downeast cooking, homemade hearty breakfasts including blueberry pancakes, real maple syrup, and other delights.

No trip to Portland is complete without an Italian sandwich from **Amato's Sandwich Shop** (74 India Street; ((207) 773-1682 or 1379 Washington Avenue; ((207) 767-5916; delicatessen and take-out; inexpensive). Amato's is the original home of the Italian sandwich, made the way it used to be.

Another Portland tradition is **Three Dollar Dewey's** (446 Fore Street; ((207) 772-3310; inexpensive), a fine drinking emporium with many excellent Maine-brewed and other beers on tap, and famous chili, lunch and dinner specialities

AROUND PORTLAND

CASCO BAY AND ISLANDS

A marvelous way to see Portland and its many beautiful neighboring islands is aboard a **Casco Bay Lines cruise** (Commercial and Franklin Streets; ((207) 774-7871). A variety of options is available, including a six-hour trip to **Bailey's Island**, a circumnavigation of the Bay stopping at all major islands including **Peaks**, **Great and Little Diamond**, and **Chebeague**, on the Mail Boat, and sunset and musical cruises. The

islands are excellent for bicycling, strolling, and getting away fom the metropolis.

Portland is also the gateway to the Canadian province of Nova Scotia via the *Prince of Fundy* cruises, departing nearly every day from May through October, an 11-hour overnight voyage. High season (June to September) rates are $68, and half price for children, with an additional $93 to carry your car. A cabin for two people varies from $40 to $160 one way. In Portland call ((207) 775-5616, or within Maine toll-free (800) 482-0955, and outside Maine toll-free (800) 341-7540.

Finally, just south of the city is the historic **Portland Headlight**. This lighthouse dates from 1791, the first authorized by the United States, upon an order from George Washington.

SEBAGO LAKE

About 12 miles (19 km) north of Portland is lovely Sebago Lake. The 14-mile (23-km) lake, second largest in Maine, lies in rolling hills of birch, maple, oak, and pine, and offers swimming, boating, fine salmon and trout fishing.

Sebago Lake State Park, at the north end of the lake, is a prime summer swimming area with wide sandy beaches, although it tends to be very crowded on weekends and holidays.

Where to Stay

Migis Lodge (off Route 302; ((207) 655-4524; 30 rooms; moderate to expensive) is on the lake shore in South Casco. There are many motels and lakeside cabins for rent in the area.

FREEPORT AND L.L. BEAN

North of Portland on U.S. 1 is **Freeport**, once a sleepy village promoted to notoriety by L.L. Bean. For 365 days a year, 24 hours a day, L.L. Bean parking lots are crammed with the cars of shoppers who are confronted inside the building with an overwhelming array of fashions, camping gear, hunting and fishing goods, wilderness and outdoor clothing, and accessories.

It all started in 1912, when founder Leon L. Bean promoted a better boot for Maine hunters. His money-back guarantee earned him a lot of goodwill, and soon the store

Sebago Lake and Sebago Lake State Park provide natural opportunities for fishing, swimming and boating.

began to grow, reaching almost legendary status by the 1980's. Now, the outlet's "wilderness clothes" are much sought-after by the yuppie generation. With success comes imitators. L.L. Bean has drawn a rabble of fashionable designer outlets and retailers to Freeport, transforming what was once a lovely colonial town into a shopper's wasteland.

Tourist Information

The **Freeport Merchants Association** has prepared a free brochure that list outlet stores, restaurants, bed and breakfasts,

country inns, and campgrounds. It is available in all the stores in Freeport. For a copy, write to the Association (P.O. Box 452 DL, Freeport, ME 04032; ((207) 865-1212).

AUGUSTA

Inland, just off Interstate 95, about 30 miles (48 km) north of Brunswick, is **Augusta**, the state capital. A small city of less than 25,000, Augusta is situated on the banks of the Kennebec River in the heart of the Kennebec Valley. Primarily a residential community

ABOVE: The placid bay of Freeport provides docking for many of the town's inhabitants.
OPPOSITE: Wild Mountain Man and his resume.

with little industry or manufacturing, Augusta is largely dependent for its livelihood on the many offices of the state government.

Well worth a visit is the **Maine State House** designed by Charles Bullfinch, who was also the architect of the Boston State House. Located at State and Capitol Streets, the Maine State House was completed in 1832, and is topped by an impressive cupola. Across from it is the **State Museum** (admission free; open Monday to Saturday, 9 am to 5 pm) which has dioramas that integrate live animals and plants and many interesting historical displays.

Fort Weston, on Bowman Street, is a restored eighteenth century, stockade. It is the site from which, in 1775, Benedict Arnold set out with his troops on the ill-fated march through the wilderness to attack Quebec.

From Augusta many scenic Kennebec Valley villages are an easy drive, including **Hallowell** and **Gardiner**. Further north is historic **Waterville**, home of prestigious Colby College.

WHERE TO STAY

There are many inexpensive to moderate motels in the Augusta area. One of the best is the **Best Western Senator Inn** (284 Western Avenue; ((207) 622-5804. 85 rooms; moderate). Also adequate is the **Holiday Inn** (Western Avenue and Interstate 95; ((207) 622-6371. 128 rooms; moderate).

EATING OUT

The **Best Western Senator Inn**, mentioned above, is also recommended for fine cuisine and "Downeast" food.

DOWNEAST MAINE

"Downeast" may be a confusing term to non-Mainers. It refers to the upper northern portion of the Maine coastline. But confused or not, once you travel north to Brunswick, you are down east. (The term was coined by sailors who were blown "down" the coast in their sailing ships by the region's prevailing winds.)

Lobster taken from the frigid waters off downeast Maine's rocky coastline has become a must for many travelers. Regional restaurants prepare the delicy in every possible fashion, but perfectly steamed lobster dipped in melted butter is hard to beat. Lobster, however, is far less consumed by Mainers than by tourists; the natives tend to find it too expensive, and are apt to prefer baked beans, corn bread, fish, and other traditional fare.

TOURIST INFORMATION

For more information, contact The **Down East Maine Association** (Box 662, Ellsworth, Maine 04605; ((207) 667-3615).

The town's most important landmark is **Bowdoin College**. A private college established in 1794, it is considered one of the best in the United States, and claims alumni such as writer Hawthorne, poet Longfellow, President Franklin Pierce and polar explorer Admiral Robert Peary. The school's **Walker Museum of Art** offers a fine collection of paintings, including a Gilbert Stuart portrait of Thomas Jefferson; its **Peary-MacMillan Arctic Museum** houses artifacts from historic Arctic expeditions.

BRUNSWICK

Brunswick is an attractive town best known for its wide avenues, tall trees shading Federal mansions, and the Bowdoin College campus. **Maine Street** is the state's widest at 198 ft (60 m). Locals explain that the wide street was built to give marauding Indians fewer places in which to hide.

The **Federal Street** area contains some of Brunswick's most impressive and historic homes, including the 1806 **Stowe House**, where Harriet Beecher Stowe wrote *Uncle Tom's Cabin*. Nearby, the **Pejepscot Historical Society Museum**, housed in an 1858 sea captain's home, has a display of local seafaring artifacts.

Where to Stay and Eating Out

Stowe House, an 1807 home, has been converted into a comfortable inn (63 Federal Street; ((207) 725-5543; 48 rooms; moderate to expensive).

For dining, **The Bowdoin Steak House** (115 Maine Street; ((207) 725-2314; moderate) is excellent.

BATH

In the last 200 years, more than 5,000 ships have been launched from Bath's historic shipyards at the mouth of the Kennebec River. Today, the **Bath Iron Works** continues the tradition. Since 1889, the company has made not only pleasure boats and freighters, but also destroyers, patrol boats, and battleships; it remains one of the busiest boatyards in the nation for U.S. Navy ships. While national security interests keep the boatyard closed to visitors, boat launchings are still festive events in the town.

Bath's shipbuilding legacy comes alive at the **Maine Maritime Museum** (Washington Street, just off U.S. 1; ((207) 443-1316). Several buildings exhibit models, gadgets, and other seafaring artifacts; a working apprentice boatyard demonstrates various stages of boatbuilding. In summer months

boat rides are scheduled to the mouth of the Kennebec River.

BOOTHBAY HARBOR

During the summer season, more than 60,000 visitors flock to Boothbay Harbor, a fishing town that lies at the end of a rugged peninsula between the Sheepscot and Damariscotta Rivers. Its streets are lined with small shops and seafood restaurants. At nearby wharves, fishermen unload catches of fish and lobster. In warm weather, dozens of ships and boats fill the harbor, creating an unmatched spectacle of masts, sails, and colors. Special celebrations in the self-proclaimed "boating capital of New England" include **Windjammer Days** and **Friendship Sloop Days**, both held in July.

Charter boats such as the *Maranbo II* and *Balmy Days* offer **harbor cruises** that include stop-over island clambakes, seal

Boothbay Harbor shops, crowded with trinkets, cater to summer's influx of tourists.

watching, lobster hauling, scenic sunsets, and more.

Back on dry land, the **Boothbay Railway Museum** (on Route 27, one mile or 1.6 km north of Boothbay Center; ((207) 633-4727) features a ride on a narrow gauge steam railway through a replica of an old New England village.

Where to Stay

There are many hotels in the Boothbay area, but in the summer they are in great demand and rooms can be difficult to find. Don't wait until dusk to begin looking.

The following provide good accommodations: **Brown Brothers Wharf Motel and Marina** (Atlantic Avenue; ((207) 633-5440; 70 rooms; moderate to expensive); **Fisherman's Wharf Inn** (40 Commercial Street; Z (207) 633-5090; 54 rooms; moderate to expensive); **Rocktide Inn** (45 Atlantic Avenue; ((800) 762-8433; 98 rooms; expensive); and **Spruce Point Inn** (Spruce Point on Route 27; ((207) 633-4152; 56 rooms; moderate to expensive).

Eating Out

For fresh lobster and local seafood, the **Brothers Wharf Restaurant** (Atlantic Avenue; ((207) 633-5440; moderate to expensive) is the best in town.

The **Lawnmeer Inn Dining Room** (Route 27, Southport; ((207) 633-2544; moderate) specializes in Downeast meals.

PEMAQUID POINT

The **Pemaquid Point Light**, built in 1827, might be the most painted, photographed and sketched lighthouse in the country. It sits on a bluff at the tip of Pemaquid Point, a ledge jutting into the sea.

The lighthouse's image is reflected in shallow pools of water left by the retreating surf. A small fishermen's museum is located in the lightkeeper's house.

The Point, south of Damariscotta on Route 130, is also home to colonial **Pemaquid**. In 1965 amateur archaeologists uncovered here the foundations of seventeenth-century houses and other artifacts which included a human skeleton outfitted in armor, believed to be a Viking. These discoveries are displayed at the tiny archae-ological museum.

MONHEGAN ISLAND

Near **Port Clyde**, nine miles (15 km) off the coast, rise the dramatic cliffs of **Monhegan Island**, a ledge of rock and forest less than two miles (three kilometers) long and one mile (one and a half kilometers) wide. The ocean scenery and boulder-strewn coast are spectacular when viewed from atop **Lighthouse Hill** There are 17 miles (27 km) of **hiking trails** along the 150-ft (46-m) cliffs. The open meadows are blanketed with wildflowers, and **Cathedral Woods** display majestic pines and firs.

Leif Ericsson is said to have walked this island more than 1,000 years ago. English explorer John Cabot referred to it on his journeys. Its headlands were reputed to be hideaways for pirates, who plundered ships off the Maine coast.

The easiest way to get to Monhegan is aboard the *Laura B.*, a converted trawler which ferries passengers from Port Clyde (at the bottom of Route 131). Along the way, the captain of the *Laura B.* will stop to let his passengers watch dolphins and whales. From a distance, the island itself resembles a huge floating whale. No cars are permitted on the island.

PENOBSCOT BAY

Rockland

Continuing north on U.S. 1, travelers pass through Rockland (north of Owls Head on the western edge of Penobscot Bay), a modern-day seaport that is the leading lobster distribution center in Maine. It is perhaps best noted for its **Maine Seafood Festival**, a three-day-long event held annually during the first weekend in August. Everything revolves around the catch — there are lobster boils, harvesting excursions, and even displays of lobster trap building.

A windjammer fleet, ☎ (207) 596-0376, offers week-long cruises along the coast, and handsome schooners ply the waters on three- to six-day island cruises from May to October. **Owls Head Lighthouse**, four miles (six and a half kilometers) south of Rock-

land, sits atop a 100-ft (30-m) cliff, and for lighthouse fans it is worth the short drive.

Camden

Camden, at the base of the Camden Hills with a long view of Penobscot Bay and its picturesque harbor, is a Maine classic. It is a yachting center and one of the loveliest towns in New England, it is also in its quiet, undemonstrative way an oasis of downeast wealth and glamour.

For a majestic panorama, head to **Camden Hills State Park** (two miles or just over three kilometers north of Camden on U.S. 1) where Mt Battie (800 ft or 244 m high) stands sentinel over the town; a stone viewing tower on top of the mount provides a spectacular view of the coast.

Camden is also a Maine publishing center, home to periodicals such as the *Down East Magazine*. It is also a renowned summer resort, attracting businessmen, Hollywood celebrities, and tourists.

Sailing is the primary attraction. In summer the harbor is filled with graceful yachts, sailboats with colorful canvases, and every other kind of floating vessel imaginable.

Sightseeing cruises and sailing trips on old schooners depart from the **Town and Public landings** (for schedules call ☎ (207) 236-4404), offering tours of Penobscot Bay and views of Mounts Battie and Megunticook.

In winter, bitter winds laden with moisture sweep in from Penobscot Bay, which means plenty of snow for the **Camden Snow Bowl**, ☎ (207) 236-3438, offering both downhill and cross-country runs. You can also ice skate on the vast **Lake Megunticook**. (If you are in Camden during early spring, you can enter a local gambling pool, centered on the day that the ice will break on the lake.)

At any time of year, you can browse through the expensive shops that cater to Camden's decidedly upscale clientele and to unwary tourists.

For those city and suburb dwellers anxious to prove themselves outdoorsmen, there is always the **Outward Bound School** on **Hurricane Island** in Penobscot Bay. This training school for wilderness survival skills claims that students should be prepared for the "most miserable, most wonderful days of your life." Two weeks of backpacking, rock climbing, or maneuvering tiny boats past bay islets is standard curriculum.

Where to Stay
Camden Harbor Inn (83 Bayview Street; ((207) 236-4200; 22 rooms; expensive) and the old colonial**Whitehall Inn** (52 High Street; ((207) 236-3391; 54 rooms; expensive), are the best accommodations in Camden.

Eating Out
Dinners at the **Whitehall Inn** (expensive) are unforgettably good and **Aubergine** (6

"Mount Desert" is certainly a misnomer. Sixteenth-century French explorer Champlain noticed its treeless mountain peaks, and gave the island its name. However, it is a place of dense forests, quiet bays and inlets, and has the highest mountains on the Atlantic coast.

BAR HARBOR

Bar Harbor is the gateway to the Acadia National Park, and a good base for visiting the only national park in New England. It is

Belmont Avenue; ((207) 236-8053; moderate to expensive) serves excellent French-style meals.

Rockport
Located on U.S. 1 between Rockland and Camden, **Rockport** is a fishing town with carefully landscaped grounds along its waterfront.

MOUNT DESERT ISLAND

Even in Maine, a land of intense natural beauty, Mount Desert Island and its largest town, Bar Harbor, are unusual. The name

Dining at one of Bar Harbor's colonial mansions.

a town which once rivaled Newport, Rhode Island, for its wealth and extravagance.

In the late nineteenth-century the island attracted artists who came to paint its incredible beauty. They were soon followed by rich East Coast families, such as the Rockefellers and Vanderbilts, who built mansions and elegant summer "cottages," transforming Mount Desert, and more specifically Bar Harbor, into their own personal playground. (One mansion featured a massive banquet table that would descend from a retractable hole in a dining room ceiling — completely set for the meal, including food and drinks!)

In 1947, a great forest fire burning out of control for nearly a month destroyed much of the island, including most of the mansions. They were replaced by more modest motels and hotels, and the island opened up to accommodate tourists of all means.

The few mansions that survived have been transformed into elegant inns, such as Cleftstone Manor in Bar Harbor, a 33-room house built in the late nineteenth century by the Blairs of Washington, D.C. (the same family that built the Washington landmark house across the street from the White House where dignitaries stay when visiting the capital).

Today, almost three million people visit Mount Desert Island (pronounced "des-SERT") annually. They come primarily to see Acadia National Park, for the yachting, and for the sightseeing cruises that leave from Municipal Pier at West Street for the Bar's scenic bays and inlets.

Tourist Information

With year round outdoor recreation opportunities in the area, the **Bar Harbor Chamber of Commerce** (Bar Harbor, ME 04609; ℂ (207) 288-5103) has prepared several free brochures and maps for vacation planning.

Where to Stay

There is no lack of good accommodations here, although they do tend to fill up during peak summer months: **Atlantic Eyrie Lodge** (Highbrook Road; ℂ (207) 288-9786; 57 rooms; expensive); **Bar Harbor Inn** (Newport Drive; toll free ℂ (800) 248-3351; 115 rooms; expensive); **Bay View Inn** (111 Eden Street; ℂ (207) 288-3173; 32 rooms; expensive); **Cleftstone Manor** (92 Eden Street; ℂ (207) 288-4951; 16 rooms; expensive); **The Ledgelawn Inn** (66 Mount Desert Street; ℂ (207) 288-4596; 34 rooms; expensive); **Stratford House Inn** (45 Mount Desert Street; ℂ (207) 288-5189; 10 rooms; moderate to expensive); and **Wonder View Motor Lodge** (Eden Street; ℂ (207) 288-3831; 82 rooms; moderate to expensive).

EATING OUT

Lorenzo Creamer's Lobster Pound (West Street; ℂ (207) 288-5033; expensive) is a cut above the other seafood restaurants in town.

ACADIA NATIONAL PARK

33,000-acre (13,350-hectare) Acadia National Park occupies most of Mount Desert Island

and is certainly one of the nation's unique national parks. Small by comparison with Yellowstone or Yosemite, it has nonetheless an equally grand diversity of landscapes, colors, geology, flora, and fauna. It is the home of 250 different bird species and over 500 varieties of wildflowers. In ecological zones it varies from sandy and rock-strewn beaches to coastal coniferous forests to montane rock and lichen. Miles of Park Service trails crisscross the island from beach to peak, through pine forest and meadows. Dominating Mount Desert Island above the bare granite of lesser peaks is majestic Cadillac Mountain, at 1,530 ft (466 m), the highest mountain on the East coast.

Much of the land comprising the park, which was established in 1916, was given by a wealthy Bostonian, George B. Dorr, and by John D. Rockefeller, Jr., who also paid for construction of many of the Park's roads. A good place to begin a tour of the Park is at the **Visitor Center** (Hull's Cove, Route 3; ℂ (207) 288-3338; open June to November).

Seeing the Park

Park rangers can help in planning tours, including **naturalist-led hiking treks** or self-guided 56-mile (90-km) auto tours, enhanced by prerecorded cassette tapes which describe points of interest, history, and geography. **Guided bus tours** motor through the park (depart from Main Street, Bar Harbor; ℂ (207) 288-5218). You can also hop aboard a **sightseeing plane** of Air Acadia, Inc. (along Route 3). Another option is to hike or bike the nearly 200 miles (322 km) of footpaths and trails. Unfortunately, Park Service budget cuts by the Reagan and Bush administrations have closed many of the Park's trails, so check with Rangers for the latest details.

The 30-mile (48-km) **Loop Road** tour of the park offers memorable views. The Loop's Ocean Drive section is one-way for 11 miles (18 km) along the Park's eastern perimeter with the Champlain Mountain's pink cliffs ahead. A hike up the **Precipice Trail**, using ladders and handrails, is rewarded by a summit-top mountain vista. On the Loop's southeastern section, **Otter Cliffs** rise precipitously more than 100 ft (30 m) above the ocean.

The Park's most spectacular site is **Cadillac Mountain**, with its unparalleled views of breathtaking ocean views and rugged island interiors, including Mt Katahdin, Maine's highest peak. For those who prefer not to walk there is an automobile road to the top.

EASTERNMOST UNITED STATES

LUBEC

Visitors often travel no further up the Maine coast than Bar Harbor. However, if they continue up U.S. 1, then detour at Route 189 toward Lubec, and **Quoddy Head State Park** (just south of Lubec), the easternmost patch of land in the United States. "Sunrise County," as it likes to be called, receives the warming rays of the sun earlier than any other point in the nation. The country's greatest variation in tides is found here, with differences ranging to almost 30 ft (nine meters).

CAMPOBELLO ISLAND

Lubec is also the gateway to **Campobello Island**, New Brunswick (Canada). Linked to the mainland by a bridge stretching over Lubec Narrows, Campobello is the location of President Franklin D. Roosevelt's family summer home. There is an 11-acre (four hectare) estate surrounding the house, which is furnished with family memorabilia, ((207) 752-2922.

WAY UP NORTH

There are entire sections of Maine, basically the larger top half of the state, that most travelers never see. It is a vast wilderness of pines, balsam firs, spruce swamps, and birch, pocketed with sandy-bottomed lakes and drained by countless trout-filled streams.

BANGOR

On route to these northern wilds via the seacoast and Interstate 95, Bangor is the first stop, and the last urban center south of Canada. This city on the west bank of the Penobscot River, once the "lumber capital of the world," was the brawling center of a young logging industry back in the days when Maine still had tall trees. In those boisterous times, lumbermen would come in after weeks in the woods, sailors would sail upriver after weeks or years at sea, and a wild and often bruising time was had in "Devil's Half-acre," the city's bar and brothel district.

Now, in more temperate times, the city maintains a giant statue of mythical lumberjack Paul Bunyan on Main Street opposite the Civic Center. Bangor still relies on the wood industries and pulp processing as the mainstay of its economy, although it is now diversifying rapidly. A Bangor Victorian mansion is the home of "horror" novelist Stephen King.

Above Bangor, the roads fan out northeast to **Moosehead Lake**, north to **Millinocket** and **Baxter State Park**, beyond to **Aroostook County**, and west to Maine's major ski areas, **Sugarloaf** and **Saddleback Mountain** near Lake Mooselookmeguntic.

Where to Stay
Holiday Inn-Main Street (500 Main Street; ((207) 947-8651; 125 rooms; moderate to expensive), and **Ramada Inn** (357 Odlin Road; ((207) 947-6961; 116 rooms; moderate to expensive).

MOOSEHEAD LAKE

Moosehead, the largest lake in Maine, lies some 90 miles (145 km) beyond Bangor. It covers more than 120 sq miles (310 sq km), with a shoreline of 420 miles (677 km). Much of the shore is inaccessible except by canoe or float plane, both of which are available for hire or charter at **Greenville** at the south end of the lake. The region remains rich in wildlife, including, deer, bear, and moose; the lake's waters abound with lake salmon and trout. For the hunter and fisherman, there are many lodges and hunting camps.

The less adventurous can get a panoramic view of the north woods from the scenic chair lift at **Big Squaw Mountain Ski Area**, ((207) 695-2272, about five miles (eight kilometers) northwest of town, off Route 15; the view in the fall is spectacular.

The craggy shores of Acadia National Park.

Tourist Information
The **Moosehead Lake Region Chamber of Commerce** (P.O. Box 581D, Greenville 04441; ((207) 695-2702) claims no visitor will be dissappointed with facilities in the area and provides free maps and brochures.

ALLAGASH WILDERNESS WATERWAY

Not for the average traveler, this wonderland of lakes, rivers, and forest is a remnant of the north woods as they used to be. Accessible by canoe, it is best known for the 98-mile (158-km) **Allagash Wilderness Waterway**, a superlative chain of lakes, some up to 20 miles long, linked by the thundering rapids and slick current of the Allagash River. Here the traveler goes at his or her own pace, paddling the long lakes and riding down the fast-moving river, camping at night with the song of loons and the Northern Lights for company. Hundreds of miles of rivers and lakes can be traveled this way, like the voyagers of old, portaging one's canoe between watersheds. Many canoeists put in on the Penobscot River just east of Moosehead Lake, cross over into the Allagash drainage at Mud Pond, and paddle all the way to the St John River, or even down to **Calais** and the Atlantic.

Again, this is only for experienced canoeists, and not to be done alone. Parts are definitely Class V whitewater and difficult even for the most experienced; the worst of Allagash Rapids and Falls is portaged even by the best. But if you think you'd some day like to try it, spend part of this visit canoeing, and plan to try the Allagash later, when you've gained the necessary skills.

An even longer voyage can be made down the **St John River**. This tends to become shallow by late summer, and is even wilder than the Allagash in early summer. Trips on the Penobscot and Kennebec Rivers can also begin here. Canoe tours are available for those not sufficiently experienced to

Northern Maine is spotted with pristine lakes which offer a haven from the civilization of the south.

try it on their own. For those who are, canoes can be rented at Greenville, and then carried by car back to Greenville when you leave the River. Two cars are an advantage: one to leave at your destination, and the other to bring back to Greenville or wherever you begin, or "put in," as Mainers say. As with any trip to the North Woods, black flies are a major problem in May and June, and mosquitoes in June through September. For further information, contact the **Moosehead Lake Vacation and Sportsmen's Association** (Rockwood, Maine 04478; ((207) 534-7300).

BAXTER STATE PARK

Percival Proctor Baxter, Governor of the State of Maine, was an early environmentalist. Knowing that civilization would one day doom the wilderness, he dreamed to set aside great tracts of land in central Maine as a nature preserve in order that generations to come might enjoy the land as it once had been.

Unable, during his two terms as governor, to persuade the Legislature to support his intent, Baxter undertook, nonetheless, to make his dream a reality. A man of considerable wealth, he devoted his life to the purchase and consolidation of 200,000 acres (81,000 hectares) of wild land which he then deeded to Maine as a state park on condition that the land remain "forever wild."

The state park that bears this extraordinary man's name is located 18 miles (29 km) north of **Millinocket**, and 75 miles (121 km) north of Bangor. It is an area of dense forests, pristine streams, lakes, and mountains, and shelters abundant wildlife. Apart from a few narrow unpaved roads, access to its interior is chiefly by the many hiking trails across it.

Mt Katahdin
Baxter State Park is dominated by Mt Katahdin, at 5,267 ft (1,605 m) the highest peak in the state, second highest in New England, and one of the highest points east of the Rockies. The Abenaki Indians' god Pamola lived on the summit, hurling thunderbolts and conjuring up fierce storms in times of anger. You can cross Pamola Peak by trekking the **Hunt Trail**, an 11-mile (18-km) path leading to the top of Katahdin. It is an

all-day, very demanding hike; beware of high winds and treacherous weather.

Most of Baxter's wilderness attractions require hiking to reach them, but the park's 162-mile (261-km) trail system guarantees access. One of the Park's loveliest sights, **Chimney Pond**, is accessible by a three-hour moderate hike from the Chimney Pond parking lot. There is a campground at the Pond (reservations normally necessary in summer), and the view of Katahdin's sheer, massive granite walls towering straight up from the far side of the Pond cannot be described.

On **Sandy Stream Pond Trail** there are often moose lingering at the pond; **Cathedral Trail** demands serious rock climbing techniques to reach the Katahdin summit; and the northern portion of the **Appalachian Trail** leads to both **Big** and **Little Niagara Falls**.

Baxter Peak is one of four Katahdin summits, the others being Hamlin, Pamola, and South. The latter two are connected by one of the park's most extraordinary geologic features: the **Knife Edge**, an extremely narrow, serrated wall of granite 4,000 ft (1,219 m) high.

Park Information
For more park information, contact the Reservation Clerk, **Baxter Park Headquarters** (64 Balsam Drive, Millinocket, Maine 04462.)

AROOSTOOK COUNTY

Still farther northeast (from the Baxter Park access road, hook up with Interstate 95, go north to U.S. 1, and continue north) is **Presque Isle**, the commercial center of Aroostook County, Maine's prime potato-growing country. Just south of town is **Aroostook Farm — Maine Agricultural Station**, 375 acres (152 hectares) devoted to potato growing research. By calling ℂ (207) 768-8341, one can arrange a free tour.

Potato Blossom Festival
Fort Fairfield, eight miles (13 km) north of Presque Isle on U.S. 1, just a stone's throw from New Brunswick, Canada, holds its annual Potato Blossom Festival in July. This is the height of the potato blossom season, and Aroostook is awash with pink, white, and lavender blooms.

SKIING IN MAINE

Two of Maine's major ski areas, Sugarloaf and Saddleback Mountains, lie 80 miles (128 km) west of Bangor, near Lake Mooselookmeguntic.

SUGARLOAF MOUNTAIN

Sugarloaf is one of the highest peaks in the east with a summit of 4,237 ft (1,291 m). With an annual snowfall of 14 ft (4.3 m), it seems, as skiers say, "to have been created especially for skiing." A lattice-work of 50 ski

trails totaling more than 30 miles (48 km), with a vertical drop of 2.637 ft (804 m), offer something for every skier.

Novice runs drop off the hills into the center of the ski village, which is filled with shops, restaurants, and watering holes. Along the mountain's western edge, the intermediate Tote Road run stretches an incredible three miles (4.8 km), and the Narrow Gauge, a famous World Cup run, offers the ultimate skiing experience for the expert.

Sugarloaf USA, ((207) 237-2861, is Maine's premier ski resort, and among the most popular in New England. It is a blend of old-time Yankee, deep-woods wilderness, refined hospitality, and superb skiing guaranteed to make any skier feel at home.

SADDLEBACK MOUNTAIN

Saddleback Mountain, ((207) 864-5364, Maine's second-largest ski resort, is about a one-hour drive south from Sugarloaf. Its summit rises to 4,116 ft (1,255 m), with a vertical drop of 1,826 ft (557 m). There are more than 40 runs, including Rustler's Range and Bronco Buster — both steep, mogul-filled slopes. Saddleback sponsors an annual ski contest here in March — anyone who can cruise Bronco from top to bottom without falling or stopping earns free ski passes.

Sunset at Acadia

New Hampshire

IN HIS poem "New Hampshire," Robert Frost wrote,

Just specimens is all New Hampshire has,
One each of everything as in a show case,
Which naturally she doesn't care to sell.

Travelers to this state quickly discover what the poet meant. Despite its small size (180 miles, or 290 km, from north to south, and 100 miles, or 160 km, at its widest point), New Hampshire has a variety of geographical and scenic features.

SEVEN DISTINCTIVE AREAS

The **Hampshire seacoast**, less than an hour's drive from Boston, follows the Atlantic Ocean for 18 miles (29 km) between Maine on the north and Massachusetts to the south.

The **Merrimack River Valley** has a colorful history but is often now referred to as "The Golden Corridor" because of the many financial institutions and high-tech industrial firms which have located there.

The **Monadnock** region, on the other hand, is reminiscent of Currier and Ives prints: a rolling countryside of small villages, the land crisscrossed with hiking paths and ski trails.

Along the western border of the state, the **Hanover and Lake Sunapee** region is the home of venerable Dartmouth College and the locale, as well, of popular winter resorts that attract skiers from all over the East.

In the **Lakes region**, Lake Winnipesaukee draws many of the state's summer visitors. Its broad expanse, wooded shores, and 274 islands offer a variety of summer pleasures for the vacationer.

The **White Mountains**, tallest in the East, tower over the Maine border and extend southwest through the center of the state. The scenery here is rugged and dramatic, with the mountains' granite faces staring down at the valley towns far below. It is a region of forests and whitewater streams that, with the changing colors of the autumn leaves, takes on a particular beauty.

The **Far North** area near the Canadian border is almost totally unspoilt and contains one of the most scenic waterways in the State.

These regions, each distinctive, can be found within the confines of a state that can be traversed from south to north in little more than three hours.

TOURIST INFORMATION

The **State of New Hampshire, Office of Vacation Travel** (P.O. Box 856-RC, Concord, NH 03301; ((603) 271-2666) has free maps and information, which it will mail to you upon request. For travel information, call toll-free (800) 258-3608.

"LIVE FREE OR DIE"

Somewhat isolated geographically from the other New England states, New Hampshire was the only one of the thirteen colonies not invaded by British troops during the Revolution. The people of the state had then, and still retain, a determined sense of independence, and have embraced conservative democracy with a particular fervor. One of New Hampshire's major newspapers, *The Manchester Union-Leader*, has in its editorial policies and news coverage embraced one

ABOVE: A commemoration of emancipation from tyranny. OPPOSITE: A New Hampshire country hotel and its tranquil setting.

of the most ferocious right-wing stances in the nation. Although many New Hampshire residents would disagree, such attitudes seem to have filtered down into the daily attitudes of the population.

New Hampshire's strong-willed, independent attitudes manifest themselves in other substantive ways. New Hampshire has no state income tax or sales tax. State revenues are generated through so-called "sin" taxes on lottery tickets and liquor and cigarette sales. Most notably, the state's Bill of Rights recognizes "revolution" as a legit-

imate means of carrying out the will of the people, hence the state motto: "Live Free or Die" found also on its license plates.

Political awareness and self-determination are also evident in New Hampshire's form of local government, the town meeting. Established early in New England's history, the town meeting was, in a sense, the genesis of American democracy, giving each man and woman in the community an equal voice in local affairs. Town Meeting Day remains an important element of that process throughout New Hampshire. In the state government, more than 420 legislators constitute one of the largest legislative assemblies in the world.

PRESIDENTIAL PRIMARIES

New Hampshire's Presidential primary, the nation's first in a presidential election year, has become the forecast of success or failure

A New Hampshire license plate, the state's motto rooted in American Revolution history, and a friendly invitation.

for candidates for that office, a mega-media event that has somehow achieved "make or break" status on the political scene. Candidates who might otherwise have difficulty pointing out New Hampshire on a map of the United States descend quadrennially upon the state to offer political platitudes to this independent people.

But platitudes do not seem to work in New Hampshire. Its residents are straightforward, unpretentious Yankees who cut to the political quick of issues. They also have an uncanny record of reflecting the national mood. Around 75 percent of the time, New Hampshire Primary winners have become presidential candidates of both the Republican and Democratic parties. Witness 1988, when both former Vice President George Bush and former Massachusetts governor Michael Dukakis gained victories.

BACKGROUND

It is not surprising that New Hampshire residents relish their tough streak of independence. Ever since Englishman David Thomsom and a small group of fishermen made the dangerous journey across the Atlantic, landing at Odiornes's Point (the town of Rye) in 1623 to establish a fledgling fishing industry, independence and self-reliance have been traits vital to survival.

Early settlers experienced severe hardships: the land had only a thin layer of topsoil, with a profusion of rocks and boulders (that's why you see so many old stone walls in the region); it was also heavily forested, requiring much hard labor to clear it before food crops could be planted; and winters were bitter, with sub-zero temperatures and mounds of snow.

Apart from subsistence farming, there were two basic means of support for the new settlement. Fishing fleets set sail from the state's only deep water port, now Portsmouth, to seek cod on the west Atlantic, while loggers cut down New Hampshire's 1,000-year-old pines for use as masts and shipbuilding timber.

By 1641, the struggling settlements had agreed to consolidate with the flourishing Massachusetts Bay Colony to the south. But the year-long King Phillip's War (named for

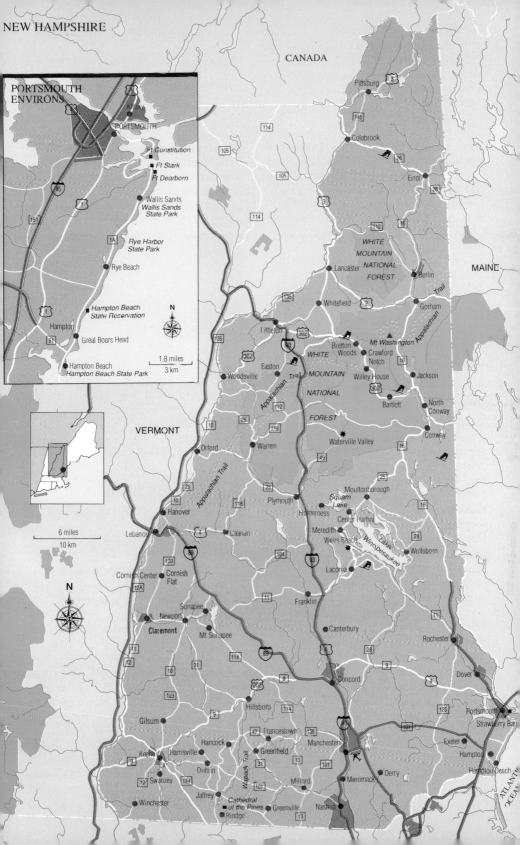

NEW HAMPSHIRE

CANADA

PORTSMOUTH ENVIRONS

Kittery

PORTSMOUTH

Ft Constitution
Ft Stark
Ft Dearborn

Wallis Sands
Wallis Sands
State Park

1A   Rye Harbor
State Park

Rye Beach

N

Hampton Beach
State Reservation

Hampton

51   Great Boars Head

Hampton Beach
Hampton Beach State Park

1.8 miles
3 km

VERMONT

N

6 miles
10 km

MAINE

Pittsburg

Colebrook

Errol

WHITE
MOUNTAIN
NATIONAL
FOREST

Lancaster

Berlin

Whitefield   Gorham

Appalachian Trail

Littleton

Bretton
Woods   Mt Washington

WHITE   Crawford
Notch

MOUNTAIN   Jackson

Easton   Willey House

NATIONAL   Bartlett   North
Conway

FOREST   Conway

Woodsville

Orford   Waterville Valley

Warren

Plymouth   Moultonborough

Holderness   Squam
Lake

Hanover   Center Harbor

Lebanon   Meredith

Caanan   Weirs Beach   Wolfeboro

Lake Winnipesaukee

Laconia

Cornish Center   Cornish
Flat   Franklin

Sunapee   Canterbury

Newport   Rochester

Claremont   Mt Sunapee

Concord   Dover

Portsmouth
Strawberry Bank

Gilsum

Hillsboro

Francestown
Hancock

Harrisville   Greenfield   Manchester   Exeter

Keene   Hampton

Dublin   Hampton Beach

Swanzey   Milford   Derry   ATLANTIC OCEAN

Merrimack

Jaffrey   Nashua

Winchester   Cathedral
of the Pines   Greenville

Rindge

a Wampanoag Indian chief) caused much disruption when it began in 1675, and the settlements did not recover until just before the American Revolution.

INDEPENDENCE

New Hampshire received its "independence" from Massachusetts in 1679, when King Charles II declared it a royal province. John Wentworth, a successful merchant, was appointed to govern the colony in 1717; it prospered for a time, with Portsmouth taking on an English elegance that is still apparent today.

Later, the colony became caught up in the fervor for independence and Wentworth was forced to leave Portsmouth in 1775. One year later, on January 5, 1776, New Hampshire drew up its own constitution, and declared its independence from England six months before the Declaration of Independence of July 4, 1776.

ECONOMIC DIVERSIFICATION

In the 1800's, New Hampshire changed gradually from a logging, fishing, and farming economy into a manufacturing center for cotton and wool.

Manufacturing continued to grow well into the twentieth century, attracting thousands of French Canadians from poor farms across the border. Many factories, including the Amoskeag Manufacturing Company, then one of the largest mills in the country, drew immigrant workers from around the world who toiled long, grueling hours. The mills are said to have produced more than one mile (1.6 km) of cloth every working minute. However, the Great Depression, labor strikes, and the changing economy combined to deal New Hampshire's economy a serious blow.

Today, a revitalized (and diversified) manufacturing industry combines with tourism, a relaxed lifestyle, and a favorable tax climate to make New Hampshire an attractive place in which to live and work.

ABOVE Portsmouth's historic churches and expansive mansions OPPOSITE were built when the town was a flourishing seaport during the eighteenth century.

THE NEW HAMPSHIRE SEACOAST

PORTSMOUTH

New Hampshire's only seaport, Portsmouth was once the capital of the state and home port to a long-lived dynasty of merchant seamen. Great riches were amassed from their trade, which then were used to build handsome houses befitting their status, bringing to the settlement a veneer of refinement and culture. The city has since

experienced wildly changing fortunes and its "Golden Age" has long passed.

Tourist Information

Travelers can still sample a bit of Portsmouth's colonial past by following the **Portsmouth Trail**, which tours six of the city's finest seventeenth- and eighteenth-century homes. Tour guides (wearing period costumes) relate the history of the houses and tell anecdotes of their original owners. The city's **Historic Associates**, ((603) 436-1118, offers combination tickets (sold at any of the houses) and tour maps. For more information contact the **Portsmouth Chamber of Commerce** at 500 Market Street, Portsmouth, NH 03801.

The **Seacoast Council on Tourism** (Box 4669, Portsmouth, NH 03801; ((603) 436-7678) is actively promoting tourism to the coast.

Portsmouth Trail

On Market Street, is the **Moffatt-Ladd House**, built in 1763 by Captain John Moffatt as a wedding gift for his son, Samuel, and noted for its elegant furnishings and eighteenth-century architectural style. Visitors are also welcome in the formal gardens, where peonies blossom in colorful splendor each June.

Pleasant Street, "the handsomest house in Portsmouth." Built in 1784 for a prominent Revolutionary War political leader who has twice governor of New Hampshire, and first president *pro tempore* of the U.S. Senate, this elegant Georgian mansion remains one of the finest eighteenth-century homes in New England. The exterior proportions are enormous, while the gracious interiors contain some of the finest hand carving in the city. The gardens have been restored to their original state, with rose and grape arbors, perennial garden beds, and a handsome

The **Warner House** (next to the Town Hall on Daniel Street), built in 1715 by another wealthy sea captain, was occupied by the old salt's descendants as late as 1930. It has been called "one of the finest urban brick residences of the first quarter of the eighteenth century" in America today. It is one of New England's most beautiful Georgian houses, with several historic murals hanging in their original positions along the staircase. Especially noteworthy is the lightning rod on the west wall, said to have been installed by Benjamin Franklin in 1762. There are also several portraits by Blackburn, including one of Polly Warner.

No less than George Washington called the **Governor John Langdon House**, on

gazebo. Washington, Lafayette, and other statesmen of the time were entertained here.

Other houses on the tour include the 1758 residence of famed American naval leader **John Paul Jones** (who, when beckoned by the British to surrender during one high-seas battle, uttered the renowned line, "We have just begun to fight"); the grand 1807 Federal mansion called the **Rundlet-May House**; and the **Wentworth Gardner House**, whose grand woodcarvings are said to have kept a master craftsman busy for more than a year.

A different way to see all six houses is on the evening candlelight tour, held once a year, which features special trolley car transportation and accompanying guides in period costume.

Strawberry Banke

Named for the wild strawberries that grew here in abundance when early settlers arrived, Strawberry Banke is a 10-acre (four-hectare) outdoor museum preserving the historic waterfront neighborhood that was the site of the original Portsmouth settlement. About 35 historic buildings, dating from 1695 to 1940, are being restored. Seven are completed (including the 1780 Captain John Wheelwright House) and are furnished with period antiques. The restoration is so well done it appears as though people still

live and work here, but are momentarily absent. Also undergoing restoration is the 1766 William Pitt Tavern, a former stagecoach stop and hotbed of Revolutionary politics. George Washington often came here when visiting local state officials.

Not only can you stroll among the historic structures (in many cases watching actual restoration taking place), but you can also participate in a number of interesting activities. Several of the historic homes have been transformed into workshops, where programs geared to the family offer educational seminars on colonial crafts (including hands-on demonstrations), lectures, and special events such as the December candlelight tour through the "village." Other houses contain craft shops of working artisans who display their handiwork. Even historic landscapes have been recreated, including eighteenth-century herb and vegetable gardens. Set your own pace; all tours are self-guided. Strawberry Banke is at Hancock and Marcy streets (((603) 433-1100; open daily May to October).

Old Harbor

The Portsmouth area has several other historical attractions, including **Fort Constitution**, the 1632 site of a British fort captured by the Sons of Liberty in 1774 (the gunpowder seized here was used in the battle of Bunker Hill); **Fort Stark State Historic Site**, the remains of a seacoast defense system dating from 1746; and the **Old Harbour Area**, located on the waterfront, now filled with crafts and antique shops and restaurants.

Both **"Viking"** and **"Heritage"** Portsmouth Harbor cruises offer narrated boat tours down the **Piscataqua River**, where 90 sawmills once cut the virgin pine trees used for masts in the Royal Navy, and out into the Atlantic, bound for the historic **Isles of Shoals**. Contact **Star Island Cruises** (P.O Box 311, Portsmouth, NH 03810; ((603) 431-4620) and **Portsmouth Harbor Cruises** (64 Ceres Street; ((603) 436-8084).

Summer Festivals

Portsmouth also attracts the **Tall Ships Festival** in summer, when visitors are welcome to climb aboard these historic vessels. The **Prescott Park Arts Festival** is another major summertime attraction, with its all-day, all-night free entertainment.

Where to Stay

EXPENSIVE

Anchorage Motor Inn (Portsmouth Traffic Circle, Portsmouth; ((603) 431-8111; 46 rooms); there are also several fine hotels located in nearby Hampton Beach.

MODERATE

There is a wide variety of accommodations in this category. In the summer, they are frequently booked; reservations are recommended.

A few recommendations are: **Holiday Inn** (300 Woodbury Avenue, Portsmouth; ((603)

431-8000;130rooms);**Howard Johnson Hotel** (Interstate 95, exit 5, Portsmouth; ((603) 436-7600; 135 rooms); **Inn at Christian Shore** (335 Maplewood Avenue, Portsmouth; ((603) 431-6770; six rooms); **The Port Motor Inn** (Portsmouth Traffic Circle, Portsmouth; ((603) 436-4378; 56 rooms); and **Sheraton Portsmouth Hotel** (Interstate 95, exit 7, 256 Market Street, Portsmouth; ((603) 431-2300; 148 rooms).

Eating Out
EXPENSIVE
Ashworth By The Sea (295 Ocean Boule-

HAMPTON BEACH

Hampton Beach is located about eight miles (13 km) south of Portsmouth. This long, sandy beach provides excellent swimming, with arcades and rides for children and the **Hampton Beach Casino,** which features top-name entertainment.

Where to Stay
EXPENSIVE
The following inns with access to the ocean

vard; ((603) 926-6762) is the state's premier seacoast restaurant featuring lobster, seafood, and steaks. **Blue Strawberry Restaurant** (29 Ceres Street, Portsmouth; ((603) 431-6420) serves six-course gourmet fixed-price dinners.

On the waterfront in Portsmouth are two fine restaurants: **The Oar House** (55 Ceres Street, Portsmouth; ((603) 436-4025) and **Pier II** (next to Memorial Bridge, Portsmouth; ((603) 426-0669).

MODERATE
Located in the Old Harbour area next to the tugboat docks in Portsmouth, **The Dolphin Striker** (15 Bow Street, Portsmouth; ((603) 431-5222) has a good ambiance and excellent food.

are recommended: **Hampton Beach Regal Inn** (162 Ashworth Avenue, Hampton Beach; ((603) 926-7758; 36 rooms); and **Kentville on the Ocean** (315 Ocean Boulevard, Hampton Beach; ((603) 926-3950; 37 rooms).

MODERATE
Some recommendations: **Ashworth By The Sea** (295 Ocean Boulevard, Hampton Beach; ((603) 926-6762; 100 rooms); **Best Western Seabrook** (Route 107, Hampton Beach; ((603) 474-3078; 107 rooms); **Hampton House** (333 Ocean Boulevard, Hampton Beach; ((603) 926-1033; 51 rooms); and

Strawberry Banke, an outdoor museum and restored neighborhood, OPPOSITE preserves Portsmouth's past. ABOVE: Portsmouth's harbor.

Lamie's Inn and Tavern (490 Lafayette Road, Hampton Beach; ((603) 926-0330; 30 rooms).

Eating Out

Lamie's Tavern (Hampton Beach; ((603) 926-0330) specializes in New England dishes, and **Lincoln House** (95 Ocean Boulevard, Hampton Beach; ((603) 926-6069) where one can enjoy spectacular ocean views and excellent meals.

For seafood, the **Galley Hatch** (Route 1, Hampton Beach; ((603) 926-6152) is the best in the area.

THE MERRIMACK RIVER VALLEY

More than half of New Hampshire's population resides in the Merrimack Valley, which offers the traveler everything from high-tech industry to superb colonial architecture, clear streams, and forests.

NASHUA

Just a short distance from either Portsmouth Boston is Nashua, home of the University of New Hampshire. There are many hotels and restaurants in the area, including **Best Western Hallmark Motor Inn** (Route 3, exit 1; ((603) 888-1200; 81 rooms; expensive); **Sheraton Tara Hotel** (Route 3, exit 1; ((800) 325-3535; 345 rooms; expensive); **Comfort Inn** (Route 3, exit 7E; ((800) 228-5150; 104 rooms; moderate); and **Howard Johnson Lodge & Restaurant** (Everett Turnpike, exit 5E; ((603) 889-0173; 72 rooms; moderate).

Green Ridge Turkey Farm Restaurant (Daniel Webster Highway; ((603) 888-7020)

serves traditional Thanksgiving roast turkey dinners year-round for a moderate price.

MYSTERY HILL

Of more interest is Mystery Hill, which unashamedly compares itself to the massive stone structures found at England's Stonehenge. Located east of Nausha on Route 111, less than three miles (five kilometers) east of Interstate 93, it is proclaimed to be one of the oldest building sites in North America. Radiocarbon testing pinpoints the origin of these eerie stone buildings, walls, chambers, and carvings at 4,000 years ago; numerous ancient hieroglyphics have been found, but few have been deciphered.

The question of who built them has sparked heated debate. Some argue for North American Indians, and others for ancient seafarers such as the Phoenicians, or the Celts from the Iberian Peninsula. Whoever was responsible for constructing this awesome complex, they were masters of astronomy. Scientists have determined that the rings of carefully arranged stones pinpoint solstices, equinoxes, and other astronomical phenomena. Trails to the astronomical stones, viewing ramp, and self-guided tour map (allow at least one hour) are available at the site headquarters, ((603) 883-8300. Guided tours are offered in summer, and on weekends during spring and fall.

MANCHESTER

Manchester, 16 miles (26 km) south on the Everett Turnpike, is worth the drive if only for the **Currier Gallery of Art** (192 Orange Street; ((603) 669-6144; open daily except Mondays and holidays). It is a fine small art museum with a choice collection of American and European paintings.

The city — one of the state's textile centers — has attracted large numbers of French Canadians, who crossed the border to work in the mills here. A large proportion of the city's population is bilingual.

Nine miles (15 km) further south down the turnpike is the **Budweiser Brewery** in Merrimack, with its famous Clydesdale horses. (Tours can be arranged by calling ((603) 889-6631.)

Where to Stay

With the exception of **Howard Johnson Hotel** (Interstate 293, exit 4, Queen City Avenue; ((603) 668-2600; 104 rooms; moderate), accommodations in this area are expensive: **Holiday Inn Center of New Hampshire** (700 Elm Street; ((603) 625-1000; 251 rooms); **Holiday Inn West** (Amoskeag Bridge; ((800) 465-4329; 120 rooms); and **Koala Inn** (Interstate 293, exit 1; ((603) 668-6110; 125 rooms).

Eating Out

The most elegant restaurant in the city is the **Renaissance** (1087 Elm Street; ((603) 669-8130; moderate to expensive) serving Greek and Italian specialties.

CONCORD

Concord (40 miles or 65 km west of Portsmouth along U.S. 4), in the center of the valley region, is the state capital. It is a rather sleepy town, founded as a trading post in 1659, then later granted a royal charter in 1725, when its name was changed to the Plantation of Penacook. Today, its most notable landmark is the golden dome of the **State Capital** (on Main Street; ((603) 271-2154), with its hall of historic New Hampshire battle flags, and statues of political favorite sons such as Daniel Webster and former president Franklin Pierce.

The **New Hampshire Historical Society** has an interesting collection of Concord Coaches dating from 1827. Many of the wagons that helped to open the American West were manufactured here.

South and west of Concord are the villages of **Hopkinton**, with its placid streets, and **Henniker**, with its double-arched stone bridge — both are pleasant towns with handsome colonial homes.

Where to Stay

The **Ramada Inn** (Interstate 93, exit 14; ((603) 224-9534; 99 rooms) is the most expensive of the hotels in Concord.

Moderately priced are **Concord Coach Motor Inn** (Interstate 93, exit 12S; ((603) 224-2511; 40 rooms) and **New Hampshire Highway Hotel & Convention Center** (Crossroads of Route 14, Interstate 93 and Route 9; ((603) 225-6687; 140 rooms).

Eating Out

Land 'N Sea Restaurant (across from State Capitol; ((603) 224-7420; moderate) is called "Concord's seafood experience."

The **Red Blazer Restaurant & Pub** (72 Manchester Street; ((603) 224-7779; moderate) serves a continental menu in a rustic atmosphere.

For those with a sweet tooth, there is **Thursday's Restaurant** (6 Pleasant Street; ((603) 224-2626; moderate) where the meals are like homemade and the desserts excellent.

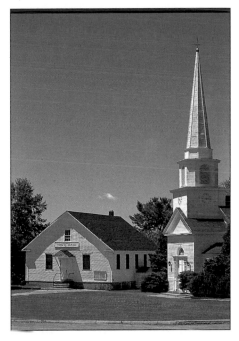

CANTERBURY SHAKER VILLAGE

Located about 17 miles (27 km) north of Concord off Interstate 93, Canterbury Shaker Village (((603) 783-9511; open May to October, Tuesday through Saturday) was once home to 300 farmers and craftspeople who led a simple life governed by their belief in God, a communal lifestyle, and a "Hands to Work and Hearts to God" philosophy.

The Shakers, a religious sect founded in eighteenth-century England, shunned contact with the outside world, and demanded

ABOVE: New Hampshire's Mystery Hill is one of the oldest building sites in North America. OPPOSITE: The Canterbury Shaker Village.

celibacy of their followers. As a result, they have all but disappeared from the modern American scene, but settlements such as Canterbury convey the eloquent simplicity of their world — a world that has become much-admired for ingenious solutions to complicated problems.

The Canterbury Shakers' two surviving members offer walking tours of the 22 historic Shaker buildings which date back to the 1780's. Tours last about 90 minutes. A museum displays Shaker crafts (famed for woodworking, basket making, and sewing), and offers workshops. The Creamery Restaurant offers Shaker food specialties.

THE VALLEY'S HISTORIC HOMES

Daniel Webster's birthplace is off Route 127, just south of Franklin. The small frame house where this noted political leader was born in 1782 is filled with family artifacts. Other historic Merrimack Valley homes open to tourists include **President Franklin Pierce's manse** in Concord, the **Pierce Homestead** in Hillsboro, and poet **Robert Frost's** 1880s white-clapboard **farmhouse** in Derry.

THE MONADNOCK

This small region in southwest New Hampshire shares its border with Massachusetts to the south and the Connecticut River with Vermont to the west. Many of New Hampshire's 54 covered bridges can be found here, and eighteenth-century villages are showcased against the backdrop of majestic Mt Monadnock. When it snows, these towns literally glow with the "Currier & Ives" imaginary romantic quality of colonial America.

KEENE

The region's finest museum is located in Keene, which also has a 172-ft (52-m)-wide, oak tree-lined Main Street, believed to be the widest paved street in the world. **Colony House Museum**, the 1819 home of Keene's first mayor (104 West Street Keene, NH 03431; ((603) 357-0889), contains a fine collection of nineteenth-century Stoddard glass and Staffordshire pewter.

Where to Stay
The Coach & Four Motor Inn (Route 12, Keene; ((603) 357-3705; 22 rooms; moderate) is a well-run small motel, providing good service and clean rooms, as do the larger **Ramada Inn** (401 Winchester Street, Keene; ((603) 357-3038; 130 rooms; moderate to expensive) and **Winding Brook Lodge** (Park Avenue, Keene; ((603) 352-3111; 90 rooms; moderate).

Eating Out
Millside Cafe (Colony Mill Marketplace on West Street, Keene; ((603) 357-4353;

moderate) is set in the warehouse of a restored woolen mill and serves continental cuisine.

For something more American, there is the **Black Lantern** (Route 12, Keene; ((603) 357-1064; moderate) whose speciality is fried chicken.

AROUND KEENE

Other Attractions
Other attractions in the region include **Francestown**, with its old colonial houses dating back to the town's 1772 beginnings; **Gilsum**, which has a stone arch bridge, and offers maps of 56 local abandoned mines; **Jaffrey Center's Old Town Burying Yard**, where novelist

Willa Cather is buried; and **Hancock**, with its Revolutionary War graves in Pine Ridge Cemetery and a splendid covered bridge spanning the Contoocook River. In **Milford**, an 1802 Paul Revere bell in the town hall tower tolls every hour. **Dublin** is a resort colony that once attracted Mark Twain and other literary figures. It is the highest town in New England, at 1,439 ft (439 m) above sea level. **Swanzey** has four covered bridges, and its theater continues to perform the 100-year-old play *Old Homestead* annually. Nearby **Winchester** has two covered bridges. And **Har-**

risville has been called the "most paintable, photogenic mill town in the United States."

On Route 119 in **Rindge**, you will find the **Cathedral of the Pines**; thousands of visitors annually visit this pine forest memorial dedicated to a son lost in World War II.

Hiking and Biking

The area provides some of New Hampshire's best hiking country, with trails through a variety of picturesque landscapes. The best is the **Wapack Trail**, which offers spectacular vistas along a 21-mile (34-km) marked path (look for yellow paint on the trees) following a high ridge from Mt Watatic in Massachusetts to the 2,280-ft (695-m) North Pack Monadnock near Greenfield.

Using Keene as a hub, the Monadnock has several scenic bicycle trails on roads with little or no traffic. One of the best follows the **Ashuelot River**, and crosses many covered bridges. The **Keene Chamber of Commerce** (c/o NEG, 8 Central Square, Keene, NH 03431; ((603) 352-1301) has regional biking trail maps.

A warning to European cyclists: American drivers tend to be far less courteous to bicycles than European drivers, so be cautious, wear a helmet, and by all means avoid well-traveled roads!

Monadnock State Park

Monadnock State Park (off Route 124, west of Jaffrey, then follow the signs) offers several trails leading to the summit of **Mt Monadnock**, one of the most-climbed mountains in the world. It is about a three- to four-hour round trip to the 3,165-ft (965-m) summit, but you will be rewarded by a commanding vista of the surrounding region. Among those who have climbed Monadnock are Emerson and Thoreau. The summit is quite barren, the trees and bush having been burned off in the 1820's by farmers. **New Hampshire Division of Parks and Recreation** (Box 856, Concord, NH 03301; ((603) 271-3254) has maps of the parks.

HANOVER AND LAKE SUNAPEE

Dartmouth Lake Sunapee is a region of lakes, picturesque villages lining the Connecticut River, and gentle mountains and hills.

HANOVER

Dartmouth College, founded in 1769, dominates every phase of life in Hanover, and is the cultural anchor for the entire region. Originally founded by Reverend Eleazar Wheelock "for the instruction of the Youth of Indian tribes," it now attracts well-heeled "youths" of every persuasion from all over the country.

Its handsome campus retains much colonial flavor, with stately Federal and Georgian buildings and an attractive village

ABOVE: Dartmouth College, at Hanover.
OPPOSITE: Robert Frost's mailbox and his home.

green. **Dartmouth Row**, located on the east side of the Green, has several white brick buildings dating from 1784, and the **Baker Memorial Library** displays frescoes by the famed Mexican artist Orozco. Guided campus tours are offered during summer only.

In town, the **Webster Cottage** on North Main Street was the residence of Daniel Webster during his final year at Dartmouth. **Lebanon Street** offers handiwork by the League of New Hampshire craftsmen. Hanover's streets are lined with bookstores, restaurants, and shops.

Where to Stay
The best accommodations in Hanover are at the 200-year-old **Hanover Inn** (Main and Wheelock Streets; ((603) 643-4300; expensive).

Eating Out
There are many good restaurants in the Hanover area. Recommended are **Bentley's** (11 S. Main Street; ((603) 643-4075; moderate to expensive) and **Jesse's** (Route 120; ((603) 643-4111; expensive).

Tourist Information
For maps of the area contact the **Hanover Chamber of Commerce** (Box 930, Hanover, NH 03755; ((603) 643-3115).

AROUND HANOVER

Orford
The hamlet of Orford, about 17 miles (27 km) north of Hanover, has an interesting area called "The Ridge," with a half-dozen stately homes dating from the 1770's to the 1830's.

Cornish
South of Hanover is the **Saint-Gaudens National Historic Site**, ((603) 675-2175, located on Route 12A north of the Cornish-Windsor covered bridge. Here are the summer home, gardens, and studio of American classical sculptor Augustus Saint-Gaudens, and many examples of his work.

The town of **Cornish** was home to the famed **Cornish Colony** for artists and writers; set up in 1885, it "officially" lasted for 50 years. Reclusive J.D. Salinger, author of *The Catcher in the Rye*, still lives in this town. Cornish also has the longest remaining

covered bridge in the United States. Built in 1866, it stretches 466 ft (142 m) over the Connecticut River to Vermont.

Still farther south is the **Fort at No. Four**; ((603) 826-7751, a reconstruction of an original 1746 fortified settlement which defended the region during the French and Indian Wars. Its buildings appear much as they did in the eighteenth century. Colonial craft demonstrations (candle making, weaving, etc.), and reenactments of a soldier's life in the colonial militia are part of the "living history" show.

Mt Sunapee State Park, outside **Newbury** (on Route 103), offers gondola rides up to the mountain's 2,700-ft (823-m) summit, with panoramic views of Lake Sunapee, known for its fine salmon and lake trout fishing, the Green Mountains in the distance to the west, and the White Mountains to the northeast.

THE LAKES REGION

With its more than 600 lakes and ponds, east-central New Hampshire is justifiably termed The Lakes Region. With their romantic Indian names, deep fish-filled waters, and good harbors, the lakes invite a leisurely, unhurried pace of life. **Lakes Region Association** (Box 300, Wolfeboro, NH 03894; ((603) 569-1117) has brochures about recreation in the area.

OPPOSITE and ABOVE: New Hampshire's larger lakes are well-used by pleasure boaters and fishermen in summer.

and **Wolfeboro Inn** (44 N Main Street, Wolfeboro; ((603) 569-3016; 43 rooms; moderate)

In Laconia, the largest town in the area, there are several good establishments: **The Anchorage on Lake Winnisquam** (RFD#1, Laconia; ((603) 524-3248; 32 rooms; moderate); **Christmas Island Resort** (Route 3, Laconia; ((603) 366-4378; 27 rooms; moderate to expensive); **The Margate at Winnipesaukee** (Route 3, Laconia, ((800) 258-0304; 146 rooms; expensive);and **Shalimar**

Resort Motel and Spa (Route 3, Laconia; ((800) 742-5427; expensive).

WOLFEBORO

Wolfeboro, on Route 28 between Lakes Winnipesaukee and Wentworth, is the heart of the lake region, although Laconia, on Route 3 to the southwest of Lake Winnipesaukee, is the region's largest town.

Wolfeboro claims to be the country's oldest summer resort. Governor John Wentworth built a summer mansion here on **Lake Wentworth** in 1771. The **Wolfeboro Railroad** offers 24-mile (39-km) two-hour round-trip tours, with antique steam engines, along Lake Winnipesaukee's southeastern shore. These trips are especially rewarding during the fall foliage season.

WHERE TO STAY IN THE LAKES REGION

The Pick Point Lodge (on Lake Winnipesaukee, Route 109 Wolfeboro; ((603) 569-1338; 12 rooms; expensive) has individual cottages.

Winnipesaukee (Route 11D, Wolfeboro; ((603) 875-5005; 24 rooms; moderate); **Lakeview Inn & Motor Lodge** (Route 109, Wolfeboro; ((603) 569-1335; 17 rooms; moderate);

EATING OUT IN THE LAKES REGION

Wolfeboro Inn (Route 109; ((603) 569-3016; expensive) serves excellent New England dinners, as does **Blackstone's, At the Margate** (76 Lake Street, Laconia; ((603) 524-7060; moderate to expensive) in nearby Laconia. **Hickory Stick Farm** (Southeast of Laconia; ((603) 524-3333; moderate) is a three-star restaurant renowned for its roast duckling.

LAKE WINNIPESAUKEE

Lake Winnipesaukee covers 72 sq miles (186 sq km), with 283 miles (456 km) of shoreline and coves, 274 habitable islands,

Faces of New Hampshire.

and eight towns on its shores. Winnipesaukee is an Indian word meaning "smile of the great spirit."

Perhaps the most active lakeside town is tacky, overbuilt **Weirs Beach**, on the western shore, a taste of Atlantic City in New Hampshire. In addition to visual pollution, it also offers the jaded traveler an assortment of band concerts, fireworks, boat races, seaplane rides, water skiing shows, arcades, miniature golf links, slot cars, a surfcoaster water park, and a 325-ft (99-m) water slide where revelers plummet down flumes to the pool below.

This is, however, great boating country, whether you own, charter, rent, or take public cruises. The largest boat on the lake is the 230-ft (70-m) *Mt Washington*, which offers narrated 50-mile (81-km) **cruises** departing

from **Weirs Beach** and ending at nearby Wolfeboro. There are also breakfast, lunch, dinner, and moonlight cruises, and several so-called theme trips — Fabulous 50's, Hawaiian Luau, Buccaneers Ball and Irish Fling. For information and booking, call ((603) 366-5531.

Another Weirs Beach option is a cruise on the *SS Mail Boat*, which makes two-hour mail trips to islands on the western side of the lake. Excellent lake trout and salmon

fishing can also be found here, but you will need a boat to escape the crowded and noisy docks.

Another way to get away from the crush of summer visitors is by biking around Lake Winnipesaukee along a series of back roads and uncrowded highways.

Summer Music

Professional musicians have gathered at Center Harbor on the northern end of Lake Winnipesaukee for six weeks each summer since 1952 to perform orchestral concerts, chamber music, and original commissioned pieces at the **New Hampshire Music Festival** (c/o NEG, P.O. Box 147, Center Harbor, NH 03226; ((603) 253-4331).

SQUAM LAKE

Squam Lake (just northwest of Winnipesaukee) — the filming location for the Henry / Jane Fonda melodrama *On Golden Pond* — is the second largest lake in the state. The Manor in **Holderness** (northeast shore of Squam Lake; ((603) 968-3348) offers two-hour cruises that take you to "*On Golden Pond*" film locations and provide commentary on the lake's loon population. Hiking trails in the area lead to the summit of the Squam Mountain.

OTHER LAKE REGION ATTRACTIONS

Moultonborough

Just north of Center Harbor on Route 25 is Moultonborough, known for the **Castle in the Clouds**, a 6,000-acre (2,430-hectare) mountaintop country estate built in 1910 by eccentric millionaire Thomas Gustav Plant at a cost of $7 million. It provides a 75-mile (121-km) panorama of Lake Winnipesaukee.

Plymouth

North of Laconia just off Interstate 93 in Plymouth are the **Polar Caves**, glacial caverns that are said to have been a last refuge for the Pemigewasset Indians when they were attacked by settlers in colonial times.

WHITE MOUNTAINS

No visitor to New Hampshire should miss its breathtaking White Mountains. Long a wild, forbidding region almost inaccessible from the rest of the state, these grand mountains are now one of New England's prime natural vacation areas, with year-round attractions.

WHITE MOUNTAIN NATIONAL FOREST

The White Mountain National Forest, which covers much of the White Mountain region, extends over 760,000 acres (307,700 hectares). Access is facilitated by more than 100 miles (160 km) of roads, which cut across whitewater rivers (totaling 650 miles or 1,048 km of fishing streams), dense forests with mountain lakes, ponds, and deep valleys. It is also a hiker's paradise, with nearly 1,200 miles (1,935 km) of foot trails.

And the standard United States Forest Service policy of clearcutting huge patches out of the forest to prevent their being designated as Wilderness Areas seems less active here, with the logging generally in smaller areas, and even European-style selective cutting being practiced.

Here the **Appalachian Trail** snakes across some of its most spectacular scenery, including several of the tallest peaks in the

East. The Appalachian Mountain Club (Pinkham Notch, Gorham, NH 03581; ((603) 466-2727) provides information about hikes and lodging along the Trail; the **Mt Washington Valley Chamber of Commerce** (Box 385S, North Conway, NH 03860; ((603) 356-3171) has more general information about the area.

MT WASHINGTON

Mt Washington, the tallest peak in the White Mountain chain, is 6,288 ft (1,916 m) high; seven other peaks rise to more than a mile (1,609 m) high; and 22 others reach more than 4,000 ft (1,219 m). But despite such imposing statistics, the White Mountains are not that difficult for the traveler to negotiate. Most highways are well-maintained, including the 90-minute round-trip road leading to the summit of Mt Washington (but eight miles, or 13 km, of braking can be tough on some cars). If you have any doubts, leave your car at the foot of the mountain and take a shuttle (chauffeured van service) to the top.

While several hiking trails accommodate even the casual stroller, some leading to the Mt Washington summit may require more than a few hours of moderate to tough hiking. The climb to the summit is not a casual climb. Although the terrain is neither too rough nor too steep, the mountain peak is susceptible to sudden weather changes that bring in sudden blizzard conditions that have resulted in the death of unprepared hikers. Rewards include spectacular views of waterfalls, deep gorges, rushing streams, and peaceful valleys.

However, mountain weather can be treacherous. Even in the middle of summer, violent blizzards and freezing temperatures do occur; winds of 231 mph (372 kph), the highest ever measured in the world, have been recorded at the summit. Unless you are an experienced, well-supplied hiker, it is advisable to keep to the short, heavily-used trails. The White Mountain National Forest, Forest Supervisor's OfficeForest Supervisor's Office (719 Main Street, P.O. Box 638, Laconia, NH 03247; ((603) 524-6450) will gladly advise hikers on trail conditions and assist in selecting the best routes for day outings or longer treks.

Fall in the White Mountains.

Mount Washington Cog Railway

Another option for a visit to the White Mountains is a ride on the Mt Washington Cog Railway. (((603) 846-5404, toll-free (800) 922-8825m, fare $27). It operates April to mid-October and leaves from the Base Station, one mile (1.6 km) north of Crawford Notch on U.S. 302. Since the mid-nineteenth century, the train has hauled tourists to the summit of the White Mountains' tallest peak — the highest north of the Carolinas and east of the Rockies.

Hailed in 1869 as a marvel of "modern" technology, this was the world's first moun-

tain climbing cog railway. The "cog" is a toothed or notched wheel that latches on to a center track, pulling and lowering the train up and down the mountain.

Today the train, powered by steam locomotives, climbs a three-mile (five-kilometer) route to the summit on the second steepest railway track in the world. (Only a track in the Swiss Alps beats it.) One trestle, "Jacob's Ladder," registers an incredible 37 percent grade. Each locomotive consumes a ton of coal and 1,000 gallons (3,785 liters) of water while making the one-hour climb to the top.

On clear days the view from the summit's observation center spans four states. Often, however, the mountain is shrouded in gray clouds and thick mist, and the train literally climbs through the fog.

CRAWFORD NOTCH

Crawford Notch, a narrow, rugged mountain pass off U.S. 302 (north of Bartlett), offers some incomparable views of the Presidential Range, including the 4,052-ft (1,235-m) Jackson Mountain. The Saco River also runs through the Notch, creating some of the tallest and most spectacular waterfalls and cascades in New Hampshire. **Arethusa Falls**, the state's highest, a is 50-minute walk from the parking area; **Silver Cascade**, a 1,000-ft (305-m) cataract, is visible from the highway.

A plaque marks the site of **Willey House**, an historic stopover for wagon teams traveling between northern New Hampshire and the seacoast. The Willey family was killed here in 1826 when they fled their home during a rockslide; ironically, the home was untouched.

Crawford Notch is also the site of the White Mountains, first attempt at a tourist industry. It is named for Abel and Ethan Crawford, who in 1819 blazed the first footpath to the summit of Mt Washington, then advertised their services as tour guides and arranged for visitor lodging.

NORTH CONWAY

There are few interstate or major highways in New Hampshire, so travelers wishing to explore the heart of the White Mountains region must abandon the four-lane roads and continue their journey on country back roads. This is actually more a bonus than an inconvenience, since "Sunday driving" is one of the most enjoyable ways to explore the state's natural wonders.

North Conway is the heart of the Mt Washington Valley region, with several touring options available. Go north from Manchester on I 93, then east on one of several roads until you reach Route 16, and turn north to North Conway.

Perhaps the easiest way to get a quick overview of the region is by boarding the **Conway Scenic Railroad** (open May to October; (((603) 356-5251) at the Main Street depot, a canary yellow building built in the 1870s. Steam locomotives puffing billows of black smoke pull restored turn-of-the-century coach cars through the **Saco River Valley** on one-hour train rides. The 11-mile (18-km) round trip also offers first-class service on an 1898 Pullman observation car.

Another option is to take a short drive to **Mt Cranmore** and board the *skimobile*

(Routes 16 and 302; ((603) 356-5543). In operation for more than 50 years, it is the oldest operating ski lift in the country. Its colorful cars glide smoothly up a trestle to the summit of Mt Cranmore, which also provides fine winter skiing.

Those with more time might consider a guided whitewater or a calmer canoe tour on the **Saco River**, which winds through the splendid wilderness scenery of Mt Washington Valley. The Saco Bound Northern Waters, two miles (three kilometers) east of Conway Center on U.S. 302, (P.O. Box 113,

Yet another way to experience the region is from the air. Scenic flights aboard a jet helicopter operate out of North Conway's **White Mountain Heliport** (P.O. Box 679, North Conway, NH 03860; ((603) 356-2930 or 356-2946).

Autumn Foliage

In addition to its other attractions, the region offers a dramatic display of fall foliage. While the weather can play havoc with the change of seasons, the most colorful time is traditionally the first two weeks in October. More than a half-million people jam New Hampshire's

Conway Center, NH 03813; ((603) 447-2177) provides guide services.

Several stables in the region offer guided trail rides through the mountains. For example, **The Riding Place** in Bretton Woods, ((603) 278-1836, tours the 75 miles (121 km) of scenic bridle paths belonging to the venerable Mount Washington Hotel. And the **Nestlenook Inn and Equestrian Center** in Jackson, ((603) 383-9443, offers all-day trail rides over Black Mountain and through local farmlands.

If mountain biking from country inn to country inn is more your style, consider one of the special weekend tours put together by **New Hampshire Bicycle Touring** (10 Maple Street, Henniker, NH 03242; ((603) 428-3147).

roads each year to have a glimpse of nature's annual color extravaganza, so it is advisable to take the back roads to avoid the crowds.

But before you leave North Conway itself, make certain to catch the view of Mt Washington from the middle of Main Street; it has been called "one of the great views in the East."

Where to Stay

EXPENSIVE

Attitash Mountain Village & Conference Center (Route 302 at Attitash Mountain; toll-free (800) 862-1600; 225 rooms) origi-

ABOVE: Indian summer in New Hampshire. OPPOSITE: An engineer for the Mount Washington Cog Railroad.

nally built for the ski season now stays open year-round. Of a similar style is **Red Jacket Mountain View Motor Inn** (Route 16; ((603) 356-5411, toll-free (800) 752-2538; 152 rooms). Ask about package deals at both of these resorts.

Peacock Inn (Kearsarge Road; ((603) 356-9041; 18 rooms) and **Stonehurst Manor** (Route 16; ((603) 356-3271; 24 rooms) are traditional New England country inns. A mile and a half (2 km) from the center of town is **Cranmore Mountain Lodge** (Kearsarge Road; ((603) 356-2044; 17 rooms). The

10 rooms in the old lodge have shared baths and are less expensive. The remaining seven are in the recently renovated loft of the barn.

MODERATE

Eastern Slope Inn Resort & Conference Center (Routes 16 and 302; ((603) 356-632, toll-free (800) 258-47091; 125 rooms) is next door to the summer theater and has clay tennis courts. Children stay free here.

The Riverside (Route 16A; ((603) 356-9060) is a small country inn with only seven rooms (four have shared baths). Rates include breakfast.

In nearby Gorham is the **Tourist Village Motel** (130 Main Street; ((603) 466-3312; 68 rooms).

INEXPENSIVE

With only seven rooms, it is more like staying at home than a hotel at the **Old Red Inn** (Main Street; ((603) 356-2642).

Eating Out

The inns all have their own dining rooms which also serve non-residents. **Stonehurst Manor** is noted for its Beef Wellington, but there are other fine restaurants in the area.

As its name would indicate, the **Scottish Lion** (Route 16; ((603) 356-6381; moderate) serves Scottish-American cuisine. **Welsh's Restaurant** (88 Main Street, Gorham; ((603) 466-2500; inexpensive to moderate) is New Hampshire's oldest family-owned restaurant.

FRANCONIA NOTCH STATE PARK

Franconia Notch State Park is another New England tourist shrine, but well worth a visit nonetheless. The Notch is a deep valley cut between the towering peaks of the Franconia and Kinsman mountain ranges, with the granite-walled, 4,200-ft (1,280-m)-high **Cannon Mountain** on the east, and the twin 5,000-ft (1,524-m) peaks of **Mounts Lafayette and Lincoln** to the west. It also contains some of the region's most familiar landmarks.

Flume Gorge

The spectacular Flume Gorge extends for 800 ft (244 m) at the base of **Mt Liberty**, down which cascades the **Pemigewasset River**, flanked by 90-ft (27-m) granite walls. Close up views (accessible by stairs and walkways) yield glimpses of rare mountain flowers and luxuriant mosses that cling to the moist walls. Nearly a half-million travelers visit the gorge annually.

Great Stone Face

Old Man of the Mountain (also known as the Great Stone Face) is a natural granite profile of a man's finely detailed face jutting from a sheer cliff 1,200 ft (366 m) above **Profile Lake**. Carved by nature over millions of years, it is formed by five separate ledges of granite, and measures 40 ft (12 m) from jutting brow to bearded chin.

Other Park Features

Panoramic views of the mountains and distant valleys are provided by the **Aerial Tramway**, which carries tram cars more than a mile (1.6 km) at an average height of 2,022 ft (616 m) to the summit of Cannon Mountain at 4,180 ft or 1,263 m.

South of the Notch are three other natural phenomena. **The Basin** has a deep glacial pothole 20 ft (six meters) in diameter at the foot of a waterfall. **Indian Head** is a 98-ft (30-m)-high profile carved by the elements in granite; its scowling visage is likened to

that of an Abenaki chief. **Lost River** and the **glacial caves**, both west of Lincoln, owe their existence to the passage of glaciers which gouged out depressions and then receded north, leaving unique boulder-strewn ravines and tunnel-like caves.

American Indian Crafts

Today, in a kind of legacy from New Hampshire's native Algonquin Indians, who crafted birch bark canoes, split ash baskets, and snowshoes, the White Mountain region offers works by some of the state's finest craftspeople. At the **Franconia League of New Hampshire Craftsmen** (on Access Road, off U.S. 3; ((603) 823-9521) one can find fine displays of their handiwork.

Where to Stay

EXPENSIVE

At the top of the line in Franconia is the **Franconia Inn** (Easton Road; ((603) 823-5542; 32 rooms) and **Sugar Hill Inn** (Route 117; ((603) 823-5621; 16 rooms) where rates drop to moderate in the off-season. Guest are required to take dinner at the inn.

MODERATE

In this category the traveler can find the following: **Gale River Motel** (Route 18; toll-free (800) 255-7989; 13 rooms); **Ledgeland**

(Route 117; ((603) 823-5341; 21 rooms), **Lovett's by Lafayette Brook** (Routes 18 and 141; ((603) 823-7761, toll-free (800) 346-3806; 32 rooms); **Stonybrook Motor Lodge** (Route 18N; ((603) 823-8192; 24 rooms); and **Sunset Hill House** (Route 117; ((603) 823-5522; 35 rooms).

INEXPENSIVE

Pinestead Farm Lodge (Route 116; ((603) 823-8121; nine rooms) is the best buy in the area and is often fully booked for the summer.

OPPOSITE: Steam engine on display at Clark Trading Post in Franconia. The Old Man of the Mountains ABOVE LEFT and Flume Gorge RIGHT in the White Mountains.

Eating Out

For a river view and good seafood meals, the **Rivagale Inn** (Main Street; ((603) 823-7044; moderate) is recommended.

The **Horse and Hound Inn** (off Route 18; ((603) 823-5501; expensive) has an excellent wine list to complement its continental cuisine.

The **Franconia Inn** (Route 116; ((603) 823-5542; expensive) serves local veal and excellent desserts, and **Lovett's Inn** (Routes 18 and 141; ((603) 823-7761; expensive) also has an excellent dining room.

SKI THE WHITE MOUNTAINS

The White Mountains provide the best skiing, both alpine and nordic, in the state. Ten full-service "Ski the White Mountains" resorts offer a panorama of slopes and cross-country ski trails against a backdrop of snowcapped peaks and serene New England scenery. **Attitash**, in Bartlett, offers some of the most consistently fine skiing in the state and is one of six nationwide United States Ski Team training centers. In **Bretton Woods** (in the shadow of Mount Washington), snow squalls known as "Bretton Woods flurries" blanket a landscape that offers some of the best views in the east. **Waterville Valley**, after a new $30 million expansion, even has its own snowboarding park — the newest rage in American winter sports. Then there's **Tuckerman Ravine**, about 12 miles (19 km) north of Jackson, a huge, precipitous, steep-walled bowl that is regarded as the only authentic Swiss-style alpine ski area in the east.

Tourist Information

Package plans include lift tickets and lodging, with several midweek specials. For more ski information, contact the **Mount Washington Valley Chamber of Commerce** (Main Street, P.O. Box 385, North Conway, NH 03860; ((603) 356-3171).

Where to Stay

In a class by itself is **Mount Washington Hotel** (Route 302, Bretton Woods; ((603) 278-1000; 185 rooms; luxury). In 1944 the Bretton Woods conference that established an international monetary system for the post-war era was held here. The same company operates the Victorian **Bretton Arms** (Route 302, Bretton Woods; ((800) 258-0330; 34 rooms; expensive) and **The Lodge at Bretton Woods** (Route 302, Bretton Woods; ((800) 258-0330; 50 rooms; moderate), and guests can use Mount Washington Hotel facilities.

Waterville Valley is a four-season vacation resort with inns, luxurious condominiums, spa and fitness programs, free lodging for kids 12 years and under, and other facilities. The Lodging Bureau (Box LD, Water-

ville Valley, NH 03215, ((603) 236-8371) has many listings and can help make reservations for short or long visits.

In addition to the resorts there are the following:

EXPENSIVE

The Valley Inn and Tavern (Tecumseh Road, Waterville Valley; ((603) 236-8336; 50 rooms); **Christmas Farm Inn** (Route 16B, Jackson; ((603) 383-4313; 38 rooms); and **Wentworth Resort Hotel** (Route 16A, Jackson; ((603) 383-9700; 65 rooms).

The Mount Washington Hotel OPPOSITE, one of New Hampshire's most stylish hotels. ABOVE: The quietly simple style of North Woodstock.

MODERATE

Covered Bridge Motel (Route 16, Jackson; ((603) 383-9151; 28 rooms); **Dana Place Inn** (Route 16, Jackson; ((603) 383-6822; 14 rooms); **Eagle Mountain House**, a historic 1897 resort, Carter Notch Road, Jackson; ((603) 383-9111, toll-free (800) 527-5022; 94 rooms; **The Inn at Thorn Hill** (Thorn Hill Road; ((603) 383-4242; 20 rooms); **Nestlenook Inn** (Dinsmore Road, Jackson; ((603) 383-9443); and **Wildcat Inn & Tavern Main Street, Jackson**; ((603) 383-4245; 18 rooms).

Eating Out

The **Mount Washington Hotel** has the best dining room (expensive) in the area, serving traditional American cuisine.

Darby's in the Lodge at Bretton Woods is fine dining at a moderate to expensive price.

Fabyan's Station (Route 302 Bretton Woods; ((603) 846-2222; moderate) is a restored train depot that serves seafood and steaks.

For excellent prime rib, there is **O'Keefe's Restaurant and Speakeasy Lounge** (Waterville Valley, Interstate 93, exit 28, then to Route 49; ((603) 236-8331; moderate).

THE FAR NORTH

Pittsburg, only six miles (10 km) from the Canadian border, is the heart of New Hampshire's northernmost wilderness. The township comprises 300,000 acres (121,500 hectares) of timberlands, mountains, streams, and the Connecticut Lakes (headwaters of the Connecticut River), making it easily the largest township in the United States, as well as one of the most isolated.

This is largely uninhabited country. The roads through this remote area border sections of the **Androscoggin River**, one of the most scenic waterways in the state. You may even catch glimpses of moose grazing in the meadows and swamplands. Waterfalls sparkle down granite cliffs, the stars are bright in the unpolluted night, and the hunting and fishing are among the best in the state.

Where to Stay

Near Pittsburg on U.S. 3 toward the Canadian border is **The Glen** (First Connecticut Lake; ((603) 538-6500; 18 rooms; moderate to expensive), a fine New Hampshire country inn.

In New Hampshire, fly-fishing purists ABOVE enjoy luxurious accomodations as well as the state's rivers and streams. OPPOSITE: A meeting house in the town of Sugar Hill.

Vermont

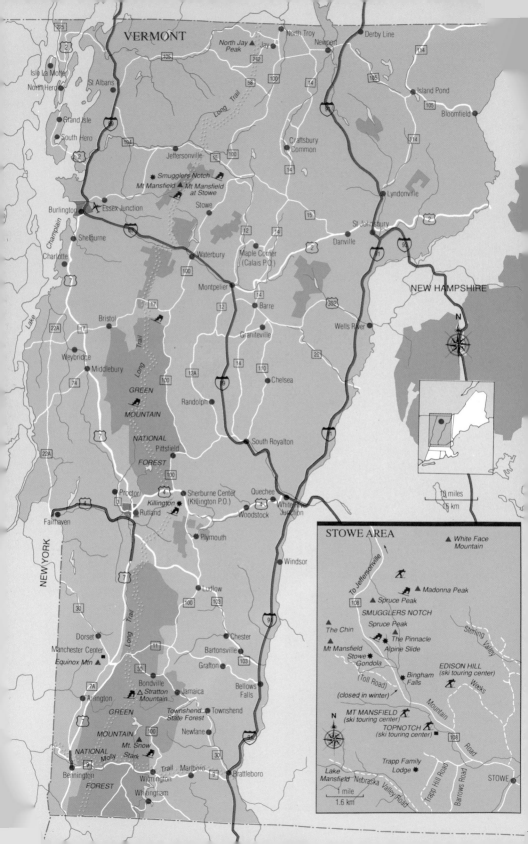

VERMONT

225

2

North Jay
Peak ▲ Jay ▲   North Troy   Newport   Derby Line

Isle La Motte
North Hero

114

St Albans

105   242

100   58

14

105   Island Pond

Grand Isle
South Hero

Long Trail

2

89

104

Jeffersonville   15   100

Craftsbury
Common

14

Lyndonville

114

Bloomfield

✽ Smugglers Notch ⛷
Mt Mansfield ▲ ▲ Mt Mansfield
at Stowe
Stowe

12

14   15

St Johnsbury

2

Danville

91   93

NEW HAMPSHIRE

Burlington   Essex Junction

89

Shelburne

Waterbury

100

Maple Corner
(Calais P.O.)

2

302

Wells River

N

Charlotte

Champlain

17

Montpelier

14

Barre

Graniteville

25

Bristol

22A   7

Lake

Weybridge

Long Trail

Middlebury

74

GREEN

MOUNTAIN

7

NATIONAL

12   12A

110

89

Randolph

Chelsea

South Royalton

91

FOREST   Pittsfield

100

Proctor   4

Sherburne Center
(Killington P.O.)

Quechee

White River
Junction

10 miles
16 km

22A

3

⛷ Killington
Rutland

4   Woodstock   4

Plymouth

Windsor

STOWE AREA

▲ White Face
Mountain

7

Fairhaven

NEW YORK

Ludlow

100   103

89

To Jeffersonville

108

⛷ ✽ Madonna Peak

▲ Spruce Peak

30

Dorset

Manchester Center

Equinox Mtn ▲

2A

11

Chester

Bartonsville

103

Grafton

103

Bellows
Falls

The Chin ▲

▲ Mt Mansfield
Stowe
Gondola ✽

SMUGGLERS NOTCH
Spruce Peak ▲

⛷ ✽ The Pinnacle
Alpine Slide

Sterling Valley

EDISON HILL
(ski touring center) ⛷

30

Bondville

Stratton
Mountain ▲

Jamaica

Townshend
State Forest   Townshend

✽ Bingham
Falls

Mountain Road

Weeks

Arlington

GREEN

100

Newfane

MOUNTAIN

Mt. Snow ▲

Molly Stark ⛷

Trail   Marlboro

9

Brattleboro

N

MT MANSFIELD
(ski touring center) ⛷

TOPNOTCH ✽
(ski touring center) ⛷

108

Barrows Road

STOWE

NATIONAL

Bennington

FOREST

Wilmington

Whitingham

Lake
Mansfield   Nebraska Valley Road

✽ Trapp Family
Lodge

1 mile
1.6 km

Trapp Hill Road

VERMONT is a rural state of farms, gentle hills, and mountains with picturesque towns that look as if they were illustrations for storybooks. Its pastoral landscapes are relatively free of sizable cities or centers of industry; Burlington, Vermont's largest community, has a population of less than 40,000.

White steeples dominate the colonial villages, and forests and pastures rise above country roads. More than 200 covered bridges add a charm to the countryside as do the maple groves which give rise to the state's claim to be the maple syrup capitol of the world.

Vermont's Green Mountains are the ski center of New England, offering a variety of downhill and cross-country trails at places like the modern complex at Killington or the traditional Stowe. Hikers, as well, can follow the 260-mile (419-km) Long Trail that tops the Green Mountain ridge all the way from Massachusetts to Canada and intersects with the Appalachian Trail near Killington.

Vermont's size only 151 miles (243 km) long and 40 to 90 miles (64 to 145 km) wide makes it a perfect place to enjoy classic New England at your own pace.

The state is bicycle-rider's dream with long stretches of back roads dotted with historic inns and lodges. Vermont's fall color extravaganza is a major attraction.

Abraham Lincoln and his family, in the mid-nineteenth century, discovered the state's special qualities. They often vacationed in the Green Mountain resort town of Manchester, in southern Vermont. (In fact Lincoln had reservations at Manchester's historic Equinox Hotel when he was assassinated in 1865.) Noted British historian Lord Bryce was also smitten with Vermont's charm when he called it the "Switzerland of North America."

Vermonters are keen to keep their state's unspoiled, serene image. The state legislature has enacted some of the toughest land use, zoning, and environmental protection laws in the nation. Even billboards are prohibited throughout the state.

TOURIST INFORMATION

Both the **Vermont Travel Division** (134 State Street, Montpelier, VT 05601; ℂ (802)

828-3236) and the **Vermont Chamber of Commerce** (P.O. Box 37, Montpelier, VT 05602; ℂ (802) 223-3443) have free maps and travel information.

BACKGROUND

In 1609 French explorer Samuel de Champlain described what he saw from the lake that now bears his name as *les verts monts* (the green mountains). However, when the French pulled ashore, his Algonquin Indian

guides attacked their enemy, the Iroquois, and Champlain was forced to lend aid with his armed troops. Verts monts became a bloody battleground between the French, the Indians, and the colonial-minded British for the next 150 years. Only after the English defeated France at Quebec in 1759 did large numbers of colonists begin to settle in the territory.

THE GREEN MOUNTAIN BOYS

Colonial Vermont was long embroiled in a territorial dispute with neighboring New York over land beyond Vermont's present borders. Ethan Allen's Green Mountain Boys, a self-styled militia, was formed to defend Vermont's position.

The same band of intrepid fighters helped the New World colonists to rid themselves of British rule and proclaim their independence. Vermont then declared itself

Vermont farm near Peacham.

an "independent nation" in 1777 because of continuing land disputes with New York.

Vermont remained independent for 14 years, conducting affairs with the United States as with a "foreign power." Finally, in 1791, it became the 14th state.

During the Civil War, Vermont lost more men proportionately than any other state in the Union. When, during the nineteenth century, many of its settlers joined the great westward migration, Vermont seemed destined to remain a small, sparsely populated farm state, albeit a beautiful one.

SOUTHEASTERN VERMONT

BELLOWS FALLS

Bellows Falls, in southeastern Vermont on the banks of the Connecticut River, is a good place to start a visit to Vermont. The first canal in America was built here in 1802; the **Old Stone Gristmill** (paper mill) museum preserves the town's logging legacy; centuries-old "stone face" petroglyphs attributed to Pennacook Indians are carved into rocks about 50 ft (15 m) downstream from the Vilas Bridge on the Vermont side of the river; and three covered bridges can be found nearby.

The Green Mountain Flyer

The Green Mountain Flyer, ((802) 463-3069, is a diesel-engine train with authentic 1930s passenger cars that rambles 13 miles (21 km) from Bellows Falls through two scenic river valleys before stopping in **Chester**; it often continues for another 14 miles (23 km) to **Ludlow**. The train crosses the old canal, follows the Connecticut River for a distance, then twists inland up the Williams River Valley; it also traverses the deep Brockway River Gorge, and passes both the **Warrel** and **Bartonsville** covered bridges, slowing down here and there for the photographers on board.

VICTORIAN CHESTER

Fans of Victoriana might make a quick stop at Chester to explore two historic districts Main Street's stately homes along its village

green and North Street's "Stone Village" which has more than 25 pre-Civil War houses faced with gneiss ledgestone.

COLONIAL GRAFTON

Grafton, founded in pre-Revolutionary times under George III, has been called the perfect New England village. Historic buildings, high-steepled churches, old inns, specialty shops (most circa 1805), and a little creek meandering through town make it interesting for photographers and browsers alike. Grafton's historic **Old Tavern** has operated since 1801, hosting people like Daniel Webster, Rudyard Kipling, Woodrow Wilson, and Teddy Roosevelt.

NEWFANE — THE TOWN THAT MOVED

Newfane, south of Bellows Falls on Route 30, is widely recognized for its architecture. The 1825 **Windham County Courthouse**, on the elm-shaded village green, is among the finest Early Republic buildings in the East. In 1825, the entire village moved two miles (3.2 km) south to its present location. Buildings were dismantled timber by timber and moved on ox-drawn sleighs to their new locations.

Where to Stay and Eating Out

Two historic inns, the **Four Columns Inn** (230 West Street, on the Village Green; ((802) 365-7713; 13 rooms; moderate to expensive) and the **Old Newfane Inn** (Village Green; ((802) 365-4427; 10 rooms; moderate to expensive), are located on the Green. The Four Columns Inn serves Vermont lamb and veal in its restaurant, and the Old Newfane Inn has Louisiana frogs' legs on its menu.

The Inn at South Newfane (Dover Road, South Newfane; ((802) 348-7191; moderate to expensive) features traditional New England specialities.

TOWNSHEND

About five miles (eight kilometers) north on Route 30 is **Townshend**, one of the most

OPPOSITE TOP: The spacious Common at Townshend. BOTTOM: A colonial-style porch at the Old Tavern

photographed villages in Vermont. Especially handsome is the town green surrounded by historic buildings.

Townshend's **Scott Covered Bridge**, just off Route 30, is the longest single-span covered bridge in Vermont; built in 1870, it stretches 165 ft (50 m) over the West River. At **Townshend State Forest**, a very steep 2.7-mile (4.5-km) hiking trail leads to the 1,580-ft (482-m) summit of Bald Mountain. A 10-minute drive north brings you to **Jamaica State Park**, noted for whitewater rafting on the West River.

1777, one of the campaign's most important clashes. Prior to the battle, Stark told his men, "There stand the redcoats, and they are ours, or this night Molly Stark sleeps a widow".

BRATTLEBORO

One can start the Molly Stark Trail from Brattleboro, in the southeast corner of the state on the Connecticut River. Vermont's first settlement was just south of here at Fort Dummer in 1724. (The Vernon Dam and hydroelectric plant, built in 1907, flooded

ACROSS SOUTHERN VERMONT

THE MOLLY STARK TRAIL

The Molly Stark Trail (Route 9) is the main thoroughfare across southern Vermont, stretching for 39 miles (63 km) from Brattleboro to Bennington. It is a two-lane road that is often crowded even during the off-season, but it is an interesting drive that passes through several picturesque villages and reveals some of the most dramatic fall colors in the state.

Molly Stark's husband, Revolutionary War hero General John Stark, led troops against the British at the Battle of Bennington in

the site.) Brattleboro is perhaps best known as the one-time residence of Rudyard Kipling, who married a town girl and lived here (actually in Dummerston) during the 1890's. In his unusual boat-shaped mansion, he wrote the *Jungle Books* and *Captain Courageous*.

The **Brattleboro Museum and Art Center** (the old Union Railroad Station at Canal and Bridge Streets) has a fine collection of Estey organs, a nineteenth-century mainstay in those American homes that could afford one.

South of Brattleboro on the New Hampshire border is Vernon's nuclear power plant, which is open for tours.

The **Creamery Bridge**, west of Brattleboro on Route 9, is a handsome covered bridge built in 1879; from here the Molly

Stark Trail leads into high Green Mountain country.

Clinging to the top of 2,347-ft (715-m) Hogback Mountain is the **Skyline**, a well-known restaurant overlooking **Marlboro** and offering distant views of mountain ranges in Massachusetts and New Hampshire.

The town's noted music festival, directed by Rudolph Serkin, is held in July.

Where to Stay and Eating Out

For accommodations, there is the **Quality Inn** (Putney Road, U.S. 5; ☎ (802) 254-8701; 100 rooms; moderate to expensive), and **Dalem's Chalet** (South Street; ☎ (802) 254-4323; moderate to expensive) serves excellent Swiss-German meals.

WILMINGTON AND WHITTINGHAM

Wilmington is the gateway to southern Vermont's ski areas, including Haystack, Hogback, Dutch Hill, Prospect Mountain, Corinthia, and Mt Snow. Detour south on Route 100 to drive through some remarkable New England scenery, especially during the fall; the tiny hamlet of Whittingham has a monument marking the birthplace of Mormon religious leader Brigham Young.

BENNINGTON

Back on the Molly Stark Trail, continue west through the high mountain scenery until you reach Bennington, historic headquarters of Ethan Allen's Green Mountain Boys.

The **Bennington Museum** has a collection of Revolutionary War artifacts and "Grandma Moses" primitives. Anna Mary Robertson Grandma Moses started painting simple country scenes at 70 years of age and achieved instant fame; she continued working until her death at 101.

The **Old First Church**, built in 1805 with a three-tiered steeple, is an oft-photographed Bennington landmark. Behind the church, a cemetery contains the graves of soldiers who fell in the Battle of Bennington, and that of poet Robert Frost, whose simple white marble tombstone is engraved with the epitaph: "I had a lover's quarrel with the world."

But the **Bennington Battle Monument** dominates every view of the village. The 306-ft (93-m) blue limestone obelisk was completed in 1889 at a cost of $112,000; it marks the site of an important colonial supply point that was defended in a three-hour clash that was a turning point in the Revolutionary War. From its observation tower there are superb views of Massachusetts' Berkshires, the Green Mountains, and New York.

Bennington College in North Bennington, situated on a lovely, rambling campus, is one of the nation's leading non-traditional or experimental colleges. Emphasizing lit-

erature, dance, and the other arts, it is known for its wealthy, non-conformist students, and for innovative approaches to education.

Nearby, surrounded by the Taconic and Green Mountains, **Old Bennington** offers lovely village scenes.

Tourist Information

The **Bennington Area Chamber of Commerce** (Veterans Memorial Drive, Bennington, VT 05201; ☎ (802) 447-3311) has any information you might want about the town and the surrounding area.

OPPOSITE AND ABOVE: Like much of New England, Vermont has remained largely a rural state.

Where to Stay

Hotels in Bennington are reasonably priced; many are in the moderate category. Always reliable are **Best Western New Englander** (220 Northside Drive; ((802) 442-6311, toll-free (800) 528-1234; 51 rooms); **Kirkside Motor Lodge** (250 W. Main Street (next to the Old First Church); ((802) 447-7596; 23 rooms); and **Ramada Inn** (U.S. 7 at Kocher Drive; ((802) 442-8145; 104 rooms).

Eating Out

For a fine French-style meal, you can dine at

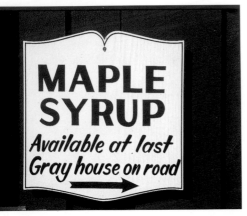

Four Chimneys Inn and Restaurant (Route 9; ((802) 447-3500; expensive). The **Publyk House** (Harwood Hill on Route 7A; ((802) 442-8301) serves inexpensive steak and seafood dinners.

NORTH TO RUTLAND

NEW ENGLAND HERITAGE TRAIL

Route 7 takes the traveler through the villages and scenic valley of the **Green Mountains National Forest**. There, in the tranquil hamlet of **Arlington**, once a gathering place for the Green Mountain Boys, artist Norman Rockwell made his home. The **Norman Rockwell Exhibition Gallery** in Arlington has hundreds of Saturday Evening Post covers and prints on display. Often, the models who posed for his works lead gallery tours.

ABOVE: There's no substitute for the real thing. OPPOSITE: The stunning Quechee Gorge and the Ottauquechee River.

MANCHESTER

Manchester, a summer resort since the 1800s, was enjoyed by Abraham Lincoln, who was drawn here by its beauty and serenity. It is a picture-postcard village nestled in the Valley of Vermont, between the Taconic and Green Mountains. Mount Equinox, the tallest peak in the Taconic Range, rises high above a town where Federal and colonial Revival mansions line its shaded streets.

Nearby, Robert Todd Lincoln, the President's son, built a 24-room manor on a large estate which he called "Hilldene". The site commands a splendid view of the surrounding countryside. He summered here from 1904 until his death in 1926 and many of the original family furnishings remain in his home **Hilldene** (admission $5.00 adults, $2.00 children; open daily, mid-May to October from 9:30 am to 5:30 pm; ((802) 362-1788).

Ernest Hemingway often tried his luck on the **Battenkill River**, one of New England's premiere fly-fishing streams. The **American Museum of Fly Fishing** (Route 7 and Seminary Avenue; ((802) 362-3300; admission is $2.00 adults, children under 12 are free; open daily 10 am to 4 pm, May to October, and Monday through Friday the rest of the year, closed on major holidays) has books, files, displays, and equipment of famous fishermen, including Hemingway, Daniel Webster, Winslow Homer, Presidents Hoover and Eisenhower.

The **Southern Vermont Art Center** is located off West Road (admission $3.00 adults, $.50 students, children under 13 free; open May 26 to October 14, Tuesday through Saturday, 10 am to 5 pm; Sunday 12 pm to 5 pm).

One of the best views in the area is found along the **Equinox Sky Line Drive**, five miles (eight kilometers) south of Route 7A. It is a six-mile (9.7-km) paved road that climbs from 600 to 3,835 ft (183 to 1,169 m) and offers panoramas from the summit of Mt Equinox.

From the **Lye Brook Wilderness Center**, hikers can follow a two-mile (3.2-km) trail leading to the Lye Brook Waterfalls, or pick up the Long Trail for a trek among the abandoned marble quarries leading to the 3,186-ft (971-m) Mt Aeolus. Maps can be picked up at the **Manchester-in-the-Mountains Chamber of Commerce** in Manchester Center, ((802) 362-2100.

Where to Stay and Eating Out

The best accommodations are in the country inns of Manchester, all of which have fine dining rooms.

The Inn at Manchester (Route 7A; ((802) 362-1793; 20 rooms; expensive) is a Victorian inn and converted carriage house. Nearby are the **1811 House** (Route 7A; ((802) 362-1811; 14 rooms; expensive),and the **Panther Inn** (Route 7A in Manchester Village; ((802) 362-2568; 13 rooms; expensive) whose chefs create five course dinners that usually include trout and quail.

On a slightly larger scale are the **Manchester View** (U.S. 7 in Manchester Center; ((802) 362-2739; 29 rooms; moderate to expensive), **Palmer House** (U.S. 7 in Manchester Center; ((802) 362-3600; 36 rooms; moderate to expensive), an **Willburton Inn** (off Route 7A; ((802) 362-2500; 32 rooms; expensive).

For moderately priced meals, **Chantecleer** (U.S. 7 in East Dorset; ((802) 362-1616) has Swiss Provincial dishes and the **Sirloin Saloon** (Route 11 in Manchester Center; ((802) 362-2600), as its name suggests, serves steaks.

DORSET

Dorset, just a few miles north of Manchester, is an artists' colony in a beautiful mountain setting. Its annual **summer theater festival** offers Actors' Equity productions featuring Actors Equity players from June to Labor Day, ((802) 867-5777.

Where to Stay and Eating Out

The **Dorset Inn** (Church and Main Streets; ((802) 876-5500 or 876-9392; 34 rooms; expensive), located on the green, has been in operation for 200 years.

On the outskirts of town is the **Barrows House Inn** (Route 30; ((802) 867-4455; 31 rooms; expensive) whose restaurant serves fresh fish and calf's liver and has its own bakery.

Village Auberge (Route 30; ((802) 867-5715; moderate to expensive) has a classic French-style menu.

CENTRAL VERMONT

RUTLAND

Rutland is Vermont's second largest city, with a population of less than 20,000. It was once known as the "Marble City" because of the quarries in the vicinity. The Vermont Marble Company supplied marble from these quarries for construction of the Tomb of the Unknown Soldier and the Kennedy Memorial in Washington, D.C., as well as for the Lincoln Memorial and the Supreme Court Building.

In Rutland, too, along Main and Center Streets and on Merchants Row and Strongs Avenue, there are buildings of historic significance embellished with marble. The **Vermont Marble Exhibit** in nearby Proctor has displays of marbles from all over the world, a working sculptor, and a sculpture garden with a bas-relief "Gallery of Presidents" (admission $2.50 adults with reductions for students and children; open daily late May to October, 9 am to 5:30 pm).

Rutland is also only 10 miles (16 km) from the large **Killington ski resort**, (see page 160).

Where to Stay and Eating Out

Rutland has several good motels, including the **Best Western Hogge Penny Motor Inn** (U.S. 4; toll-free (800) 828-3334; 96 rooms; moderate to expensive), and the **Holiday Inn**

Centre of Vermont (S. Main Street; ((802) 775-1911; 151 rooms; moderate to expensive).

The best dining in the area is found at **Countryman's Pleasure** (Townline Road in Mendon; ((802) 773-7141; moderate to expensive), where the veal and lamb dishes are complemented with home-baked goods.

Royal's Hearthside (U.S. 7; ((802) 775-0856; moderate to expensive) serves a standard New England fare, and the Italian sandwiches at **Gill's Deli** on Strongs Avenue are among the best anywhere.

PLYMOUTH

In the early morning of August 3, 1923, in Plymouth (about 30 miles or 48 km east of Rutland on Route 100A), Vice-President Calvin Coolidge was sworn in as the 30th president of the United States by his father in the parlor of the Coolidge homestead. These unusual circumstances arose when Coolidge was notified of President Warren Harding's death while visiting his home town; his father, a notary public, did the honors.

A visit to Plymouth, a typical rural Vermont village nestled among the Green Mountains, should include a walk through the historic district which includes the **Coolidge Homestead** and his birthplace home.

Nearby is the family cheese factory operated by Calvin's son, John. Founded by the president's father, it still specializes in the curd cheese so favored by "Silent Cal." Other Coolidge sites include the steep hillside cemetery where Coolidge and six generations of his family are buried.

Where to Stay
The **Salt Ash Inn** (junction of Routes 100 and 100A; ((802) 672-3748; 15 rooms; moderate) is an historic country inn still in operation today.

WOODSTOCK

Woodstock exudes a peaceful nineteenth-century charm. The oval-shaped town green is surrounded by fine examples of Federal, Greek Revival, and Romanesque-style homes.

The Town Crier bulletin board, at Elm and Central Streets, still informs residents of important announcements and events. Of the 87 remaining Paul Revere-made bells,

four hang in Woodstock churches; three of these continue to toll as well as ever.

The successful Gold Rush lawyer, Frederick Billings, is credited with generating an interest in village preservation in the 1870s. Sample Woodstock's nineteenth-century charm during the two-hour guided walking tours of the historic district; for information; call ((802) 457-1830. Or visit the **Billings Farm & Museum** (admission $5.00 adults, with reductions for children and senior citizens; open daily May 7 to October, 10 am to 5 pm), a living history of Vermont farm life

a century ago. The last covered bridge built in Vermont (1969) is in the village center.

Skiing is big in Woodstock, with **Suicide Six** and **Sonnenberg** ski areas nearby. The village is credited with the invention of the tow rope (pulling skiers up Mt Tom, powered by a "Model T" Ford engine) which revolutionized the ski industry.

Quechee Gorge, six miles (10 km) east of Woodstock on Route 4, is a sheer 165-ft (50-m) chasm dropping down to the Ottauquechee River; a steep one-mile (1.6-km)-long hiking trail leads to the bottom of the gorge. An obelisk marks the 1805 birthplace of Mormon Church founder Joseph Smith just outside **South Royalton**, 18 miles (29 km) north, and a museum there displays early church artifacts. **Brookfield's floating bridge**, built in 1812, is a structure of weathered timbers floating on 300 barrels spanning tiny **Sunset Lake**, 18 miles (30 km) north of Woodstock.

OPPOSITE. Locals seek recreation in a Woodstock park. ABOVE: A covered bridge in Woodstock. Once a common sight in Vermont, few of these bridges now remain.

Where to Stay and Eating Out

Woodstock Inn and Resort (14 At the Green; ((802) 457-1100; 120 rooms; expensive) has facilities for almost every sport imaginable and its restaurant is moderately priced.

The **Braeside Motel** (U.S. 4; ((802) 457-1366; 12 rooms; moderate), situated on a hillside, includes breakfast in the price of its rooms. There is also **The Kedron Valley Inn** (106 S. Woodstock Street; ((802) 457-1473; 29 rooms; expensive).

Parker House (16 Main Street in Quechee; ((802) 295-6077; expensive), serves French-

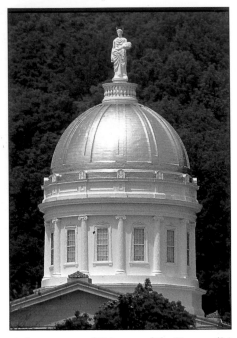

style menus, and **Prince and the Pauper** (24 Elm Street; ((802) 457-1818, expensive), also serves French-style menus.

MONTPELIER THE TINIEST CAPITAL

Montpelier, with less than 9,000 residents, is the smallest state capital in the nation. It is a pleasant town, set in a valley of the Winooski River. The gold-leaf dome of the **Vermont State House** is stunning when viewed against a backdrop of hills ablaze with fall foliage.

On the State House Lawn is the **Vermont State Museum** (admission free; opening

The gold-domed state capital building ABOVE and Ben and Jerry's ice cream OPPOSITE are two of Montpelier's biggest attractions.

times variable), fashioned to resemble the old Pavilion Hotel, a landmark demolished in 1966. Collections are eclectic and include the last panther shot in Vermont in 1881.

Those with a sweet tooth should head up Interstate 89 to the Stowe exit, then go about half a mile (800 m) to the headquarters of "the best ice cream in the world," according to *Time* magazine. **Ben & Jerry's** all-natural ice cream, ((802) 244-5641, offers guided factory tours, but most fun is the sample scoop of ice cream offered before you leave.

AROUND MONTPELIER

Barre The Granite Capital

Barre is the center of the country's granite industry. For a better understanding of just how difficult and dangerous granite mining can be, visit **Rock of Ages Quarry**, four miles (6.4 kilometers) south of Montpelier on Route 14. This is the world's largest granite quarry, 350 ft (107 m) straight down to the bottom of the open rock mine. Huge machines lift 100-ton granite slabs out of the pit, while at the Craftsmen Center, workers cut and polish the rock, then carve it into memorial gravestones or sculptures. A quarry train offers a 20-minute ride through the mining complex. (((802) 476-3115; admission $2.00 adults, $1.00 children; open June 1 to October 15, Monday through Friday, 9:30 am to 3:30 pm.)

The town's granite legacy can also be viewed at **Hope Cemetery** on the edge of town, where the headstones are said to rival the finest granite carvings anywhere.

The Green Mountains

Stretching from Montpelier south to Rutland and north to Underhill State Park, the Green Mountains offer some of the best skiing on the east coast.

MAJOR SKI RESORTS

MT MANSFIELD AT STOWE

One of Vermont's two premier ski areas, Mt Mansfield at Stowe, is about an hour's drive east of Burlington. There is always snow at Stowe, is a much-repeated refrain. The Civilian Conservation Corps built Stowe in 1933 when workers carved a trail on Mt Mansfield, Vermont's highest peak (4,393 ft or 1,339 m); since then, Mt Mansfield at Stowe has created more challenging and scenic runs, and is often called "the ski capital of the East."

Located at the foot of Mt Mansfield, the village of **Stowe** is also one of New England's most varied resort communities, with its white-steepled churches, colonial-style buildings, and Swiss chalets.

Mt Mansfield's fabled "Front Four" have been called "the toughest expert proving grounds in the East." Beginning at elevations of 4,000 ft (1,339 m), with vertical drops of 2,350 ft (716 m), these slopes challenge a skier's ability with steep, mogul-filled, tree-lined chutes.

There are plenty of intermediate slopes providing wide-open touring, and a Nordic system that meets with three other trails to offer more than 100 miles (161 km) of interconnected backcountry trails.

Stowe has several beginners' trails, so new skiers need not be scared away by its "expert" reputation. For example, the novice run called the Toll Road is more than four miles (six kilometers) long.

Year-Round Attractions at Stowe

Four-season attractions make Stowe an enjoyable summer resort. The **Mount Mansfield Toll Road** ($6.00 car and passengers) off Route 108 is a five-mile (eight-kilometer) gravel road leading to a lookout point near the summit; from there one can follow a two-mile (3.2-km) hiking path to the top. Mt Mansfield's **gondola ride** (admission $6.00; open daily June to early September, Saturday and Sunday from September to October) also provides near-summit panoramas. Nearby Spruce Peak has an **alpine slide**, a kind of warm-weather luge with wheels, that barrels down the slopes along an aluminum chute.

It is also renowned for its charming inns and lodges. One of the most famous is the **Trapp Family Lodge**, run by the family of the *The Sound of Music*. The site of their Tyrolean-style lodge is said to remind them of their native Austria.

SMUGGLERS' NOTCH

At **Smugglers' Notch Ski Area**, about eight miles (13 km) north of Stowe in Jeffersonville, the three mountains — **Morse, Sterling**, and **Madonna** — are interconnected by winding trails and lifts. Some trails run from the village center.

Smugglers' main attraction is Madonna, 3,668 ft (1,118 m) high with a vertical rise of 2,610 ft (796 m). This is expert skier territory, with giant moguls requiring a high degree

of skill. Yet Smugglers' (named after the contraband that was smuggled through the pass during the war of 1812) also has a special children's center which offers day care, ski schools, and camps — there is even a Club Med-type program headquartered in the newly completed **Village Center** with a swimming pool.

Smugglers' Notch auto road, open summers only, is a narrow, twisting road that climbs to the scenic notch (mountain pass) between Mt Mansfield and Spruce Peak.

WHERE TO STAY

Expensive

The **Trapp Family Lodge** (off Route 108; toll-free (800) 826-7000; 93 rooms) is the most prestigious of the lodges in Stowe. Breakfast and dinner are included in the price of rooms.

The **Golden Eagle Motor Inn** (Route 108; ℂ (802) 253-4811, toll-free (800) 626-1010; 68 rooms) rents moderately-priced apartments and has every facility imaginable.

Also recommended are **Mount Mansfield Resort** (Mountain Road; ((802) 253-7311; 80 rooms) and **Salzburg Motor Inn** (Route 108; ((802) 253-8541; 51 rooms).

Moderate
Alpine Motor Lodge (Mount Mansfield Road; ((802) 253-7700; 29 rooms); **Stoweflake Resort Motor Inn** (Mountain Inn; ((802) 782-9009; 73 rooms; on the expensive end of the range); **Stowehof Inn** (Edison Hill Road; ((802) 422-9722; 46 rooms); and **Topnotch at Stowe** (Mountain Road; ((802) 253-8585; 107 inn rooms).

EATING OUT

Expensive
The **Trapp Family Lodge** (((802) 826-7000) serves traditional Austrian fixed-price menus). The **Topnotch at Stowe** (((802) 253-8585) and **Ile de France** (Route 108; ((820) 253-7751), both serve French-style meals.

Inexpensive
The **Shed** (Mountain Road; ((820) 253-4364) serves hearty hamburgers dubbed Shedburgers.

KILLINGTON

Central Vermont's largest ski resort is Killington, 10 miles (16 km) east of Rutland on Route 4. One word describes it BIG. It has six separate but interconnected mountains (Killington Peak is the highest at 4,241 ft or 1,293 m), with 107 ski trails and moguls the size of small hotels in all, twice as much skiing as any other Eastern ski resort. And it claims the longest ski lift in the world, stretching more than three miles (4.8 km) over the Green Mountains.

Bear Mountain is expert terrain, with one trail, Outer Limits, at an incline of 62 percent; it is easily the steepest in New England. Beginners should try the 10-mile (16-km)-long Juggernaut trail, the longest Alpine run in the United States.

Another Killington drawing card is the long ski season. With more than 240 inches (six meters) of snow annually and vast snowmaking capacity, the resort's season often extends from October to June.

Killington's outstanding ski school and Children's Center attract many families. Besides special programs, activities, and day care, its "family ski workshop" allows Mom, Dad, and the kids to receive lessons and ski together under the tutelage of a single instructor.

Tourist Information
Killington and Pico Areas Association (P.O. Box 114, Killington, VT 05751; ((802) 773-4181) and **Killington Lodging Bureau** (((802) 422-3711) can help find lodging and provide information of recreational facilities in the area.

Where to Stay
Specifically recommended accommodations are **Cortina Inn** (Route 4, Mendon Mountain; ((802) 773-3331; 98 rooms; expensive); **Grey Bonnet Inn** (Route 100; ((802) 775-2537; 40 rooms; moderate); **Killington Village** (718 Killington Road; ((800) 343-0762; 96 rooms, more than 600 condominiums; moderate to expensive); **Shelburne-Killington Motel** (U.S. 4; ((802) 773-9535; 18 rooms; moderate to expensive); and **The Vermont Inn** (U.S. 4; ((802) 775-0708; 16 rooms; expensive).

Eating Out
For Vermont country-style food, the restaurant at **Vermont Inn** (Route 4; ((802) 773-9847; moderate to expensive) is excellent.

Other popular restaurants, serving - Vermont lamb and fresh trout, include **Annabelle's** (Junction of Routes 100 &107; ((802) 746-8541; moderate to expensive) and **Hemingway's** (U.S. 4; ((802) 422-3886; expensive).

OTHER SKI RESORTS

Other popular ski areas include **Mt Snow**, 14 miles (22,5 km) north of Wilmington, which has old New England charm. It offers several open snow-field downhill runs, and a five-mile (eight-kilometer)-long Nordic touring trail skirting craggy ridges along six peaks of the Green Mountains, making it the highest-elevation cross-country trail in Vermont.

Stratton Mountain, about 15 miles (24 km) north of Mt Snow, has a European atmosphere, and Tyrol-style vaudeville entertainment ("better than Kitzbuhel's.")

Jay Peak lies eight miles (13 km) south of North Troy and the Canadian border.

LAKE CHAMPLAIN

Lake Champlain stretches for 125 miles (201 km) down Vermont's northwest border, separating the state from New York. Nestled in a huge valley with the Adirondacks to the west and the Green Mountains on the east, the lake is one of the most popular resort areas in Vermont.

MIDDLEBURY

An easy place to begin a Champlain valley tour is at Middlebury (on Route 7, about 46 miles, or 74 km, north of Rutland), a little town whose female academy, now **Middlebury College**, was founded in 1800; tours of the campus take in the handsome 1806 Congregational Church on the Common, and the Starr Library, with its collection of works by Robert Frost.

Just north of Middlebury in **Weybridge** is the University of Vermont's **Morgan Horse Farm**. You can watch more than 50 Morgans being put through training drills, and guided tours will take you into the handsome Victorian barns.

MAD RIVER VALLEY

Bristol is the gateway to the remote Mad River Valley, known for its rolling mountain terrain. Three ski areas and a scenic road leading to the 2,356-ft (718-m) tip of the **Appalachian Gap** are highlights of the valley. Bristol also operates the only freshwater windjammer cruises in America; here you may sail one of these tall-masted ships on Lake Champlain with Vermont's mountains in the background.

At **Charlotte**, there is an 18-minute ferry ride across Lake Champlain to Essex, N.Y., a charming nineteenth-century town.

The **Shelburne Museum and Heritage Park**, ((802) 985-3344, is five miles, or eight

kilometers, south of Burlington. It has been called a collection of collections, with 45 acres (18 hectares) of Americana. The enclave includes 37 buildings: a horseshoe-shaped barn which houses more than 150 horse-drawn carriages and sleighs; the 1783 Stagecoach Inn, with its collection of American folk art; the 1840 Dorset House, featuring more than 1,000 hand carved duck decoys; and even Lake Champlain's historic sidewheeler steamboat *Ticonderoga*, docked alongside the old Colchester Reef Lighthouse.

Another fascinating stop is **Shelburne Farms**, ((803) 985-3222, a beautiful nineteenth-century agricultural estate on the shores of Lake Champlain. The old farm buildings include Shelburne House, the estate's 110-room mansion with views of both the lake and the Adirondacks in New York. The gorgeous estate grounds are attributed to landscape architect Frederick Law Olmstead. Today it is a working experimental farm and learning center.

LAKE CHAMPLAIN'S ISLANDS

The three islands in the northern end of Lake Champlain **Grand Isle**, **North Hero**, and **Isle la Motte** are sometimes referred to as "Vermont's Cape Cod." Isle la Motte is the best of the three, with its St Anne shrine marking the site of a 1666 French fort. All islands can be reached via highway U.S. 2.

There is also "Champ," the Loch Ness monster of Lake Champlain. The humpbacked creature, first "sighted" by Champlain in the 1600's, has been "seen" several times by ferry boats and pleasure craft from both Vermont and New York. However, much like Scotland's Loch Ness "monster", it has never shown itself to scientific research expeditions.

BURLINGTON

Burlington, Vermont's largest city with 38,000 residents on the shore of Lake Champlain, is the commercial and industrial center of the state. It hosts the annual **Champlain Shakespeare Festival** and the **Vermont Mozart Festival** presented by the University of Vermont (UVM) in July and August.

Some Burlington landmarks are the **University of Vermont** (founded in 1791), located at the top of a hill on the eastern edge of town, and the **Old Mill** building, which has a cornerstone laid by Lafayette in 1825. **Battery Park**, on Pearl Street, is where American guns defeated the British during the War of 1812; now it affords great views of the lake. And **Ethan Allen Park** preserves part of the Allen's historic farmstead.

You can sail Lake Champlain on the *Ethan Allen;* ((802) 862-9685, a vintage stern-

wheeler that takes in the mountain scenery along the shoreline.

WHERE TO STAY

Expensive

The **Sheraton Inn** (870 Williston, S. Burlington Street; ((802) 862-6576, toll-free (800) 324-3535; 125 rooms) is built around a central greenhouse.

At the **Radisson Burlington Hotel** (60 Battery Street; ((802) 658-6500, toll-free (800) 333-3333; 257 rooms), children stay free.

Moderate

Howard Johnson Motor Lodge (U.S. 2, S. Burlington; ((802) 863-5541, toll-free (800) 654-2000; 89 rooms) has an indoor pool and tennis court, and children stay free.

Nearby is the **Best Western Redwood** (1036 Shelburne Road, S. Burlington; ((802) 862-6421; 54 rooms)

ABOVE: A still-life in Vermont.
OPPOSITE: East Orange, Vermont.

EATING OUT

The best restaurants in Burlington are moderately priced, and include the French-style **Déjà Vu Cafe** (185 Pearl Street; ((802) 864-7917); **Ice House Restaurant** (171 Battery Street; ((802) 863-9330), which serves seafood; **Pauline's** (1080 Shelburne Road; ((802) 862-1081), which also serves seafood; and **Sweetwater's** (118 Church Street; ((802) 964-9800), the yuppie favorite.

NORTHEAST VERMONT

St Johnsbury, on U.S. 2, is the gateway to the northeast, a backwoods region travelers seldom visit. It is a land of lakes, forests, small villages — and few people.

The best time to visit the area is during the fall "color" season in September, when the woods are ablaze with color, and villages celebrate with festivals, food, and fun.

Danville, west of St Johnsbury, is the headquarters of the American Society of Dowsers, people who use willow wands to find water; their fall convention draws lots of attention. **Lyndonville**, nestled in the green hills of the Passumpsic River valley, has five covered bridges within village limits, the earliest dating from 1795.

Finally, **Derby Line** is one of the most unusual hamlets in America. The United State–Canadian border passes right through the town, resulting in houses sitting astride the border between Vermont and Quebec. In the town library, the book stacks and checkout desks are in different countries.

AUTUMN FOLIAGE TOURS

Vermont's fall foliage has been called the world's finest, attracting people from all over the world. The leaves usually begin to change in early September at higher elevations in northern Vermont and along the Canadian border. This is the least-populated portion of the state, and is noted for its sweeping, panoramic views. The color season moves progressively southward, usually ending in the final weeks of October.

The compactness of Vermont (180 miles, or 290 km long, and about 60 miles, or 97 km at its widest point) makes it relatively easy to travel. Don't be afraid to get off the main highways you will often find that the back roads with their colorful canopies of leaves, lined by old stone walls, or set off against the brilliant green pastures of rolling countryside, enhance the pleasure of fall touring.

Scores of small Vermont towns celebrate the season with festivals that might include guided tours, bazaars, live entertainment, and homemade, traditional New England foods.

colors but also a wide array of cultural activities. Vermont's northern mini-metropolis follows the shore of Lake Champlain, and a walk to downtown Battery Park, where American guns turned away British warships during the War of 1812, reveals a setting that impressed even Rudyard Kipling.

• For color cruising, board *The Spirit of Ethan Allen* (℘ (802) 862-8300), a recreated paddlewheel-era boat that offers 90-minute voyages on Lake Champlain; you will have a magnificent view of Vermont's Green Moun-

TOURIST INFORMATION

The **Vermont Travel Division** operates a fall foliage hotline, ℘ (802) 828-3236, and publishes suggested fall color routes covering the entire state. Also remember that overnight accommodation anywhere along popular fall color routes should be made well in advance.

ITINERARIES

A few additional fall color tour suggestions include:

• **Burlington**, surrounded by remarkable scenery, not only offers brilliant autumn

tains in the east, and New York state's Adirondacks to the west.

• Back on shore, head 20 miles (32.3 km) southeast on Interstate 89 to reach the **Green Mountain Audubon Nature Center**, ℘ (802) 434-3068, 230 acres (93 hectares) of trails winding through beaver ponds, hemlock swamp, and retired farm fields, set in a blaze of color.

• An especially colorful 124-mile (200-km) car tour follows U.S. 7 south from Burlington, skirts **Lake Champlain** and then enters the **Green Mountain National Forest** before reaching Bennington, near the New York/Massachusetts border.

• **Smugglers Notch State Park**, near Stowe, offers some of the most spectacular color scenery in Vermont, though you may have to fight off the crowds. From Stowe, travel west on Route 108, enter the state park, and soon you will be negotiating hairpin curves along sheer cliffs and ledges leading to the 2,162-ft (659-m) "notch," named after nineteenth-century creative capitalists who smuggled illegal goods from the United States into Canada through the natural pass in the Green Mountains.

BICYCLING IN VERMONT

Vermont's rolling hills, low-road mountain passes, country backroads, outstanding state parks, and light traffic make it a cyclist's paradise. In fact, it has often been rated as the top biking state in America.

Bicycle touring is a great way to enjoy at close range the state's emerald green landscape while discovering interesting villages and historic towns. There are several Vermont cycling groups that conduct tours of varying lengths and degrees of difficulty, from leisurely rides into the countryside to grueling off-road mountain touring. Most not only provide experienced guides who lead the way, explaining state sights and sounds, but also make all the arrangements for overnight lodging and meals.

Or you can rent bicycles and strike out on your own, following suggested state cycling routes, or those mapped out by bike clubs that create itineraries to match your interests.

BICYCLING DIRECTORY

Guided Tours
• **Bike Vermont** (P.O. Box 207 G, Woodstock, VT 05091; ((802) 457-3553), conducts inn-to-inn bicycle tours for cyclists at all skill levels. Groups average no more than 12 to 15 people, with 20 the maximum.
• **New England Bicycle Tours** (P.O. Box 26-R, Randolph, VT 05060; ((802) 728-3261), offers two- to five-day road tours and mountain bike adventures for riders of all abilities. You will stay overnight in country inns or renowned resorts; you can even choose back country camping. Tour leaders and support vans accompany all trips. Both road and mountain bike rentals are available.

• **Outdoor Tours Limited** (P.O. Box 97, Calais, VT 05648; ((802) 229-4570) specializes in northern Vermont trips which include weekend and five-day, camping and inn-to-inn tours. Rentals are available.

Vermont Back Roads Bike Tours (Box 31, Craftsbury Common, VT 05827; ((802) 586-7767), includes three-day and six-day tours on back roads, averaging 10 to 20 miles (26 to 32 km) per day using mountain bikes.
• **Vermont Bicycle Touring** (Box 711-GX, Bristol, VT 05443; ((802) 453-4811) offers easy to challenging tours for adults and

families, with special emphasis on overnighting at country inns, and sampling home-cooked meals. Two- to five-day trips; others can be booked for extended periods. A support van assists with luggage transportation, picnic lunches, and repairs on the five-day trips. Rentals and custom-planned trips are also available.
• **Vermont Country Cyclers** (P.O. Box 145-VT3, Waterbury Center, VT 05677; ((802) 244-5215) conducts two- to nine-day biking vacations for cyclists of all abilities. Country inn overnight accommodation includes some of the finest Vermont has to offer, and evening

ABOVE: Cycling in the White Mountains.
OPPOSITE: A country-store shopping opportunity in Peacham.

meals consist of gourmet cuisine. Two tour leaders and a support van accompany every group, which is limited to 20-plus cyclists.

• **Vermont Mountain Bike Tours** (P.O. Box 526, Pittsfield, VT 05762; ((802) 746-8943) offers mountain adventures for cyclists who desire an out-of-the-ordinary cycling experience. Only back country is traveled, including seldom-used dirt roads, old farm lanes, logging trails, and staying overnight at country inns. Two- to five-day tours, for beginners and intermediate levels. Mountain bikes required; rentals available.

Self-Guided tours
• **Bicycle Holidays** (Road 3 Box 2394, Middlebury, VT 05753; ((802) 388-7347), plan personalized self-guided tours that might include country inn or bed and breakfast overnight accommodation, attractions, and service along the route.
• **Country Inns Along the Trail** (Road 3, Brandon, VT 05733; ((802) 247-3300) prides itself on custom-planned biking itineraries based on length of trip and degree of difficulty desired. Their program includes the participation of more than 25 country inns in western and central Vermont.

MORE CYCING INFORMATION

• The **Vermont Travel Division** (134 State Street, Montpelier, VT 05602; ((802) 828-3236), provides up-to-date information about biking in the state, including suggested routes and material on attractions, accommodation, and restaurants along the way.
• The *Handbook on American Youth Hostels, Inc.*, provides information on budget accommodation; you must become a member to use the hostels. Send a self-addressed envelope to **Greater Boston Council, American Youth Hostels** (1020 Commonwealth Avenue, Boston, MA 02215; ((617) 731-5430).
• One of the most popular information sources over the years has been *25 Bicycle Tours in Vermont*, available through Vermont Bicycle Touring, listed above.

Weathered wood at Waits River.

Connec-
ticut

FOR MORE THAN three centuries, Connecticut has welcomed travelers. George Washington visited the state a number of times; the bedroom his hosts decorated at Webb House for his visit to Wethersfield in 1781 still looks the same today.

Mark Twain stopped in Connecticut on business in 1873, and stayed for a good portion of his life, writing such classics as *Tom Sawyer* during his time in Hartford. His flamboyant "Steamboat Gothic" home still stands in Hartford.

Even P.T. Barnum, the master of hype who traveled the world with his Greatest Show on Earth, put all that aside when he returned to his home in Bridgeport. The Barnum Museum there provides lots of entertainment courtesy of the master showman.

However, travelers on Interstate 95 often pass straight through Connecticut on their way to holiday spots elsewhere in New England, missing out on a unique part of New England which is best explored along its picturesque back roads.

It is not hard to get around in Connecticut. The state is a rectangle measuring only 90 miles (145 km) by 55 miles (89 km), bordered by New York on the west, Massachusetts to the north, and Rhode Island to the east.

Its southern boundary stretches along Long Island Sound; protected by Long Island, New York, these shores have long sandy beaches and historic port towns. Both the Connecticut River, which bisects the state, and the Housatonic in the northwest provide spectacular scenery, and the Litchfield Hills, which rise in northern Connecticut, are dotted with villages perfect for leisurely touring.

TOURIST INFORMATION

Since no two places in the state are more than a two-hour drive apart, it is possible to enjoy the best of what Connecticut has to offer in a few days. The **Connecticut Department of Economic Development** (210 Washington Street, Hartford, CT 06611; ((203) 566-3385 or 566-3977) provides free maps and guides to help plan your trip. For **travel information**, call toll-free (800) CT-BOUND.

BACKGROUND

Adriaen Block, a Dutch navigator, was the first recorded European explorer to sail along Connecticut's coast in 1614. He traveled up the Connecticut River, where the Dutch later established a trading post near today's Hartford, for dealing in the region's lucrative beaver trade.

However, by 1635, English settlers from the already crowded Massachusetts Bay Colony, driven by a search for farmland, were flowing into the Connecticut River valley.

The Massachusetts colonists established three towns along the Connecticut River Hartford, Wethersfield, and Windsor known jointly as the Hartford Colony. On January 14, 1639, the colony proclaimed the Fundamental Orders of Connecticut which, some historians contend, is the world's first written democratic constitution; hence the state's nickname, "The Constitution State."

Connecticut revolutionaries played important political and military roles in the American Revolution. Among these were General Israel Putnam, who ordered troops on Bunker Hill not to fire "until you see the whites of their eyes," and the revolutionary Nathan Hale, hanged as a spy by the British, who said before he died, "I regret that I have but one life to give to my country."

Commerce, trade and manufacturing took root thereafter. Banks were established in Hartford by 1792, and the insurance industry began in Norwich in 1795. Samuel Colt

Southern Connecticut is more commercial OPPOSITE, than the northeast "Quiet Corner" ABOVE.

of Hartford developed the Colt .45; Gideon Roberts made Bristol the clock capital of the United States; everyone wore Danbury hats; and Meriden silver services were treasured.

This level of prosperity endures today, as indicated by the state's per capita income which is the highest in the nation.

HARTFORD

Mark Twain once said, "Of all the beautiful towns it has been my fortune to see, Hart-

ford is chief." The capital of Connecticut, Hartford, can look back on 350 years of history from its setting on the banks of the Connecticut River. The **Center Church burying ground** has gravestones dating from 1640. The **Old State House**, built in 1796, is the oldest in the nation, and Mark Twain's eccentric mansion still stands on a small green surrounded by skyscrapers.

The state's second largest city has recently undergone a boom that has transformed downtown Hartford into a mixture of high-rise architecture, new riverfront developments, restorations such as Pratt Street, sophisticated stores and cafés set into refurbished buildings, and Constitution Plaza.

The national headquarters of 40 insurance companies, Hartford has been an insurance haven since an eighteenth-century ship owner took out a policy on his boat and cargo. When the tragic fire of 1835 de-

The State Capitol reflects Hartford's wealth, much of which has been amassed by its numerous insurance companies.

stroyed more than 600 buildings in New York City, many insurance companies could not honor claims and went bankrupt. The Hartford Insurance Company's president visited every New York policyholder, assuring them that their claims would be quickly settled. Since then, its financial stability, despite disasters such as the Great Chicago Fire and the San Francisco earthquake of 1906, have enhanced Hartford's reputation as the insurance capital of the nation.

THE CHARTER OAK

Hartford's riverside location drew early attention. The "city" began as a Dutch trading post named Fort Good Hope in 1633. Massachusetts Bay Colony Puritans settled here two years later, and the village eventually formed one-third of the Hartford Colony, its independence guaranteed by the Royal Charter of 1662.

Legend has it that when the royal governor demanded return of the charter 25 years later, it was stolen and hidden in the trunk of a massive oak tree, the famous "Charter Oak," that stood until felled by a storm in the 1850s. (The oak's location is now marked by a plaque.) The governor was recalled, and the threat to independence overcome.

TOURIST INFORMATION

For a quick orientation and free maps and guides of the city, you can stop at the **Tourist Information Center** in the Old State House (800 Main Street, Hartford, CT 06103; ℂ (203) 522-6766) which is open Monday through Saturday, 10 am to 5 pm.

A WALKING TOUR

The Walk is a self-guided journey through Hartford's historic sites and new landmarks. Begin at the **Old State House** in the downtown district. Tours of the handsome 1796 Federal structure, the first public building designed by Charles Bulfinch, include the restored Senate chamber with its Gilbert Stuart portrait of George Washington and original furnishings.

North on Main Street is the **Richardson**, a brownstone designed by Henry Hobson

Richardson, one of America's foremost architects of the nineteenth century. It is considered an architectural landmark, now restored to its original condition, with restaurants, specialty shops, and apartments.

Across the street, **Christ Church** is made conspicuous by its elegant spire. Then at State and Market Streets is **Constitution Plaza**, a unique, 12-acre (five-hectare) urban park where on sunny days some of Hartford's 100,000 downtown workers take café-style lunches on the green.

The plaza's two-sided boat-shaped building, home to Phoenix Mutual Life Insurance, is already a Hartford landmark. New employees are greeted with "Welcome aboard!" (The Phoenix company was established in 1851 to insure only teetotalers.)

Travelers Tower, off Main Street, has a 527-ft (161-m)-high observation deck offering splendid views of the city and the Connecticut River Valley. It is home to its namesake company, which started in 1863 by insuring Colonel James Bolter for $5,000 on his trips from the post office to his home. His premium? Two cents.

Just ahead is the **Wadsworth Atheneum** (((203) 278-2670), one of the country's first public art museums. It holds 165 permanent and visiting exhibits that include 40,000 art objects. Its collections include Egyptian and Roman artifacts, paintings by masters such as Goya and Rembrandt, and a large selection of works by American artists of the Hudson Valley School.

By far the most impressive building is the **State Capitol**, near Bushnell Park. The golden-domed capitol, with its many turrets, gables, and towers, was built 1879. The **Hartford Civic Center** (Asylum and Trumbull Streets) is home to the Hartford Whalers, the city's team in the National Hockey League.

Among other "Walk" attractions is **City Place**, the tallest office building in Connecticut, with a high-tech system of sensors, scanners, and silicon chips that automatically control most of the building's functions.

MARK TWAIN'S NOOK FARM

Mark Twain (Samuel Clemens) is perhaps America's most oft-quoted writer. Born and raised in Hannibal, Missouri, on the Mississippi River, he came to Hartford in the 1870s. His home at **Nook Farm** (Farmington Avenue and Forest Street), built in 1874 for $131,000, reflects the grand style of its owner. The many gabled, orange-red colored house caused scandalous comments in its time because of its stylistic excesses.

It is Victoriana and Gothic — a tangle of gingerbread, pointy towers, intricate woodworking, even decorating gems fashioned by Louis Comfort Tiffany. It still contains much of Twain's original furnishings, including the huge hand-carved bed purchased on his travels through Europe. He became so enamored of the delicate headboard hand carvings that he often slept with his head at the foot of the bed to gaze at the head board.

Upstairs in the billiards room is where Twain did much of his writing and entertaining. He wrote *Tom Sawyer, The Adventures of Huckleberry Finn*, and other masterpieces here.

Twain left the house in 1891 after bad business investments forced him to embark on a quick European lecture tour to raise money. Novelist **Harriet Beecher Stowe's** modest Victorian home is just across the lawn. For tour information, call (((203) 525-9317.

WHERE TO STAY

Expensive
The large, modern **Parkview Hilton** (One Hilton Plaza; (((203) 249-5611, toll-free (800) 445-8667; 400 rooms) and **Sheraton-Hartford Hotel** (315 Trumbull Street; (((203) 728-5151, toll-free (800) 325-3535; 400 rooms) frequently offer weekend specials to attract travelers. At the Hilton children stay free.

The weekend specials at the **Holiday Inn Downtown** (50 Morgan Street; (((203) 549-2400; 359 rooms) drop this hotel to the moderate category.

For a touch of Old Hartford, try the **Summit Hotel** near the Old State House (5 Constitution Plaza; (((203) 278-2000; 285 rooms).

For excellent accommodations outside the city, Marriott operates the **Hartford Marriott Hotel/Farmington** (15 Farm Springs Road, Farmington; (((203) 678-1000, toll-free (800) 321-2211; 381 rooms)

and the **Courtyard by Marriott Hotel** (1 Day Hill Road, Windsor; ℂ (203) 683-0022, toll-free (800) 321-2211). Both offer excellent weekend rates.

Moderate
In Hartford, the best buy is the **Howard Johnson Motel** (7 Weston Street; ℂ (203) 525 4441; 80 rooms). On the outskirts of town is the **Super 8 Motel** (57 W. Service Road; ℂ (203) 246-8888, toll-free (800) 843-1991; 104 rooms) that includes breakfast in the price of the rooms.

Close by in East Hartford are several smaller, moderately priced motels: **Executive Motor Lodge** (490 Main Street, East Hartford; ℂ (203) 569-1100; 85 rooms); **Holiday Inn** (363 Roberts Street; ℂ (203) 528-9611, toll-free (800) 465-4329; 130 rooms); and **Ramada Inn** (100 E. River Drive, ℂ (203) 528-9703, toll-free (800) 272-6232; 199 rooms).

Four Seasons International Bed & Breakfast (11 Bridlepath Road, West Simsbury, Connecticut; ℂ (203) 651-3045) is a booking service for bed-and-breakfast lodging in the Hartford area. Most of their listings are in nearby small towns.

Inexpensive
The best bargain in the greater Hartford area is **Motel 6** (Silas Deane Highway, Wethersfield, CT 06109; ℂ (203) 563-5900; 146 rooms).

EATING OUT

Expensive
Terrace on the Park (1 Hilton Plaza; ℂ (203) 249-5611) in the Hilton serves as elegant a meal as you can find in Hartford.

Moderate
Featuring Northern Italian cuisine, **Carbone's Ristorante** (588 Franklin Avenue; ℂ (203) 249-9646) is a popular Hartford eatery.

In nearby Glastonbury, you can dine in the Colonial atmosphere of **Blacksmith's Tavern** (2300 Main Street, Glastonbury; ℂ (203) 659-0366).

Inexpensive
The eating-out experience in Hartford is **Shelly's Downtown Deli** (Hartford Civic Center; ℂ (203) 278-1510) with its 300-item

menu including every type of sandwich available and kosher favorites. Breakfast is served at all hours.

HARTFORD AREA EXCURSIONS

Farmington
Just 10 miles (16 km) west of Hartford on Route 10, Farmington is an elegant colonial town often referred to as "one of New England's museum pieces." Its rich eighteenth-century architecture includes the **Stanley-Whitman House**, parts of which date from

1663. The village's **Hill-Stead Museum** contains several French Impressionist paintings.

Wethersfield
In Hartford's suburban south, Weathersfield has more than 150 houses pre-dating the mid-nineteenth century, including the 1752 **Webb House**, where George Washington and French commander Jean Baptiste Donatien de Vimeur, Count of Rochambeau, met in 1781 to plan the Yorktown campaign that led to America's victory in the Revolutionary War.

Hartford mixes modern and traditional.
OPPOSITE: An Alexander Calder sculpture.
ABOVE: The Harriet Beecher Stowe house.

Bristol

In 1790, Gideon Roberts started selling his clocks here, just 18 miles (29 km) west of Hartford. Soon the town became the clockmaking capital of the United States. The **American Clock and Watch Museum** (Maple Street, off Route 6; ((203) 583-6070) displays more than 2,000 fine timepieces made in Connecticut.

CONNECTICUT RIVER VALLEY

The Connecticut River (from the Indian

name Quinnituckett or long tidal river) flows for 410 miles (660 km) from its headwaters near the Canadian border in New Hampshire to Long Island Sound, neatly bisecting Connecticut into east and west. **Essex**, **Ivoryton**, **Old Lyme**, **Chester** and **East Haddam**, a cluster of little towns 10 to 15 miles from Long Island Sound, are within easy reach of the area's attractions and where you can stay in one of the Valley's country inns

---

ESSEX

A gateway to the valley, Essex is also the terminus of the **Valley Railroad,** ((203) 767-0103, which offers 55-minute tours of the river valley aboard turn-of-the-century steam

trains to **Deep River Gorge** near picturesque **Chester**. From Deep River Gorge, riders take an hour-long **riverboat cruise** up the Connecticut River past some of the valley's best scenery, including Gillette's famous castle and the Goodspeed Opera House, before returning by rail to the Essex Depot.

GILLETTE CASTLE

A five-minute ride by car ferry from **Chester** brings one to **Hadlyme** and an eccentric hilltop fieldstone mansion dubbed **Gillette**

Castle, ((203) 526-2336. Built by actor William Gillette, a Hartford native famous for his portrayal of Sherlock Holmes, the 122-acre (49-hectare) medieval castle commands a sweeping view of the Connecticut River and countryside.

Construction of the 24-room mansion began in 1914, and took five years to complete. Built to Gillette's design, the castle has granite walls that are four feet (1.3 meters) thick at the base, and interior trim hand hewn from southern white oak. Huge oak doors are fastened by complicated wooden locks; some bedroom furniture is built into the castle's structure, and other furnishings slide on metal tracks. Electric light fixtures are decorated with bits of colored glass gathered by his friends. He could even see who was entering the house by a series of angled mirrors starting outside his bedroom door. Outside, Gillette built a large railroad, with a "Grand Central" depot starting at the entrance gate and winding to "125th Street" at the property's eastern terminus; he delighted in manning the throttle while treating visitors to rides through his estate. The train was dismantled long ago.

In his will, Gillette instructed his executors "to see to it that the property [does] not fall into the hands of some blithering saphead who has no conception of where he is or with what surrounded." In 1943, Gillette Castle was acquired by the state.

EAST HADDAM

Just north of Gillette Castle on Route 82, East Haddam is an old riverboat landing and the site of the **Goodspeed Opera House**, ((203) 873-8668. This 1876 building on the banks of the Connecticut River cuts a dashing figure when viewed from the water; inside, the beautifully-restored Victorian auditorium now offers equity productions of American musicals from mid-April to December.

The Victorian-style town is also the location of the **Nathan Hale Schoolhouse** (where Hale taught in 1773). Also available are afternoon **sightseeing cruises** and evening music excursions on the river (board in Haddam; ((203) 345-4507).

WHERE TO STAY AND EATING OUT

Part of the experience of visiting the Connecticut River Valley is staying in one of its many country inns. For centuries New Yorkers have come here to escape the hustle and bustle of America's largest city. In the summer, reservations are essential; most of these inns are in the expensive category.

Essex

The **Griswold Inn** (48 Main Street, Essex; ((203) 767-0991; 23 rooms) is almost a tourist attraction in itself. Reservations to stay in the 212-year-old country inn are made months in advance. In spite of its popularity, its rates are reasonable, at the high end of the moderate range. They do, however, include breakfast. To dine on its wild game specialties, you will

have to make reservations and those who wait till the last minute to call are often disappointed. On Sundays from 11 am to 2:30 pm, you can feast at a Hunt Breakfast for $12.00. Children under six eat free.

Ivoryton

The **Copper Beach Inn** (Main Street, Ivoryton; ((203) 767-0330; 13 rooms) is an excellent alternative to the Griswold. Food critics claim it has the best restaurant in southern Connecticut.

For a change of pace in dining, the **Fine Bouche** (Main Street, Centerbrook; ((203)

767-1277), a couple of miles away serves French meals at about the same price as the Copper Beach Inn.

Chester

The **Inn at Chester** (318 W. Main Street; ((203) 526-4961; 48 rooms) is in a lovely rural setting. This late-eighteenth century farmhouse is adjacent to the state forest and has access to miles of hiking trails.

Old Lyme

Old Lyme has two excellent inns: **The Old Lyme Inn** (85 Lyme Street; ((203) 434-2600),

OPPOSITE LEFT: The Connecticut Valley Railroad. OPPOSITE RIGHT: Gillette Castle. ABOVE: Essex.

a stately 1850's mansion with five rooms in the main building and nine in the new addition, and **Bee and Thistle Inn** on the banks of the Lieutenant River (100 Lyme Street; ((203) 434-1667), which serves seafood and duck specialties in its dining room.

MYSTIC AND NEW LONDON

Facing Long Island Sound and the sea, Mystic and New London attracted restless, venturesome Yankees, who became sailors, and sailed

them around the world in search of whales, rum, spices, and the riches of the China Trade.

MYSTIC

Since the seventeenth century, Mystic has been building boats. Its elegant clipper ships made Mystic one of the country's top whaling centers — with nearly 20 whalers in its fleet. Later, its vessels formed the backbone of America's Navy in World War II.

Mystic Seaport

This recreated nineteenth-century seafaring village and living-history museum is at the

Fog and sun at Mystic Seaport.

mouth of the Mystic River and has a whaleboat demonstration, oystering displays, and sailors tending the sails aboard an elegant whaler.

The 17-acre (seven-hectare) Seaport, begun in 1929, contains more than 60 historic waterfront buildings, 300 ships and boats, and artifacts of nineteenth-century maritime America.

America's sole surviving wooden whaling ship, the *Charles W. Morgan*, is the Seaport's master attraction. Visitors may walk the main deck, explore the cargo hold which still smells of whale blubber, and see where the crew of more than 90 men lived and worked. The 113-ft (35-m)-long, three-masted *Morgan*, built in 1841, sailed the seas for nearly 80 years, making 37 whaling voyages, some lasting up to five years. A fascinating 30-minute program on nineteenth-century whaling at the Meeting House includes rare footage of an actual whaling voyage.

You can also explore the decks of the square-rigged *Joseph Conrad*, an iron-hulled Dutch training vessel built in 1882; today it serves as a training ship for the Seaport's special sailing program. The *L.A. Dunton Fishing Schooner* (1921) illustrates the days of Grand Banks fishing aboard a two-masted Gloucester schooner. And the coal-fired *Sabino Passenger Steamboat* (1908) provides pleasant cruises down the Mystic River.

Along Gravel, Clift, and High Streets, among others on the west bank of the river, are a number of historic sea captains' homes. Especially interesting is 13 Gravel Street, an 1836 "spite house" built into the street to deliberately block the neighbor's view. (Ninety-minute self-guided audio-cassette tour tapes are available for rent or sale at Olde Mistick Village shops.)

Stonington

Don't leave the area without visiting Stonington, just east of Mystic, off Alternate Route 1A. It has been called "one of the prettiest coastal villages in Connecticut."

The **Old Lighthouse** on Stonington Point reminds visitors of Stonington's past as a whaling and sealing port; inside, a small museum contains seafaring artifacts, and the lighthouse tower has a view of three

states (Fisher's Island, N.Y., Rhode Island to the east, and Connecticut), as well as breathtaking vistas across the sound.

Where to Stay

Overlooking the harbor, atop a hill at the junction of U.S. 1 and Route 27, **The Inn at Mystic** (Route 27; ((203) 536-9604; 68 rooms; expensive) is an old-style New England inn, housed in a cluster of Victorian buildings. On its spacious grounds are tennis courts, a pool, and a boat dock.

In town is another traditional inn,

Whaler's Inn (20 E. Main Street; ((203) 536-1506; 45 rooms), as well as the larger, more modern **Mystic Hilton** (Coogan Boulevard; ((203) 572-0731, toll-free (800) 445-8667; 187 rooms). At the Hilton, children stay free in their parents' room, and special weekend rates are often available.

Comfort Inn (132 Germanville Avenue; ((203) 572-8531; toll-free (800) 228-5150; 120 rooms; moderate) and **Days Inn of Mystic** (Route 27; ((203) 572-0574; 122 rooms; moderate) have less luxurious rooms at a more modest rate. The Days Inn has designated no-smoking rooms.

Just east of Mystic in Stonington, you can find bread-and-breakfast accommodations. **The State of Connecticut Tourism Division Information Center** at the North Stonington southbound exit off I-95 has a listing of these homes and will help make reservations.

Eating Out

EXPENSIVE

If you don't stay at the Inn at Mystic, you may want to dine at its **Flood Tide Restau-**

rant (junction of U.S. 1 and Route 27; ((203) 536-8140) on Long Island roast duck or Maine lobster.

For a French-style meal, **J.P. Daniels** (Route 184, Old Mystic; ((203) 572-9564) is the best in the area.

MODERATE

Actually three restaurants in one, **Seamen's Inne** (Germanville Avenue; ((203) 536-9649) caters New England meals to suit your price range. You can have an inexpensive snack at the bar, a moderately-priced meal at the cafe, or a more expensive, larger meal in the dining room.

Nearby in North Stonington is **Randall's** (Route 2; ((203) 599-4540), which serves fixed-price meals that feature New England specialties.

INEXPENSIVE

To the south in Noank is **Abbot's Lobster in the Rough** (117 Pearl Street; ((203) 536-7719) where you get the best buy for your money. There are no waiters; you order at the window, pay the tab, and wait for your number to be called. In addition to steamed lobster, the menu includes whatever seafood is in season.

NEW LONDON

At one time, New London was the second busiest whaling port on the East Coast. The mansions built by her sea captains testify to their successes. Especially interesting is Huntington Street's **"Whale Oil Row"**, where wealthy seamen built four white-columned Greek Revival mansions in the 1830s. The Pennsylvania oil boom in the late 1850s ended the whaling industry's profitability.

New London is still a seafaring town; its fine deep water port is home to the **United States Coast Guard Academy**, ((203) 444-8270, one of the nation's four service academies that train military officers. You can take a walking tour of the grounds; cadet dress parades are held in spring and fall, and the training barque *Eagle*, a three-masted square rigger built in 1936, is open for weekend tours when in port. New London also has several historic buildings, including the 1774 **Nathan Hale School House**, and **Monte**

Cristo Cottage, boyhood home of Nobel Prize-winning playwright Eugene O'Neill.

Groton

Across the Thames River from New London is Groton, home port of the **United States Navy's Atlantic Submarine Fleet**. You can take a one-hour submarine base tour aboard sightseeing buses, ((203) 449-4779, with the possibility of seeing docked submarines being repaired along the river.

A better way to immerse yourself in submarine lore is by climbing aboard the *SS Nautilus*, the world's first nuclear-powered submarine, built in 1954 by Groton's Electric Boat Division of General Dynamics. The ship's claustrophobic quarters were crammed with 111 officers and crew during its journeys, which included cruising under the Arctic ice cap, from the Bering Strait to the Greenland Sea, in 1958.

The **Submarine Force Library**, ((203) 449-3174, is filled with interesting displays and exhibits that trace the development of United States submarines from the Revolutionary War, through World War II, to today's sleek nuclear-powered ships.

It's also possible to take a sightseeing cruise on the Thames aboard the **River Queen II** (board at The Harbour Inn, 193 Thames Street; ((203) 445-9516). You will pass the *SS Nautilus* and other submarines at their riverside berths, sight Trident submarines being constructed at Groton, pass the submarine base and Coast Guard Academy, and perhaps even see a submarine or two returning to home port.

Tourist Information

Maps and guides of the area are available from the **Southeastern Connecticut Tourism District** (Ye Olde Town Mill, 8 Mill Street, New London, CT 06320; ((203) 444-2206).

NORTHWEST CONNECTICUT

Quiet country back roads, peaceful colonial villages, great hiking trails, including part of the Appalachian Trail, make touring in this region quite special. **Canaan**, on Route 7 near the state line with Massachussets in the north and **Kent**, further south also on Route

7 near the New York State line are the access pointes to the region. From Hartford, **Litchfield**, 30 miles (50 km) away on U.S. 202, is perhaps the best base for a visit to the region.

CANAAN TO KENT

At Canaan, just south of the Massachusetts border, one can ride the **Housatonic Railroad** along the Housatonic River through the green hill country. Board at the 1872 **Union Station** (Routes 7 and 44; ((203) 824-0339), America's oldest train

depot in continuous use. Six miles (10 km) east on U.S. 44 at Norfolk is the site of **Indian burial grounds** Nearby **Haystack Mountain** and the 34-ft (10-m)-high stone tower at the summit (1,716 ft or 523 m) offers views of Long Island Sound, the Berkshires in Massachusetts and mountain peaks in New York. A road one mile (1.6 km) north of Norfolk on Route 272 leads halfway up the mountain; a quick 30-minute hike gets you to the top. The June mountain laurel and fall foliage are spectacular.

OPPOSITE: Groton, home port of the U.S. Navy's Atlantic Submarine Fleet and the Submarine Force Library. ABOVE: Lobster, the New England seacoast specialty

Another summit pavilion, in **Dennis Hill State Park** south of Norfolk on Route 272, provides views of Haystack Mountain, the Green Mountains, and part of New Hampshire; even New Haven Harbor can be seen on the horizon on a clear day.

West Cornwall

West Cornwall, 13 miles (21 km) south of Canaan, has a **covered bridge** (Route 128) that has been in continuous service since 1837. If you are here at meal time, **Fresh-**

field's (Route 128, West Cornwall; ((203) 672-6601) serves moderately-priced meals.

Housatonic Meadows

South of West Cornwall on Route 7 and located in the heart of the rock-strewn valley of the Housatonic, Housatonic Meadows lies amid rugged hills. Tall pines shade the banks of the river, which is known for its fly fishing.

Kent

Another **covered bridge** spanning the Housatonic River is south on Route 7 in Kent, where the **Sloane-Stanley Museum** displays handmade tools used by early settlers. The covered **Bull's Bridge** also spans

the Housatonic, stretching into New York state; it is four miles (six kilometers) south of Kent.

Kent Falls

North of Kent on Route 7, Kent Falls whitewater cascades draw thousands of visitors. A gentle stepped pathway runs parallel to the waterfalls. It is also one of the most photographed natural sites in the state.

Macedonia Brook

At Macedonia Brook, north of Kent, two 1,400-ft (427-m) peaks offer stunning views of the Catskills and Taconics.

LITCHFIELD

Many historians consider Litchfield the finest unrestored colonial town in the country. George Washington and General Lafayette both visited here. In fact, the entire borough of Litchfield has been declared a National Historic District.

The eighteenth-century, white-clapboard mansions lining its peaceful, wide streets are not museums but homes. Historic buildings on serene South Street include the 1753 **home of Oliver Wolcott**, signer of the Declaration of Independence; the birthplace of the revolutionary Ethan Allen; and the **Tapping Reeve House**, the first law school in America, founded in 1774. Tapping Reeve claims as alumni two vice-presidents of the United States (Aaron Burr and John C. Calhoun), 101 members of Congress, 34 Chief Justices of the United States, 28 U.S. Senators, and 14 governors. The beautiful white-steepled **Congregational Church** presides over the town's lovely village green.

Tourist Information

Free information is available from the **Litchfield Hills Travel Council** (P.O. Box 1776, Marble Dale, CT 06777; ((203) 868-2214).

Where to Stay and Eating Out

The best accommodations in town are at the **Litchfield Inn** (Route 202; ((203) 567-4503; 31 rooms) and **Tollgate Hill Inn** (Route 202; ((203) 567-4545; 10 rooms), which was established as a tavern in 1789, but was located on a nearby hill. In 1923 it was moved to its present site. Both inns serve excellent meals and are in the expensive category.

Black Rock State Park

West of **Thomaston** on Route 6, Black Rock State Park is a hiker's paradise, with the scenery of the Western Highlands dominating the blue-blazed **Mattatuck Trail**.

Lake Waramaug and New Preston

Five miles (eight kilometers) north of New Preston, is an autumn delight, with bright hues mirrored in the unrippled surface of

For those entering Connecticut from New York on Interstate 95, it will be hard to tell just when the Empire State ends and the Constitution State begins. That's because coastal cities and villages such as affluent **Greenwich**, **Stamford**, **Riverside**, and **Darien** are more suburbs of New York City than Connecticut towns.

An endless number of New Yorkers talk about owning a little farmhouse in Darien, to

Lake Waramaug. **Mt Tom**, near Bantam, boasts hiking trails leading to a summit tower. Overlooking the lake is the **Hopkin's Inn** (Hopkins Road, New Preston; ((203) 868-7295; 10 rooms; moderate), famous for its restaurant which serves Austrian and Swiss specialties.

HIKING AND CANOEING

Serious hikers might want to trek part of the **Appalachian Trail** that stretches from Kent to Canaan, while canoeists can look forward to flatwater or **whitewater adventures** on the Housatonic (contact Clarke Outdoors, West Cornwall; ((203) 672-6365).

get away from the Big Apple's problems at the end of the work day. Only 50 to 90 minutes from Manhattan, some of these towns have evolved into dormitory communities.

BRIDGEPORT

Farther up the coast is Bridgeport, an important manufacturing city with a population of 150,000, and P.T. Barnum, creator of the Greatest Show on Earth, wintered in Bridgeport. He also discovered one of his greatest acts here namely 28-in (71-cm)-tall General Tom Thumb, a Bridgeport native.

ABOVE: Pig farm in Litchfield county.
OPPOSITE: Norwich Connecticut's Leffingwell Inn preserved as it was in 1735.

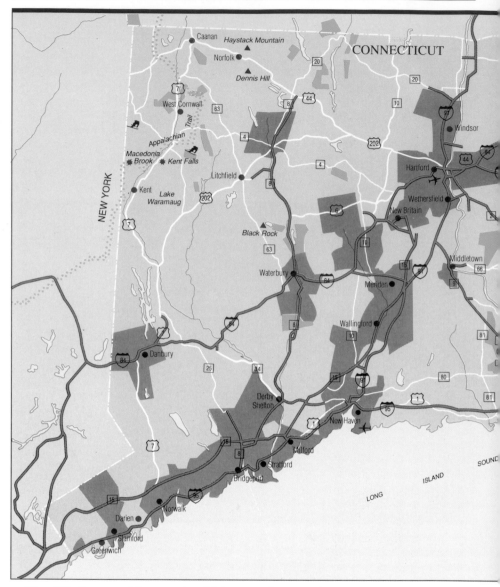

The **P.T. Barnum Museum** (on Main Street; ((203) 576-7320) has just undergone a $6 million renovation. It boasts much circus lore and many curiosities that made Barnum famous, including personal memorabilia of Thumb and others.

Bridgeport's **Beardsley Zoological Gardens** is the only zoo in Connecticut. And the city **Summer Music Festival** hosts the New York Philharmonic.

Stratford, just east up the Sound, is the home of the **American Shakespeare Theater**, which offers the Bard's plays all summer,

and pre- and post-Broadway productions the rest of the year.

WHERE TO STAY

As this area is just across the state line from New York, many visitors to New York City elect to stay in Connecticut where rates are more reasonable and train service to Manhattan is good.

Expensive

At the top of the line are the **Hyatt Regency Greenwich** (1800 East Putnam Avenue, Old

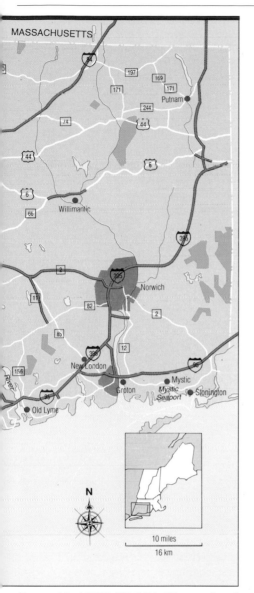

10 miles

16 km

The **Showboat Inn** (500 Steamboat Road, Greenwich; ((203) 661-9800 or toll-free (800) 243-8511; 103 rooms) is a good medium-sized hotel.

Moderate

Bridgeport Hilton Hotel (1070 Main Street, Bridgeport; ((203) 334-1234, toll-free (800) 465-4329; 234 rooms); **Howard Johnson Motor Lodge** (150 Ledge Road, Darien; ((203) 655-3933; 72 rooms). **Ramada Inn** (50 Ledge Road, Darien; ((203) 655-8211; 100 rooms); and **Ramada Inn** (19 Clarks Hill Avenue, Stamford; ((203) 327-4300; 87 rooms).

EATING OUT

Most of the hotels in the area have their own restaurants, but for distinctive Italian dining in Bridgeport **Meghan's** (2068 E. Main Street, Bridgeport, ((203) 576-1283; expensive) and **Paris Bistro** (3546 Main Street, Bridgeport; ((203) 374-6093, expensive) are recommended.

Greenwich has many good French restaurants: **Cinquante-cinq** (55 Arch Street; ((203) 869-5641; expensive); **Jean-Louis** (61 Lewis Street; ((203) 622-8450; moderate to expensive); **La Grange** (420 Field Point Road; ((203) 869-7500; expensive); **Tapestries** (554 Old Post Road #3; ((203) 629-9204; moderate to expensive); and **Swan Court** (26 Mill River Street; ((203) 325-1900; expensive) which serves a fixed-price traditional French meal.

NEW HAVEN

Founded in 1638 on the Connecticut coast, New Haven began as a Puritan settlement at the end of a harbor four miles (6.5 km) from Long Island Sound. Three rivers flow into the sound here — the Quinnipiac, the Mill and the West. Around the village, low meadows give way to gently sloped hills. The prominent landmarks then, as now, were two isolated peaks known as East Rock and West Rock.

The town was planned in classic fashion with nine squares. The center square today is New Haven's public Green, once a market-place and pastureland. It is surrounded by

Greenwich; ((203) 637-3691; 35 rooms) and **The Inn at Mill River** (26 Mill River Street, Stamford; ((203) 1900, toll-free (800) 325-0344 in Connecticut or (800) 325-0345 outside Connecticut; 94 rooms). Both are old-style country inns.

Also in Stamford in this category are **Le Pavilion Hotel** (60 Strawberry Hill Road; ((203) 357-8100; 176 rooms); **Crowne Plaza Hotel** (700 Main Street; ((203) 358-8400, toll-free (800) 465-4329; 381 rooms); and **Stamford Marriott Hotel** (2 Stamford Forum; ((203) 357-9555; 505 rooms).

three historic churches built between 1812 and 1815, all exhibiting distinctive architectural styles: Federal, Georgian, and Gothic Revival.

In the nineteenth century, worn out farmlands forced people into cities and towns; by the end of the Civil War, more than half of Connecticut's population lived in urban areas. After Eli Whitney created a mass-production line for manufacturing his cotton gin, New Haven gradually became a manufacturing center; that tradition continues today.

Guided one-hour walking tours of the historic campus start at **Phelps Gateway** on College Street, across from the New Haven Green, ℂ (203) 432-2300. One of the most interesting areas is the **Old Campus**, containing Yale's oldest buildings, including Connecticut Hall, where Nathan Hale studied. One of the most unusual campus buildings among those designed by famous architects is the **Ingalls Hockey Rink** by Eero Saarinen, inspired by the shape of a whale.

The **Yale University Art Gallery**, on Chapel Street, is one of the finest small

In 1716, the Collegiate School of Saybrook, established 15 years earlier, moved to New Haven, changing its name to **Yale University** to honor a generous donor, Elihu Yale. The earliest Yale buildings were built just west of the Green; the campus now covers 160 acres (65 hectares) in the central city and dominates New Haven. The distinguished Ivy League school has nearly 12,000 students divided among its 12 colleges — each with its own library, dormitories, and dining halls. Historically, about 15 graduates each year eventually become U.S. Congressmen. Renowned alumni include Nathan Hale, William Howard Taft, Noah Webster and George Bush.

galleries in the country. In addition to a collection of French Impressionist paintings, it has on show many works by patriot painter John Trumbull, including the original *Bunker Hill* and *Declaration of Independence*.

New Haven's **Shubert Performing Arts Center** features Broadway-bound productions and road shows. The New Haven Symphony Orchestra performs at Yale's **Woolsey Hall**.

Where to Stay

At graduation and matriculation (May and September), hotels in New Haven can be completely booked. If your trip takes you here during these times, you will have to make your reservations well in advance.

EXPENSIVE

The best accommodations in New Haven, without doubt, are at **The Inn at Chapel West** (1201 Chapel Street; ((203) 777-1201; 13 rooms). In fact, the excellent service raise this above the category of expensive to luxury.

Also in the heart of downtown is **Park Plaza Hotel** (155 Temple Street; ((203) 772-1700; 300 rooms), which has a rooftop restaurant.

Less expensive and close to Yale is the **Colony Inn** (1157 Chapel Street; ((203) 776-1234; 86 rooms).

MODERATE

Children stay free with their parents at the **Holiday Inn at Yale** (30 Whalley Avenue; ((203) 777-6221, toll-free (800) 465-4329).

There are two Howard Johnson's in the area. The **Howard Johnson's** north of New Haven in Hamden (2260 Whitney Avenue, Hamden; ((203) 288-3831, toll-free (800) 654-2000) is less expensive than the more centrally located **Howard Johnson's Long Wharf** (400 Sargent Drive, New Haven; ((203) 562-1111, toll-free (800) 654-2000; 154 rooms).

Eating Out

The best restaurants in New Haven are in the expensive category and serve ethnic dishes.

For Greek dining, you won't be disappointed by **Basel's** (993 State Street; ((203) 624-9361).

Blessings (45 Howe Street; ((203) 624-3557) serves tasty northern Chinese specialties, and **Delmonaco's** (232 Wooster Street; ((203) 865-1109) prepares northern Italian-style meals.

If you want something more traditional, there is **Robert Henry's** (1032 Chapel Street; ((203) 789-1010).

Less a place to eat, and more an attraction, is **Atticus Bookstore-Cafe** (1082 Chapel Street; ((203) 776-4040), where you can have coffee and pastries for breakfast or tea and cakes for afternoon tea in the presence of one of the best selections of books in the state.

New Haven's Yale University, among the nation's most distinctive in learning and architecture.

Rhode
Island

A CASUAL glance at a map of the United States reveals that Rhode Island at 1,212 sq miles (3,144 sq km), even with the many islands of Narragansett Bay, is the smallest state in the nation. But the "Ocean State," as it calls itself, with its 400 miles (664 km) of shoreline, has a variety of coastal land and undeveloped beaches. (It also claims the longest official name of any state — "Rhode Island and Providence Plantations."

It was the seacoast that brought the bluebloods of America to Newport, a harbor town transformed into a haven for the millionaires of the "Gilded Age." They built magnificent estates (referred to as "summer cottages") along the cliffs and ledges that border the ocean. Many of these structures remain today as a testament of Newport's affluent past.

BACKGROUND

The Florentine navigator Giovanni da Verrazano explored Narragansett Bay in 1524 under commission from the King of France. He is said to have named the area Rhode Island because of its resemblance to the island of that name in the Aegean Sea. One hundred years were to pass before the first colonists would arrive — from England, not from France. Among the first of these was Reverend William Blackstone, a nomadic preacher who came to Rhode Island when his lands on the Shawmut Peninsula, near Boston, were taken over by Puritan settlers.

Roger Williams, who founded Providence Plantations in 1636, had been driven out of Salem, Massachusetts, for advocating religious freedom and tolerance. His convictions were to have a benign and continuing effect on the development of the new colony. Ann Hutchinson, who helped to establish Portsmouth in 1638, soon followed, as did others anxious to be free of the rigors of Boston Puritanism. By the nineteenth century, immigrants in large numbers were coming to Rhode Island to seek a new life.

Religious freedom, rich farmlands, and sheltered harbors provided, for Rhode Island, an environment in which tolerance and liberty could prosper.

THE TRIANGLE TRADE

Providence and Newport became leading seaports and centers of the infamous, "Triangle Trade" in the New World. Their merchants sent ships loaded with rum to Africa, traded the rum for slaves, then sailed to the West Indies where they traded slaves for sugar and molasses, the ingredients from which, in home ports, rum could again be distilled. By 1760, Newport had become New England's major port for slave-trading

ships — a dubious distinction in a colony founded on tenets of religious and individual freedom.

In the same century, Rhode Island's craggy coastline, islands, and coves sheltered pirates and privateers who raided ships far out in the Atlantic; later in life, these scoundrels and their crews returned, often, to reside ashore in respectable affluence. The search for legendary pirate treasure, said to be buried somewhere in Jamestown, continues today.

STATEHOOD AND THE TWENTIETH CENTURY

In 1772, the resistance of Rhode Islanders to British rule became increasingly overt, as witnessed by the burning of the British ship, *Gaspee*. After the Revolutionary War broke out, the colony joined wholeheartedly in the long struggle for independence that culminated in the final American-French victory at Yorktown.

Boating and fishing: holiday pastimes on Rhode Island's rugged coast.

Despite its passion for independence, Rhode Island was the last of the original 13 states to ratify the United States Constitution. Subsequently, the state enjoyed rapid growth and prosperity, becoming, in time, a major industrial center. By 1793, a large-scale textile industry had been established in Pawtucket and, by the mid-nineteenth century, it was producing almost 20 percent of the nation's cloth. By the turn of the century, immigrant workers and their families accounted for almost 70 percent of the state's population. When textile factories

were drawn to the south by cheaper labor after World War II, the state was forced to diversify its economy.

TOURIST INFORMATION

Today, with nearly 950,000 people squeezed into 1,214 sq miles (3,144 sq km), Rhode Island is a bustling, energetic state and a popular summer resort in which Newport continues to enjoy preeminence. The state's compactness — only 48 miles or 77 km long, and 37 miles or 60 km wide — makes it easy for visitors to enjoy its quiet coves and beaches, wildlife-filled salt marshes, open meadows, and big cities. The **Rhode Island Division of Tourism** (7 Jackson Walkway, Providence, RI 02903; ℭ (401) 277-2601, toll-free (800) 556-2484) has prepared numerous maps and brochures to help you enjoy your stay in Rhode Island.

Bellevue Avenue ABOVE and the Cliff Walk OPPOSITE in Newport have been the home of New England's nouveau riche since the Civil War.

NEWPORT

Dramatic cliffs rising out of the ocean, elegant mansions, expansive lawns, and baronial gardens are to be seen in Newport. The rich transformed this harbor town into their own summer resort, commissioning America's finest architects to recreate gaudy palaces, mansions, and ersatz chateaus along Ocean Drive and Bellevue Avenue.

Pre-Revolutionary southern plantation owners were the first to discover Newport's summer pleasures as they exchanged the intense heat of the south for refreshing ocean breezes. Following the Civil War, such scions of American wealth as the Astors and the Vanderbilts flocked to the town, entertaining their friends with picnics and parties, caviar and champagne, in keeping with the excesses of what came to be known as the Gilded Age.

Today, no visit to Newport is complete without a tour of a few of these mansions abandoned when income and property taxes and the Great Depression made their upkeep too expensive.

An option is a bus tour of Newport, a 22-mile (35-km) ride through the historic Colonial section, Ocean Drive and its spectacular coastline, Bellevue Avenue with its millionaire "cottages," and guided tours through two of the mansions, conducted by Viking Tours of Newport (101 Swinburne Row, Brick Market Place; ℭ (401) 847-6921). Or you can rent a 90-minute guided auto-tour cassette tape which covers more than 300 years of Newport history and local anecdotes. Cassettes can be purchased at local gift shops or rented at The Paper Lion on America's Cup Avenue in the Long Wharf Mall.

THE MANSIONS OF THE GILDED AGE

Although scores of mansions existed during the Gilded Age, only 50 or so remain, of which eight owned by the Preservation Society of Newport County, ℭ (401) 847-1000, are open to tours.

It is a good idea to purchase a combination ticket that allows you to visit a number of mansions at your leisure; each tour takes less than two hours.

The Breakers, on Ochre Point Avenue, is the most spectacular of the Newport mansions, and largest of the grand summer "cottages." Built in 1895 for Cornelius Vanderbilt and designed by architect Richard Morris Hunt, it replicates a sixteenth-century northern Italian palace. Seventy rooms (tended by 40 servants in its heyday) are graced with imported blue marble, alabaster pillars, gold gilt, mosaics, and stained glass, with magnificent grounds overlooking the Atlantic Ocean — all enclosed by immense wrought iron fences and gates.

sailles. Completed in 1902 for the daughter of the man who discovered Nevada's Comstock Lode, it was the scene of brilliant society balls and galas.

Hammersmith Farm, on Ocean Drive, was the site for the wedding reception of John F. Kennedy and Jacqueline Bouvier after their Newport marriage in 1953. The rambling 1887, 28-room shingled mansion, with gardens designed by Frederick Law Olmstead, was often used as a summer White House by President Kennedy, and now houses mementos from those years.

Marble House, on Bellevue Avenue, was built in 1892 as a gift for the wife of William K. Vanderbilt. Another Hunt design, it is one of the most sumptuous of Newport's "cottages," featuring a dazzling gold ballroom in the French style. (The house is thought to have been styled after the Petit Trianon in Versailles.)

The Elms, on Bellevue Avenue, was completed in 1901 for Pennsylvania coal king Edward Julius Berwind. Modeled after the Chateau d'Asnieres near Paris, it features large rooms and an awesome entrance hall, with its own fountains and formal gardens. It is perhaps the most gracefully-styled of the mansions.

Rosecliff, on Bellevue Avenue, is a 40-room mansion designed by Stanford White and inspired by the Grand Trianon in Ver-

The farm itself was established in 1640 by William Brenton of England and remains the only working farm in the city.

CLIFF WALK

To enjoy the grandeur of the mansions and the sea in a more natural setting, take the **Cliff Walk**, a 3.5-mile (5.5-km) coastal path that hugs the craggy shoreline along Rhode Island Sound. From its starting point just off Memorial Boulevard (near Newport Beach) to its terminus at Ocean Avenue, the walk is a narrow strip of public land that separates great estates such as The Breakers, Rosecliff, Marble House, and Salve Regina College from the sea.

In the nineteenth century, the rich attempted to close the path to the public. But the locals protested, and eventually the state backed them. Proceed to the end of Narragansett Avenue; there the "Forty Steps" enable you to reach the water without following the entire length of the walk.

COLONIAL NEWPORT

Among Newport's great treasures is its colonial architecture, especially evident in the Point and Historic Hill neighborhoods. The 1748 **Hunter House**, considered "one of the 10 best examples of residential colonial architecture in America," was also the headquarters of the French Navy during the American Revolution. **Trinity Church** (1726), with its tall white colonial spire, is based on a Christopher Wren design, and is a landmark visible for miles. The **Touro Synagogue** (1759) was the first ever built in America. **Old Colony House**, an eighteenth-century structure, was headquarters for George Washington as he planned the battle of Yorktown in 1781; it also became the seat of Rhode Island's colonial government. The 1699 **Quaker Meeting House** is the oldest religious building in Newport. And the **White Horse Tavern**, built before 1673, is America's oldest operating tavern.

The **Old Stone Tower**, a "mysterious" structure variously attributed to the Phoenicians, Celts, Vikings, and the Portuguese, is more probably the remains of a colonial windmill built by then-governor Benedict Arnold. The **Green Animals** on Cory's Lane in nearby Portsmouth, dating from 1880, is considered the best topiary garden in America, with 80 trees and shrubs sculpted in every animal shape imaginable.

Visitors who wish to take home a memento of Newport history should head to "**Antique Alley,**" a cluster of antique shops grouped on Thames and Spring Streets; especially good antique hunting is found on Franklin Street in the Historic Hill section of town.

THE WATERFRONT

It is not unusual to see million-dollar yachts anchored in **Brenton Cove** or sailing the waters of Narragansett Bay. Of the bay it has been written, "It is big and scenically lovely, surrounded by wooded countryside, colonial towns, big cities and history-packed shores, with sightseeing opportunities matched by few cruising grounds."

Newport and yachting are inseparable; in fact, it has often been called the yachting capital of the world, harboring countless yacht clubs, boatyards, and sail-making shops. Twenty-four America's Cup races were held in Newport waters beginning in 1851; the last Cup race held here, in 1983, saw the Australians become the first foreign country to wrestle the trophy from the United States.

Fort Adams State Park

America's Cup memorabilia is housed at the **Museum of Yachting**, worth a visit just for its spectacular waterfront location at Fort Adams State Park on Ocean Drive. It is a display of Newport's rich yachting heritage, with small craft, ship models, costumes, and photographs; the America's Cup section includes the 1930 Cup challenger, *Shamrock V*, one of the largest sailing sloops in the world at 127 ft (38.7 m) long and 160 ft (48.8 m) high. The museum also sponsors the Classic Yacht Regatta each Labor Day weekend.

Sightseeing cruises set sail daily (May to October) from Goat Island Marina, off Washington Street, and other dock areas. Cruises take you past the mansion-dotted coastline of Newport, the once pirate-infested shores of Jamestown, towering Newport Bridge, and Fort Adams, guardian of the harbor; some include a visit to Hammersmith Farm.

Another major attraction is shore surfcasting, and bottom fishing in protected bay and shoreline areas, and offshore big-game fishing for white marlin and tuna. Numerous charters are available; for licensing information, call ((401) 789-3094.

TENNIS HALL OF FAME

The **Newport Casino**, facing Bellevue Avenue, was America's most exclusive country club in the 1880s. Now it houses the **International Tennis Hall of Fame**. American lawn tennis started at the Casino some 100 years ago, and the first national championships were held on its grassy courts from 1881 until 1915, when the tournament moved to Forest Hills, New York.

Hall of Fame exhibits include Davis Cup memorabilia, historical displays, and equipment exhibits. Outside the main building, the Casino's dozen grass courts stretch across to the restored "court tennis" court, where you can see how the "sport of kings" was played in England and Europe during the thirteenth century. Each summer, a Grand Prix tennis tournament lures top international players; it is one of the few professional tennis championships played on grass in the United States.

WHERE TO STAY

The luxury **Inn at Castle Hill** (on Ocean Drive; ℂ (401) 849-3800; 9 rooms) has a beautiful view. This handsome retreat rests on 32 acres (13 hectares) of shoreline hugging Narragansett Bay and the Atlantic Ocean. Reservations should be made well in advance.

Expensive
If you prefer to stay in one of the old Newport homes, the **Guest House Association of Newport** (P.O. Box 981, Newport, RI 02840; ℂ (401) 846-5444) will help you find rooms.

Offering standard hotel and motel accommodations are **Treadway Newport Resort and Marina** (America's Cup Avenue; ℂ (401) 847-1000; 134 rooms) and **Sheraton Islander Inn and Conference Center** (Goat Island; ℂ (401) 849-2600; 254 rooms).

Moderate
There are many bed-and-breakfast establishments in the area. Contact the **Bed & Breakfast of Rhode Island** (P.O. Box 3291, Newport, RI 02840; ℂ (401) 849-1298) for reservations. Other accommodations include **Best Western Mainstay Inn** (151 Admiral Kalbfas Road; ℂ (401) 849-9880; 52 rooms); **Holiday Inn Crowne Plaza** (25 America's Cup Avenue; ℂ (401) 849-1000; 308 rooms); and **Mill Street Inn** (75 Mill Street; ℂ (401) 849-9500; 23 rooms).

EATING OUT

Newport presents a variety of dining choices.

Expensive
One of New England's most appealing French-style restaurants is **La Petite Auberge** (19 Charles Street; ℂ (401) 849-6669), with French classic and nouvelle cuisine.

The **SS Newport** (Waite's Wharf; ℂ (401) 846-1200), a restored fishing boat-turned-restaurant moored offshore at Waite's Wharf, specializes in lobster.

French-style provincial fare is the mainstay at **Le Bistro** (Bowen's Wharf; ℂ (401) 849-7778).

Interesting colonial dishes are served at the **White Horse Tavern** (Marlborough and Farewell Streets; ℂ (401) 849-3600)

The **Inn at Castle Hill** (ℂ (401) 849-3800), **The Black Pearl** (Bannister's Wharf; ℂ (401) 864-5264), and **Clark Cooke House** (Bannister's Wharf; ℂ (401) 849-2900) are also fine restaurants.

Moderate
Choices include plain and exotic seafood at **Scales and Shells** (527 Thames Street; ℂ (401) 846-3473); **The Mooring** (Sawyer's Wharf; ℂ (401) 846-2260), which serves great clam chowder; and **Puerini's** (24 Memorial Boulevard West; ℂ (401) 847-5506), where excellent pasta dishes are served.

For more restaurant suggestions, pick up a free *Newport Guide* at the town's Information Center at Brick Market Place.

NEWPORT AREA EXCURSIONS

A side trip to **Jamestown**, three miles (4.8 km) west of Newport on Conanicut Island, should include a drive along its southern tip; there are superb views across Narragansett Bay from Beaver Trail Lighthouse, including **Fort Wetherhill** — built on 100-ft (30-m)-tall granite cliffs — and Mackerel Cove.

BLOCK ISLAND

Where do Rhode Islanders go during the summer to get away from it all? Small Block Island, 11 sq miles (28 sq km), situated about 12 miles (19 km) south of the mainland off Point Judith.

A relatively unspoiled retreat of oceanside cliffs, shifting sand dunes, and spectacular annual spring and fall bird migrations, Block Island has cooler summer temperatures than on the mainland, and great beachcombing and biking. The beaches are almost deserted even at the height of the tourist season, and some of the best deep-sea fishing can be had in the island's waters.

GETTING THERE

Most visitors to the island arrive by ferry from Galilee, Providence, or New London, Connecticut. However, you can travel from **Westerly** Rhode Island on New England Airlines, ((401) 466-5953 or 5881, which operate regular 12 minute chartered flights.

Before or after your trip to Block Island, you can stay at the **Pine Lodge Motel** (Box 562; ((401) 322-0333; 80 units; moderate) and eat at **Shelter Harbor Inn** (10 Wagner Street; ((401) 322-8883; New England cuisine; moderate) or **Villa Trombino** (106 Ashway Road; ((401) 596-3444; Italian cuisine, inexpensive).

AROUND THE ISLAND

Cycling is one of the most popular ways to get around Block Island. Bicycle rentals are near the Old Harbor and Great Salt Pond ferry docks. By bike or car, head to **Mohegan Bluffs** on the island's south shore; multicolored clay cliffs of 200 ft (61m) in height stretch for several miles along the shore, offering a spectacular ocean vista, with the steep walking paths to the beaches that rim the coastline below.

Not far away is **Palatine Graves**, east off Dickens Point, said to be the burial grounds of eighteenth-century Dutch immigrants. **Settlers' Rock**, resting on the shore of Cow Cove, is the island's own Plymouth Rock, commemorating the arrival of the first pioneers on the island in 1661.

Much of the north shore is a bird and wildlife refuge, and an old stone lighthouse on Sandy Point can be reached along a sandy path. **North Light** is a prime spot for birdwatching and sunsets.

New Harbor is great for surf fishing and water sports. The best swimming is along the eastern shore, especially at **Crescent Beach**, but the deserted beaches along the windswept western shore can also be very appealing. (Be cautious of strong undertows and rugged surf.) You can also explore some of the 365 freshwater ponds in the island's interior.

Taxi island tours (pick them up near Old Harbor ferry) are gaining popularity with visitors who prefer to leave the driving to someone else. A round trip lasts little more than an hour, and drivers will usually let you stop for photographs.

The island's folklore is rich in stories of eighteenth century pirates and in tales of undiscovered treasure buried on the island by Captain Kidd and others.

Even more infamous than pirates is the island's reputation for shipwrecks. More than 1,000 ships have gone down off its fogbound coast. Folk tales tell of unscrupulous islanders who lured boats to the treacherous waters, then looted, wrecked, and sank the ships. Tourists today receive a friendlier welcome.

WHERE TO STAY

Expensive
The **1661 Inn and Guesthouse** (Old Harbor, Spring Street; ((401) 466-2421 or (401) 466-2063; 26 rooms), is a luxurious Victorian hotel with ocean views. There is also the **Samuel Peckham Inn** (New Harbor; ((401) 466-2439 or 466-2567; 17 rooms).

Moderate
Historic **Spring House** (Spring Street; ((401) 466-5844), one of the best known hotels, has been greeting visitors since 1852; its veranda offers a fine view of the Atlantic. Block Island has several other moderately priced inns and bed-and-breakfast accommodation.

EATING OUT

Block Island has several fine moderately-priced restaurants: **Ballard's Inn** (Old Harbor; ((401) 466-2231; Italian and American cuisine); **Harborside Inn** (Old Harbor; ((401) 466-5504; steaks and seafood); and **Samuel Peckham Tavern** (New Harbor; ((401) 466-2439; lobster specialties).

PROVIDENCE

This handsome city, set like Rome on seven hills and bisected by the Providence River, was founded in 1636 by Roger Williams

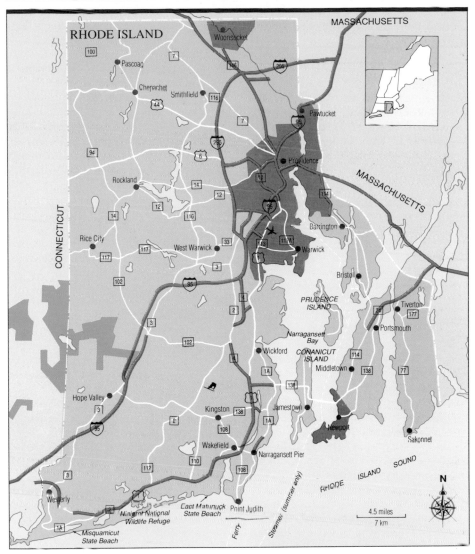

after clashes with the Puritans forced him out of Massachusetts. Williams' open, spirited humanity has endured in Providence's sunny streets and lovely homes, and in the liberal character gave rise to two of the nations finest schools, Brown University and the Rhode Island School of Design.

BACKGROUND

Early Providence earned its reputation as a seaport in the Triangular Trade (rum, slaves, and sugar). When the China Trade opened in 1781, many Providence merchants made a fortune. By 1793, with maritime fortunes

declining, Slater Mill (in suburban Pawtucket) became the first American mill to harness water power to spin cotton. (Now a historic site, the Roosevelt Street mill offers guided tours with eighteenth-century machine demonstrations.)

Textile manufacture brought the city into the nineteenth century, and Providence became an important industrial center. However, with the Great Depression and the southward shift of industry after World War II, the city fell on harder times.

Today Providence, the capital of Rhode Island and the second largest city in New England, has a revitalized downtown district and streets of Federal-style homes that haven't changed much since the nineteenth century.

TOURIST INFORMATION

Providence is a good city for walking, given its one-way streets, narrow roadways, and snarled traffic. The **Preservation Society**, ((401) 831-7440, offers several guided walking tours of various city districts. And the **Convention and Visitors Bureau** (30 Exchange Center; ((401) 274-1636) has pamphlets describing self-guided walking tours.

TOURING THE CITY

City Hall, at Kennedy Plaza in the revitalized downtown district, is designed in the manner of the Louvre and the Tuileries in Paris. The old **Biltmore Plaza Hotel** (now the **Omni Biltmore**), a 1920's showplace, has been transformed into a first-class hostelry, with a grand marble staircase in the lobby.

South of Kennedy Plaza is the ornate Majestic Theatre (now called the **Lederer Theater**), a 1917 movie house that is all terra cotta and arches; it is home to the Tony Award-winning Trinity Square Repertory Company, one of the finest in the country. East of the plaza, between Westminster and Weybosset Streets, is **The Arcade**, the country's oldest indoor shopping "mall" (1828), and sole survivor of several Greek Revival-style "temples of trade," built in America in the early 1800's. Today, it is a lively marketplace with shops and eateries.

Across the Providence River at the foot of College Hill (South Water and College Streets) is **Market House**, a red brick building built in 1773 that served as the political and commercial center of colonial Providence. It is also the site of the Providence Tea Party, where on March 2, 1775, revolutionaries burned hundreds of pounds of British tea in an act of defiance against the Crown. The house is part of the prestigious **Rhode Island School of Design**. The school maintains a museum, part of which is the elegant, mahogany-panelled Pendleton House and its collection of eighteenth-century American furniture.

North on Main Street is the **Meeting House of the First Baptist Church** in Amer-ica, a preserved 1775 colonial church designed by Joseph Brown; it is a tribute to Roger Williams, founder of Providence, who established the church in 1638. Continue north on Main and you come to the **Roger Williams National Memorial**, a park that is the site of the original Providence settlement in 1636.

Opposite is the **Cathedral of St John**, established in 1722, one of four original colonial parishes in the state. Its box pews and communion silver date to the Queen Anne period.

You are now approaching the beginnings of Benefit Street.

BENEFIT STREET — A MILE OF HISTORY

Benefit Street area is an impressive concentration of original colonial buildings. Beautifully restored eighteenth- and nineteenth-century Federal houses, churches, and museums overlook the city's historic waterfront. The Providence Preservation Society (headquarters at 24 Meeting Street) offers guided tours and pamphlets that describe some of the 100 historic homes (built largely by early sea captains and colonial merchants) that line Benefit and adjoining streets.

The street itself has a curious history. Once a meandering dirt path that led to informal graveyards behind family homes, it was straightened and "improved for the benefit" of the people, so the official proclamation reads.

Walking south, you will see several Federal homes, and the **Old State House**, where the Rhode Island General Assembly renounced allegiance to King George III, and signed their Declaration of Independence on May 4, 1776, more than two months before the 13 colonies gave their assent to liberty in Philadelphia.

Farther south is the **Providence Athenaeum**, an 1838 building that resembles a Greek temple and is one of America's oldest libraries. The modest clapboard, 1707 Quaker-style **house of Governor Stephen Hopkins**, a signatory of the Declaration of Independence (Benefit and Hopkins Streets) is open to visitors. It is said that he nudged other delegates at the Continental Congress into supporting that document. Next is the **First Unitarian Church**, built in 1816, whose steeple holds the largest and heaviest bell cast by Paul Revere & Sons.

The **John Brown House**, on Power Street just east of Benefit Street, was described by John Quincy Adams as "the most magnificent and elegant mansion that I have ever seen on this continent." Built in 1786, the three-story Georgian mansion once belonged to John Brown, one of the four Brown brothers. Another brother, Moses, developed the Slater Mill; Joseph was a noted architect who designed some of Providence's most enduring landmarks; and Nicholas was the founder of Rhode Island College, now Brown University. All brothers played an important role in shaping the future of Providence.

The Brown family collections include a display of early Rhode Island furniture. One of the best pieces, a block-front secretary, has been described as "one of the finest examples of American colonial furniture existent."

North of the Brown House, at Prospect and Cottage Streets, is the 133-acre (54-hectare) College Hill campus of **Brown University**. Chartered in 1764, it is the seventh oldest college in the United States. The university's **John Carter Brown Library** holds the world's premier collection of early and colonial Americana.

CONSTITUTION HILL

Across the river and west on Interstate 44 is the summit of Constitution Hill, upon which rests the **State Capitol**, its white marble glistening in the sun. The capitol was built in 1891 and its cupola is the second largest unsupported dome in the world, after St Peter's in Rome. The building houses an historic full-length portrait of George Washington by Gilbert Stuart, the original royal Charter of 1663, and, of course, legislative chambers and the governor's office. One-hour guided tours are offered weekdays from 9 am to 3:30 pm.

WHERE TO STAY

In a class all its own is the recently restored **Omni Biltmore** (Kennedy Plaza; ℂ (401) 421-0700, toll-free (800) 843-6664; 289 rooms). With special weekend rates, the Omni could be considered in the expensive category, but the service is always that of a luxury hotel.

In the moderate to expensive range are the 13-story **Holiday Inn Downtown** (21

Atwells Avenue; ℂ (401) 831-3900; 274 rooms) and **Marriott Inn** (Charles and Orms Streets; ℂ (401) 272-2400; 345 rooms). In nearby Pawtucket is the moderately-priced **Howard Johnson's Motor Lodge** (2 George Street; ℂ (401) 723-6700; 136 rooms), where children stay free.

EATING OUT

Expensive

The best seafood in town is found at the **Bluepoint Oyster Bar** (99 N. Main Street; ℂ (401) 272-6145).

For excellent Italian cuisine, **Camille's Roman Garden** (71 Bradford Street; ℂ (401) 751-4812) cannot be beaten.

Pot au Feu (44 Custom House Street; ℂ (401) 273-8953) serves excellent continental cuisine.

Moderate

Wes's Rib House (1 Robar Plaza; ℂ (401) 421-9090) serves hearty meals of Missouri-style barbecue ribs, chicken, pork chops, or cured ham. **Alforno** (7 Steeple Street; ℂ (401) 273-9760) features northern Italian cuisine.

Inexpensive

For an unusual dining experience, Providence has the **Haven Brothers Diner** (Fulton and Dorrance Streets; ℂ (401) 861-7777). It is a real aluminum diner that pulls up to the curb each evening, and offers American food.

Providence, Rhode Island's capital.

Travelers' Tips

GETTING THERE

New England is accessible by air, rail, and road. Major entry points are Boston, New York (only minutes away from Connecticut, the southernmost New England state), and Montreal, Canada.

BY AIR

Most major international airlines provide service to Boston, but fares are often cheaper to New York. Some United States carriers offer in country flight coupons at substantial savings to foreign travelers. These programs change from year to year, so check with you travel agent when planning your trip. In 1991, for example, a $50.00 coupon would allow you to fly anywhere in New England on U.S. Air. The coupons could only be purchased outside the Unites States by foreigners or United States citizens working abroad.

The following are the telephone numbers of the international carriers who maintain an office in Boston or at Boston's Logan International Airport:
Aer Lingus, toll-free (800) 223-6537
Air Canada, toll-free (800) 422-6232
Air France, toll-free (800) 237-2747
Air Jamaica, toll-free (800) 523-5585
Air New Zealand, toll-free (800) 262-1234
Alaska Airlines, toll-free (800) 426-0333
Alitalia Airlines, (617) 542-9060
American Airlines, (617) 542-6700
British Airways, toll-free (800) 247-9297
Continental Airlines, (617) 569-8400
El Al — Israel, toll-free (800) 223-6700
Icelandair, toll-free (800) 223-5500
Finnair, toll-free (800) 223-5700
Japan Airlines, (617) 262-8800
Lufthansa, toll-free (800) 645-3880
Northwest Orient, (617) 267-4885
Pan American, toll-free (800) 221-1111
Qantas, toll-free (800) 227-4500
Sabena, (617) 542-4296
Swissair, (617) 423-7778
TWA, (617) 367-2800
United, (617) 482-7900

Most domestic carriers fly to Boston and the other large New England cities (Hartford, Providence, Portland, etc.) To find economy flights to New England, you will have to consult your travel agent. Fares are variable. Competition among companies can cause sudden price wars that can make flying to New England quite reasonable. During the summer, it is advisable to avoid any discount packages that require you to fly standby. Flights are not only full but also overbooked. Make your seat reservations a week in advance to be assured of not being bumped off your flight, and do your fellow travelers a favor and cancel any unwanted reservations.

The following domestic airlines fly to New England and have offices in the Boston area:
Alaska Airlines, toll-free (800) 426-0333
American Airlines, (617) 542-6700
Continental Airlines, (617) 569-8400
Delta Airlines, (617) 567-4100
HubExpress, toll-free (800) 962-4744
Northwest Orient, (617) 267-4885
Pan American, toll-free (800) 221-1111
TWA, (617) 367-2800
United, (617) 482-7900
US Air, (617) 482-3160

BY RAIL

Amtrak, the only rail passenger carrier in the United States, connects a few New England cities. There is frequent service to Boston from Montreal and New York. On the New York–Boston line, there are intermediate stops in Connecticut. You can hop off the train from Montreal at Port Kennedy, New York, and take the ferry across Lake Champlain to Burlington, Vermont. For prices and schedules, call Amtrak toll-free at (800) 872-7245. To receive a free travel planner, write to Amtrak Distribution Center (P.O. Box 7717, Itasca, IL 60143).

BY GREYHOUND BUS

Greyhound Lines can get you to New England from within the United States or Canada. Its routes will usually take you into Boston or New York with connections to Maine, New Hampshire, and Vermont. Your travel agent or local Greyhound agent can provide information on schedules and fares, or contact Greyhound in New York (((212 635-0800) or Boston (((617) 423-5810).

BY ROAD

Although most New Englanders consider New England a country unto itself, there are no border crossings when driving within Unites States.

When entering from Canada, even United States citizens need to have appropriate identification (see TRAVEL DOCUMENTS below).

TRAVEL DOCUMENTS

When arriving in New England, Canadian and Mexican citizens need only show proof of identification and residence (a driver's license will do). British need only a valid passport. Other visitors need a valid passport and a United States visa. Contact the United States embassy or consulate in your country for the exact details for obtaining a visa.

Your travel agent can also be helpful in obtaining a visa. Allow 28 days for processing.

Vaccinations may or may not be required for entry into the United States. (Country of origin or recently-visited countries could alter your situation; check before you leave.)

CONSULATES

IN BOSTON

BRITISH
600 Atlantic Avenue, Boston
(248-9555

AUSTRALIAN
20 Beacon, Boston
(248-8655

CANADIAN
3 Copley Pl., Boston
(262-3760

Travelers' Tips

IRISH
535 Boylston, Boston
(267-9330

IN NEW YORK

BRITISH
145 Third Avenue, New York, NY
((212) 745-0202

AUSTRALIAN
636 Fifth Avenue, New York, NY
((212) 245-4000

CANADIAN
1251 Avenue of the Americas, New York NY
((212) 586-2400

IRISH
515 Madison Avenue, New York, NY
((212) 319-2555

CUSTOMS

Customs allows you to bring in duty-free gifts valued up to $100. For more specific information, including shopping restrictions, contact your local American embassy or consulate branch. Carrying non-prescription narcotic drugs into the country may well result in a long prison sentence. When entering the United States, foreign visitors should allow a minimum of an hour to clear customs at Boston or New York. For European travelers, the close scrutiny of customs and immigration officers is sometimes shocking and annoying. During the peak summer season, foreign passport holders have had to wait up to two hours before even reaching passport control at New York's Kennedy International Airport. At Boston this rarely happens.

WHEN TO GO

There is no best time to come to New England. Summer, fall, winter, and spring all have something to offer. However, New England has a season all its own — "Colors." This arrives in early fall when the leaves change to crimson, gold, and orange. Days are warm and evenings cool. The countryside is at its best then.

New England summers are traditionally glorious and comfortable, with lots of sun and gentle cooling breezes off the ocean, although hot and humid conditions are not altogether unfamiliar to the region. Summer is the height of the tourist season, with most attractions open from late May to October.

Winters can be bitterly cold, with snow and cutting winds. But it is rarely too severe for skiers. New England has more than 100 ski areas throughout its six states. It is neither the Alps nor the Rockies, but the slopes are good and fast, the cross country runs Olympic class, and the hospitality, warm and friendly.

Spring is often referred to as the mud season: lots of rain, with warm days and cool nights. However, several airlines offer special low fares during this traditional off-season period. Your reward is the freshness of spring with its new growth and blooming flowering wild flowers and fruit trees.

WHAT TO TAKE

New England styles tend to be casual, especially in Maine, Vermont, and New Hampshire. More traditional styles rule preppy Connecticut and Rhode Island; Massachusetts has a little bit of everything. Big cities, especially Boston, may require very formal wear, especially for business meetings and restaurant dining. Men should pack a jacket and tie, and women should bring a dress or suit.

While season dictates other clothing needs, summer visitors should bring along a warm sweater or jacket in case of cool evening temperatures — especially when visiting the coast.

Regardless of season, rain gear is appropriate.

GETTING AROUND

Rail travel is the most limited means of getting around New England (see GETTING THERE below).

AIRLINES

Airplanes can get you from city to city. In addition to the domestic carriers listed under GETTING THERE above, there are small domestic airlines that provide intra-New England flights:
Bar Harbor Airlines — for Portland, Maine; toll-free (800) 343-3210.
Pilgrim Airlines — for New Haven, Connecticut, and Provincetown, Mass.; toll-free (800) 243-0490.

BUS SERVICES

Reasonable bus services are available throughout New England, provided by the following three major companies with central offices in Boston:
Bonanza, ((617) 423-5810
Greyhound, ((617) 423-5810
Peter Pan Bus Lines Inc., ((617) 426-7838, toll free (800) 628-8468 outside Massachusetts or toll-free (800) 332-8995 in-state.

Of course, bus travel is more time-consuming than air, but it does offer the advantage of being able to see the countryside at a relaxed pace.

TAXIS AND LIMOUSINES

Taxis operate throughout New England, although they are most often found in big cities rather than the small towns. Rates vary; ask if there are standard rates for airport routes.

Limousines are another way to get conveniently from airports to major cities; rates are often comparable to taxi fares. In Boston, contact:
Carey of Boston Limousine, ((617) 623-8700
Commonwealth Limousine, ((617) 787-5575
Boston Cab, ((617) 536-5010
Checker Cab, ((617) 536-7000
Red Cab, ((617) 734-5000

AUTOMOBILES

By far the best way to see New England is at your own pace and schedule by automobile. Exploring the small country roads is to find the best New England has to offer.

Most airports, major hotels, or tourist centers have offices (or can provide information) for car rentals. Renters must have a valid driver's license and a credit card (used for deposit), be at least 21 years of age, though, in certain circumstances some companies set the minimum age at 21 years. Foreign drivers may need an international driver's license. Be sure to check out liability clauses in the rental agreement; they are not automatically included, and your personal automobile insurance or credit card may cover none, part, or all of your liability risks. Check if your airline offers car rental packages with airfare. Car rental agency telephone numbers include:

American International, toll-free (800) 527-0202

Avis, toll-free (800) 331-1212

Budget, toll-free (800) 527-0700

Dollar (in Boston), (617) 569-5300

Hertz, toll-free (800) 654-3131

National, toll-free (800) 328-4567

Foreign travelers can often get better rates when booking from abroad. "Fly and Drive" packages are often better buys than booking flights and car rentals separately.

For the most adventurous travelers, consider renting a camper. Throughout New England, in state and national forests, are well-maintained and equipped campgrounds, some of the best in the United States. There are also many private camp grounds that have luxury camping facilities — hot water, showers, pool, playground, electrical hook-ups, etc. Listings of camping facilities can be obtained from the individual state offices of tourism, whose addresses are included in the opening section of each chapter.

ACCOMMODATION

Throughout New England there are many hotels and motels that all provide the standard room with one or two double or queen-sized beds, private bath, telephone, and television. As rates often change without notice, specific prices are not noted in this guide. Hotels and motels are classified in the following categories: inexpensive, less than $35 for a double room (2 person occupancy); moderate, $35 to $85; expensive more than $80. In Boston, New Haven, and Rhode Island, there is a special category — luxury, over $200.

Also listed in the Guide are the traditional New England country inns and bed-and-breakfasts that are growing in popularity. Rates at the country inns are generally in the expensive category. However, if you book for a week-long stay or mid-week and off season, you can sometimes negotiate a more moderate price.

Bed and breakfast accommodations are in the moderate category and bring you in more individual contact with New Englanders. The bed-and-breakfast operators have a closely knit organization and will usually be more than happy to help you find a bed-and-breakfast at your next destination.

The lists of accommodations are included at the end of each destination and are not all-inclusive. State and local tourism agencies will gladly supply you with further information and help in booking rooms. On New England's backroads there are many small motels whose accommodations are good and prices reasonable. It is always best to examine the rooms before making a decision.

ABOVE: Boston's MTA subway, made famous by the Kingston Trio's lyrics in the 1950's.

EATING OUT

The most difficult thing about eating out in New England is deciding which of the many excellent restaurants to choose. Needless to say, the lists of restaurants included with each destination are far from exhaustive. Ownership, prices, chefs, and specialties do change. However, those recommended are established houses that have provided a tradition of good food over the years. Price guidelines for full meals (without liquor) are as follows: inexpensive, under $15 per person; moderate, $15 to $30; expensive, over $30. Reservations are always recommended.

TIPPING

Tips are not included on your tab. Fifteen percent is the standard. Don't hesitate to leave more if the service has been exceptional, but never leave less unless the waiter or waitress has been surly.

SHOPPING

ANTIQUES

"Antique" is generally a term bandied about in a rather casual manner. In the United States, it has often become interchangeable with the word "old." Therefore, it is best to look to United States Customs for some kind of workable definition.

In 1930, the federal government ruled that objects must be at least 100 years old to be classified as antiques and admitted into the country duty-free, and in 1966, a tariff act further ruled that there would be duty-free admission into the country of all objects 100 years old before the date of entry.

Therefore, anything at least 100 years old is "officially" given antique status, although many objects less than a century old are generally included under that term. It is to be aware of the official government distinction.

Antiquing in Litchfield County Connecticut can be a barrel of fun.

Buying Antiques

Like anything else, antique prices reflect the free enterprise marketplace. In other words, things are worth whatever someone will pay for them. You should therefore consider all antique price tags as general starting points for negotiation. You should not have to pay the asking price for an antique unless there is heavy demand or competition for the particular piece or style. (Then you might even be forced to pay more, if your heart is set on it and your wallet deep enough.)

Always attempt to bring down the price, even if you are normally a timid negotiator. Antique dealers expect you to do it; besides, the asking price probably reflects this realization.

As an educated consumer, you might want to pick up an antique price/guide book that offers background on history, styles, and general prices. One of the most consistent and respected guides is Kovel's, which can be purchased at most major bookstores.

Also remember that almost all types of Americana — whether or not they are listed in official antique guidebooks — have become sought-after collector's items.

Furniture Styles

After the wilderness was ruined and great cities sprang up along the eastern seaboard in the eighteenth century, colonial furniture took on its distinctive, elegant style. Some antiques are recognized art forms. Typical of certain time periods and much sought after today. They include:

Queen Anne (1702–1714) — walnut furniture distinguished by curved contours, often with ball and claw feet and shell carvings.

Early Georgian (1714–1745) — the Queen Anne style was elaborated with paw feet, and eagles' or lions' head carvings; a heavy baroque style came into vogue after 1735. Most of the furniture makers continued to use walnut, but mahogany was becoming increasingly popular.

Chippendale (1745–1765) — perhaps the most renowned period in American furniture styling, with the works of master cabinet maker Thomas Chippendale most prominent. Straight square legs, but a great freedom of design, with many Gothic, Chinese, and French touches, including lavish fretwork and rococo flourishes. Almost exclusive use of mahogany.

Adam Style (1760–1785) — classical, delicate with much painted decoration. This period also saw the introduction of oval and sideboard tables, and wheel back chairs. Mahogany dominated, but sycamore and other light woods were also used.

Hepplewhite Style (1780–1795) — light and graceful with much painted decorations,

shire County Massachusetts Antiques Dealers Association, and guarantee antique authenticity. Some of them are located in New England's beautiful towns, so whether you're seriously looking for antiques, just browsing, or simply wandering the region's backroads, you should have a pleasant and interesting journey.

Cautions

Be very careful about what you buy when purchasing expensive or valuable pieces. Always ask for antique authentication, or

inlay, and delicate carving that often used Prince of Wales feathers, ears of wheat, and honeysuckle motifs. Also Anglicized versions of contemporary French styles; continued use of mahogany.

Sheraton Style (1790–1810) — Thomas Sheraton was a gifted furniture designer, not a cabinet maker. His style is dominated by square back chairs, tapered legs, bow front chests and sideboards, pedestal dining tables, and much use of inlay in mahogany.

Dealer's Directory

Contact the Massachusetts State Tourism Department for a list of the antique dealers. Look out for those who belong to the Berk-

frequent dealers who take pride in their merchandise and guarantee authenticity. A simple tag description should not necessarily satisfy you unless you are knowledgeable about antiques yourself. In fact, stories are legendary about how a few unscrupulous dealers fabricate entire case histories for antiques in order to impress — and con — buyers. It is *caveat emptor* — "let the buyer beware."

HANDICRAFTS

Throughout New England are many specialty shops that sell only locally or regionally crafted merchandise. Particularly appealing are the wooden and fabric items.

Travelers' Tips

One can find a variety of children's pull toys and puzzles that are as durable as they are attractive. These are not bargains because many are one of a kind, more works of art than toys.

Hand-made cotton clothing, stuffed animals, and kitchen items are also plentiful. These are usually products of cottage industries that each year play a larger role in the economics of the small New England towns.

OUTLET STORES

Until a quarter of a century ago, all the New England factory towns had stores that sold their "accidented" products. The careful, clever shopper could save enormous amounts. A family could be dressed and shod for a fraction of retail cost, and household linens were likewise cheaper. Now most of these factories are closed, but outlet stores remain. They are not the great sources of bargains they once were, but the discounts are generally 20 to 30 percent which include seconds, remaindered stock, samples, overruns of almost every name brand sold in the United States: Fieldcrest, Dior, Barbizon, Levis, Bass, Arrow, Haynes, White Stag, Nike, Adidas, New Balance, etc.

Freeport, Maine, is the best known of the outlet store shopping areas, but there are other stores throughout New England. Each spring new guides to the outlet stores appear on the New England newsstands to help visitors and residents alike find the best bargains.

MONEY

United States dollar rates have fluctuated so wildly of late it is pointless to include any specific comparative guidelines. Trends have increased the home currency value of many European and Asian visitors.

It is advisable to purchase travelers' checks in United States dollars for your money use because many banks do not offer foreign currency exchange services. Travelers' checks can be easily replaced if stolen or lost.

WEIGHTS AND MEASURES

The United States use ounces, pounds, gallons, miles, acres, etc. It does not use the metric system. Some conversions are as follows:

1 inch = 2.54 centimeters
1 foot = 0.305 meters
1 mile = 1.6 kilometers
1 gallon – 3.78 liters
1 ounce =28.35 grams
1 pound = 0.45 kilograms.

COMMUNICATIONS

NEWSPAPERS

Pick up any local daily newspaper for the latest overview of local and national news. The *Boston Globe* is New England's leading regional newspaper. *USA Today*, a national daily, provides national news capsules. Only in Boston can you find foreign language newspapers.

MAIL

Post offices — Most post offices are open Monday through Friday from 9 am to 5 pm. There are often long lines and belligerent employees. It is just part of the system. At the time of going to press, first-class letters require a 29-cent stamp and postcards 18 cents. International rates vary with desti-

OPPOSITE: Second-hand clothing and bric-a-brac in rural Northeast Connecticut.
ABOVE: Moped rental at Martha's Vineyard.

nation, but are generally about twice the domestic tariff.

TELEPHONE

The recent breakup of AT&T has played havoc with phone users throughout the country. Now several kinds of pay phones are in operation, all requiring different steps of operation; read the directions carefully before depositing your coins. A local call is $.25 at most pay phones. To use international calling cards, you'll need to dial 0 to get the operator.

Major hotels have telefax services, at a price, as do office services stores in the larger cities.

For the electronically equipped traveler, CCITT and Bell approved modems that will work in the United States. 1200 baud is more reliable than 2400.

TELEVISION

America has four major television networks and thousands of local affiliate stations. Add cable and pay-TV to the selections, and the country becomes a TV-junkie's paradise, with scores of choices.

PUBLIC HOLIDAYS

National public holidays include the following:
New Year's Day — January 1
Martin Luther King, Jr.'s Birthday — January 15
Lincoln's Birthday — February 12
Washington's Birthday — February 22
Memorial Day — last Monday in May
Independence Day — July 4
Labor Day — first Monday in September
Columbus Day — second Monday in October
Thanksgiving Day — fourth Thursday in November
Christmas Day — December 25

During those holidays, federal, state and city offices close, and more importantly the banks. In the cities and town, stores and many restaurants are closed on Sundays, but shopping malls are usually open seven days a week.

Other holidays such as St Patrick's Day (March 17), Easter Sunday (April), Mother's Day (May), Father's Day (June), and Halloween (October 31) may be celebrated in various ways by different states and communities.

Also, state holidays vary widely. For a calendar of state events, contact the appropriate state tourism agencies.

TIME ZONES

New England is in the Eastern Time Zone, the same time of day as New York, one hour ahead of Chicago, three hours ahead of California, normally five hours behind Great Britain, and six hours behind western Europe. There is only a five hour time differential between New England and Europe for several weeks in October and April when the Europeans switch to daylight saving time before the Americans.

Bibliography

COLLECTION, *Fifty Hikes* (one book for each New England state), Woodstock, Vermont, Back Country Publications, 1983.

JUDSON HALE, *Inside New England*, New York, Harper & Row Publishers, 1982.

JOHN HARRIS, *The Boston Globe Historic Walks in Old Boston*, Chester, Connecticut., The Globe Pequot Press, 1984.

NATHANIEL HAWTHORNE, *The Scarlet Letter*.

HENRY JAMES, *The Bostonians*.

NEIL JORGENSEN, *A Guide to New England's Landscape*, Barre, Mass., Barre Publishing Co., 1980.

HERMAN MELVILLE, *Moby Dick*.

NEAL PEIRCE, *The New England States*, New York, W.W. Norton and Company, Inc. 1976.

MICHAEL SCHUMAN, *Favorite Daytrips in New England*, Dublin, N.H., Yankee Books, 1987.

ELIZABETH SQUIRE, *Guide to the Recommended Country Inns of New England*, Chester, Connecticut., The Globe Pequot Press, 1987.

NANCY WEBSTER & RICHARD WOODWORTH, *Getaways for Gourmets*, West Hartford, Connecticut., Wood Pond Press, 1988.

Photo Credits

Ellis Klarenbeek: Pages 5 *right*, 11 *right*, 20, 22, 23, 29, 32, 41, 42 *top*, 47, 48, 61, 62-63, 68, 90-91, 101, 102 left, 106, 112, 128, 135 *right*, 140, 151 *top and bottom*, 158, 188, 189, 191, 193, 203, 205

Quick Reference A–Z Guide
to Places and Topics of Interest with
Listed Accommodation, Restaurants and
Useful Telephone Numbers